YOUR PAL

FRED

LOW POWER

Michael Rex

VIKING

VIKING
An imprint of Penguin Random House LLC, New York

First published in the United States of America by Viking,
an imprint of Penguin Random House LLC, 2023

Visit us online at penguinrandomhouse.com.

Library of Congress Cataloging-in-Publication Data is available.

Manufactured in China

ISBN 9780593206355 (hardcover)

1 3 5 7 9 10 8 6 4 2

ISBN 9780593206386 (paperback)

1 3 5 7 9 10 8 6 4 2

TOPL

Design by Kate Renner
Text set in Out of Line BB

The artwork in this book was created in Photoshop.

To my wife, Teresa,
because she's the kindest,
and she's the best.

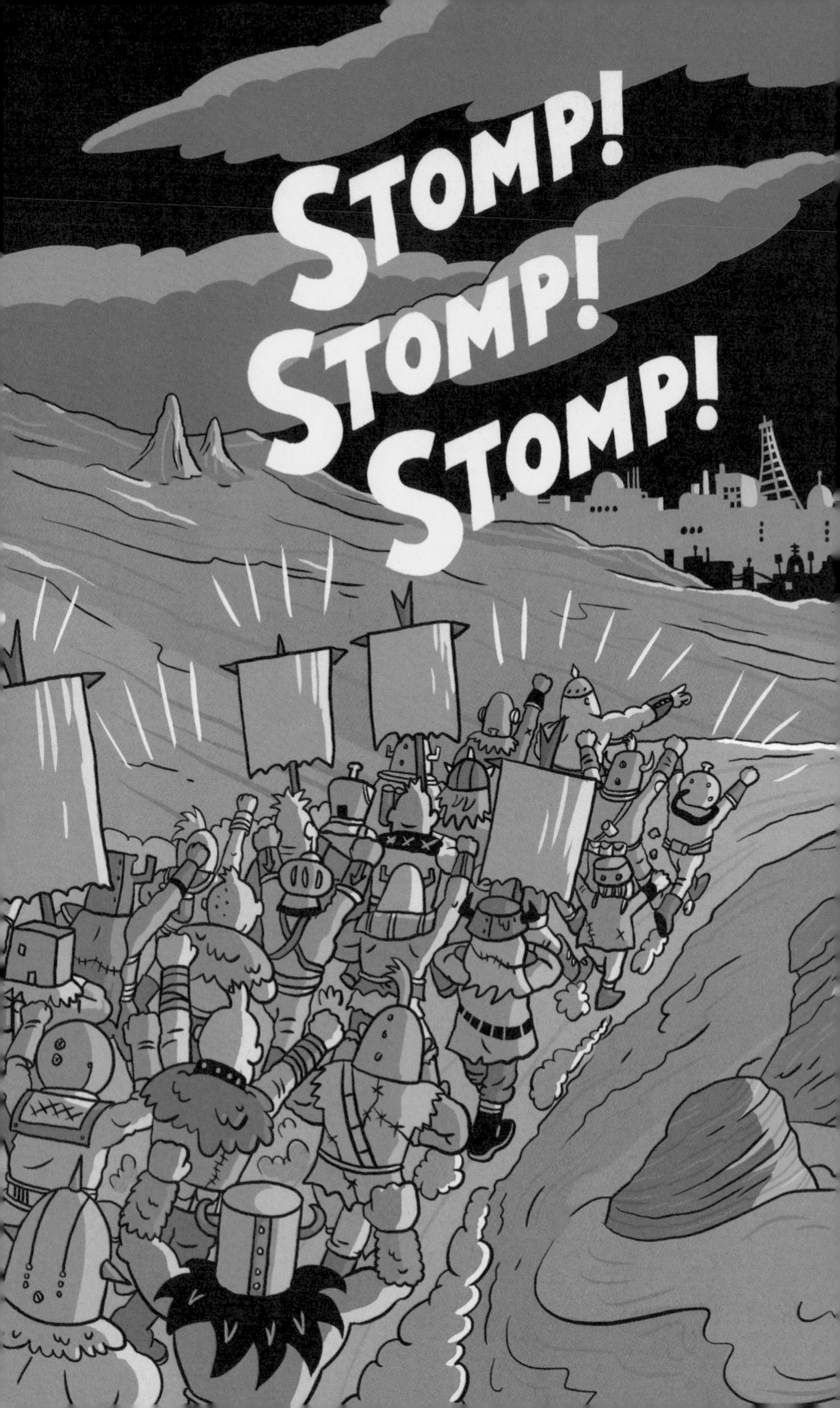
STOMP!
STOMP!
STOMP!

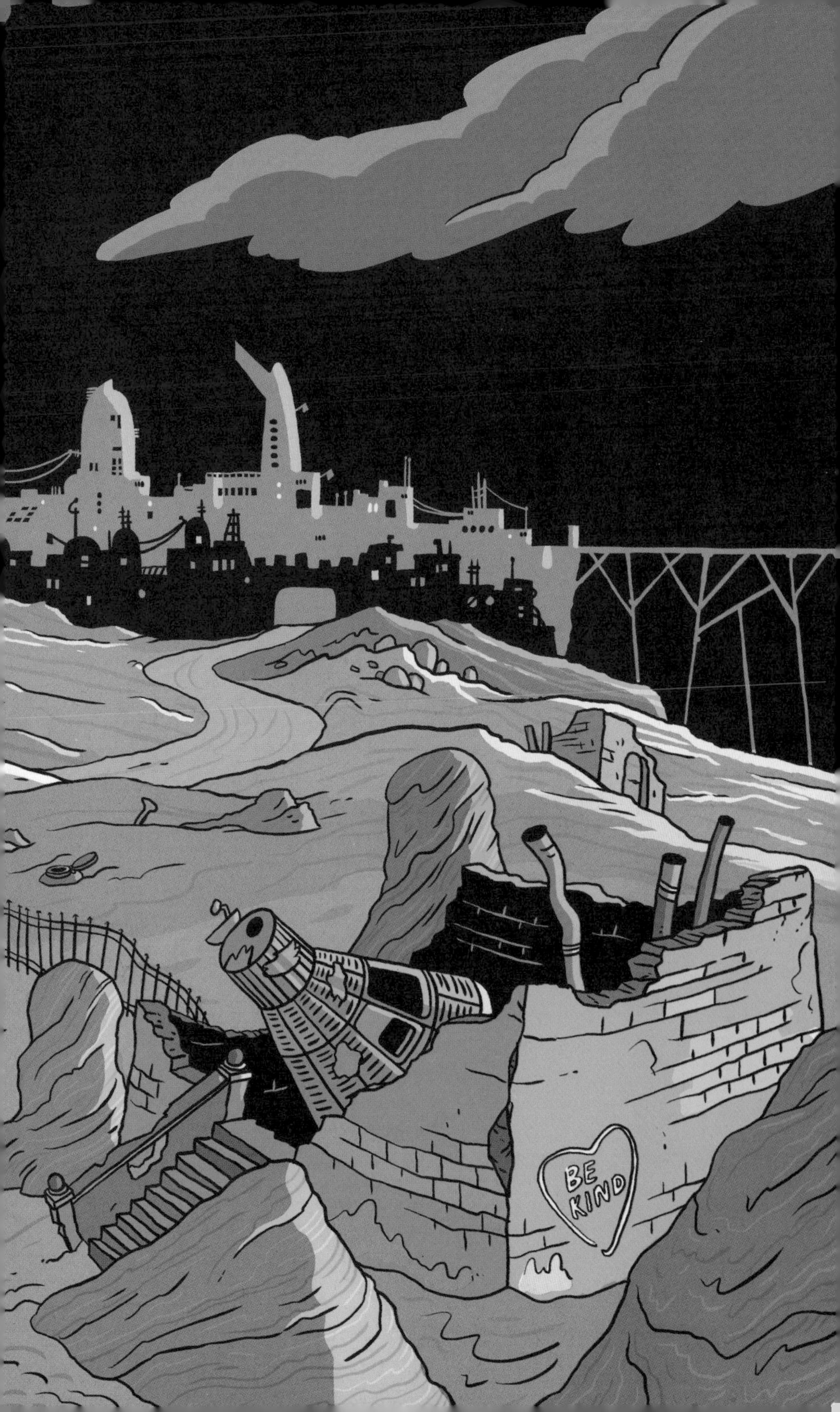
BE KIND

STOMP! STOMP!

CHAPTER 1

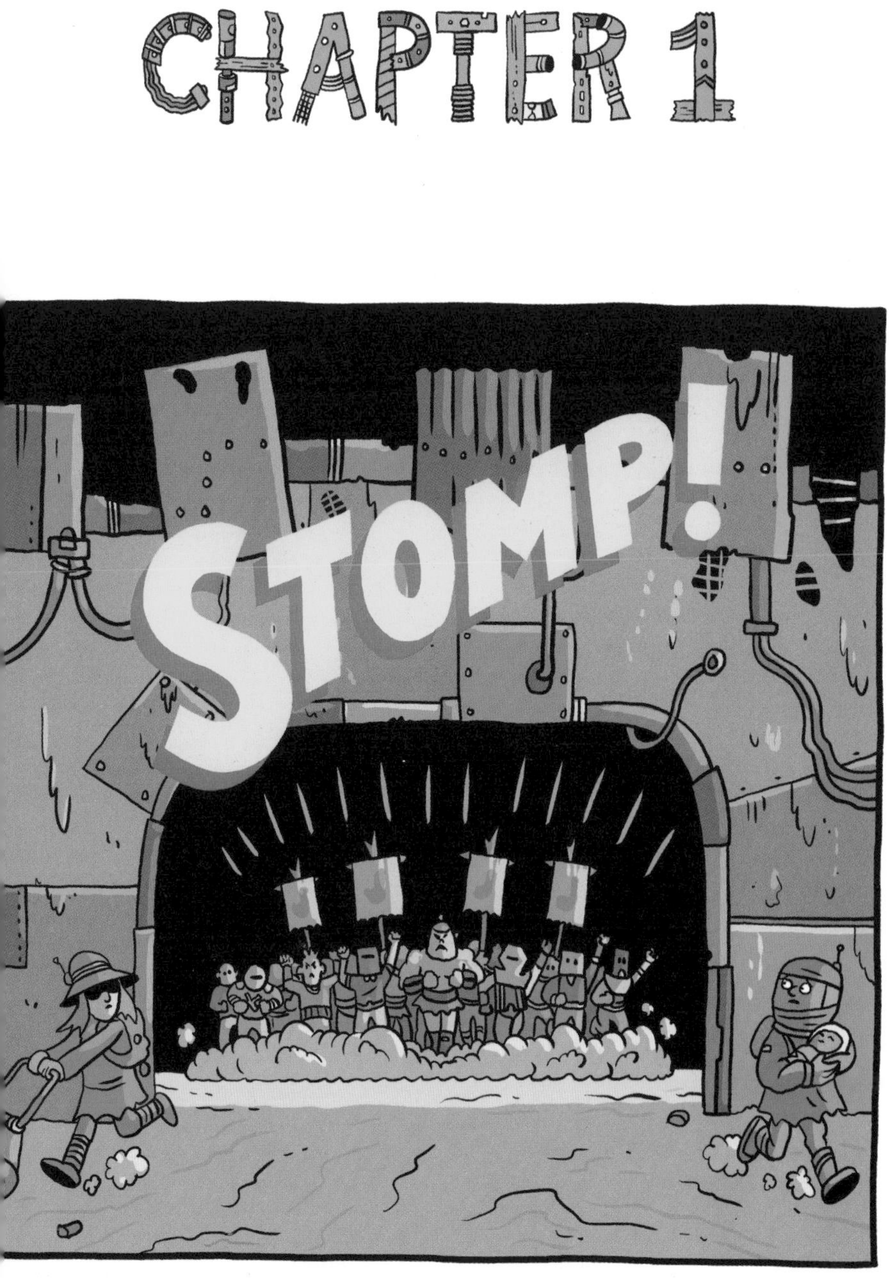
STOMP!

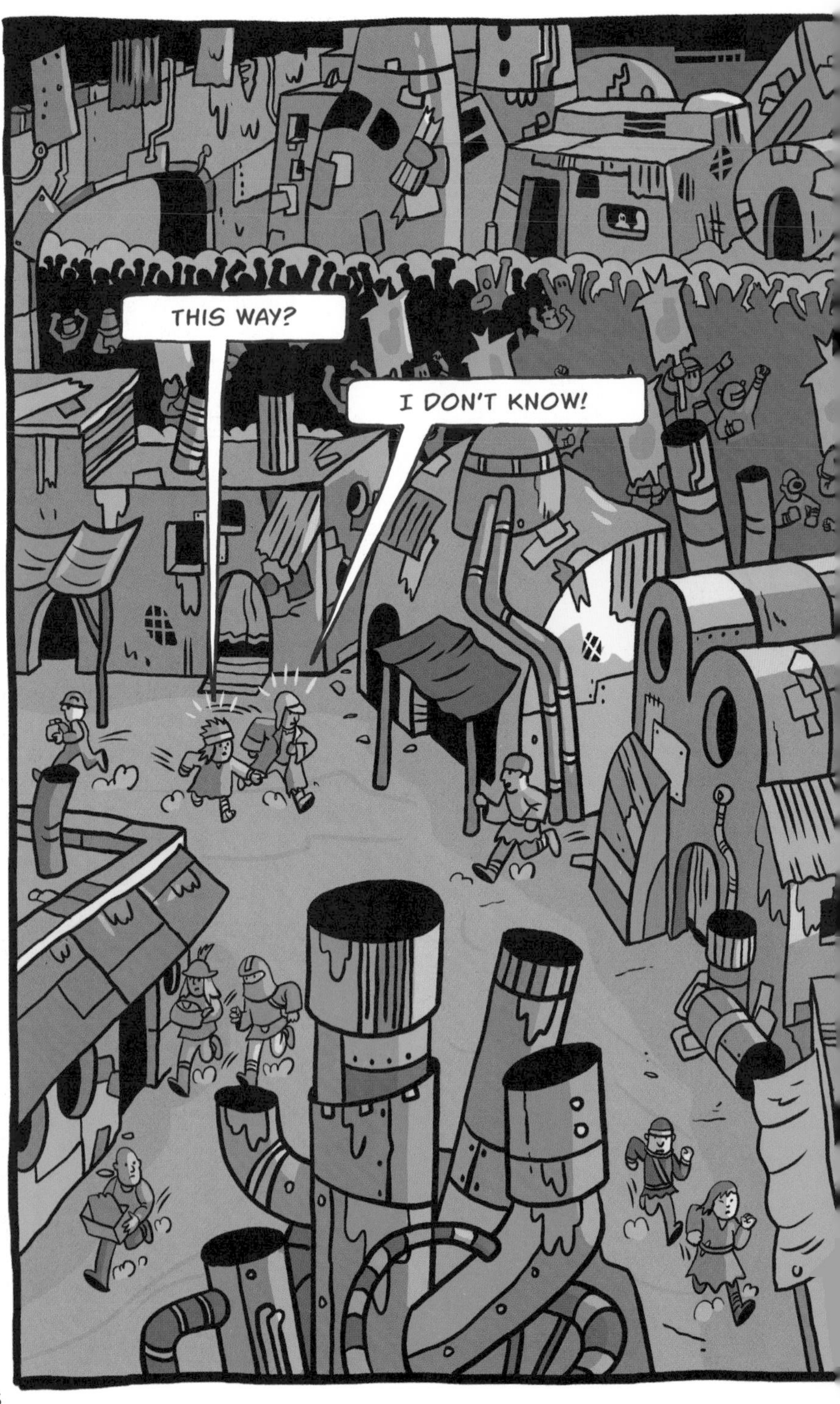
THIS WAY?
I DON'T KNOW!

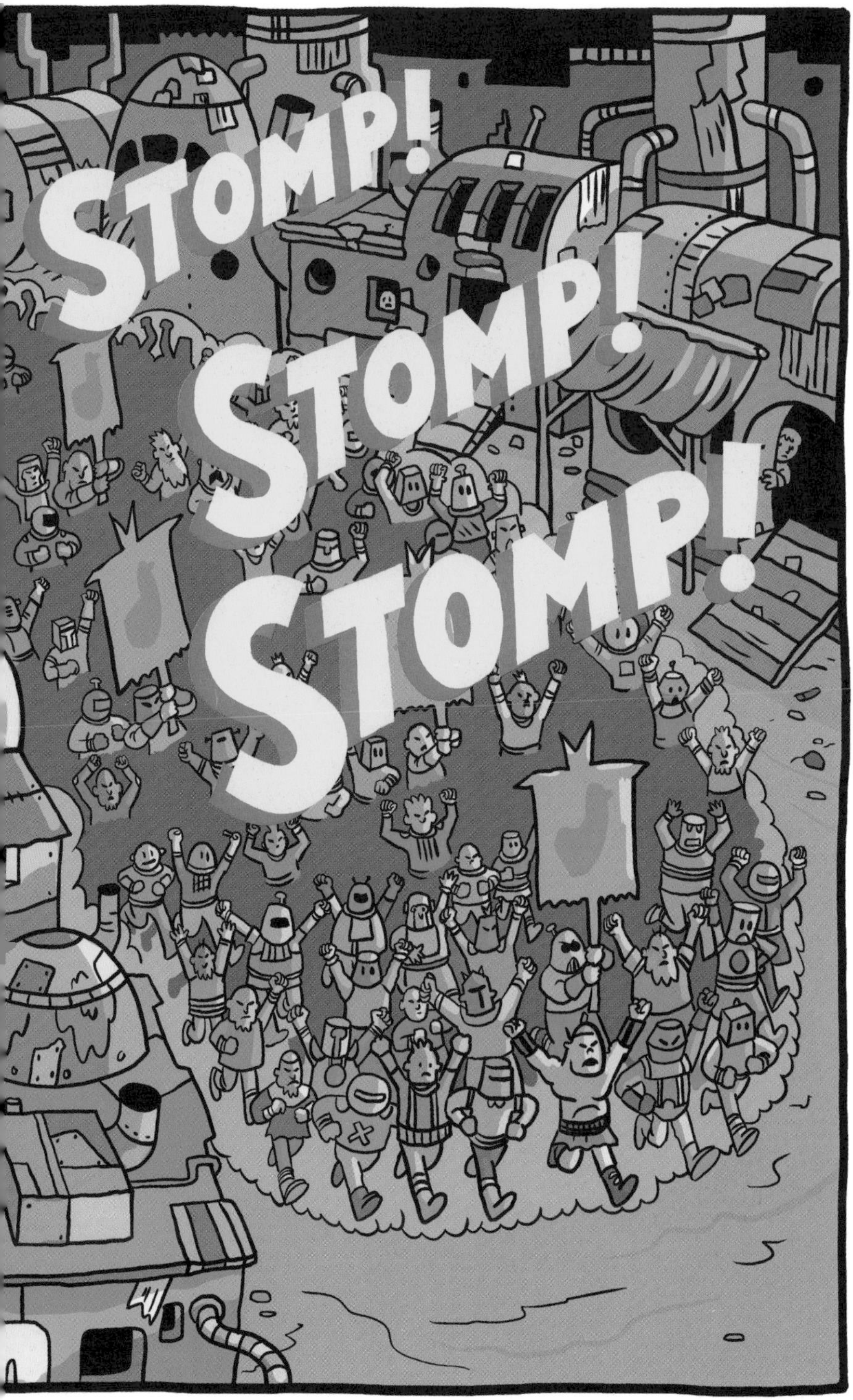
STOMP!
STOMP!
STOMP!

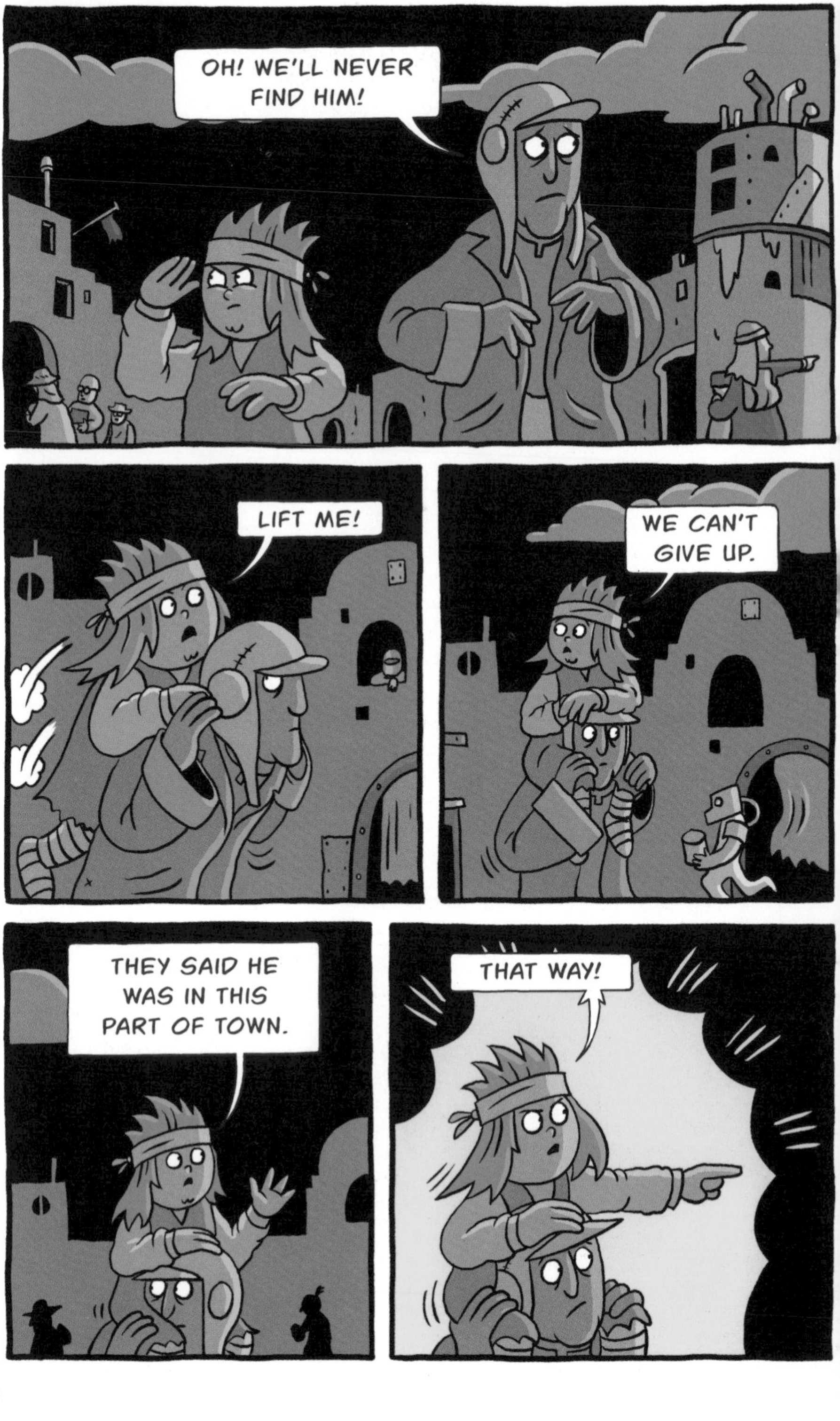
OH! WE'LL NEVER FIND HIM!
LIFT ME!
WE CAN'T GIVE UP.
THEY SAID HE WAS IN THIS PART OF TOWN.
THAT WAY!

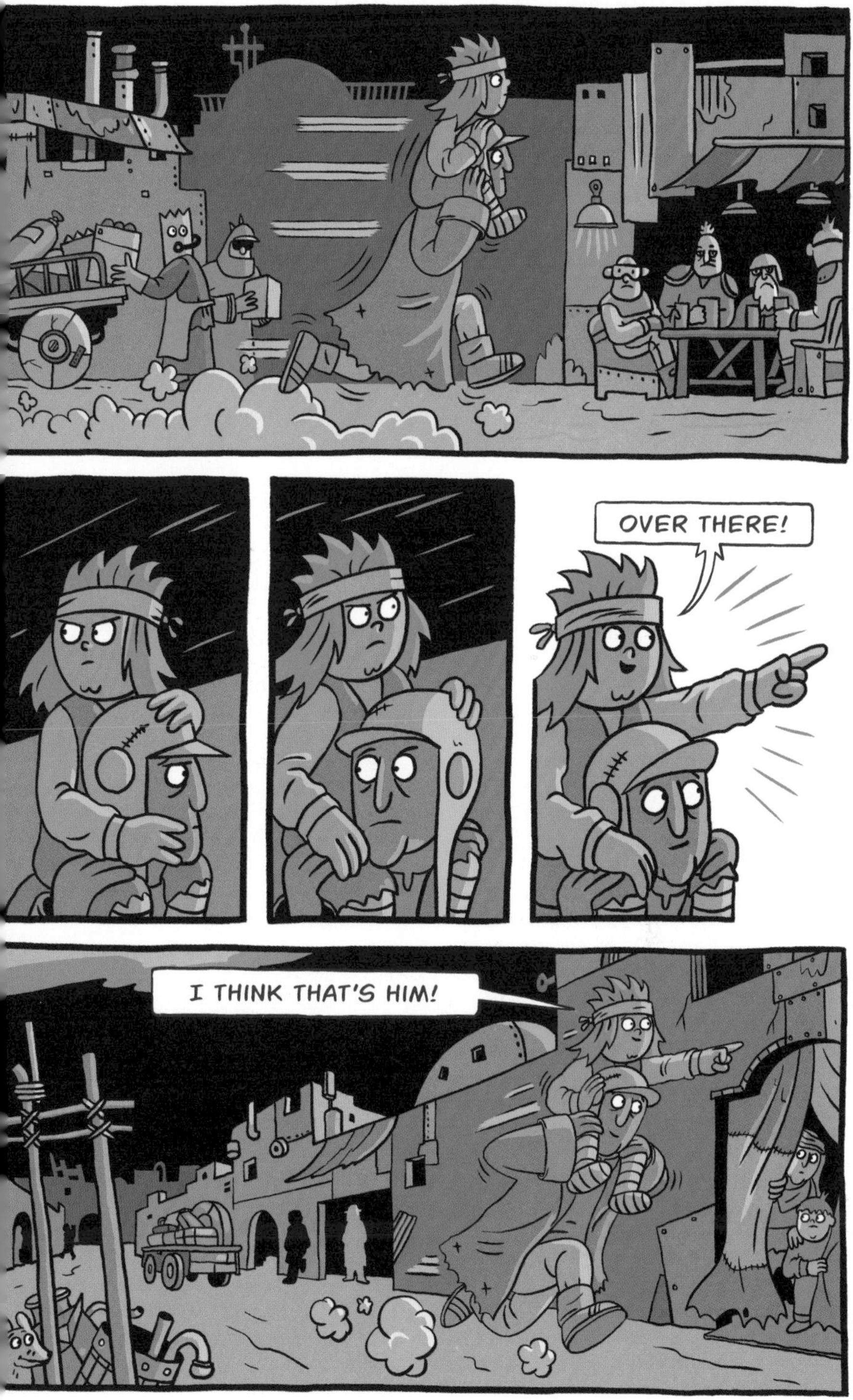
OVER THERE!
I THINK THAT'S HIM!

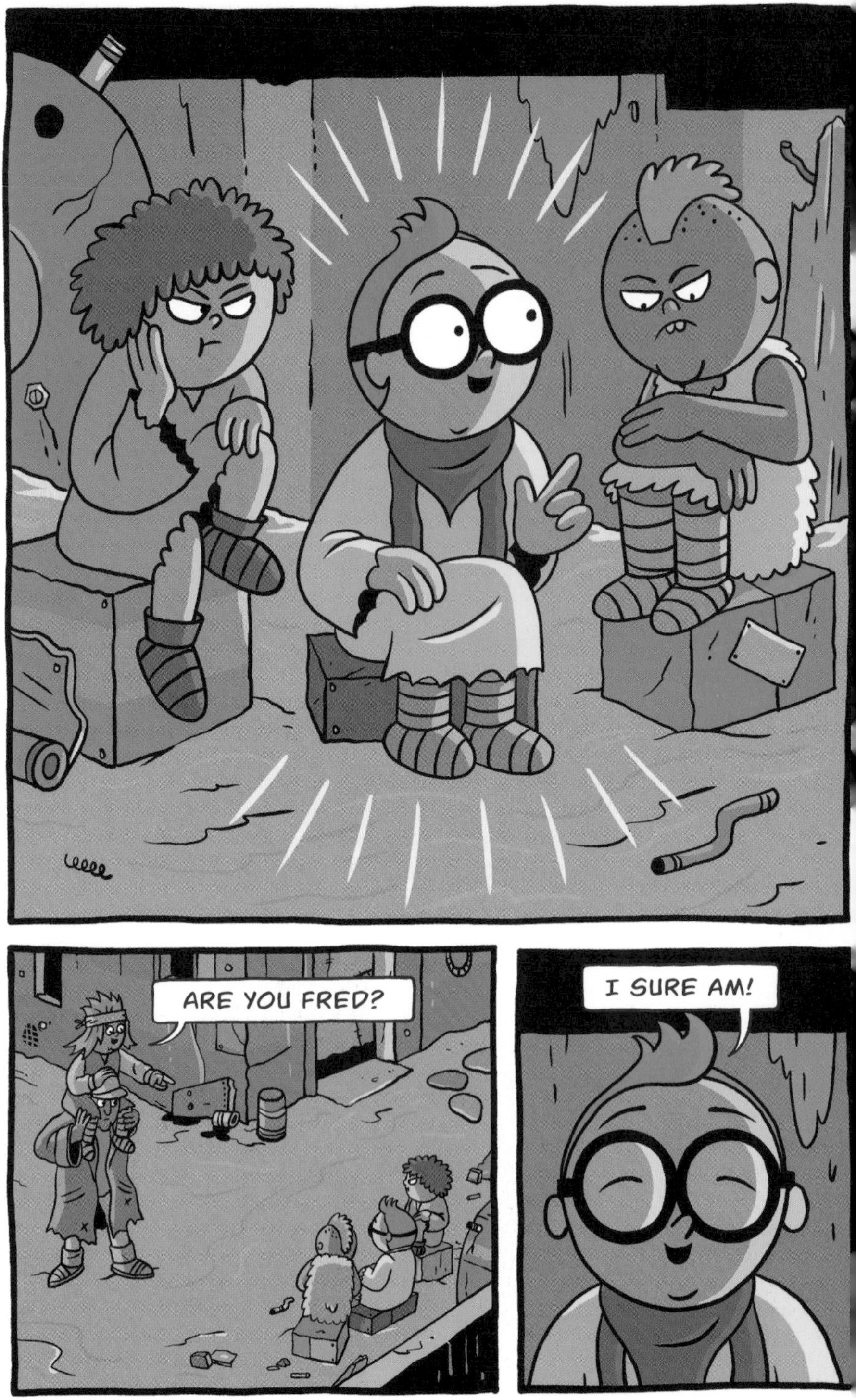
ARE YOU FRED?
I SURE AM!

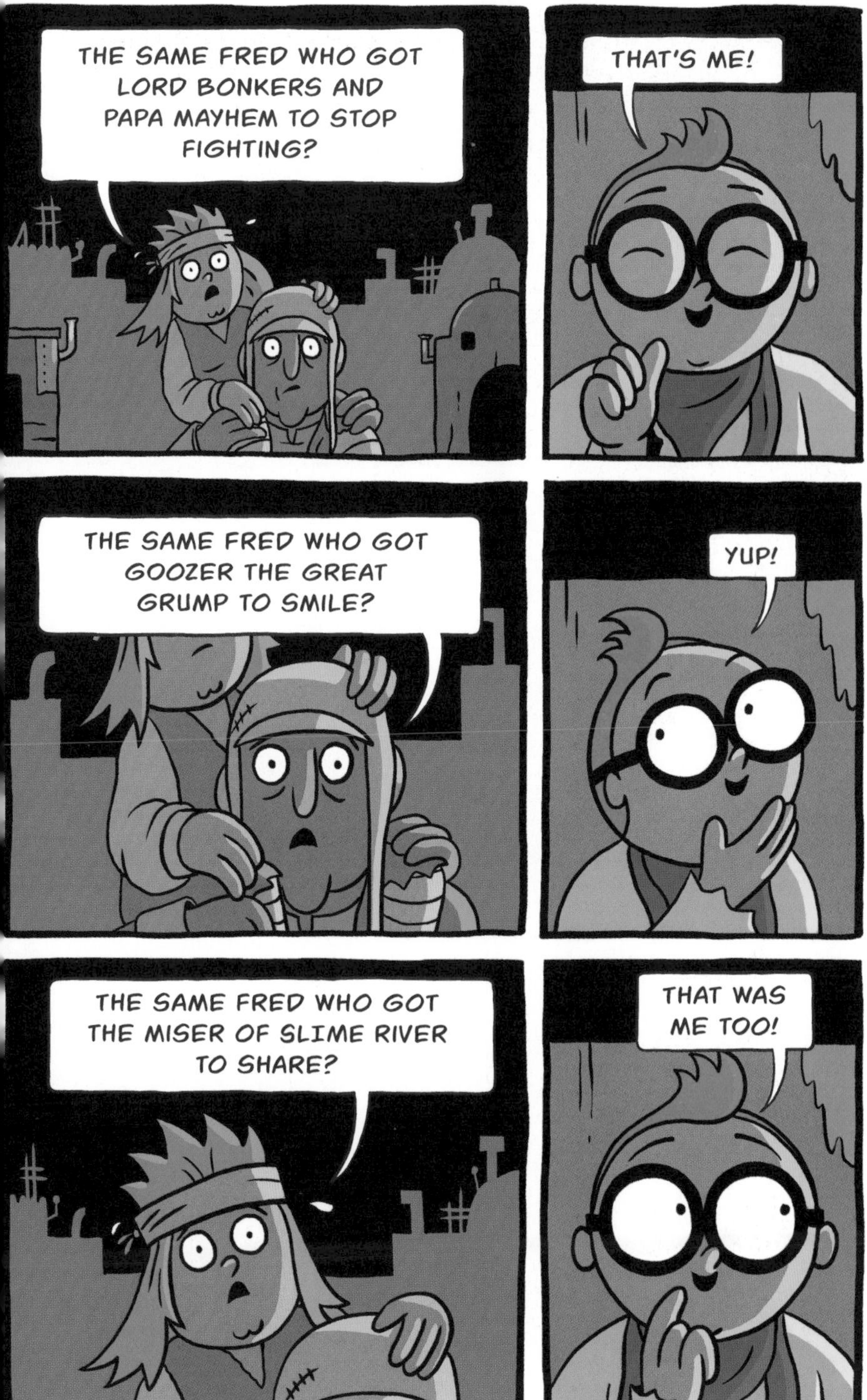
THE SAME FRED WHO GOT LORD BONKERS AND PAPA MAYHEM TO STOP FIGHTING?
THAT'S ME!
THE SAME FRED WHO GOT GOOZER THE GREAT GRUMP TO SMILE?
YUP!
THE SAME FRED WHO GOT THE MISER OF SLIME RIVER TO SHARE?
THAT WAS ME TOO!

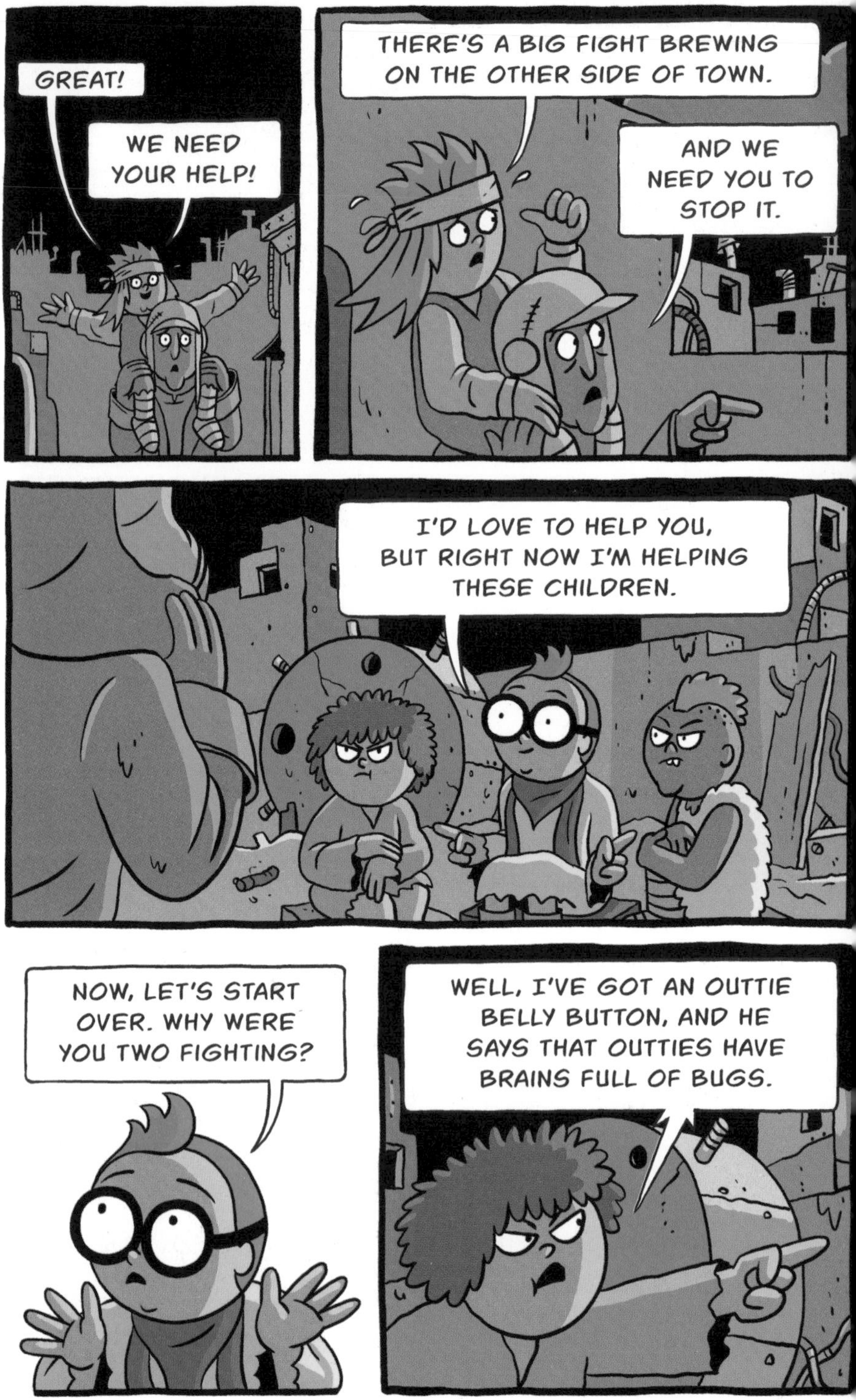
GREAT!
WE NEED YOUR HELP!
THERE'S A BIG FIGHT BREWING ON THE OTHER SIDE OF TOWN.
AND WE NEED YOU TO STOP IT.
I'D LOVE TO HELP YOU, BUT RIGHT NOW I'M HELPING THESE CHILDREN.
NOW, LET'S START OVER. WHY WERE YOU TWO FIGHTING?
WELL, I'VE GOT AN OUTTIE BELLY BUTTON, AND HE SAYS THAT OUTTIES HAVE BRAINS FULL OF BUGS.

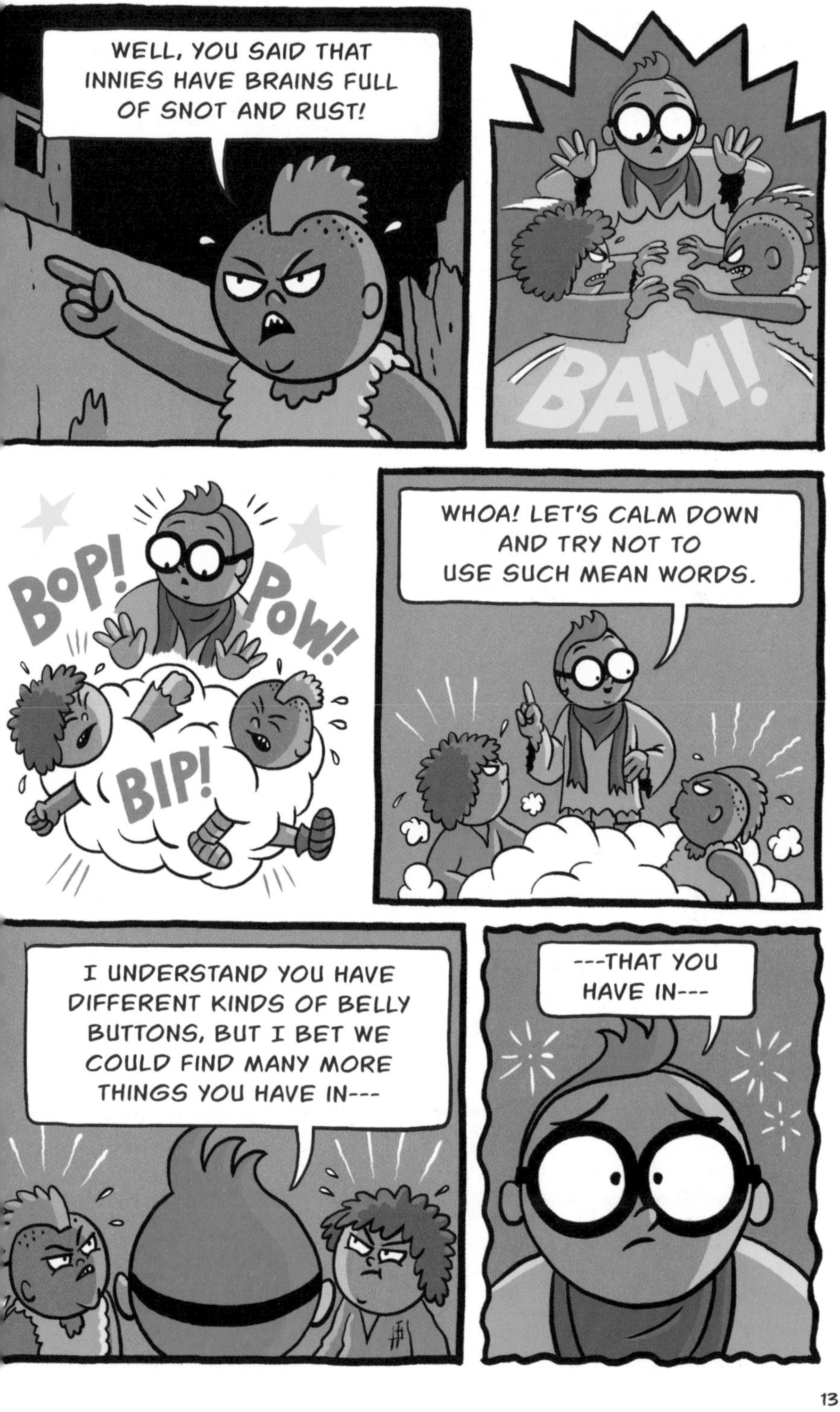
WELL, YOU SAID THAT INNIES HAVE BRAINS FULL OF SNOT AND RUST!
BAM!
BOP!
POW!
BIP!
WHOA! LET'S CALM DOWN AND TRY NOT TO USE SUCH MEAN WORDS.
I UNDERSTAND YOU HAVE DIFFERENT KINDS OF BELLY BUTTONS, BUT I BET WE COULD FIND MANY MORE THINGS YOU HAVE IN---
---THAT YOU HAVE IN---

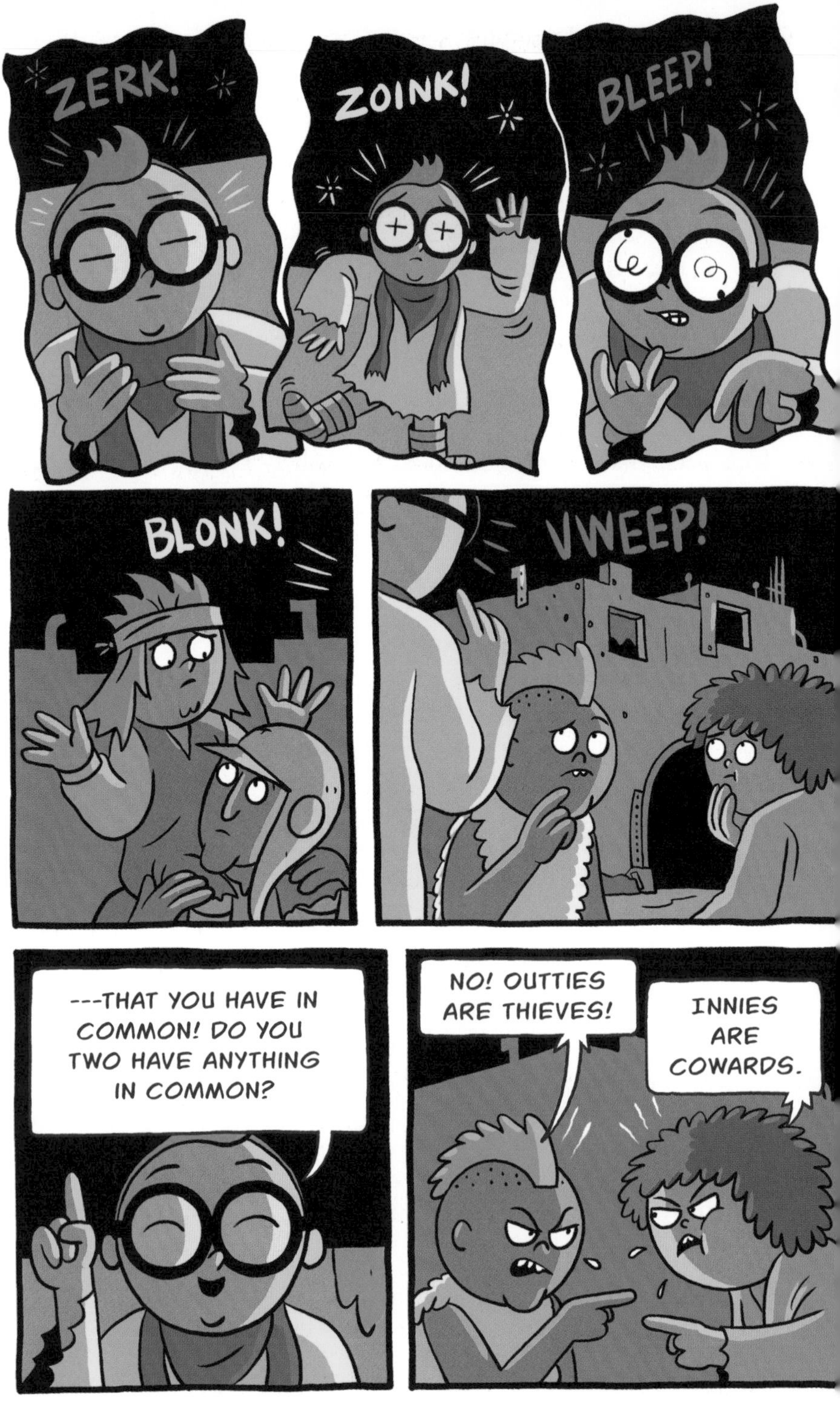
ZERK!
ZOINK!
BLEEP!
BLONK!
VWEEP!
---THAT YOU HAVE IN COMMON! DO YOU TWO HAVE ANYTHING IN COMMON?
NO! OUTTIES ARE THIEVES!
INNIES ARE COWARDS.

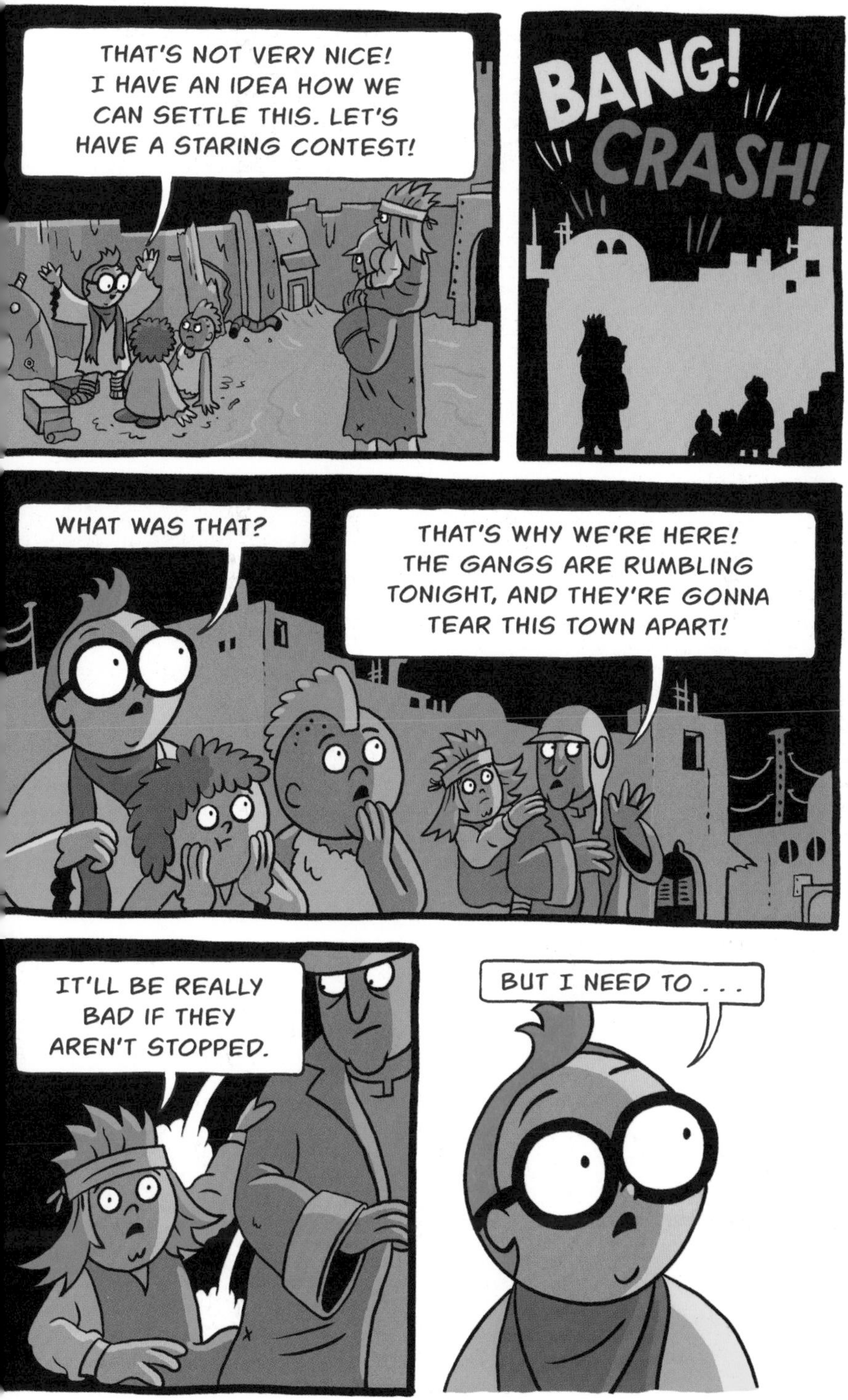
THAT'S NOT VERY NICE! I HAVE AN IDEA HOW WE CAN SETTLE THIS. LET'S HAVE A STARING CONTEST!
BANG!
CRASH!
WHAT WAS THAT?
THAT'S WHY WE'RE HERE! THE GANGS ARE RUMBLING TONIGHT, AND THEY'RE GONNA TEAR THIS TOWN APART!
IT'LL BE REALLY BAD IF THEY AREN'T STOPPED.
BUT I NEED TO . . .

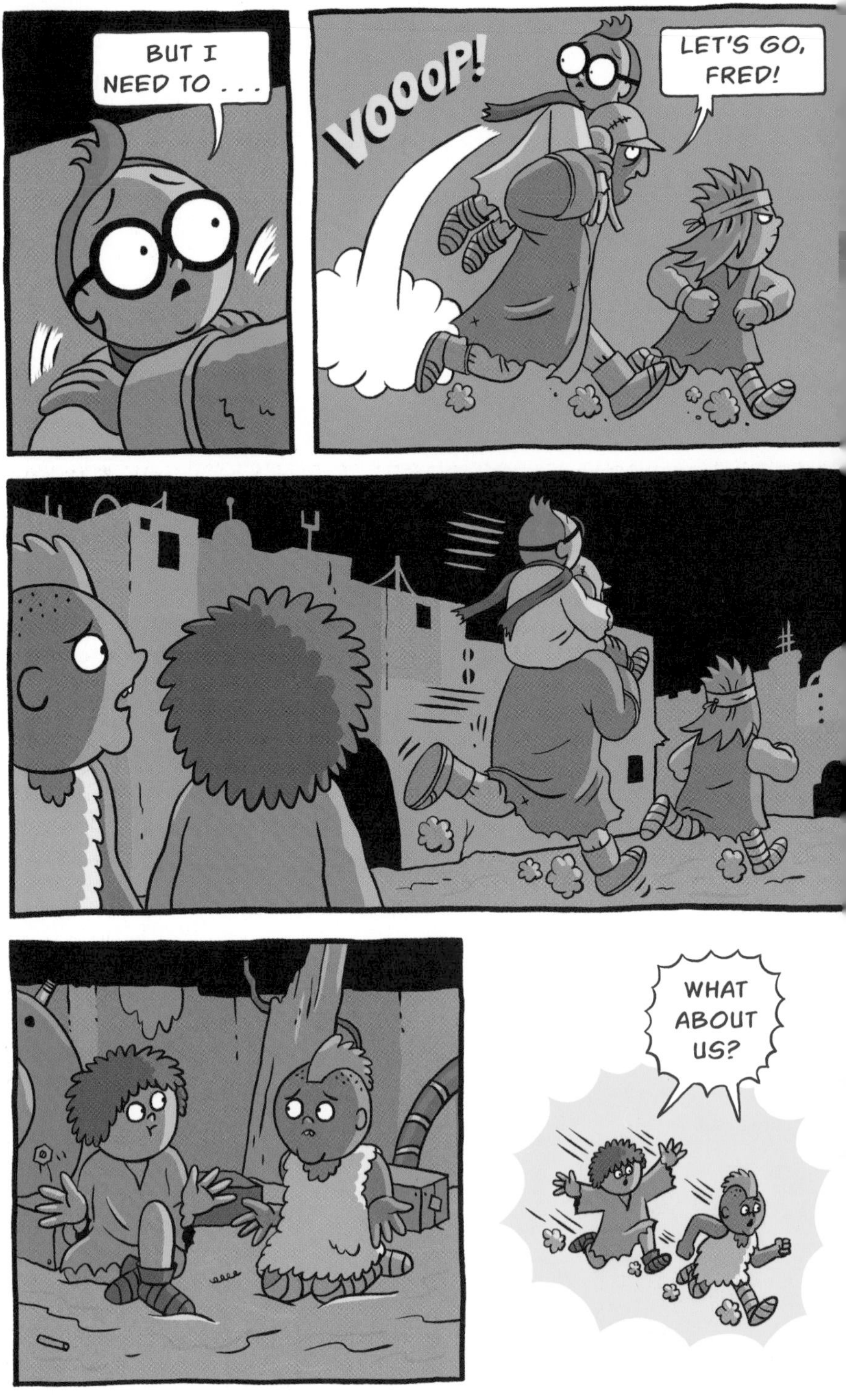
BUT I NEED TO . . .
VOOOP!
LET'S GO, FRED!
WHAT ABOUT US?

CHAPTER 2

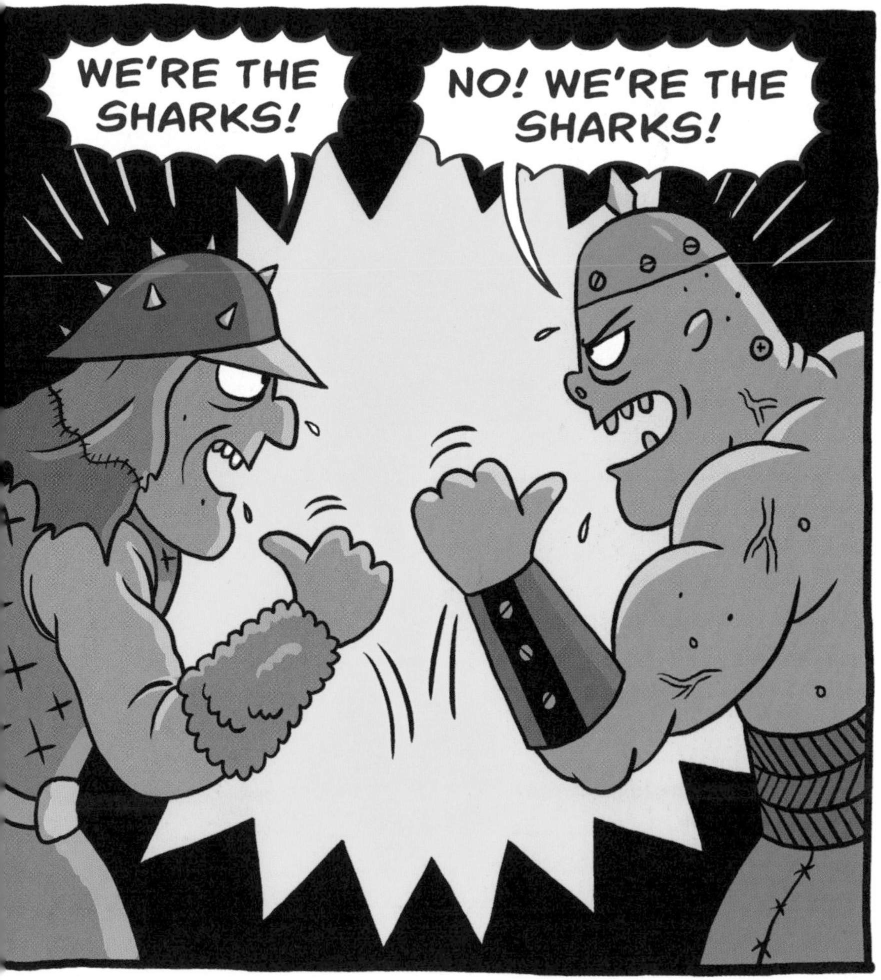
WE'RE THE SHARKS!
NO! WE'RE THE SHARKS!

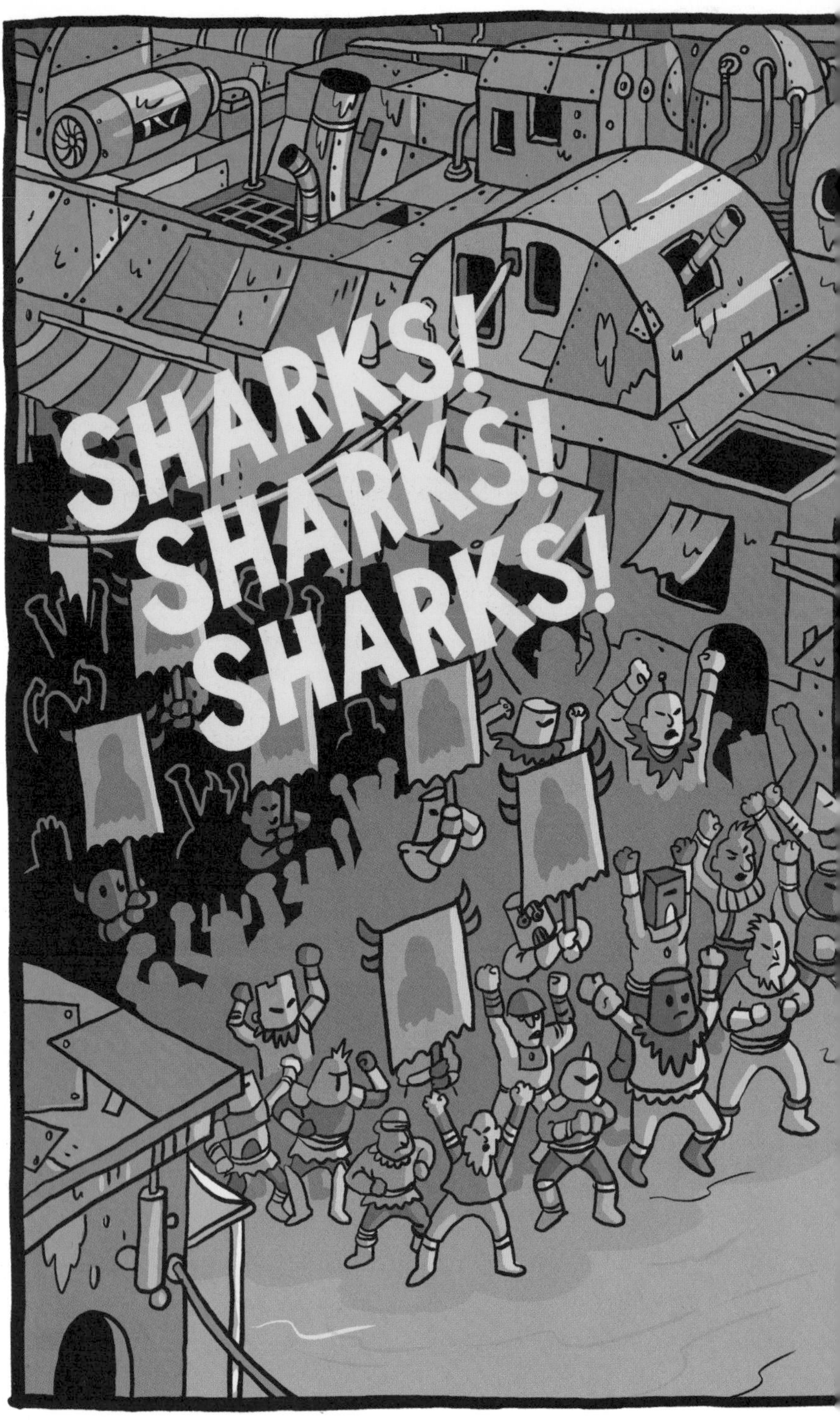
SHARKS!
SHARKS!
SHARKS!

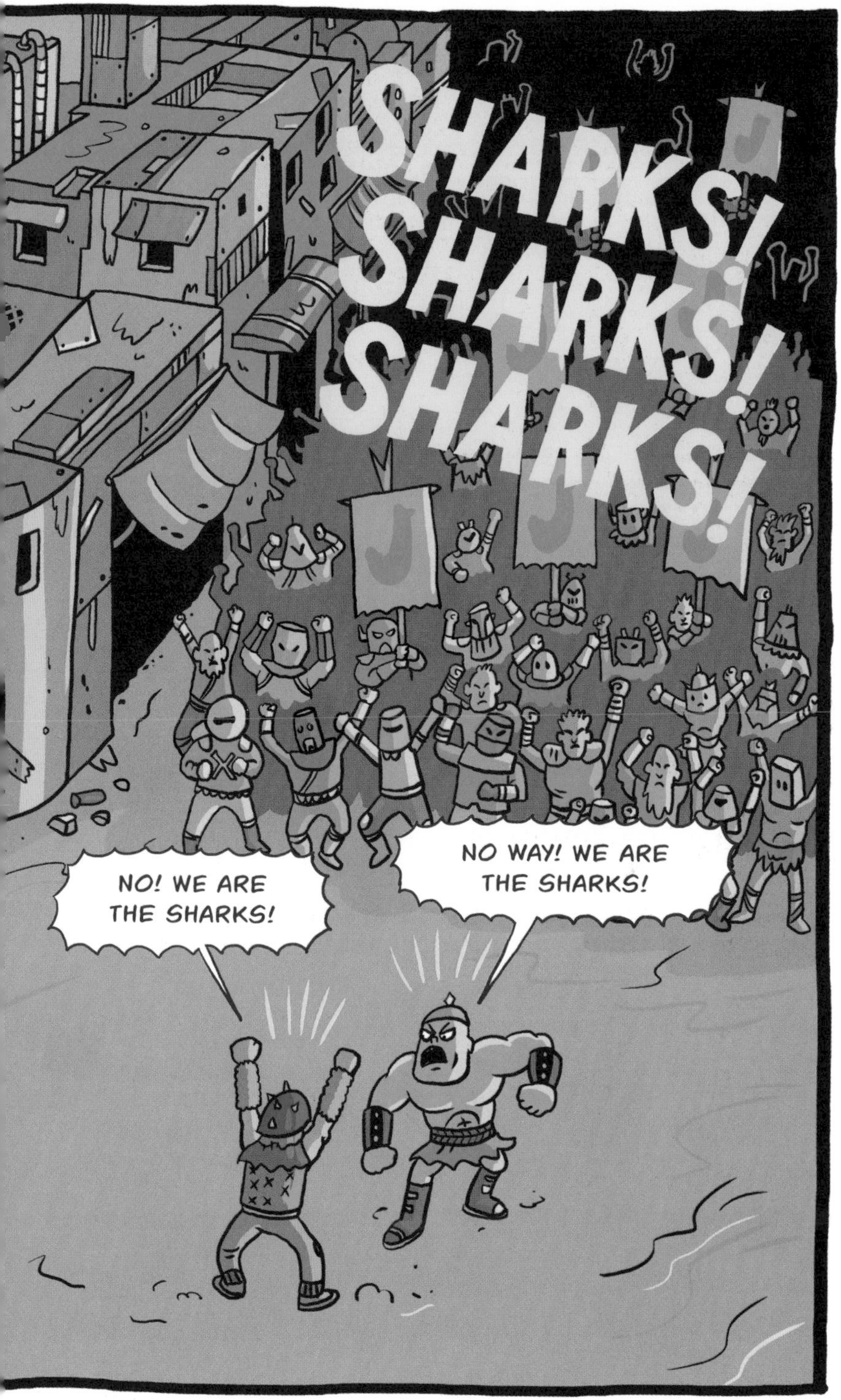
SHARKS! SHARKS! SHARKS!
NO! WE ARE THE SHARKS!
NO WAY! WE ARE THE SHARKS!

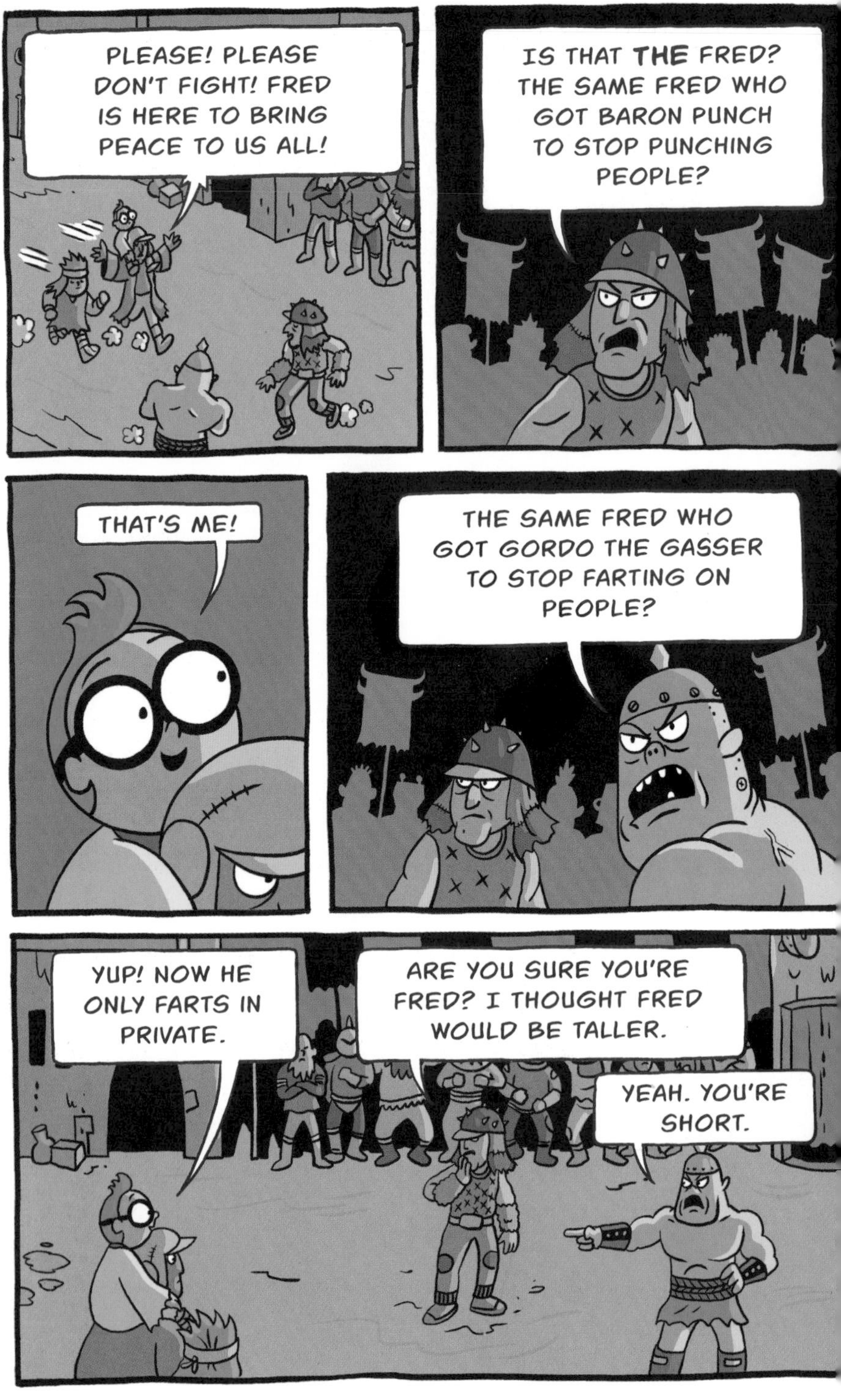
PLEASE! PLEASE DON'T FIGHT! FRED IS HERE TO BRING PEACE TO US ALL!
IS THAT **THE** FRED? THE SAME FRED WHO GOT BARON PUNCH TO STOP PUNCHING PEOPLE?
THAT'S ME!
THE SAME FRED WHO GOT GORDO THE GASSER TO STOP FARTING ON PEOPLE?
YUP! NOW HE ONLY FARTS IN PRIVATE.
ARE YOU SURE YOU'RE FRED? I THOUGHT FRED WOULD BE TALLER.
YEAH. YOU'RE SHORT.

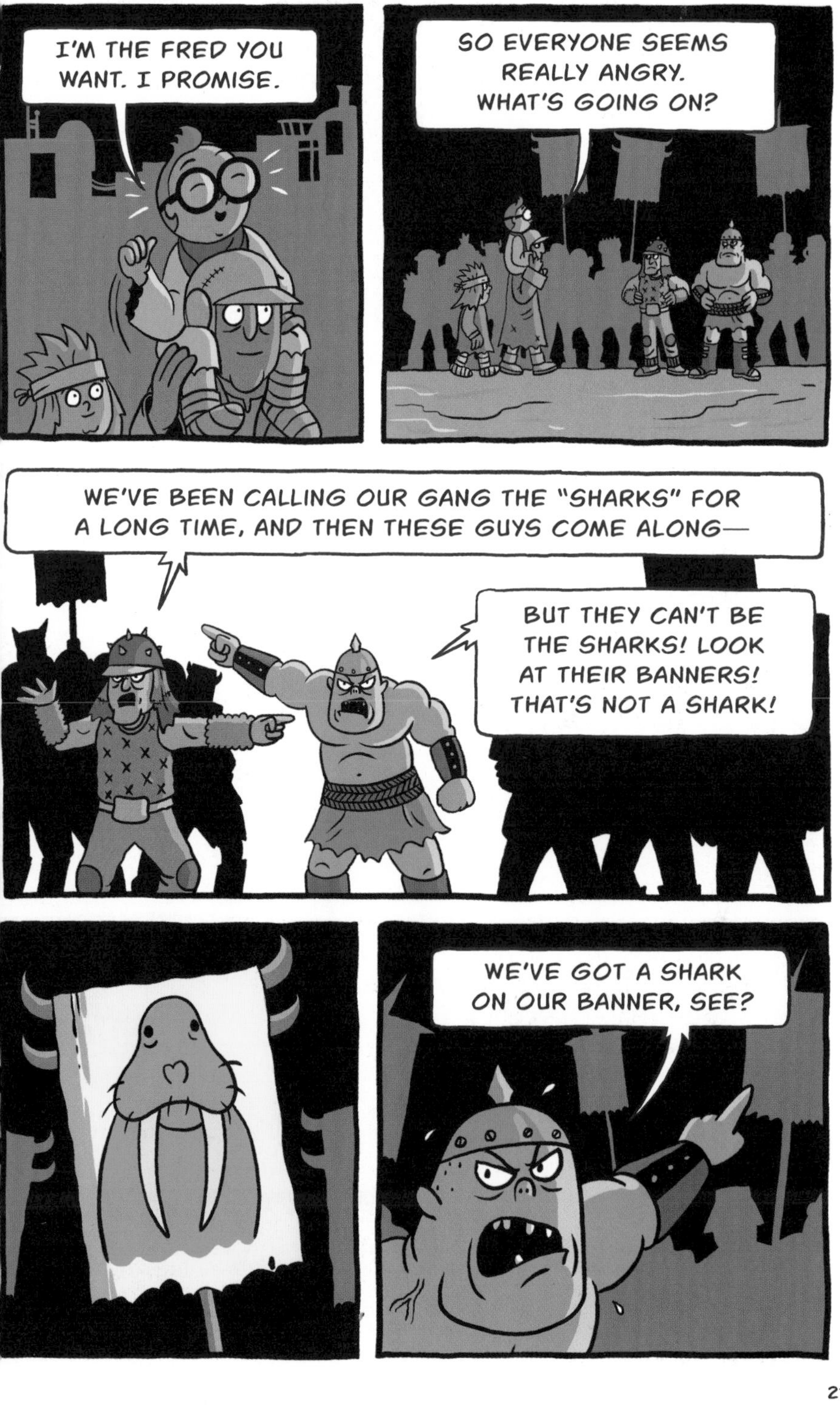
I'M THE FRED YOU WANT. I PROMISE.
SO EVERYONE SEEMS REALLY ANGRY. WHAT'S GOING ON?
WE'VE BEEN CALLING OUR GANG THE "SHARKS" FOR A LONG TIME, AND THEN THESE GUYS COME ALONG—
BUT THEY CAN'T BE THE SHARKS! LOOK AT THEIR BANNERS! THAT'S NOT A SHARK!
WE'VE GOT A SHARK ON OUR BANNER, SEE?

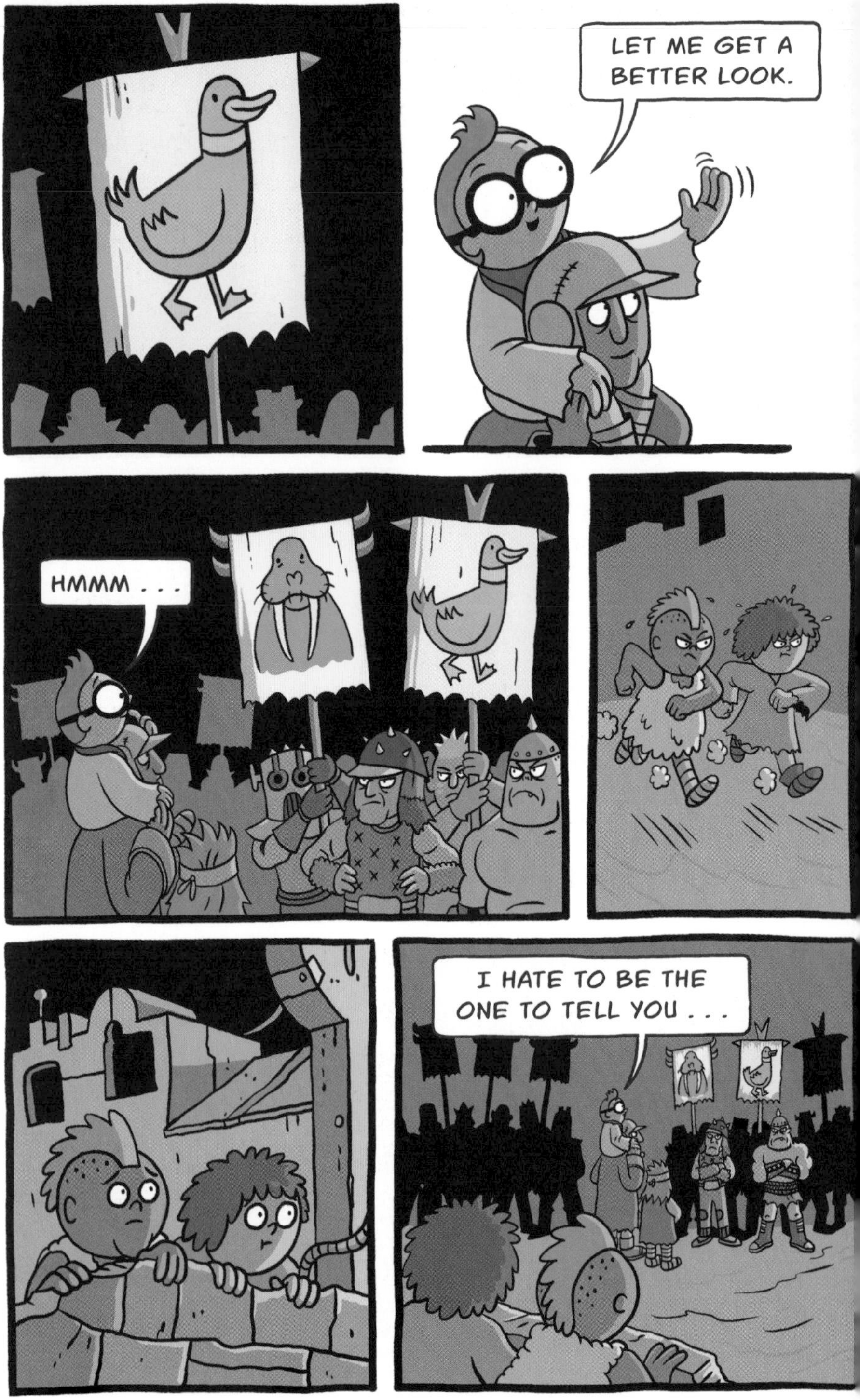
LET ME GET A BETTER LOOK.
HMMM . . .
I HATE TO BE THE ONE TO TELL YOU . . .

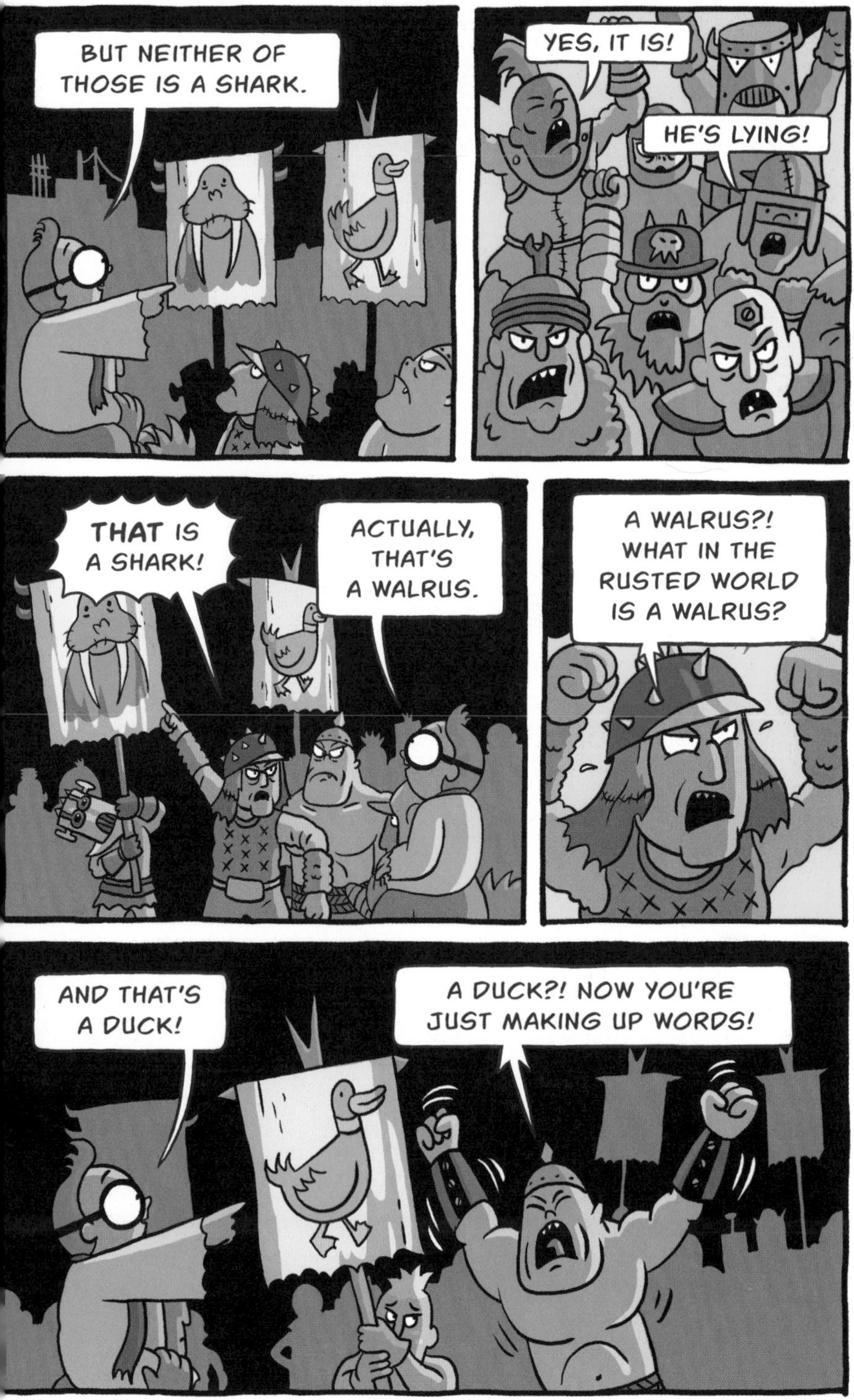
BUT NEITHER OF THOSE IS A SHARK.
YES, IT IS!
HE'S LYING!
THAT IS A SHARK!
ACTUALLY, THAT'S A WALRUS.
A WALRUS?! WHAT IN THE RUSTED WORLD IS A WALRUS?
AND THAT'S A DUCK!
A DUCK?! NOW YOU'RE JUST MAKING UP WORDS!

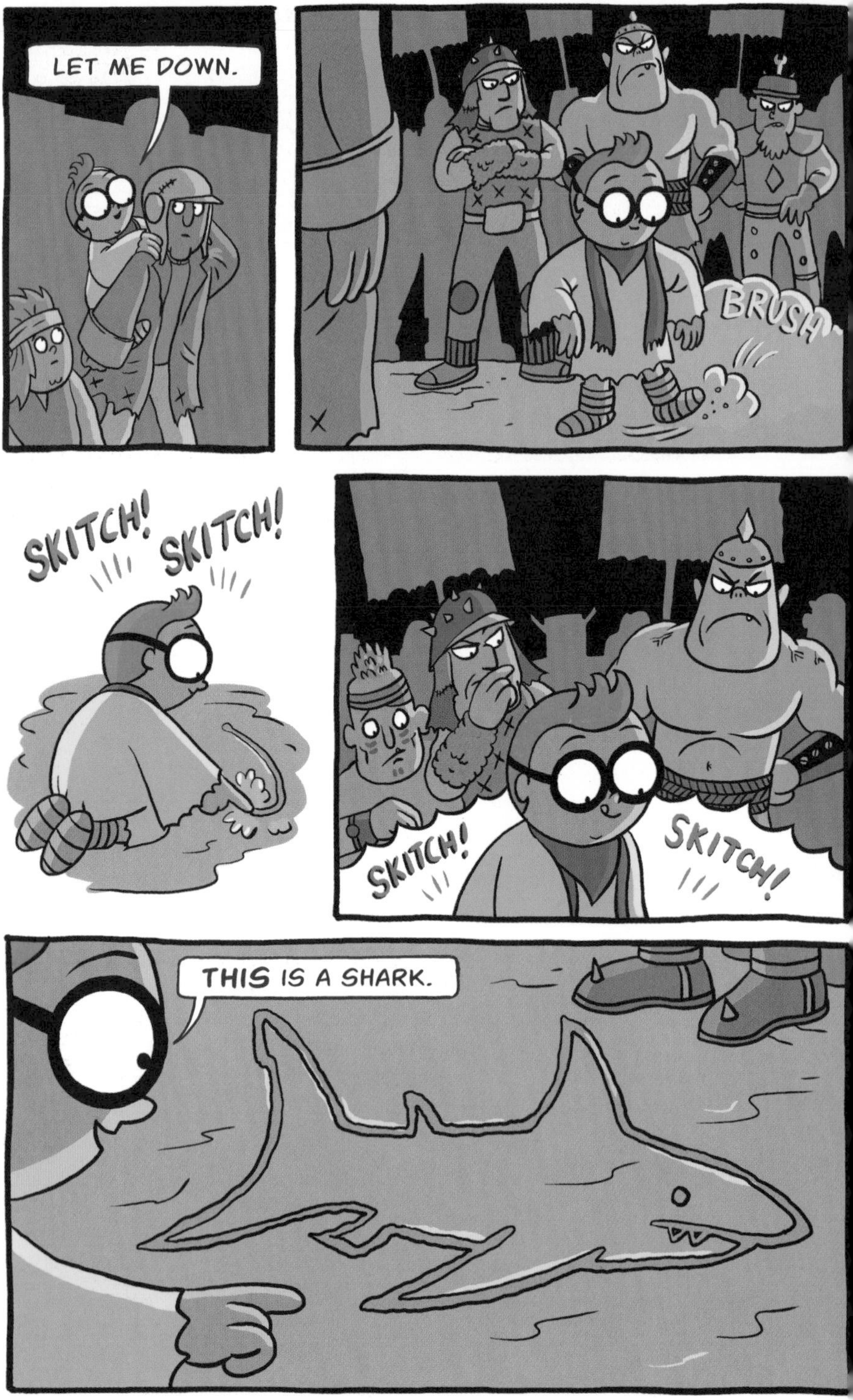
LET ME DOWN.
BRUSH
SKITCH! SKITCH!
SKITCH!
SKITCH!
THIS IS A SHARK.

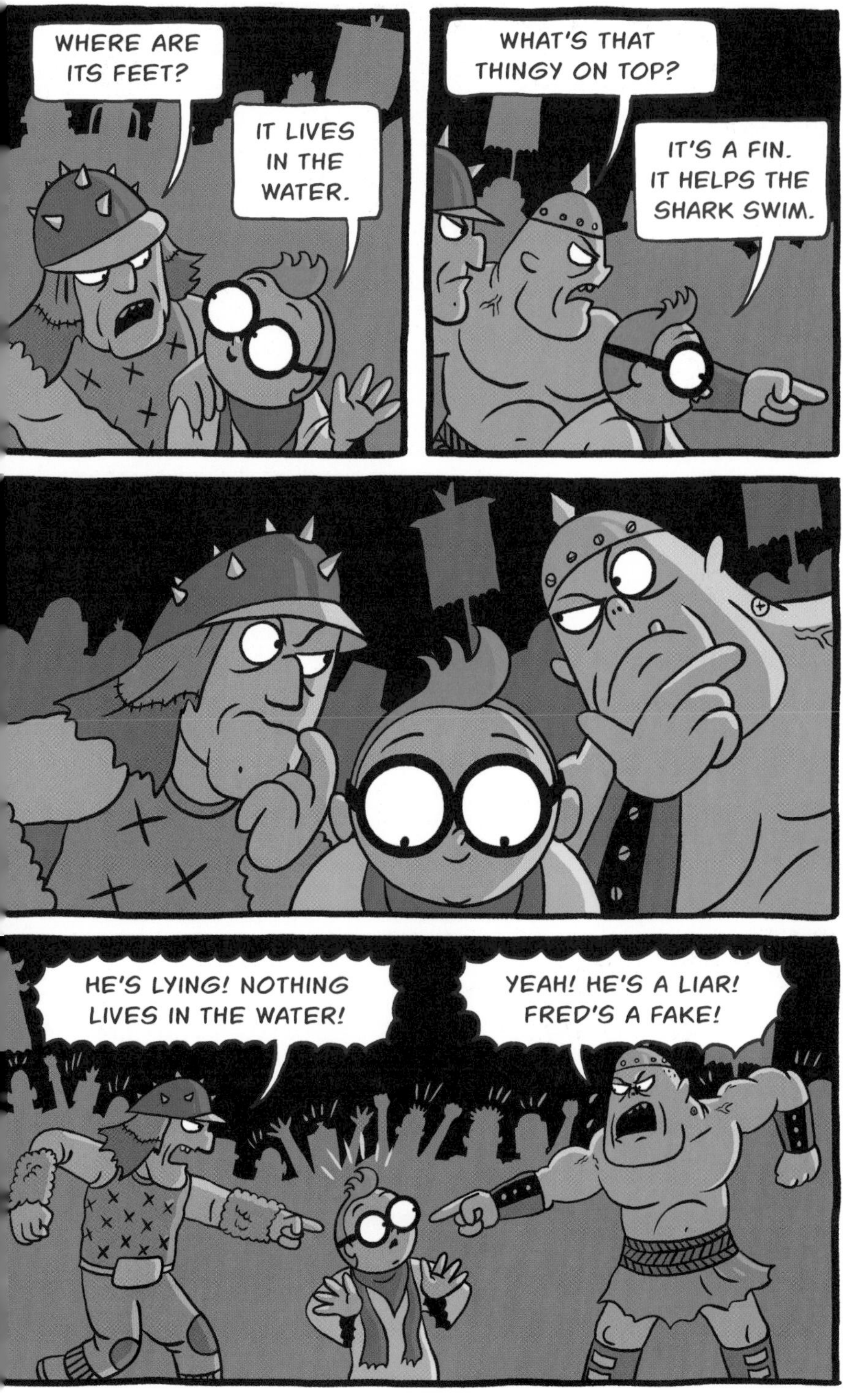
WHERE ARE ITS FEET?
IT LIVES IN THE WATER.
WHAT'S THAT THINGY ON TOP?
IT'S A FIN. IT HELPS THE SHARK SWIM.
HE'S LYING! NOTHING LIVES IN THE WATER!
YEAH! HE'S A LIAR! FRED'S A FAKE!

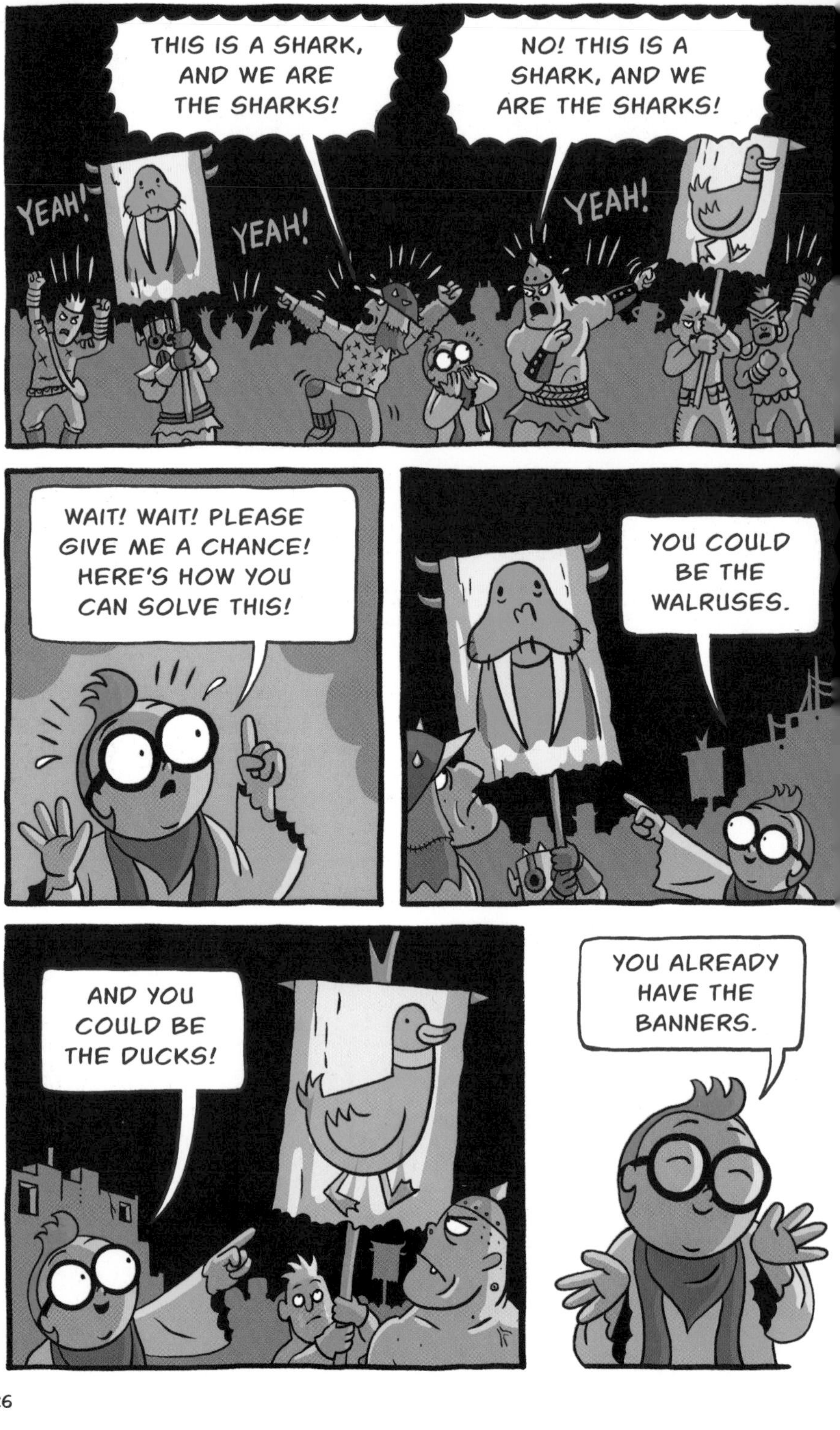
THIS IS A SHARK, AND WE ARE THE SHARKS!
YEAH!
YEAH!
NO! THIS IS A SHARK, AND WE ARE THE SHARKS!
YEAH!
WAIT! WAIT! PLEASE GIVE ME A CHANCE! HERE'S HOW YOU CAN SOLVE THIS!
YOU COULD BE THE WALRUSES.
AND YOU COULD BE THE DUCKS!
YOU ALREADY HAVE THE BANNERS.

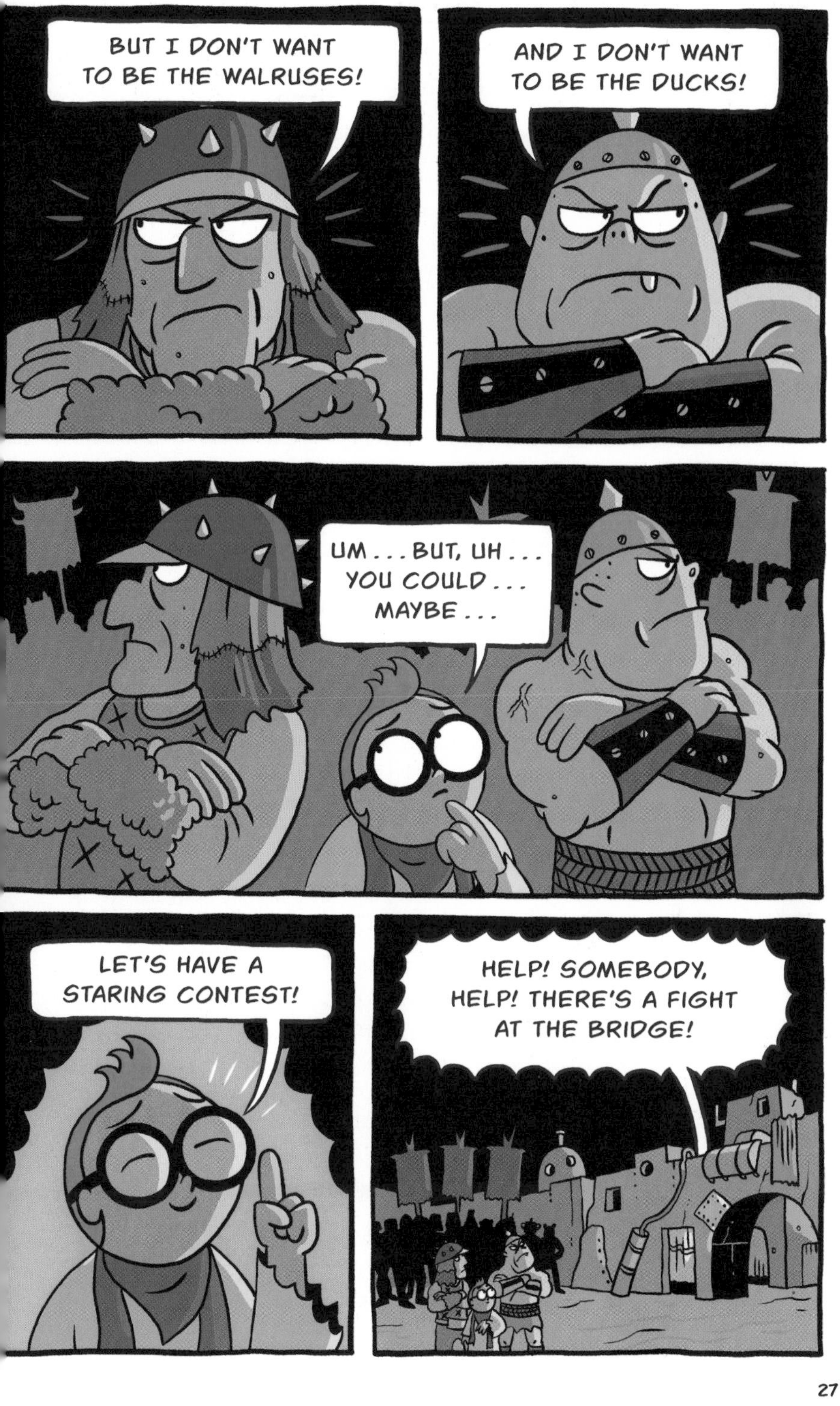
BUT I DON'T WANT TO BE THE WALRUSES!
AND I DON'T WANT TO BE THE DUCKS!
UM . . . BUT, UH . . . YOU COULD . . . MAYBE . . .
LET'S HAVE A STARING CONTEST!
HELP! SOMEBODY, HELP! THERE'S A FIGHT AT THE BRIDGE!

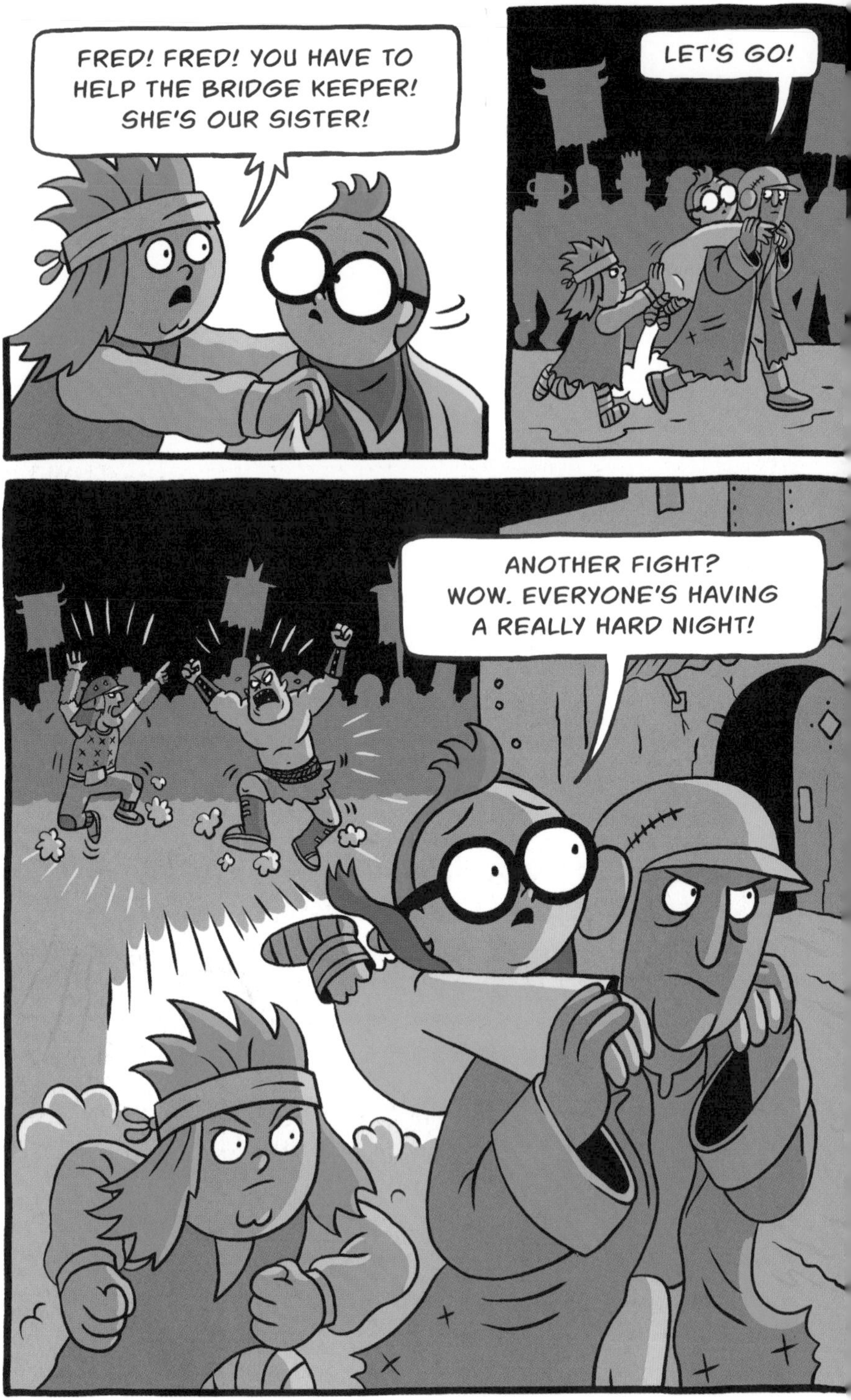
FRED! FRED! YOU HAVE TO HELP THE BRIDGE KEEPER! SHE'S OUR SISTER!
LET'S GO!
ANOTHER FIGHT? WOW. EVERYONE'S HAVING A REALLY HARD NIGHT!

CHAPTER 3

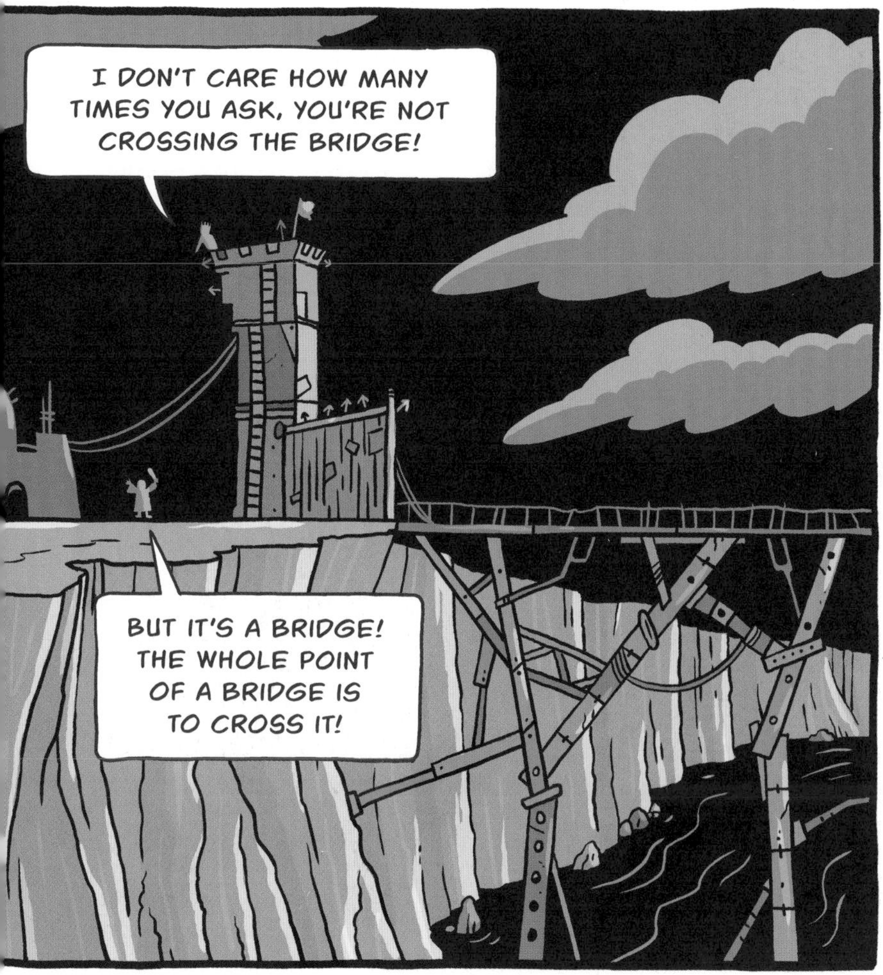
I DON'T CARE HOW MANY TIMES YOU ASK, YOU'RE NOT CROSSING THE BRIDGE!
BUT IT'S A BRIDGE! THE WHOLE POINT OF A BRIDGE IS TO CROSS IT!

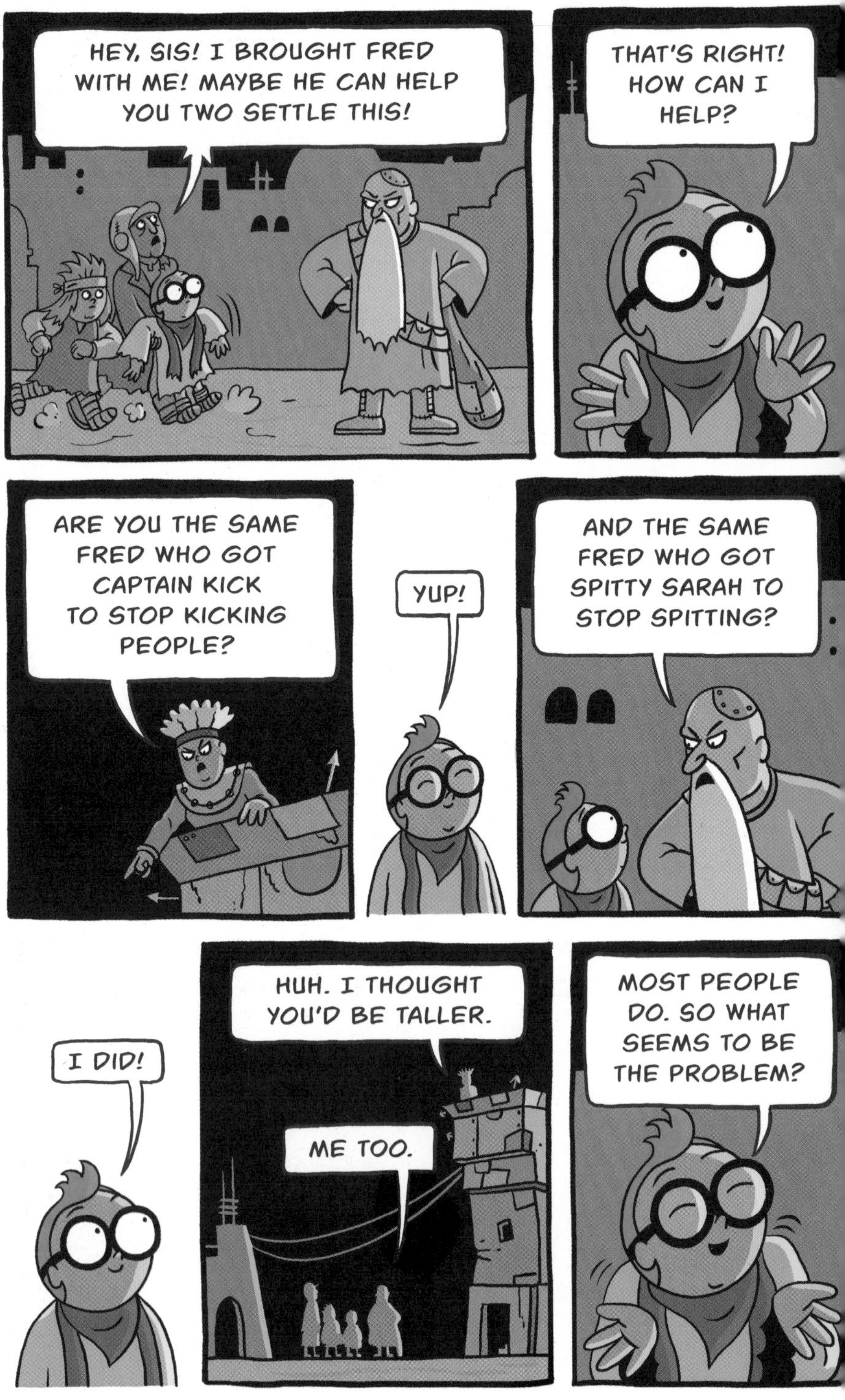
HEY, SIS! I BROUGHT FRED WITH ME! MAYBE HE CAN HELP YOU TWO SETTLE THIS!
THAT'S RIGHT! HOW CAN I HELP?
ARE YOU THE SAME FRED WHO GOT CAPTAIN KICK TO STOP KICKING PEOPLE?
YUP!
AND THE SAME FRED WHO GOT SPITTY SARAH TO STOP SPITTING?
I DID!
HUH. I THOUGHT YOU'D BE TALLER.
ME TOO.
MOST PEOPLE DO. SO WHAT SEEMS TO BE THE PROBLEM?

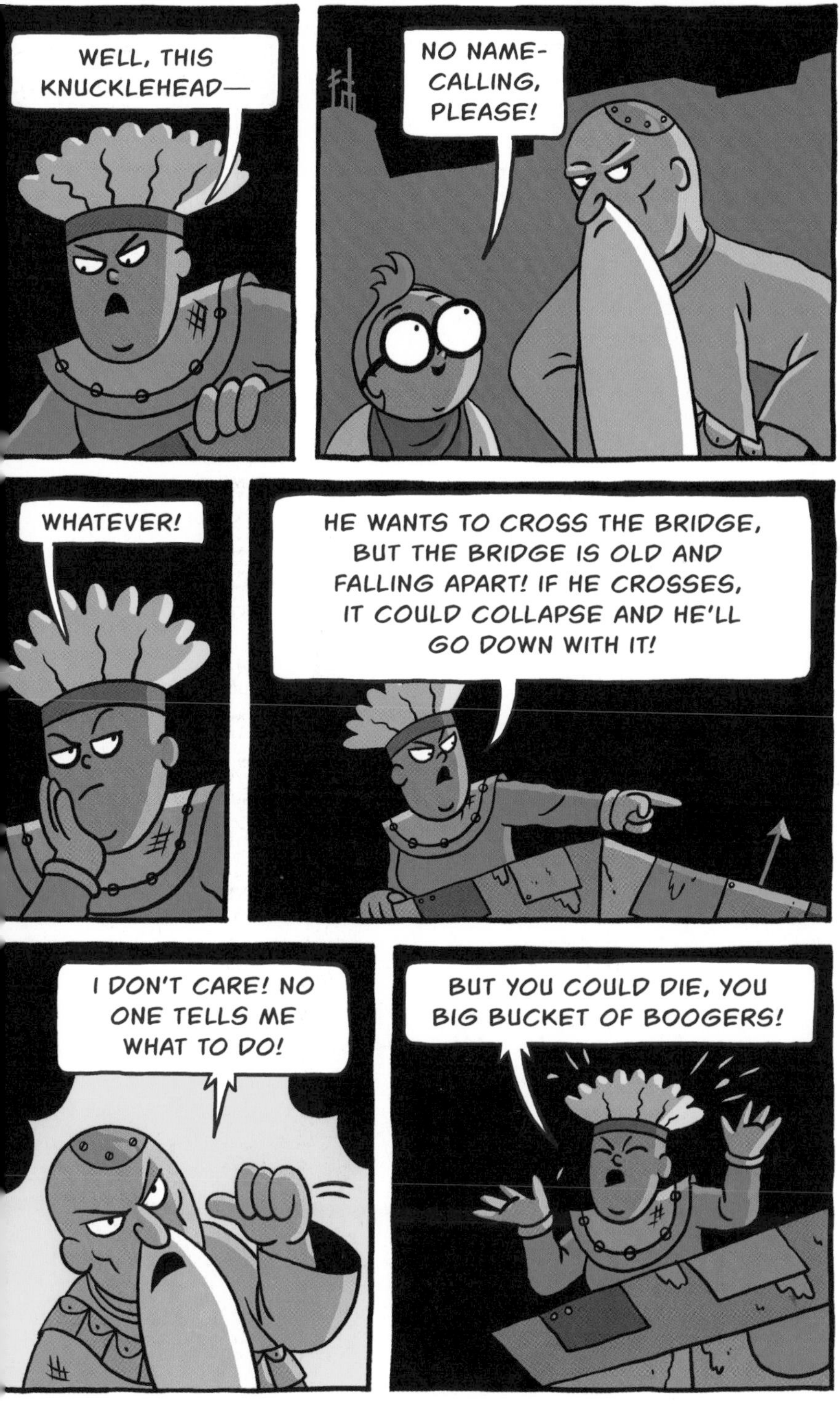
WELL, THIS KNUCKLEHEAD—
NO NAME-CALLING, PLEASE!
WHATEVER!
HE WANTS TO CROSS THE BRIDGE, BUT THE BRIDGE IS OLD AND FALLING APART! IF HE CROSSES, IT COULD COLLAPSE AND HE'LL GO DOWN WITH IT!
I DON'T CARE! NO ONE TELLS ME WHAT TO DO!
BUT YOU COULD DIE, YOU BIG BUCKET OF BOOGERS!

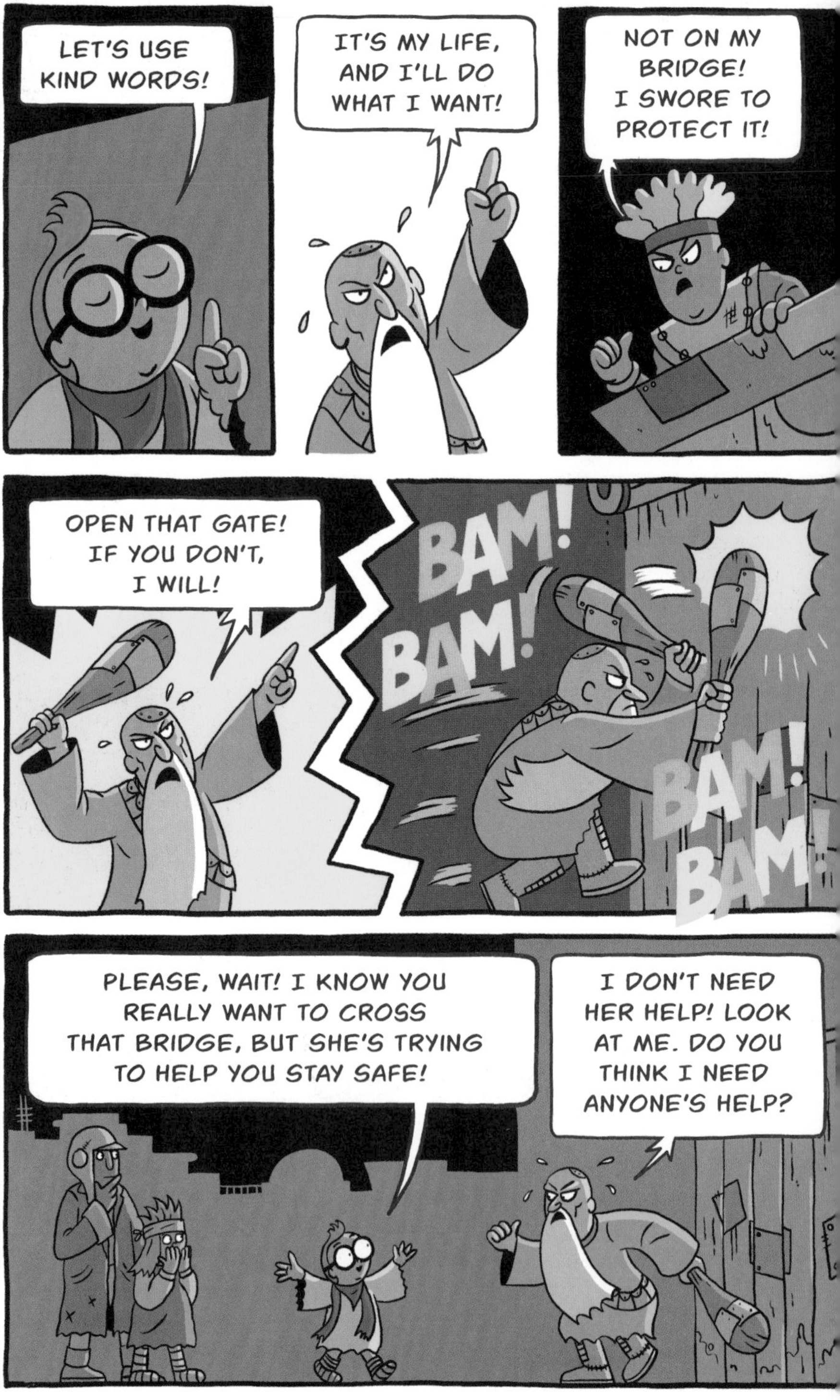
LET'S USE KIND WORDS!
IT'S MY LIFE, AND I'LL DO WHAT I WANT!
NOT ON MY BRIDGE! I SWORE TO PROTECT IT!
OPEN THAT GATE! IF YOU DON'T, I WILL!
BAM! BAM!
BAM! BAM!
PLEASE, WAIT! I KNOW YOU REALLY WANT TO CROSS THAT BRIDGE, BUT SHE'S TRYING TO HELP YOU STAY SAFE!
I DON'T NEED HER HELP! LOOK AT ME. DO YOU THINK I NEED ANYONE'S HELP?

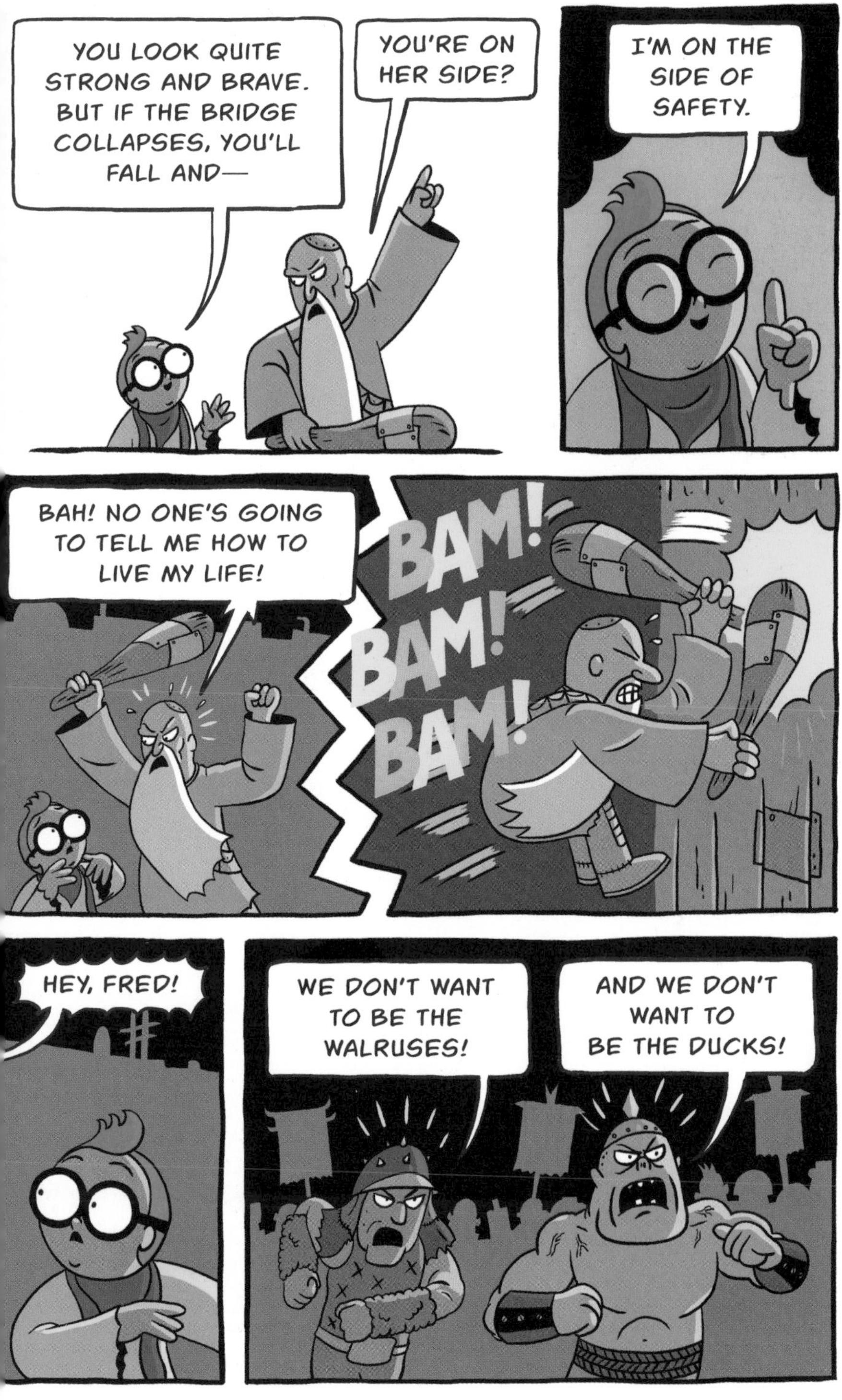
YOU LOOK QUITE STRONG AND BRAVE. BUT IF THE BRIDGE COLLAPSES, YOU'LL FALL AND—
YOU'RE ON HER SIDE?
I'M ON THE SIDE OF SAFETY.
BAH! NO ONE'S GOING TO TELL ME HOW TO LIVE MY LIFE!
BAM! BAM! BAM!
HEY, FRED!
WE DON'T WANT TO BE THE WALRUSES!
AND WE DON'T WANT TO BE THE DUCKS!

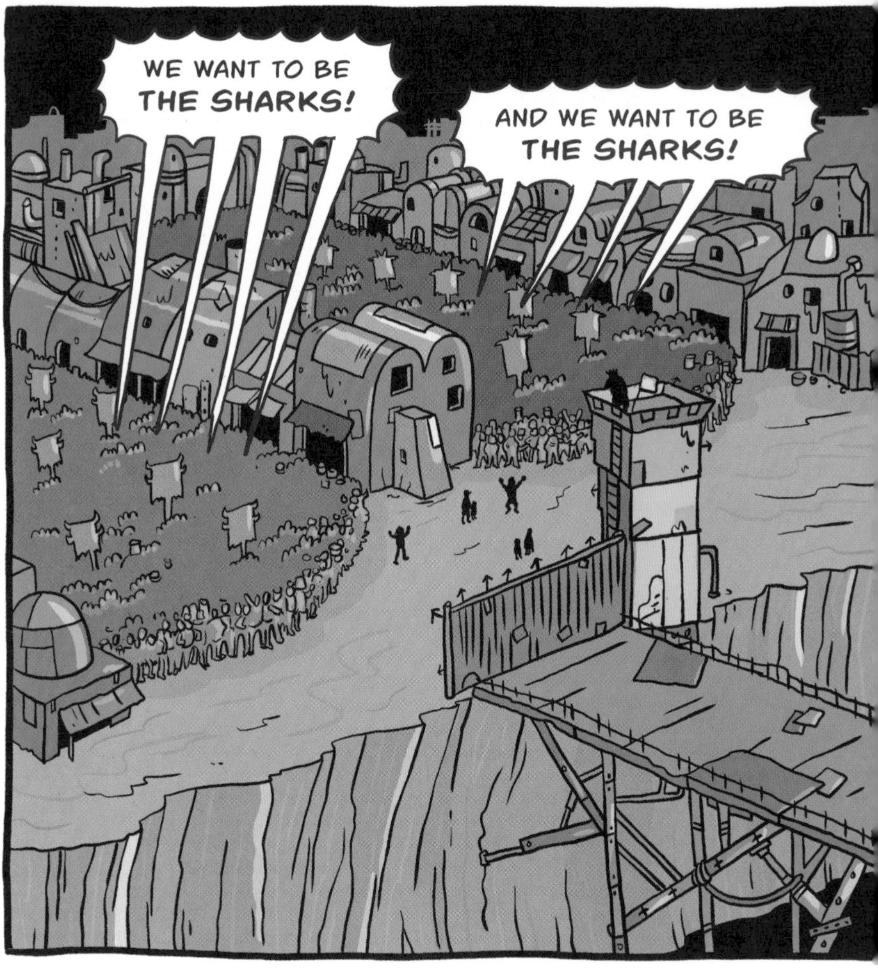
WE WANT TO BE THE SHARKS!
AND WE WANT TO BE THE SHARKS!

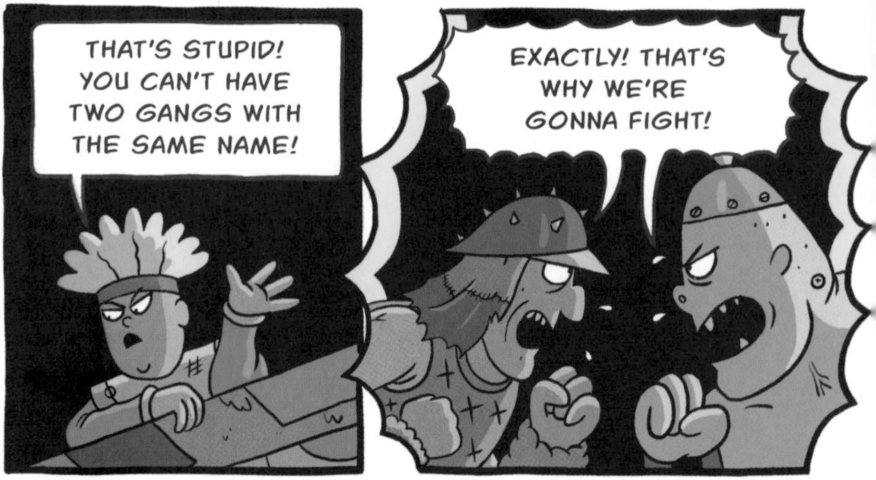
THAT'S STUPID! YOU CAN'T HAVE TWO GANGS WITH THE SAME NAME!
EXACTLY! THAT'S WHY WE'RE GONNA FIGHT!

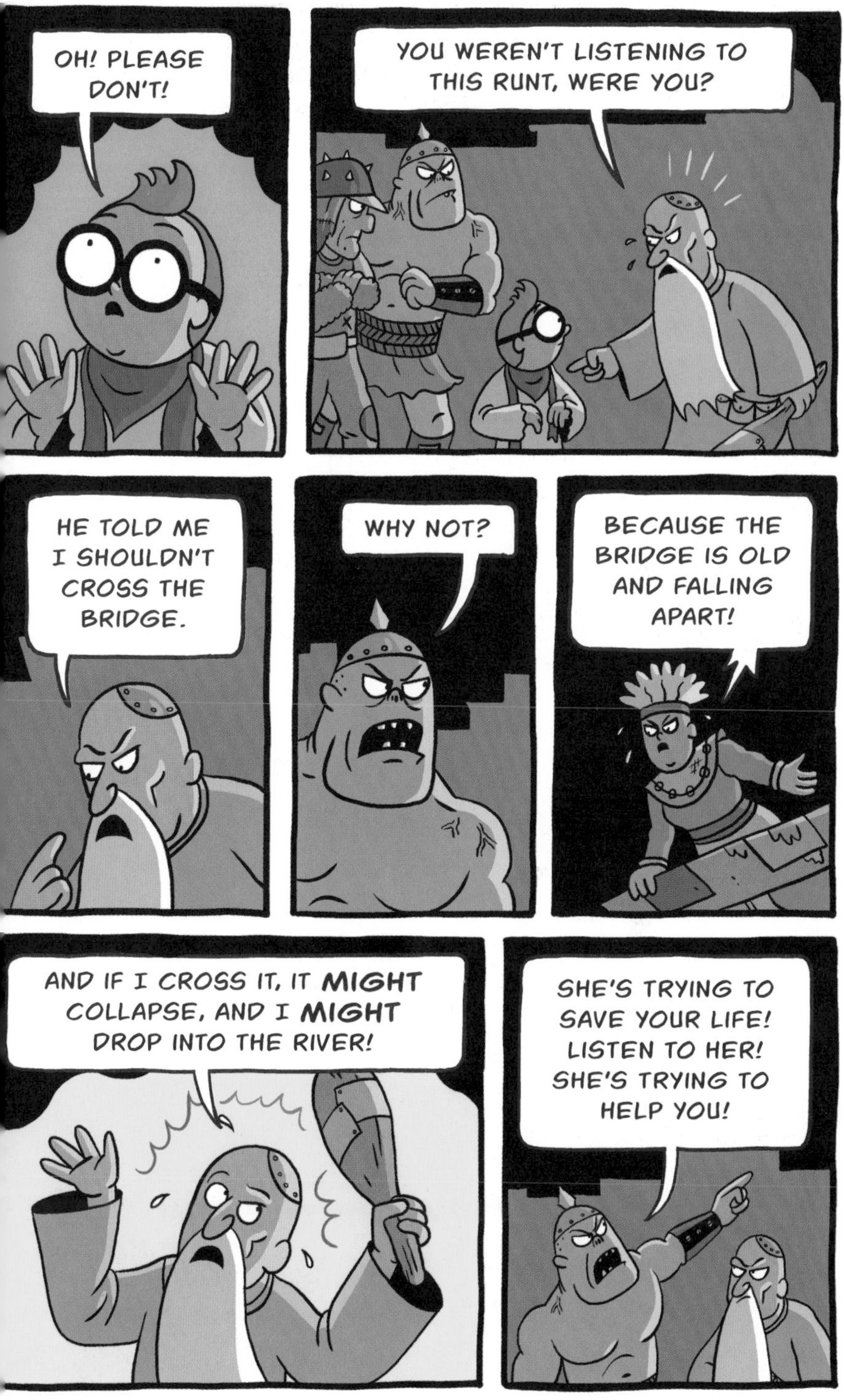
OH! PLEASE DON'T!
YOU WEREN'T LISTENING TO THIS RUNT, WERE YOU?
HE TOLD ME I SHOULDN'T CROSS THE BRIDGE.
WHY NOT?
BECAUSE THE BRIDGE IS OLD AND FALLING APART!
AND IF I CROSS IT, IT **MIGHT** COLLAPSE, AND I **MIGHT** DROP INTO THE RIVER!
SHE'S TRYING TO SAVE YOUR LIFE! LISTEN TO HER! SHE'S TRYING TO HELP YOU!

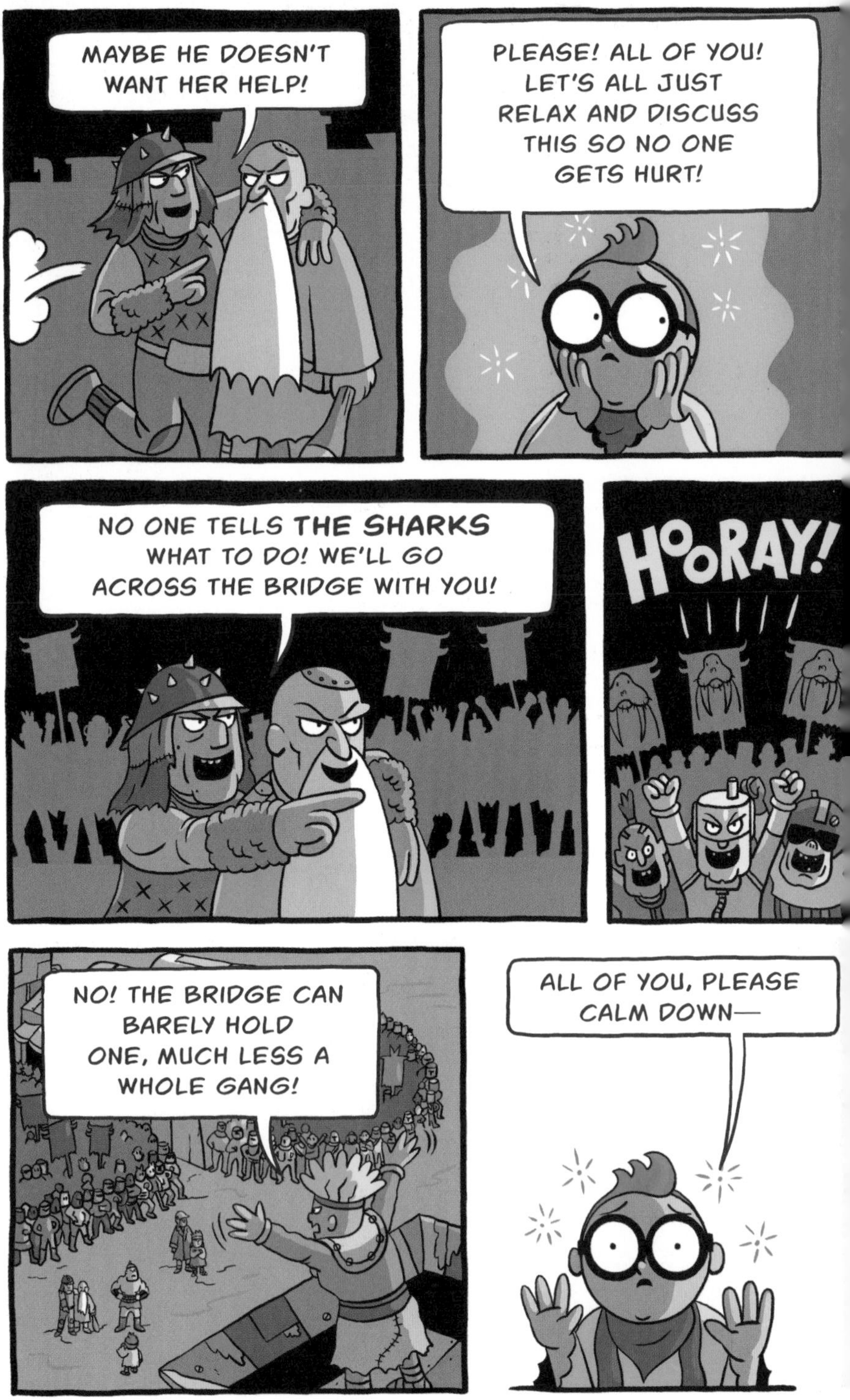
MAYBE HE DOESN'T WANT HER HELP!
PLEASE! ALL OF YOU! LET'S ALL JUST RELAX AND DISCUSS THIS SO NO ONE GETS HURT!
NO ONE TELLS **THE SHARKS** WHAT TO DO! WE'LL GO ACROSS THE BRIDGE WITH YOU!
HOORAY!
NO! THE BRIDGE CAN BARELY HOLD ONE, MUCH LESS A WHOLE GANG!
ALL OF YOU, PLEASE CALM DOWN—

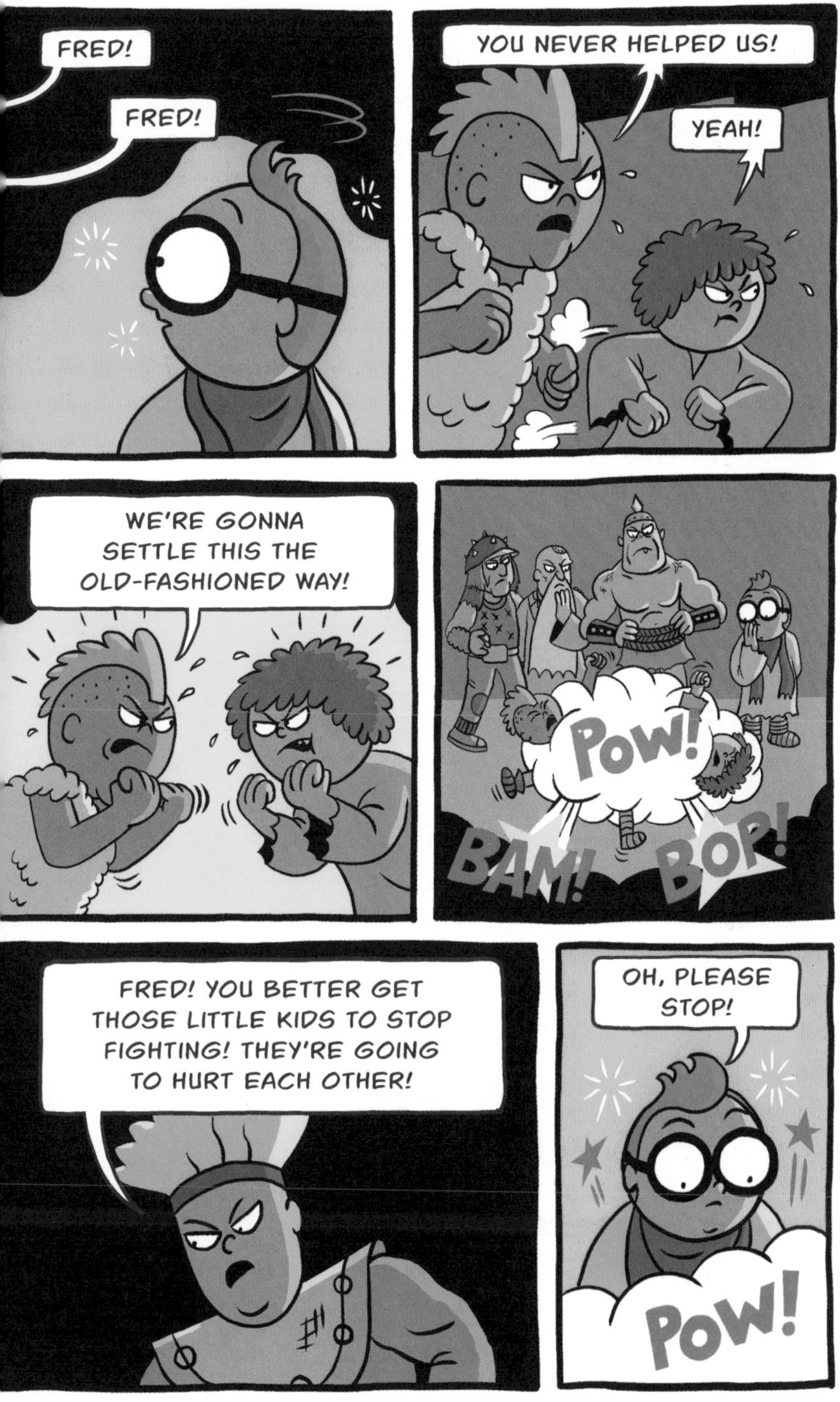
FRED!
FRED!
YOU NEVER HELPED US!
YEAH!
WE'RE GONNA SETTLE THIS THE OLD-FASHIONED WAY!
POW!
BAM!
BOP!
FRED! YOU BETTER GET THOSE LITTLE KIDS TO STOP FIGHTING! THEY'RE GOING TO HURT EACH OTHER!
OH, PLEASE STOP!
POW!

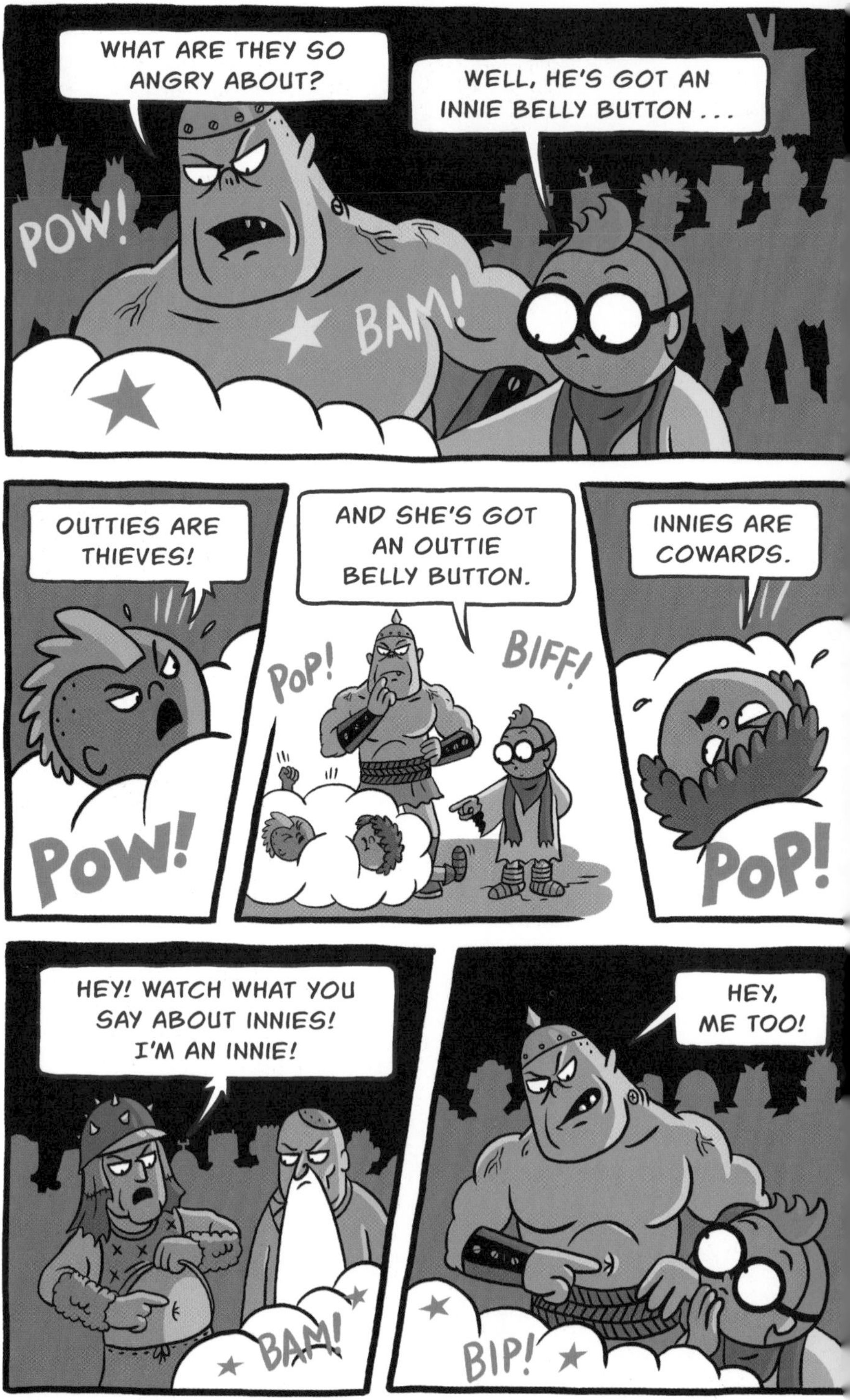
WHAT ARE THEY SO ANGRY ABOUT?
WELL, HE'S GOT AN INNIE BELLY BUTTON . . .
POW!
BAM!
OUTTIES ARE THIEVES!
POW!
AND SHE'S GOT AN OUTTIE BELLY BUTTON.
POP!
BIFF!
INNIES ARE COWARDS.
POP!
HEY! WATCH WHAT YOU SAY ABOUT INNIES! I'M AN INNIE!
BAM!
HEY, ME TOO!
BIP!

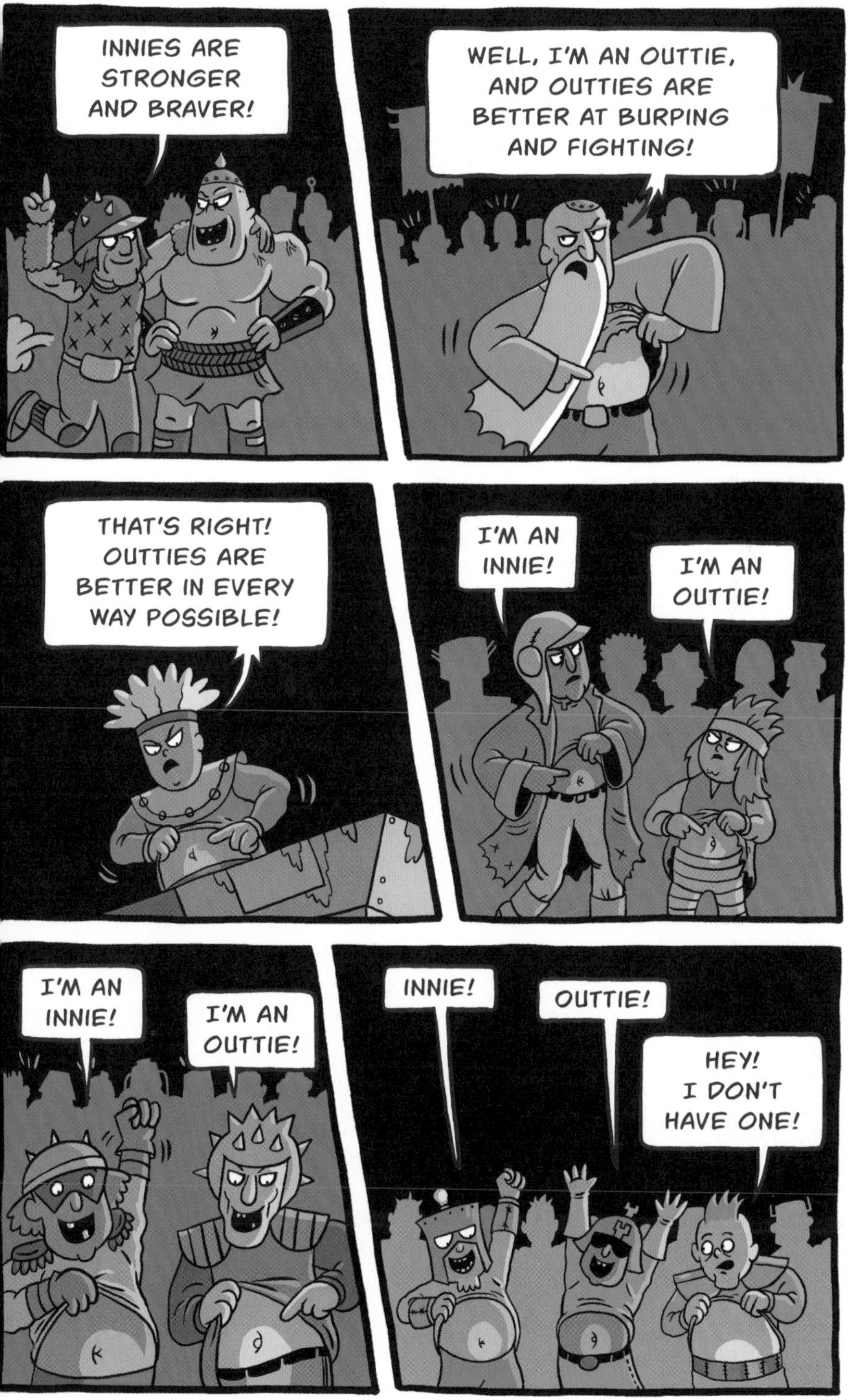
INNIES ARE STRONGER AND BRAVER!
WELL, I'M AN OUTTIE, AND OUTTIES ARE BETTER AT BURPING AND FIGHTING!
THAT'S RIGHT! OUTTIES ARE BETTER IN EVERY WAY POSSIBLE!
I'M AN INNIE!
I'M AN OUTTIE!
I'M AN INNIE!
I'M AN OUTTIE!
INNIE!
OUTTIE!
HEY! I DON'T HAVE ONE!

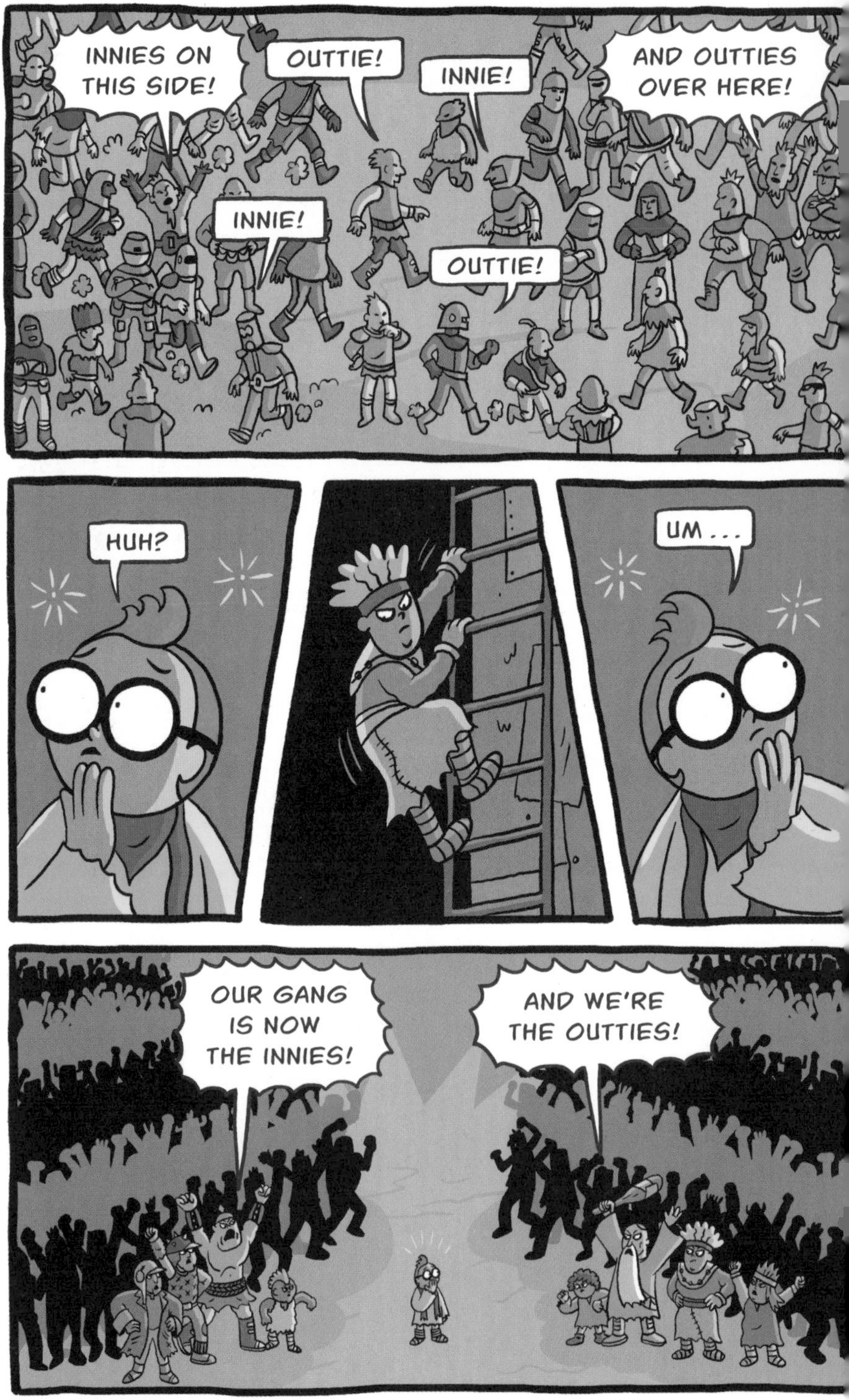
INNIES ON THIS SIDE!
OUTTIE!
INNIE!
AND OUTTIES OVER HERE!
INNIE!
OUTTIE!
HUH?
UM . . .
OUR GANG IS NOW THE INNIES!
AND WE'RE THE OUTTIES!

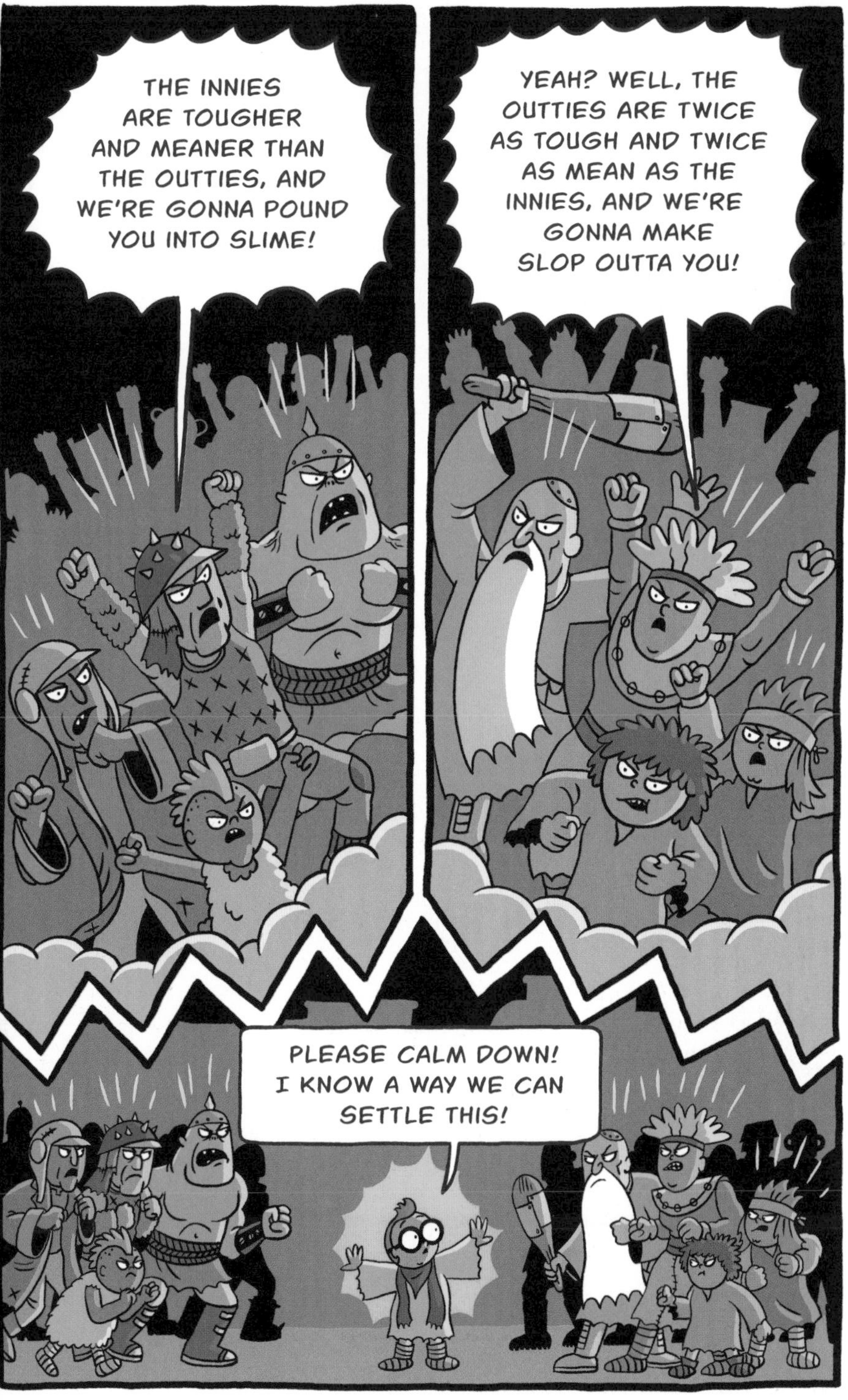

THE INNIES ARE TOUGHER AND MEANER THAN THE OUTTIES, AND WE'RE GONNA POUND YOU INTO SLIME!
YEAH? WELL, THE OUTTIES ARE TWICE AS TOUGH AND TWICE AS MEAN AS THE INNIES, AND WE'RE GONNA MAKE SLOP OUTTA YOU!
PLEASE CALM DOWN! I KNOW A WAY WE CAN SETTLE THIS!

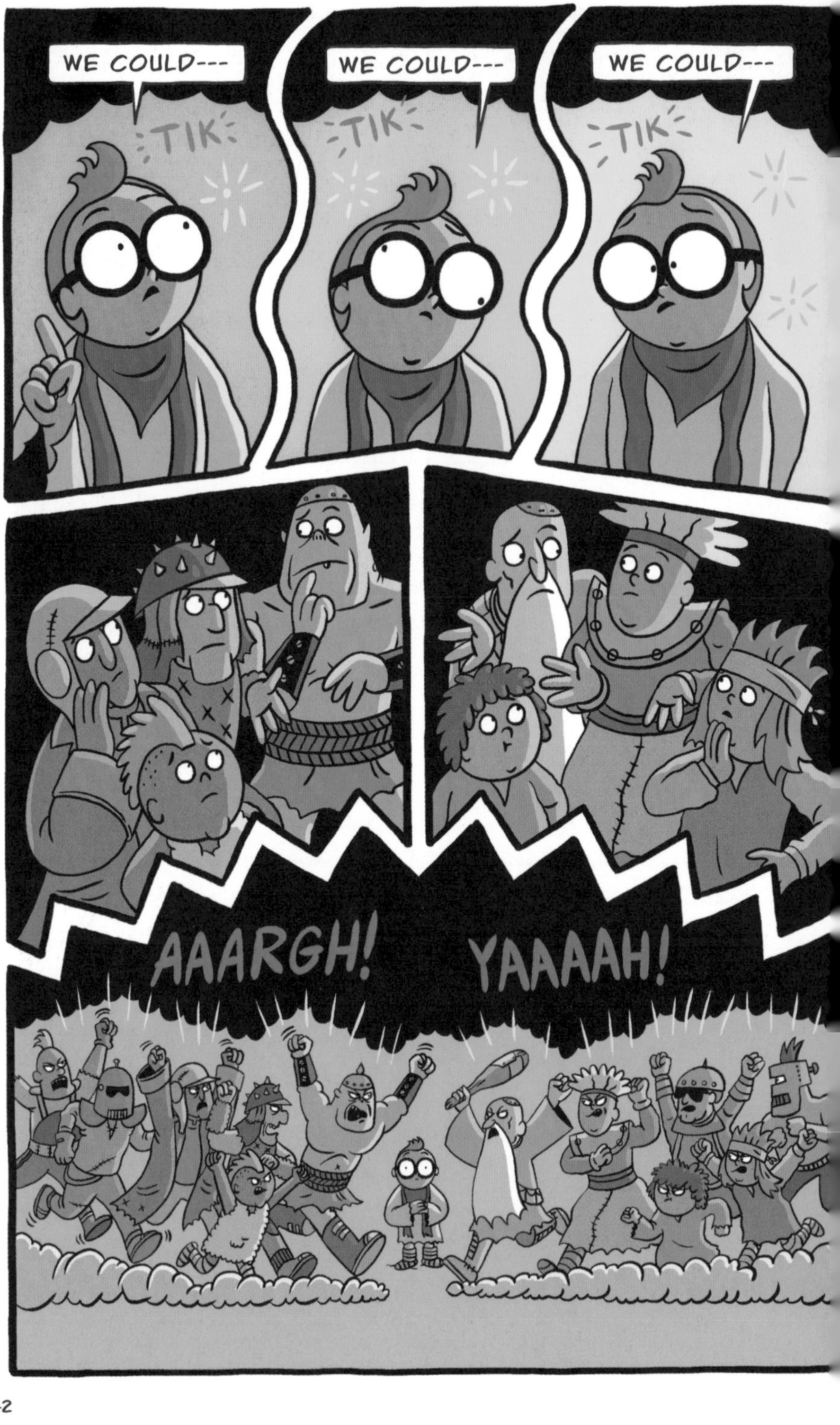
WE COULD---
TIK
WE COULD---
TIK
WE COULD---
TIK
AAARGH!
YAAAAH!

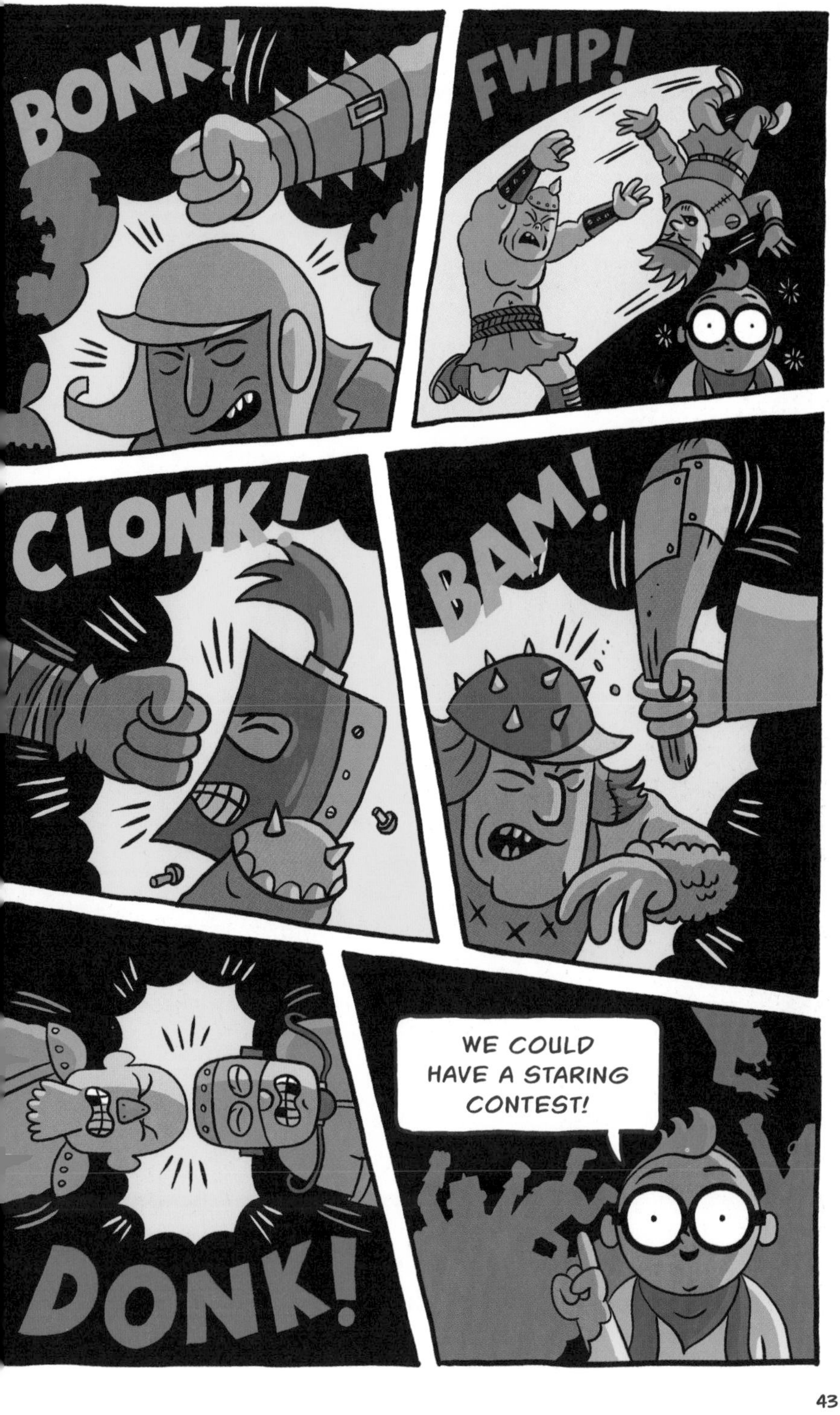
BONK!
FWIP!
CLONK!
BAM!
DONK!
WE COULD HAVE A STARING CONTEST!

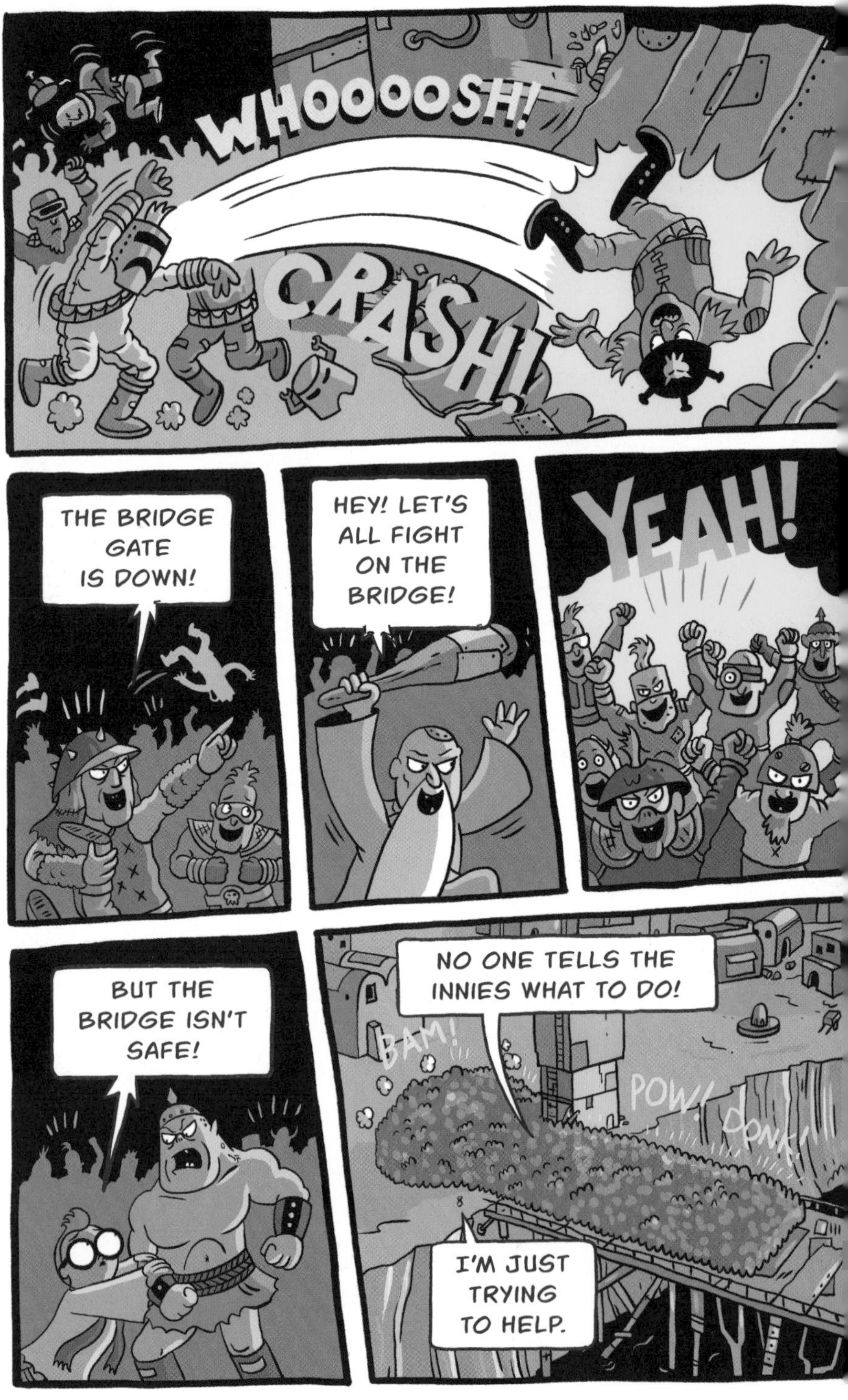
WHOOOOSH!
CRASH!
THE BRIDGE GATE IS DOWN!
HEY! LET'S ALL FIGHT ON THE BRIDGE!
YEAH!
BUT THE BRIDGE ISN'T SAFE!
NO ONE TELLS THE INNIES WHAT TO DO!
BAM!
POW!
DONK!
I'M JUST TRYING TO HELP.

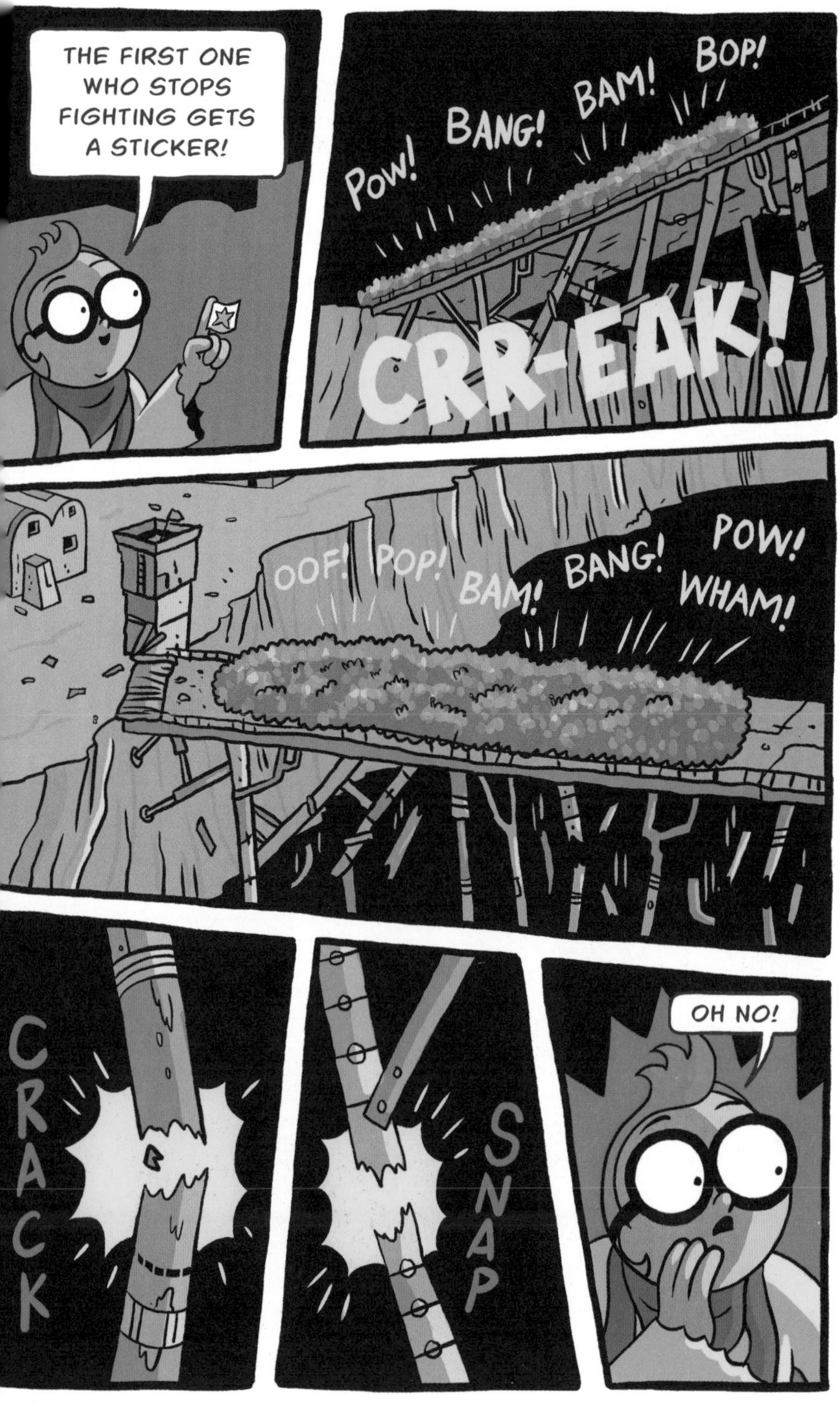
THE FIRST ONE WHO STOPS FIGHTING GETS A STICKER!
POW!
BANG!
BAM!
BOP!
CRR-EAK!
OOF!
POP!
BAM!
BANG!
POW!
WHAM!
CRACK
SNAP
OH NO!

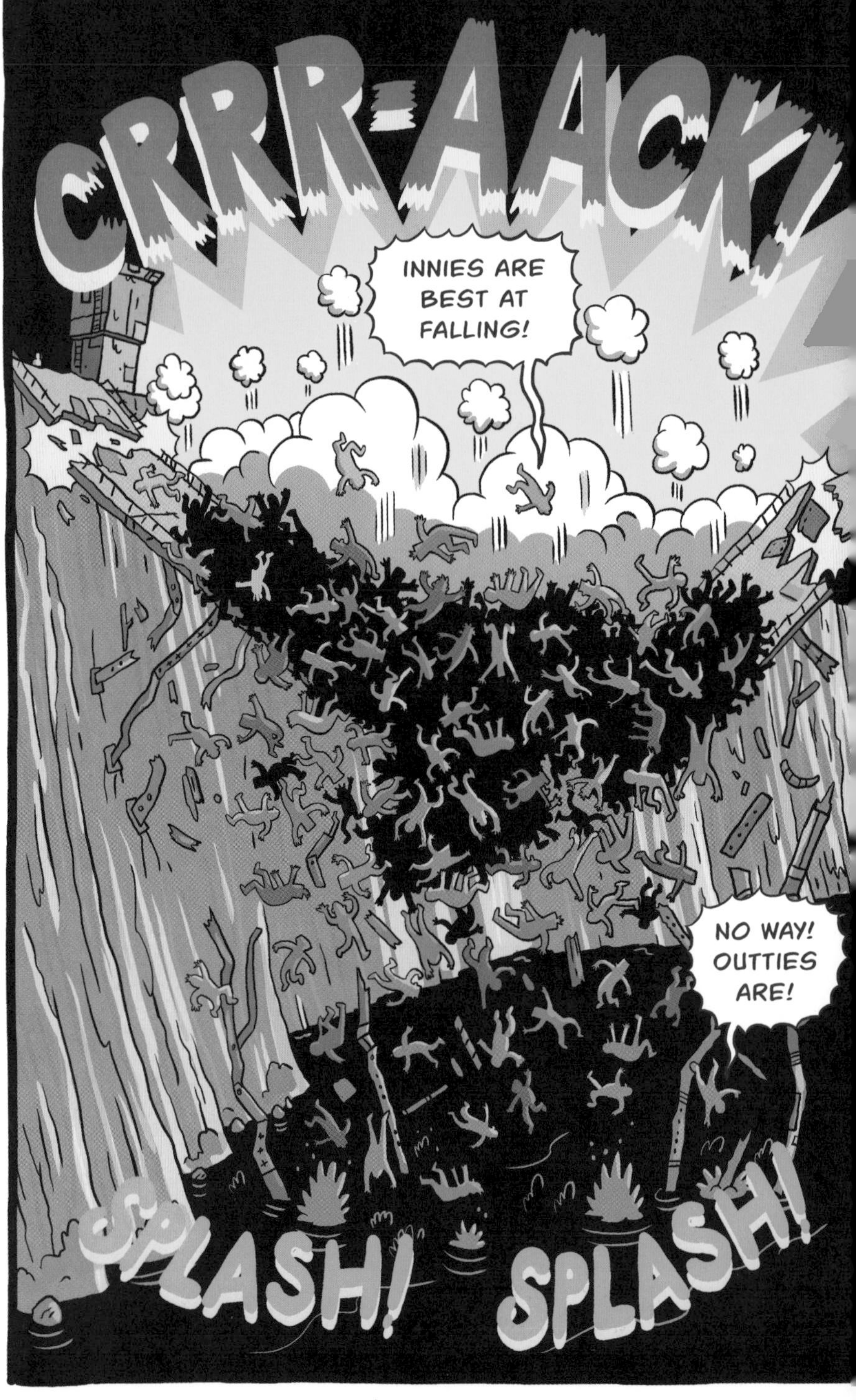
CRRR-AACK!
INNIES ARE BEST AT FALLING!
NO WAY! OUTTIES ARE!
SPLASH! SPLASH!

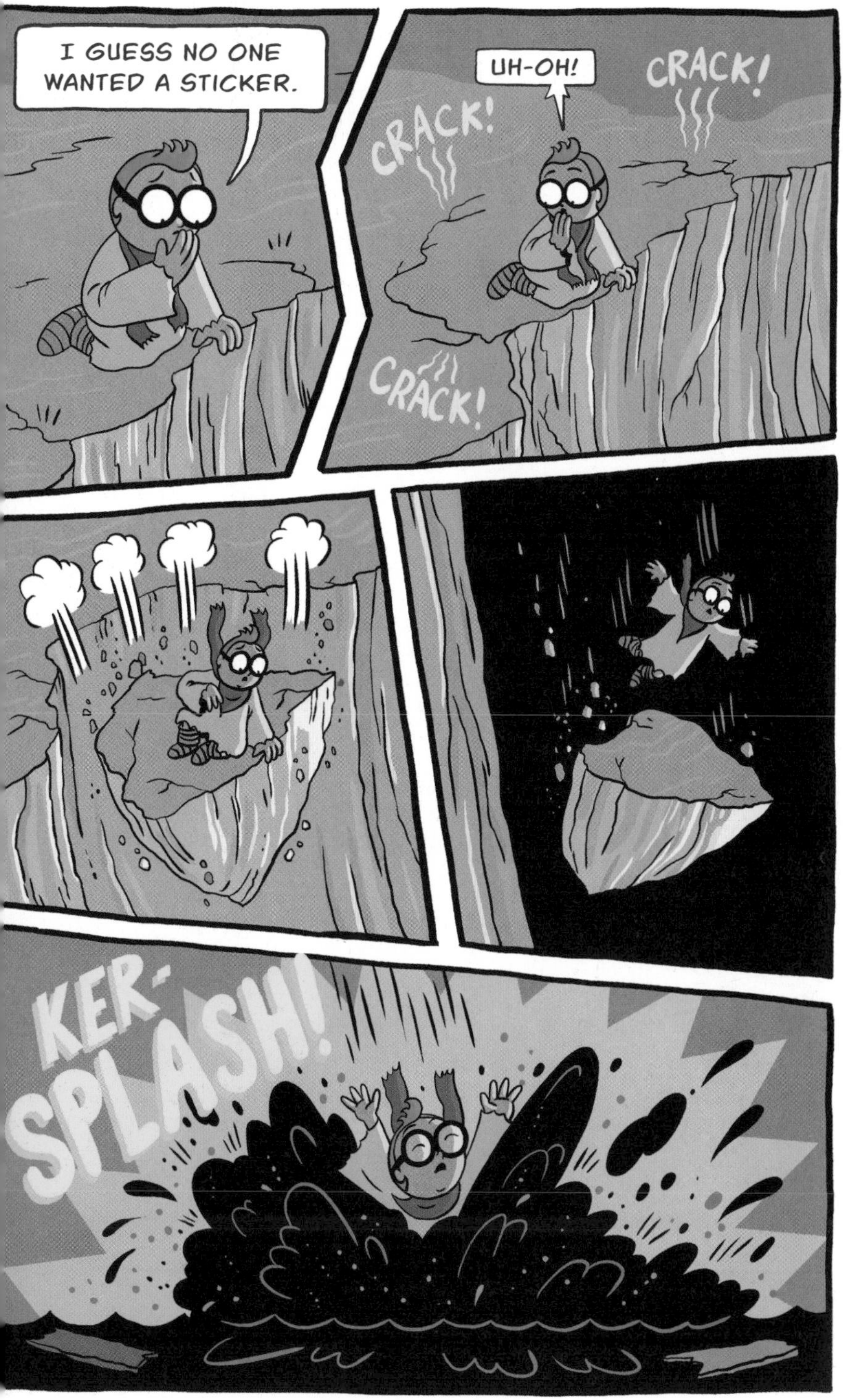
I GUESS NO ONE WANTED A STICKER.
UH-OH!
CRACK!
CRACK!
CRACK!
KER-SPLASH!

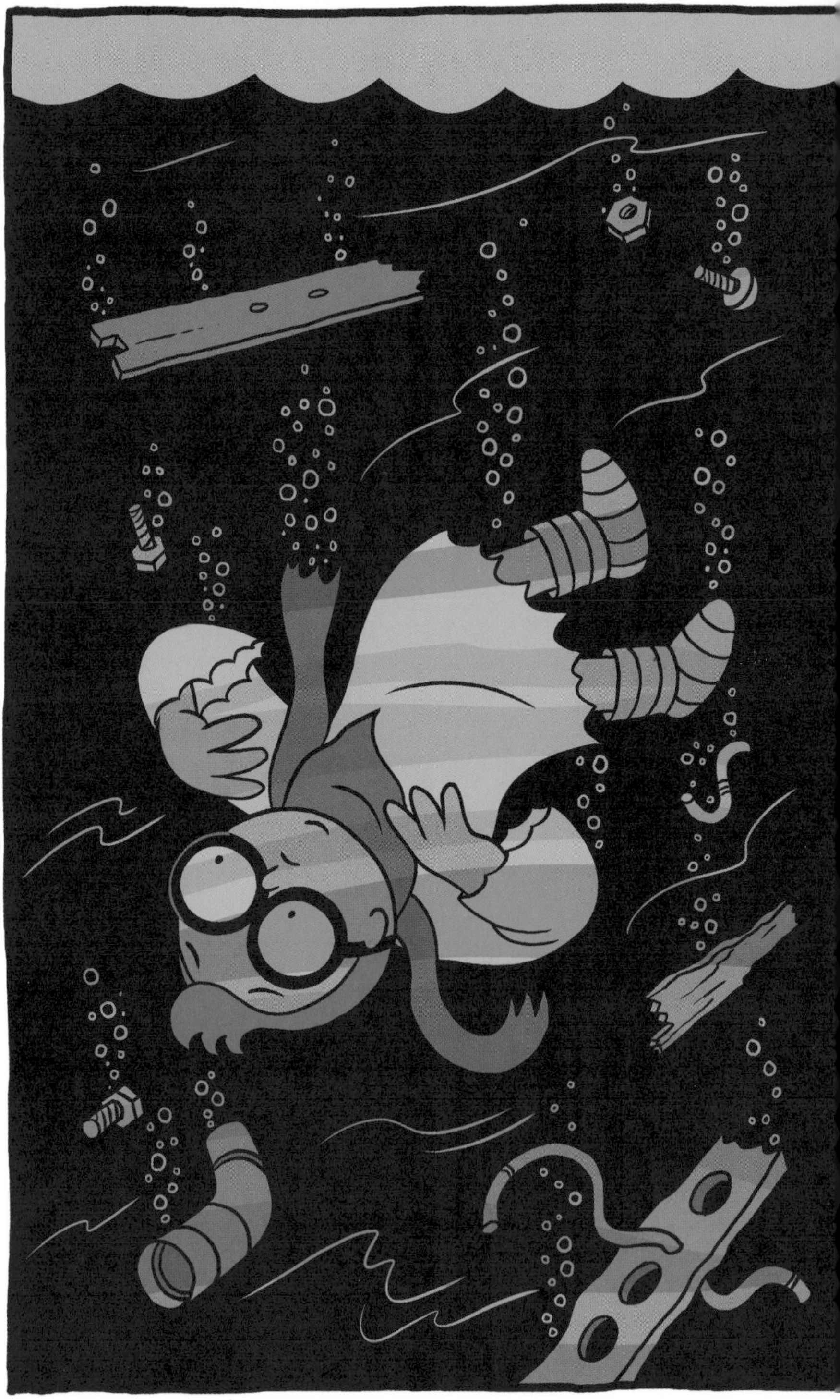

CHAPTER 4

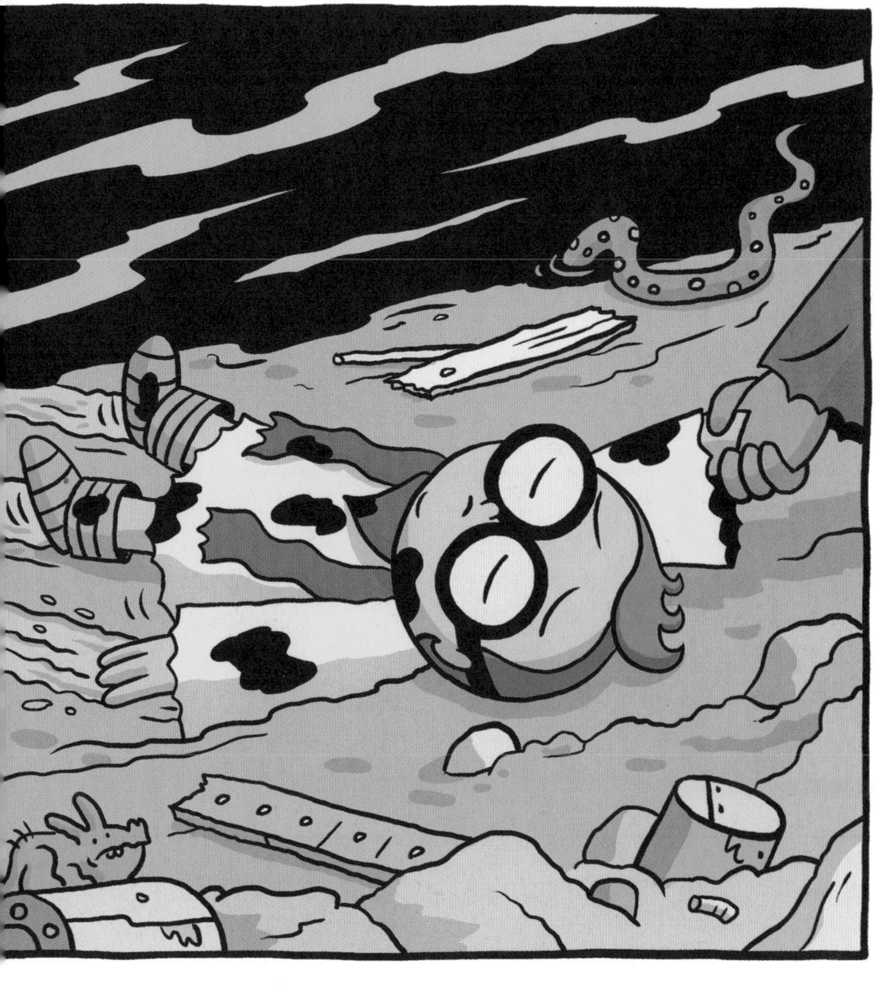

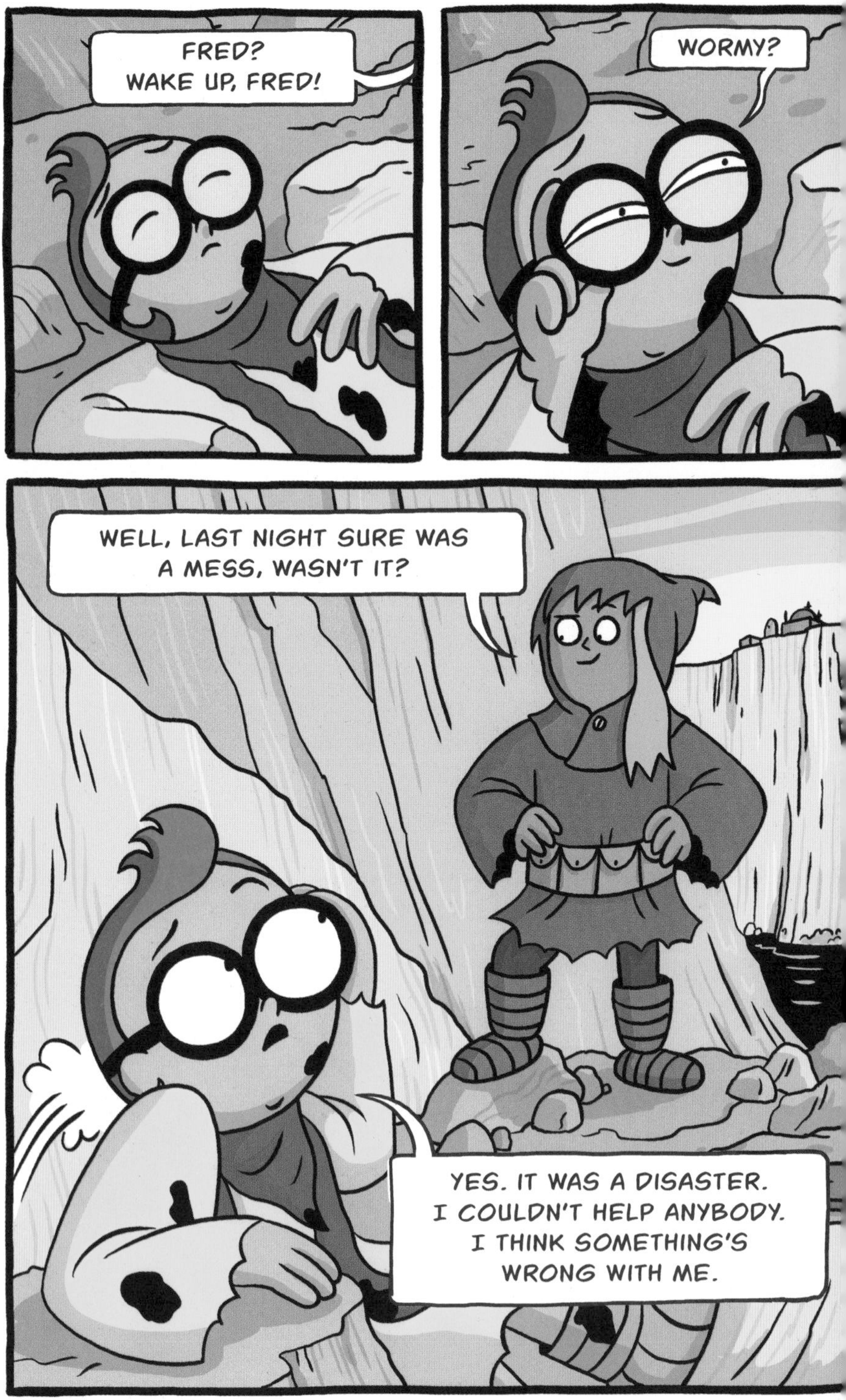
FRED?
WAKE UP, FRED!
WORMY?
WELL, LAST NIGHT SURE WAS A MESS, WASN'T IT?
YES. IT WAS A DISASTER. I COULDN'T HELP ANYBODY. I THINK SOMETHING'S WRONG WITH ME.

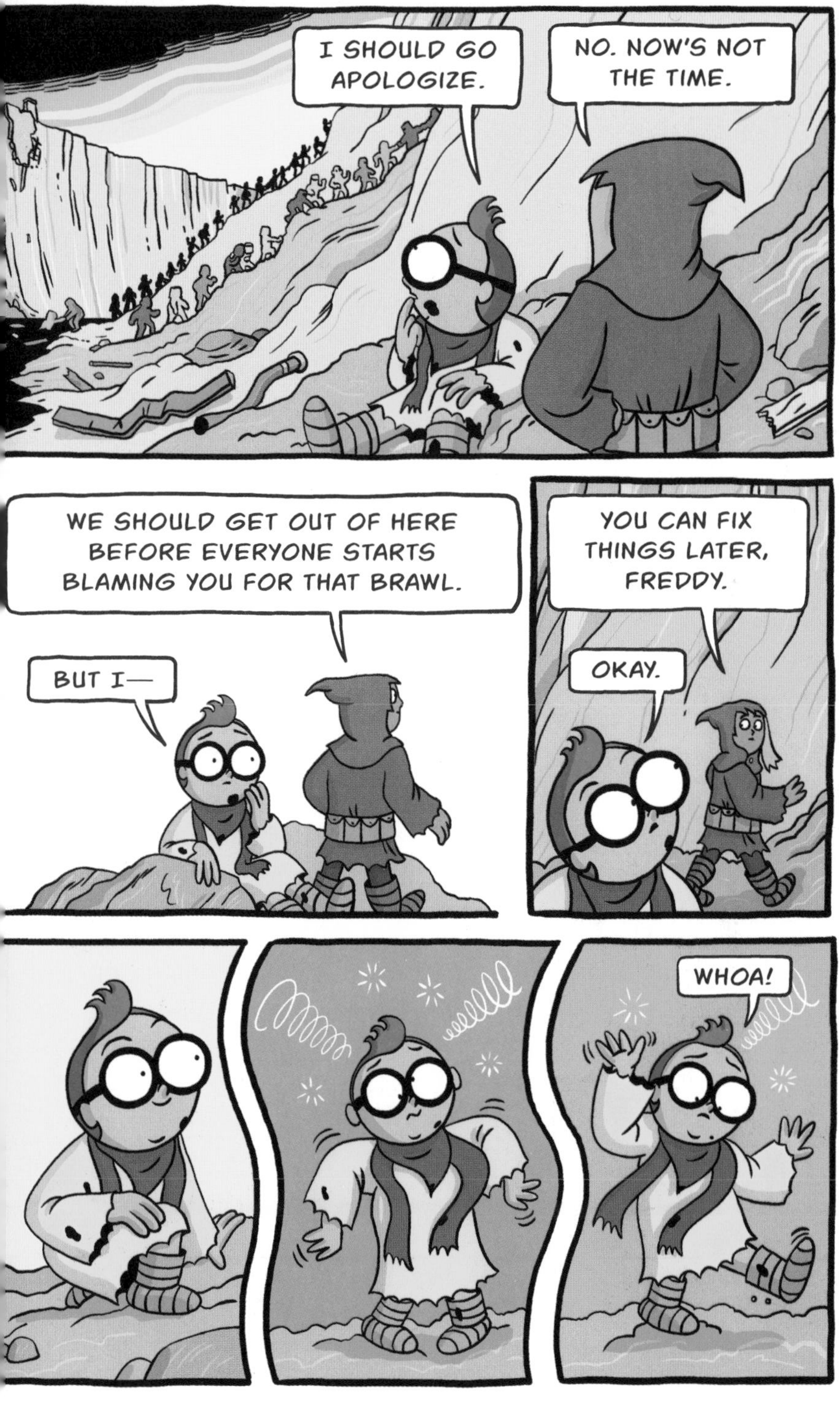
I SHOULD GO APOLOGIZE.
NO. NOW'S NOT THE TIME.
WE SHOULD GET OUT OF HERE BEFORE EVERYONE STARTS BLAMING YOU FOR THAT BRAWL.
BUT I—
YOU CAN FIX THINGS LATER, FREDDY.
OKAY.
WHOA!

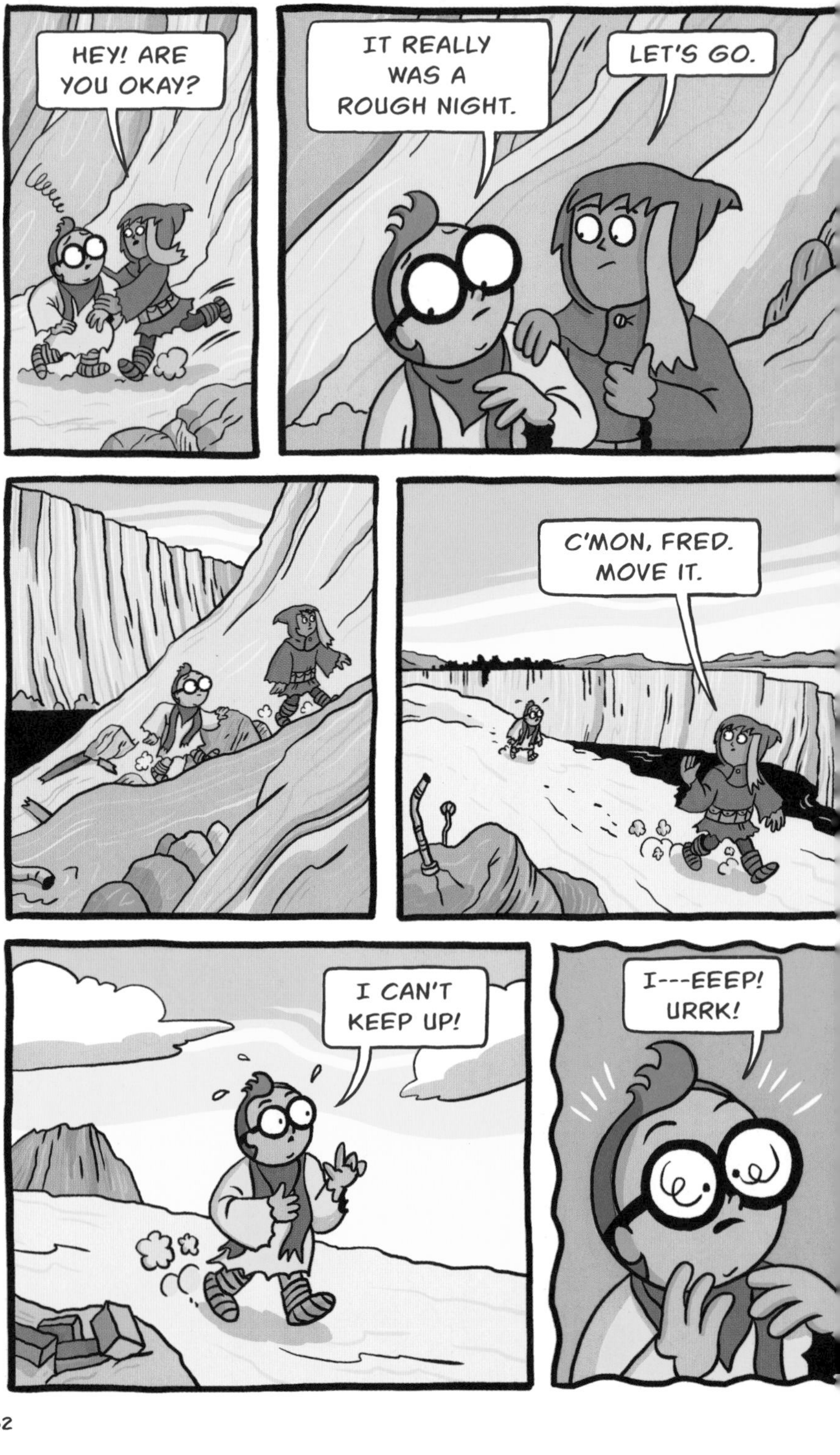
HEY! ARE YOU OKAY?
IT REALLY WAS A ROUGH NIGHT.
LET'S GO.
C'MON, FRED. MOVE IT.
I CAN'T KEEP UP!
I---EEEP! URRK!

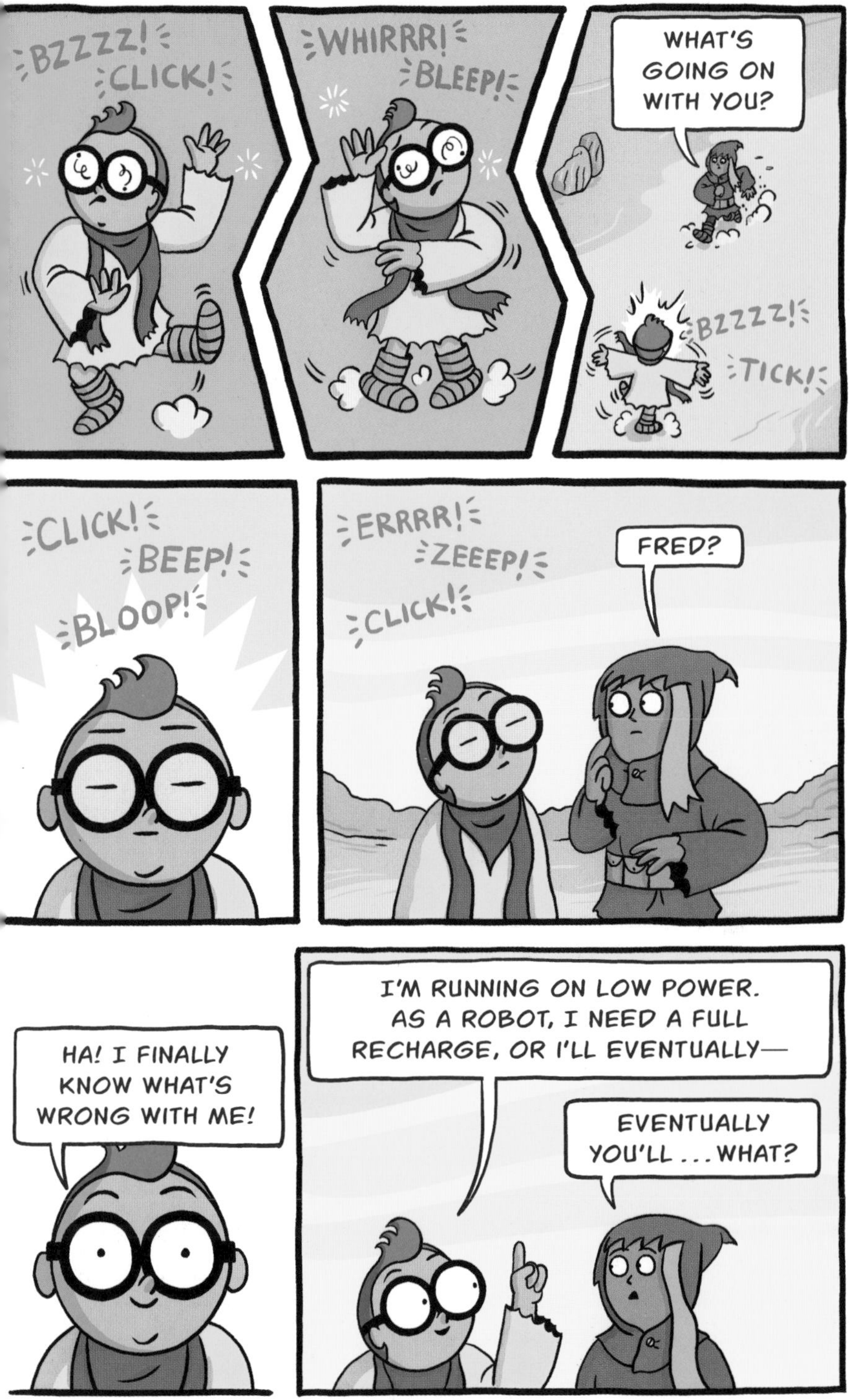
BZZZZ!
CLICK!
WHIRRR!
BLEEP!
WHAT'S GOING ON WITH YOU?
BZZZZ!
TICK!
CLICK!
BEEP!
BLOOP!
ERRRR!
ZEEEP!
CLICK!
FRED?
HA! I FINALLY KNOW WHAT'S WRONG WITH ME!
I'M RUNNING ON LOW POWER. AS A ROBOT, I NEED A FULL RECHARGE, OR I'LL EVENTUALLY—
EVENTUALLY YOU'LL . . . WHAT?

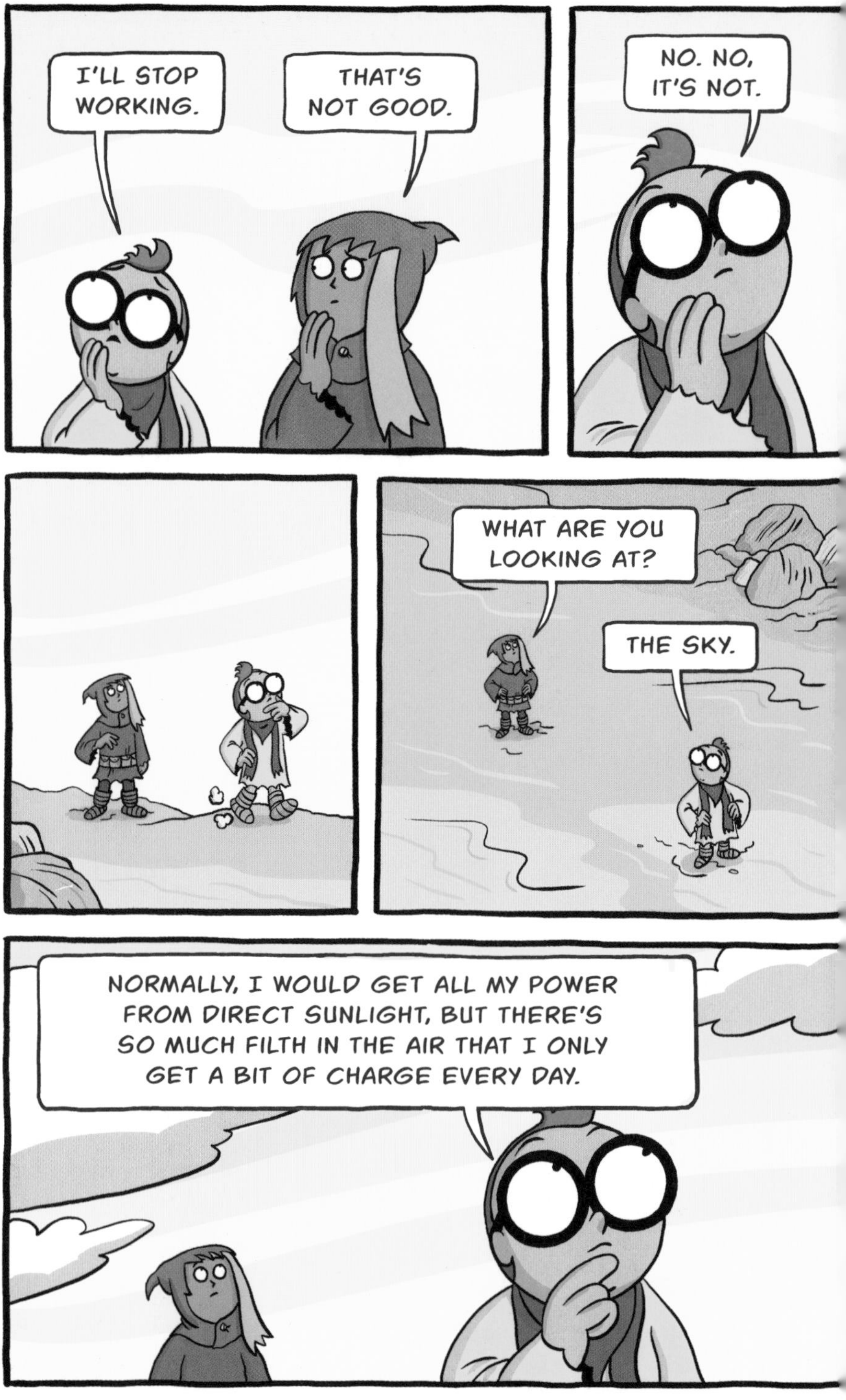
I'LL STOP WORKING.
THAT'S NOT GOOD.
NO. NO, IT'S NOT.
WHAT ARE YOU LOOKING AT?
THE SKY.
NORMALLY, I WOULD GET ALL MY POWER FROM DIRECT SUNLIGHT, BUT THERE'S SO MUCH FILTH IN THE AIR THAT I ONLY GET A BIT OF CHARGE EVERY DAY.

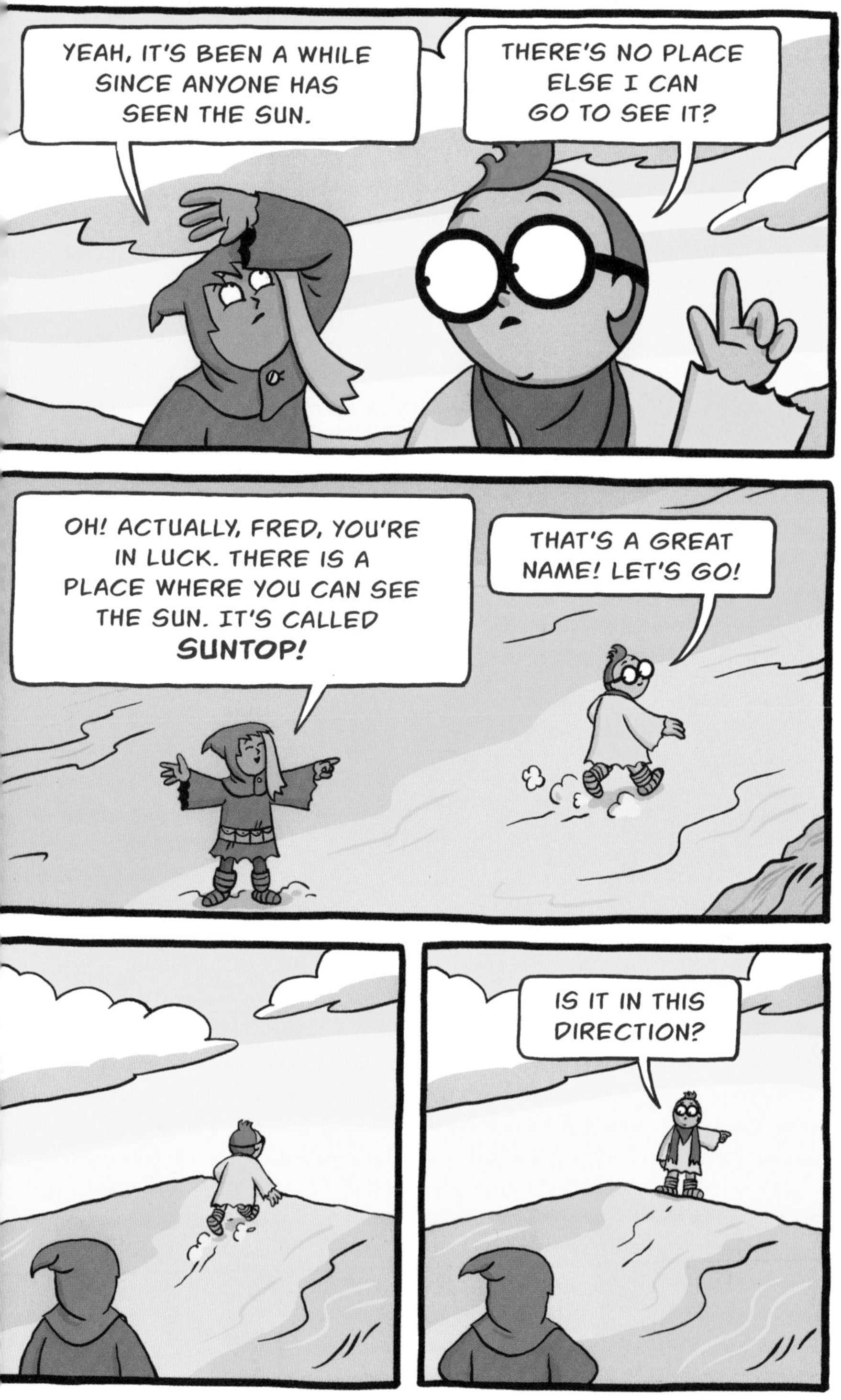
YEAH, IT'S BEEN A WHILE SINCE ANYONE HAS SEEN THE SUN.
THERE'S NO PLACE ELSE I CAN GO TO SEE IT?
OH! ACTUALLY, FRED, YOU'RE IN LUCK. THERE IS A PLACE WHERE YOU CAN SEE THE SUN. IT'S CALLED **SUNTOP!**
THAT'S A GREAT NAME! LET'S GO!
IS IT IN THIS DIRECTION?

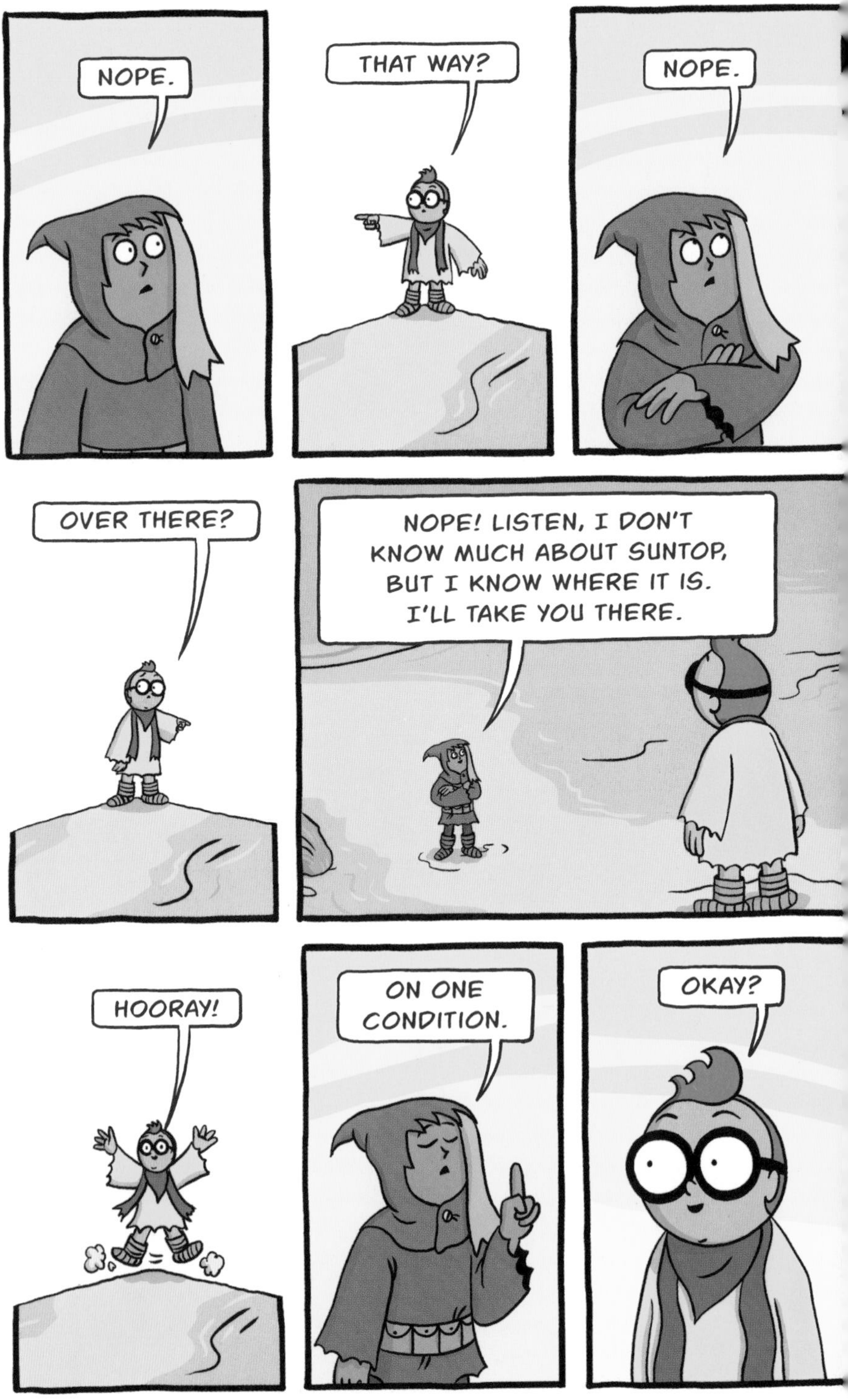
NOPE.
THAT WAY?
NOPE.
OVER THERE?
NOPE! LISTEN, I DON'T KNOW MUCH ABOUT SUNTOP, BUT I KNOW WHERE IT IS. I'LL TAKE YOU THERE.
HOORAY!
ON ONE CONDITION.
OKAY?

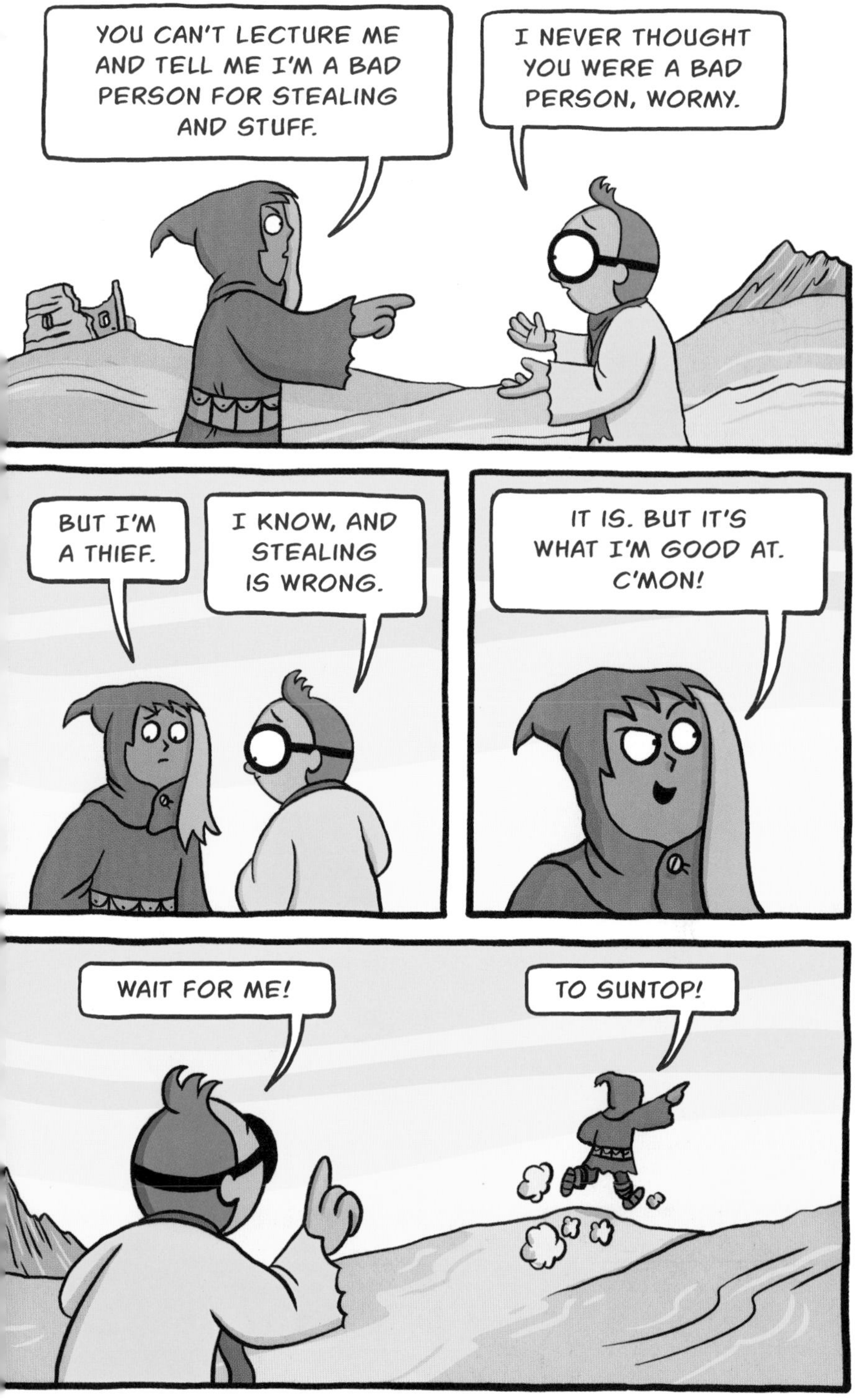
YOU CAN'T LECTURE ME AND TELL ME I'M A BAD PERSON FOR STEALING AND STUFF.
I NEVER THOUGHT YOU WERE A BAD PERSON, WORMY.
BUT I'M A THIEF.
I KNOW, AND STEALING IS WRONG.
IT IS. BUT IT'S WHAT I'M GOOD AT. C'MON!
WAIT FOR ME!
TO SUNTOP!

CHAPTER 5

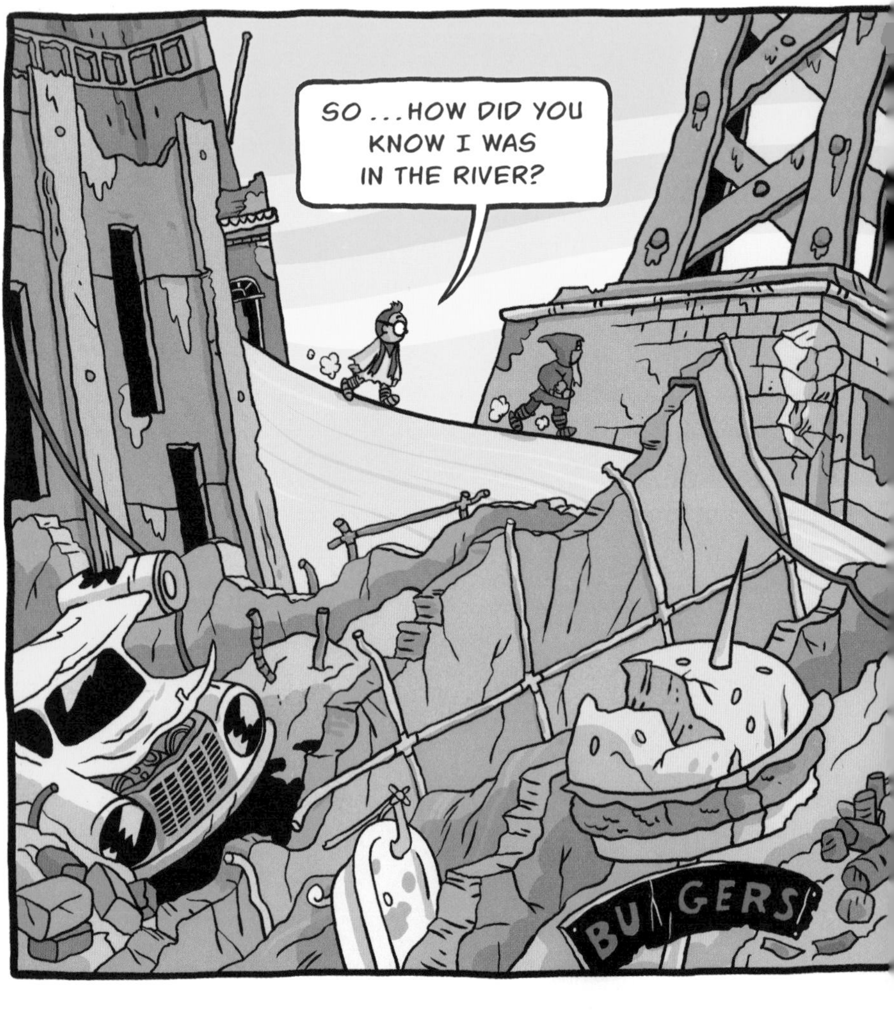

SO . . . HOW DID YOU KNOW I WAS IN THE RIVER?
BU GERS

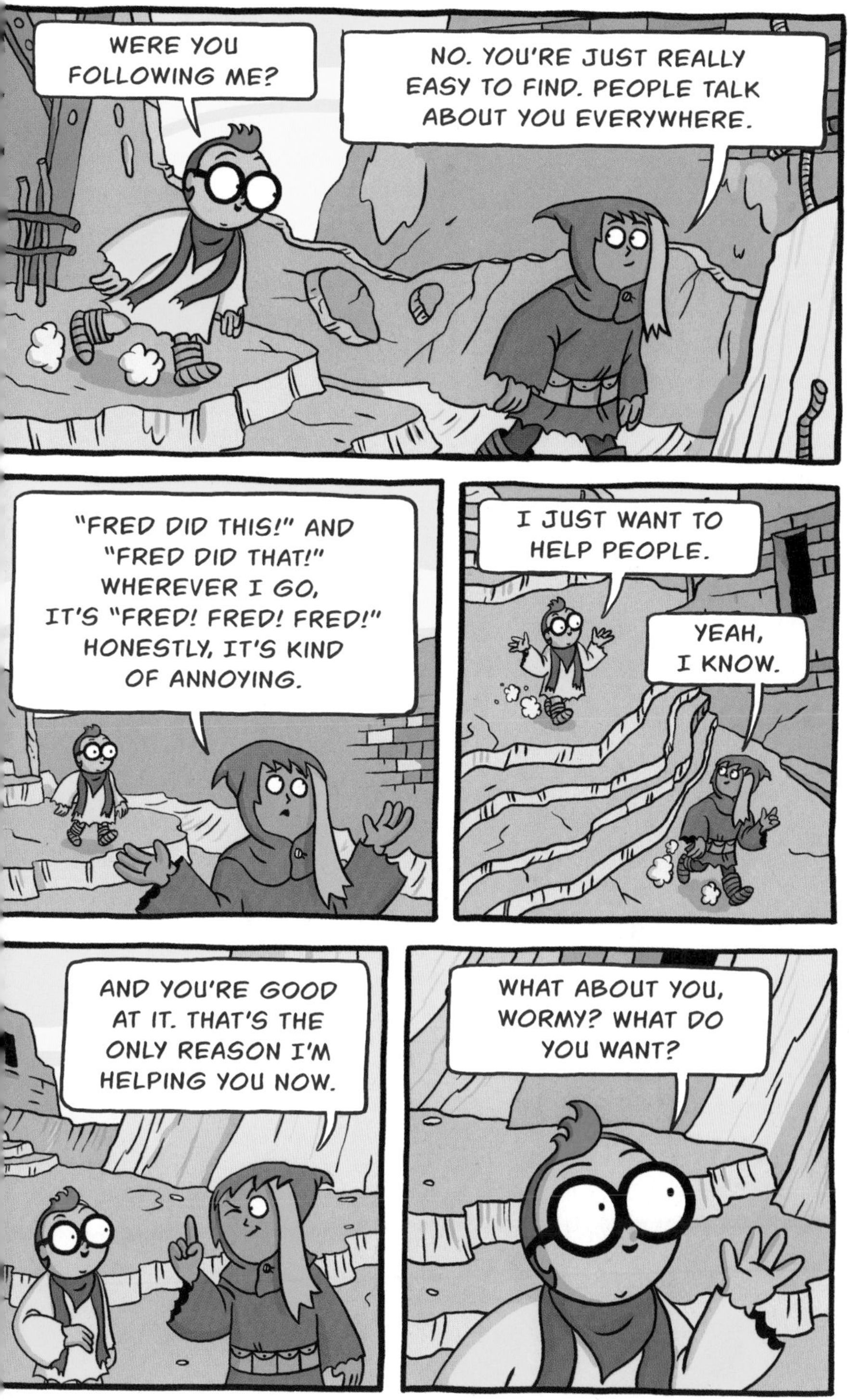
WERE YOU FOLLOWING ME?
NO. YOU'RE JUST REALLY EASY TO FIND. PEOPLE TALK ABOUT YOU EVERYWHERE.
"FRED DID THIS!" AND "FRED DID THAT!" WHEREVER I GO, IT'S "FRED! FRED! FRED!" HONESTLY, IT'S KIND OF ANNOYING.
I JUST WANT TO HELP PEOPLE.
YEAH, I KNOW.
AND YOU'RE GOOD AT IT. THAT'S THE ONLY REASON I'M HELPING YOU NOW.
WHAT ABOUT YOU, WORMY? WHAT DO YOU WANT?

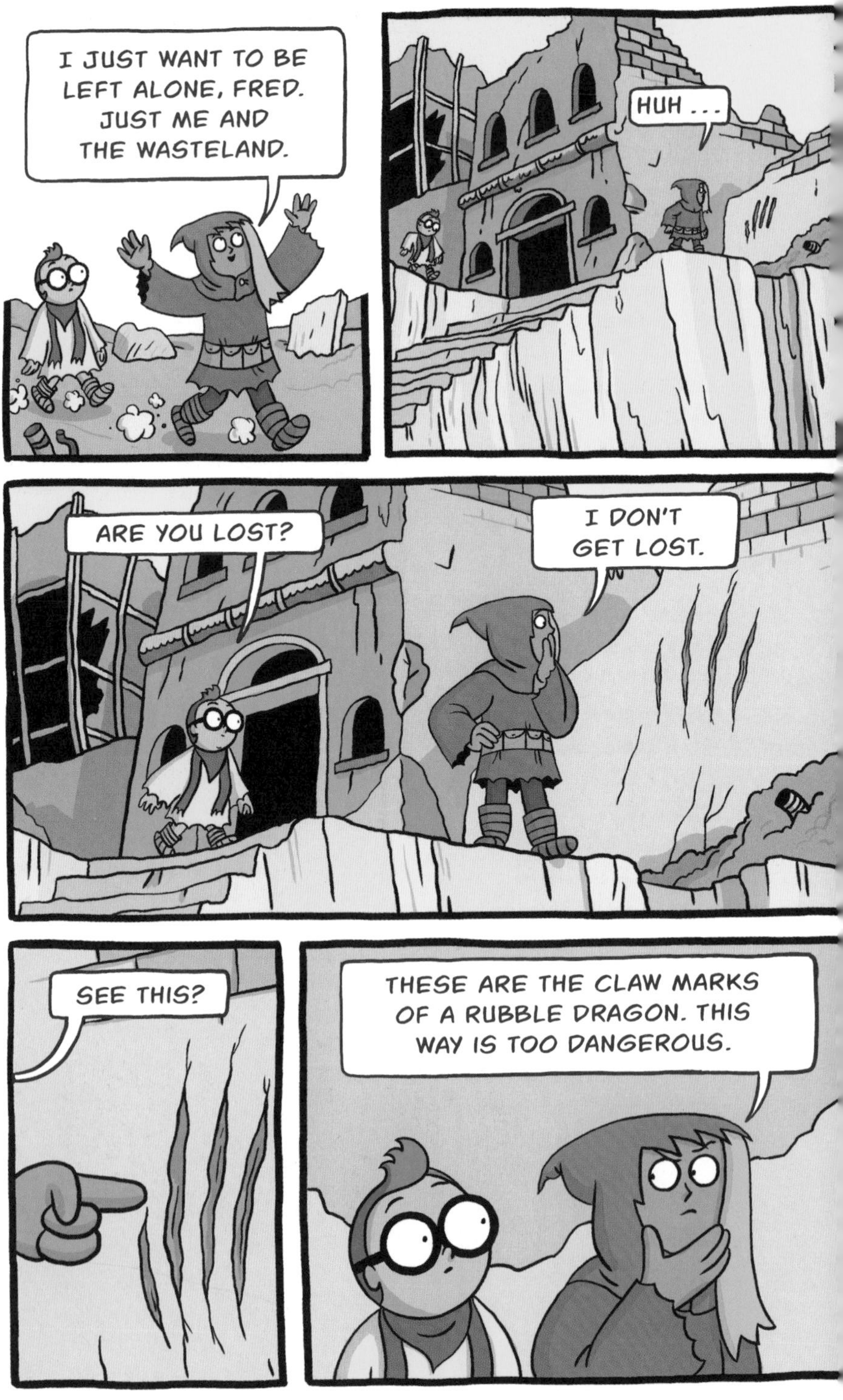
I JUST WANT TO BE LEFT ALONE, FRED. JUST ME AND THE WASTELAND.
HUH . . .
ARE YOU LOST?
I DON'T GET LOST.
SEE THIS?
THESE ARE THE CLAW MARKS OF A RUBBLE DRAGON. THIS WAY IS TOO DANGEROUS.

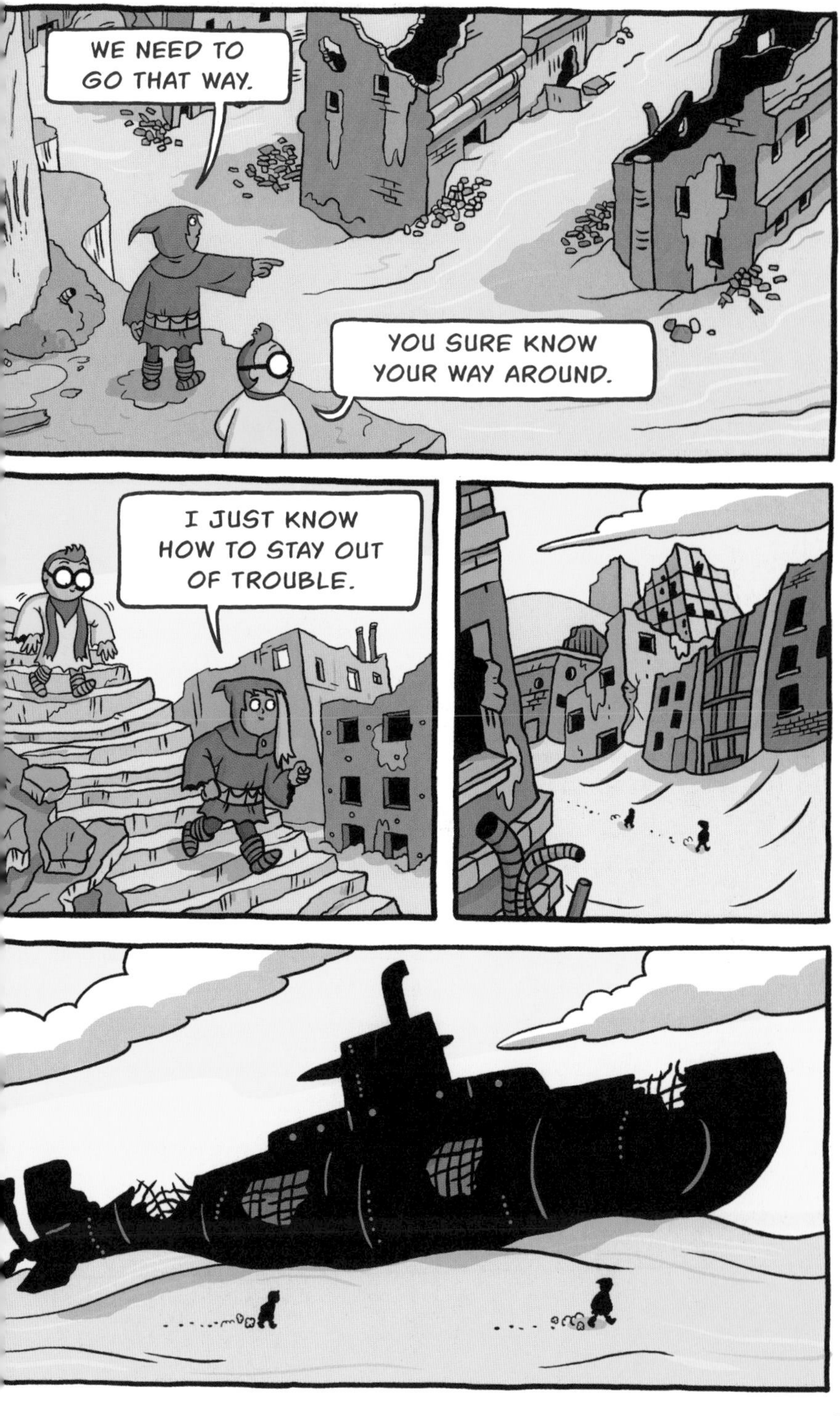
WE NEED TO GO THAT WAY.
YOU SURE KNOW YOUR WAY AROUND.
I JUST KNOW HOW TO STAY OUT OF TROUBLE.

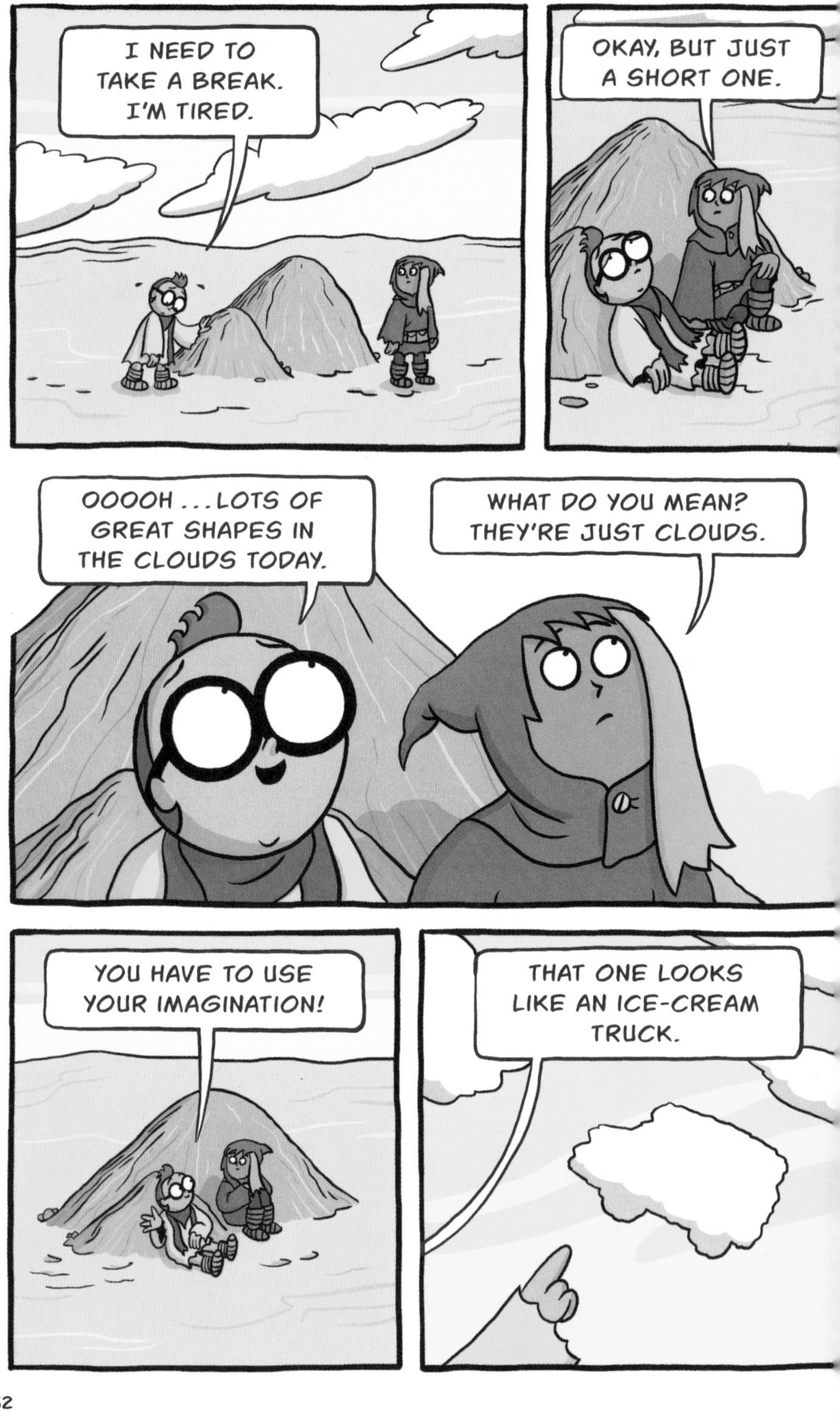

I NEED TO TAKE A BREAK. I'M TIRED.
OKAY, BUT JUST A SHORT ONE.
OOOOH . . . LOTS OF GREAT SHAPES IN THE CLOUDS TODAY.
WHAT DO YOU MEAN? THEY'RE JUST CLOUDS.
YOU HAVE TO USE YOUR IMAGINATION!
THAT ONE LOOKS LIKE AN ICE-CREAM TRUCK.

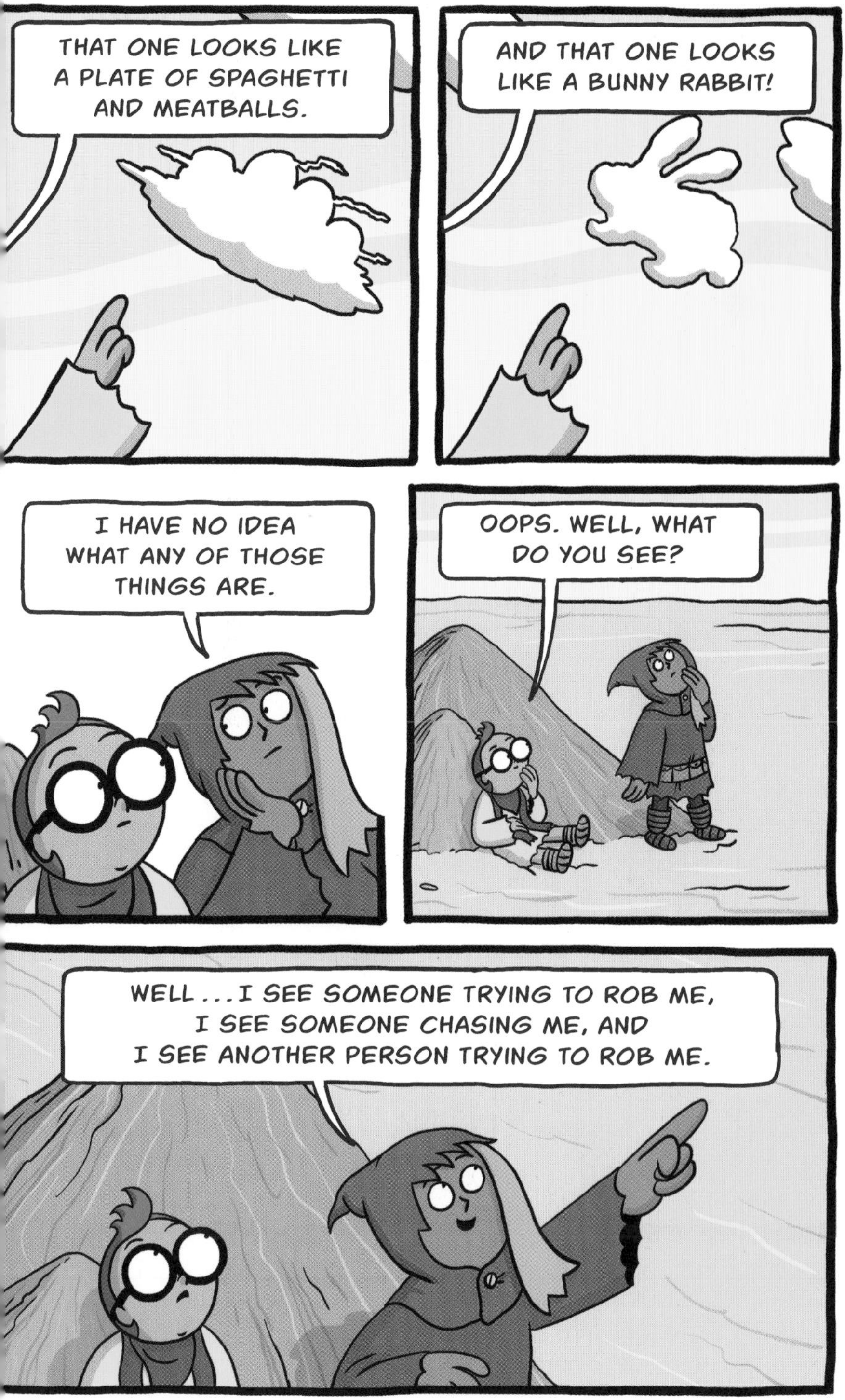
THAT ONE LOOKS LIKE A PLATE OF SPAGHETTI AND MEATBALLS.
AND THAT ONE LOOKS LIKE A BUNNY RABBIT!
I HAVE NO IDEA WHAT ANY OF THOSE THINGS ARE.
OOPS. WELL, WHAT DO YOU SEE?
WELL . . . I SEE SOMEONE TRYING TO ROB ME, I SEE SOMEONE CHASING ME, AND I SEE ANOTHER PERSON TRYING TO ROB ME.

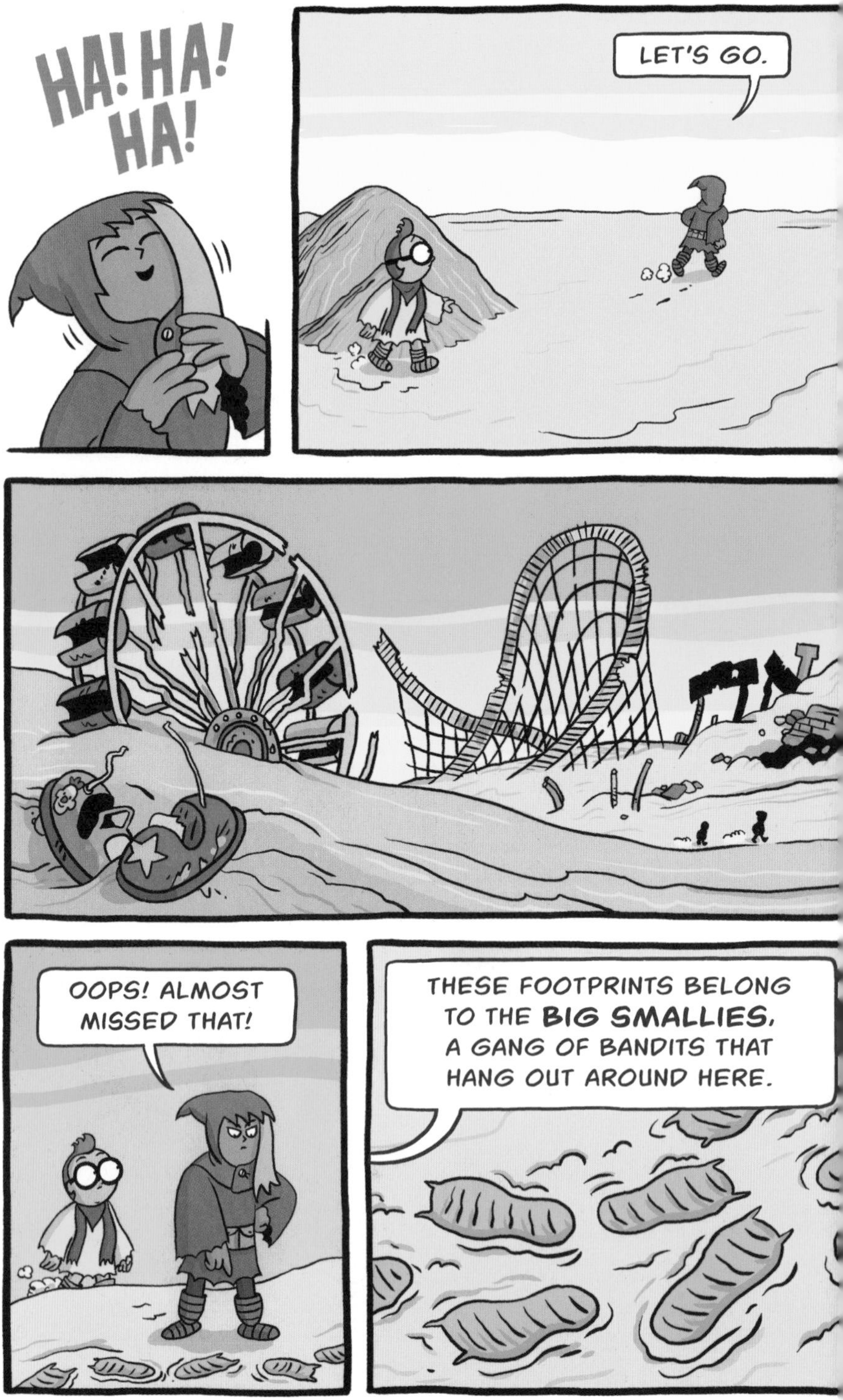
HA! HA! HA!
LET'S GO.
OOPS! ALMOST MISSED THAT!
THESE FOOTPRINTS BELONG TO THE **BIG SMALLIES**, A GANG OF BANDITS THAT HANG OUT AROUND HERE.

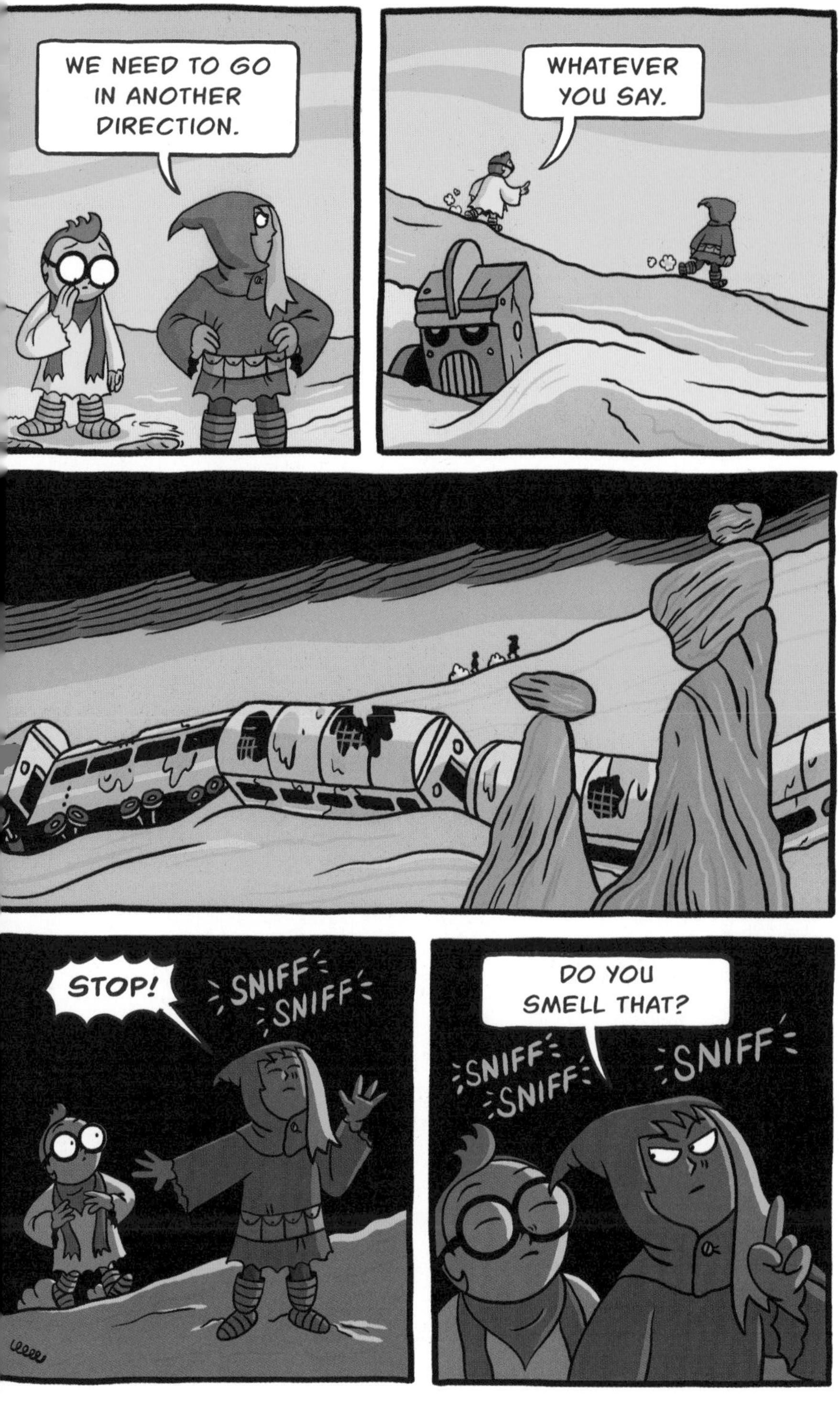
WE NEED TO GO IN ANOTHER DIRECTION.
WHATEVER YOU SAY.
STOP!
SNIFF SNIFF
DO YOU SMELL THAT?
SNIFF SNIFF
SNIFF

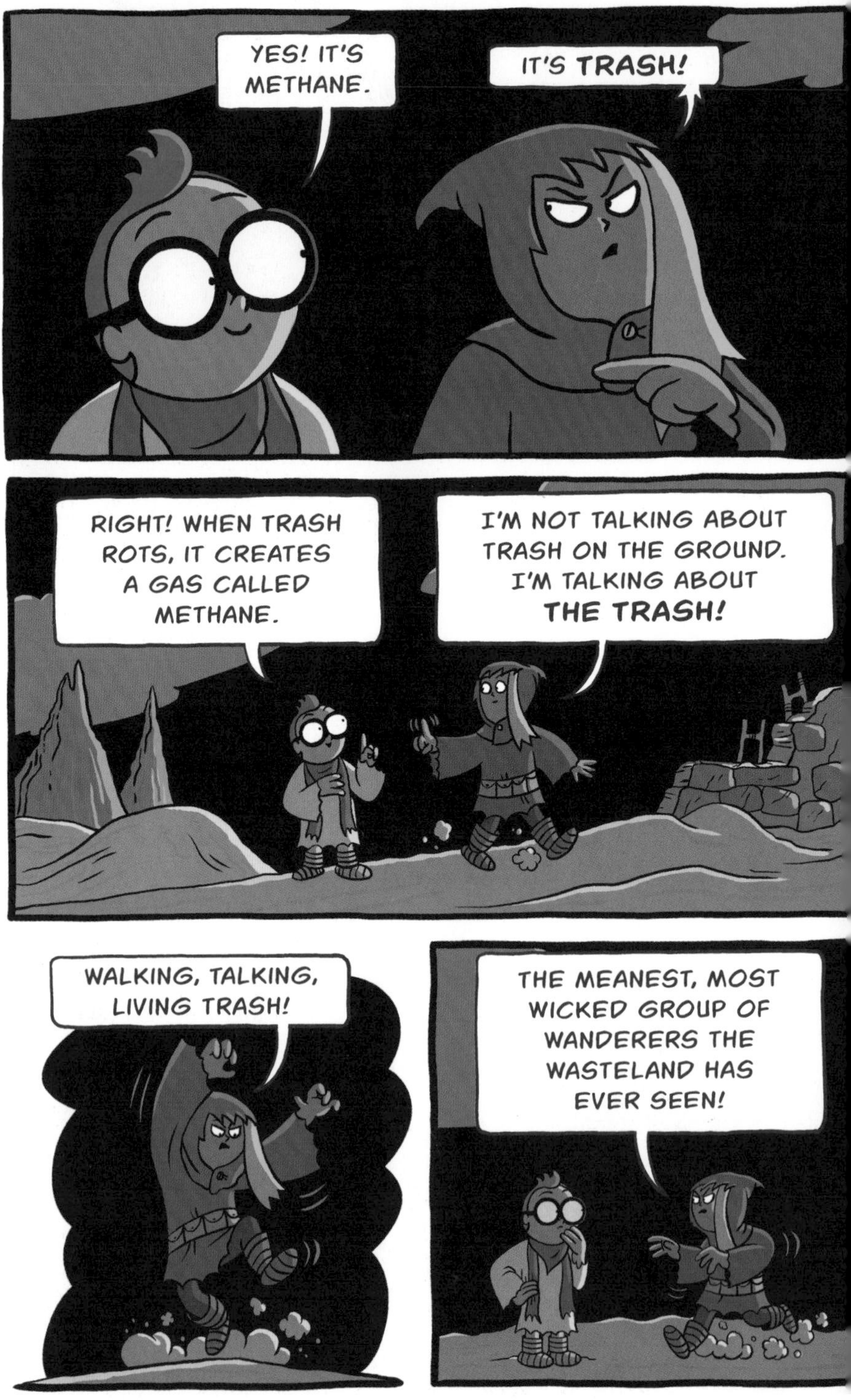
YES! IT'S METHANE.
IT'S TRASH!
RIGHT! WHEN TRASH ROTS, IT CREATES A GAS CALLED METHANE.
I'M NOT TALKING ABOUT TRASH ON THE GROUND. I'M TALKING ABOUT THE TRASH!
WALKING, TALKING, LIVING TRASH!
THE MEANEST, MOST WICKED GROUP OF WANDERERS THE WASTELAND HAS EVER SEEN!

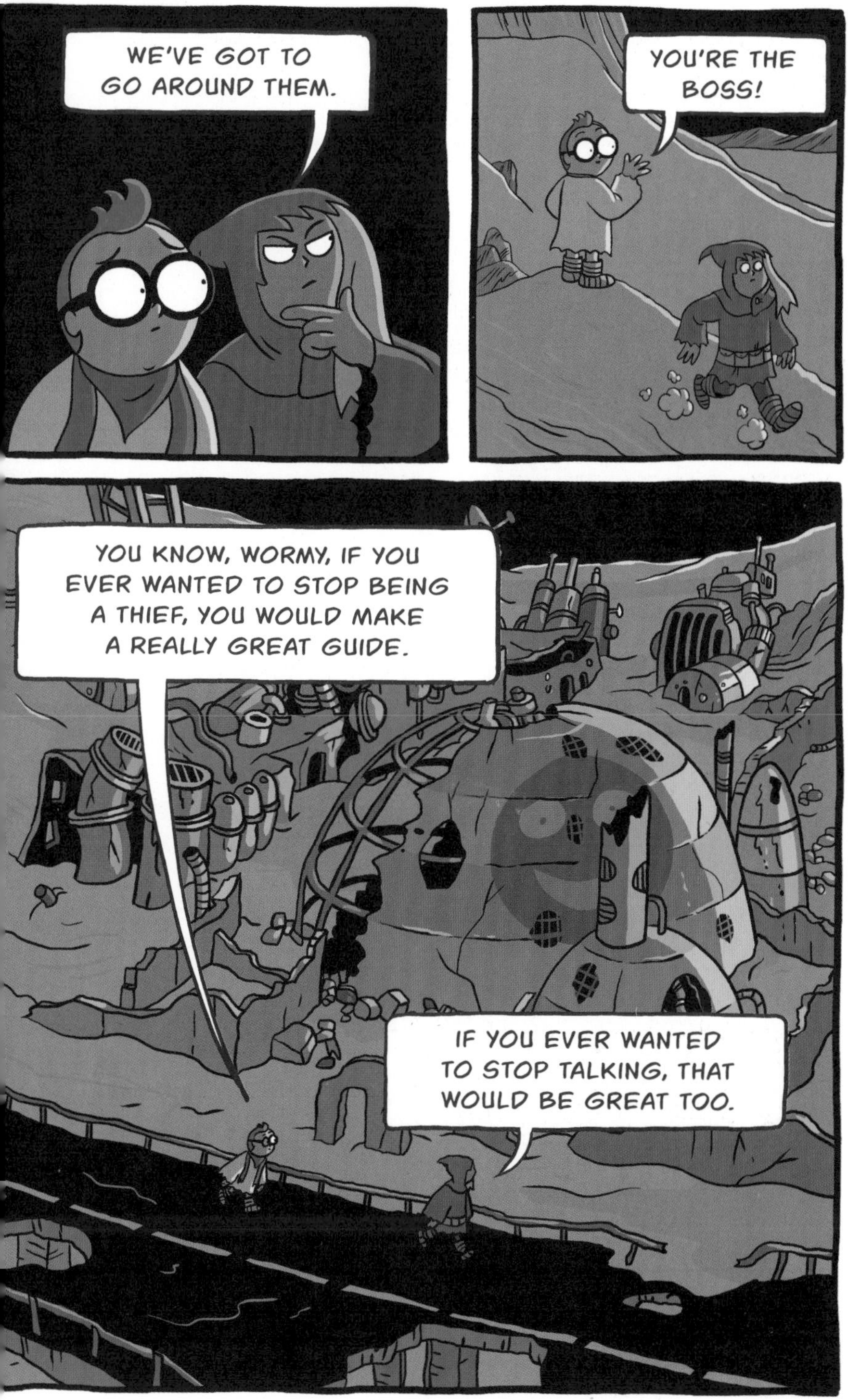
WE'VE GOT TO GO AROUND THEM.
YOU'RE THE BOSS!
YOU KNOW, WORMY, IF YOU EVER WANTED TO STOP BEING A THIEF, YOU WOULD MAKE A REALLY GREAT GUIDE.
IF YOU EVER WANTED TO STOP TALKING, THAT WOULD BE GREAT TOO.

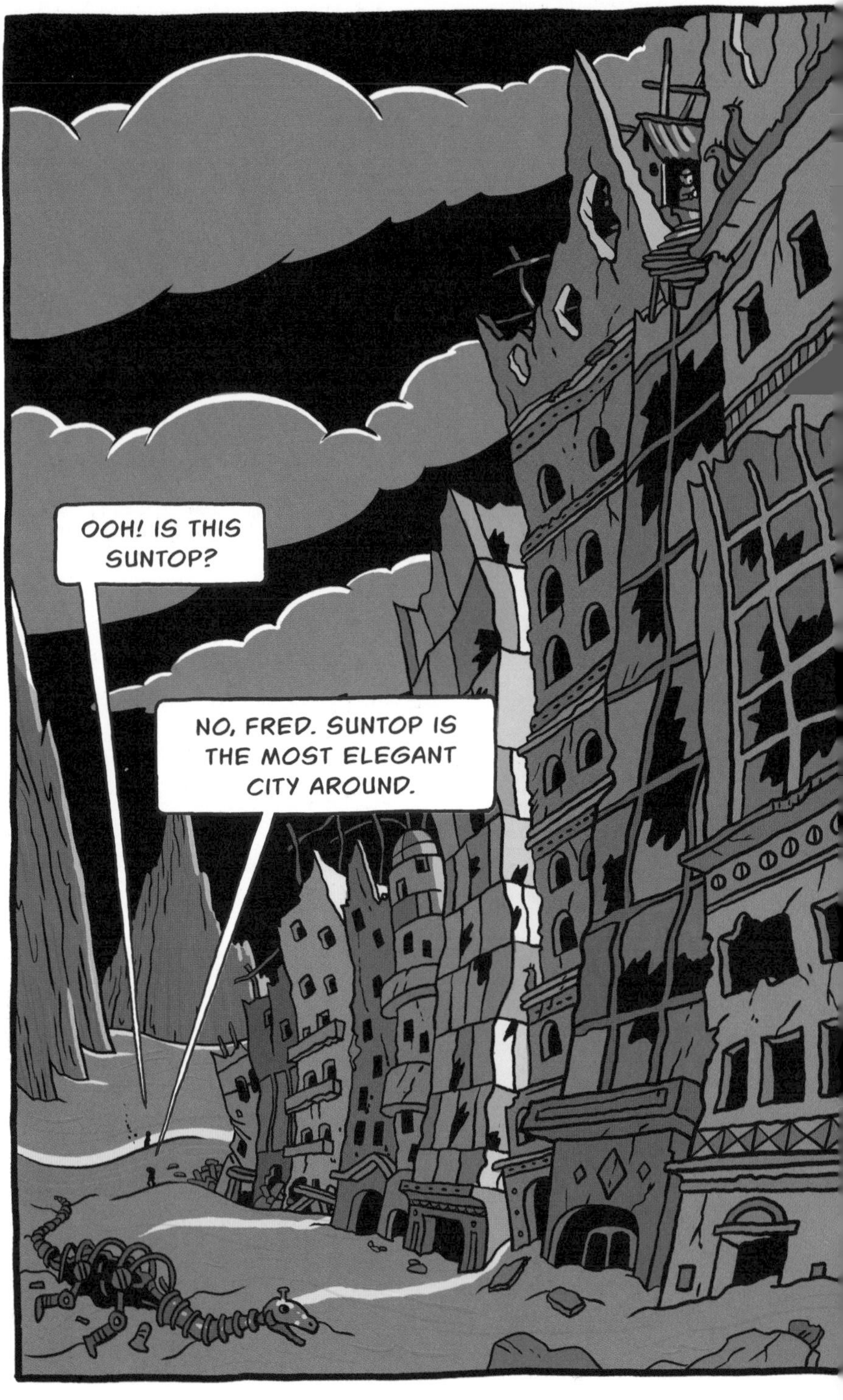
OOH! IS THIS SUNTOP?
NO, FRED. SUNTOP IS THE MOST ELEGANT CITY AROUND.

CHAPTER 6

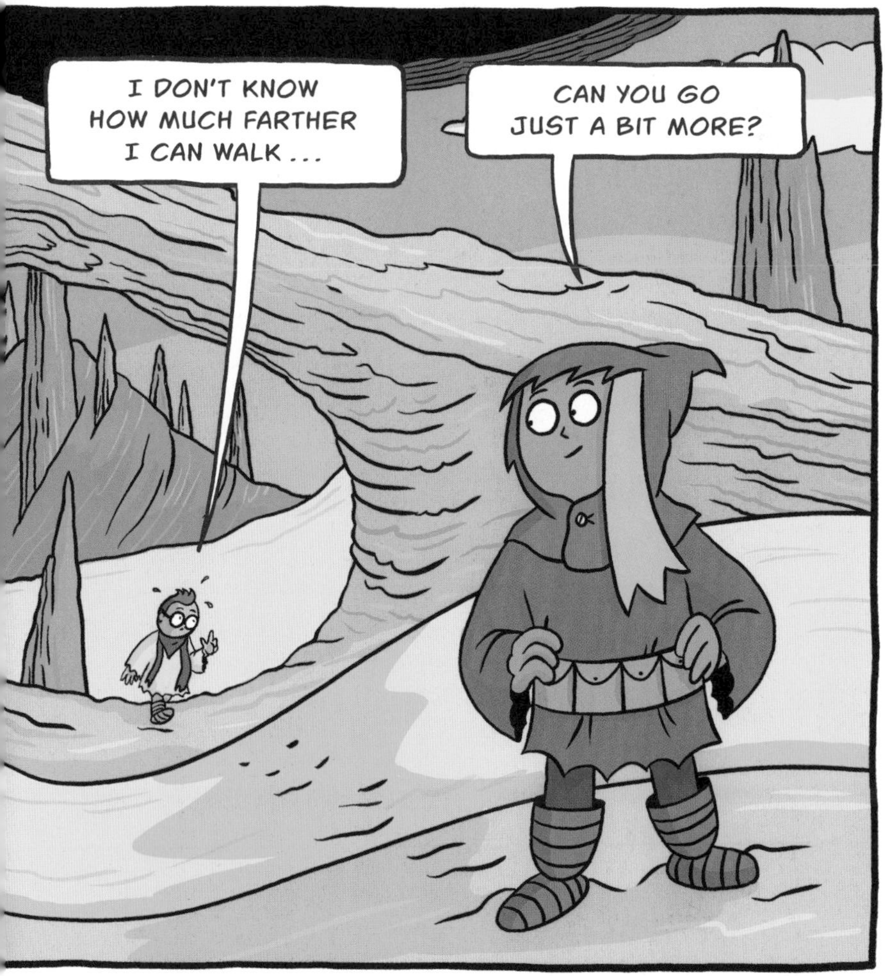

I DON'T KNOW HOW MUCH FARTHER I CAN WALK . . .
CAN YOU GO JUST A BIT MORE?

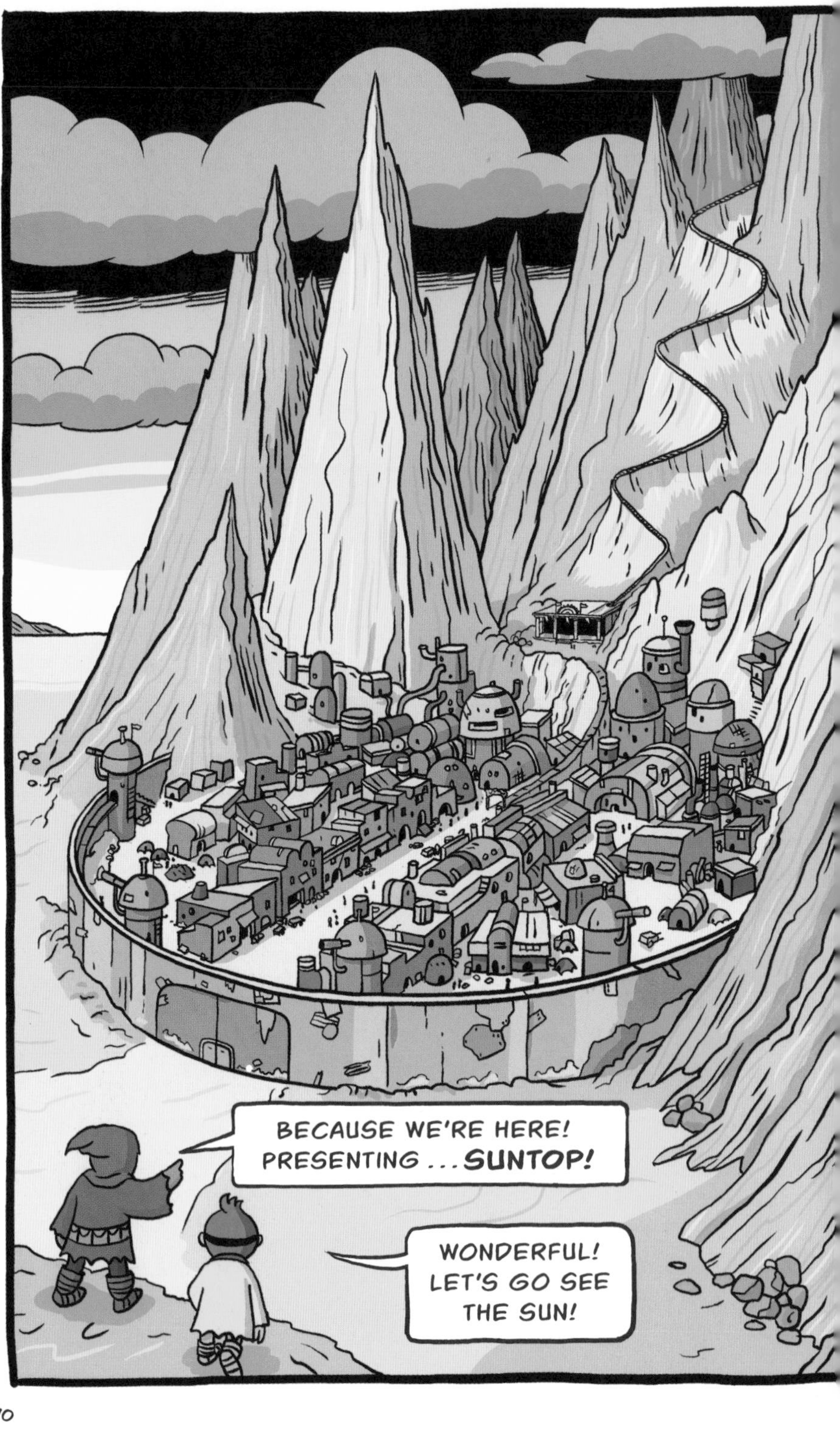
BECAUSE WE'RE HERE! PRESENTING ... SUNTOP!
WONDERFUL! LET'S GO SEE THE SUN!

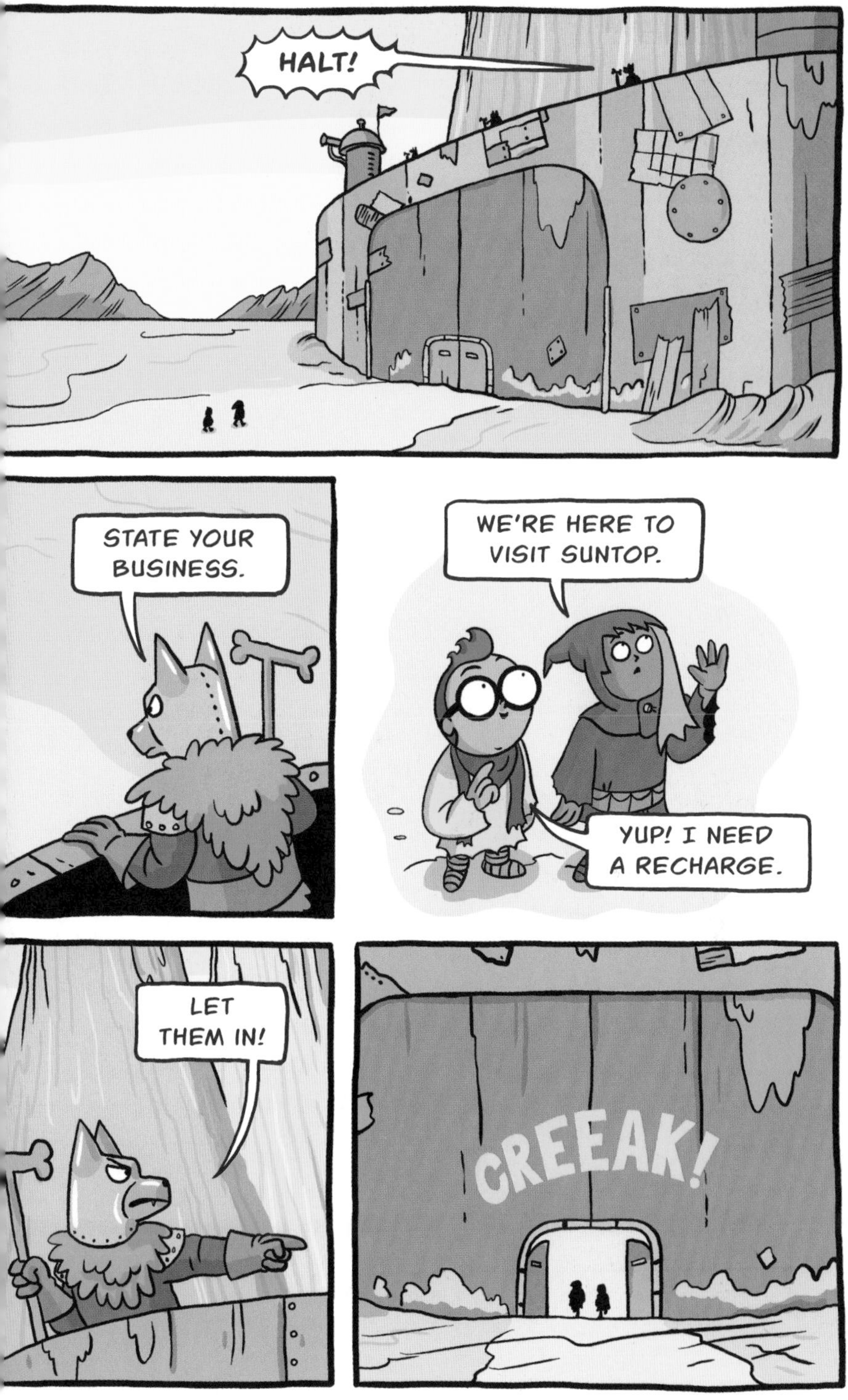
HALT!
STATE YOUR BUSINESS.
WE'RE HERE TO VISIT SUNTOP.
YUP! I NEED A RECHARGE.
LET THEM IN!
CREEAK!

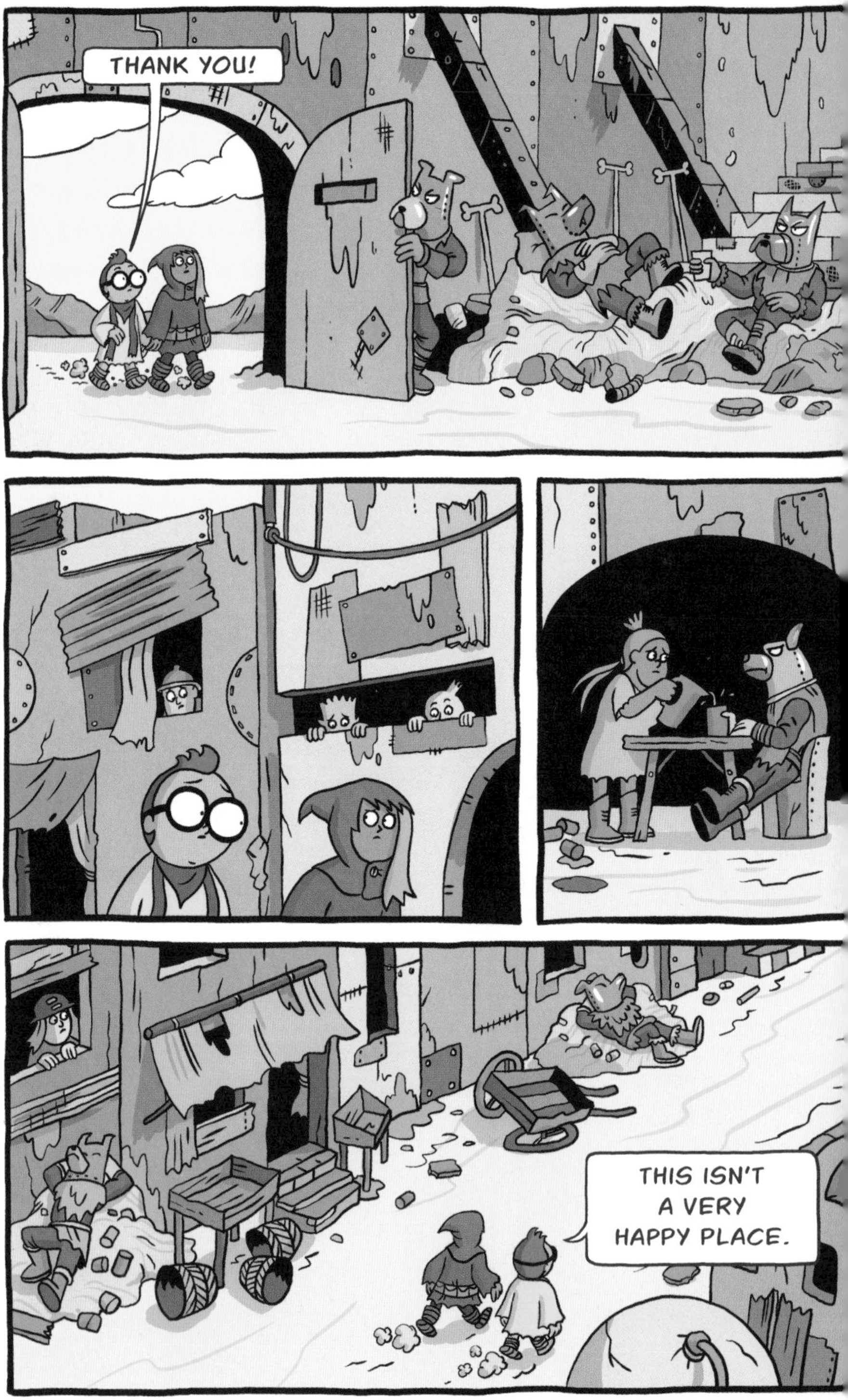
THANK YOU!
THIS ISN'T A VERY HAPPY PLACE.

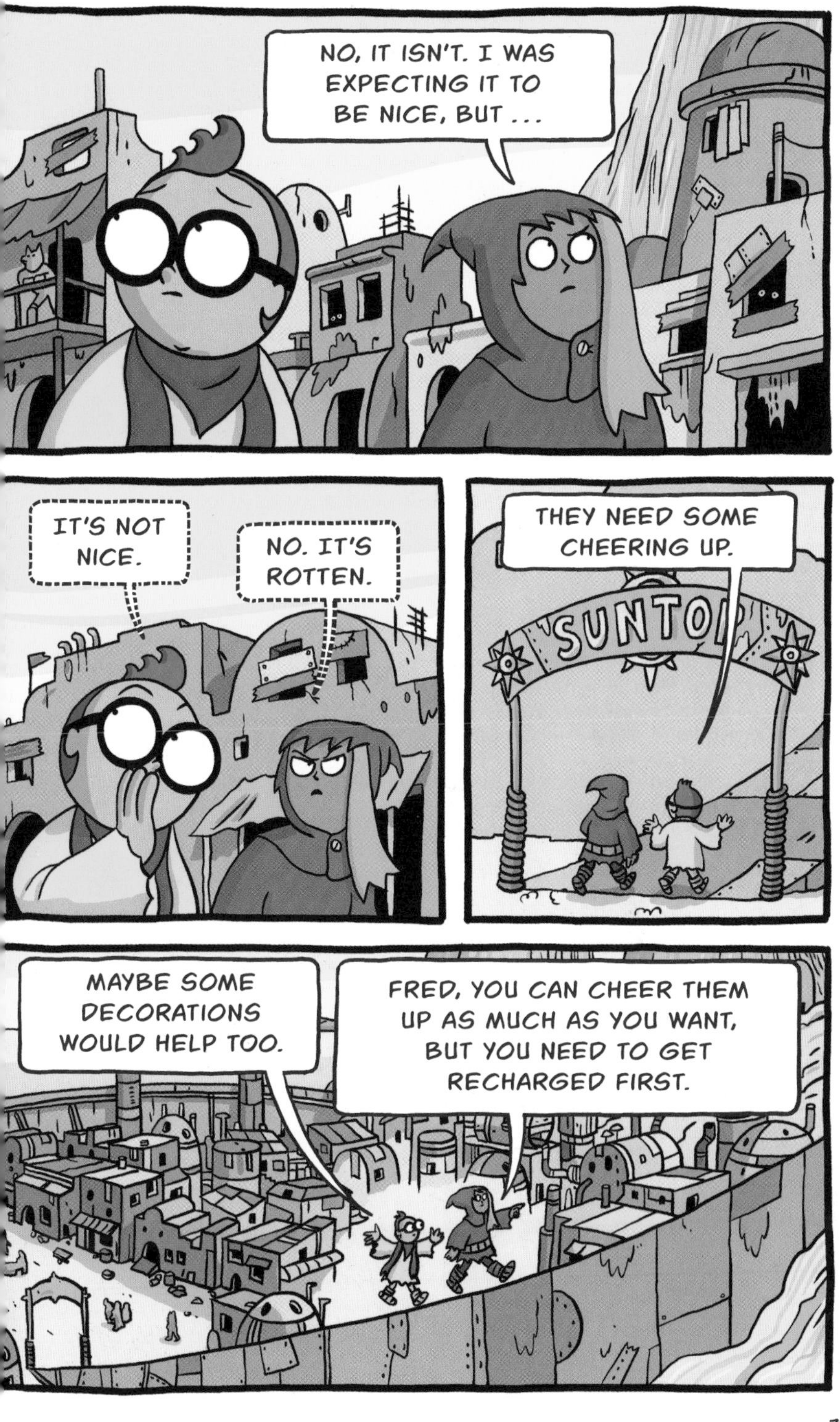
NO, IT ISN'T. I WAS EXPECTING IT TO BE NICE, BUT . . .
IT'S NOT NICE.
NO. IT'S ROTTEN.
THEY NEED SOME CHEERING UP.
SUNTO
MAYBE SOME DECORATIONS WOULD HELP TOO.
FRED, YOU CAN CHEER THEM UP AS MUCH AS YOU WANT, BUT YOU NEED TO GET RECHARGED FIRST.

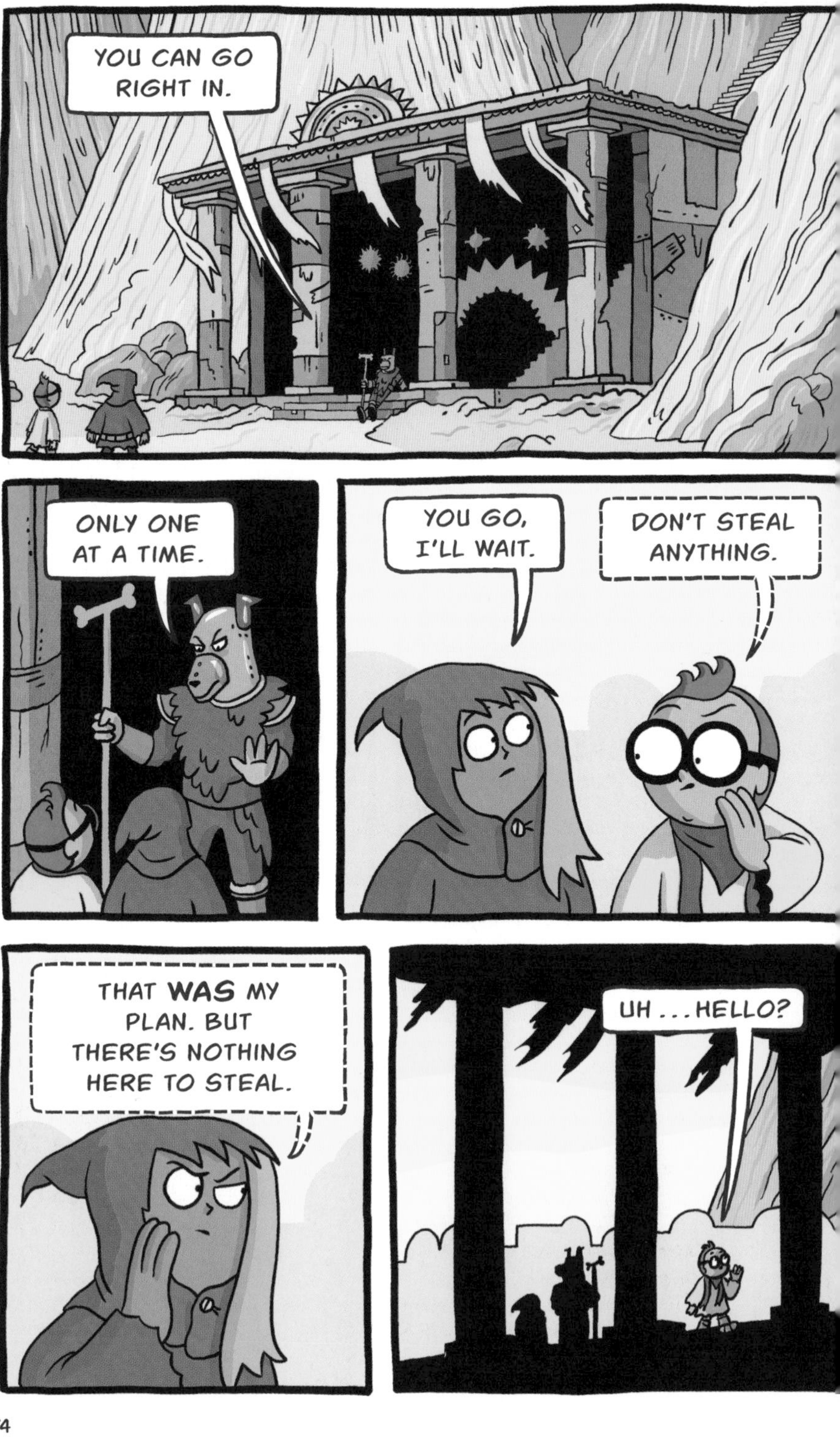
YOU CAN GO RIGHT IN.
ONLY ONE AT A TIME.
YOU GO, I'LL WAIT.
DON'T STEAL ANYTHING.
THAT **WAS** MY PLAN. BUT THERE'S NOTHING HERE TO STEAL.
UH . . . HELLO?

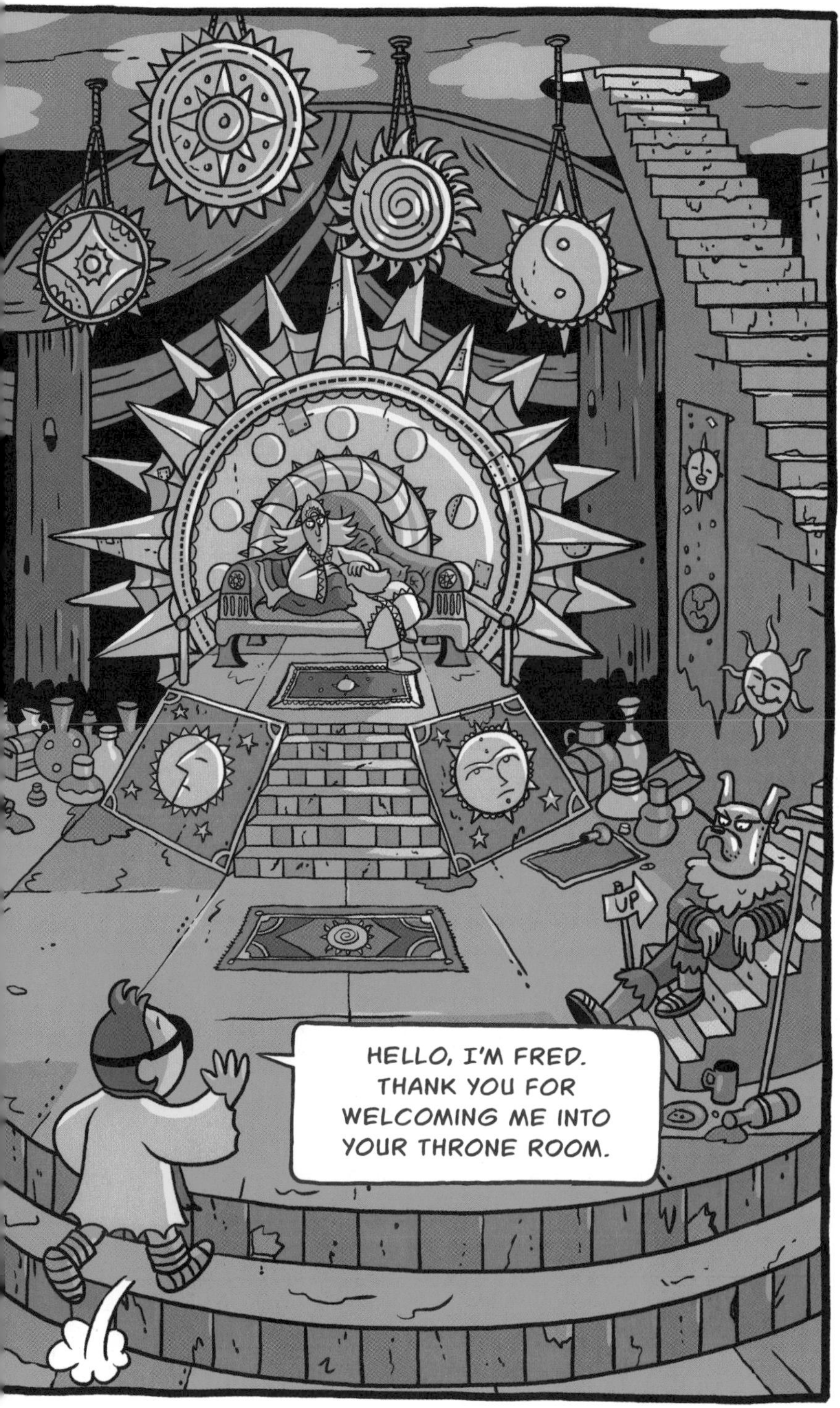
UP
HELLO, I'M FRED. THANK YOU FOR WELCOMING ME INTO YOUR THRONE ROOM.

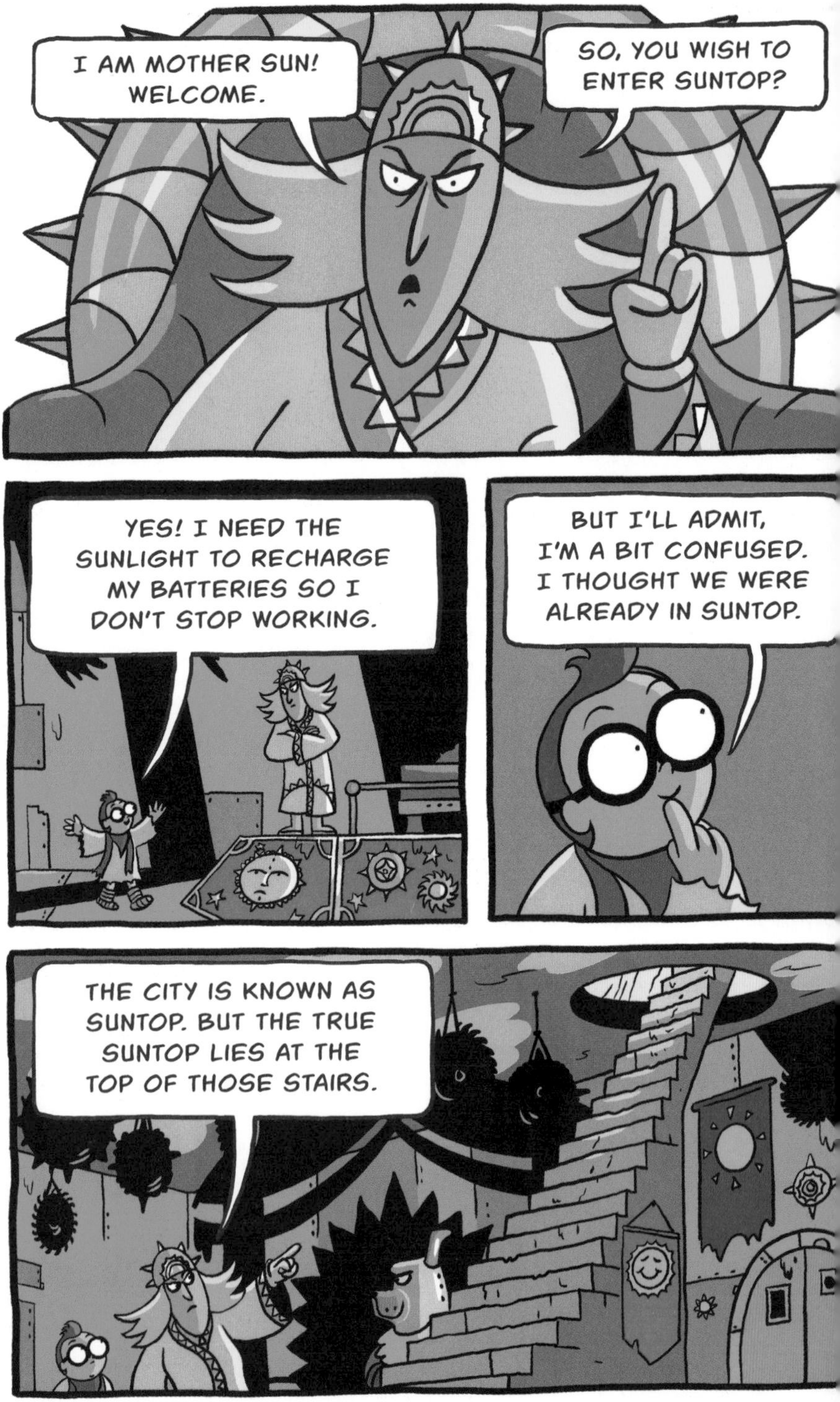
I AM MOTHER SUN! WELCOME.
SO, YOU WISH TO ENTER SUNTOP?
YES! I NEED THE SUNLIGHT TO RECHARGE MY BATTERIES SO I DON'T STOP WORKING.
BUT I'LL ADMIT, I'M A BIT CONFUSED. I THOUGHT WE WERE ALREADY IN SUNTOP.
THE CITY IS KNOWN AS SUNTOP. BUT THE TRUE SUNTOP LIES AT THE TOP OF THOSE STAIRS.

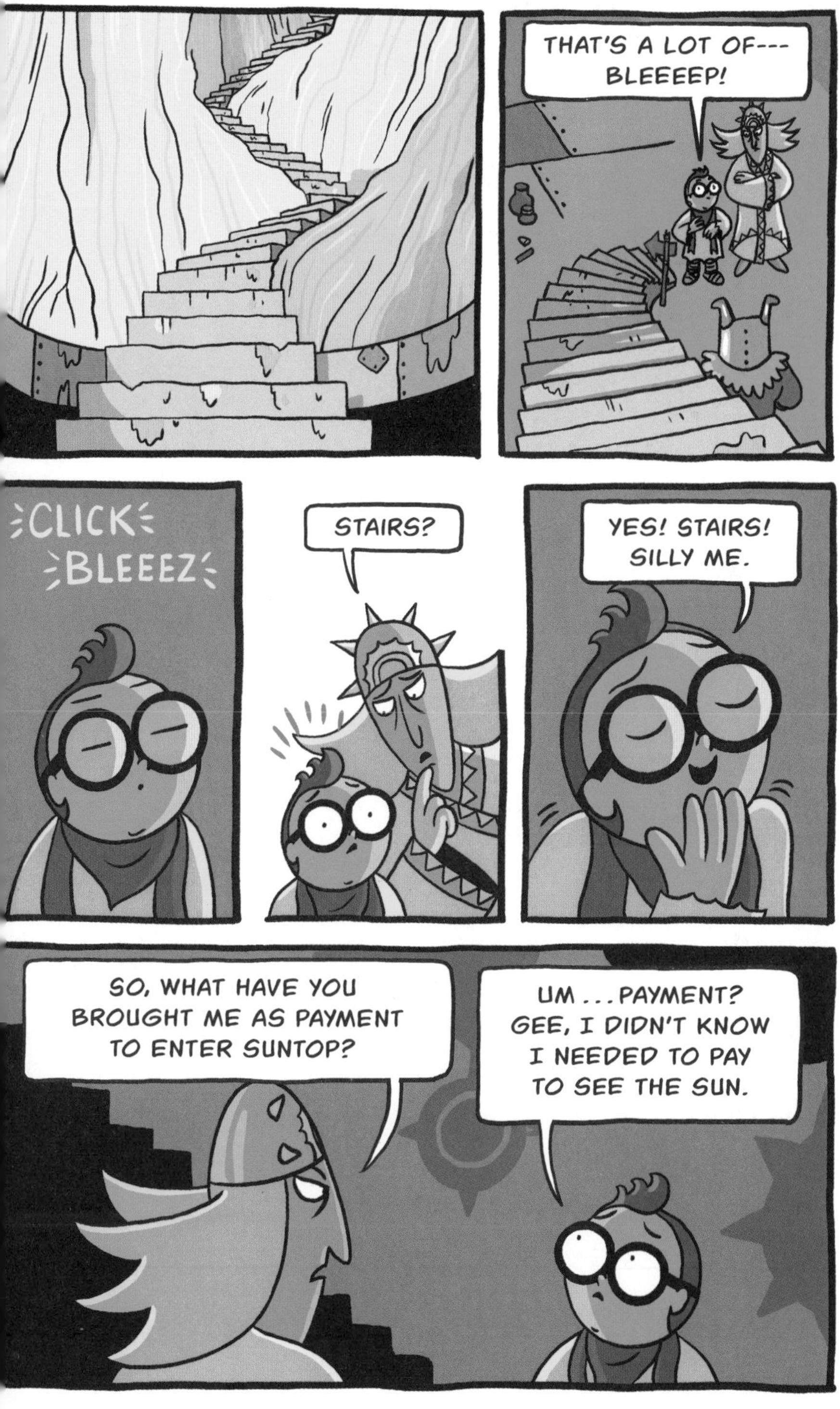
THAT'S A LOT OF---
BLEEEEP!
CLICK
BLEEEZ
STAIRS?
YES! STAIRS! SILLY ME.
SO, WHAT HAVE YOU BROUGHT ME AS PAYMENT TO ENTER SUNTOP?
UM . . . PAYMENT? GEE, I DIDN'T KNOW I NEEDED TO PAY TO SEE THE SUN.

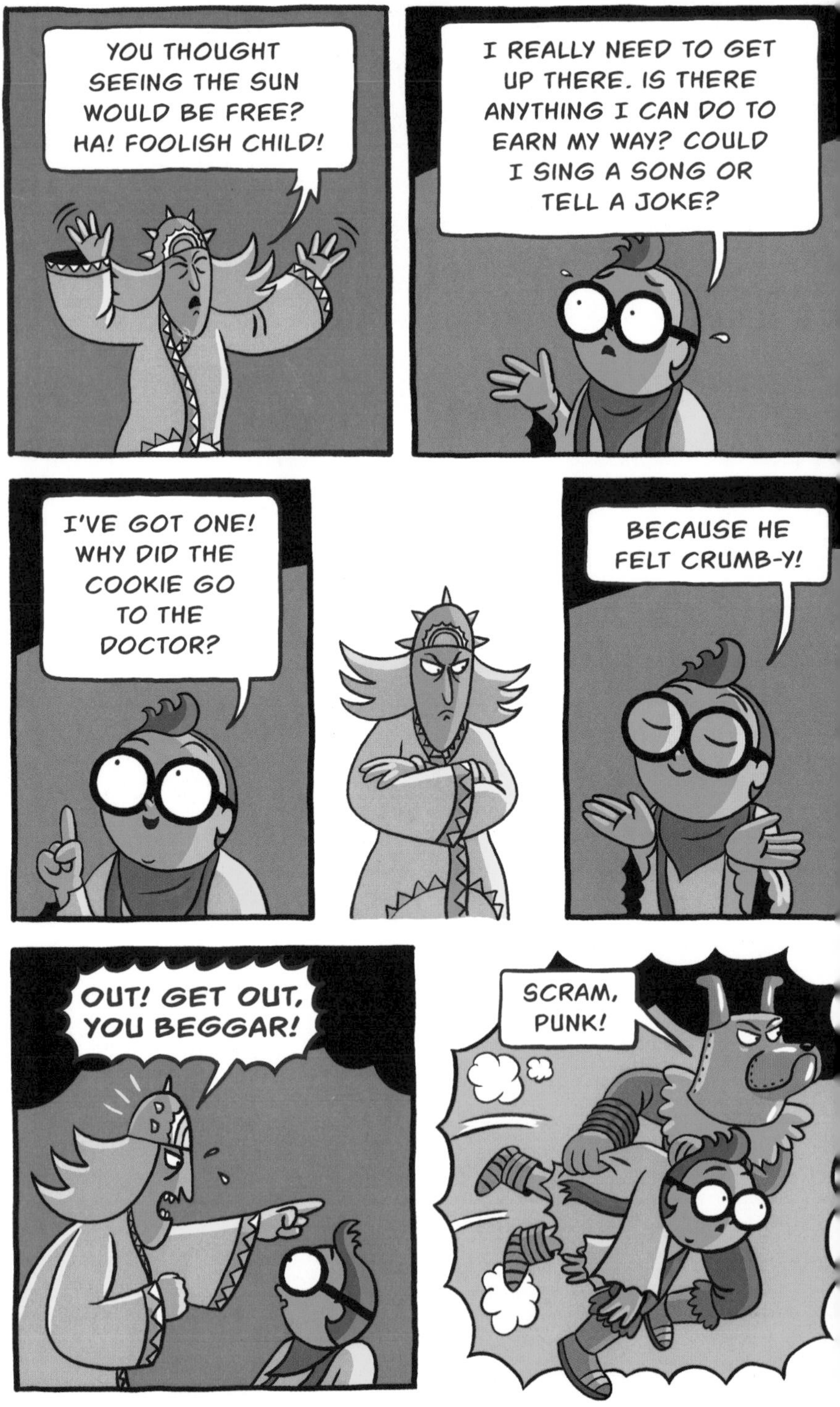
YOU THOUGHT SEEING THE SUN WOULD BE FREE? HA! FOOLISH CHILD!
I REALLY NEED TO GET UP THERE. IS THERE ANYTHING I CAN DO TO EARN MY WAY? COULD I SING A SONG OR TELL A JOKE?
I'VE GOT ONE! WHY DID THE COOKIE GO TO THE DOCTOR?
BECAUSE HE FELT CRUMB-Y!
OUT! GET OUT, YOU BEGGAR!
SCRAM, PUNK!

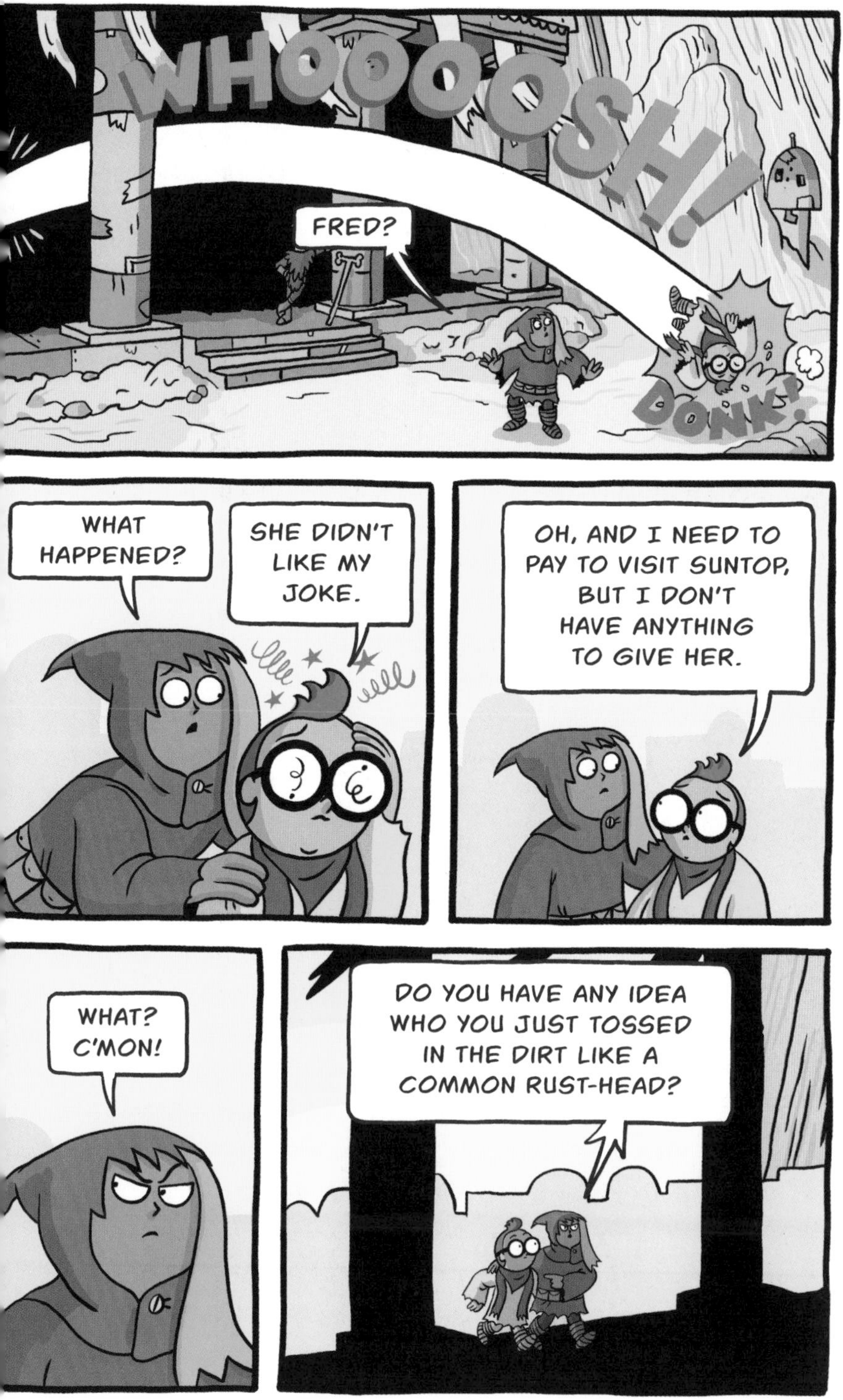
WHOOOOOSH!!
FRED?
DONK!
WHAT HAPPENED?
SHE DIDN'T LIKE MY JOKE.
OH, AND I NEED TO PAY TO VISIT SUNTOP, BUT I DON'T HAVE ANYTHING TO GIVE HER.
WHAT? C'MON!
DO YOU HAVE ANY IDEA WHO YOU JUST TOSSED IN THE DIRT LIKE A COMMON RUST-HEAD?

WHO ARE YOU?

I'M WORMY! AND THIS IS FRED. **THE** FRED!

THE FRED? THE SAME FRED WHO GOT BORGO THE INSULTER TO STOP INSULTING PEOPLE?

YUP.

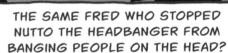

THE SAME FRED WHO STOPPED NUTTO THE HEADBANGER FROM BANGING PEOPLE ON THE HEAD?

THAT'S RIGHT.

HUH. I THOUGHT YOU'D BE TALLER.

NOPE. HE'S SHORT, BUT HE'S HERE NOW.

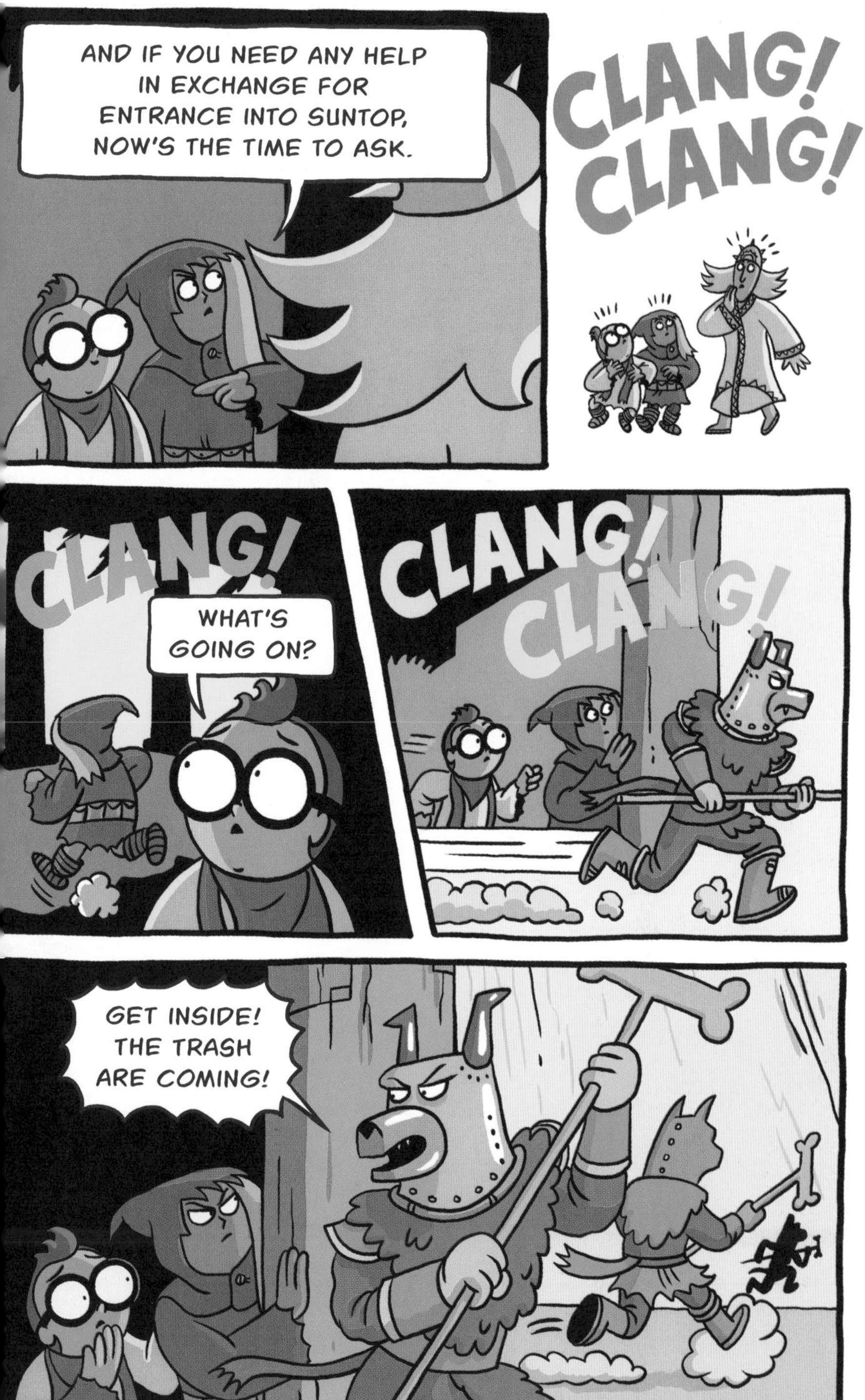
AND IF YOU NEED ANY HELP IN EXCHANGE FOR ENTRANCE INTO SUNTOP, NOW'S THE TIME TO ASK.
CLANG! CLANG!
CLANG!
WHAT'S GOING ON?
CLANG! CLANG!
GET INSIDE! THE TRASH ARE COMING!

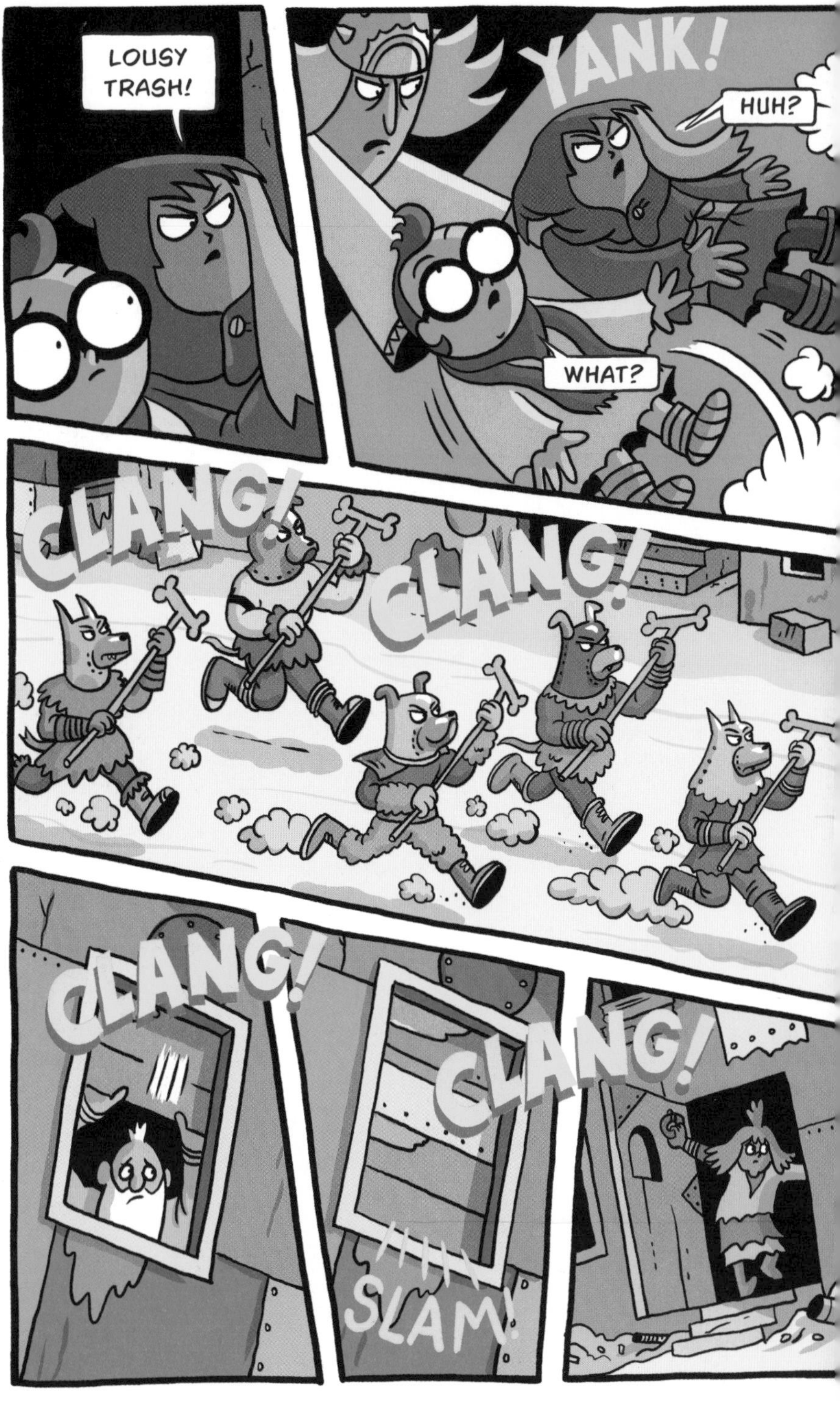
LOUSY TRASH!
YANK!
HUH?
WHAT?
CLANG!
CLANG!
CLANG!
CLANG!
SLAM!

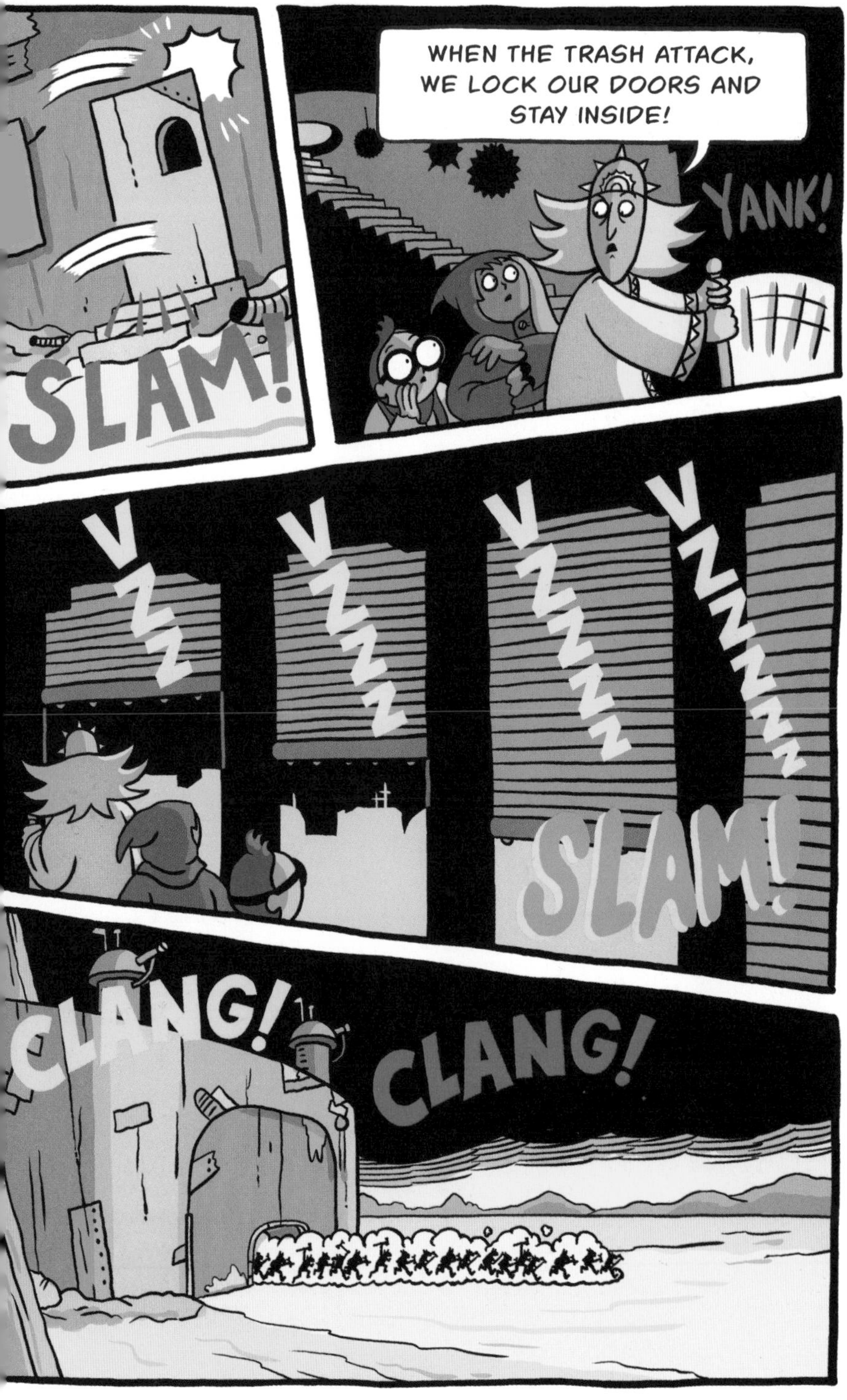
SLAM!
WHEN THE TRASH ATTACK, WE LOCK OUR DOORS AND STAY INSIDE!
YANK!
VZZZ
VZZZZ
VZZZZZ
VZZZZZZZ
SLAM!
CLANG!
CLANG!

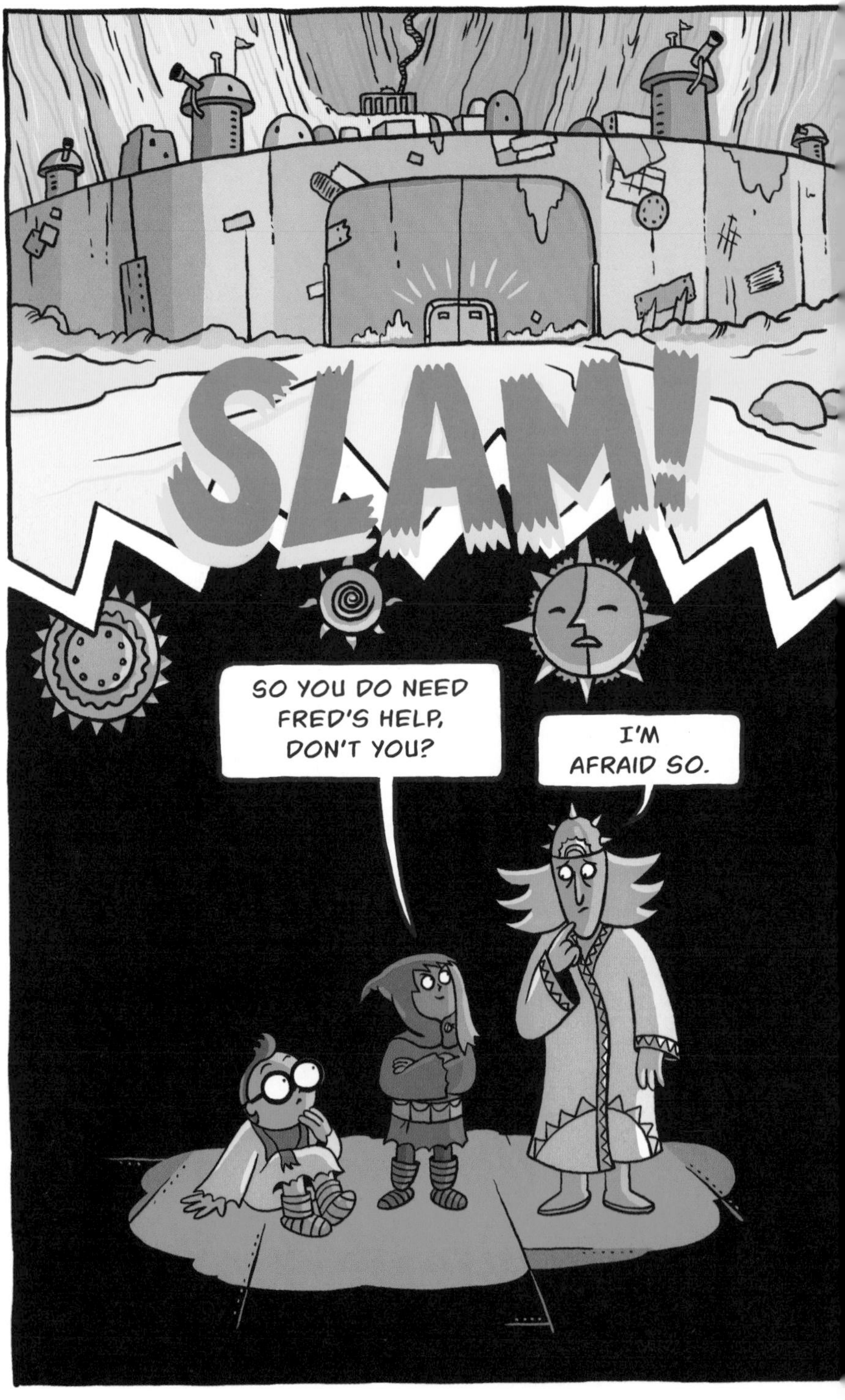
SLAM!
SO YOU DO NEED FRED'S HELP, DON'T YOU?
I'M AFRAID SO.

CHAPTER 7

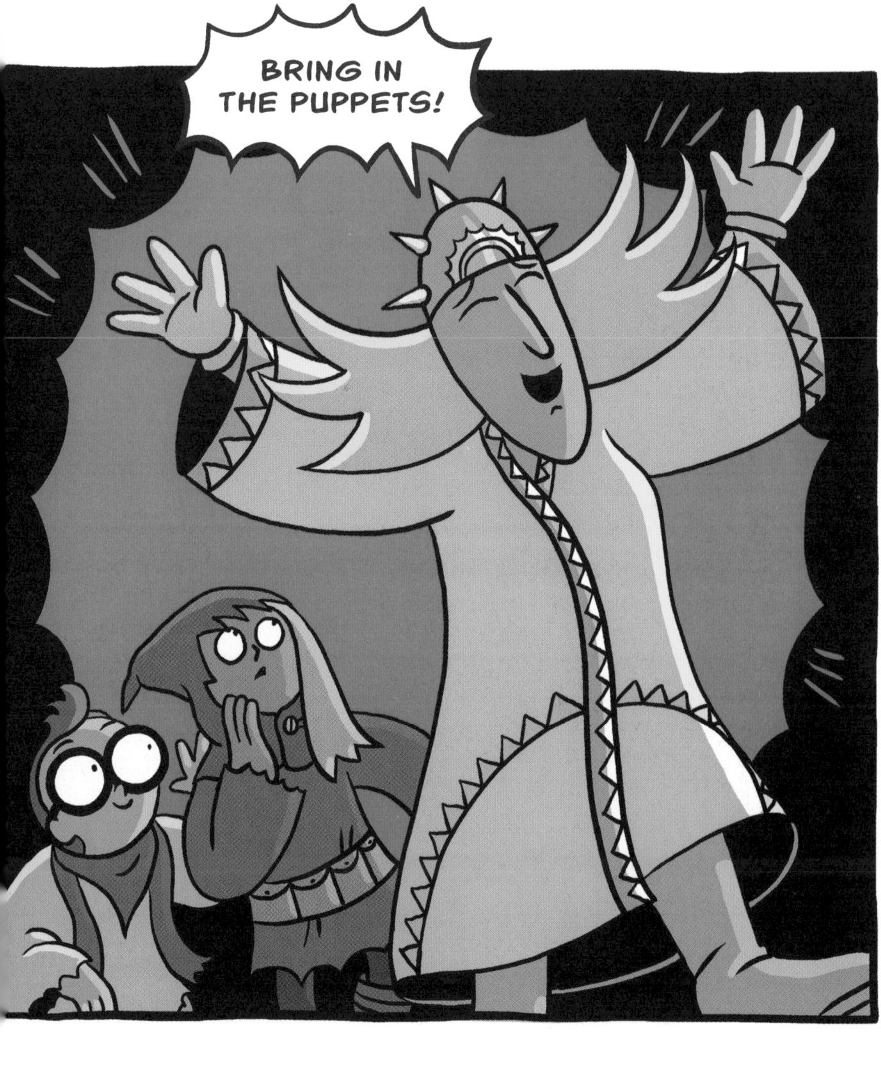
BRING IN THE PUPPETS!

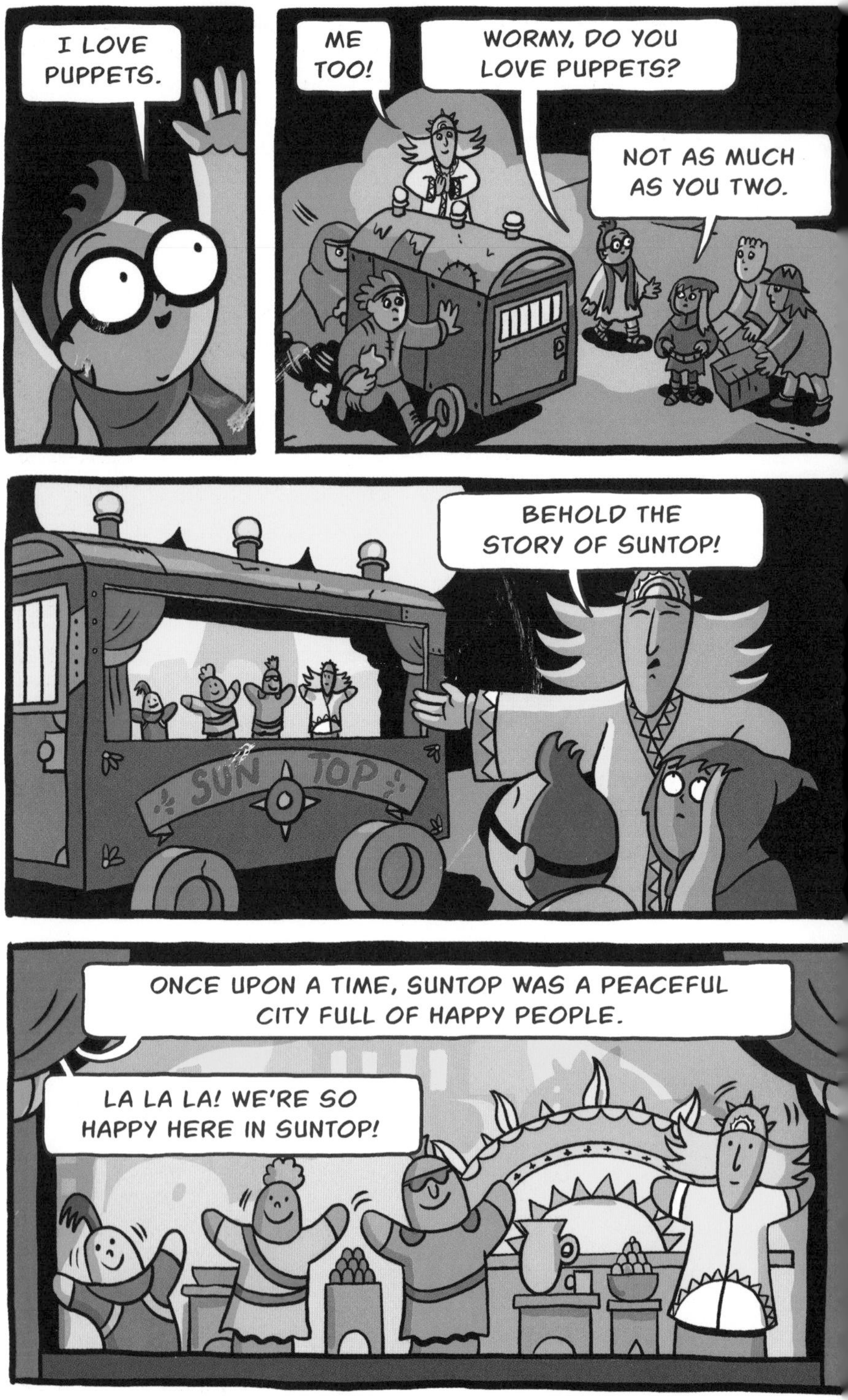
I LOVE PUPPETS.
ME TOO!
WORMY, DO YOU LOVE PUPPETS?
NOT AS MUCH AS YOU TWO.
BEHOLD THE STORY OF SUNTOP!
SUN TOP
ONCE UPON A TIME, SUNTOP WAS A PEACEFUL CITY FULL OF HAPPY PEOPLE.
LA LA LA! WE'RE SO HAPPY HERE IN SUNTOP!

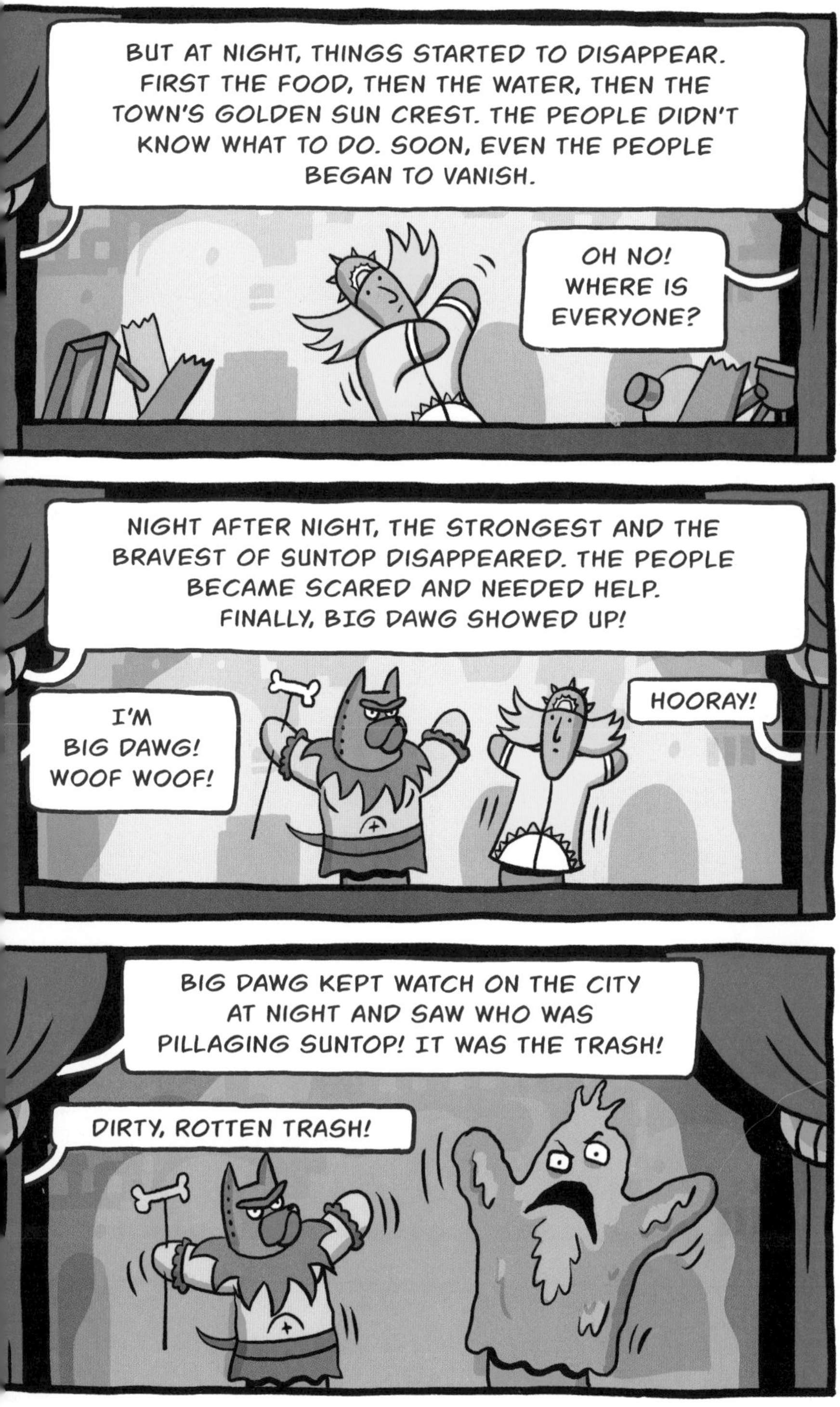
BUT AT NIGHT, THINGS STARTED TO DISAPPEAR. FIRST THE FOOD, THEN THE WATER, THEN THE TOWN'S GOLDEN SUN CREST. THE PEOPLE DIDN'T KNOW WHAT TO DO. SOON, EVEN THE PEOPLE BEGAN TO VANISH.
OH NO! WHERE IS EVERYONE?
NIGHT AFTER NIGHT, THE STRONGEST AND THE BRAVEST OF SUNTOP DISAPPEARED. THE PEOPLE BECAME SCARED AND NEEDED HELP. FINALLY, BIG DAWG SHOWED UP!
I'M BIG DAWG! WOOF WOOF!
HOORAY!
BIG DAWG KEPT WATCH ON THE CITY AT NIGHT AND SAW WHO WAS PILLAGING SUNTOP! IT WAS THE TRASH!
DIRTY, ROTTEN TRASH!

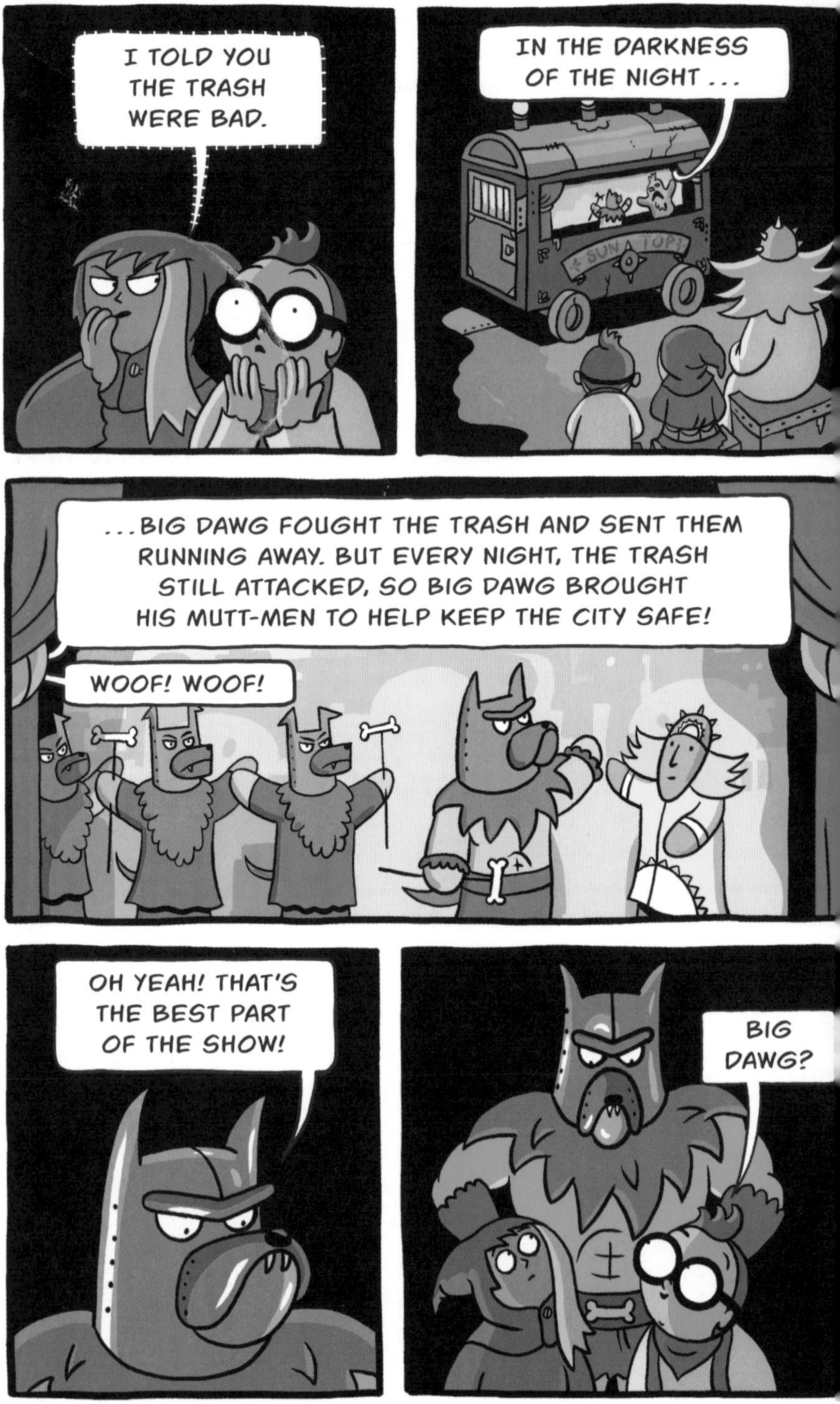
I TOLD YOU THE TRASH WERE BAD.
IN THE DARKNESS OF THE NIGHT . . .
SUN TOP!
. . . BIG DAWG FOUGHT THE TRASH AND SENT THEM RUNNING AWAY. BUT EVERY NIGHT, THE TRASH STILL ATTACKED, SO BIG DAWG BROUGHT HIS MUTT-MEN TO HELP KEEP THE CITY SAFE!
WOOF! WOOF!
OH YEAH! THAT'S THE BEST PART OF THE SHOW!
BIG DAWG?

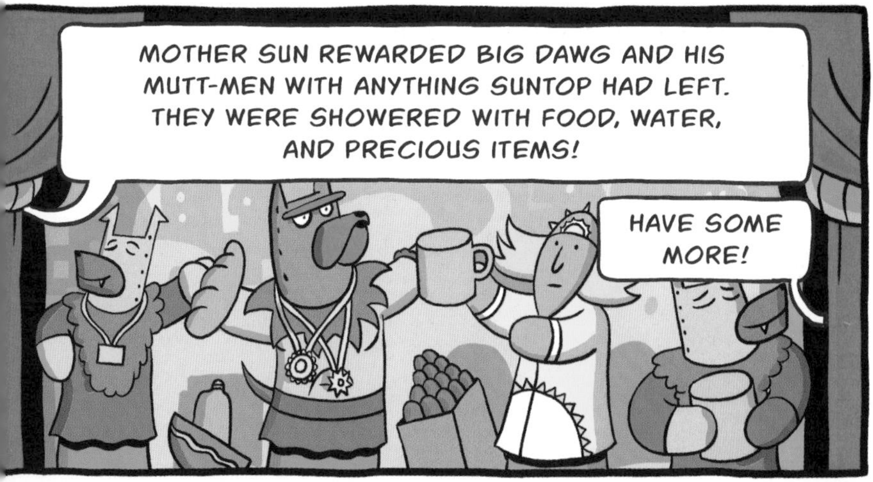
MOTHER SUN REWARDED BIG DAWG AND HIS MUTT-MEN WITH ANYTHING SUNTOP HAD LEFT. THEY WERE SHOWERED WITH FOOD, WATER, AND PRECIOUS ITEMS!
HAVE SOME MORE!

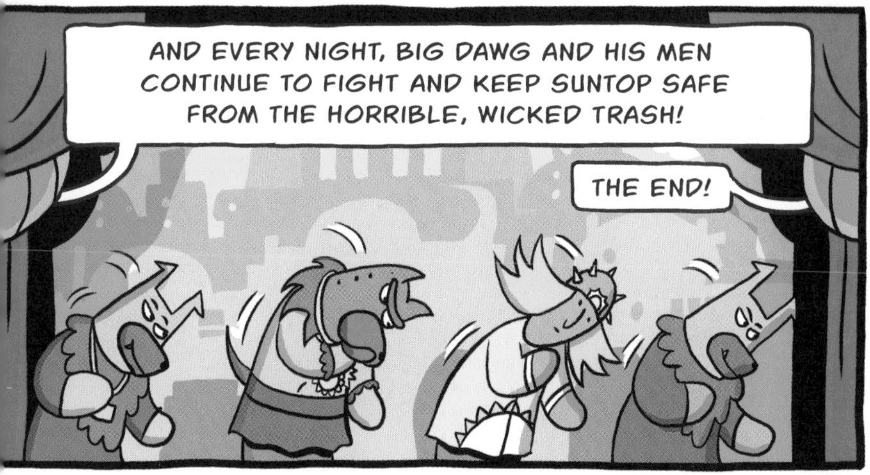
AND EVERY NIGHT, BIG DAWG AND HIS MEN CONTINUE TO FIGHT AND KEEP SUNTOP SAFE FROM THE HORRIBLE, WICKED TRASH!
THE END!

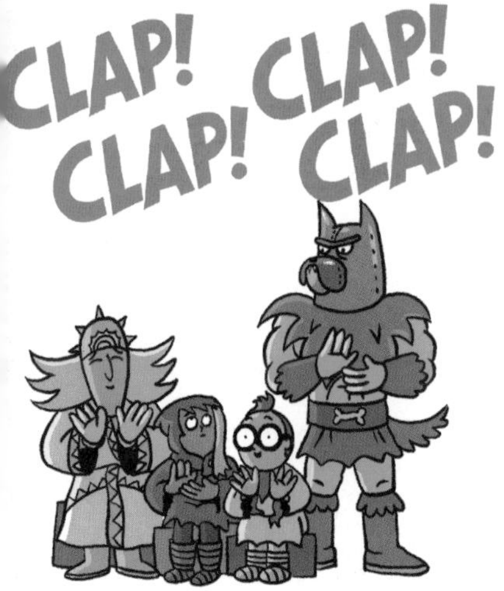
CLAP! CLAP! CLAP! CLAP!

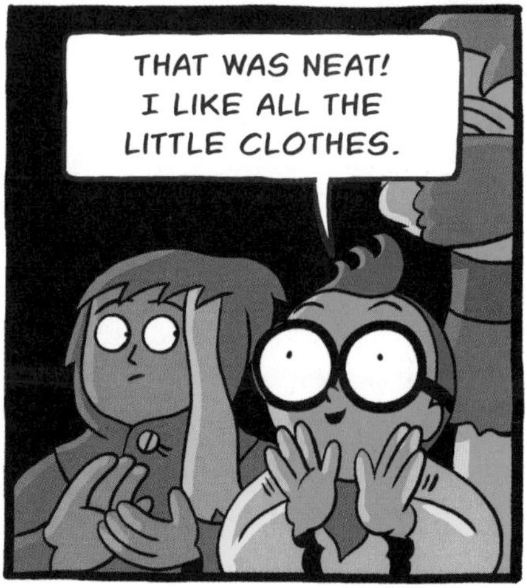
THAT WAS NEAT! I LIKE ALL THE LITTLE CLOTHES.

YOU'RE BACK EARLY.

IT WAS JUST A SMALL SKIRMISH TONIGHT. THERE WERE ONLY A FEW, SO WE TOOK CARE OF THEM QUICKLY.

BIP!

BAM!

BOOM!

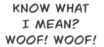

KNOW WHAT I MEAN? WOOF! WOOF!

TRUTHFULLY, FRED, I NEED YOUR HELP.

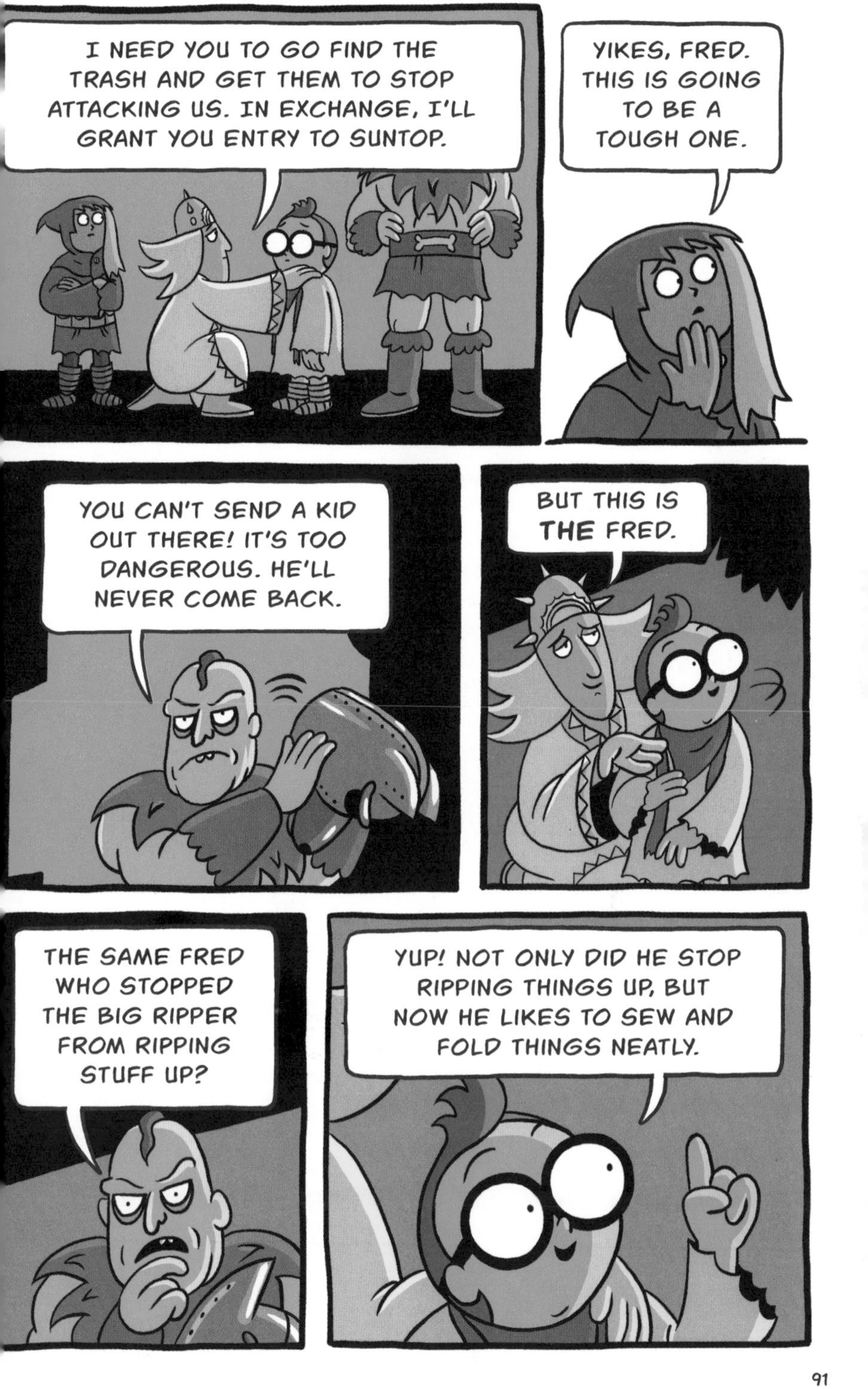
I NEED YOU TO GO FIND THE TRASH AND GET THEM TO STOP ATTACKING US. IN EXCHANGE, I'LL GRANT YOU ENTRY TO SUNTOP.
YIKES, FRED. THIS IS GOING TO BE A TOUGH ONE.
YOU CAN'T SEND A KID OUT THERE! IT'S TOO DANGEROUS. HE'LL NEVER COME BACK.
BUT THIS IS **THE** FRED.
THE SAME FRED WHO STOPPED THE BIG RIPPER FROM RIPPING STUFF UP?
YUP! NOT ONLY DID HE STOP RIPPING THINGS UP, BUT NOW HE LIKES TO SEW AND FOLD THINGS NEATLY.

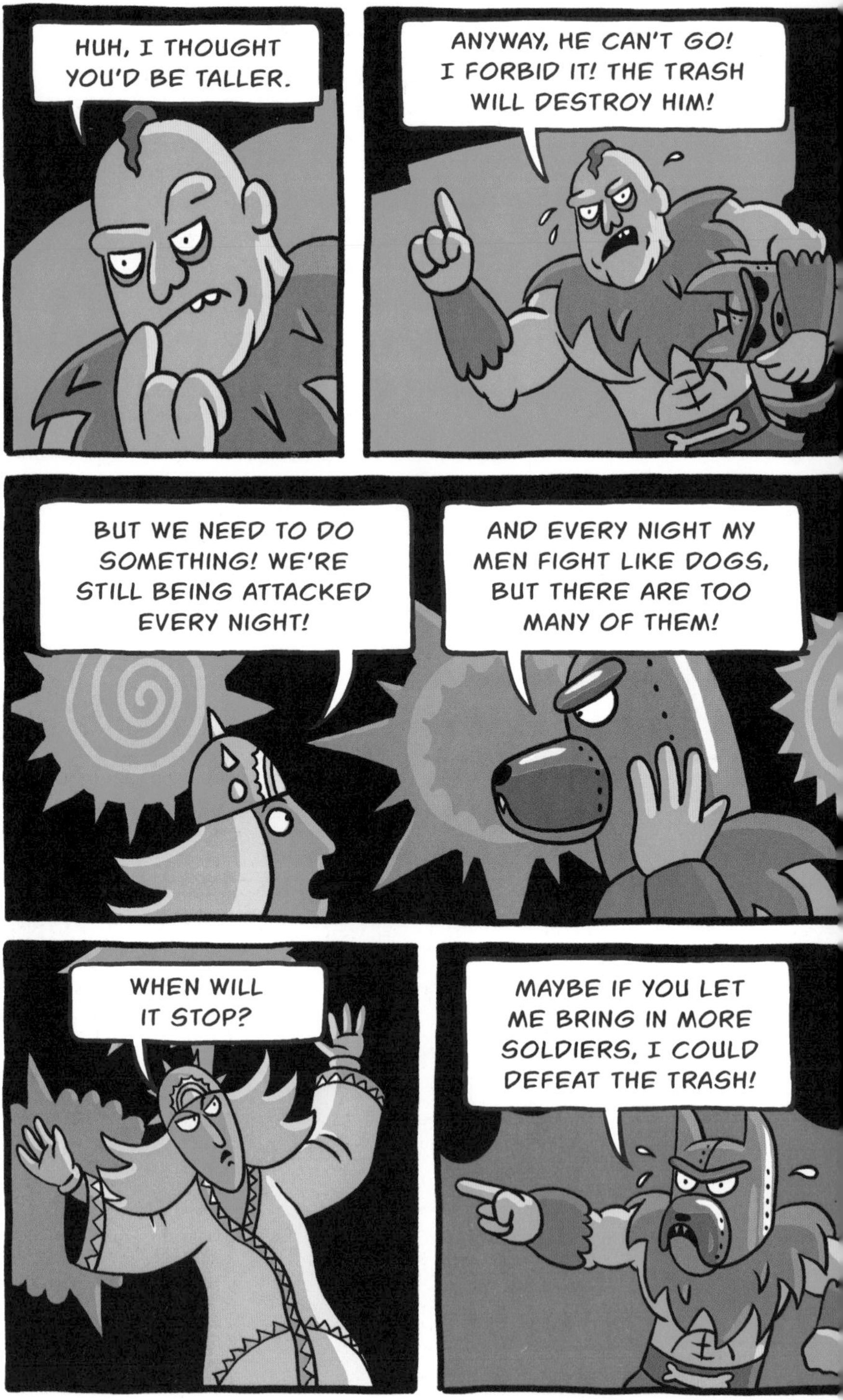
HUH, I THOUGHT YOU'D BE TALLER.
ANYWAY, HE CAN'T GO! I FORBID IT! THE TRASH WILL DESTROY HIM!
BUT WE NEED TO DO SOMETHING! WE'RE STILL BEING ATTACKED EVERY NIGHT!
AND EVERY NIGHT MY MEN FIGHT LIKE DOGS, BUT THERE ARE TOO MANY OF THEM!
WHEN WILL IT STOP?
MAYBE IF YOU LET ME BRING IN MORE SOLDIERS, I COULD DEFEAT THE TRASH!

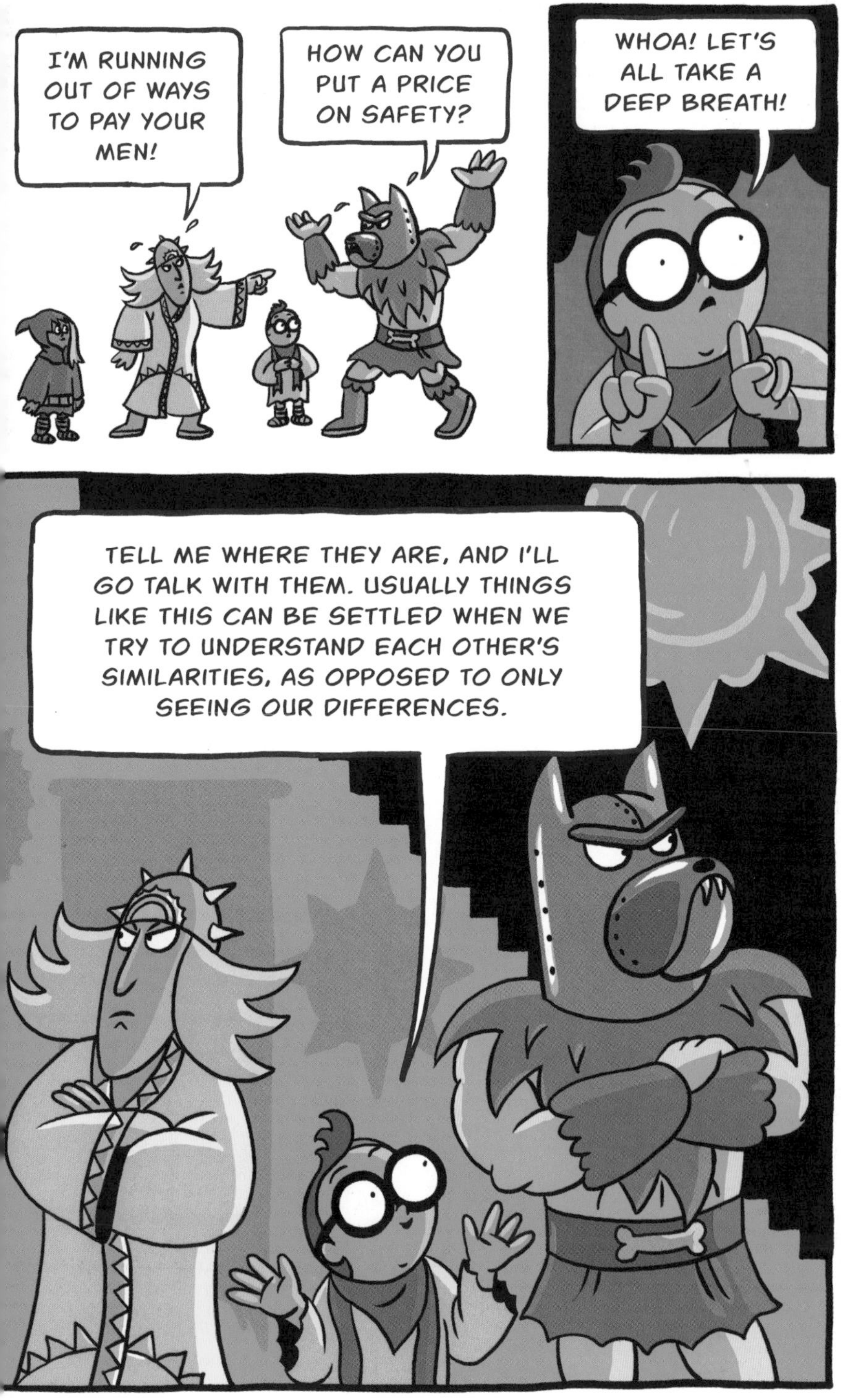
I'M RUNNING OUT OF WAYS TO PAY YOUR MEN!
HOW CAN YOU PUT A PRICE ON SAFETY?
WHOA! LET'S ALL TAKE A DEEP BREATH!
TELL ME WHERE THEY ARE, AND I'LL GO TALK WITH THEM. USUALLY THINGS LIKE THIS CAN BE SETTLED WHEN WE TRY TO UNDERSTAND EACH OTHER'S SIMILARITIES, AS OPPOSED TO ONLY SEEING OUR DIFFERENCES.

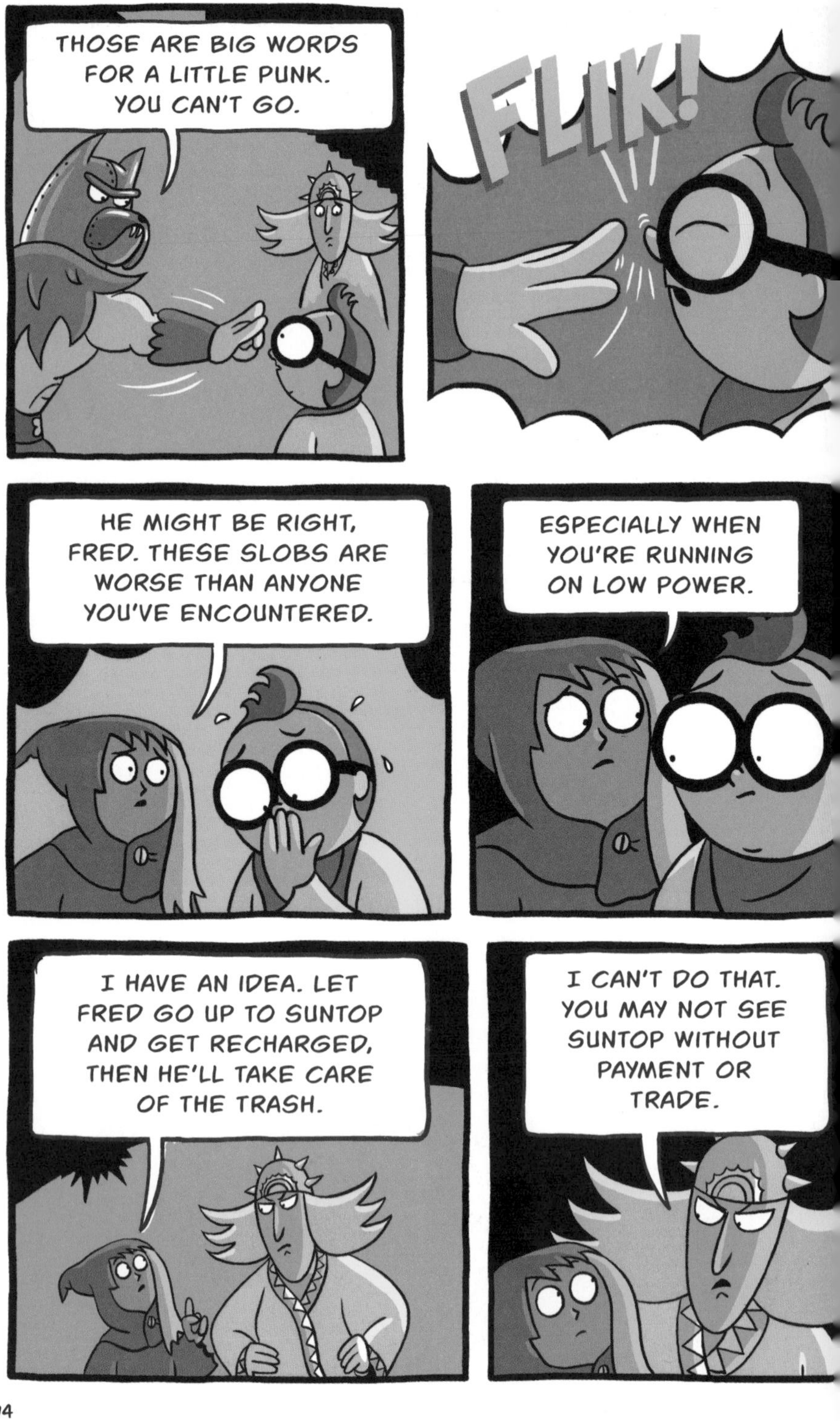
THOSE ARE BIG WORDS FOR A LITTLE PUNK. YOU CAN'T GO.
FLIK!
HE MIGHT BE RIGHT, FRED. THESE SLOBS ARE WORSE THAN ANYONE YOU'VE ENCOUNTERED.
ESPECIALLY WHEN YOU'RE RUNNING ON LOW POWER.
I HAVE AN IDEA. LET FRED GO UP TO SUNTOP AND GET RECHARGED, THEN HE'LL TAKE CARE OF THE TRASH.
I CAN'T DO THAT. YOU MAY NOT SEE SUNTOP WITHOUT PAYMENT OR TRADE.

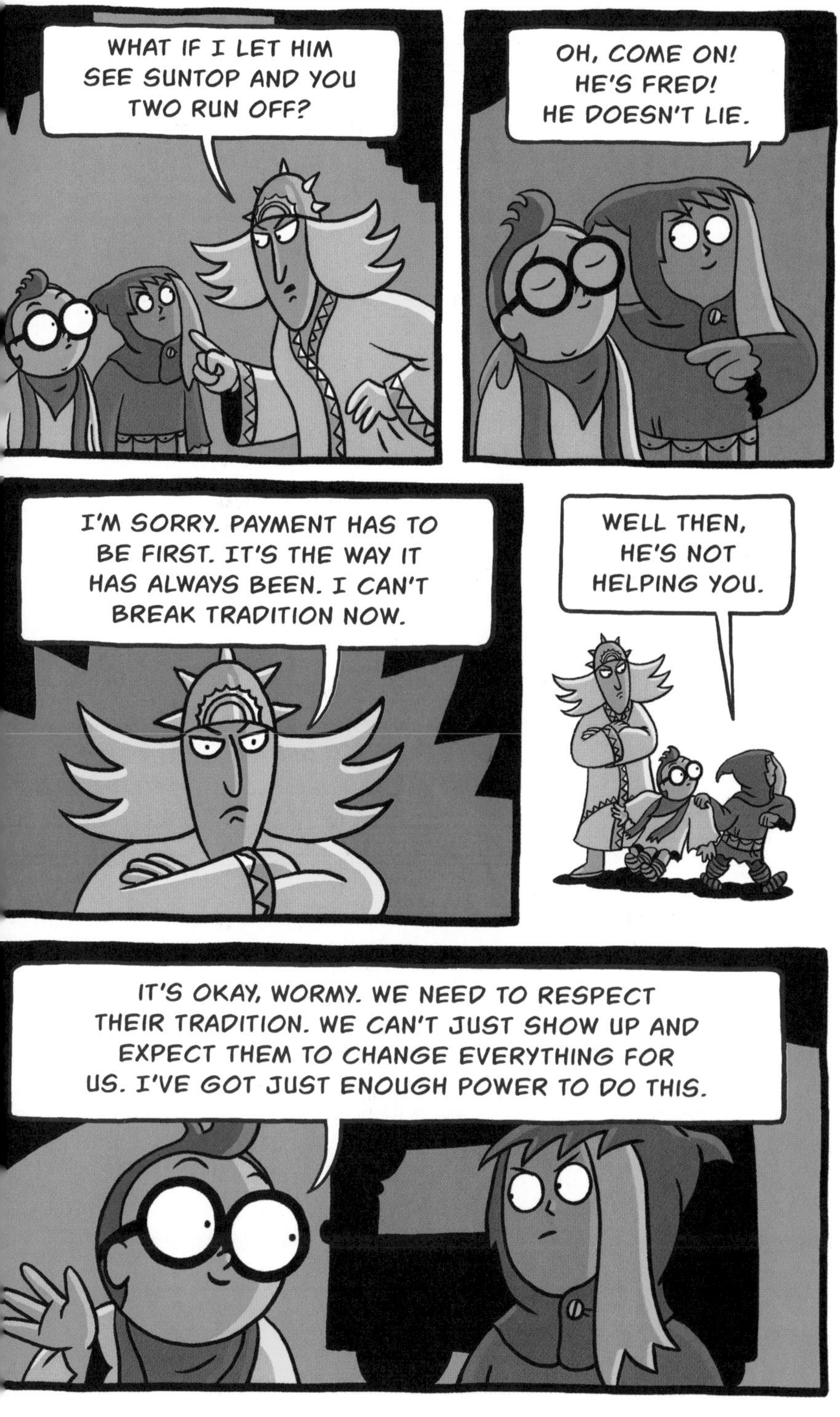

WHAT IF I LET HIM SEE SUNTOP AND YOU TWO RUN OFF?
OH, COME ON! HE'S FRED! HE DOESN'T LIE.
I'M SORRY. PAYMENT HAS TO BE FIRST. IT'S THE WAY IT HAS ALWAYS BEEN. I CAN'T BREAK TRADITION NOW.
WELL THEN, HE'S NOT HELPING YOU.
IT'S OKAY, WORMY. WE NEED TO RESPECT THEIR TRADITION. WE CAN'T JUST SHOW UP AND EXPECT THEM TO CHANGE EVERYTHING FOR US. I'VE GOT JUST ENOUGH POWER TO DO THIS.

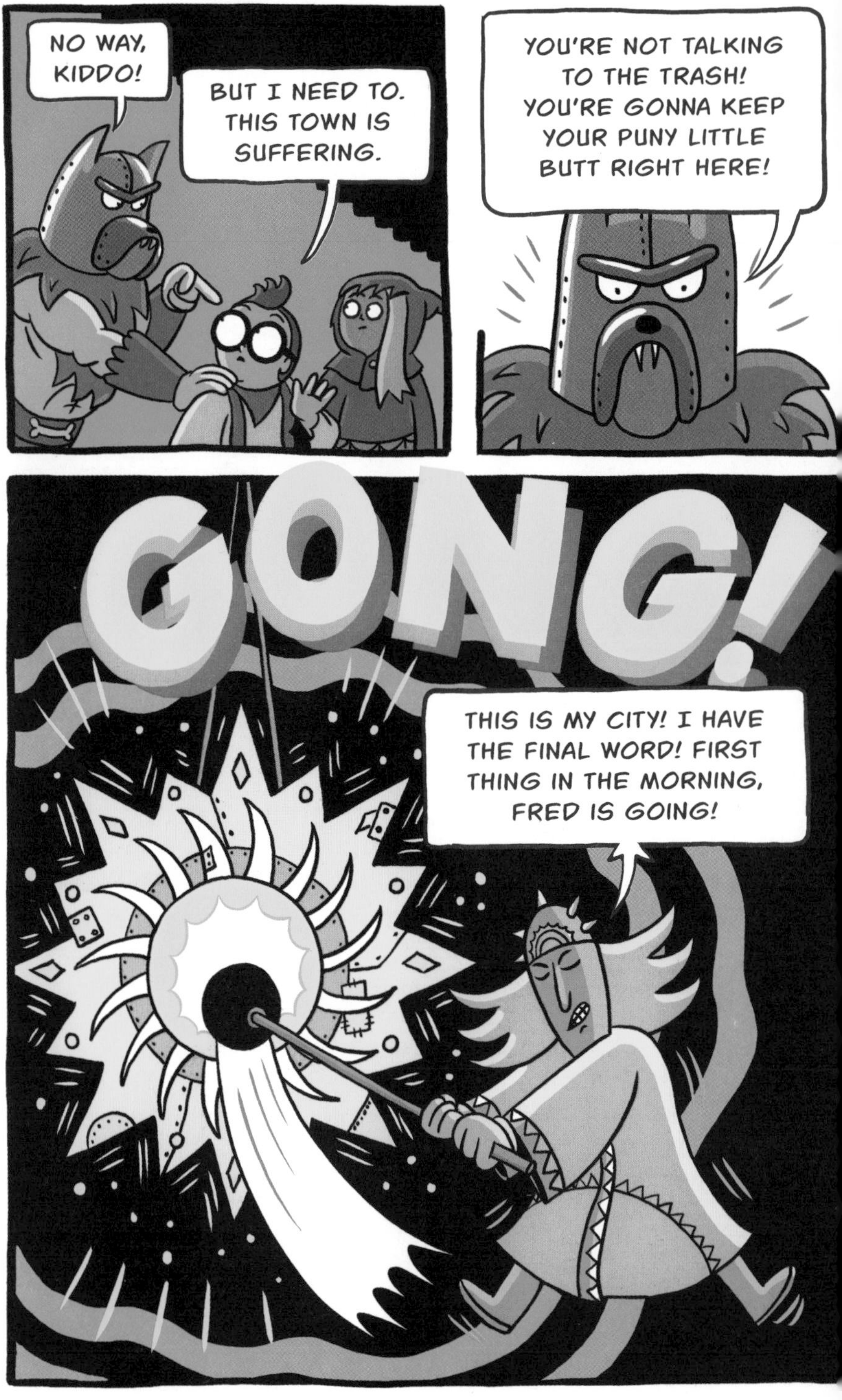
NO WAY, KIDDO!
BUT I NEED TO. THIS TOWN IS SUFFERING.
YOU'RE NOT TALKING TO THE TRASH! YOU'RE GONNA KEEP YOUR PUNY LITTLE BUTT RIGHT HERE!
GONG!
THIS IS MY CITY! I HAVE THE FINAL WORD! FIRST THING IN THE MORNING, FRED IS GOING!

CHAPTER 8

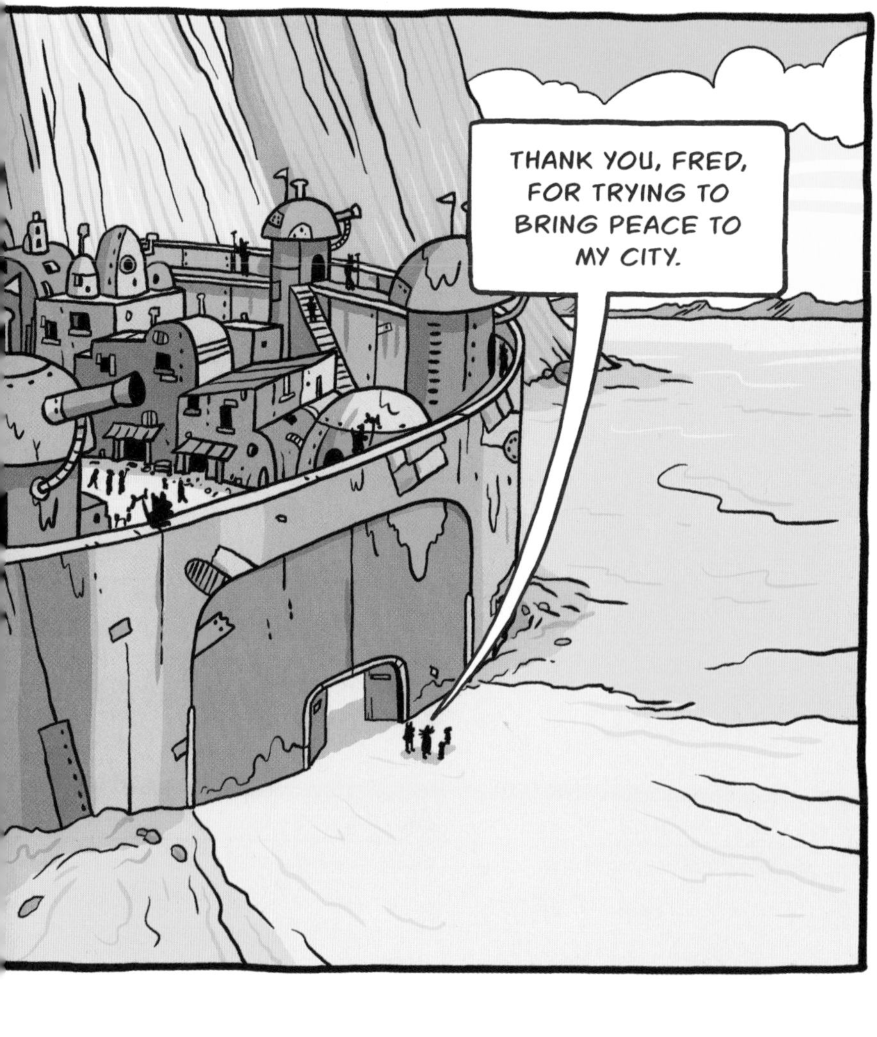
THANK YOU, FRED, FOR TRYING TO BRING PEACE TO MY CITY.

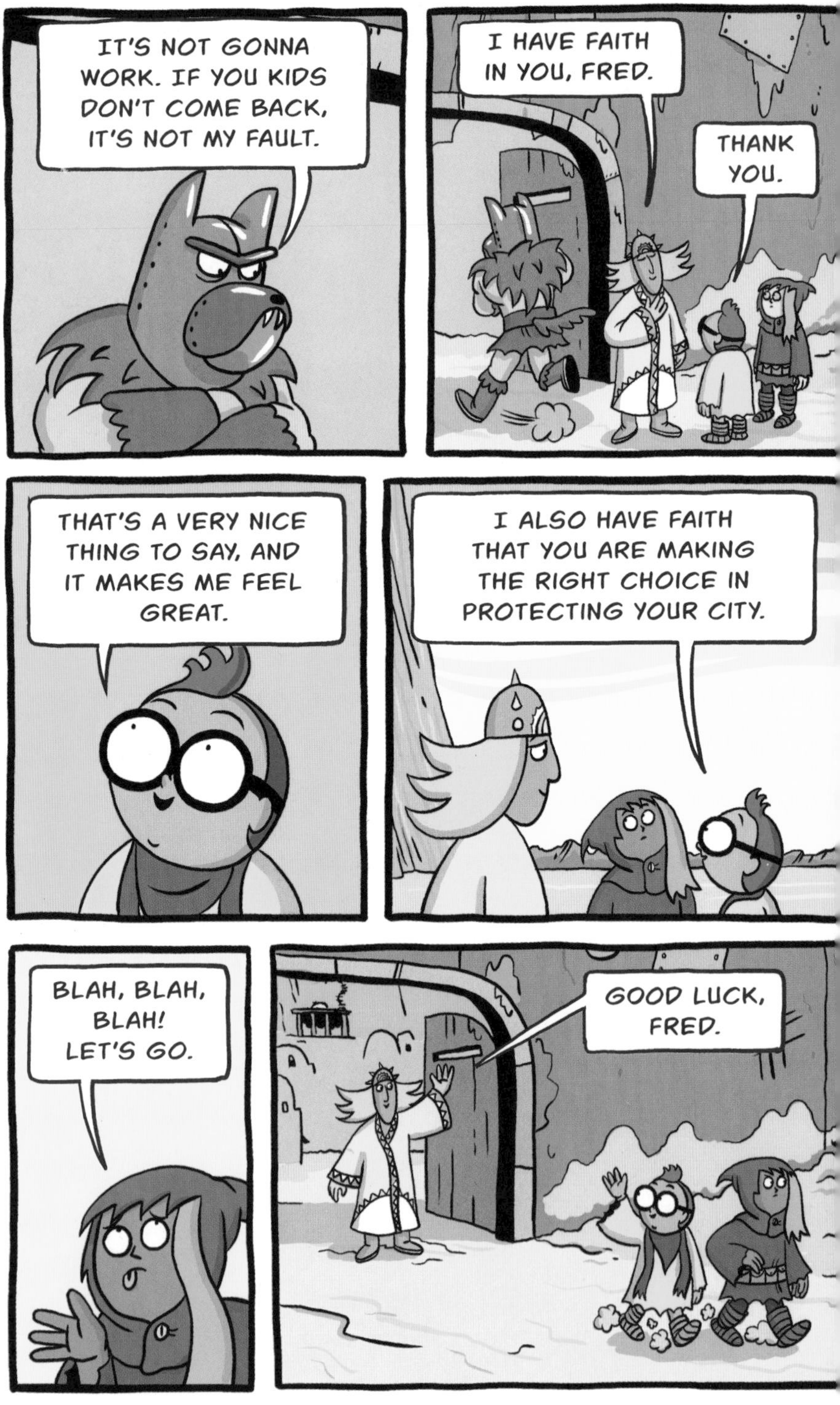
IT'S NOT GONNA WORK. IF YOU KIDS DON'T COME BACK, IT'S NOT MY FAULT.
I HAVE FAITH IN YOU, FRED.
THANK YOU.
THAT'S A VERY NICE THING TO SAY, AND IT MAKES ME FEEL GREAT.
I ALSO HAVE FAITH THAT YOU ARE MAKING THE RIGHT CHOICE IN PROTECTING YOUR CITY.
BLAH, BLAH, BLAH! LET'S GO.
GOOD LUCK, FRED.

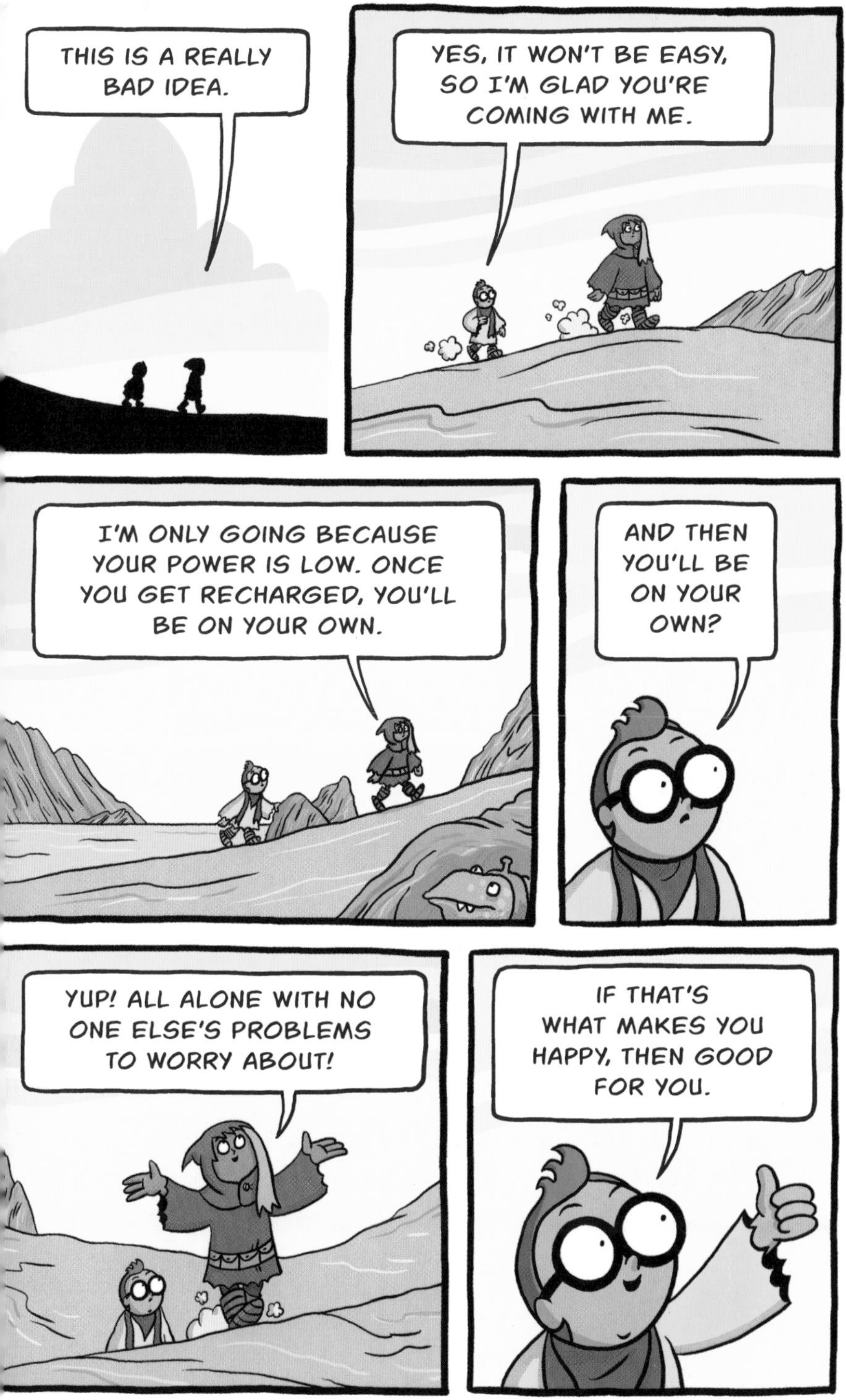
THIS IS A REALLY BAD IDEA.
YES, IT WON'T BE EASY, SO I'M GLAD YOU'RE COMING WITH ME.
I'M ONLY GOING BECAUSE YOUR POWER IS LOW. ONCE YOU GET RECHARGED, YOU'LL BE ON YOUR OWN.
AND THEN YOU'LL BE ON YOUR OWN?
YUP! ALL ALONE WITH NO ONE ELSE'S PROBLEMS TO WORRY ABOUT!
IF THAT'S WHAT MAKES YOU HAPPY, THEN GOOD FOR YOU.

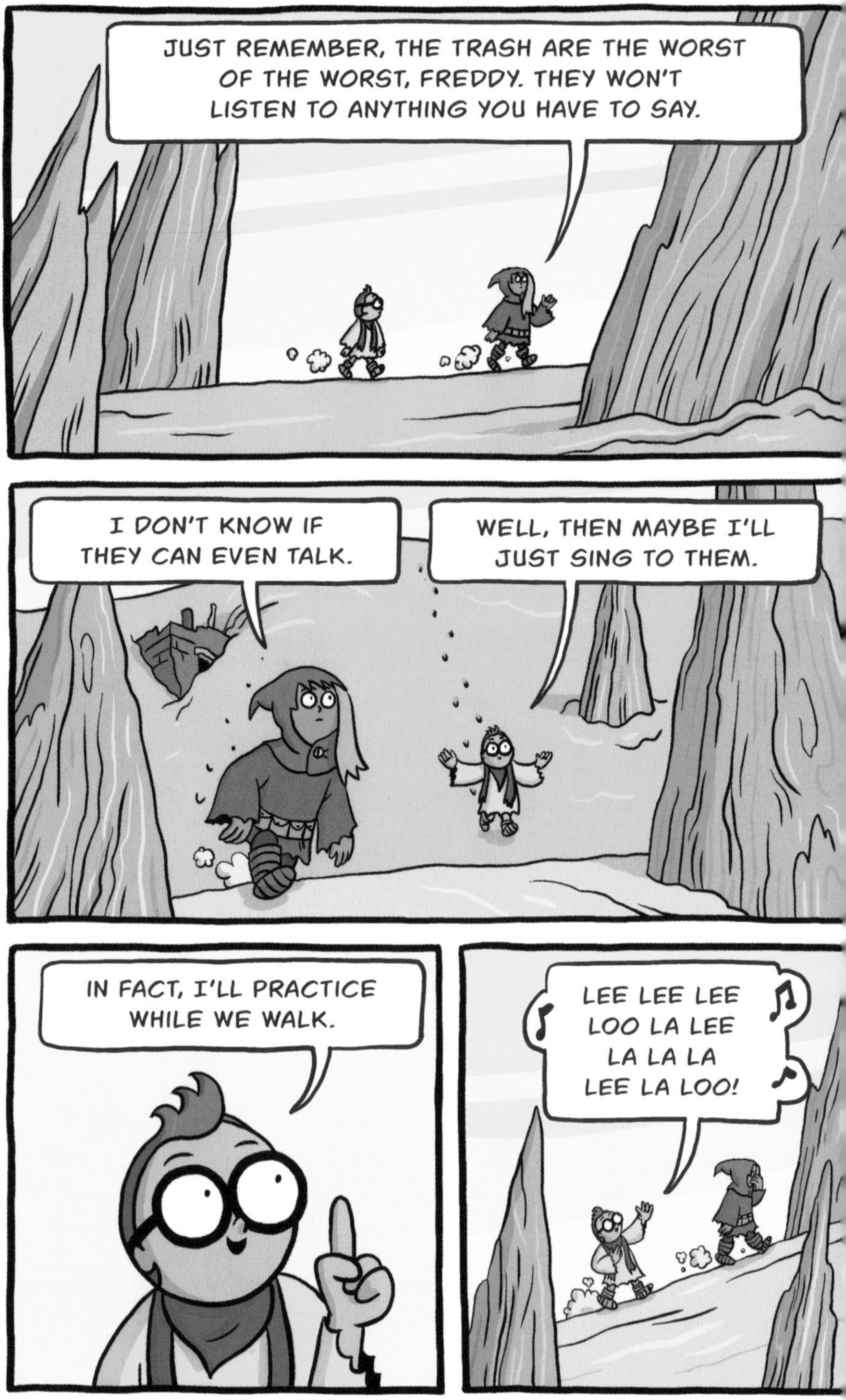
JUST REMEMBER, THE TRASH ARE THE WORST OF THE WORST, FREDDY. THEY WON'T LISTEN TO ANYTHING YOU HAVE TO SAY.
I DON'T KNOW IF THEY CAN EVEN TALK.
WELL, THEN MAYBE I'LL JUST SING TO THEM.
IN FACT, I'LL PRACTICE WHILE WE WALK.
LEE LEE LEE LOO LA LEE LA LA LA LEE LA LOO!

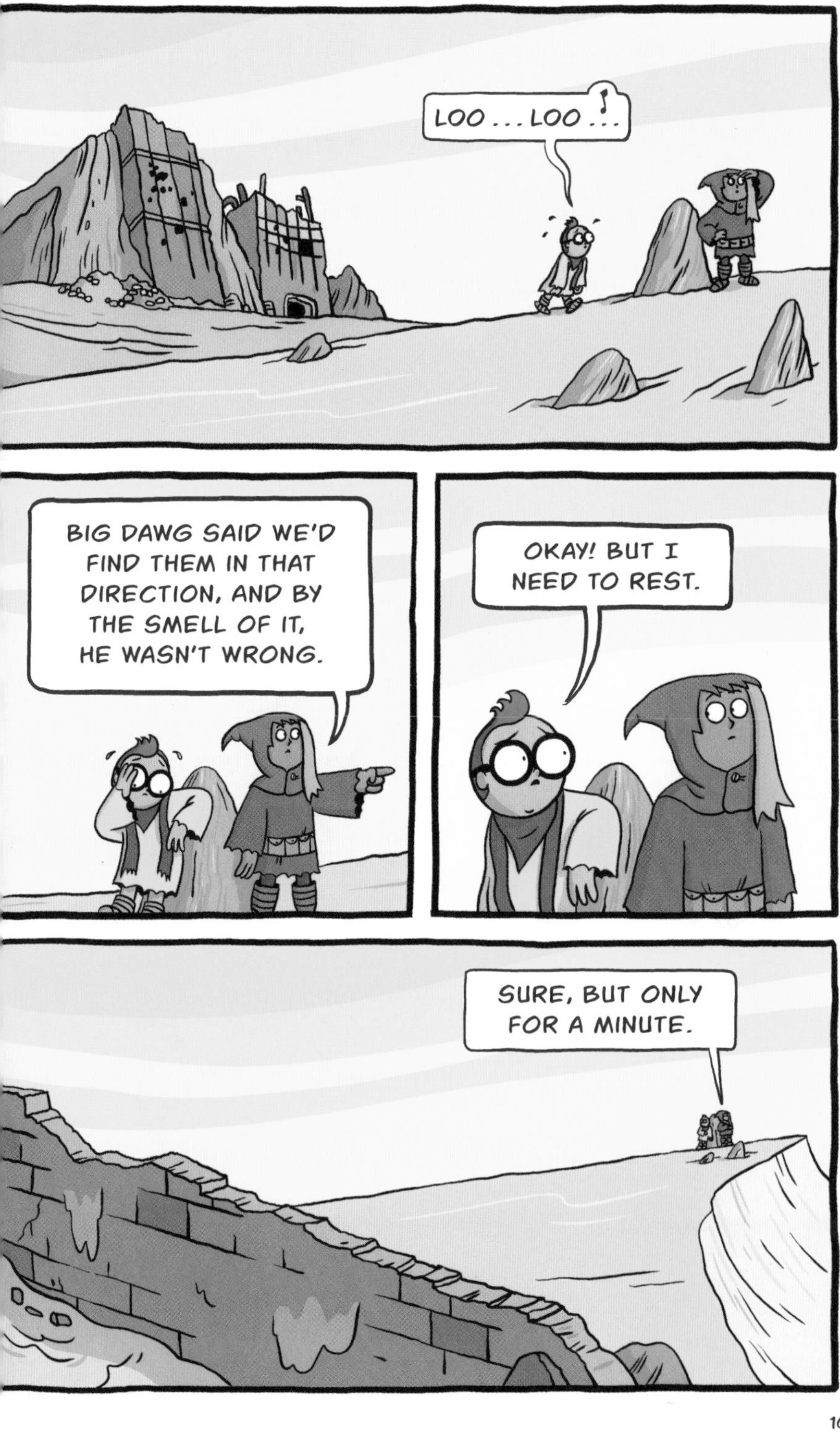
LOO . . . LOO . . .
BIG DAWG SAID WE'D FIND THEM IN THAT DIRECTION, AND BY THE SMELL OF IT, HE WASN'T WRONG.
OKAY! BUT I NEED TO REST.
SURE, BUT ONLY FOR A MINUTE.

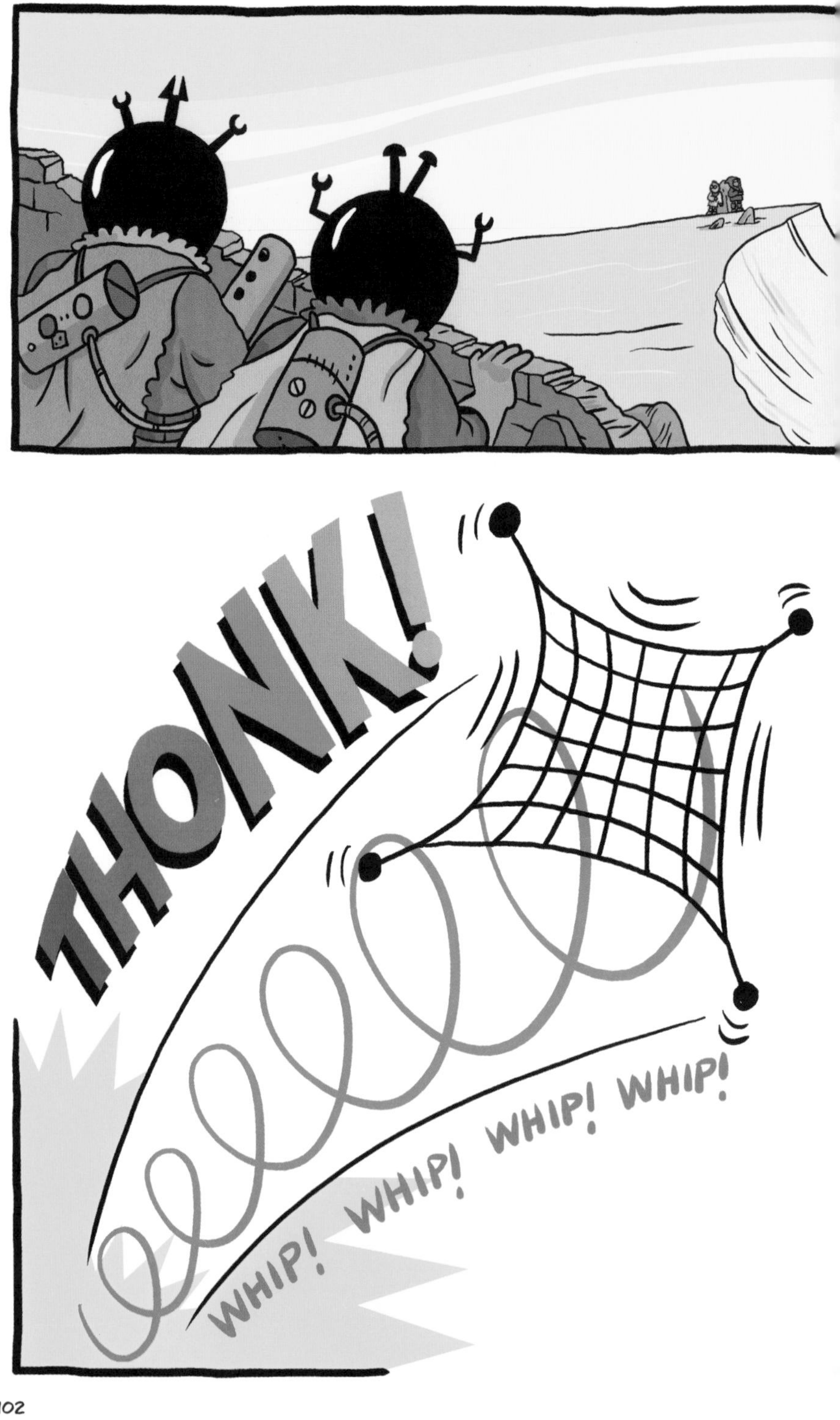
THONK!
WHIP! WHIP! WHIP! WHIP!

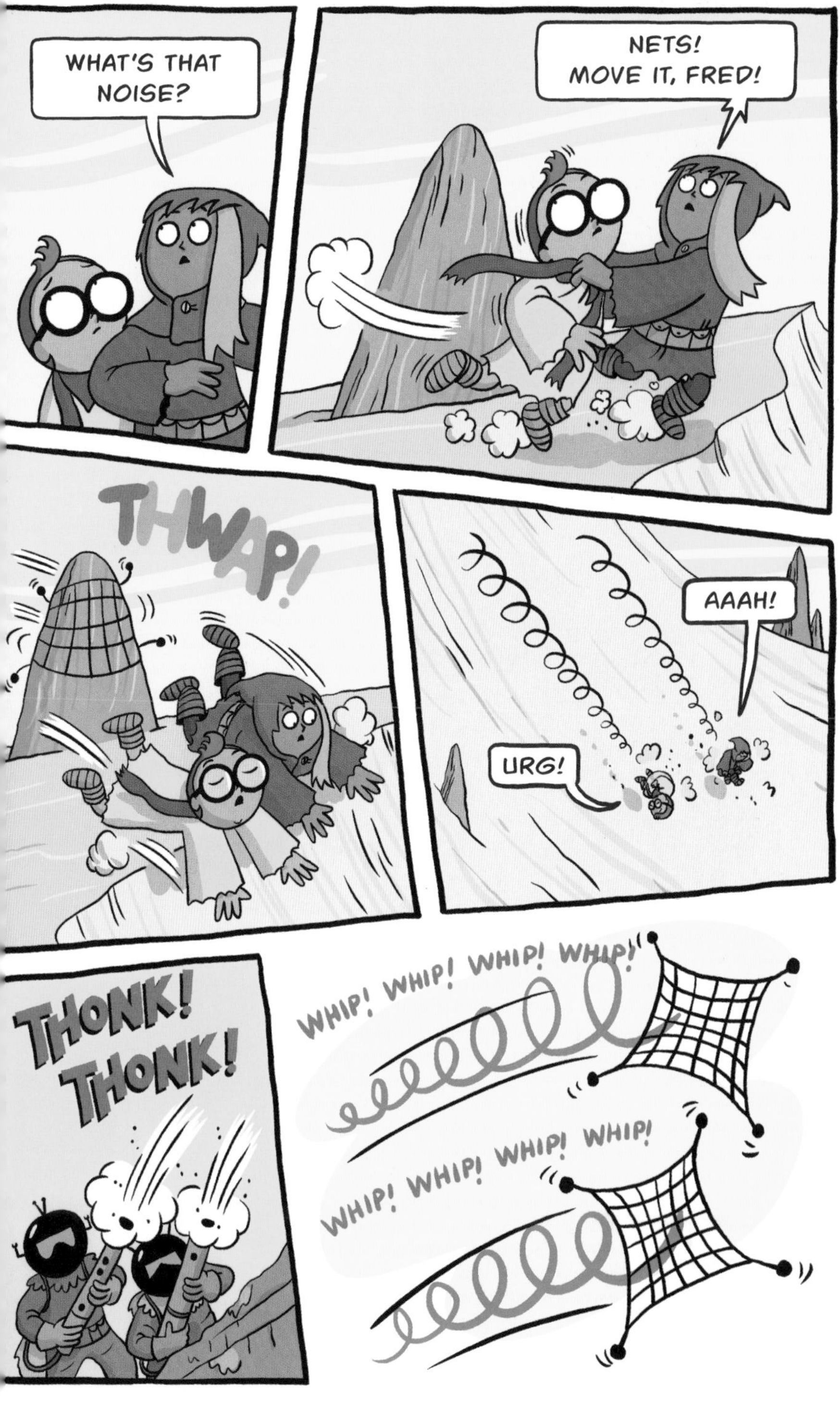

WHAT'S THAT NOISE?
NETS! MOVE IT, FRED!
THWAP!
AAAH!
URG!
THONK! THONK!
WHIP! WHIP! WHIP! WHIP!
WHIP! WHIP! WHIP! WHIP!

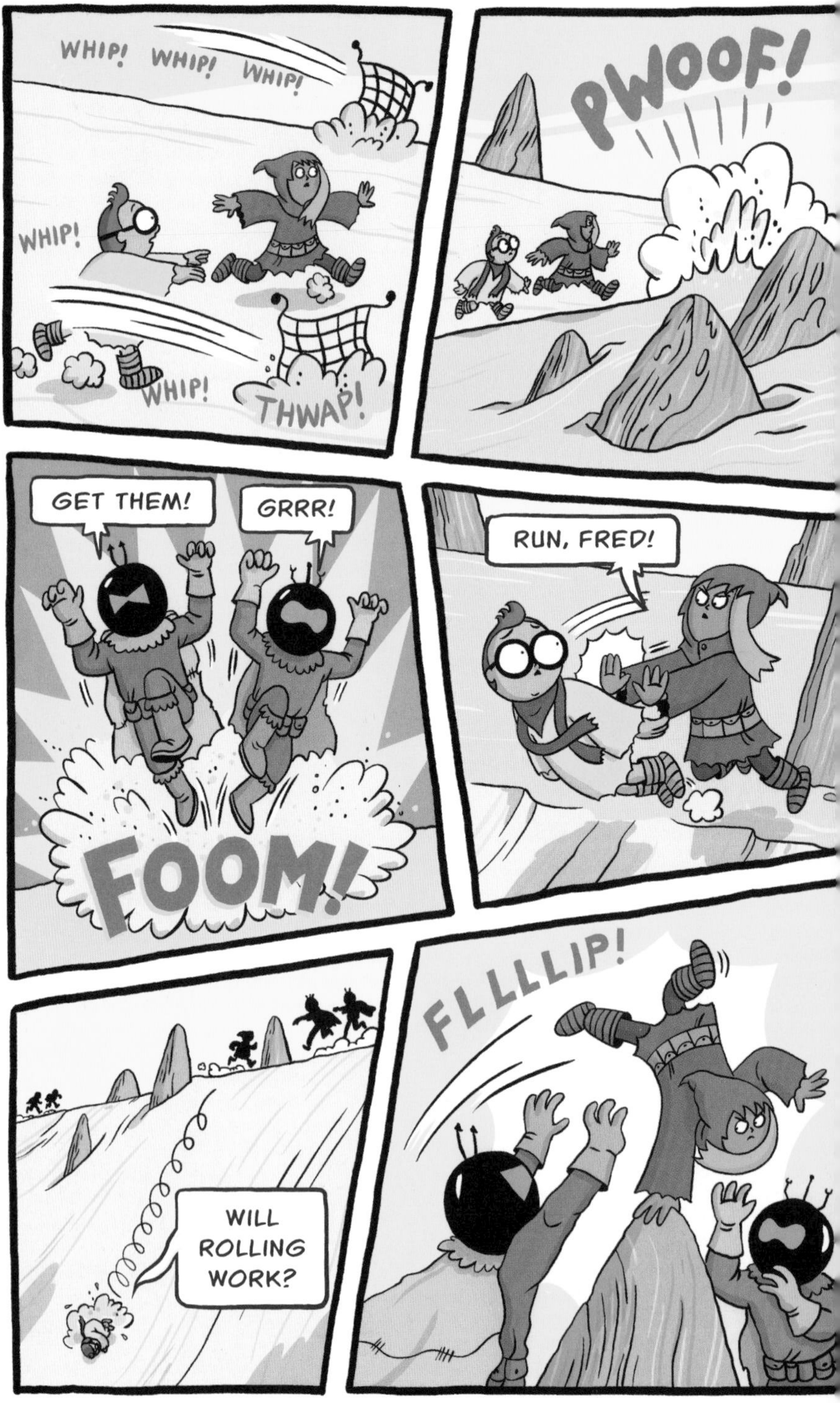
WHIP! WHIP! WHIP!
WHIP!
WHIP!
THWAP!
PWOOF!
GET THEM!
GRRR!
FOOM!
RUN, FRED!
WILL ROLLING WORK?
FLLLLIP!

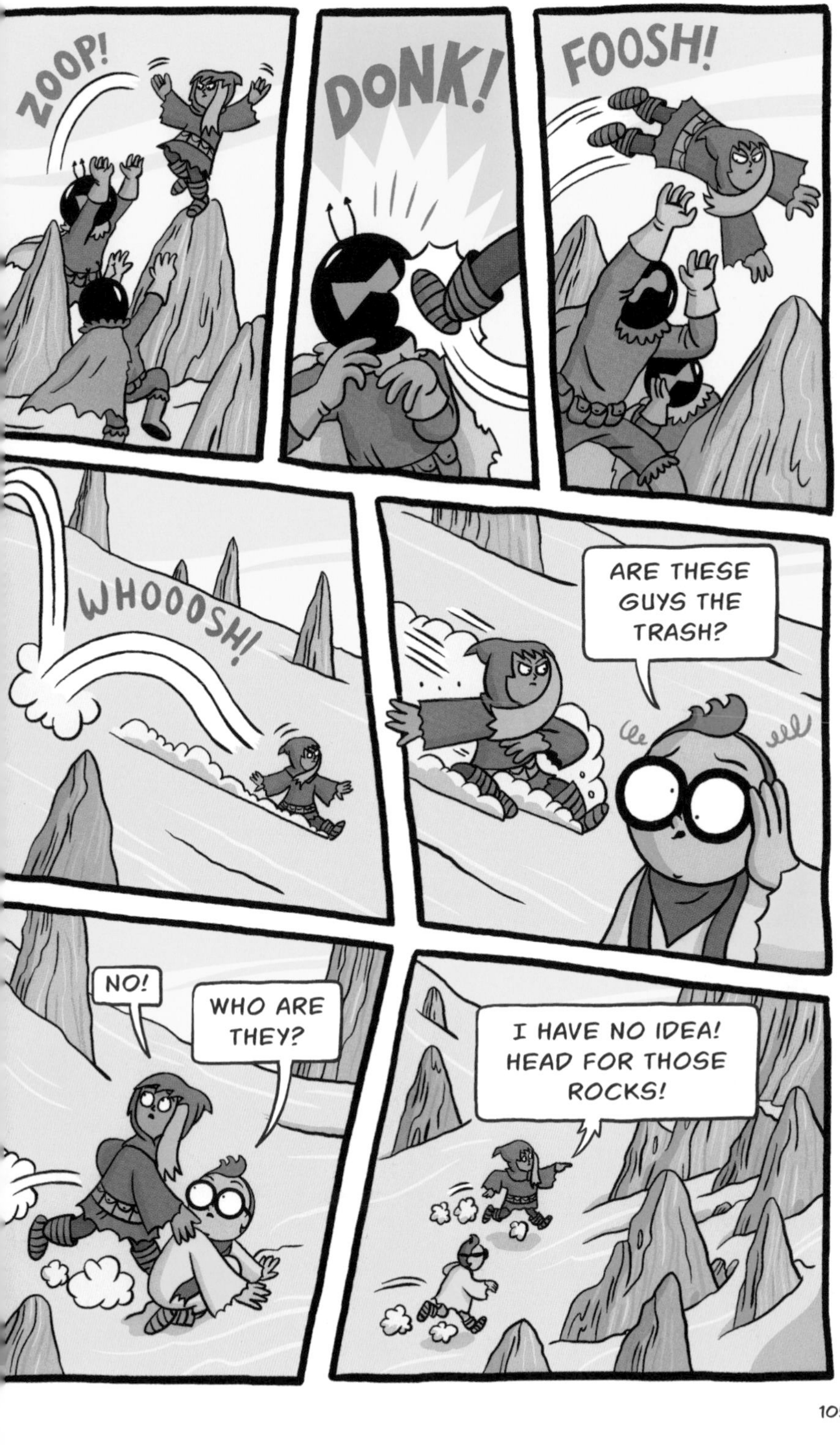
ZOOP!
DONK!
FOOSH!
WHOOOSH!
ARE THESE GUYS THE TRASH?
NO!
WHO ARE THEY?
I HAVE NO IDEA! HEAD FOR THOSE ROCKS!

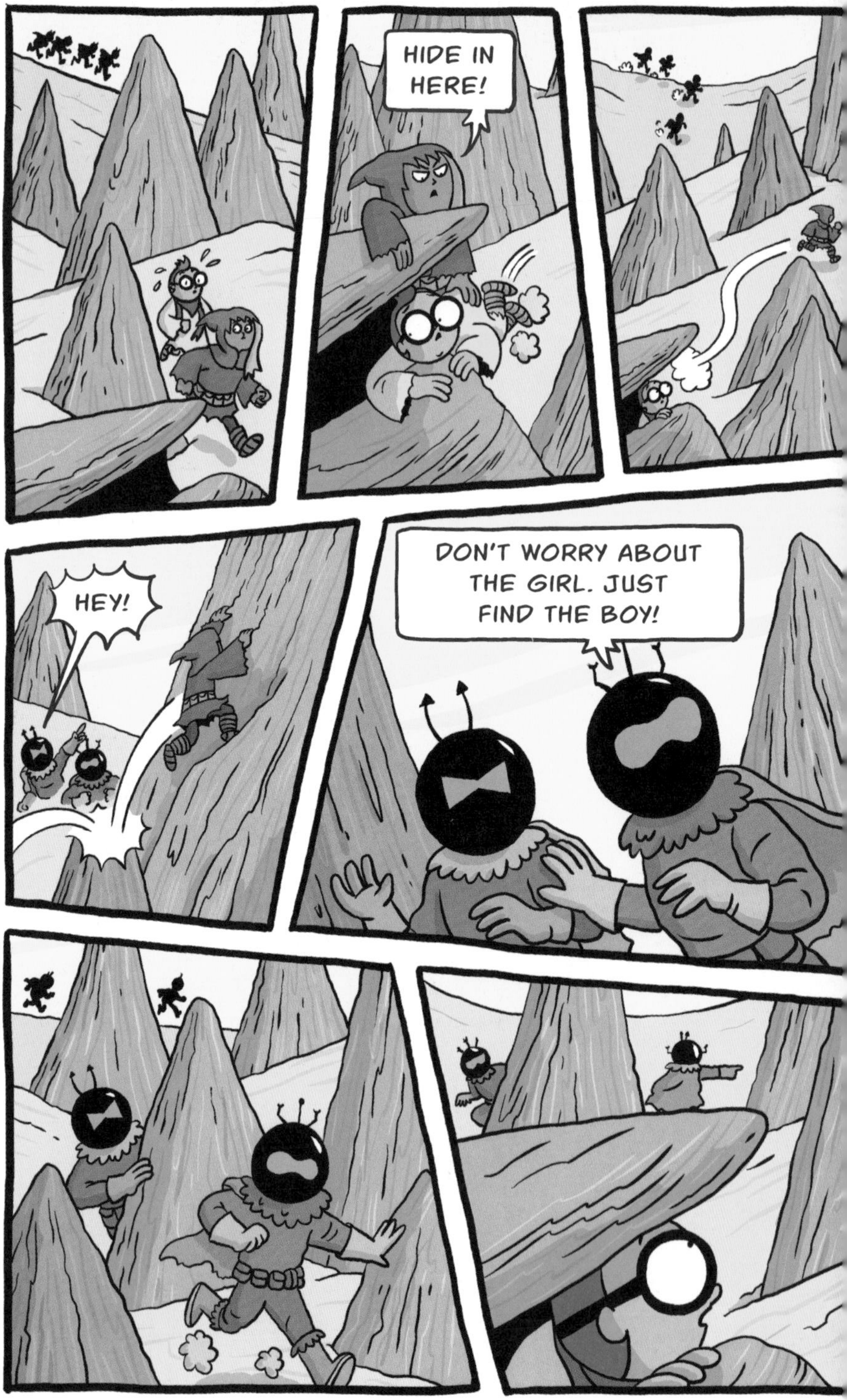
HIDE IN HERE!
HEY!
DON'T WORRY ABOUT THE GIRL. JUST FIND THE BOY!

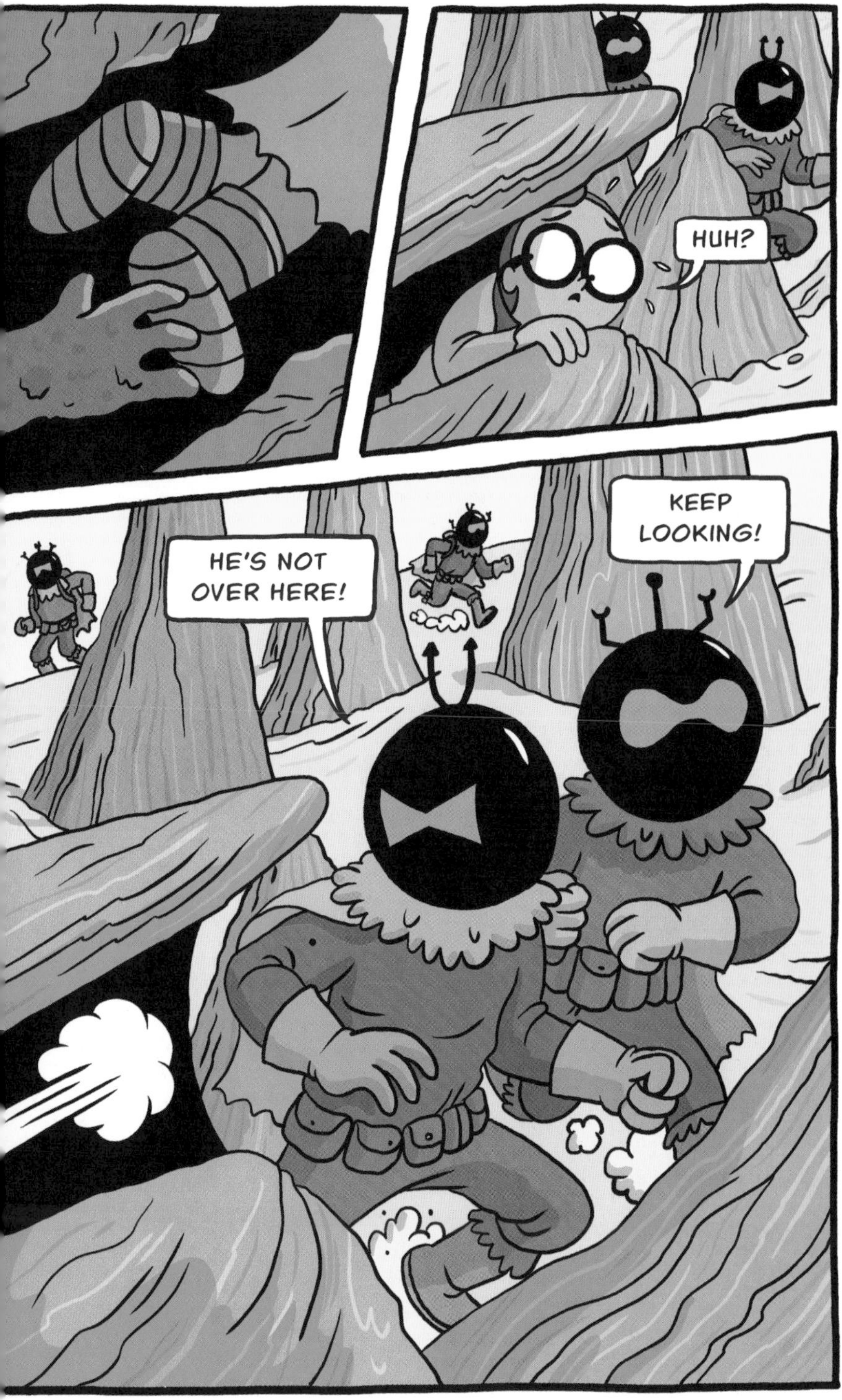
HUH?
HE'S NOT OVER HERE!
KEEP LOOKING!

CHAPTER 9

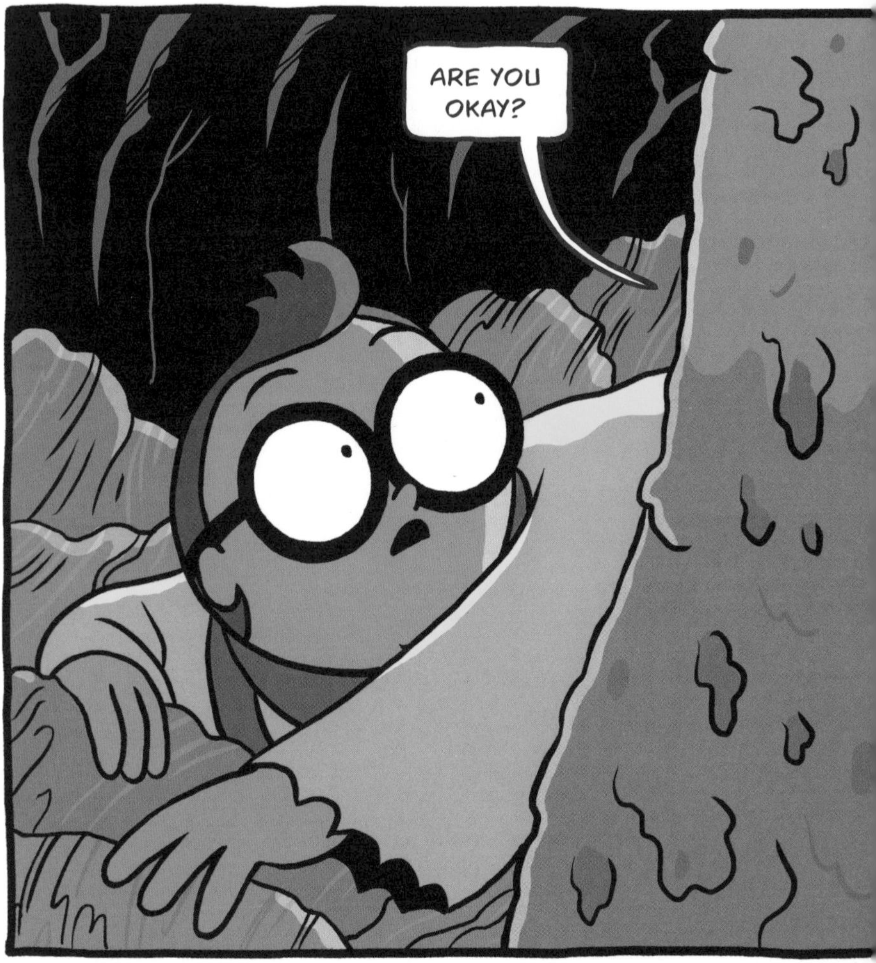
ARE YOU OKAY?

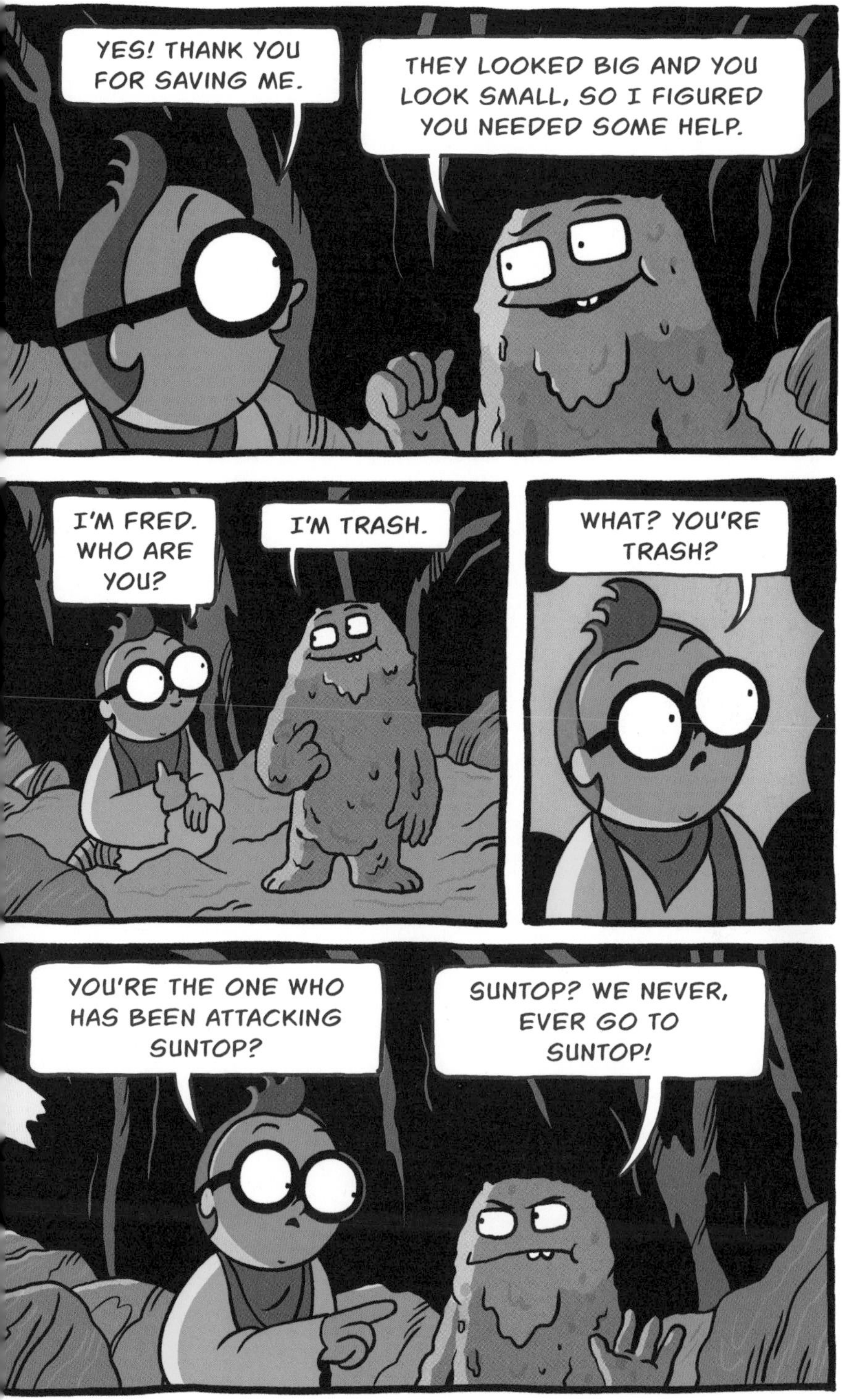
YES! THANK YOU FOR SAVING ME.
THEY LOOKED BIG AND YOU LOOK SMALL, SO I FIGURED YOU NEEDED SOME HELP.
I'M FRED. WHO ARE YOU?
I'M TRASH.
WHAT? YOU'RE TRASH?
YOU'RE THE ONE WHO HAS BEEN ATTACKING SUNTOP?
SUNTOP? WE NEVER, EVER GO TO SUNTOP!

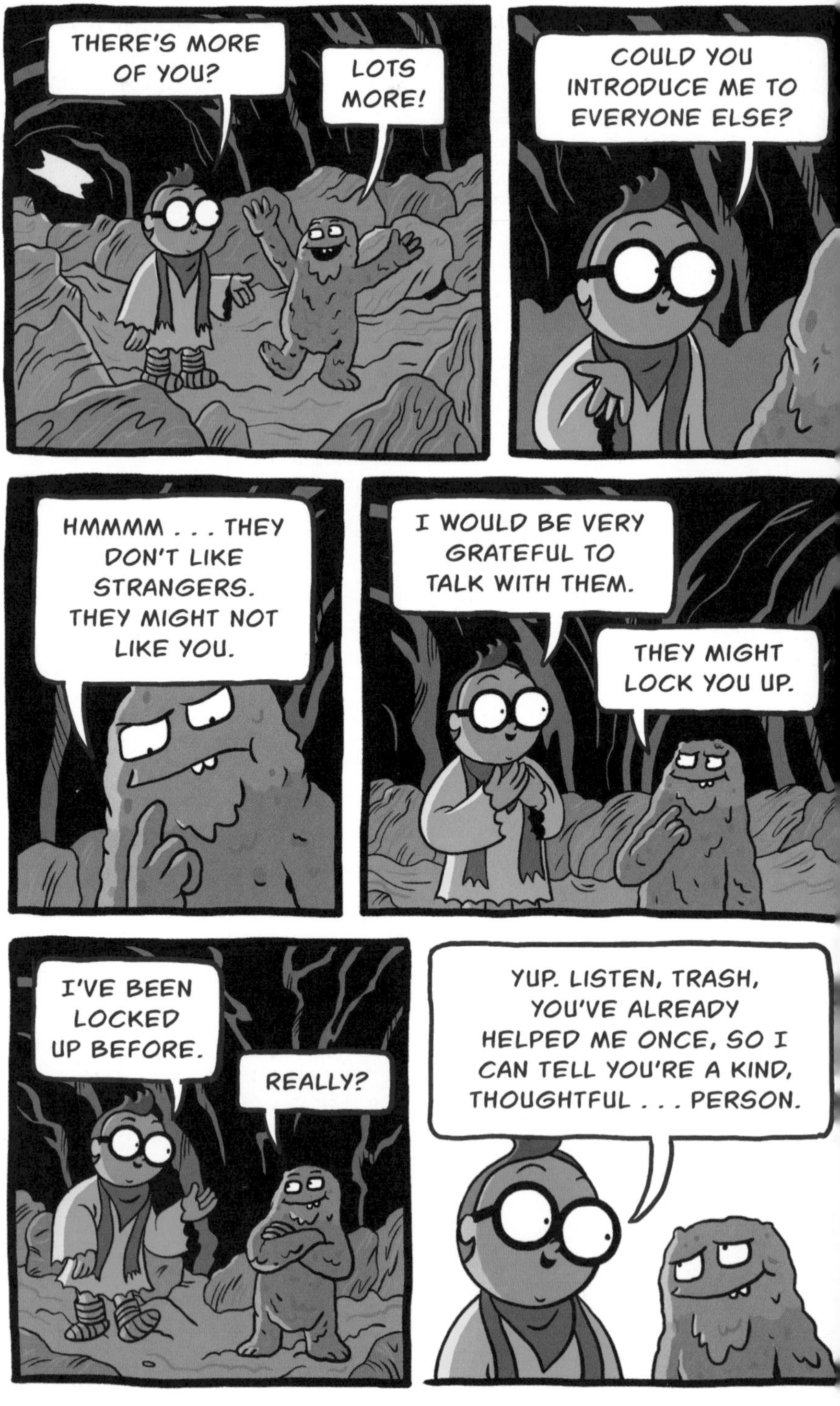
THERE'S MORE OF YOU?
LOTS MORE!
COULD YOU INTRODUCE ME TO EVERYONE ELSE?
HMMMM . . . THEY DON'T LIKE STRANGERS. THEY MIGHT NOT LIKE YOU.
I WOULD BE VERY GRATEFUL TO TALK WITH THEM.
THEY MIGHT LOCK YOU UP.
I'VE BEEN LOCKED UP BEFORE.
REALLY?
YUP. LISTEN, TRASH, YOU'VE ALREADY HELPED ME ONCE, SO I CAN TELL YOU'RE A KIND, THOUGHTFUL . . . PERSON.

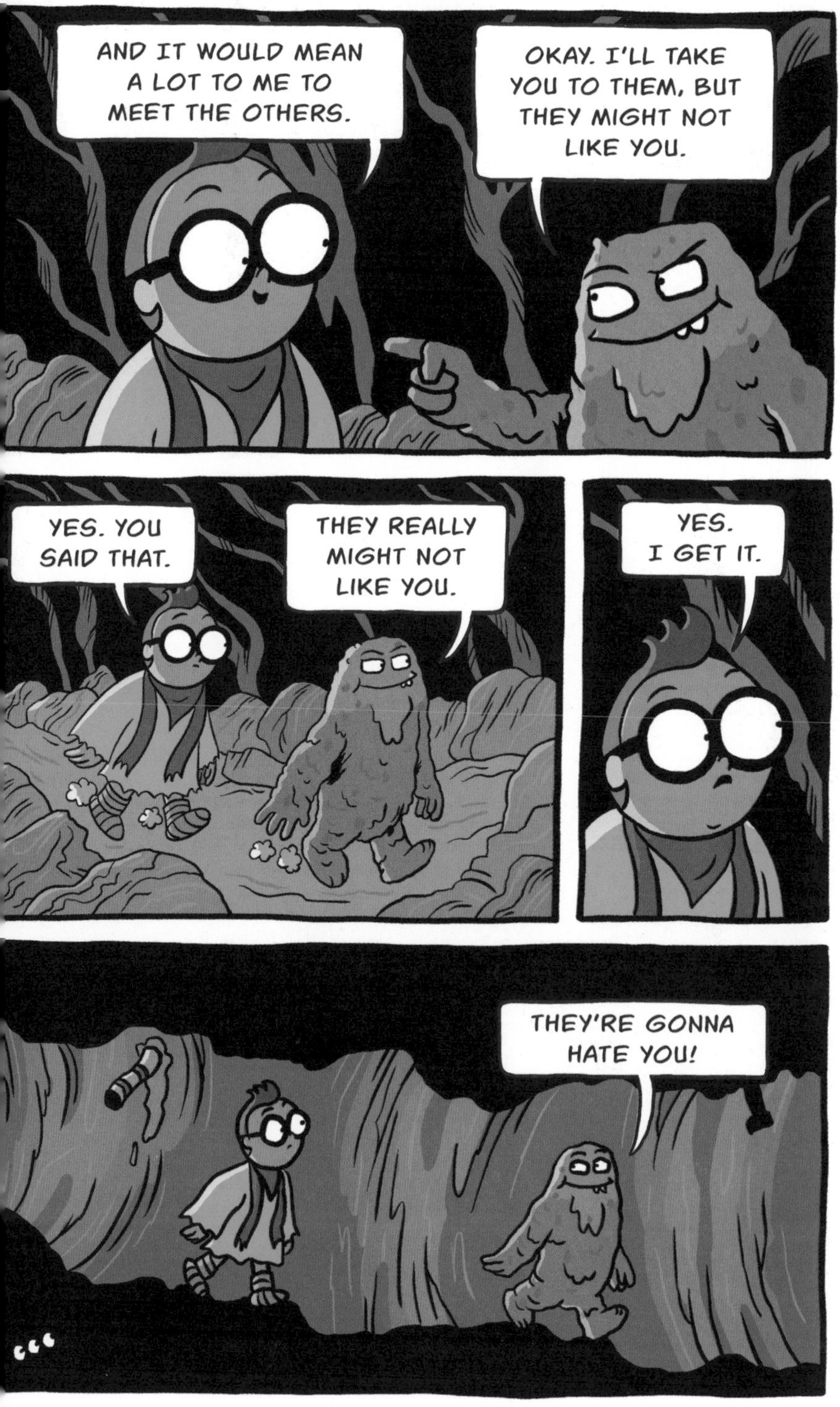
AND IT WOULD MEAN A LOT TO ME TO MEET THE OTHERS.
OKAY. I'LL TAKE YOU TO THEM, BUT THEY MIGHT NOT LIKE YOU.
YES. YOU SAID THAT.
THEY REALLY MIGHT NOT LIKE YOU.
YES. I GET IT.
THEY'RE GONNA HATE YOU!

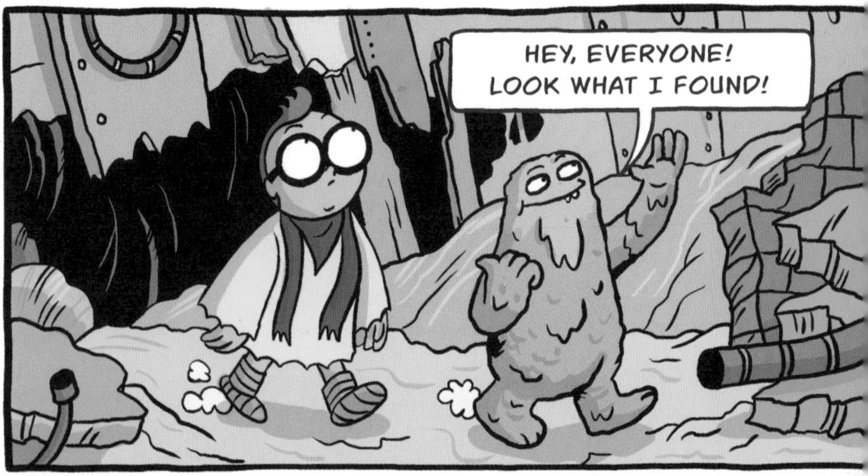
HEY, EVERYONE!
LOOK WHAT I FOUND!

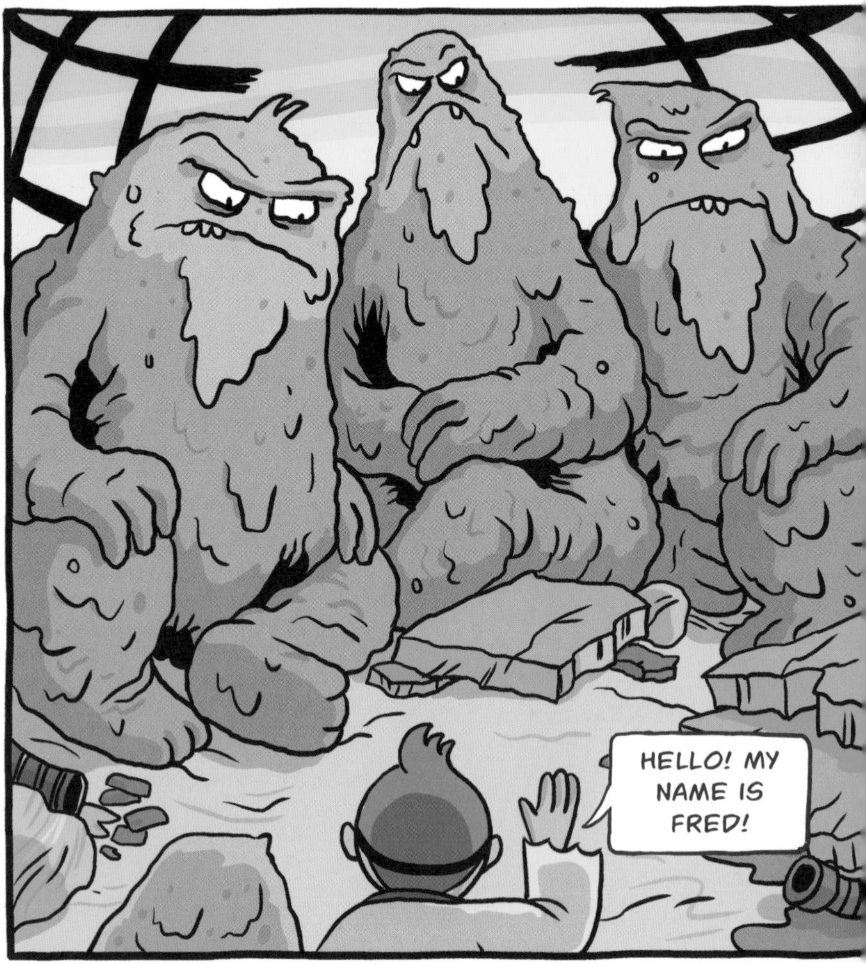
HELLO! MY
NAME IS
FRED!

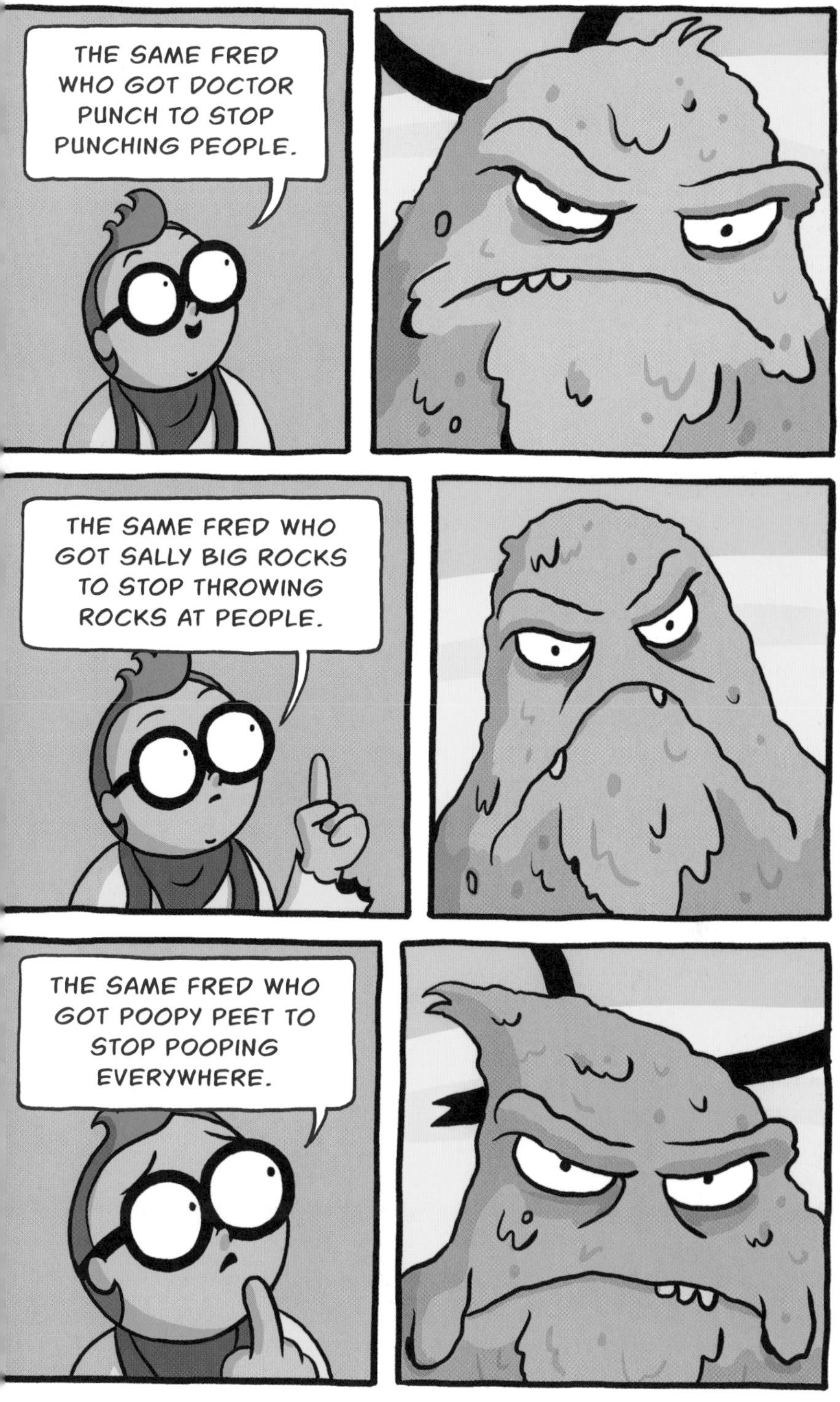
THE SAME FRED WHO GOT DOCTOR PUNCH TO STOP PUNCHING PEOPLE.
THE SAME FRED WHO GOT SALLY BIG ROCKS TO STOP THROWING ROCKS AT PEOPLE.
THE SAME FRED WHO GOT POOPY PEET TO STOP POOPING EVERYWHERE.

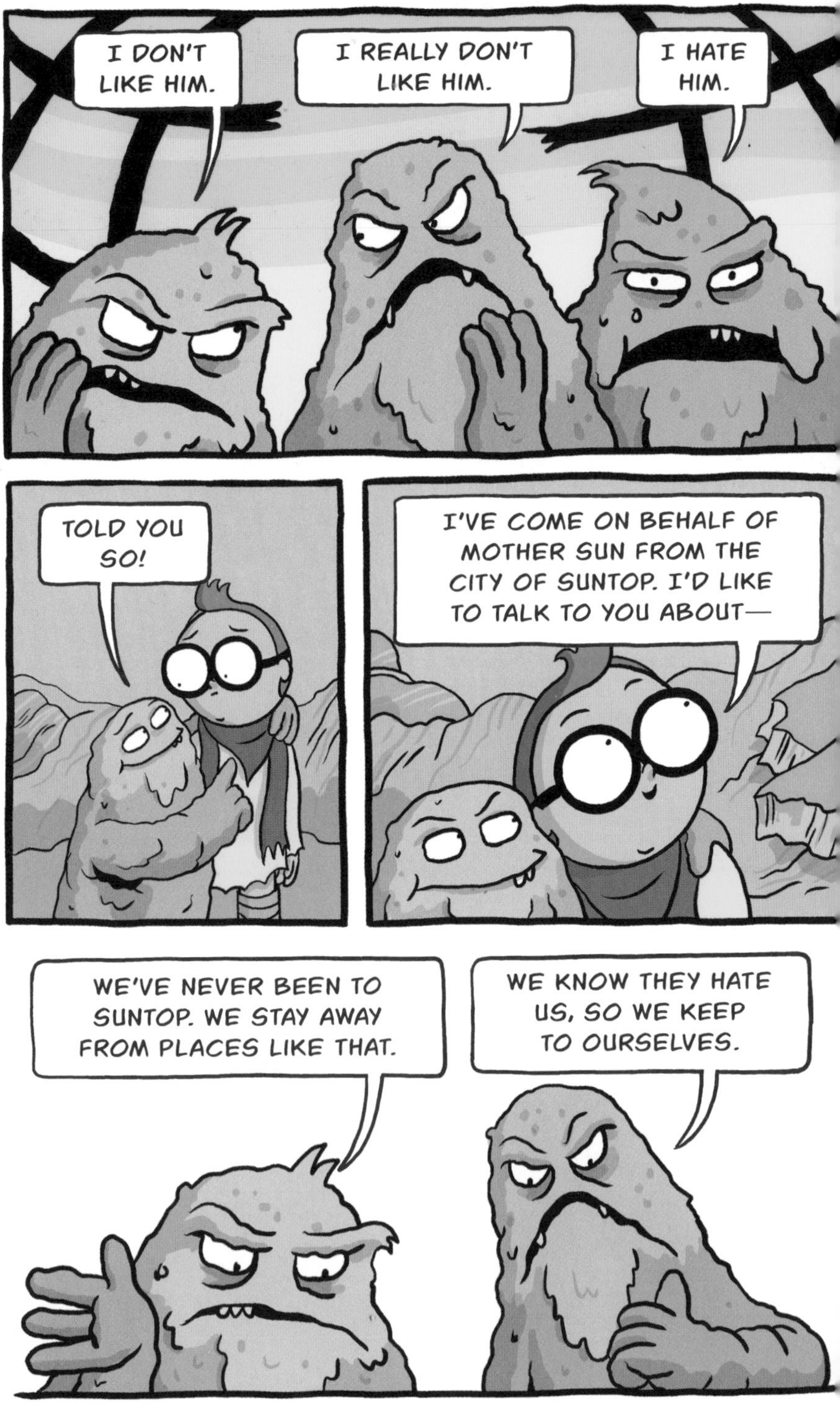
I DON'T LIKE HIM.
I REALLY DON'T LIKE HIM.
I HATE HIM.
TOLD YOU SO!
I'VE COME ON BEHALF OF MOTHER SUN FROM THE CITY OF SUNTOP. I'D LIKE TO TALK TO YOU ABOUT—
WE'VE NEVER BEEN TO SUNTOP. WE STAY AWAY FROM PLACES LIKE THAT.
WE KNOW THEY HATE US, SO WE KEEP TO OURSELVES.

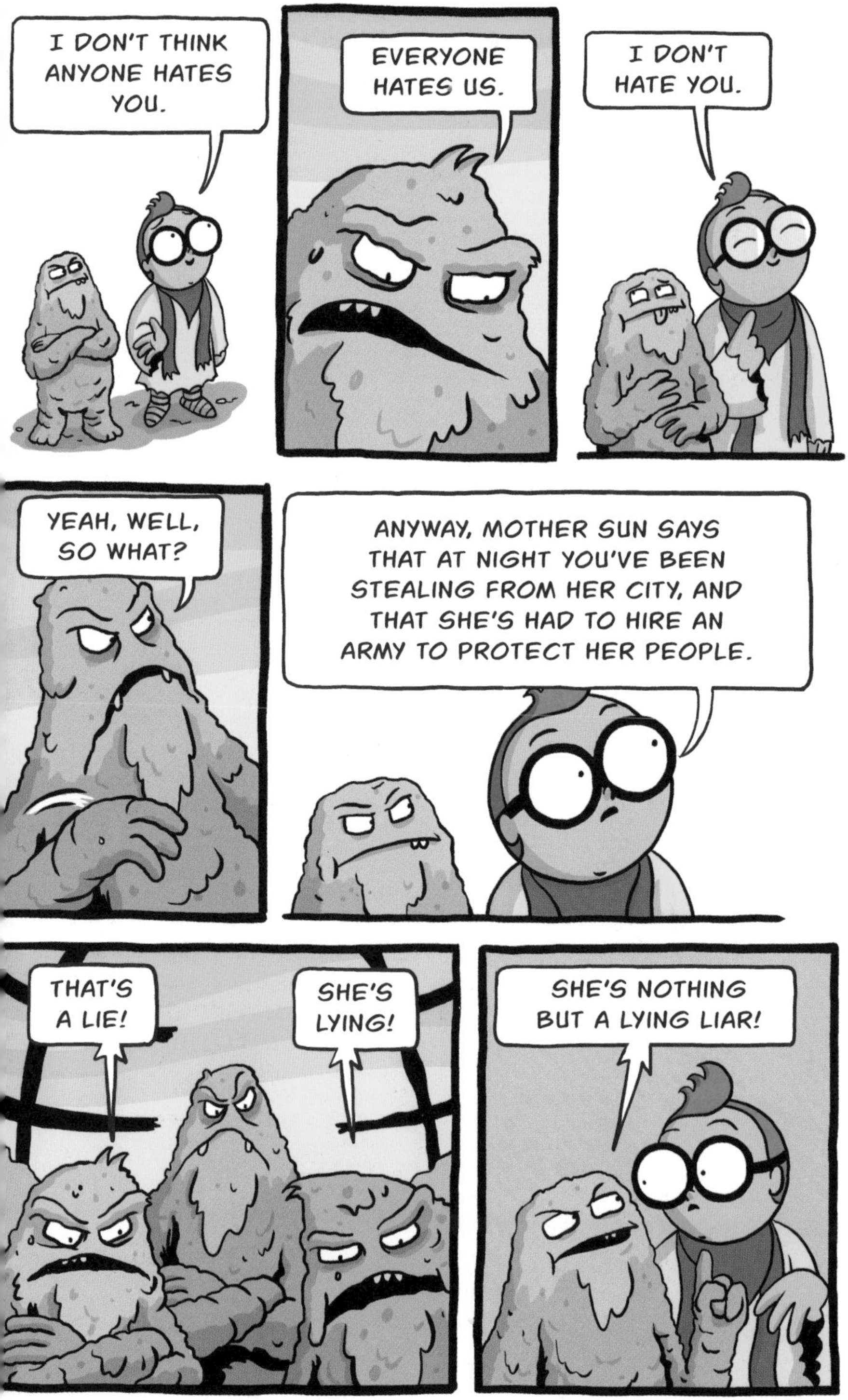
I DON'T THINK ANYONE HATES YOU.
EVERYONE HATES US.
I DON'T HATE YOU.
YEAH, WELL, SO WHAT?
ANYWAY, MOTHER SUN SAYS THAT AT NIGHT YOU'VE BEEN STEALING FROM HER CITY, AND THAT SHE'S HAD TO HIRE AN ARMY TO PROTECT HER PEOPLE.
THAT'S A LIE!
SHE'S LYING!
SHE'S NOTHING BUT A LYING LIAR!

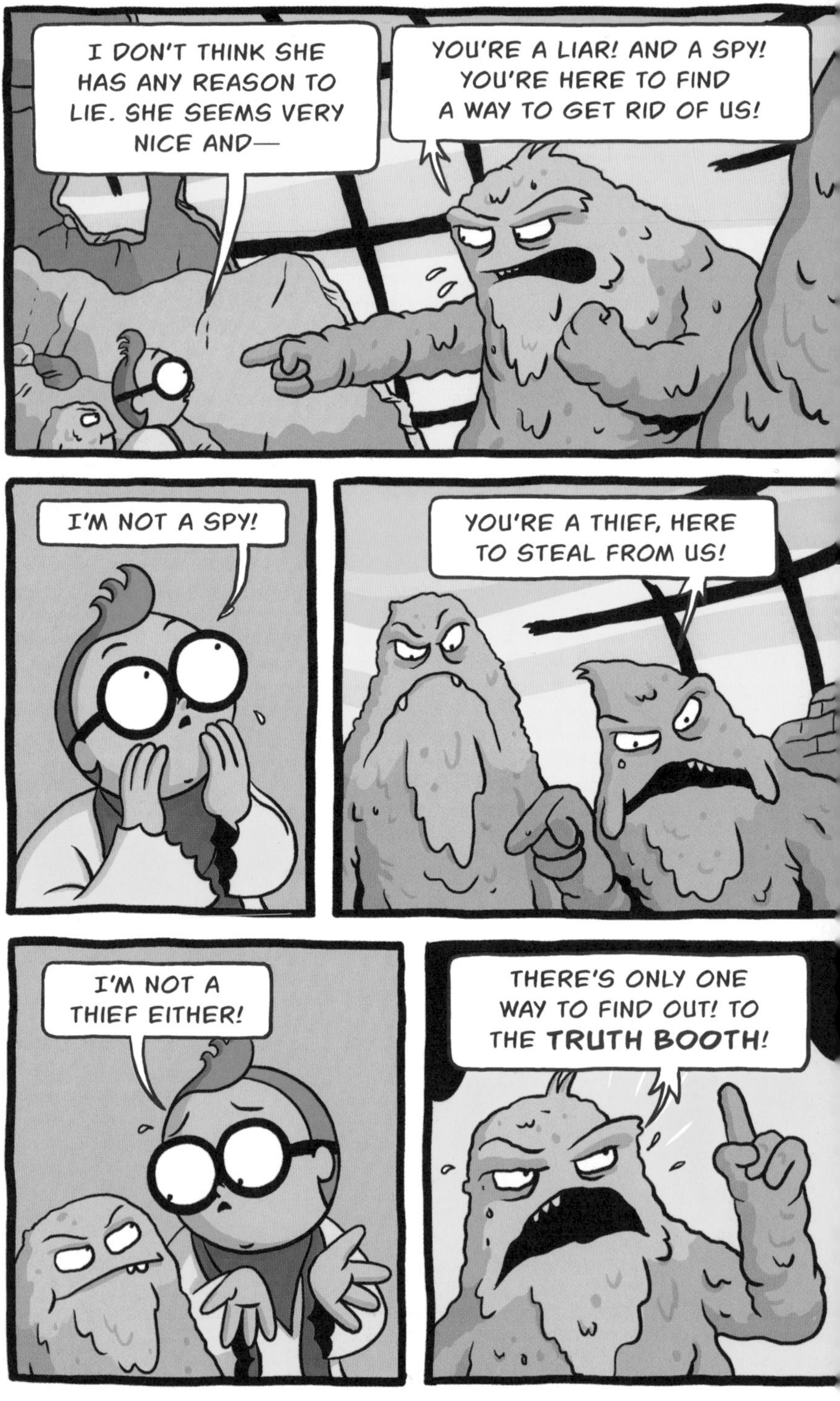
I DON'T THINK SHE HAS ANY REASON TO LIE. SHE SEEMS VERY NICE AND—
YOU'RE A LIAR! AND A SPY! YOU'RE HERE TO FIND A WAY TO GET RID OF US!
I'M NOT A SPY!
YOU'RE A THIEF, HERE TO STEAL FROM US!
I'M NOT A THIEF EITHER!
THERE'S ONLY ONE WAY TO FIND OUT! TO THE **TRUTH BOOTH**!

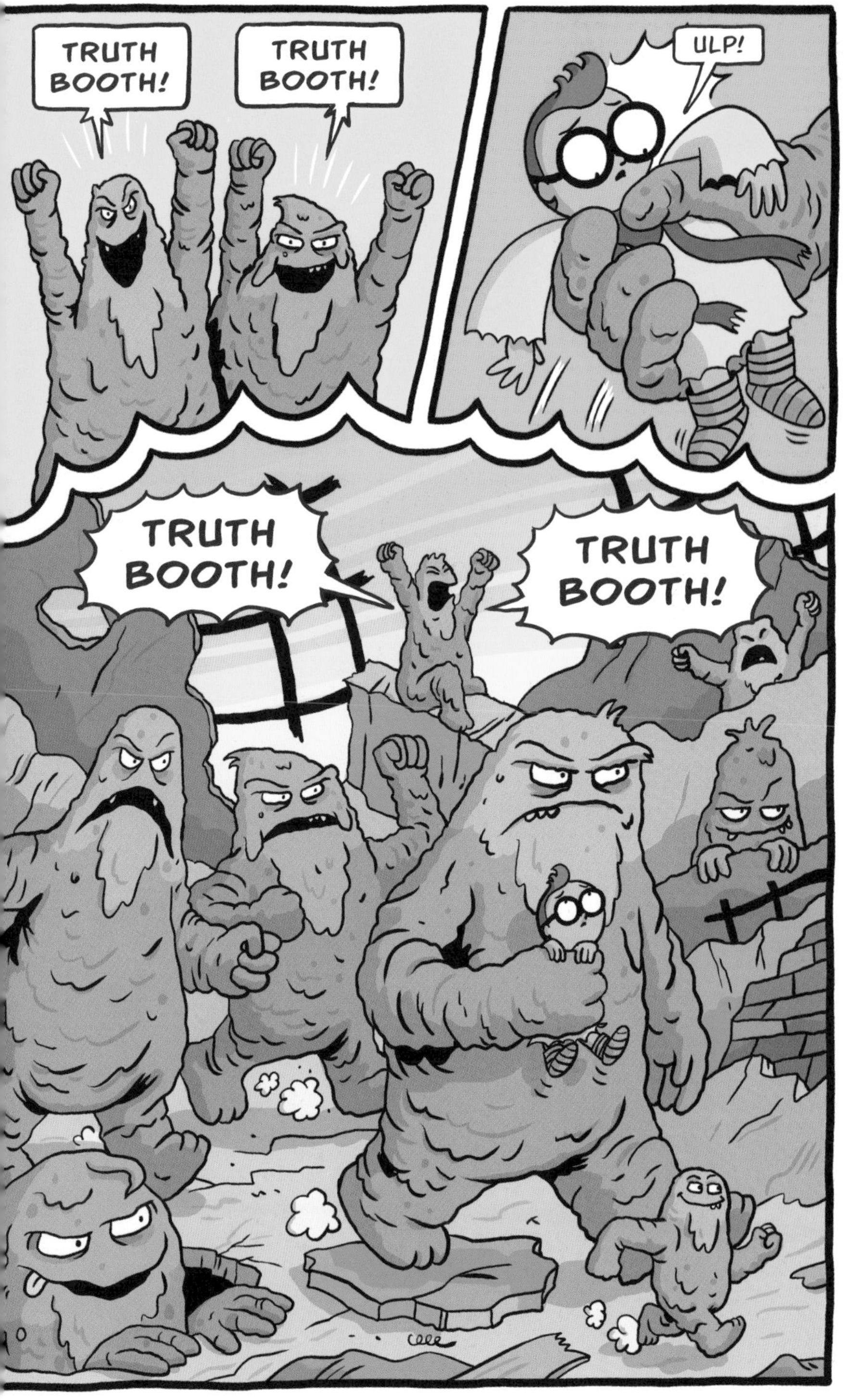
TRUTH BOOTH!
TRUTH BOOTH!
ULP!
TRUTH BOOTH!
TRUTH BOOTH!

CHAPTER 10

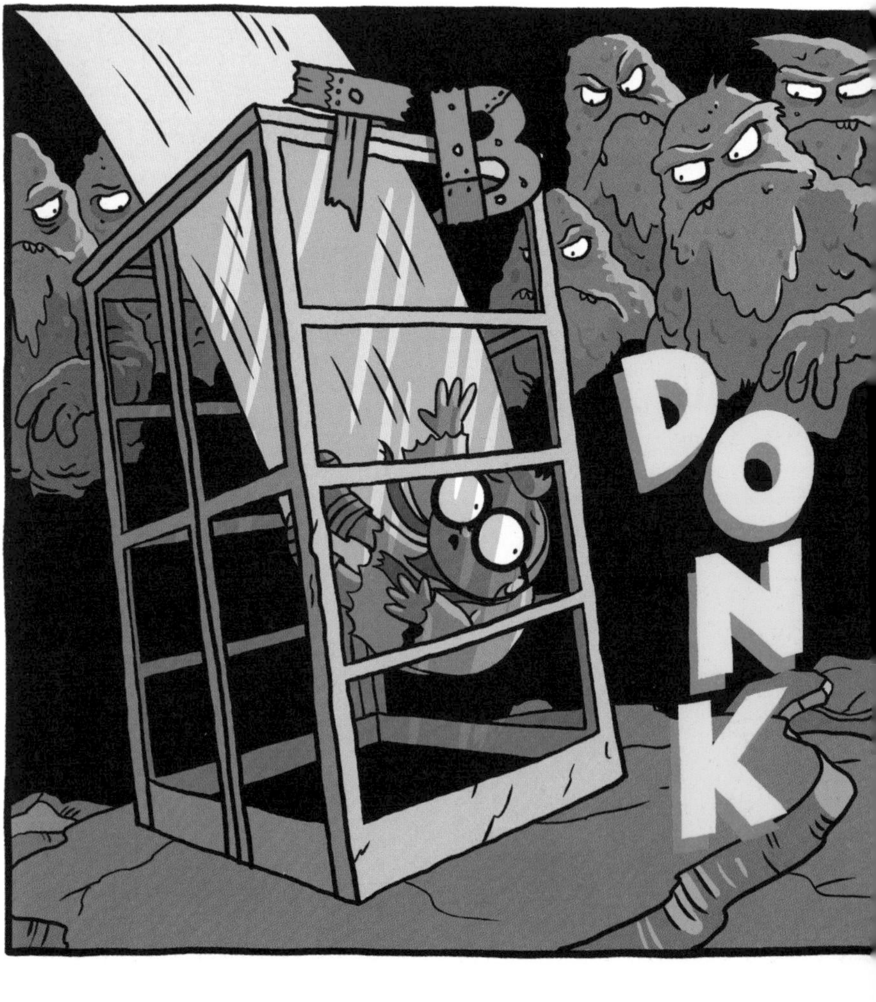

DONK

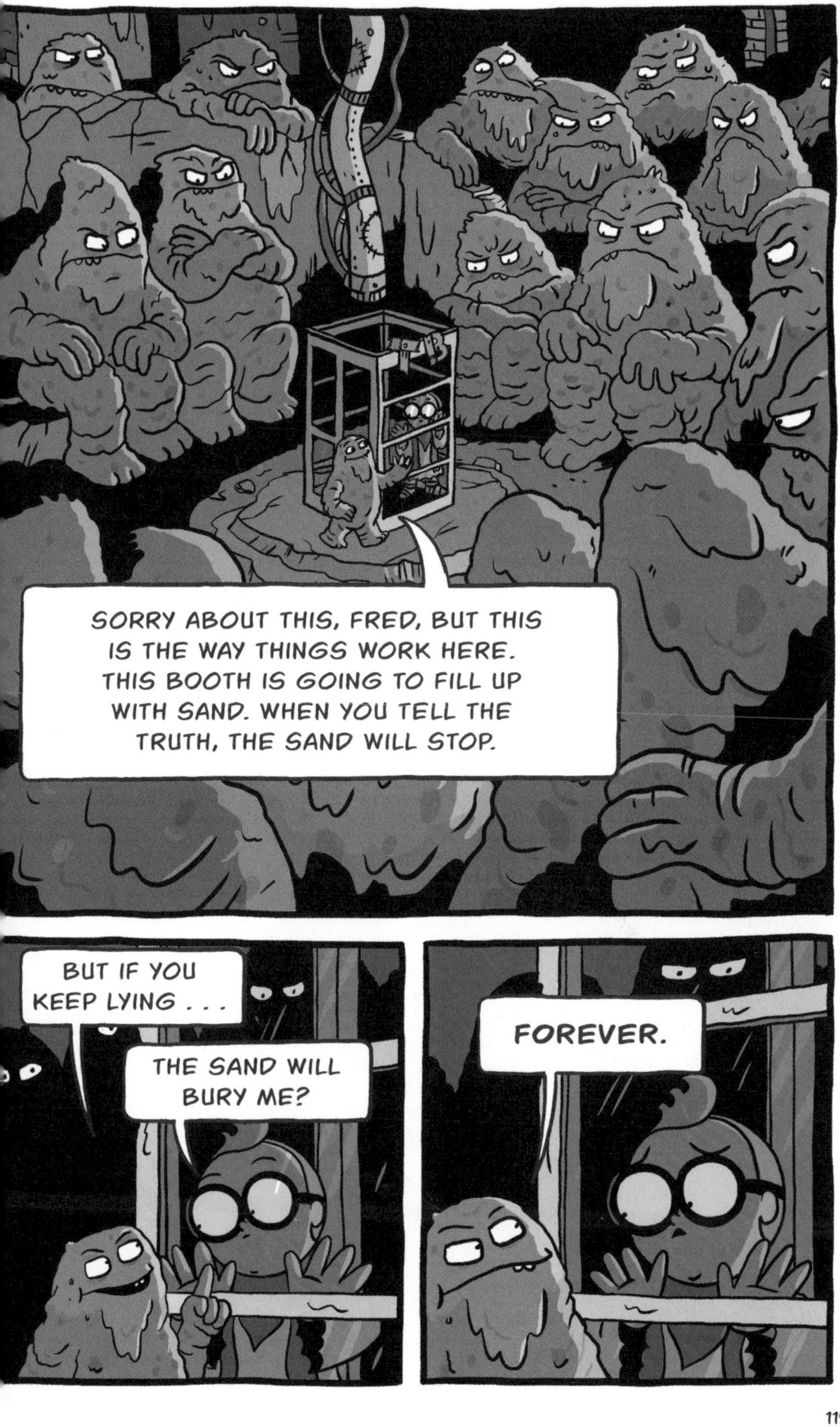
SORRY ABOUT THIS, FRED, BUT THIS IS THE WAY THINGS WORK HERE. THIS BOOTH IS GOING TO FILL UP WITH SAND. WHEN YOU TELL THE TRUTH, THE SAND WILL STOP.
BUT IF YOU KEEP LYING . . .
THE SAND WILL BURY ME?
FOREVER.

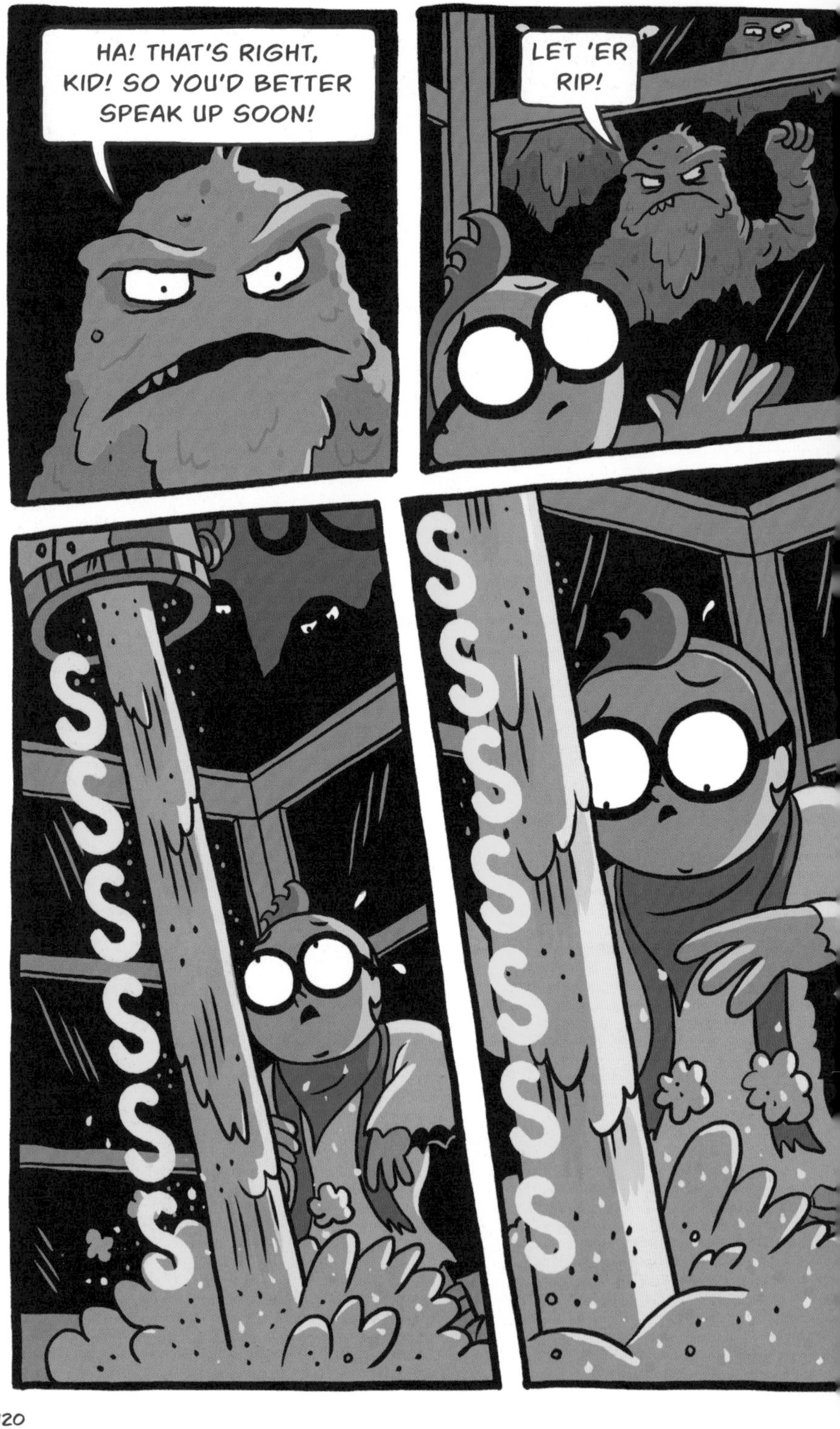
HA! THAT'S RIGHT, KID! SO YOU'D BETTER SPEAK UP SOON!
LET 'ER RIP!
SSSSSSS
SSSSSSSS

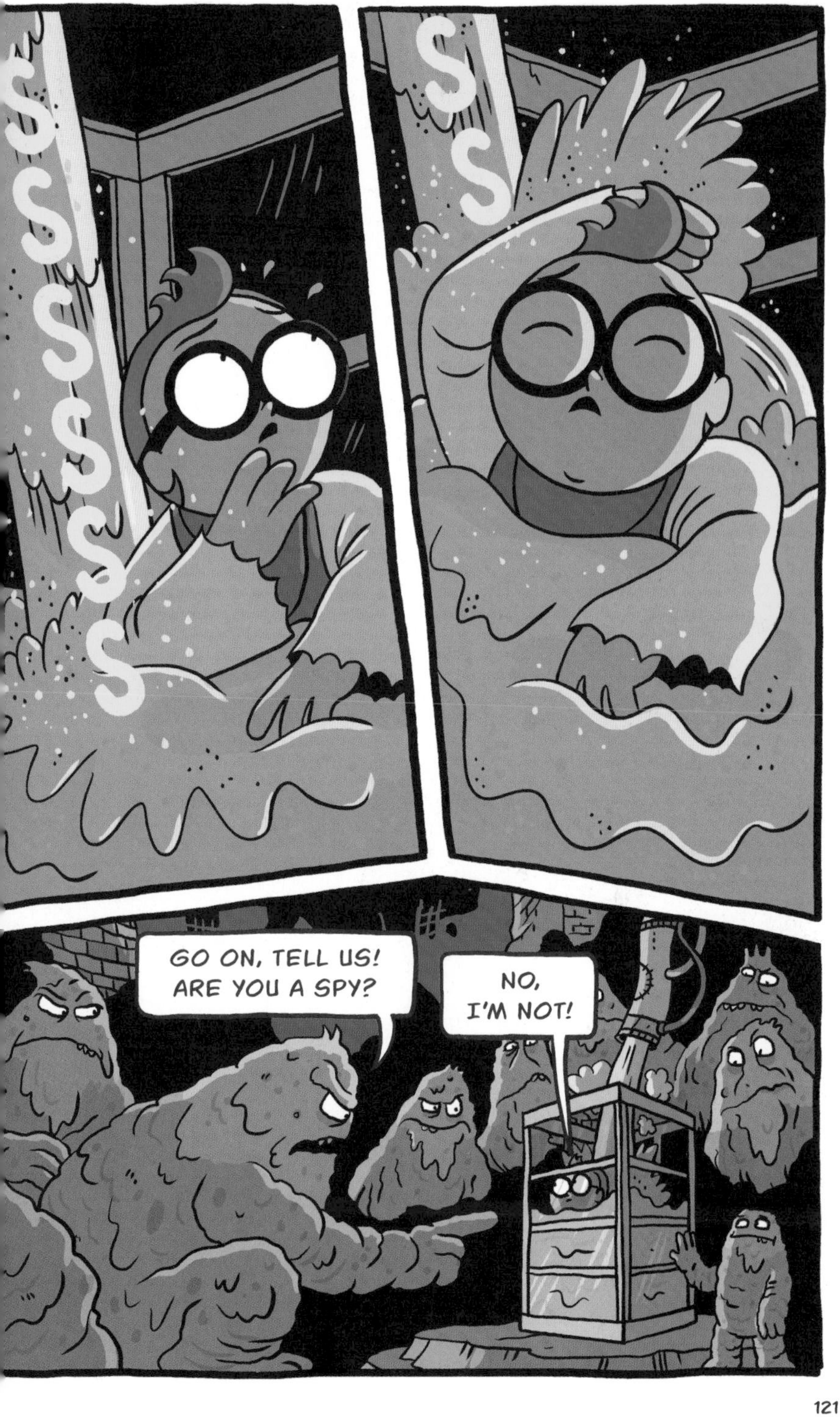
SSSSSSS
SS
GO ON, TELL US! ARE YOU A SPY?
NO, I'M NOT!

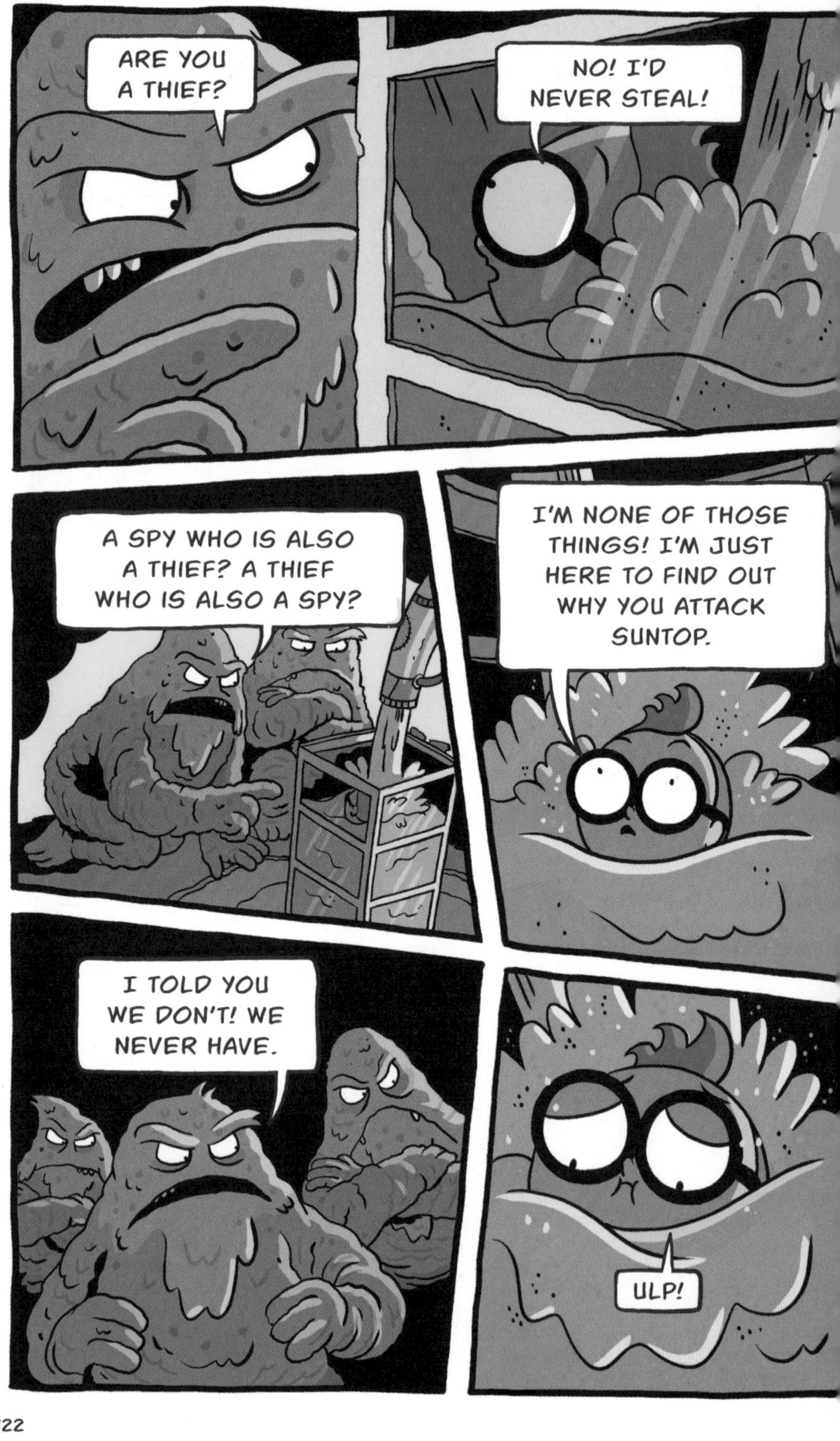
ARE YOU A THIEF?
NO! I'D NEVER STEAL!
A SPY WHO IS ALSO A THIEF? A THIEF WHO IS ALSO A SPY?
I'M NONE OF THOSE THINGS! I'M JUST HERE TO FIND OUT WHY YOU ATTACK SUNTOP.
I TOLD YOU WE DON'T! WE NEVER HAVE.
ULP!

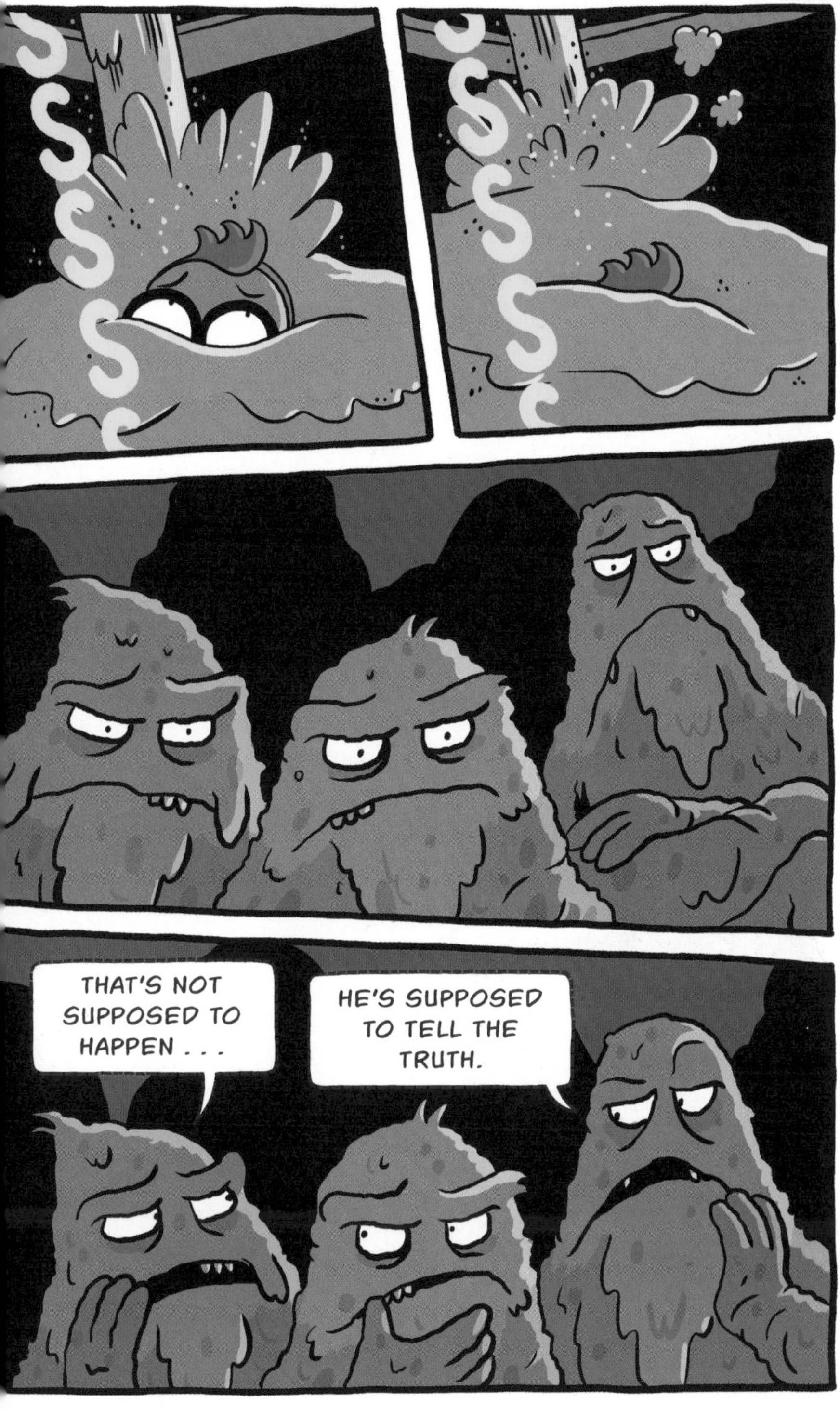
SSSSS
SSSSS
THAT'S NOT SUPPOSED TO HAPPEN . . .
HE'S SUPPOSED TO TELL THE TRUTH.

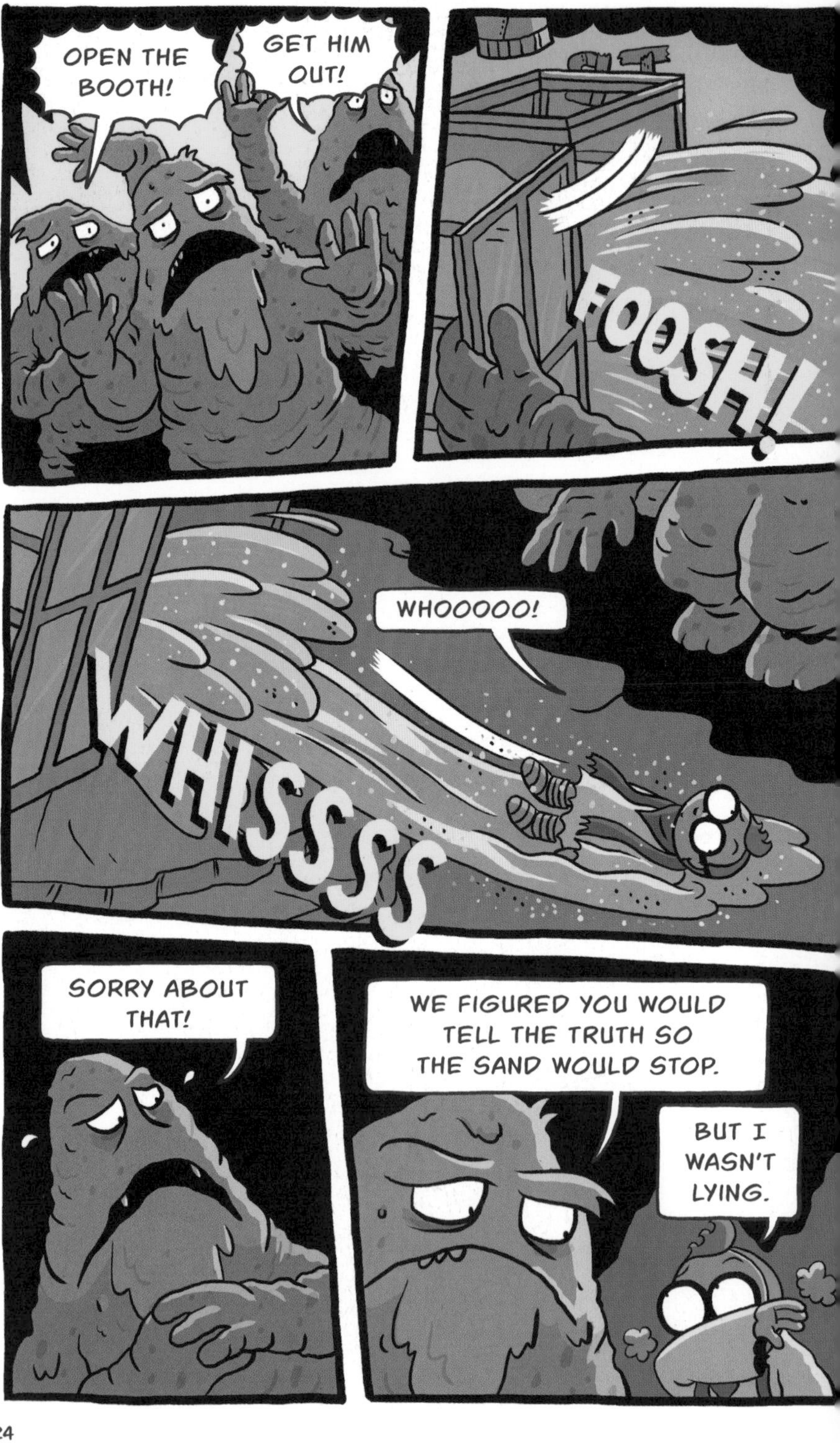
OPEN THE BOOTH!
GET HIM OUT!
FOOSH!
WHOOOOO!
WHISSSSS
SORRY ABOUT THAT!
WE FIGURED YOU WOULD TELL THE TRUTH SO THE SAND WOULD STOP.
BUT I WASN'T LYING.

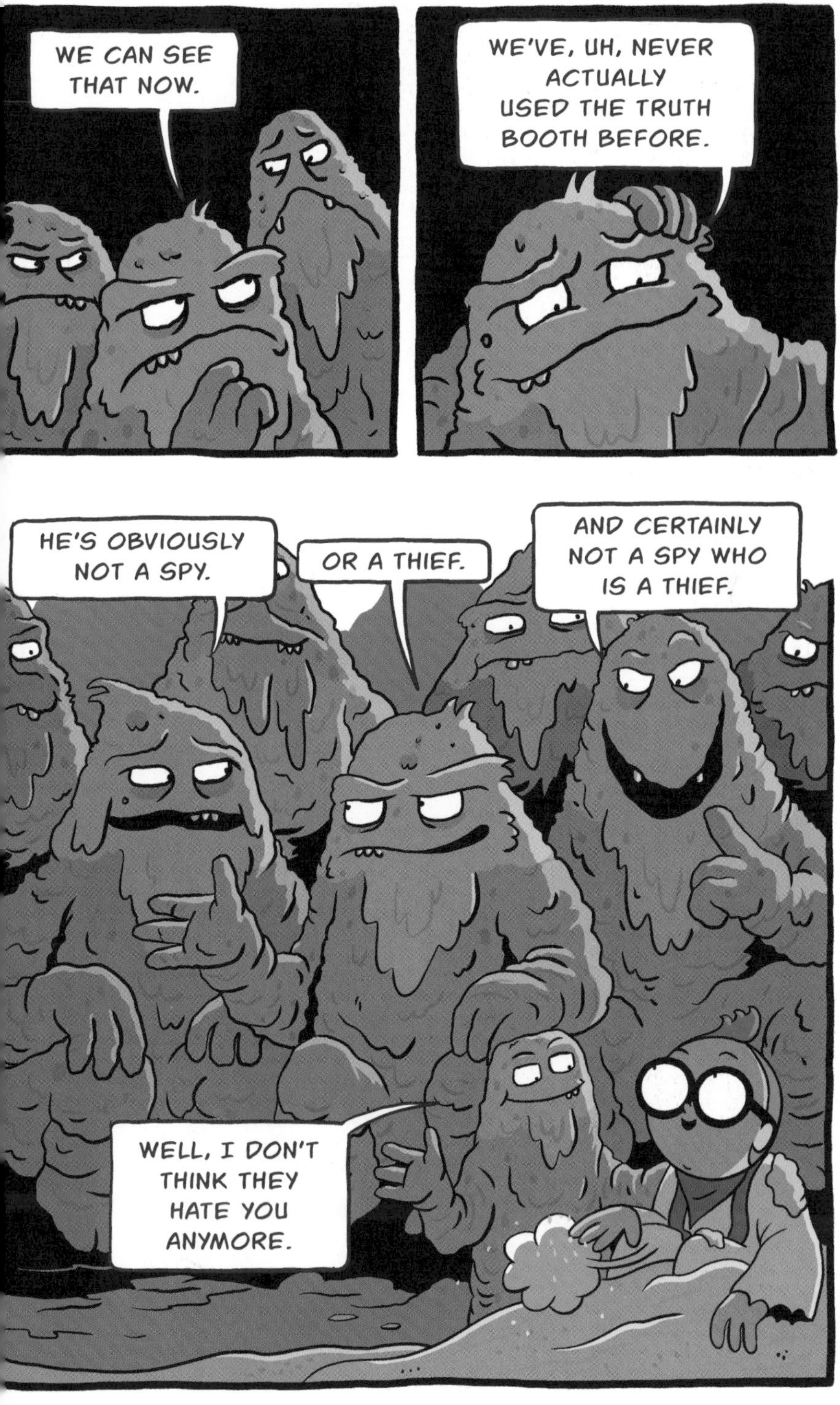
WE CAN SEE THAT NOW.
WE'VE, UH, NEVER ACTUALLY USED THE TRUTH BOOTH BEFORE.
HE'S OBVIOUSLY NOT A SPY.
OR A THIEF.
AND CERTAINLY NOT A SPY WHO IS A THIEF.
WELL, I DON'T THINK THEY HATE YOU ANYMORE.

CHAPTER 11

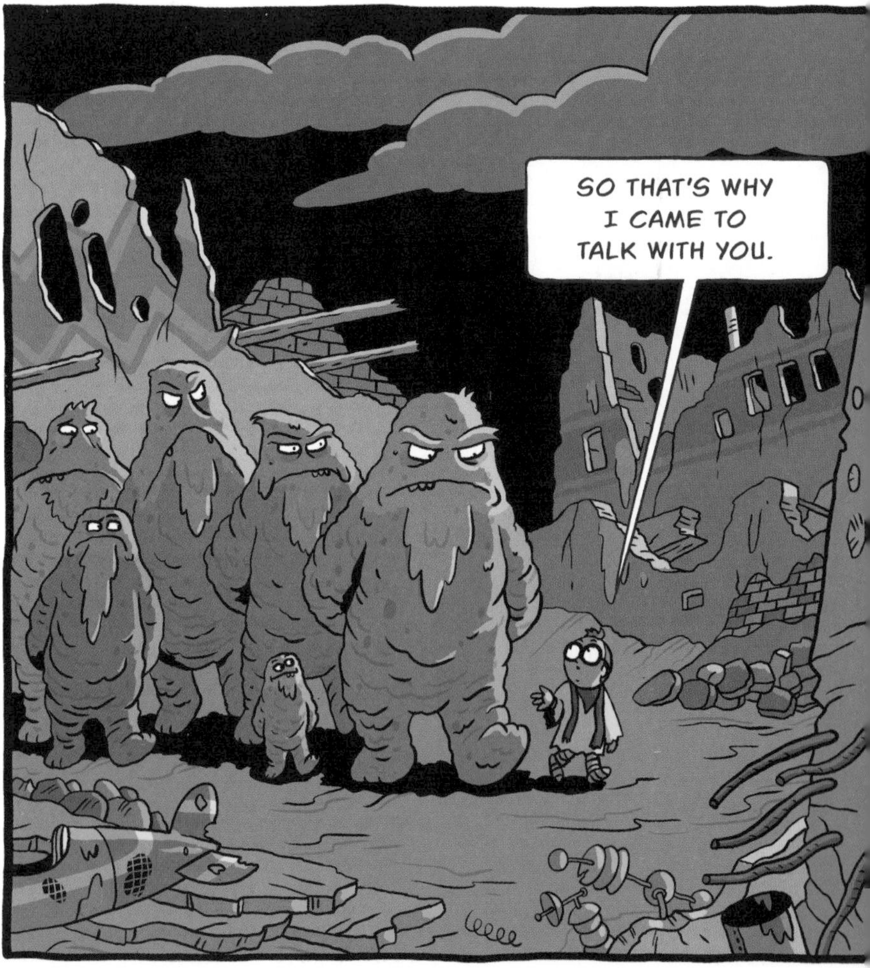
SO THAT'S WHY I CAME TO TALK WITH YOU.

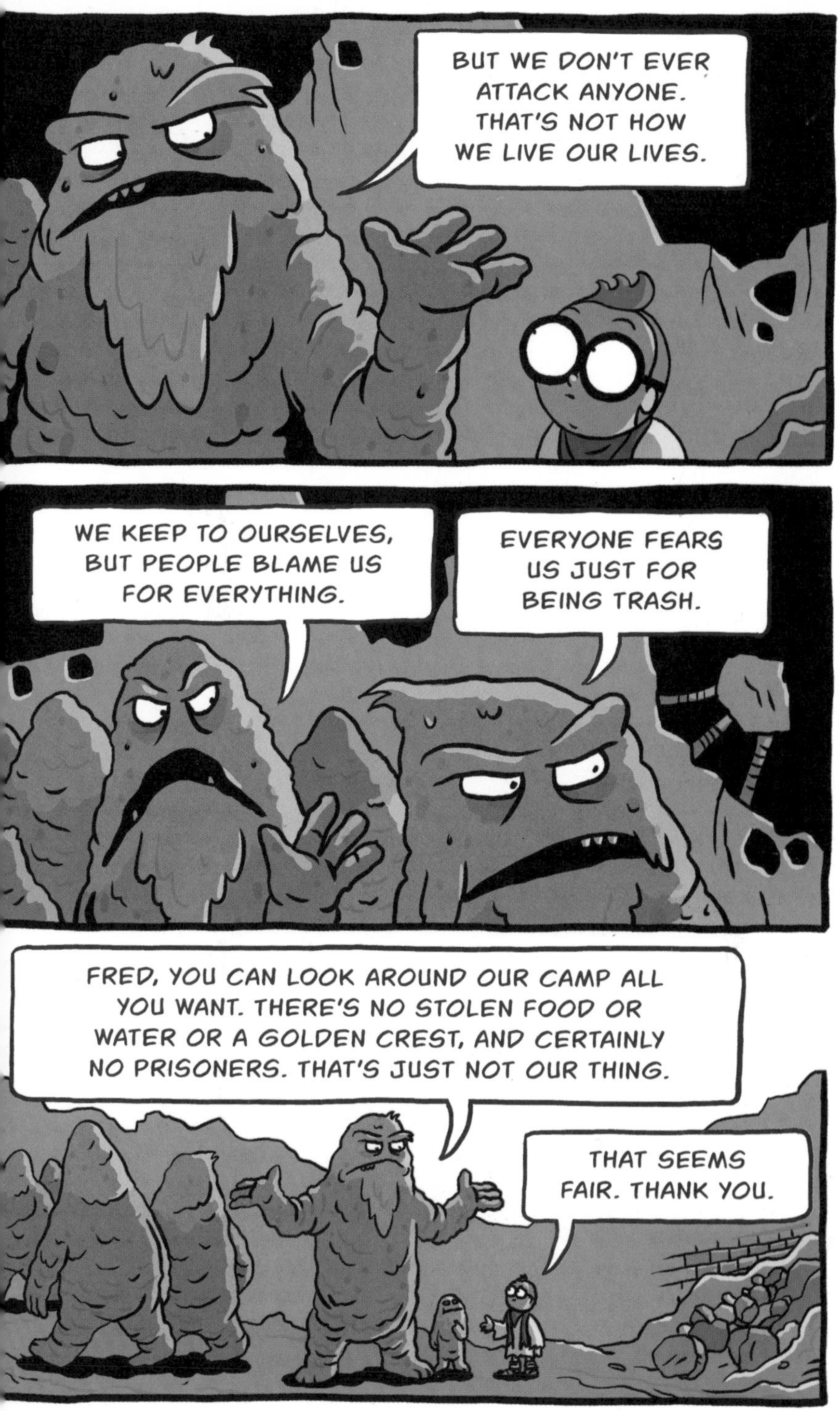
BUT WE DON'T EVER ATTACK ANYONE. THAT'S NOT HOW WE LIVE OUR LIVES.
WE KEEP TO OURSELVES, BUT PEOPLE BLAME US FOR EVERYTHING.
EVERYONE FEARS US JUST FOR BEING TRASH.
FRED, YOU CAN LOOK AROUND OUR CAMP ALL YOU WANT. THERE'S NO STOLEN FOOD OR WATER OR A GOLDEN CREST, AND CERTAINLY NO PRISONERS. THAT'S JUST NOT OUR THING.
THAT SEEMS FAIR. THANK YOU.

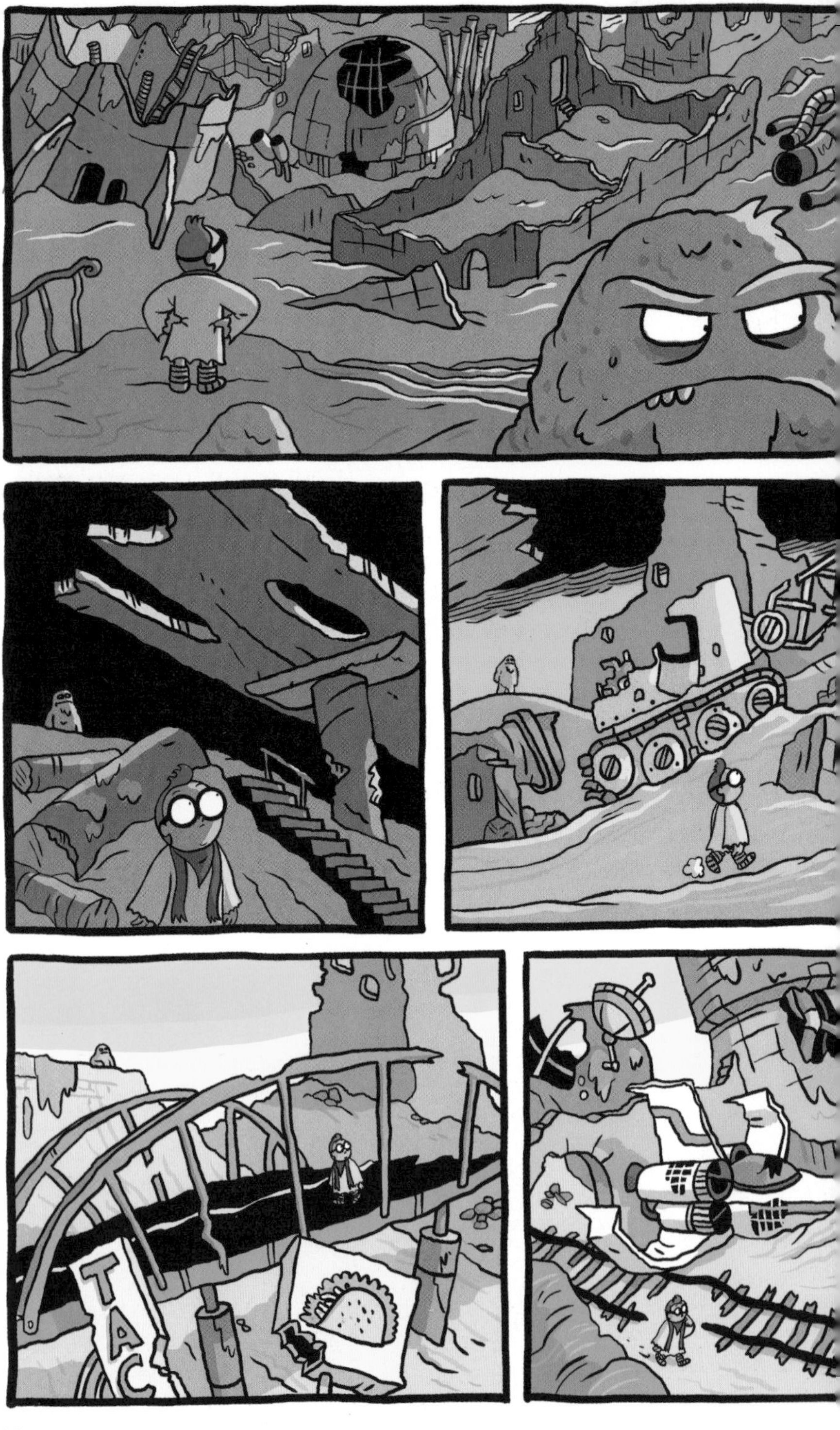
TAC

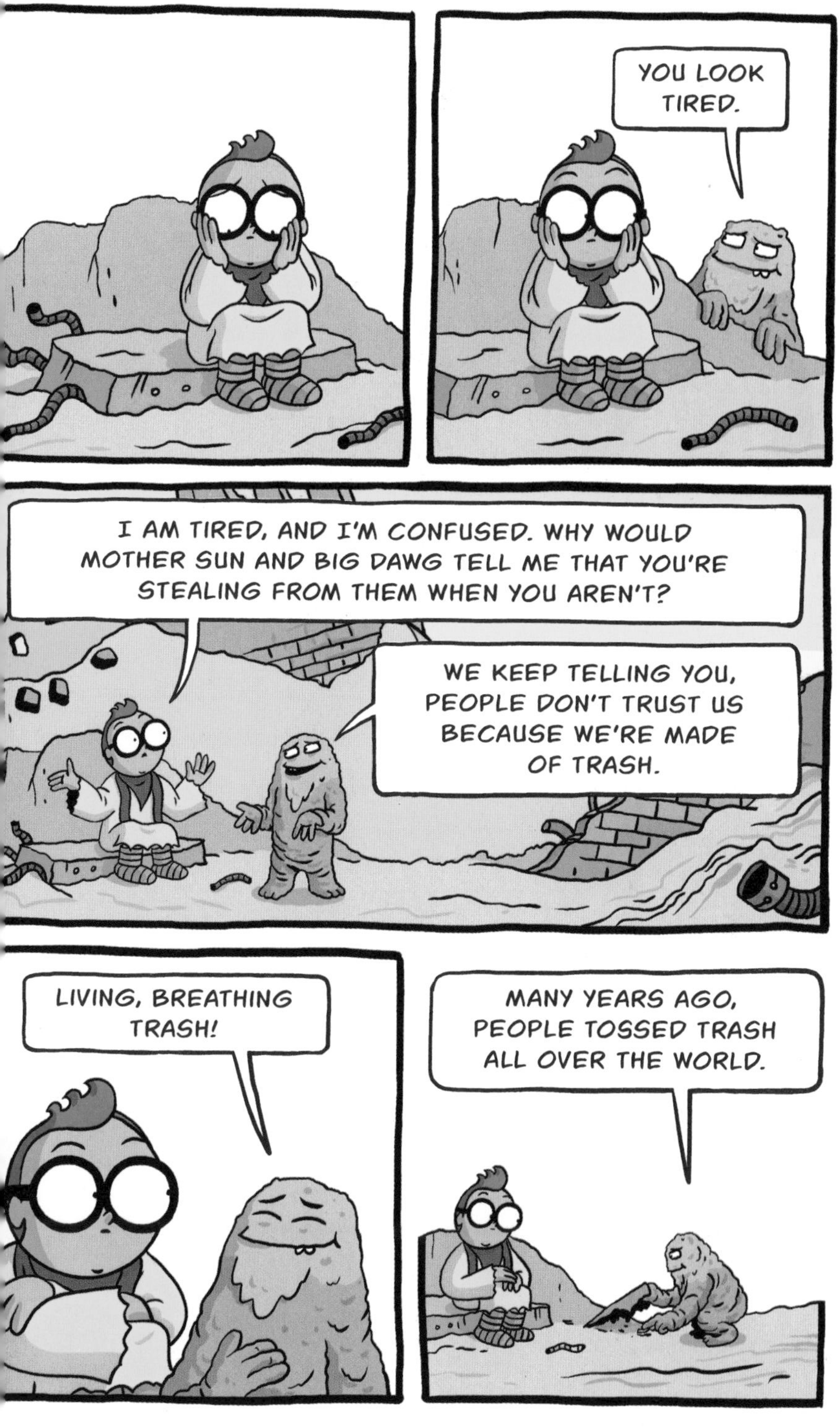
YOU LOOK TIRED.
I AM TIRED, AND I'M CONFUSED. WHY WOULD MOTHER SUN AND BIG DAWG TELL ME THAT YOU'RE STEALING FROM THEM WHEN YOU AREN'T?
WE KEEP TELLING YOU, PEOPLE DON'T TRUST US BECAUSE WE'RE MADE OF TRASH.
LIVING, BREATHING TRASH!
MANY YEARS AGO, PEOPLE TOSSED TRASH ALL OVER THE WORLD.

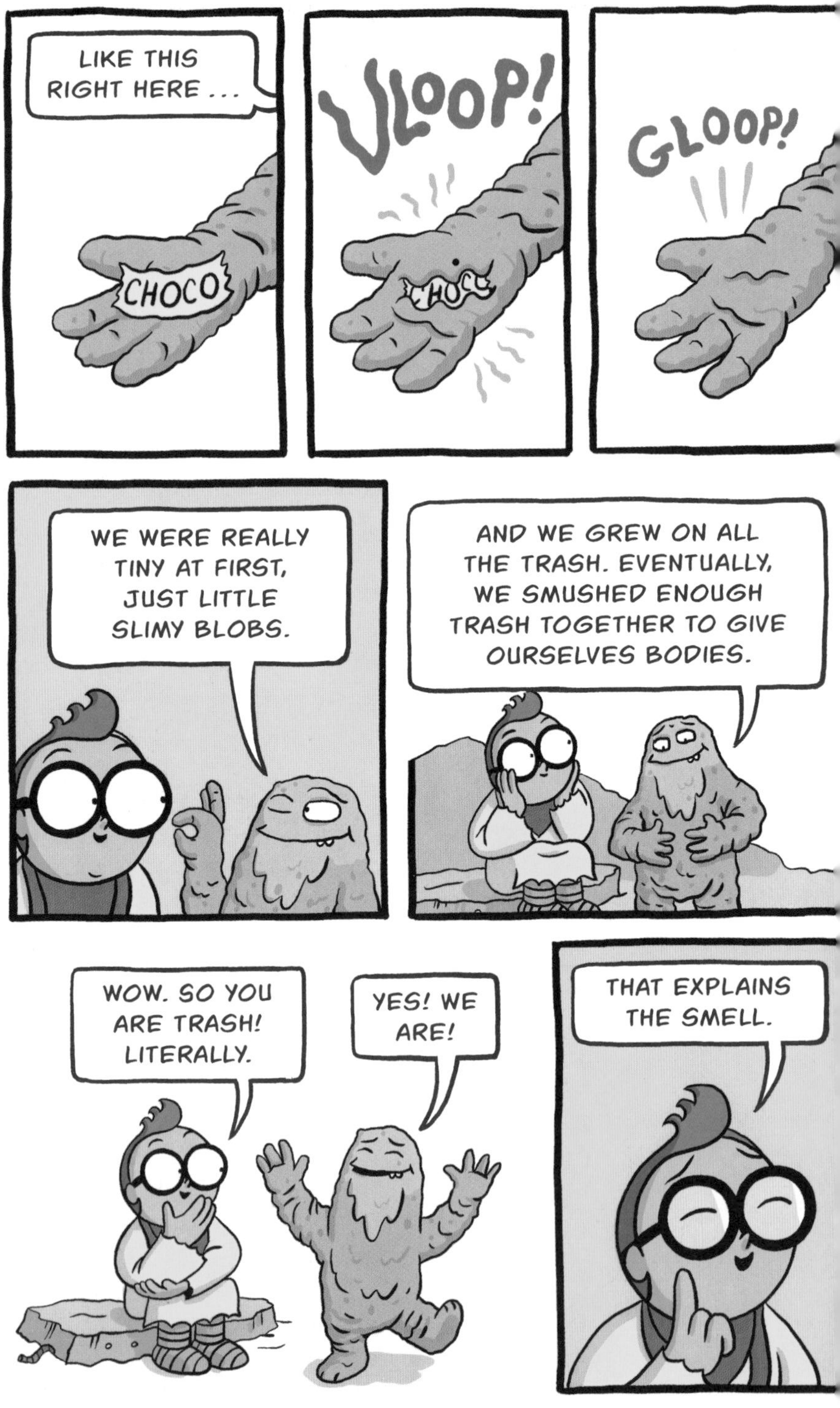
LIKE THIS RIGHT HERE . . .
CHOCO
VLOOP!
GLOOP!
WE WERE REALLY TINY AT FIRST, JUST LITTLE SLIMY BLOBS.
AND WE GREW ON ALL THE TRASH. EVENTUALLY, WE SMUSHED ENOUGH TRASH TOGETHER TO GIVE OURSELVES BODIES.
WOW. SO YOU ARE TRASH! LITERALLY.
YES! WE ARE!
THAT EXPLAINS THE SMELL.

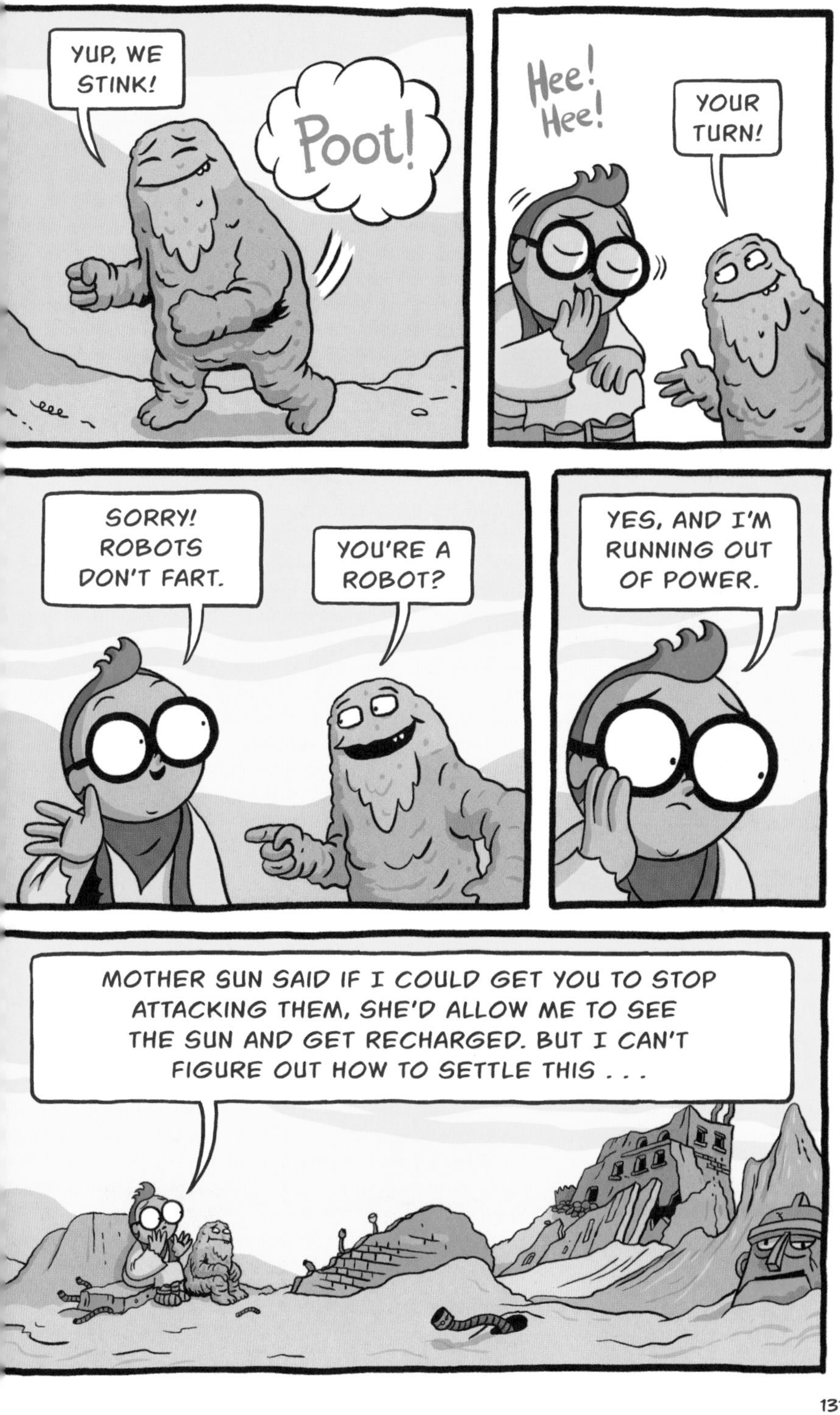
YUP, WE STINK!
Poot!
Hee! Hee!
YOUR TURN!
SORRY! ROBOTS DON'T FART.
YOU'RE A ROBOT?
YES, AND I'M RUNNING OUT OF POWER.
MOTHER SUN SAID IF I COULD GET YOU TO STOP ATTACKING THEM, SHE'D ALLOW ME TO SEE THE SUN AND GET RECHARGED. BUT I CAN'T FIGURE OUT HOW TO SETTLE THIS . . .

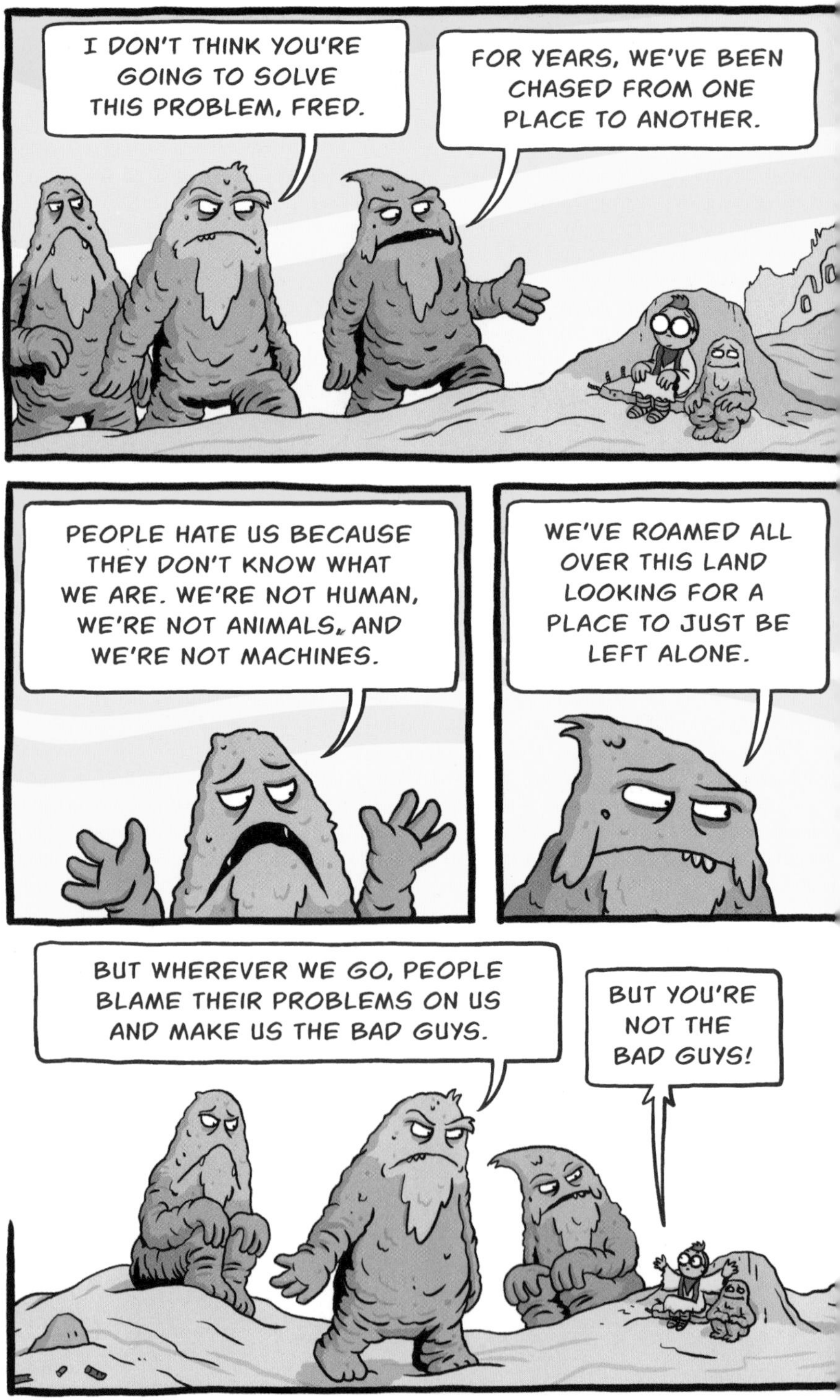
I DON'T THINK YOU'RE GOING TO SOLVE THIS PROBLEM, FRED.
FOR YEARS, WE'VE BEEN CHASED FROM ONE PLACE TO ANOTHER.
PEOPLE HATE US BECAUSE THEY DON'T KNOW WHAT WE ARE. WE'RE NOT HUMAN, WE'RE NOT ANIMALS, AND WE'RE NOT MACHINES.
WE'VE ROAMED ALL OVER THIS LAND LOOKING FOR A PLACE TO JUST BE LEFT ALONE.
BUT WHEREVER WE GO, PEOPLE BLAME THEIR PROBLEMS ON US AND MAKE US THE BAD GUYS.
BUT YOU'RE NOT THE BAD GUYS!

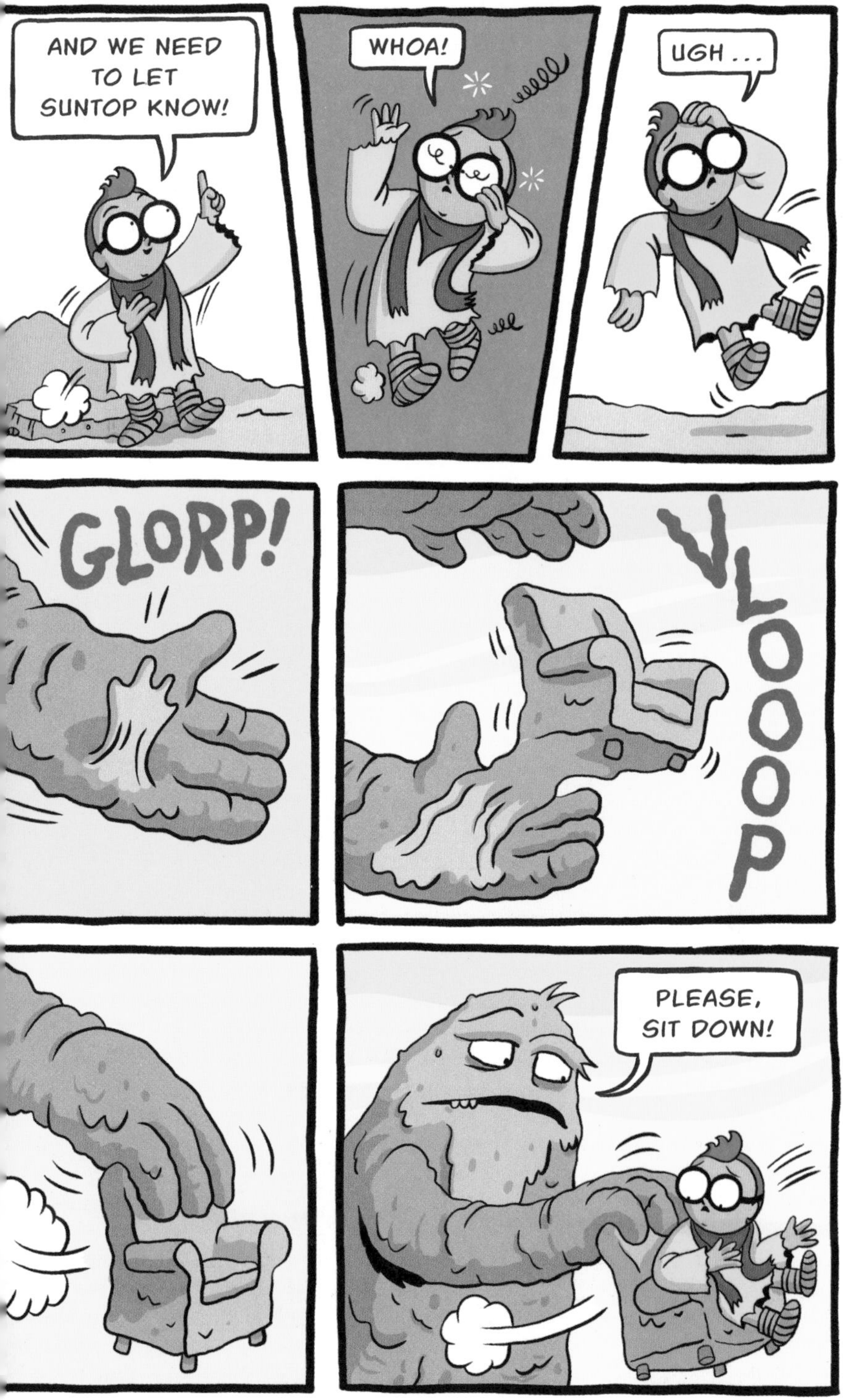
AND WE NEED TO LET SUNTOP KNOW!
WHOA!
UGH . . .
GLORP!
VLOOOP
PLEASE, SIT DOWN!

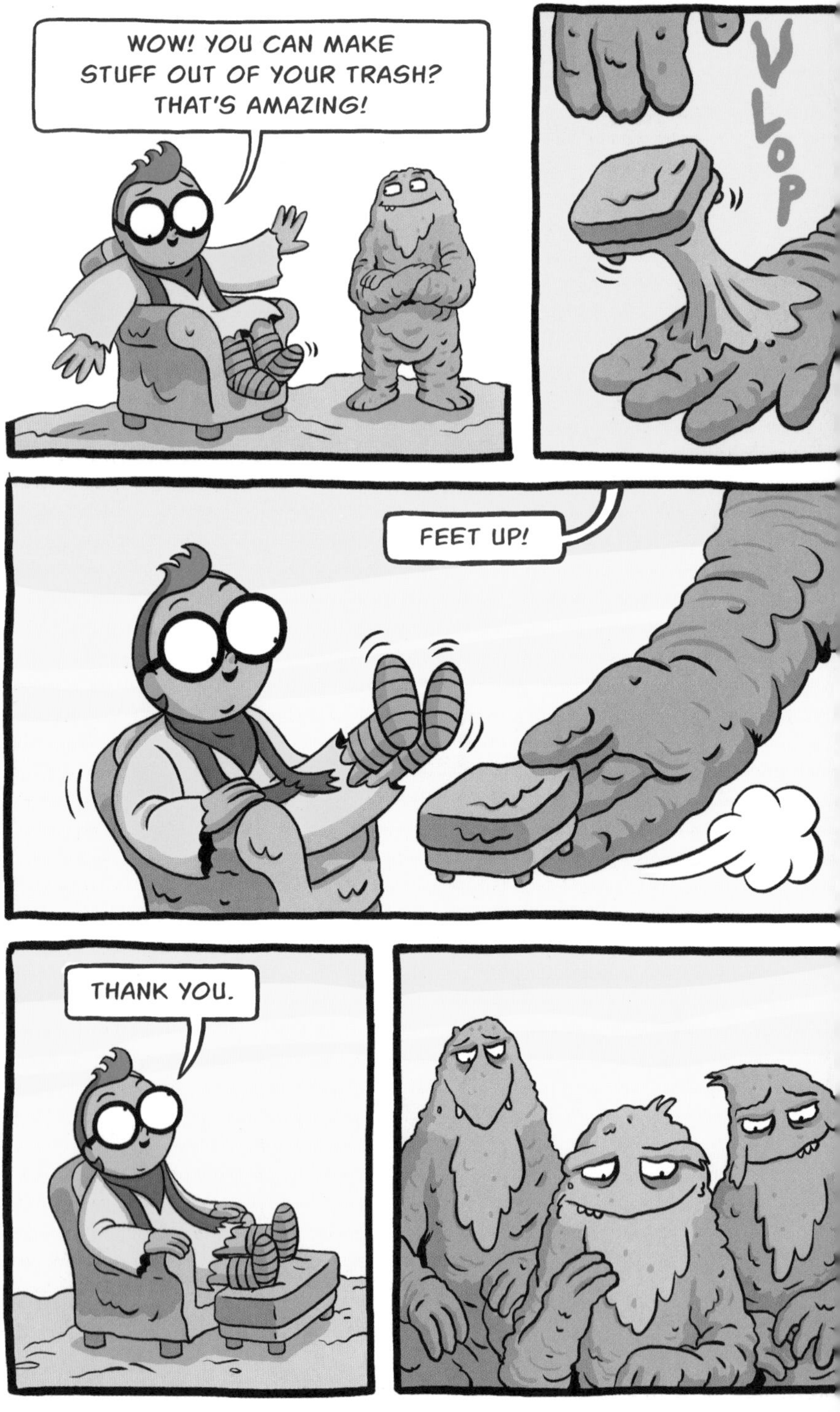
WOW! YOU CAN MAKE STUFF OUT OF YOUR TRASH? THAT'S AMAZING!
VLOP
FEET UP!
THANK YOU.

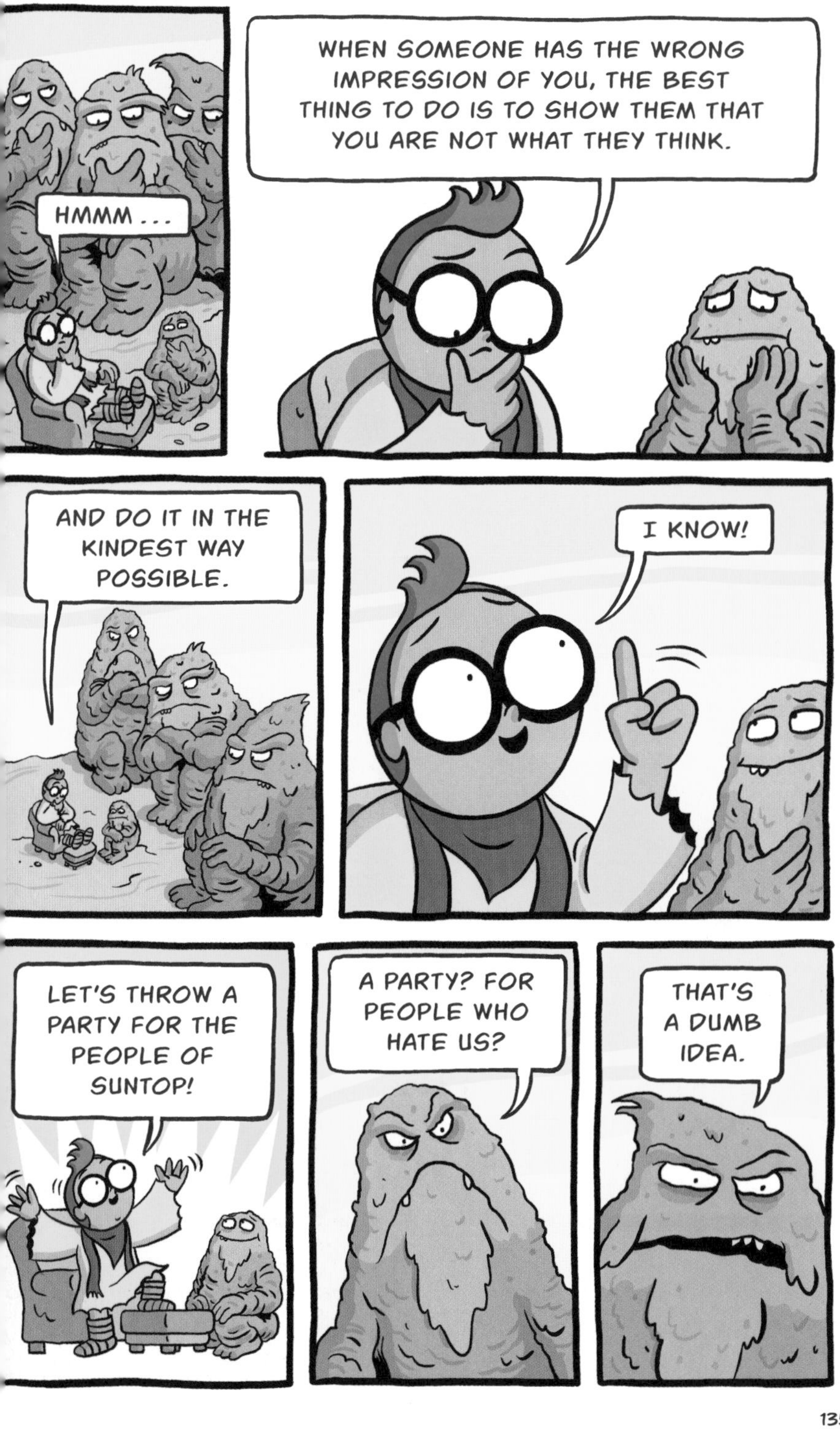

HMMM . . .
WHEN SOMEONE HAS THE WRONG IMPRESSION OF YOU, THE BEST THING TO DO IS TO SHOW THEM THAT YOU ARE NOT WHAT THEY THINK.
AND DO IT IN THE KINDEST WAY POSSIBLE.
I KNOW!
LET'S THROW A PARTY FOR THE PEOPLE OF SUNTOP!
A PARTY? FOR PEOPLE WHO HATE US?
THAT'S A DUMB IDEA.

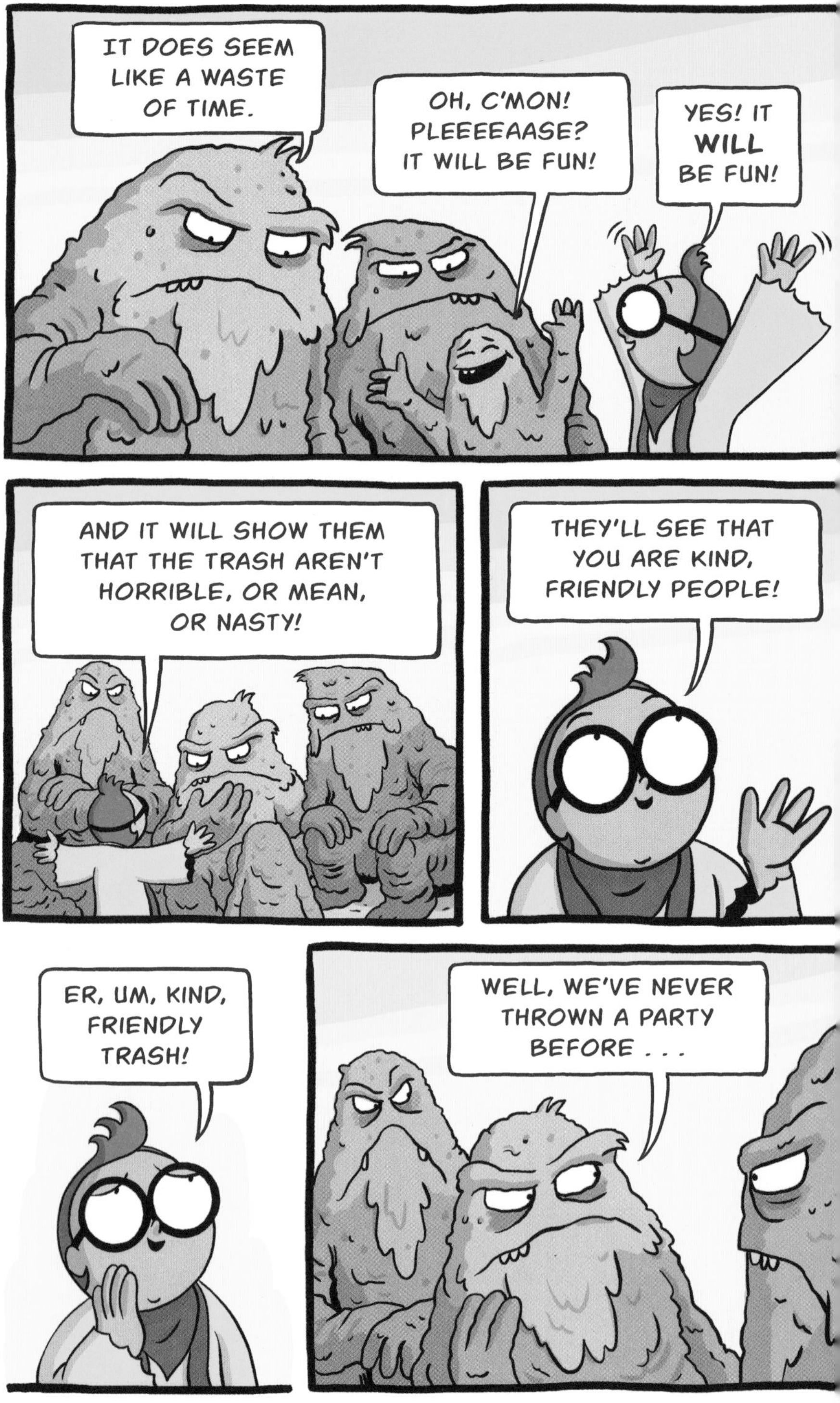
IT DOES SEEM LIKE A WASTE OF TIME.
OH, C'MON! PLEEEEAASE? IT WILL BE FUN!
YES! IT **WILL** BE FUN!
AND IT WILL SHOW THEM THAT THE TRASH AREN'T HORRIBLE, OR MEAN, OR NASTY!
THEY'LL SEE THAT YOU ARE KIND, FRIENDLY PEOPLE!
ER, UM, KIND, FRIENDLY TRASH!
WELL, WE'VE NEVER THROWN A PARTY BEFORE . . .

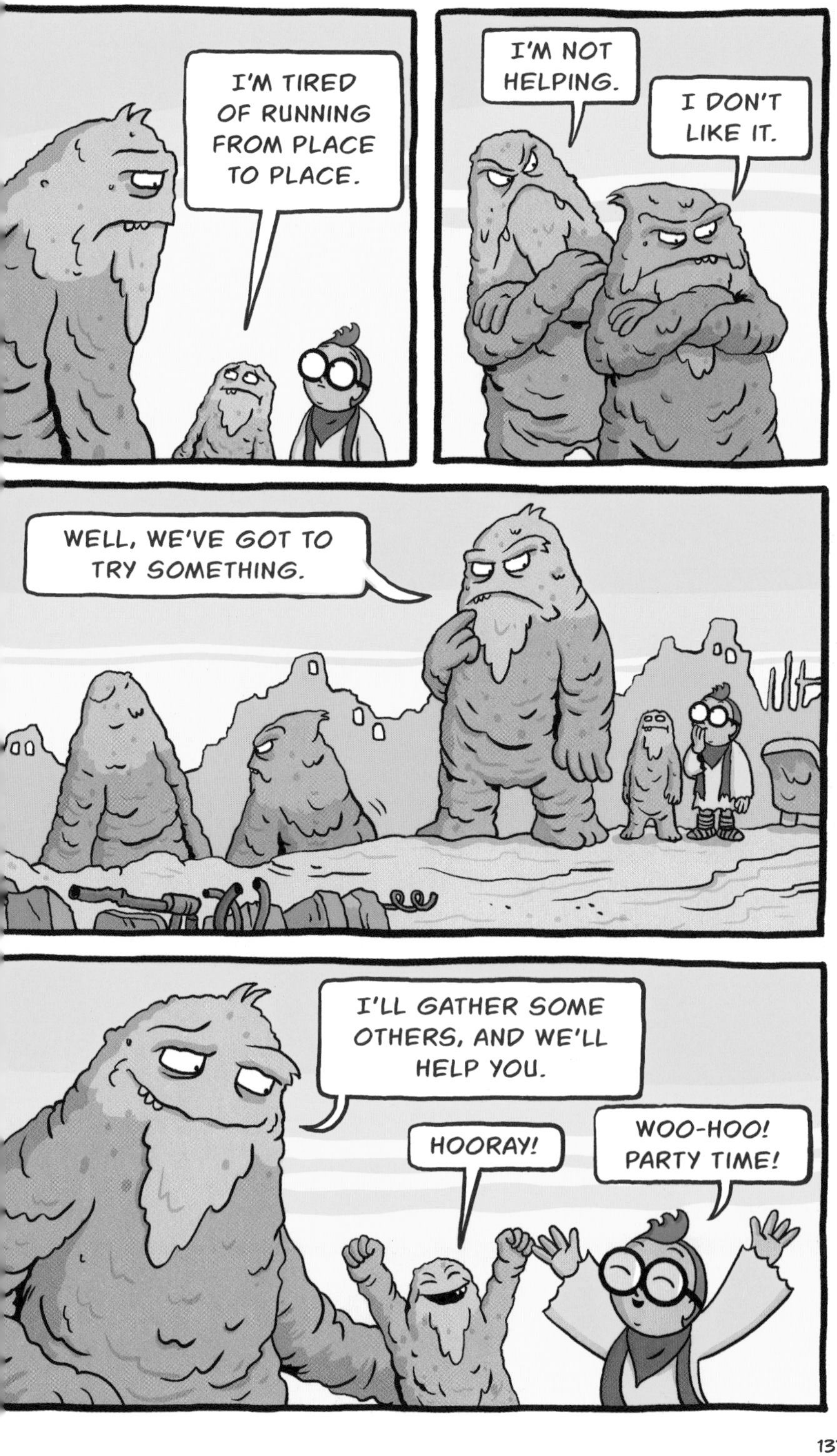
I'M TIRED OF RUNNING FROM PLACE TO PLACE.
I'M NOT HELPING.
I DON'T LIKE IT.
WELL, WE'VE GOT TO TRY SOMETHING.
I'LL GATHER SOME OTHERS, AND WE'LL HELP YOU.
HOORAY!
WOO-HOO! PARTY TIME!

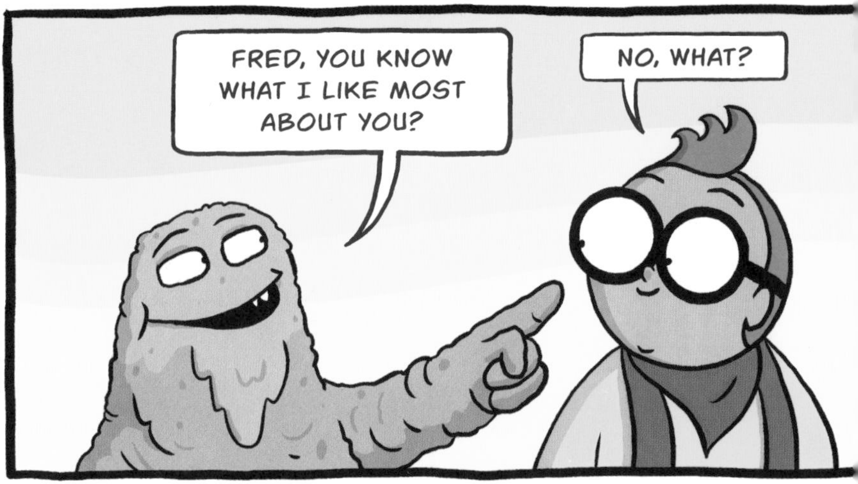
FRED, YOU KNOW WHAT I LIKE MOST ABOUT YOU?
NO, WHAT?

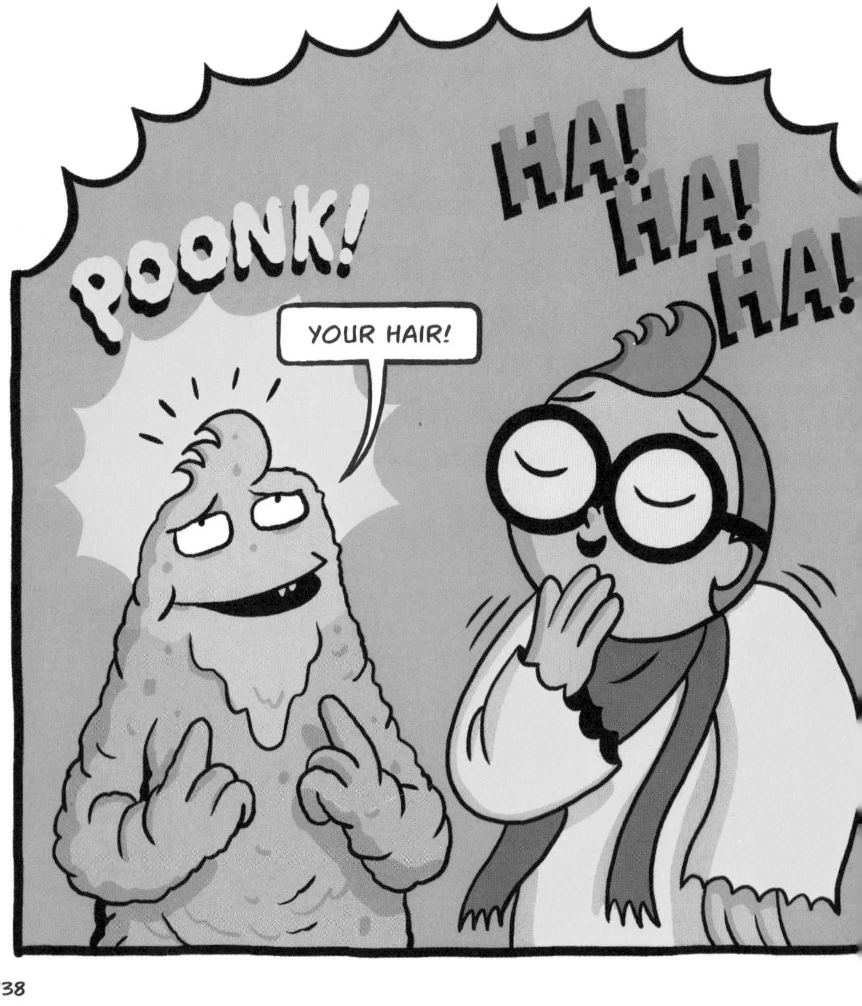
POONK!
HA! HA! HA!
YOUR HAIR!

CHAPTER 12

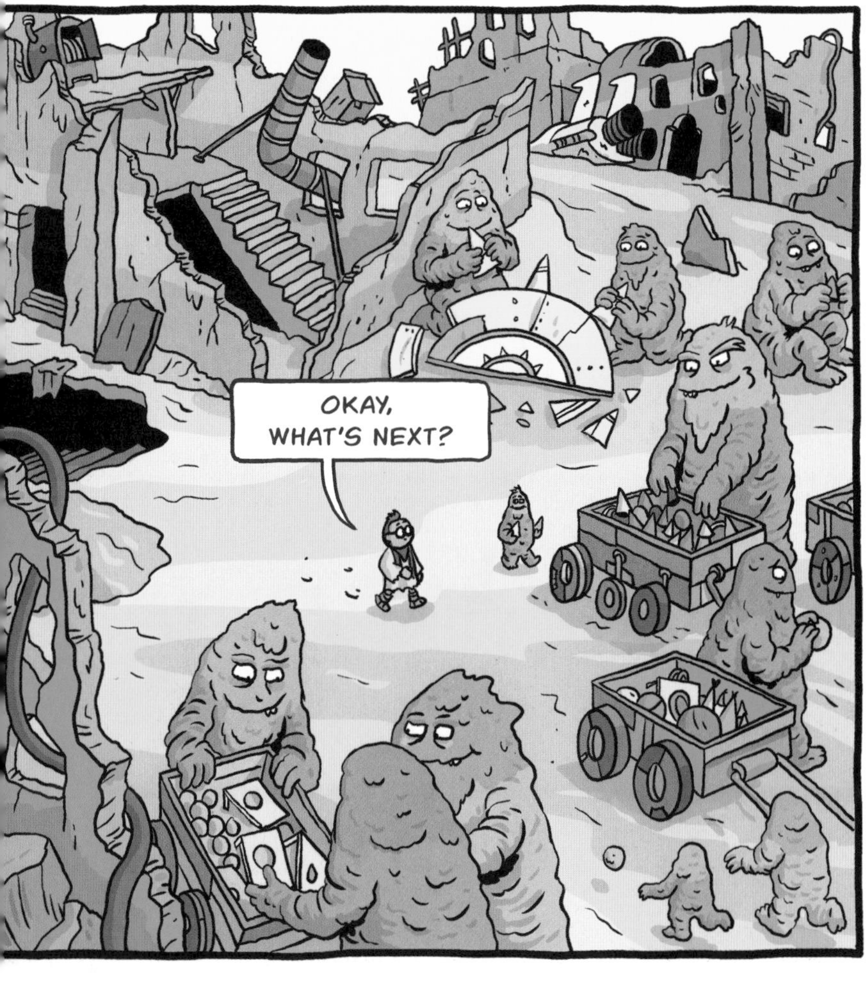
OKAY, WHAT'S NEXT?

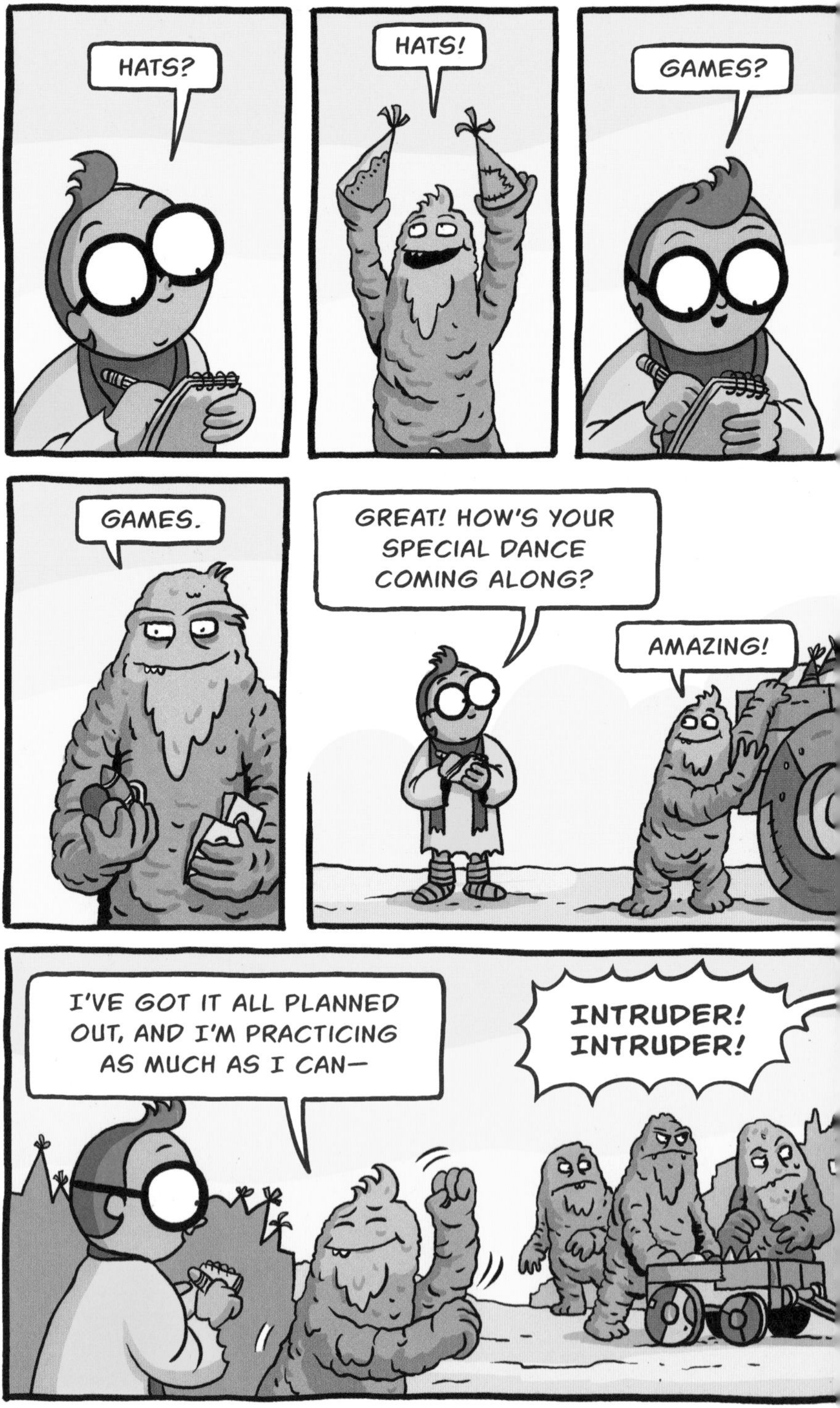
HATS?
HATS!
GAMES?
GAMES.
GREAT! HOW'S YOUR SPECIAL DANCE COMING ALONG?
AMAZING!
I'VE GOT IT ALL PLANNED OUT, AND I'M PRACTICING AS MUCH AS I CAN—
INTRUDER! INTRUDER!

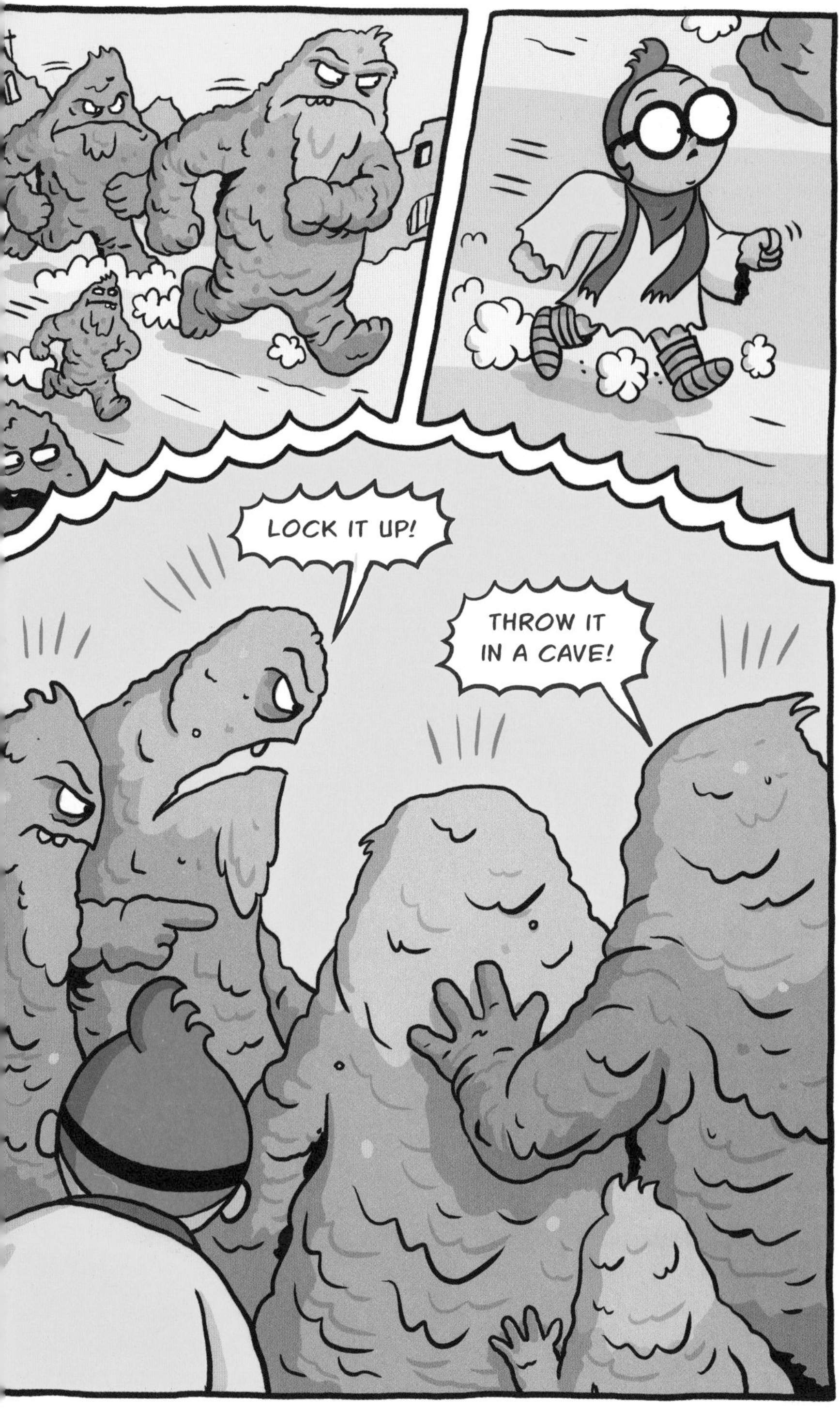
LOCK IT UP!
THROW IT IN A CAVE!

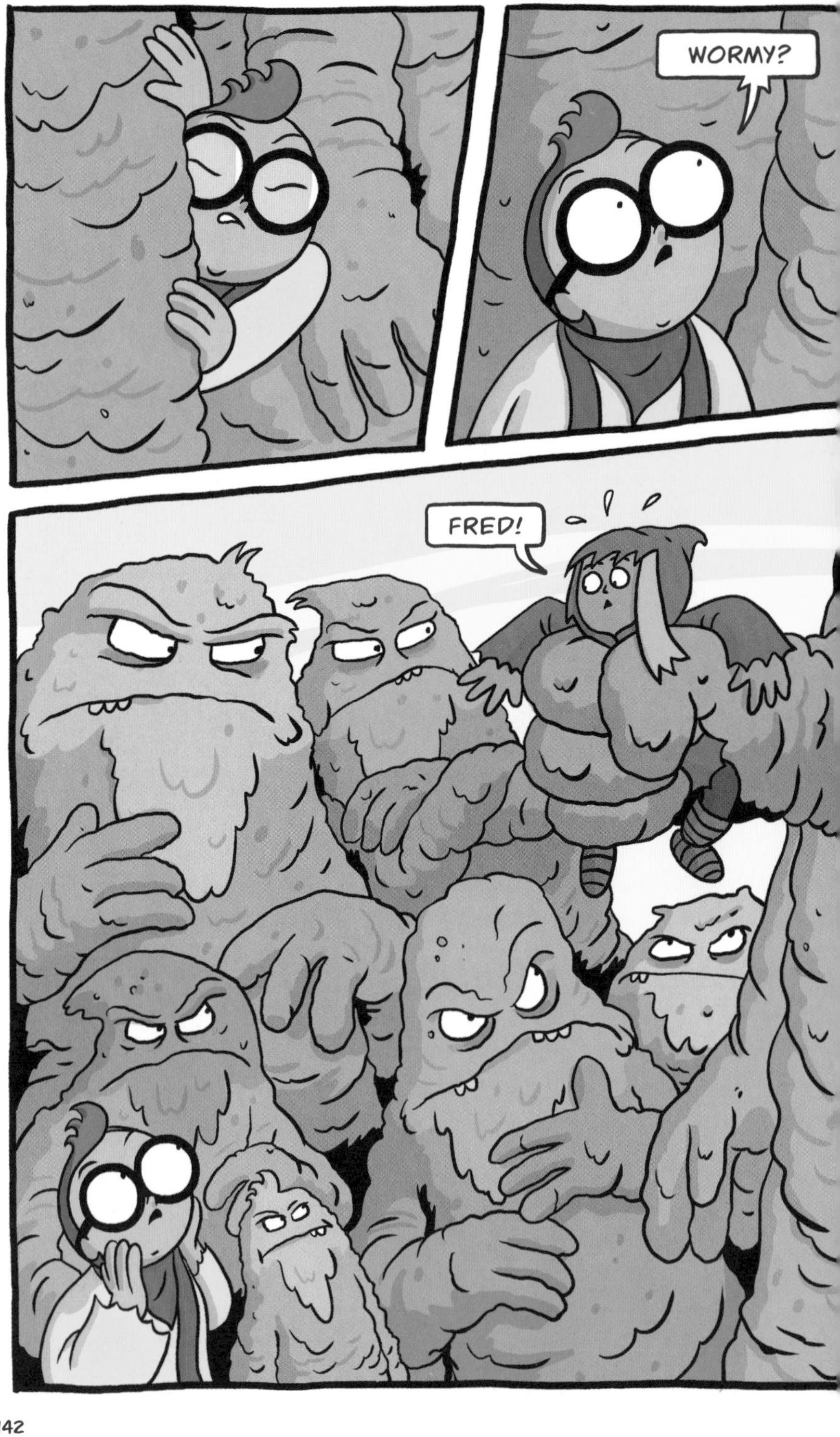
WORMY?
FRED!

DO YOU KNOW THIS INTRUDER?

YES! SHE'S MY CLOSEST FRIEND!

I'M REALLY GLAD TO SEE YOU!

DID YOU STEAL ANYTHING?

NO, I WAS LOOKING FOR YOU, YOU RUST-HEAD!

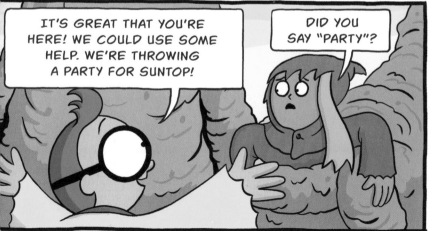

IT'S GREAT THAT YOU'RE HERE! WE COULD USE SOME HELP. WE'RE THROWING A PARTY FOR SUNTOP!

DID YOU SAY "PARTY"?

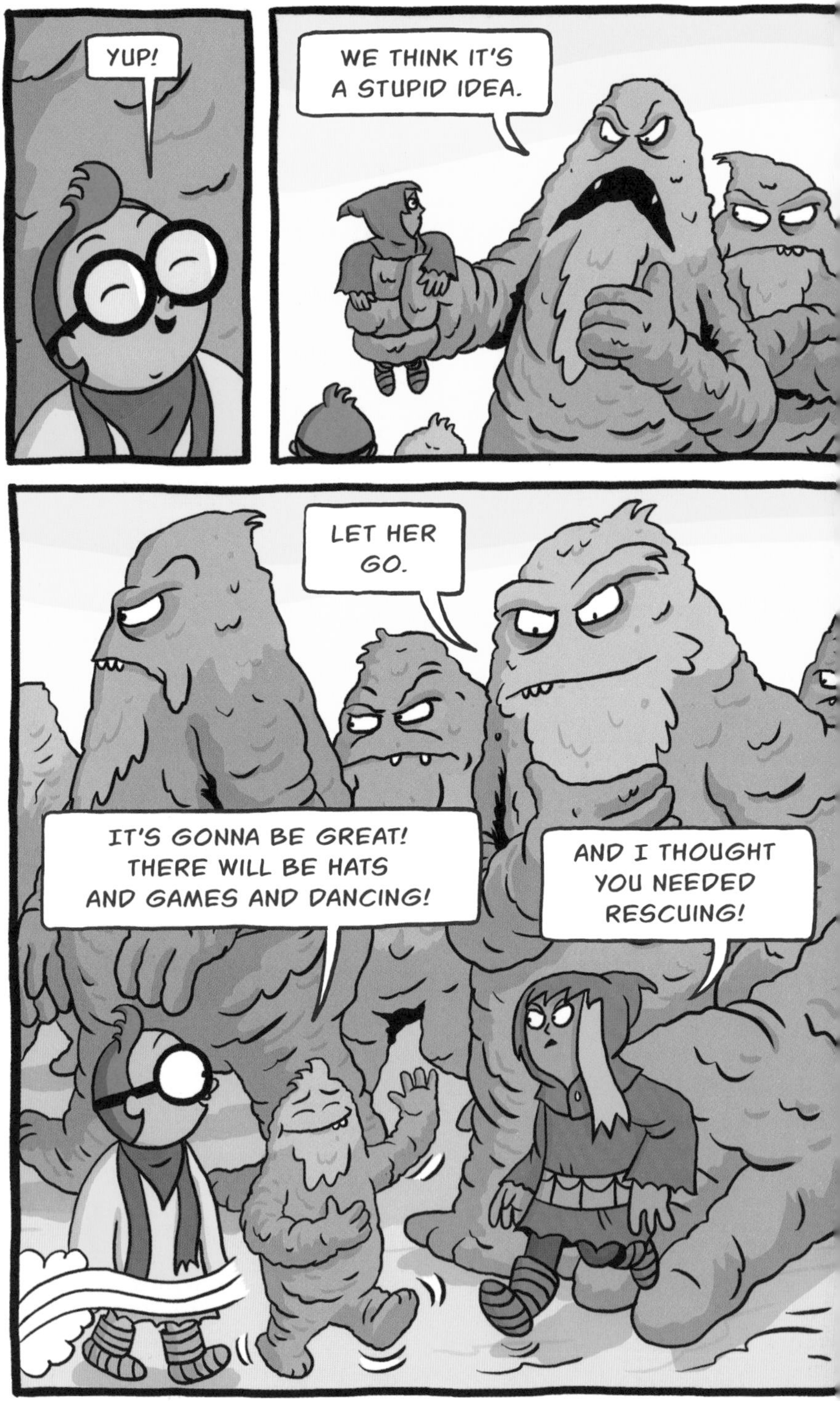
YUP!
WE THINK IT'S A STUPID IDEA.
LET HER GO.
IT'S GONNA BE GREAT! THERE WILL BE HATS AND GAMES AND DANCING!
AND I THOUGHT YOU NEEDED RESCUING!

CHAPTER 13

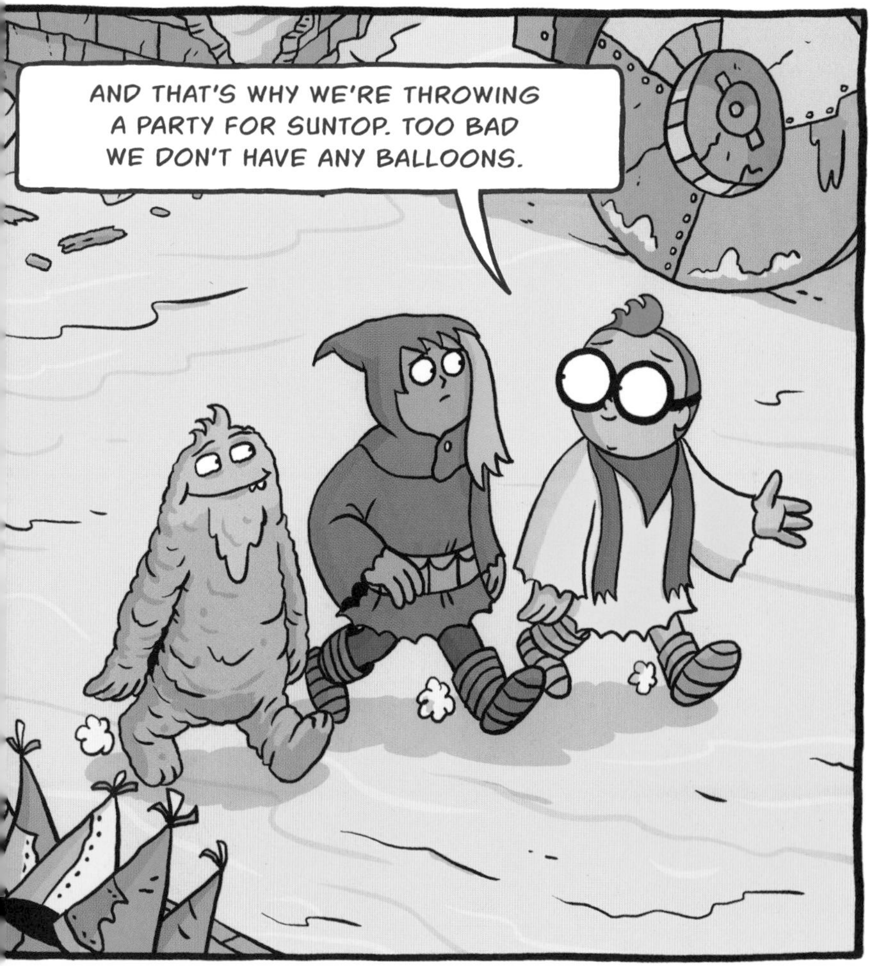
AND THAT'S WHY WE'RE THROWING A PARTY FOR SUNTOP. TOO BAD WE DON'T HAVE ANY BALLOONS.

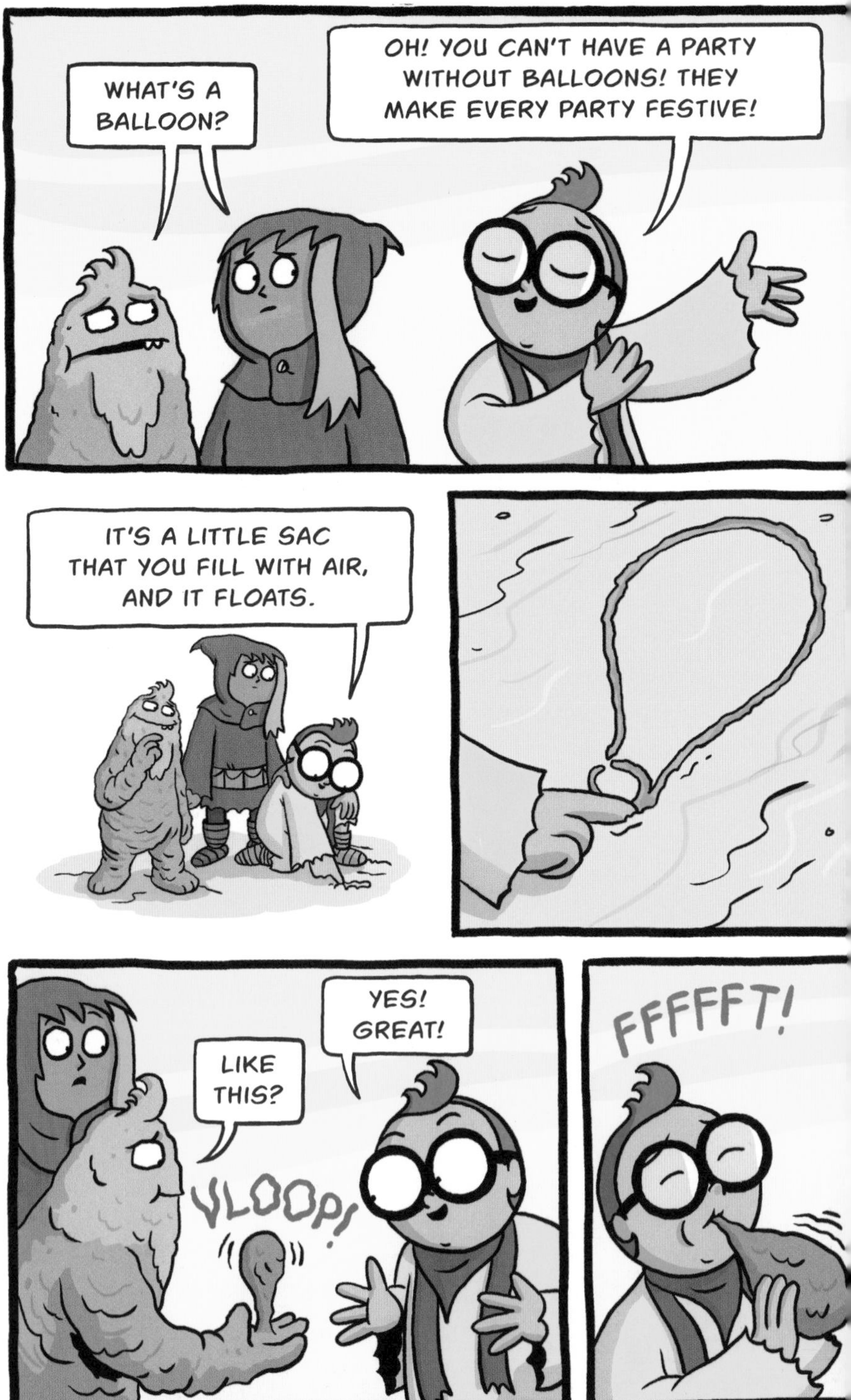
WHAT'S A BALLOON?
OH! YOU CAN'T HAVE A PARTY WITHOUT BALLOONS! THEY MAKE EVERY PARTY FESTIVE!
IT'S A LITTLE SAC THAT YOU FILL WITH AIR, AND IT FLOATS.
LIKE THIS?
YES! GREAT!
VLOOP!
FFFFFT!

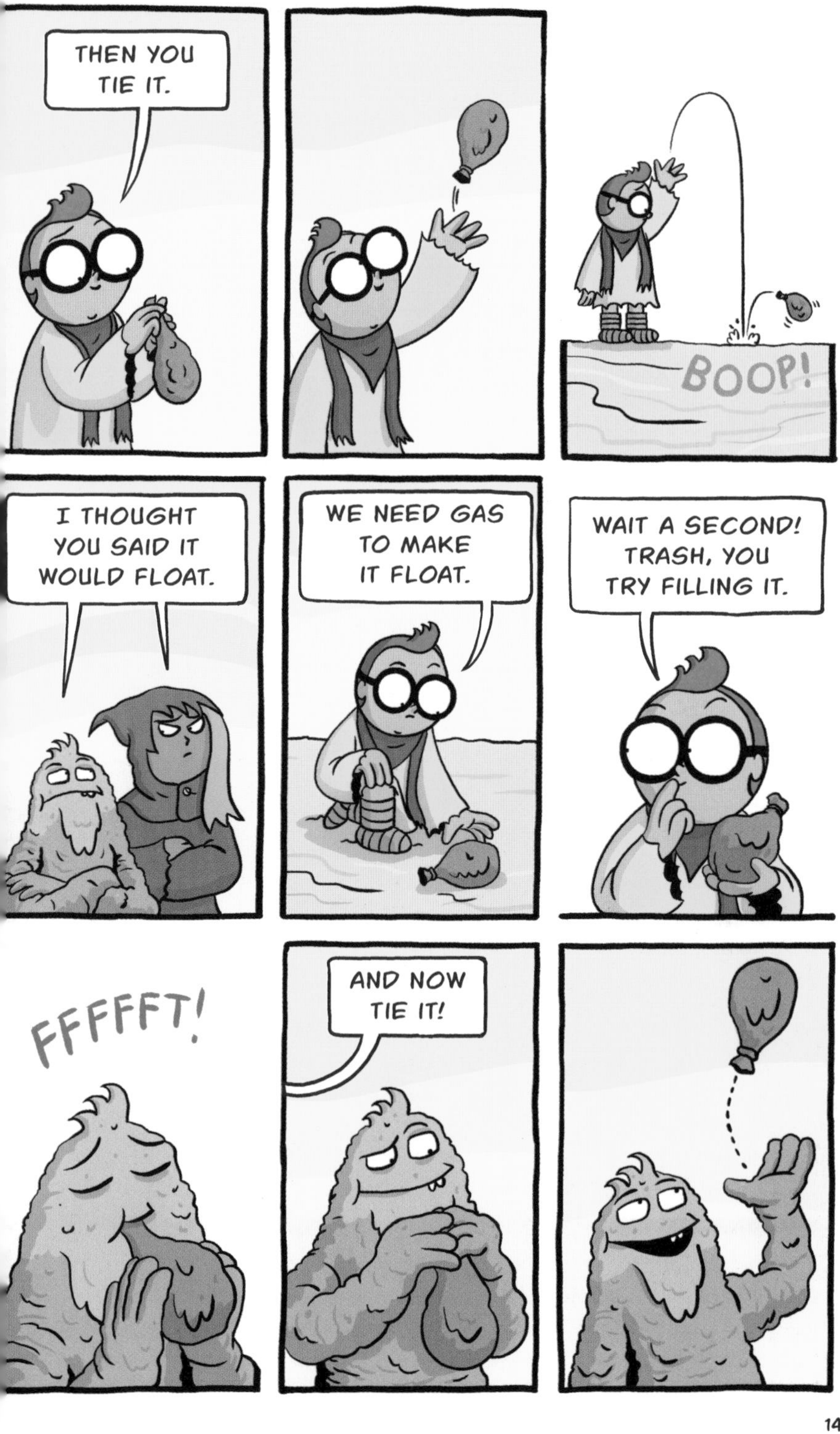
THEN YOU TIE IT.
BOOP!
I THOUGHT YOU SAID IT WOULD FLOAT.
WE NEED GAS TO MAKE IT FLOAT.
WAIT A SECOND! TRASH, YOU TRY FILLING IT.
FFFFFT!
AND NOW TIE IT!

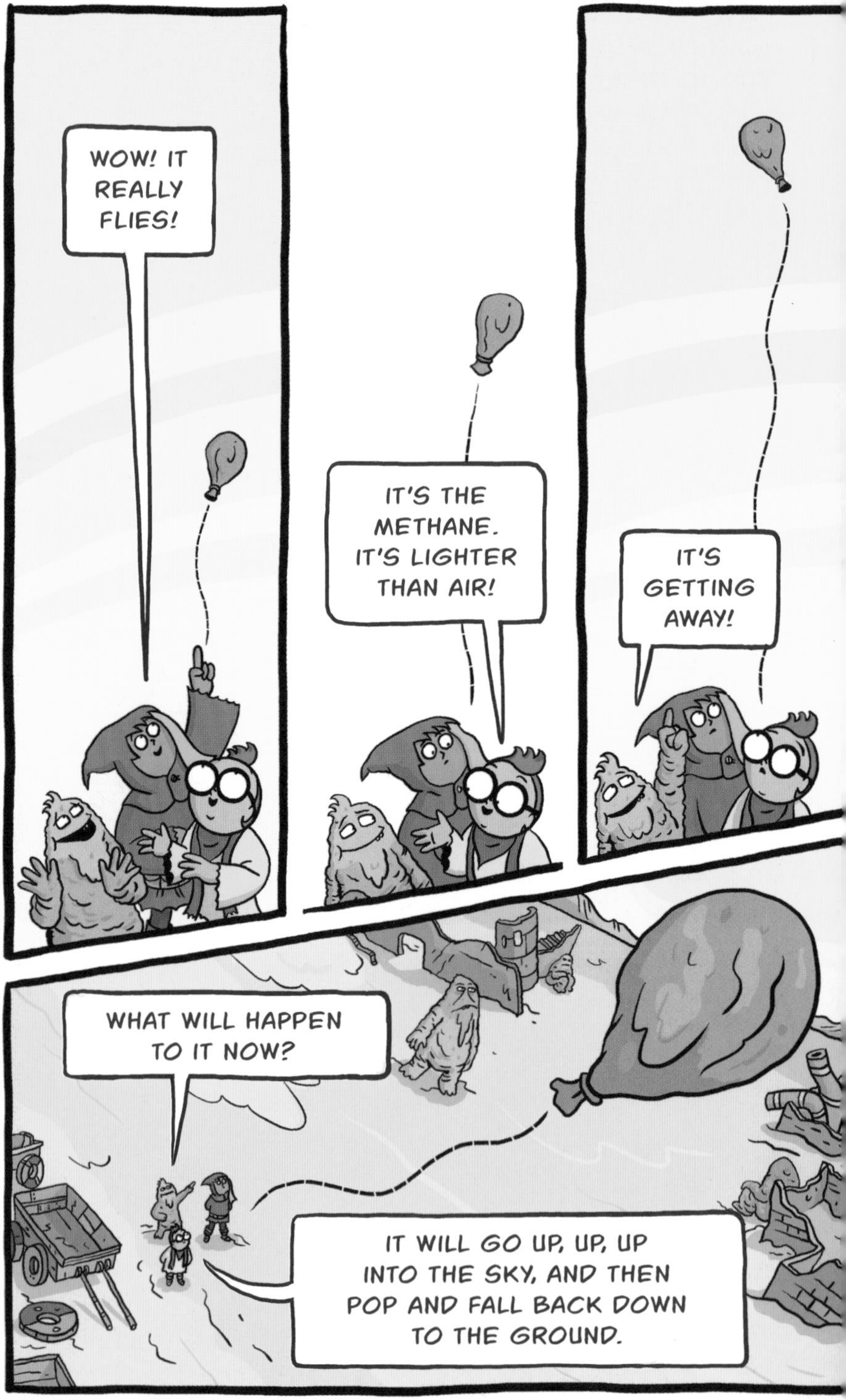
WOW! IT REALLY FLIES!
IT'S THE METHANE. IT'S LIGHTER THAN AIR!
IT'S GETTING AWAY!
WHAT WILL HAPPEN TO IT NOW?
IT WILL GO UP, UP, UP INTO THE SKY, AND THEN POP AND FALL BACK DOWN TO THE GROUND.

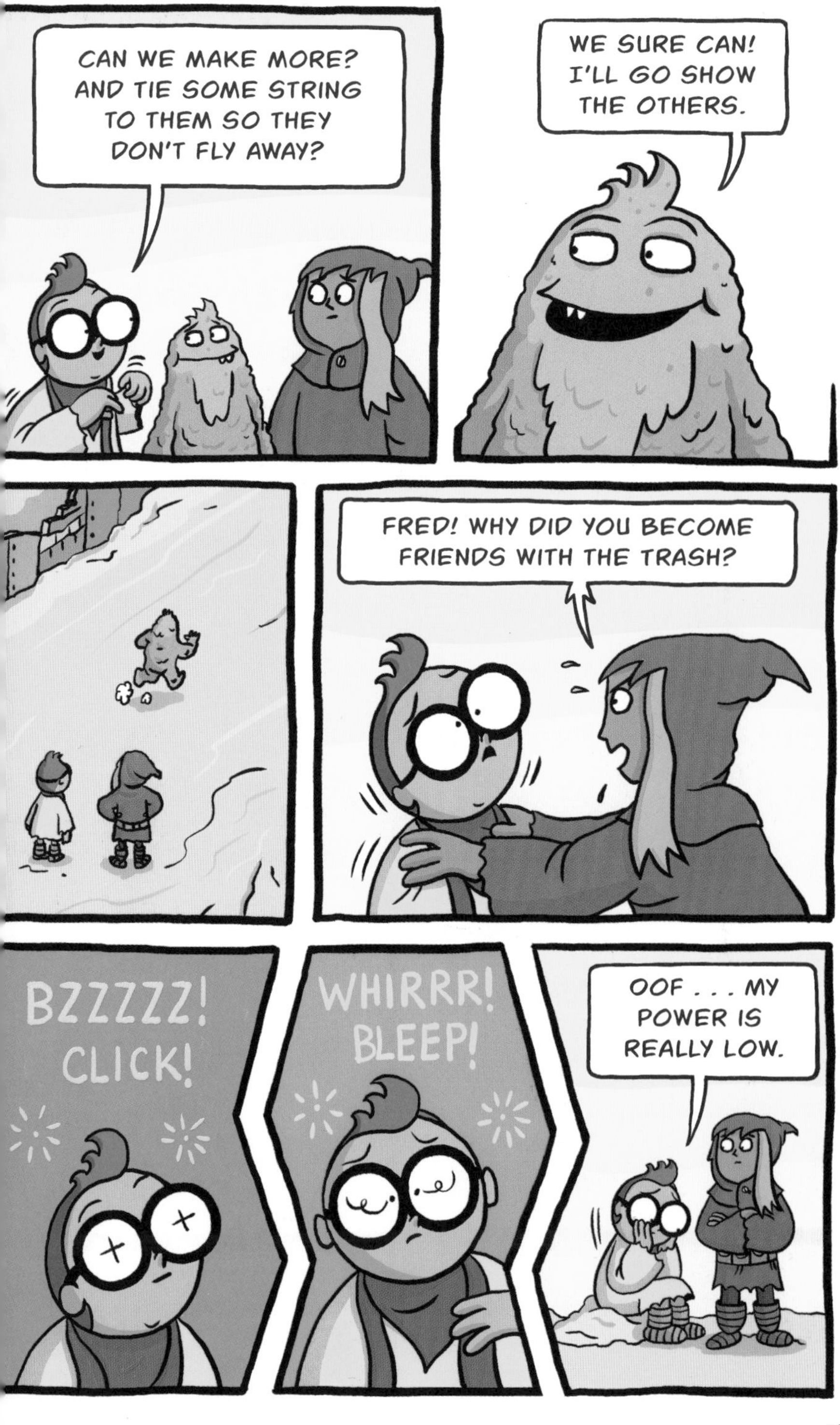
CAN WE MAKE MORE? AND TIE SOME STRING TO THEM SO THEY DON'T FLY AWAY?
WE SURE CAN! I'LL GO SHOW THE OTHERS.
FRED! WHY DID YOU BECOME FRIENDS WITH THE TRASH?
BZZZZZ! CLICK!
WHIRRR! BLEEP!
OOF . . . MY POWER IS REALLY LOW.

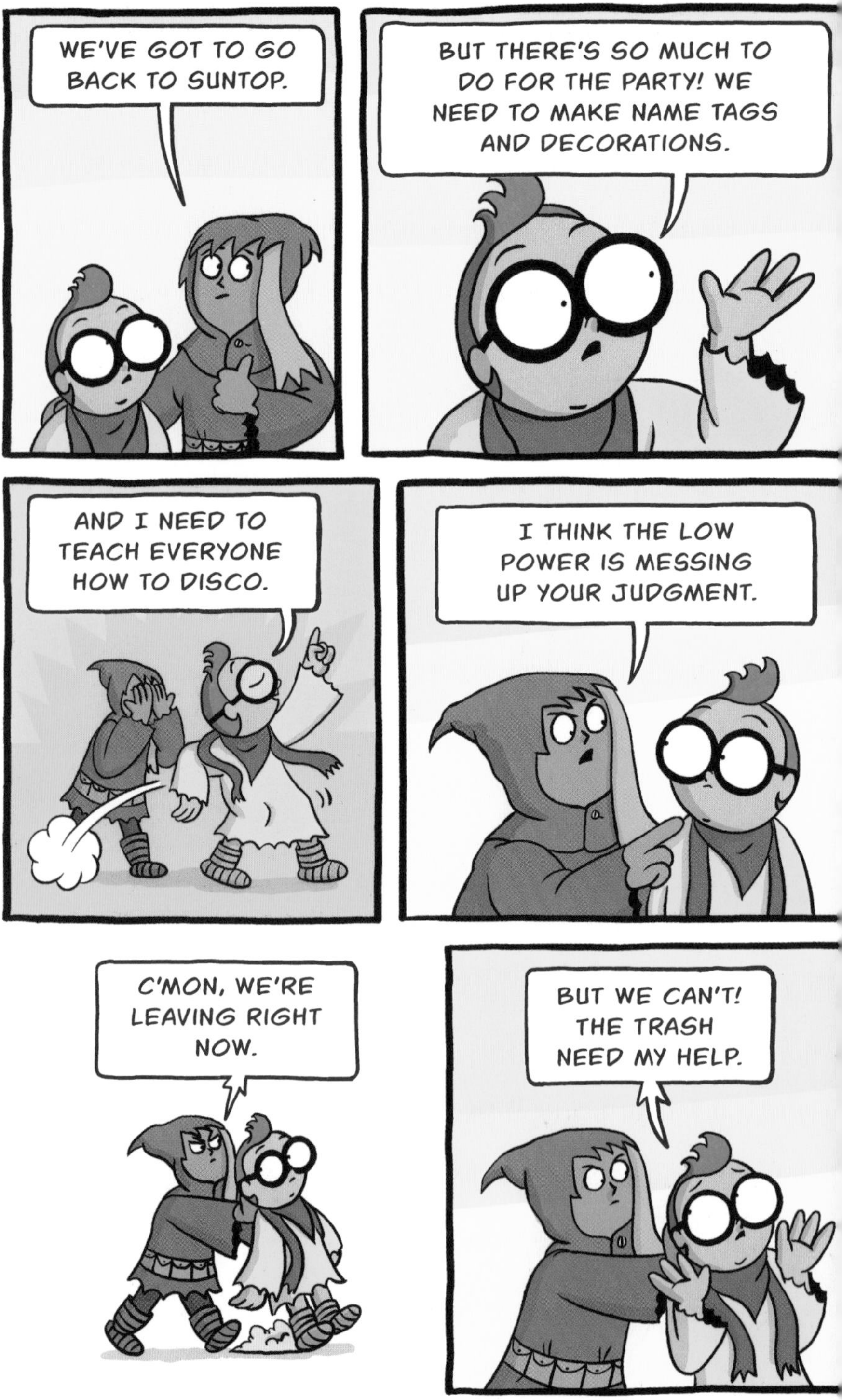
WE'VE GOT TO GO BACK TO SUNTOP.
BUT THERE'S SO MUCH TO DO FOR THE PARTY! WE NEED TO MAKE NAME TAGS AND DECORATIONS.
AND I NEED TO TEACH EVERYONE HOW TO DISCO.
I THINK THE LOW POWER IS MESSING UP YOUR JUDGMENT.
C'MON, WE'RE LEAVING RIGHT NOW.
BUT WE CAN'T! THE TRASH NEED MY HELP.

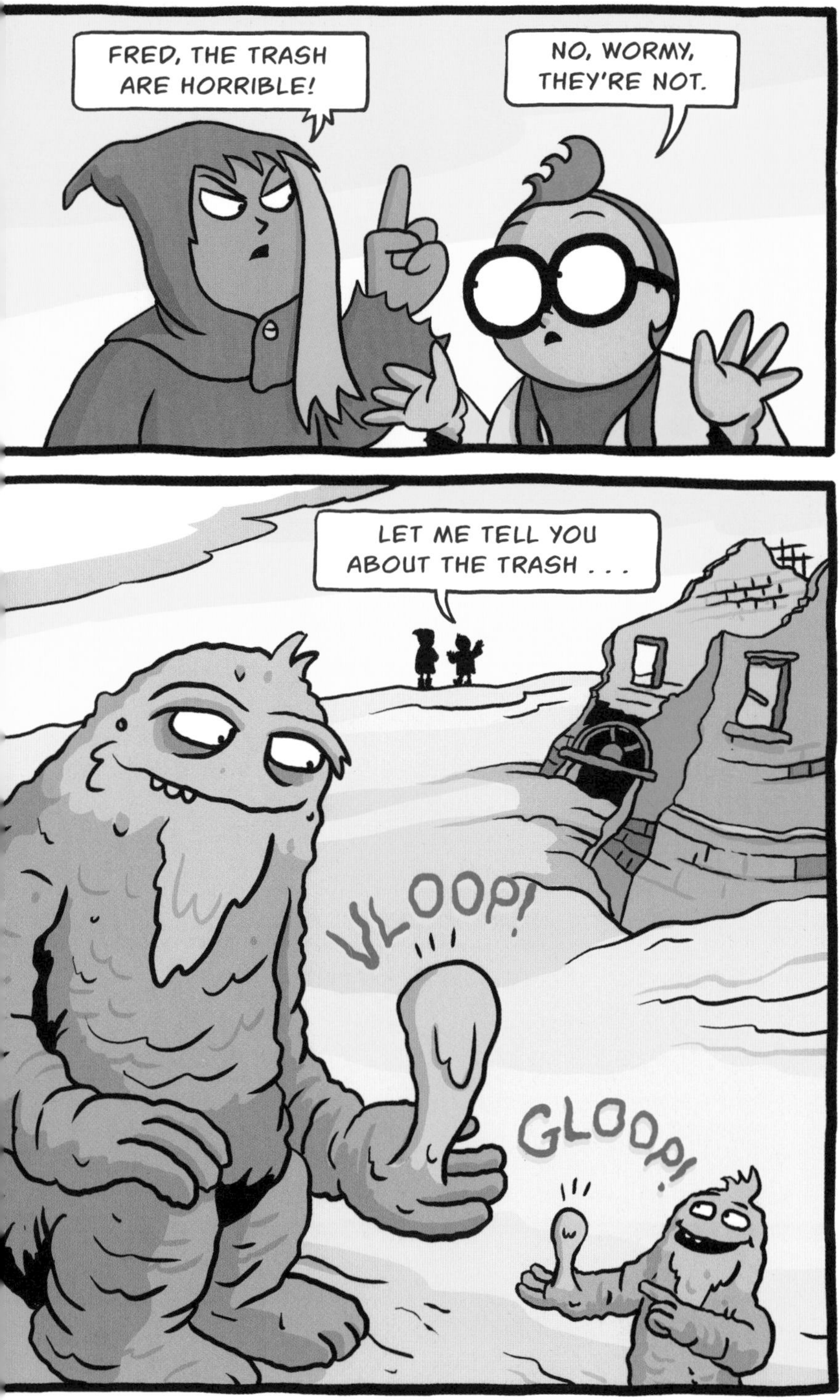
FRED, THE TRASH ARE HORRIBLE!
NO, WORMY, THEY'RE NOT.
LET ME TELL YOU ABOUT THE TRASH . . .
VLOOP!
GLOOP!

CHAPTER 14

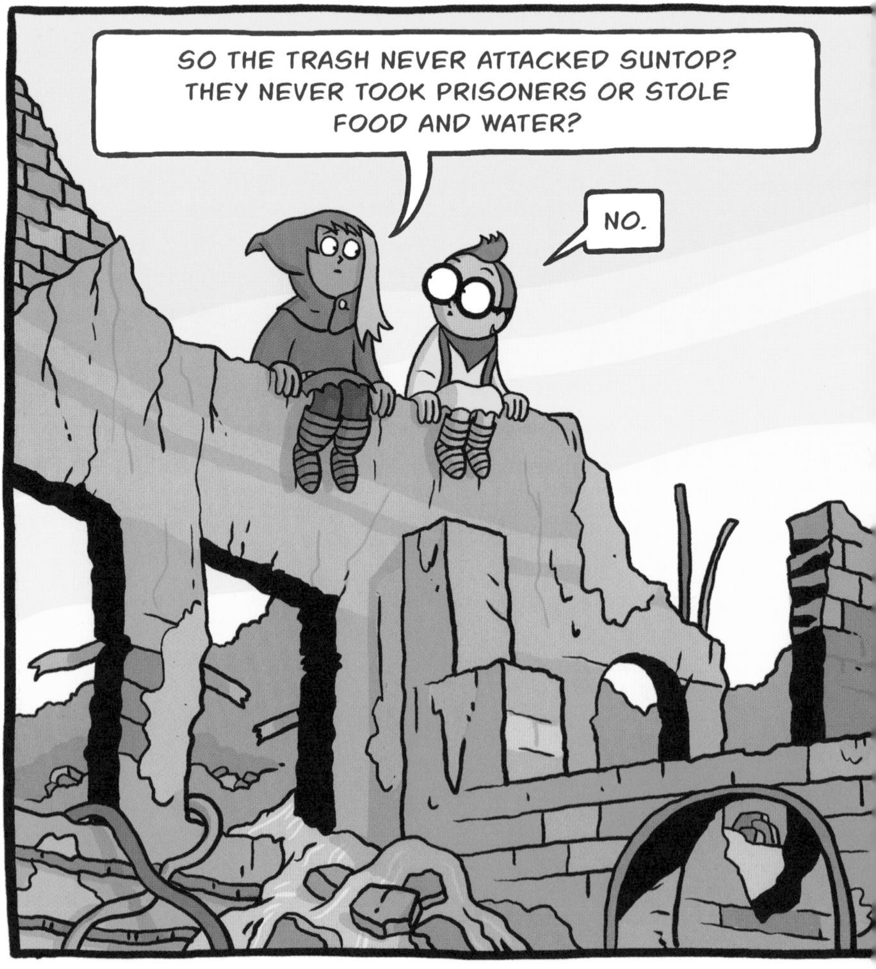
SO THE TRASH NEVER ATTACKED SUNTOP? THEY NEVER TOOK PRISONERS OR STOLE FOOD AND WATER?
NO.

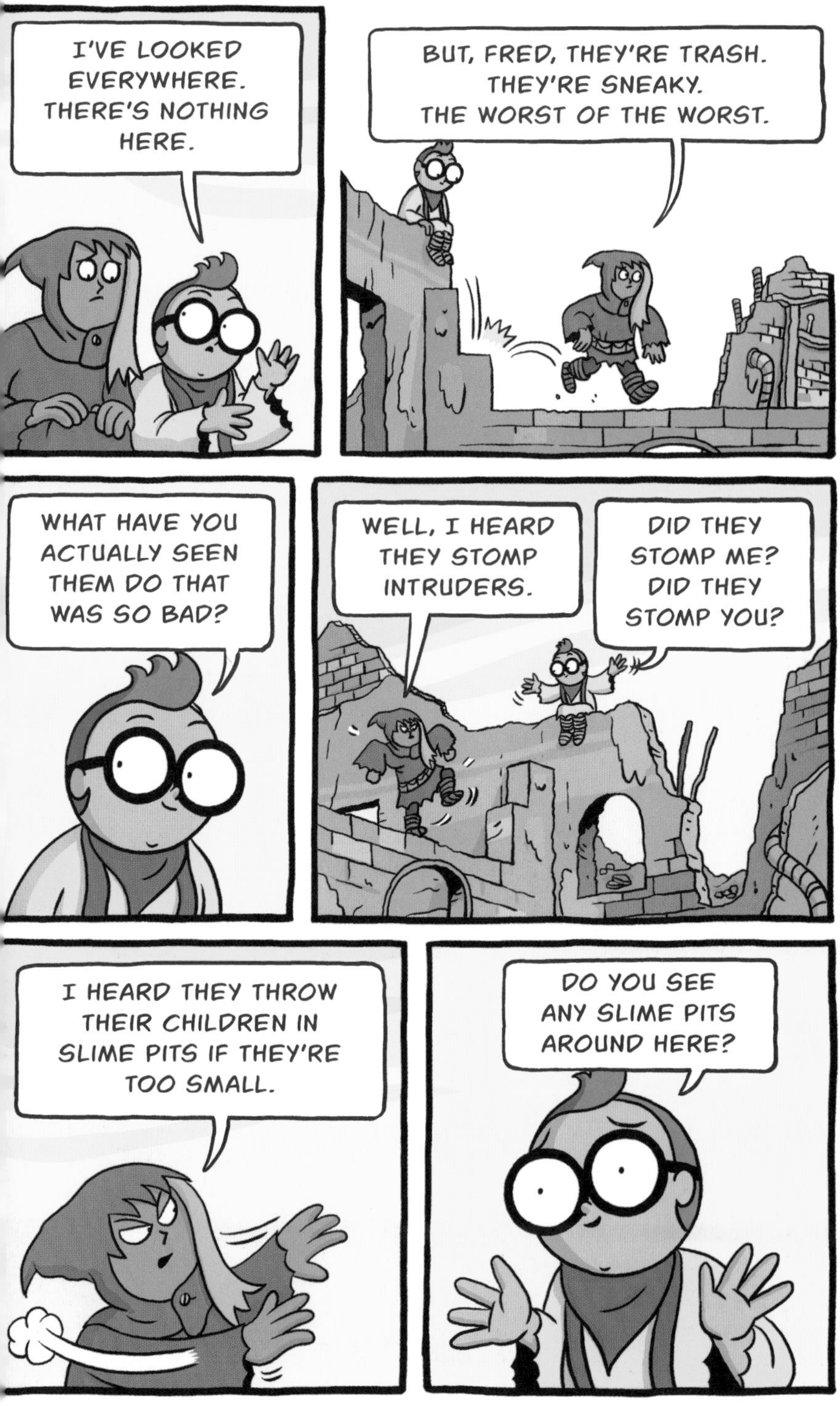
I'VE LOOKED EVERYWHERE. THERE'S NOTHING HERE.
BUT, FRED, THEY'RE TRASH. THEY'RE SNEAKY. THE WORST OF THE WORST.
WHAT HAVE YOU ACTUALLY SEEN THEM DO THAT WAS SO BAD?
WELL, I HEARD THEY STOMP INTRUDERS.
DID THEY STOMP ME? DID THEY STOMP YOU?
I HEARD THEY THROW THEIR CHILDREN IN SLIME PITS IF THEY'RE TOO SMALL.
DO YOU SEE ANY SLIME PITS AROUND HERE?

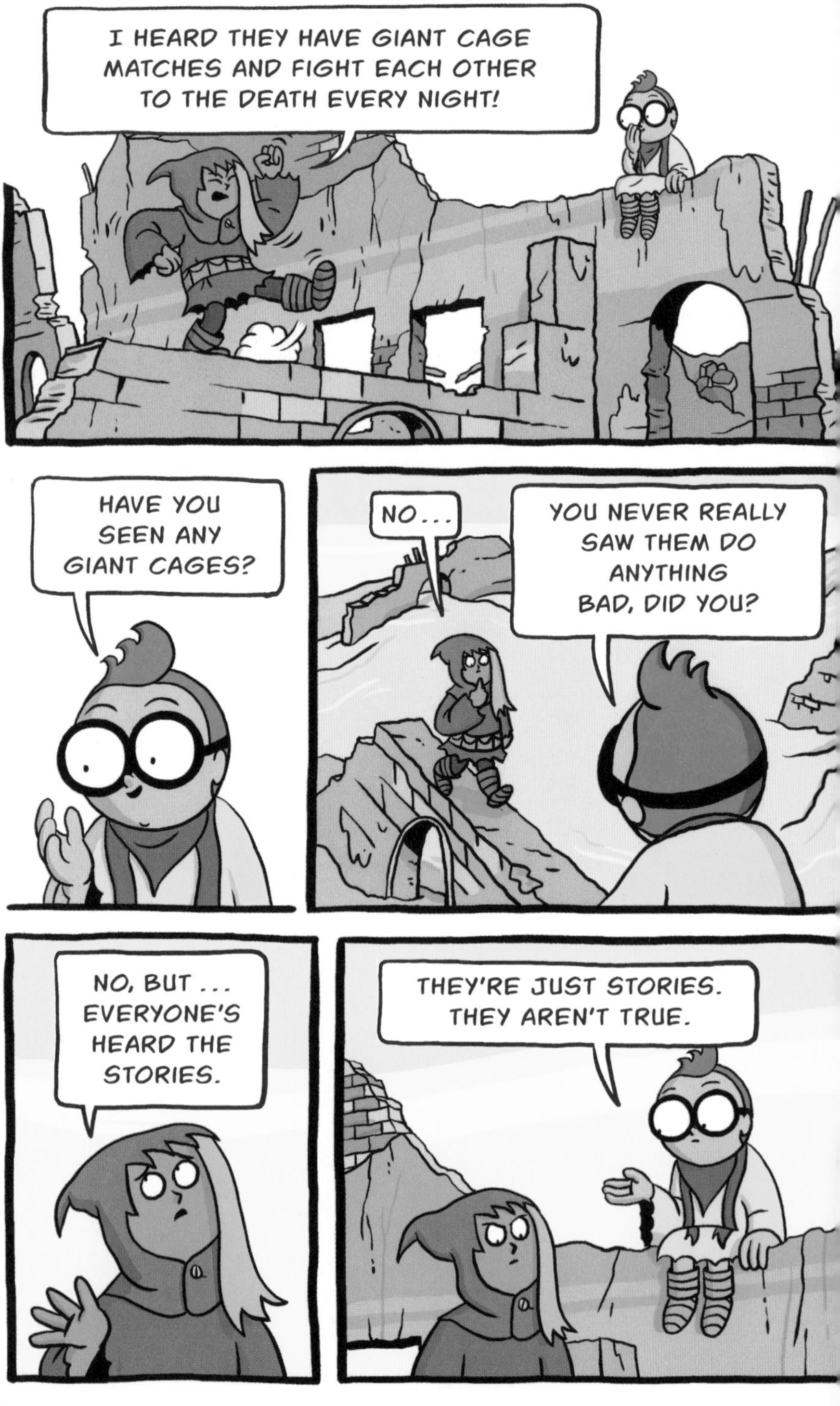
I HEARD THEY HAVE GIANT CAGE MATCHES AND FIGHT EACH OTHER TO THE DEATH EVERY NIGHT!
HAVE YOU SEEN ANY GIANT CAGES?
NO . . .
YOU NEVER REALLY SAW THEM DO ANYTHING BAD, DID YOU?
NO, BUT . . . EVERYONE'S HEARD THE STORIES.
THEY'RE JUST STORIES. THEY AREN'T TRUE.

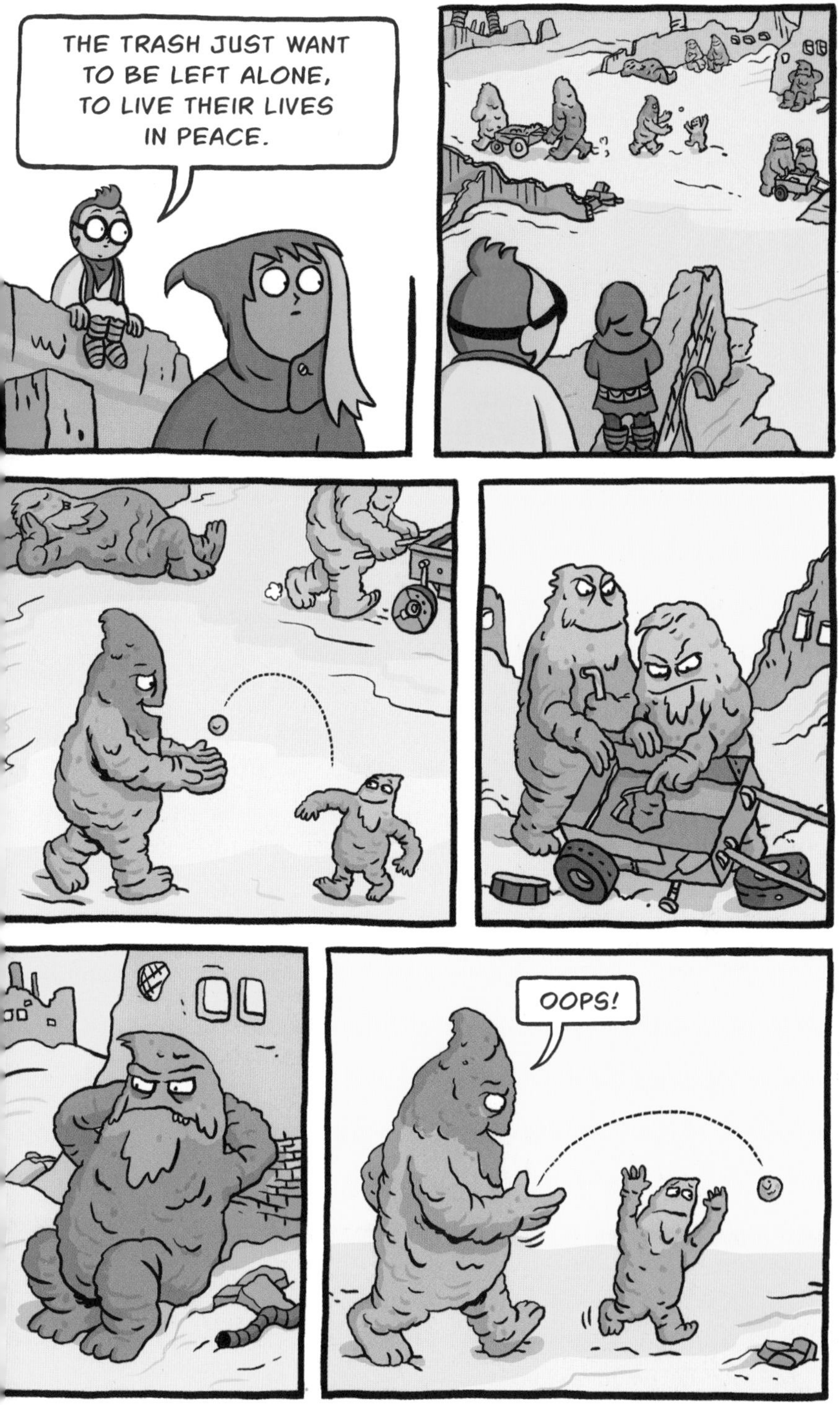
THE TRASH JUST WANT TO BE LEFT ALONE, TO LIVE THEIR LIVES IN PEACE.
OOPS!

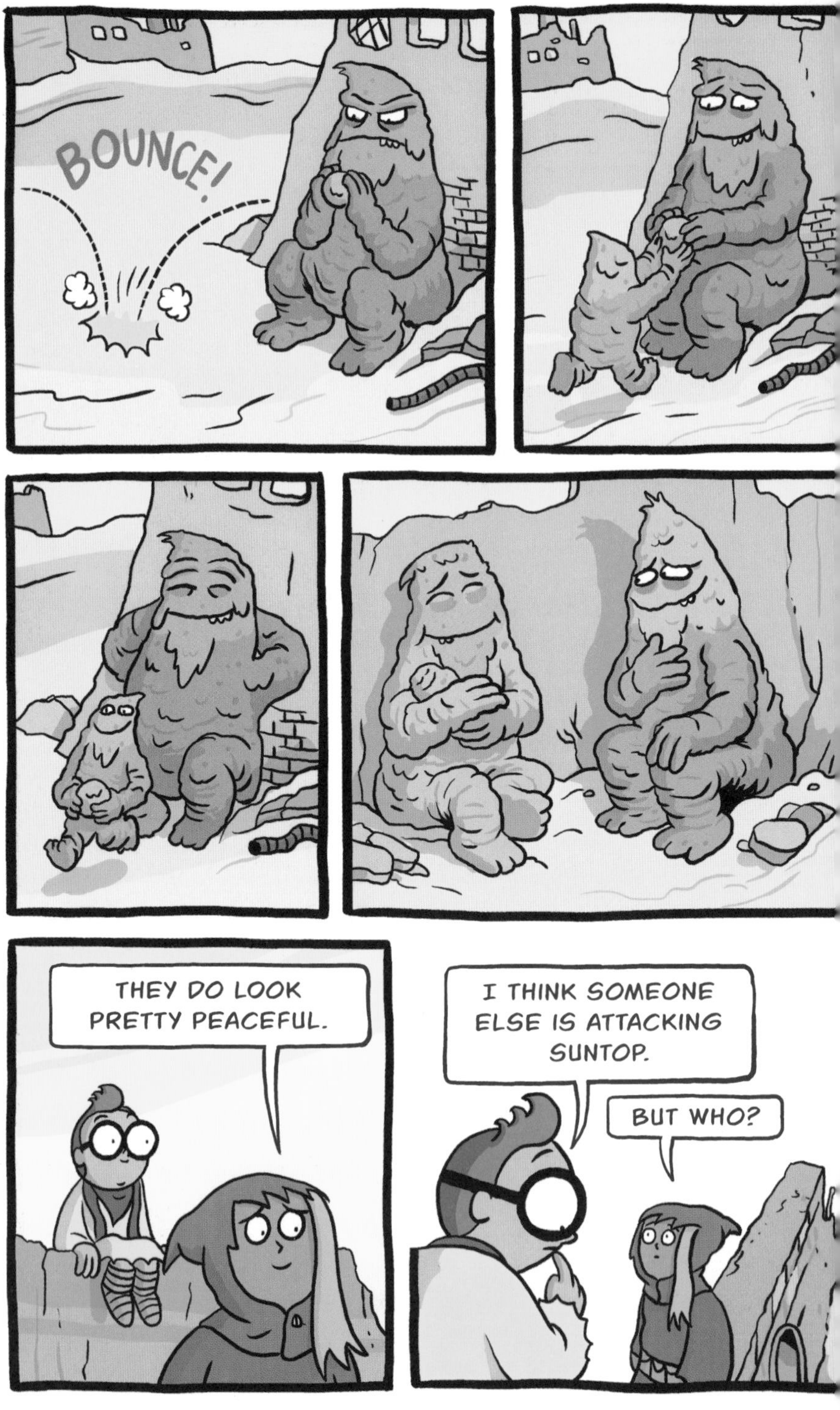
BOUNCE!
THEY DO LOOK PRETTY PEACEFUL.
I THINK SOMEONE ELSE IS ATTACKING SUNTOP.
BUT WHO?

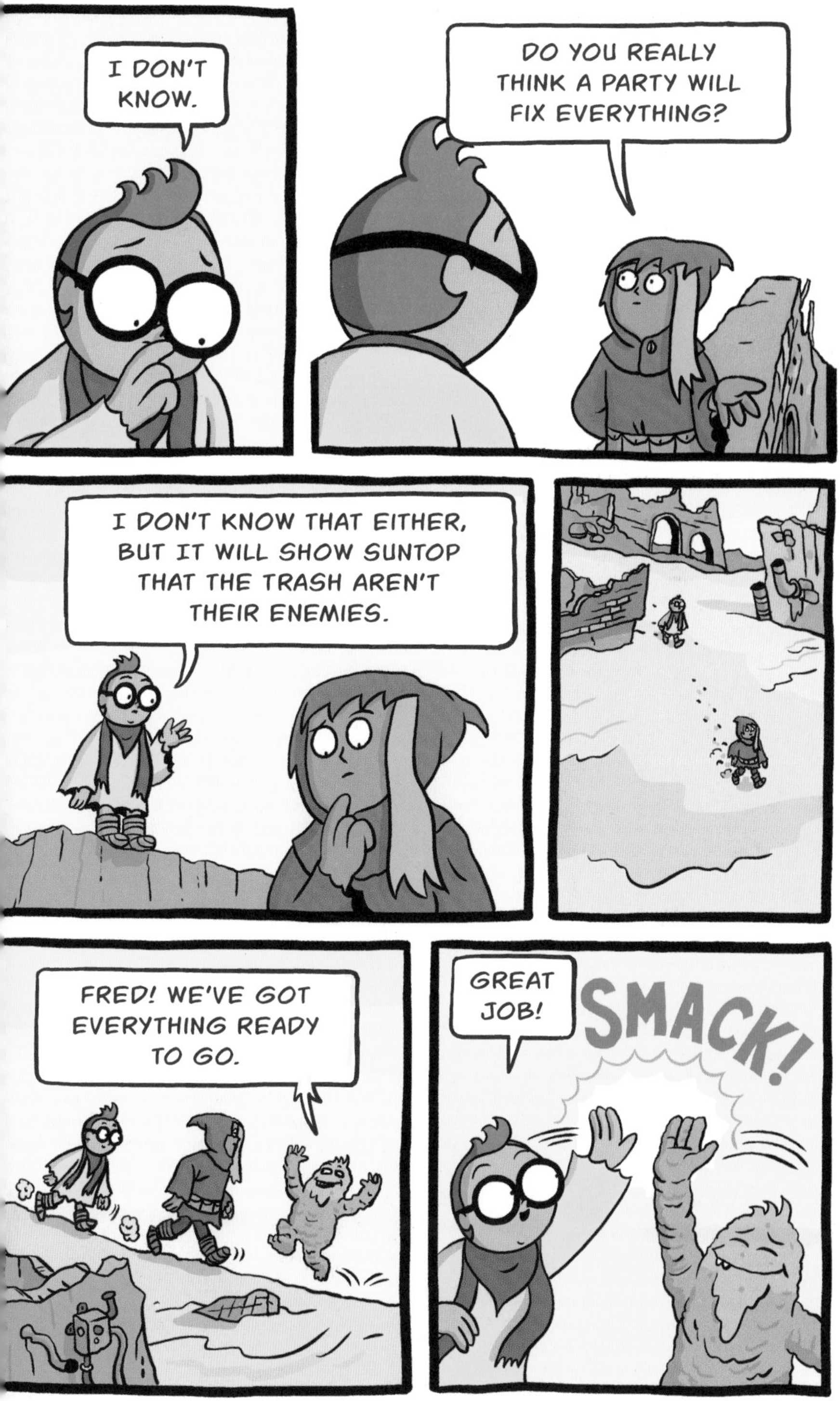
I DON'T KNOW.
DO YOU REALLY THINK A PARTY WILL FIX EVERYTHING?
I DON'T KNOW THAT EITHER, BUT IT WILL SHOW SUNTOP THAT THE TRASH AREN'T THEIR ENEMIES.
FRED! WE'VE GOT EVERYTHING READY TO GO.
GREAT JOB!
SMACK!

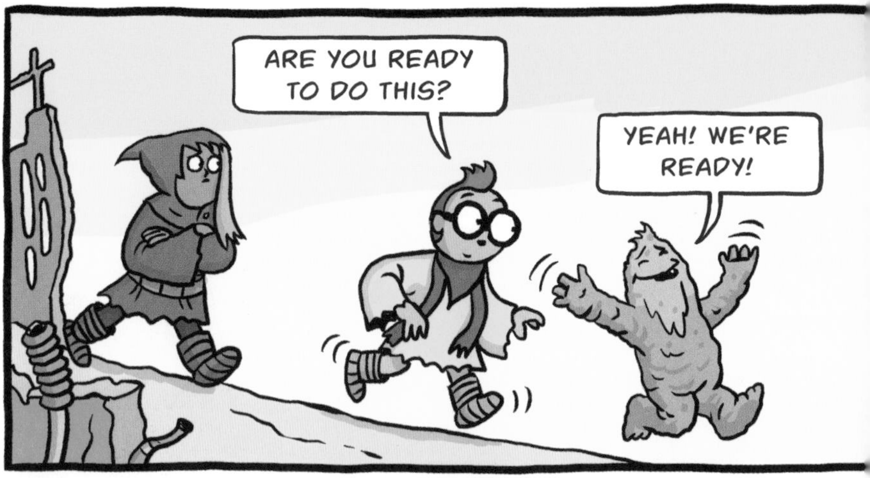
ARE YOU READY TO DO THIS?
YEAH! WE'RE READY!

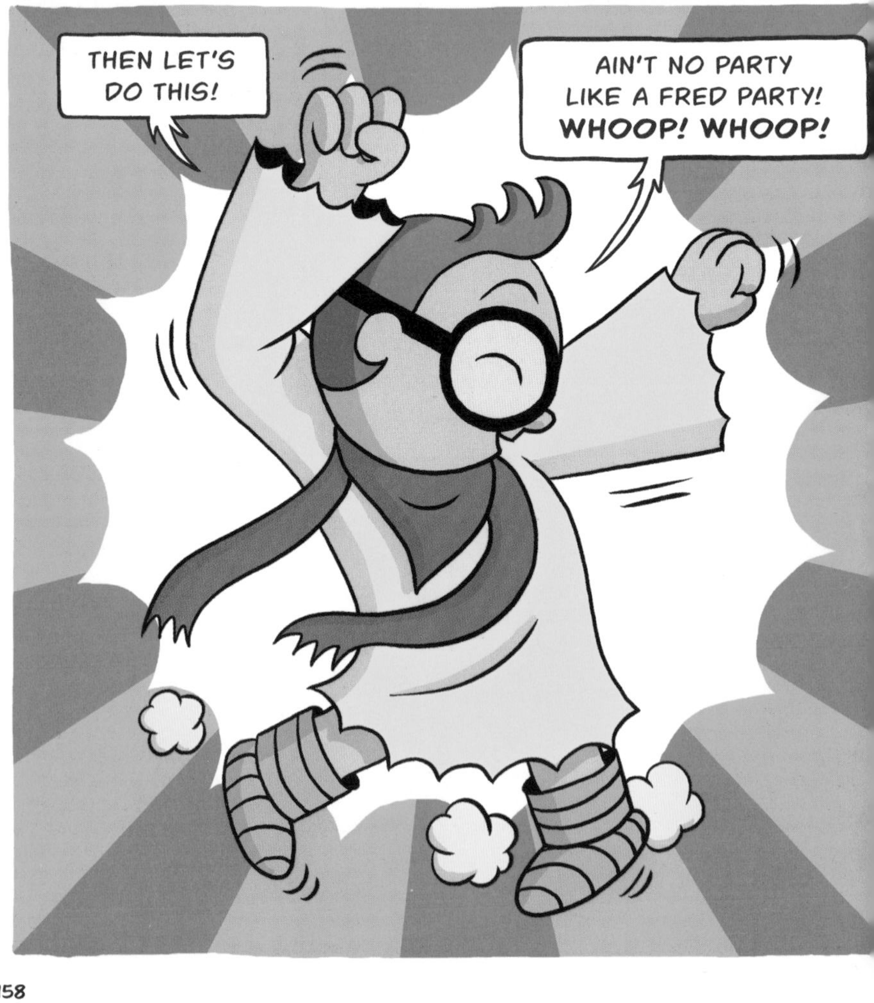
THEN LET'S DO THIS!
AIN'T NO PARTY LIKE A FRED PARTY! **WHOOP! WHOOP!**

CHAPTER 15

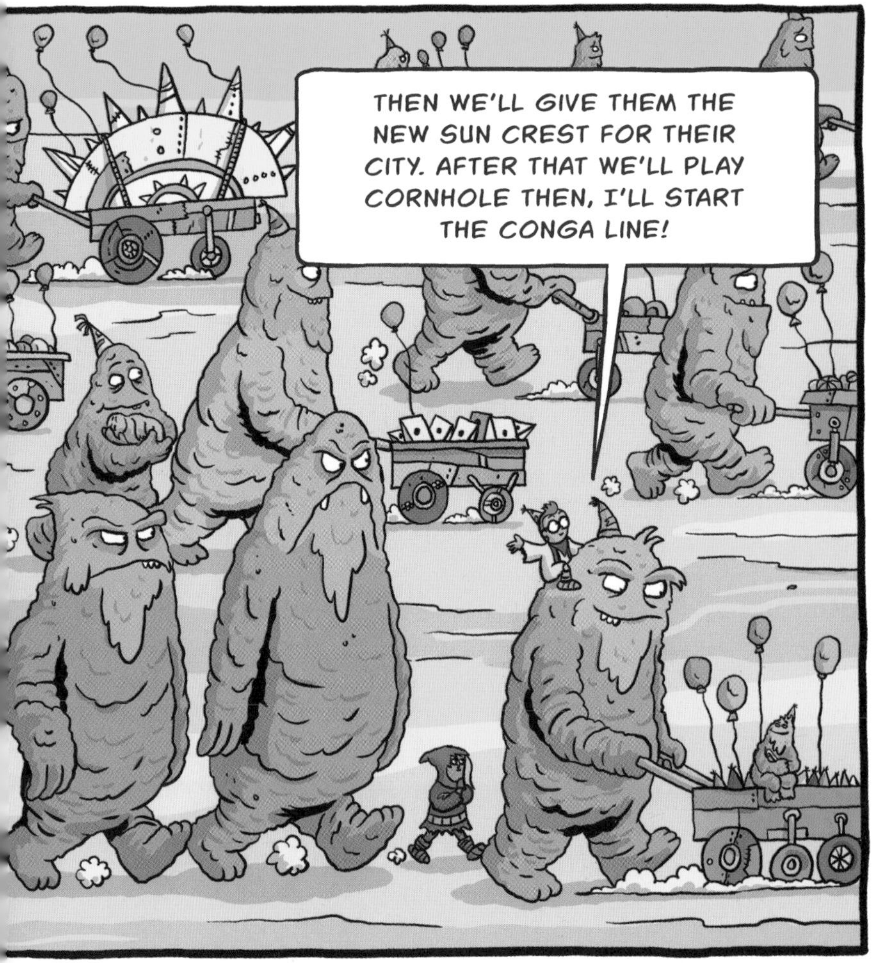
THEN WE'LL GIVE THEM THE NEW SUN CREST FOR THEIR CITY. AFTER THAT WE'LL PLAY CORNHOLE THEN, I'LL START THE CONGA LINE!

IS THAT WHEN I CAN DO MY SPECIAL DANCE?

YUP! WHO LIKES TO PARTY? **I LIKE TO PARTY!**

I STILL THINK IT'S A BIG, STUPID IDEA.

ME TOO.

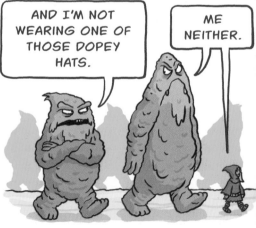

AND I'M NOT WEARING ONE OF THOSE DOPEY HATS.

ME NEITHER.

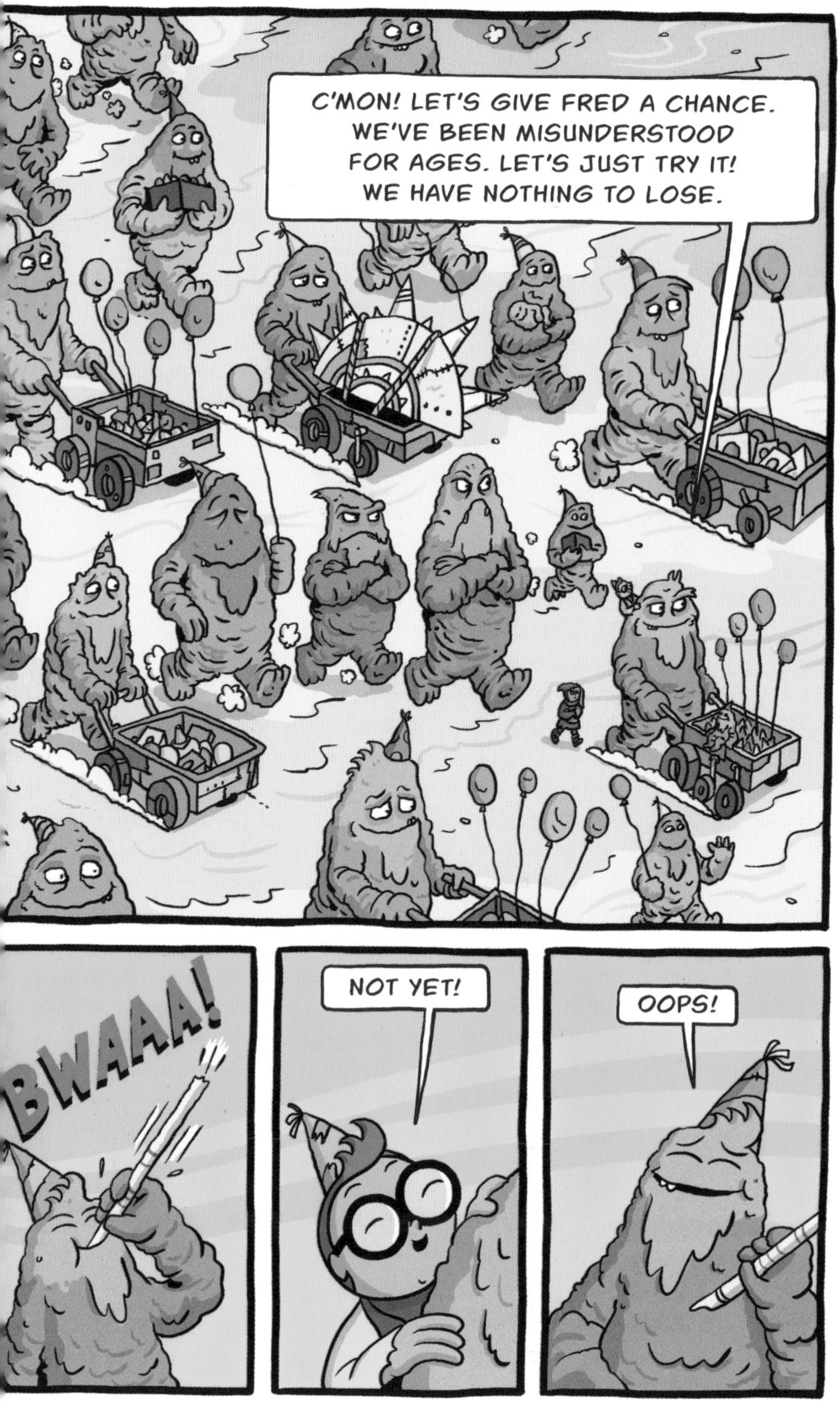
C'MON! LET'S GIVE FRED A CHANCE. WE'VE BEEN MISUNDERSTOOD FOR AGES. LET'S JUST TRY IT! WE HAVE NOTHING TO LOSE.
BWAAA!
NOT YET!
OOPS!

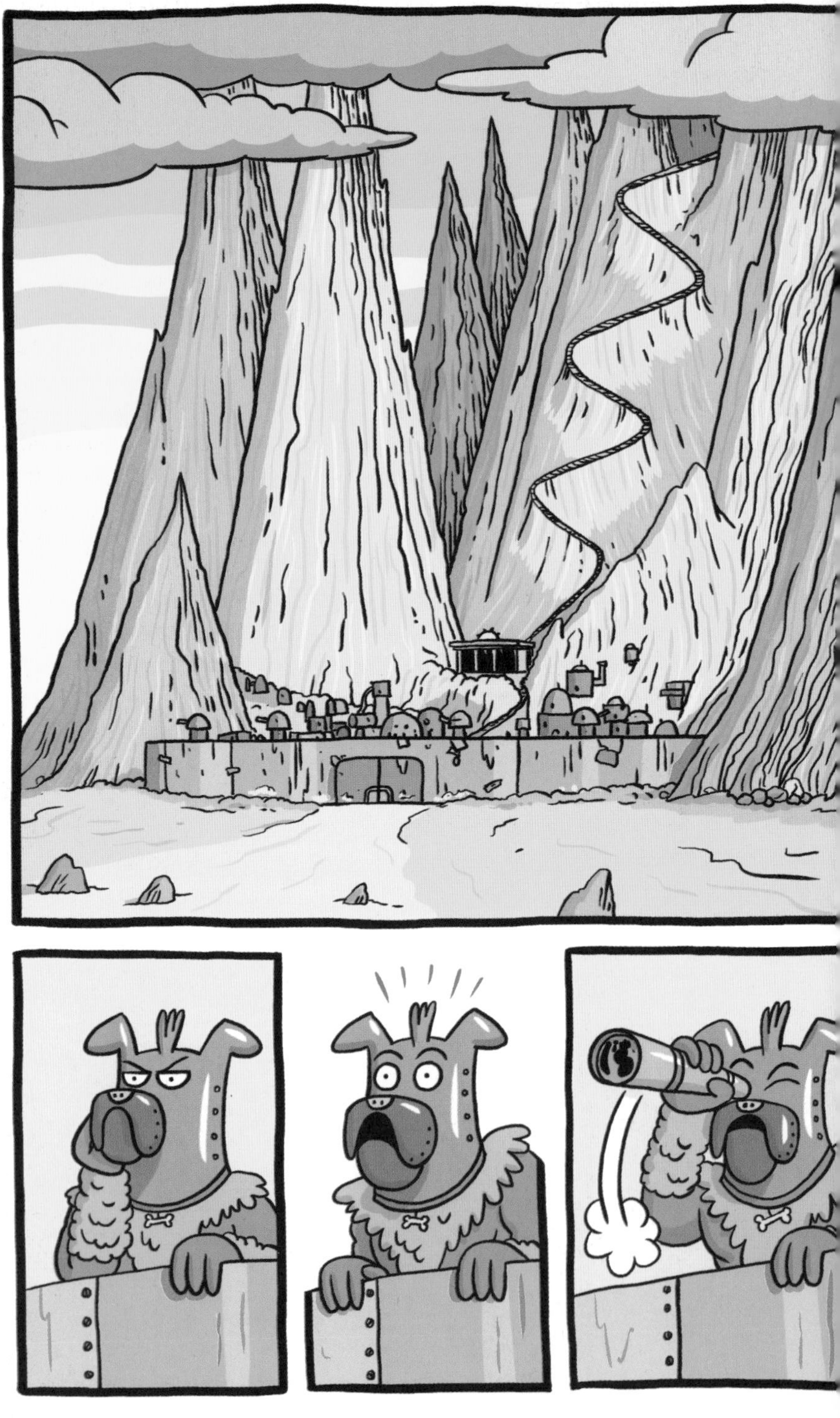

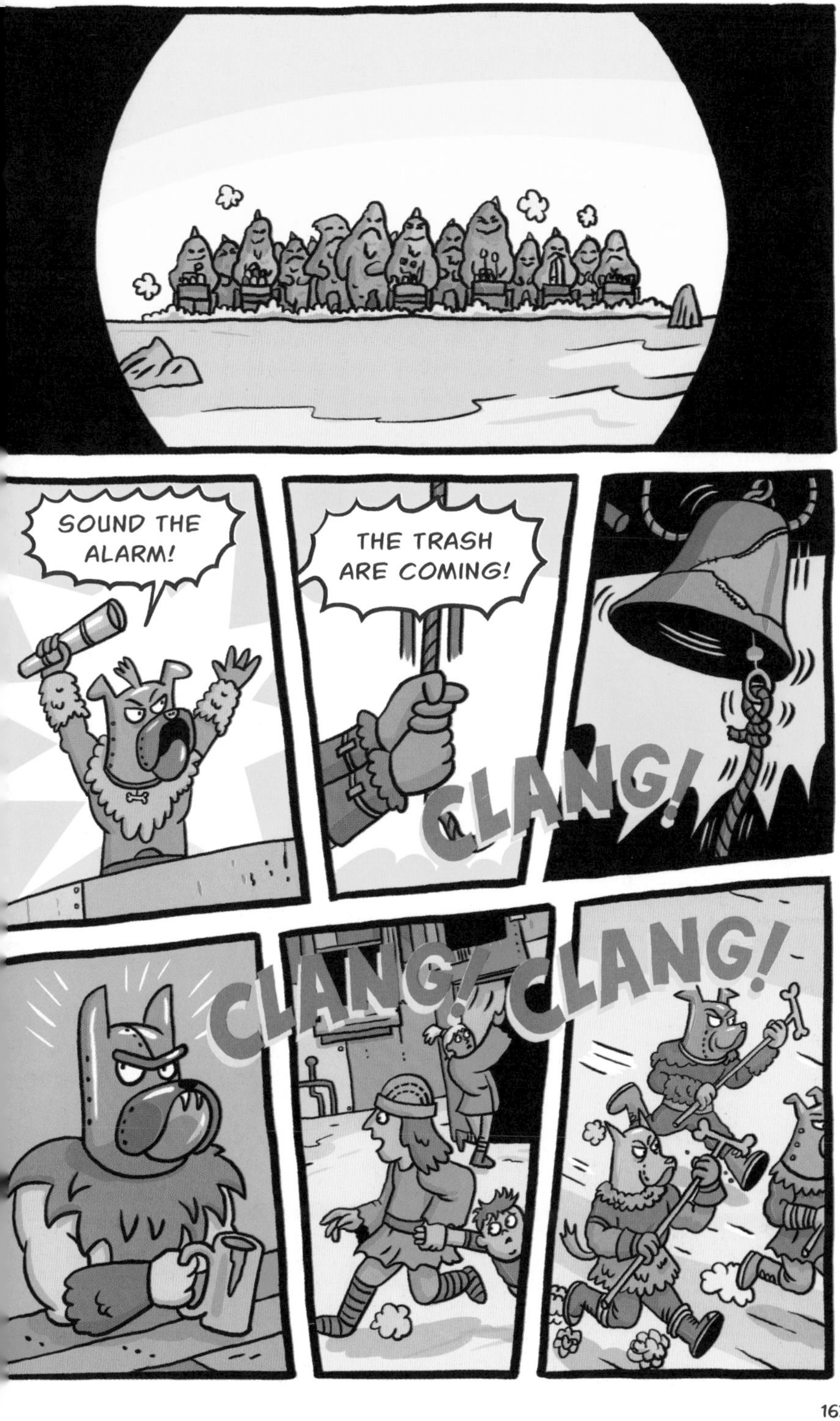
SOUND THE ALARM!
THE TRASH ARE COMING!
CLANG!
CLANG!
CLANG!

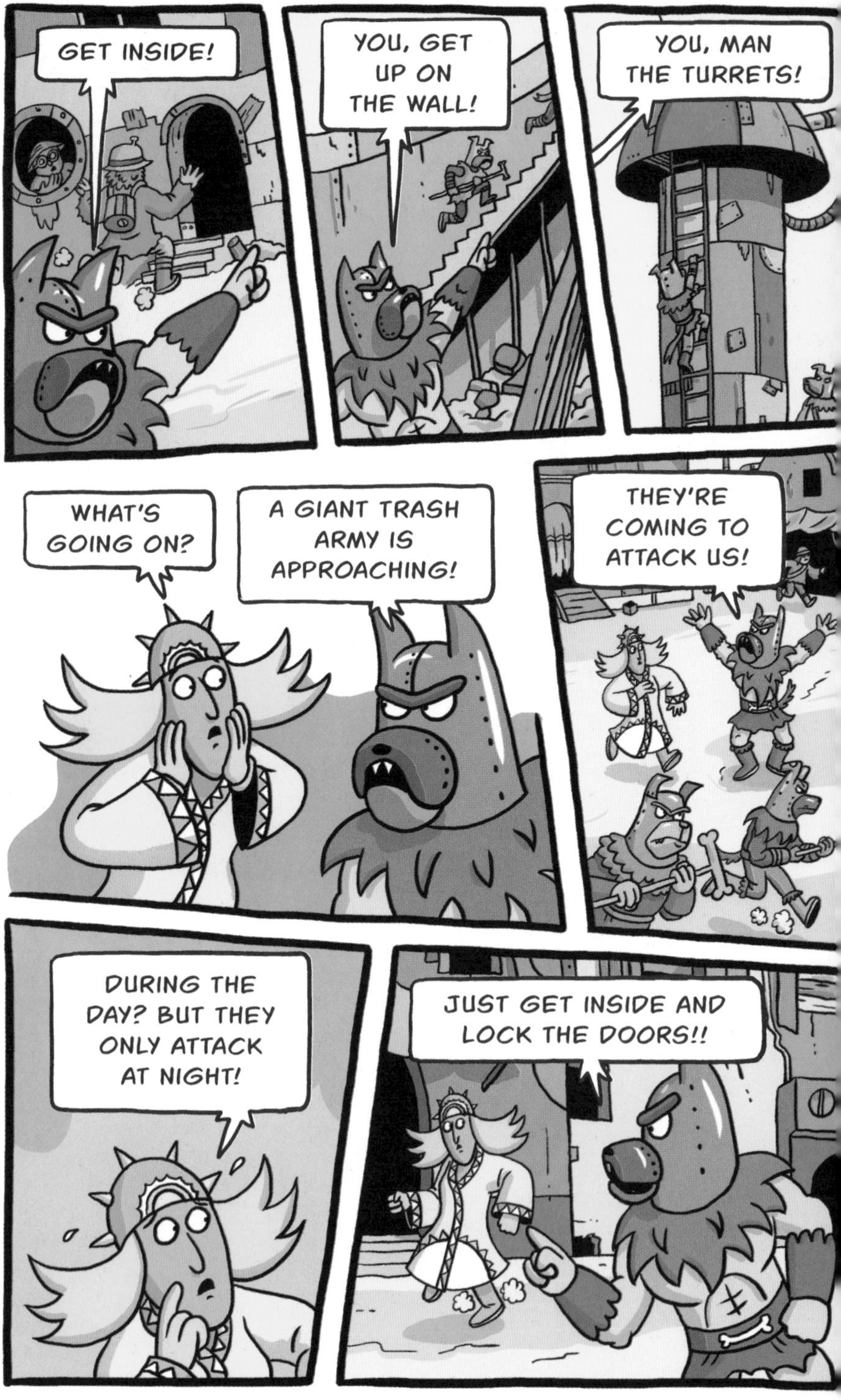
GET INSIDE!
YOU, GET UP ON THE WALL!
YOU, MAN THE TURRETS!
WHAT'S GOING ON?
A GIANT TRASH ARMY IS APPROACHING!
THEY'RE COMING TO ATTACK US!
DURING THE DAY? BUT THEY ONLY ATTACK AT NIGHT!
JUST GET INSIDE AND LOCK THE DOORS!!

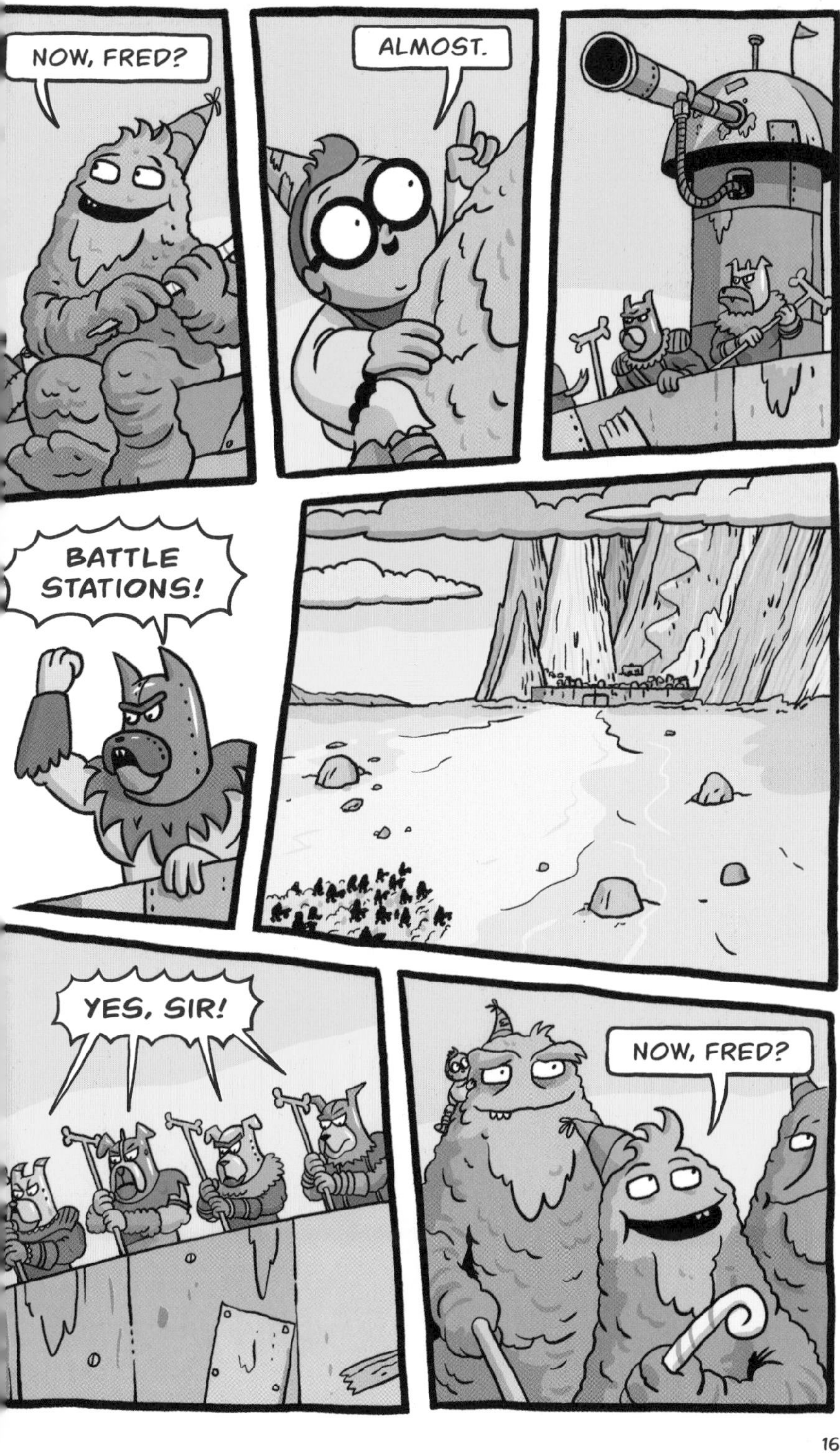
NOW, FRED?
ALMOST.
BATTLE STATIONS!
YES, SIR!
NOW, FRED?

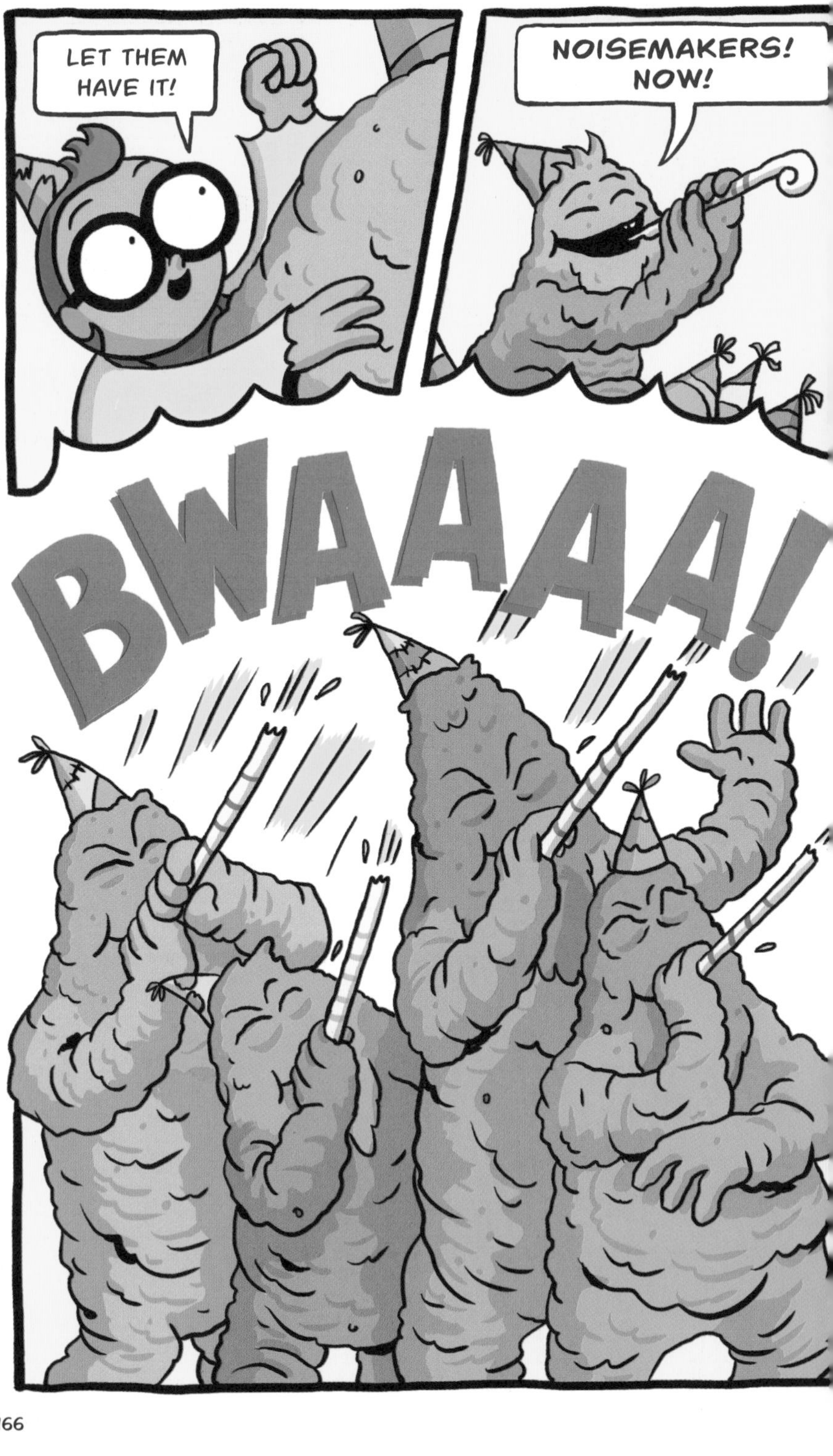
LET THEM HAVE IT!
NOISEMAKERS! NOW!
BWAAAAA!

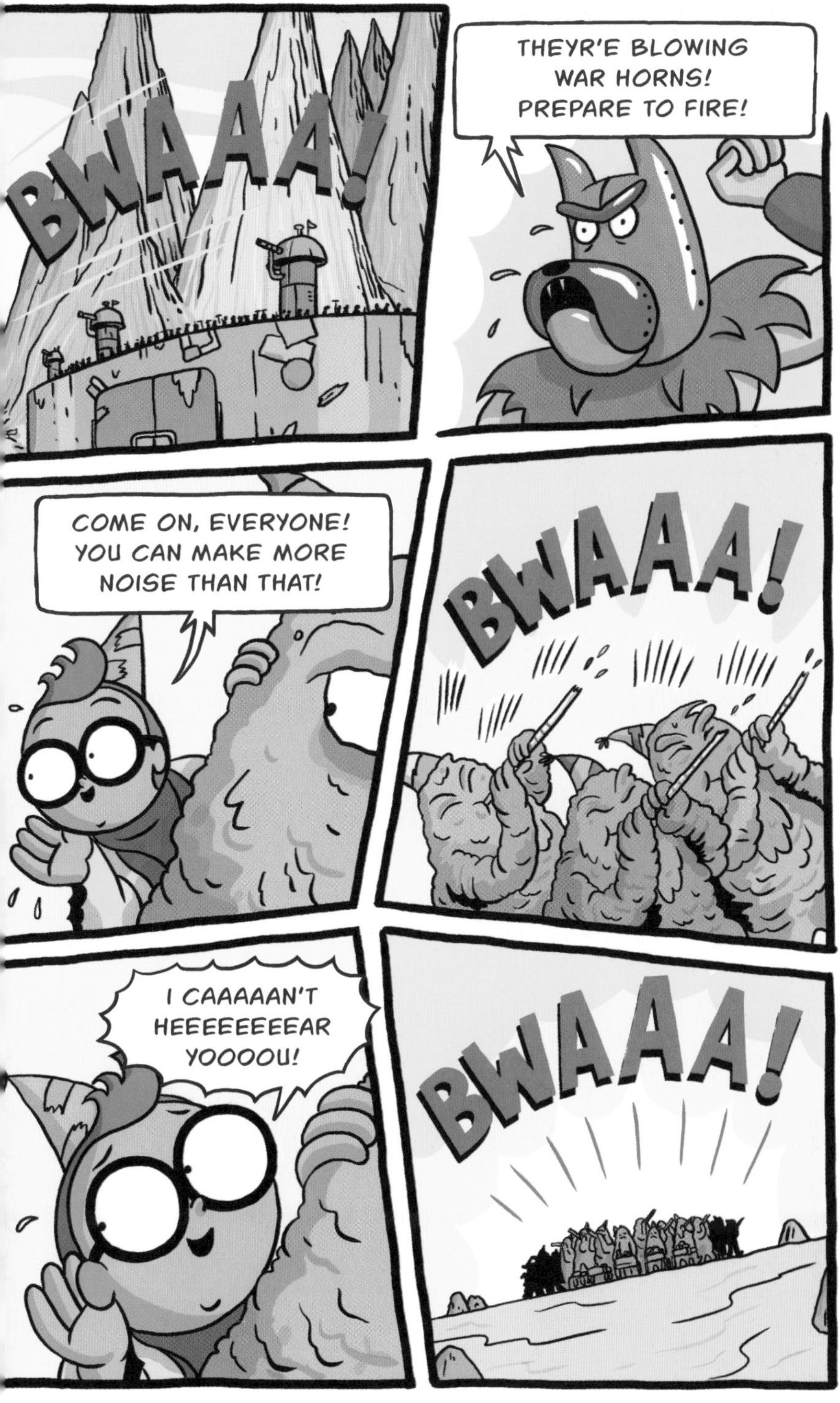
BWAAAA!
THEYR'E BLOWING WAR HORNS! PREPARE TO FIRE!
COME ON, EVERYONE! YOU CAN MAKE MORE NOISE THAN THAT!
BWAAAA!
I CAAAAAN'T HEEEEEEEEAR YOOOOU!
BWAAAA!

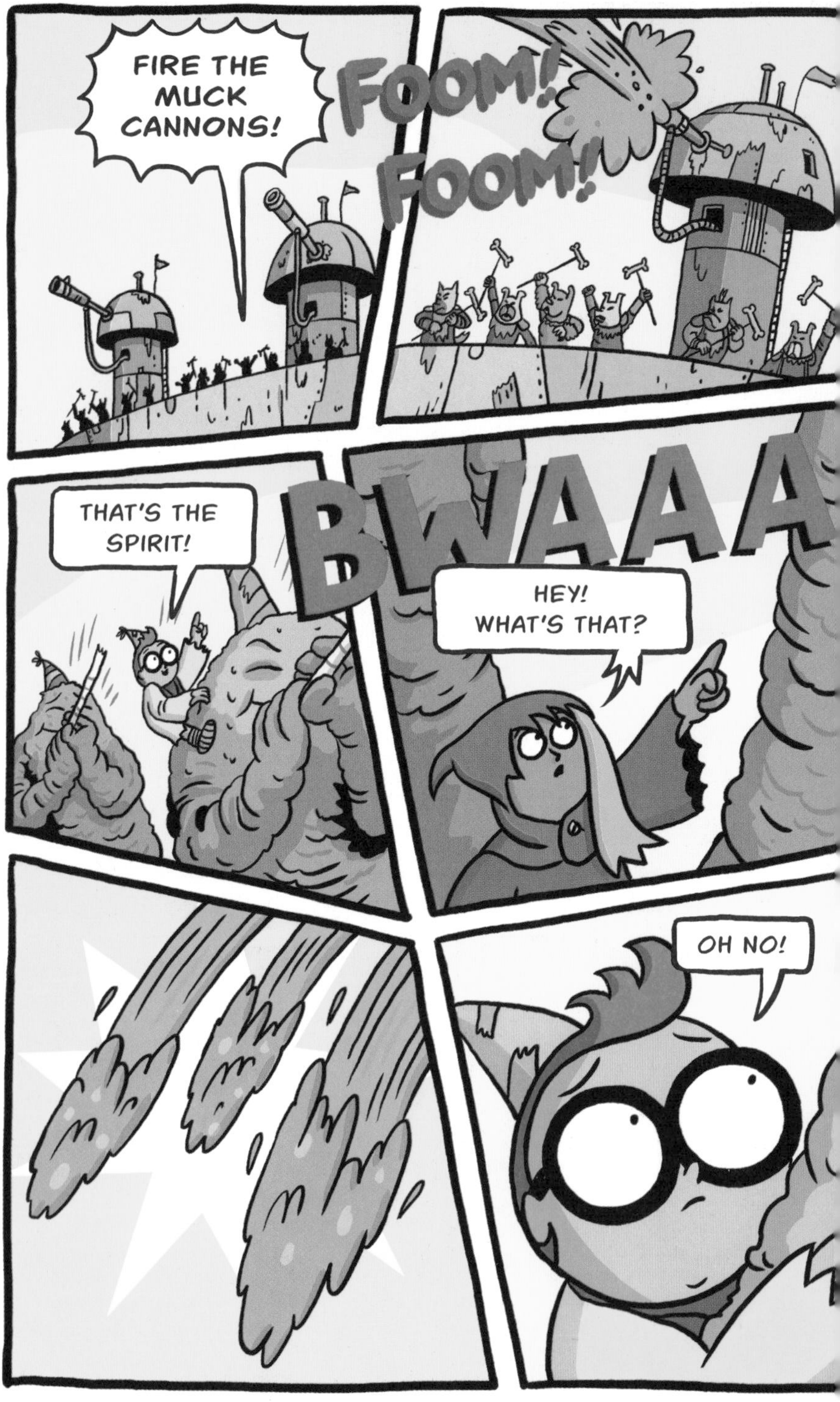
FIRE THE MUCK CANNONS!
FOOM! FOOM!
THAT'S THE SPIRIT!
BWAAA
HEY! WHAT'S THAT?
OH NO!

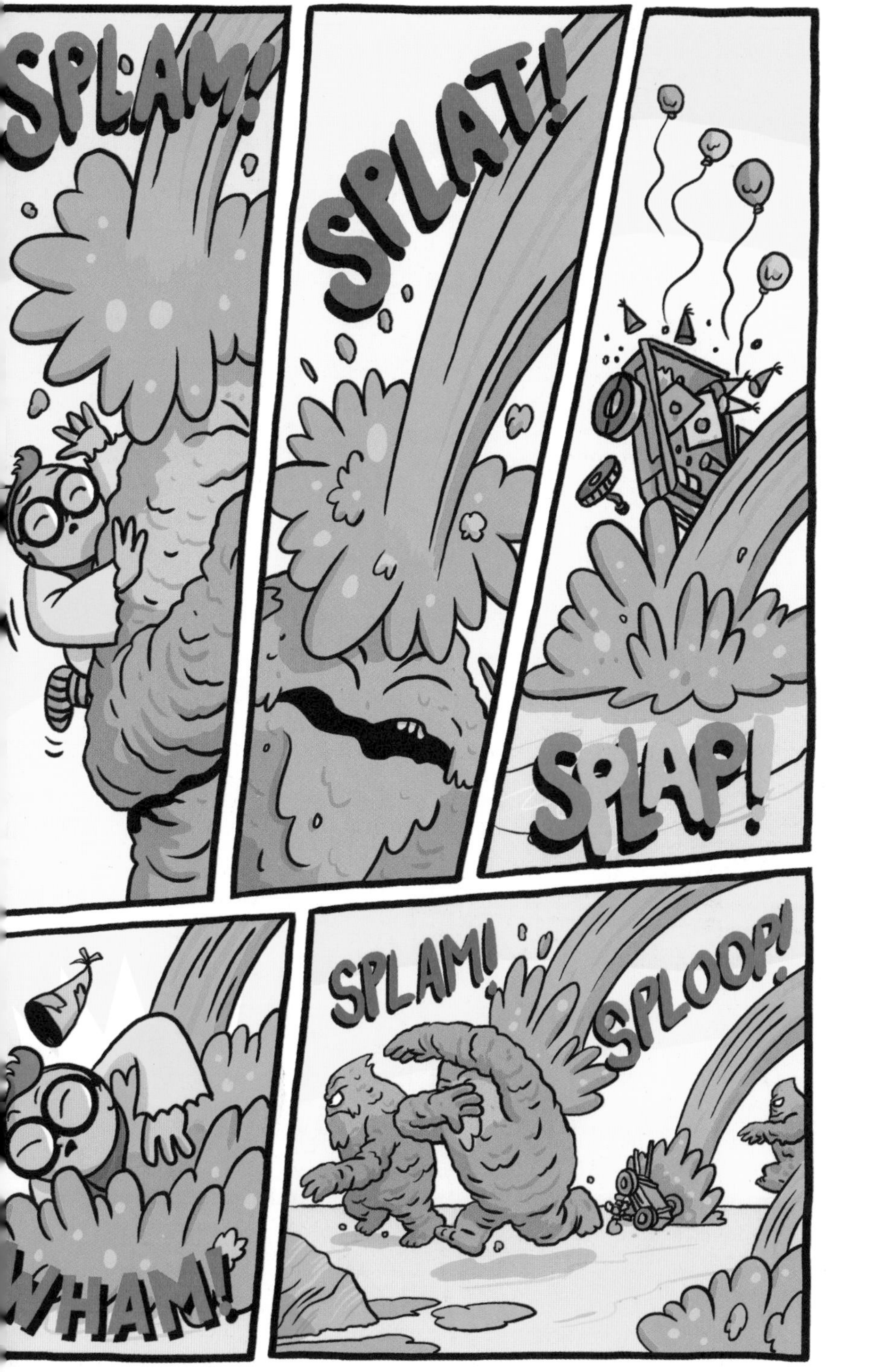
SPLAM!
SPLAT!
SPLAP!
WHAM!
SPLAM!
SPLOOP!

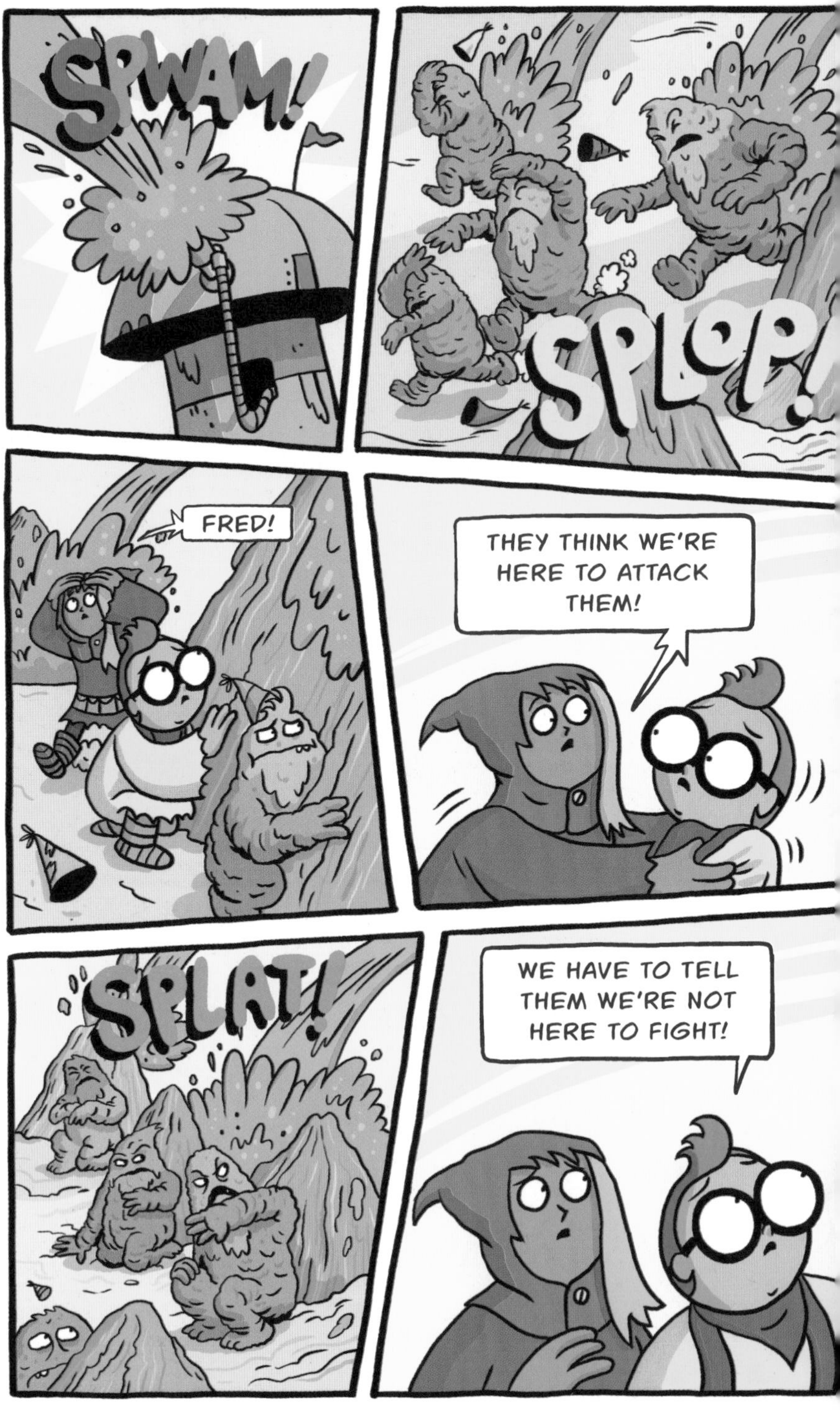
SPWAM!
SPLOP!
FRED!
THEY THINK WE'RE HERE TO ATTACK THEM!
SPLAT!
WE HAVE TO TELL THEM WE'RE NOT HERE TO FIGHT!

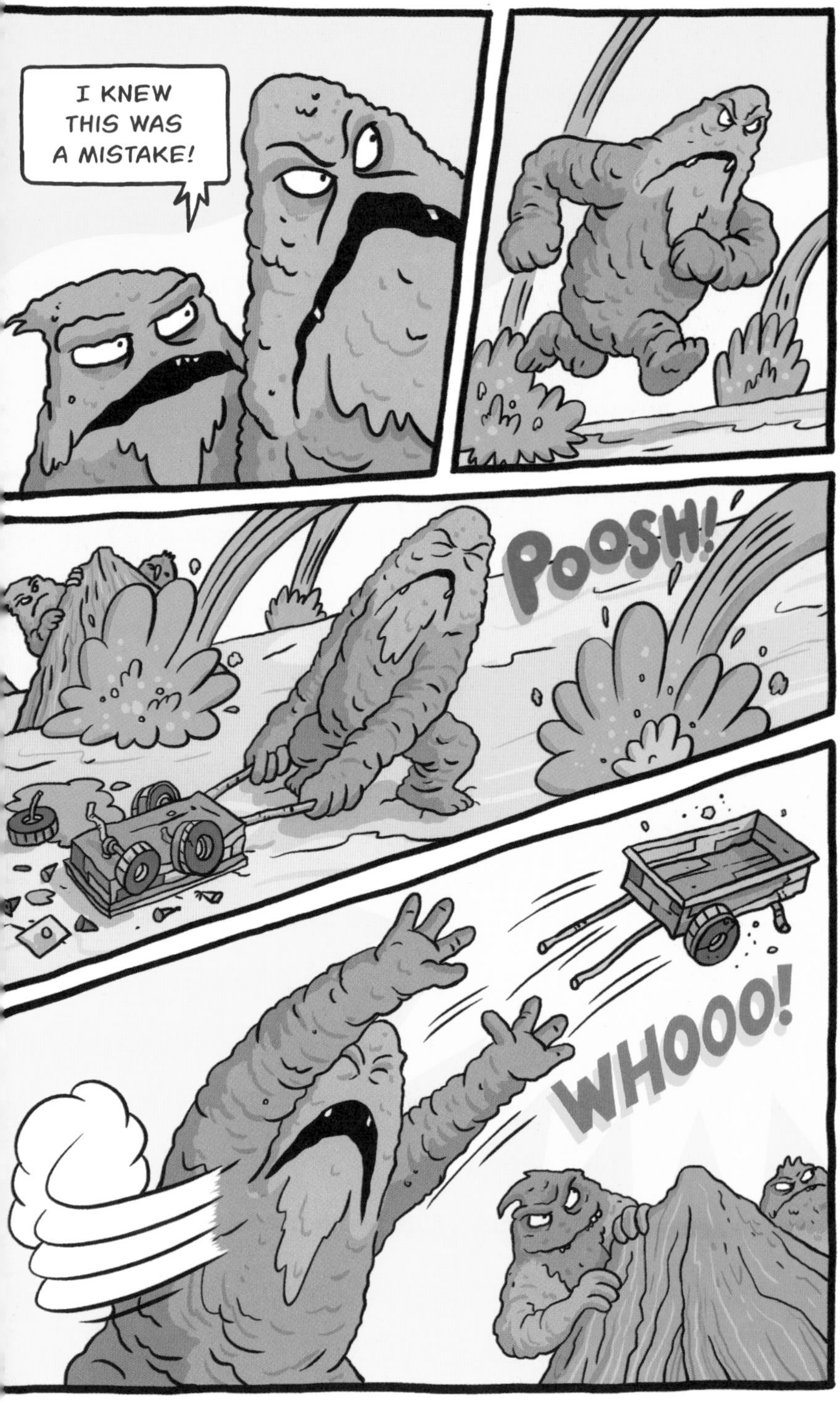
I KNEW THIS WAS A MISTAKE!
POOSH!
WHOOO!

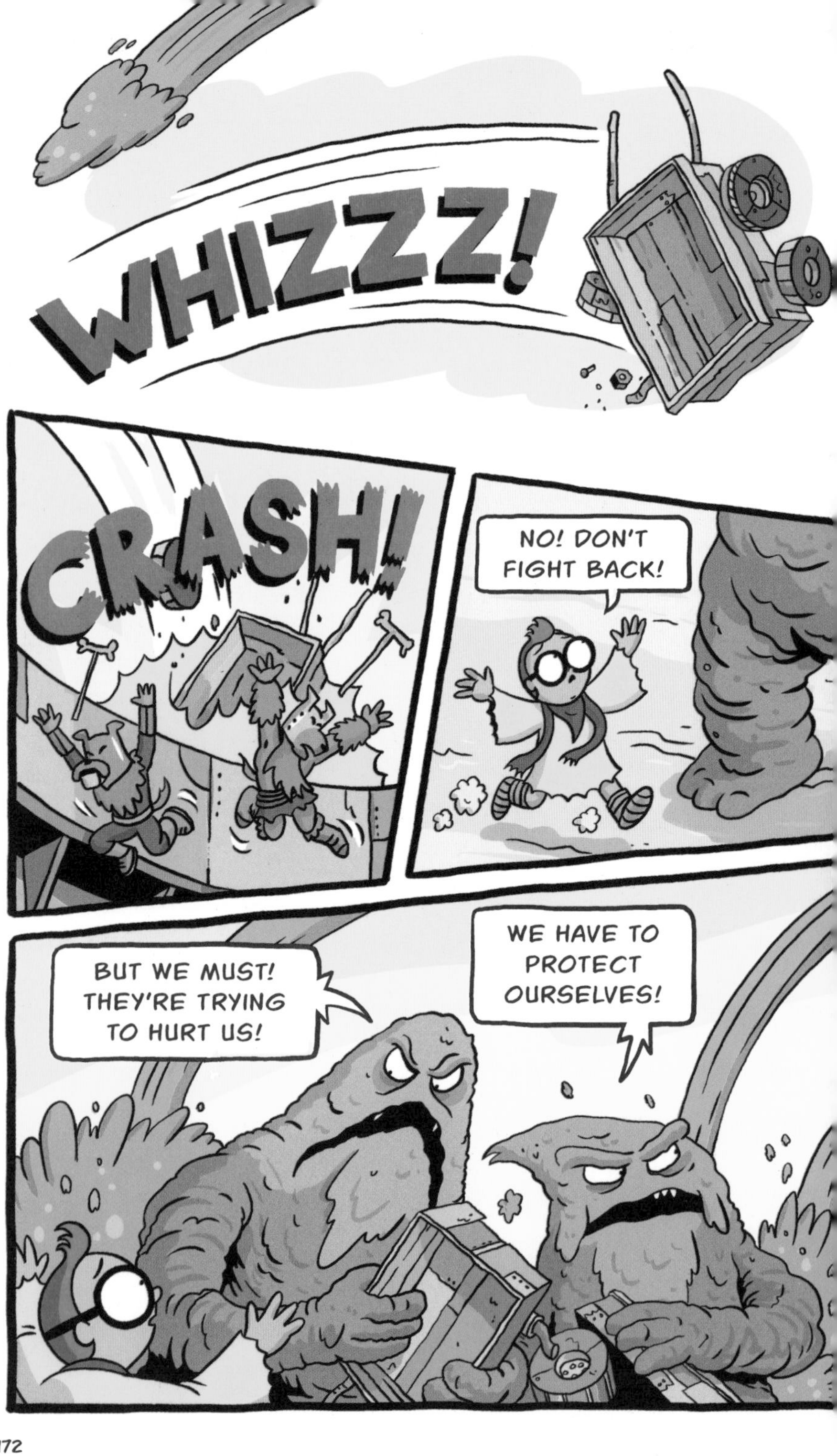
WHIZZZ!
CRASH!
NO! DON'T FIGHT BACK!
BUT WE MUST! THEY'RE TRYING TO HURT US!
WE HAVE TO PROTECT OURSELVES!

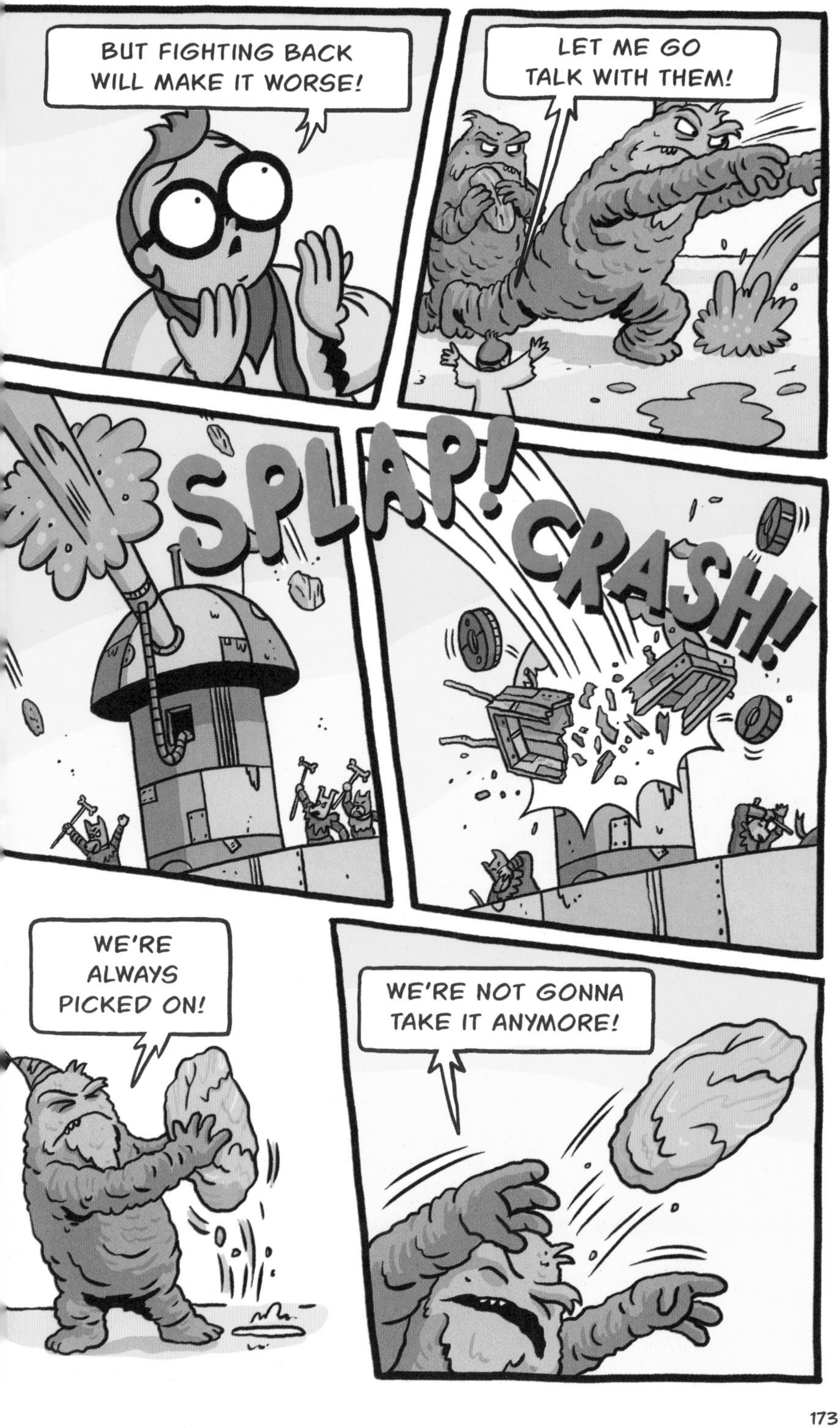
BUT FIGHTING BACK WILL MAKE IT WORSE!
LET ME GO TALK WITH THEM!
SPLAP!
CRASH!
WE'RE ALWAYS PICKED ON!
WE'RE NOT GONNA TAKE IT ANYMORE!

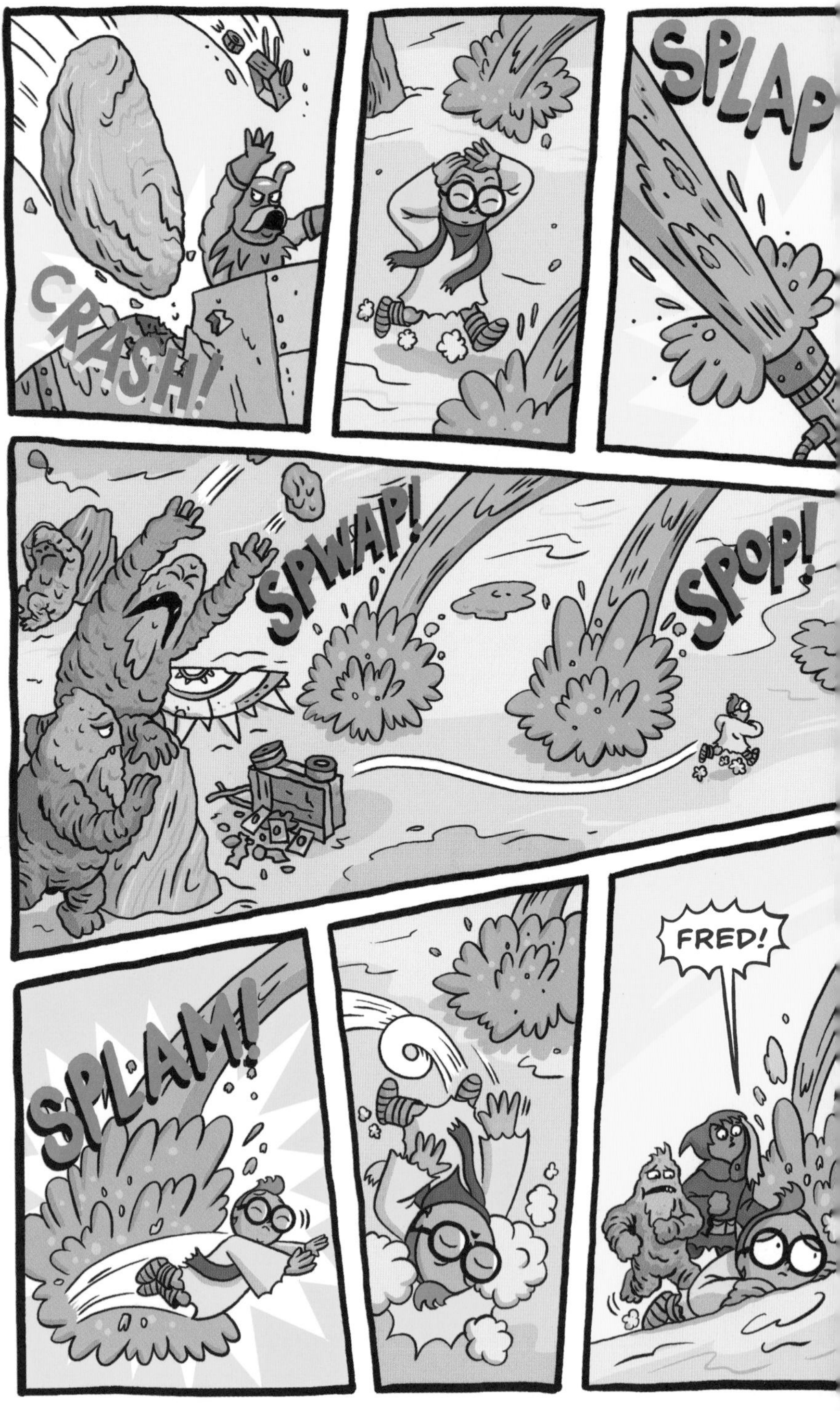
CRASH!
SPLAP
SPWAP!
SPOP!
SPLAM!
FRED!

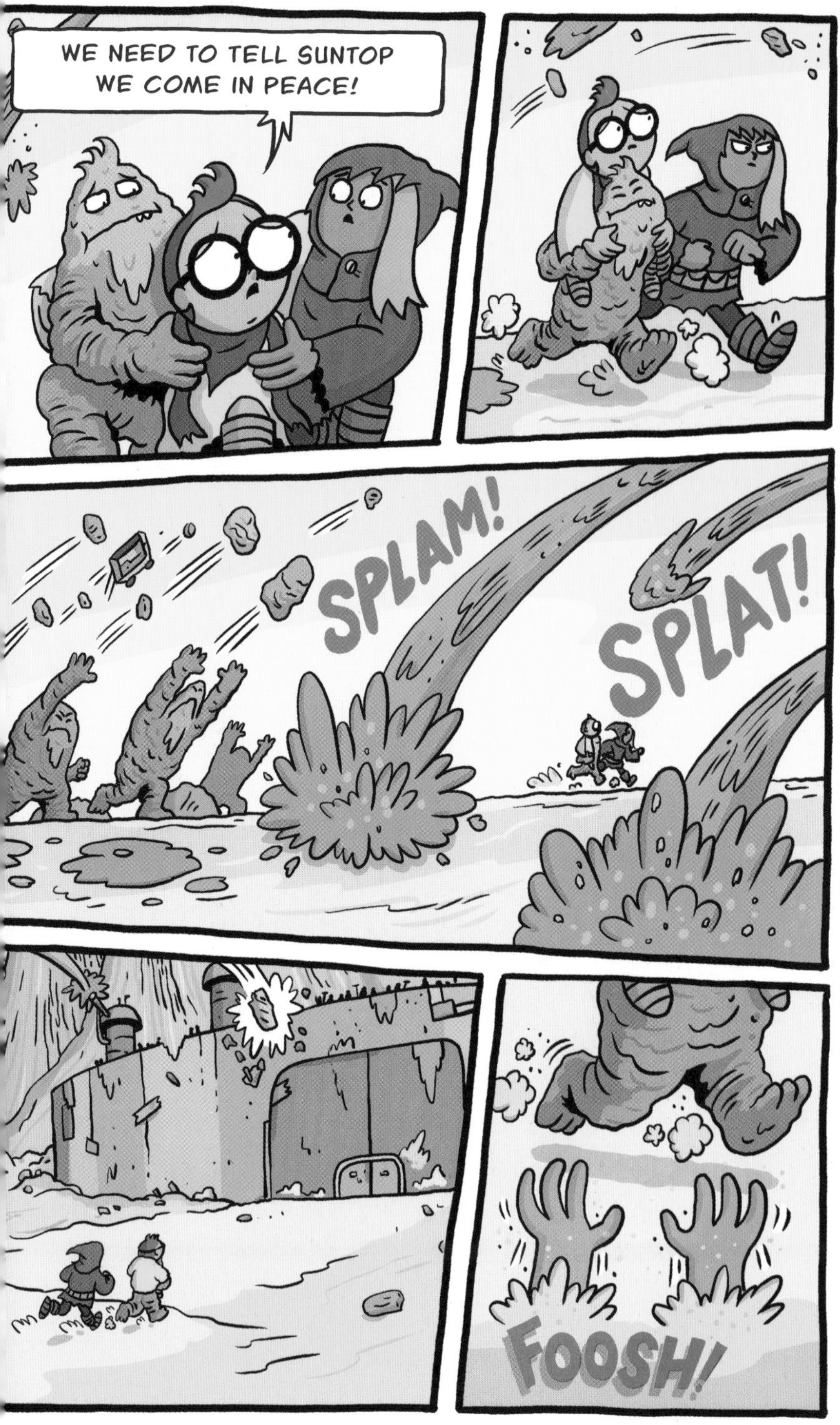
WE NEED TO TELL SUNTOP WE COME IN PEACE!
SPLAM!
SPLAT!
FOOSH!

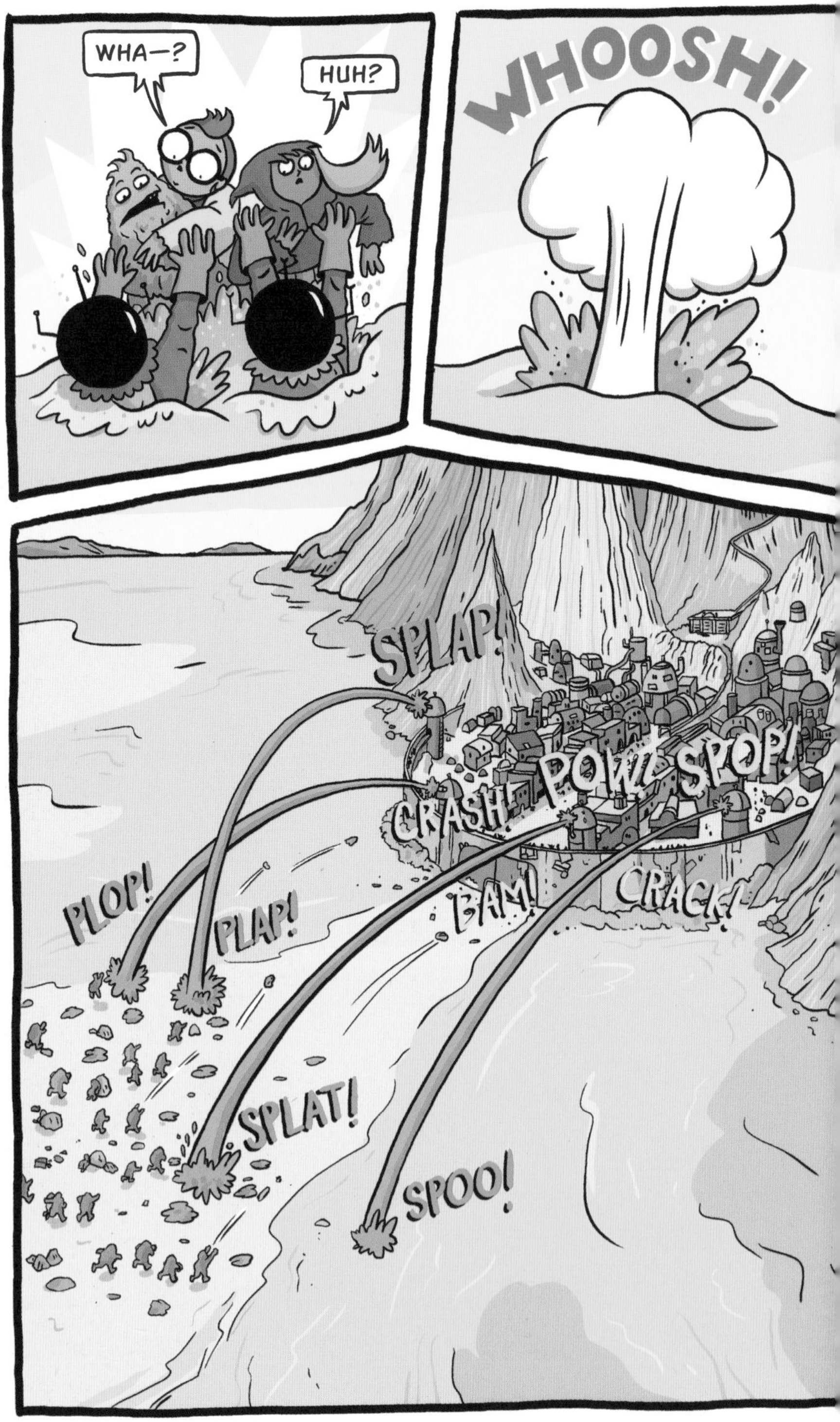
WHA—?
HUH?
WHOOSH!
SPLAP!
CRASH!
POW!
SPOP!
PLOP!
PLAP!
BAM!
CRACK!
SPLAT!
SPOO!

CHAPTER 16

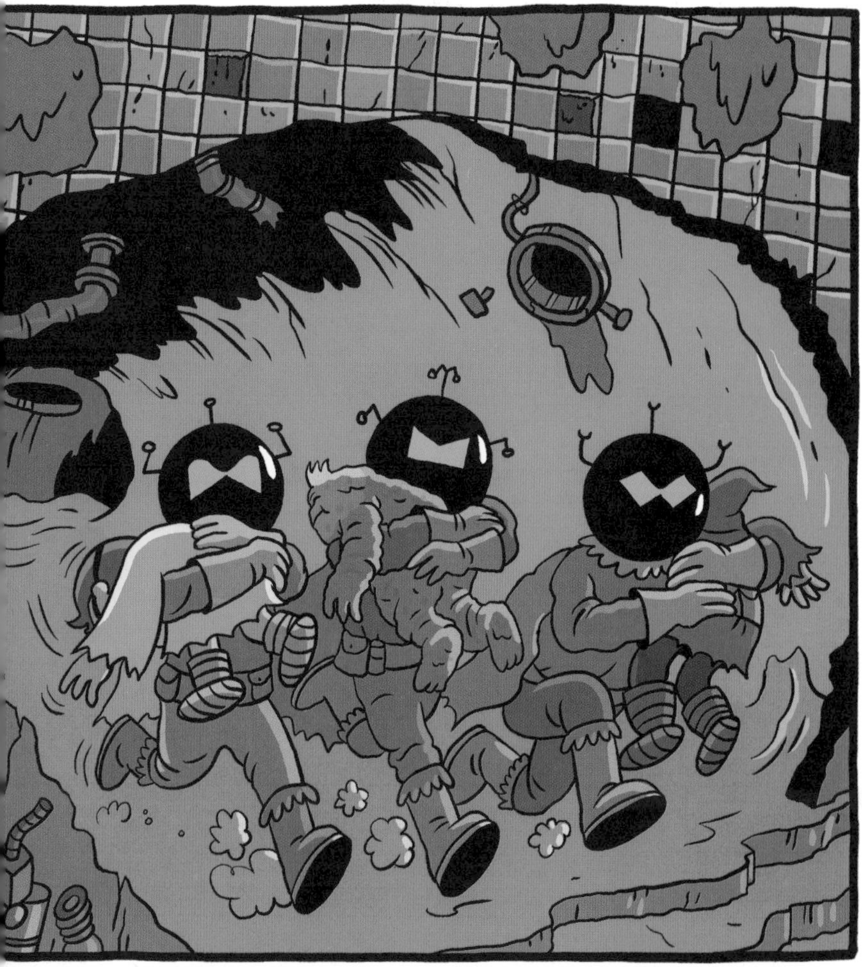

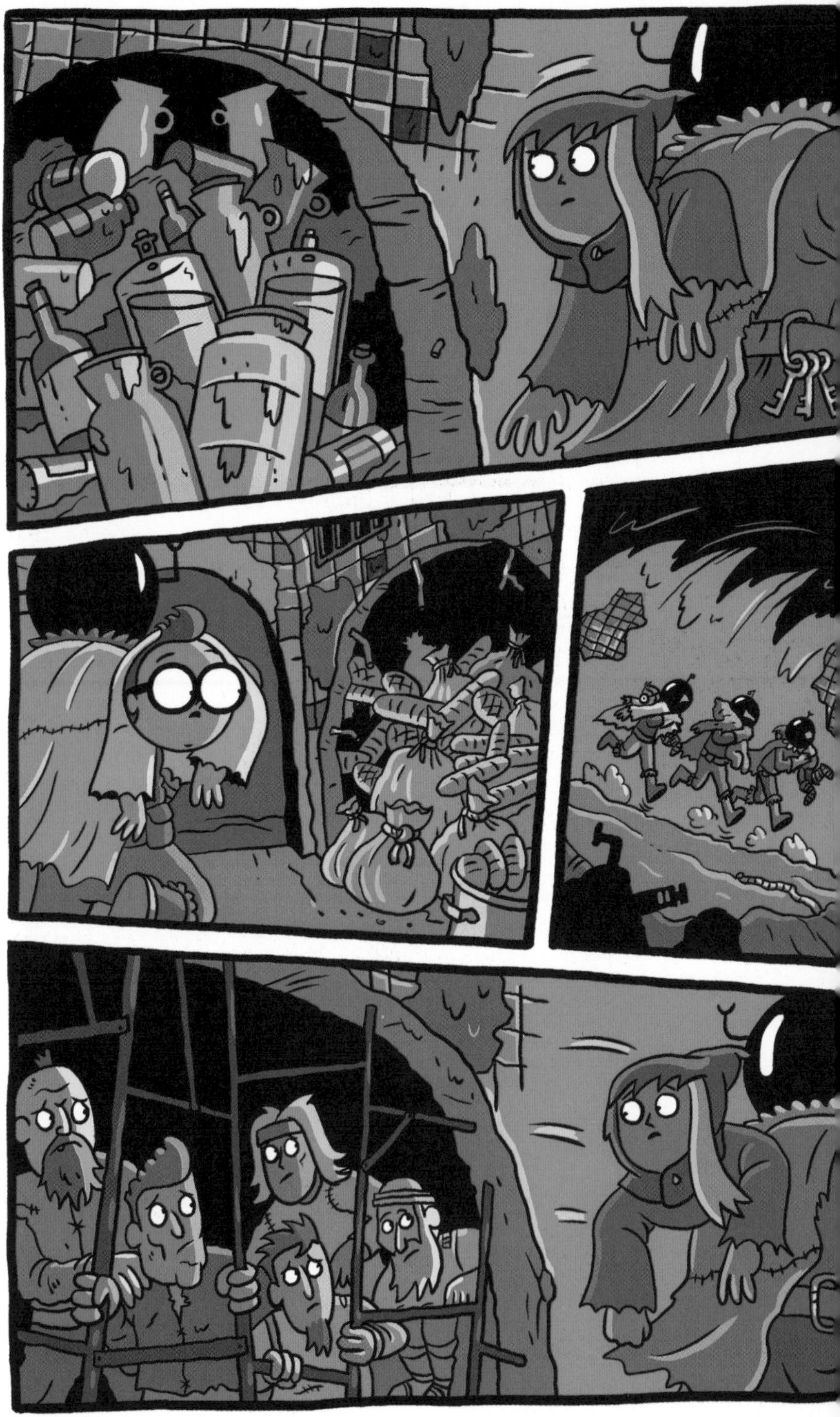

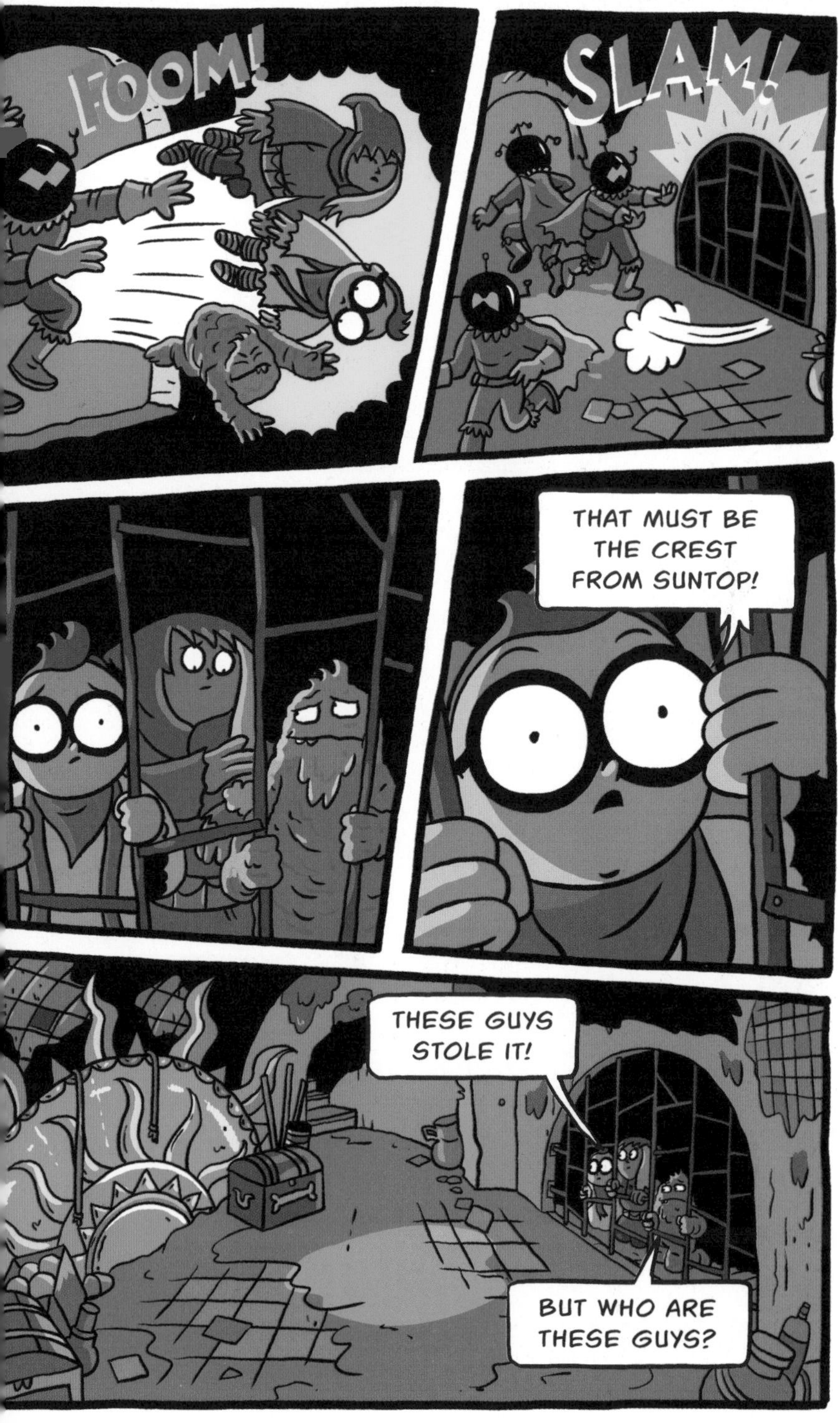
FOOM!
SLAM!
THAT MUST BE THE CREST FROM SUNTOP!
THESE GUYS STOLE IT!
BUT WHO ARE THESE GUYS?

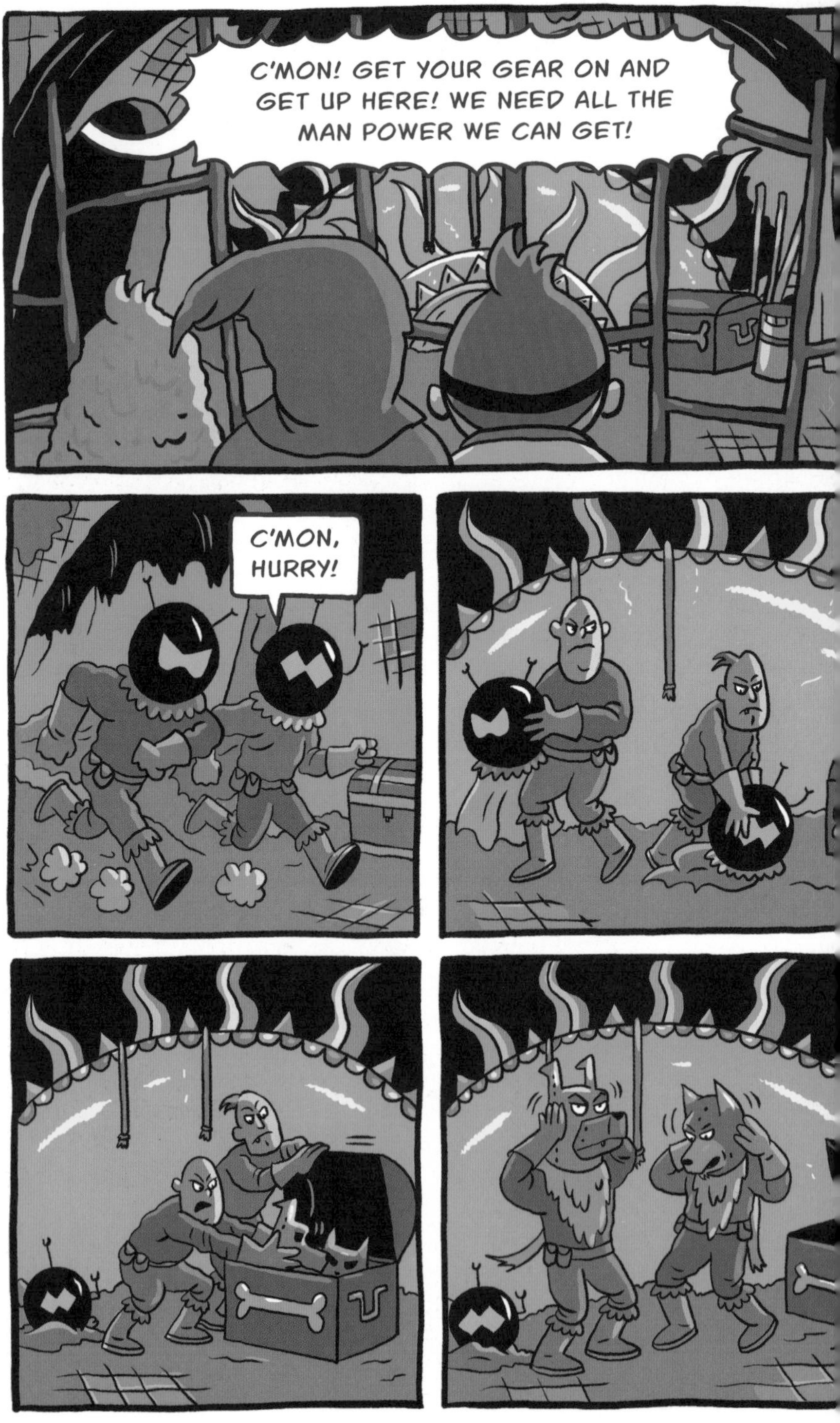
C'MON! GET YOUR GEAR ON AND GET UP HERE! WE NEED ALL THE MAN POWER WE CAN GET!
C'MON, HURRY!

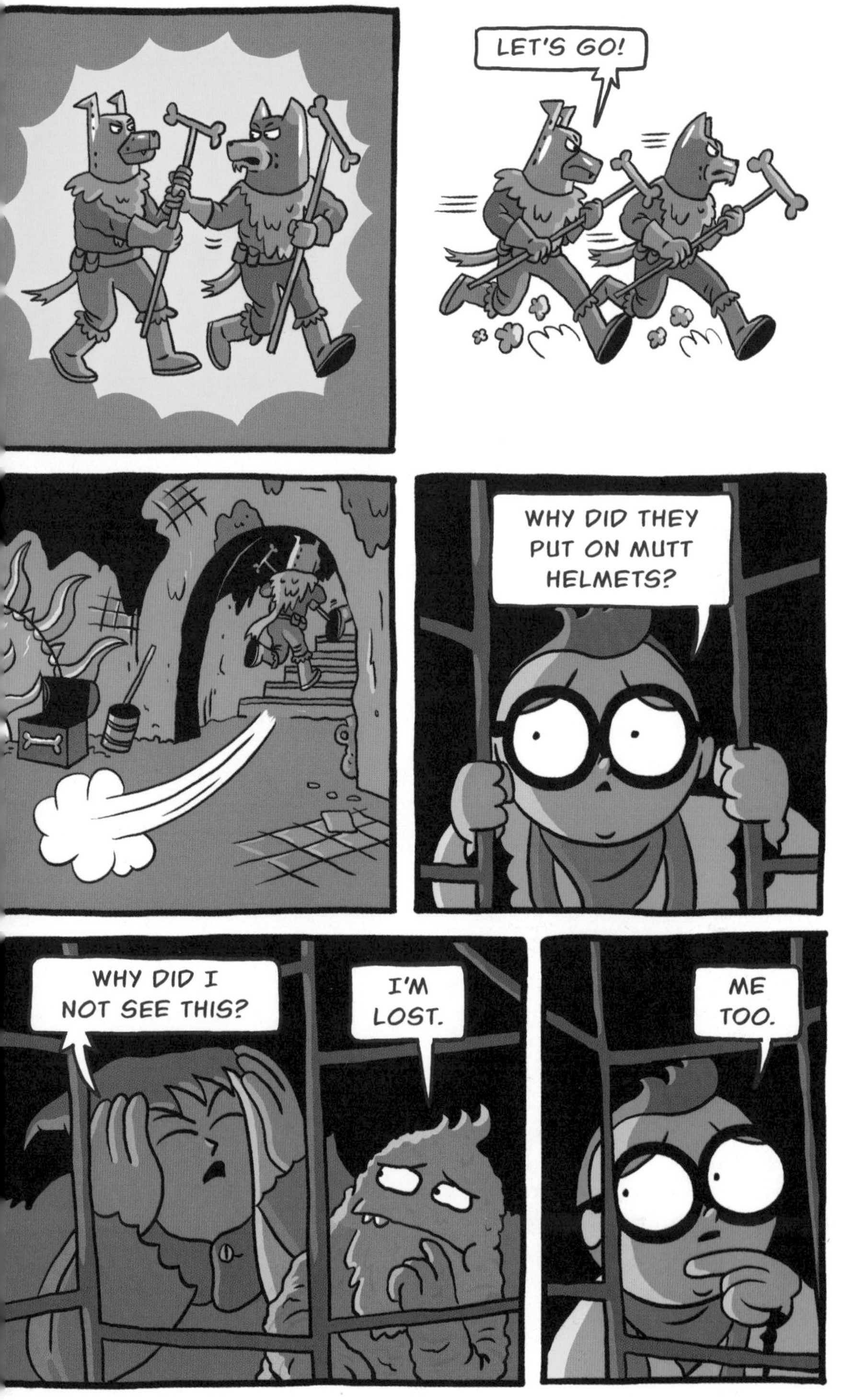
LET'S GO!
WHY DID THEY PUT ON MUTT HELMETS?
WHY DID I NOT SEE THIS?
I'M LOST.
ME TOO.

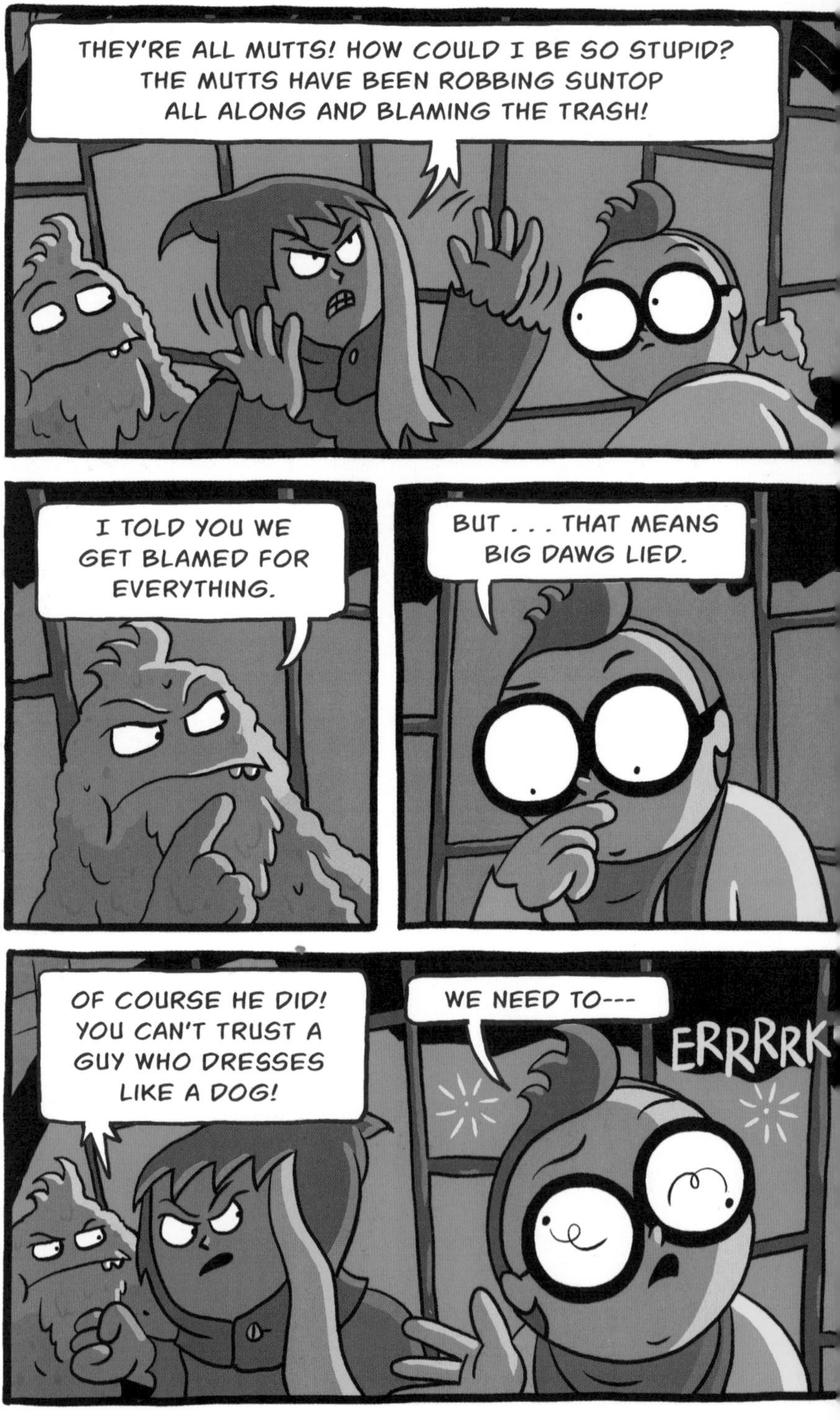
THEY'RE ALL MUTTS! HOW COULD I BE SO STUPID? THE MUTTS HAVE BEEN ROBBING SUNTOP ALL ALONG AND BLAMING THE TRASH!
I TOLD YOU WE GET BLAMED FOR EVERYTHING.
BUT . . . THAT MEANS BIG DAWG LIED.
OF COURSE HE DID! YOU CAN'T TRUST A GUY WHO DRESSES LIKE A DOG!
WE NEED TO---
ERRRRK

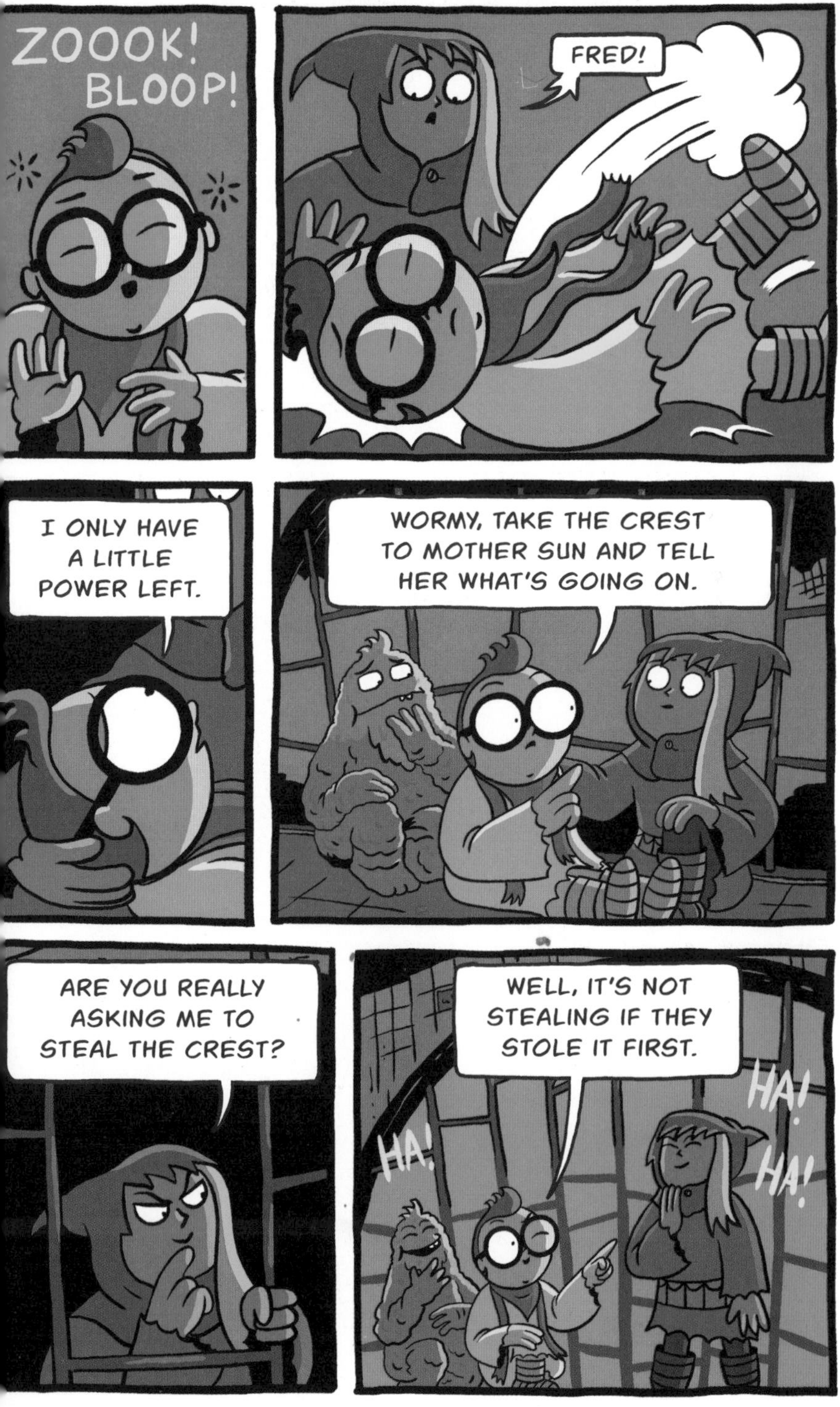
ZOOOK! BLOOP!
FRED!
I ONLY HAVE A LITTLE POWER LEFT.
WORMY, TAKE THE CREST TO MOTHER SUN AND TELL HER WHAT'S GOING ON.
ARE YOU REALLY ASKING ME TO STEAL THE CREST?
WELL, IT'S NOT STEALING IF THEY STOLE IT FIRST.
HA!
HA!
HA!

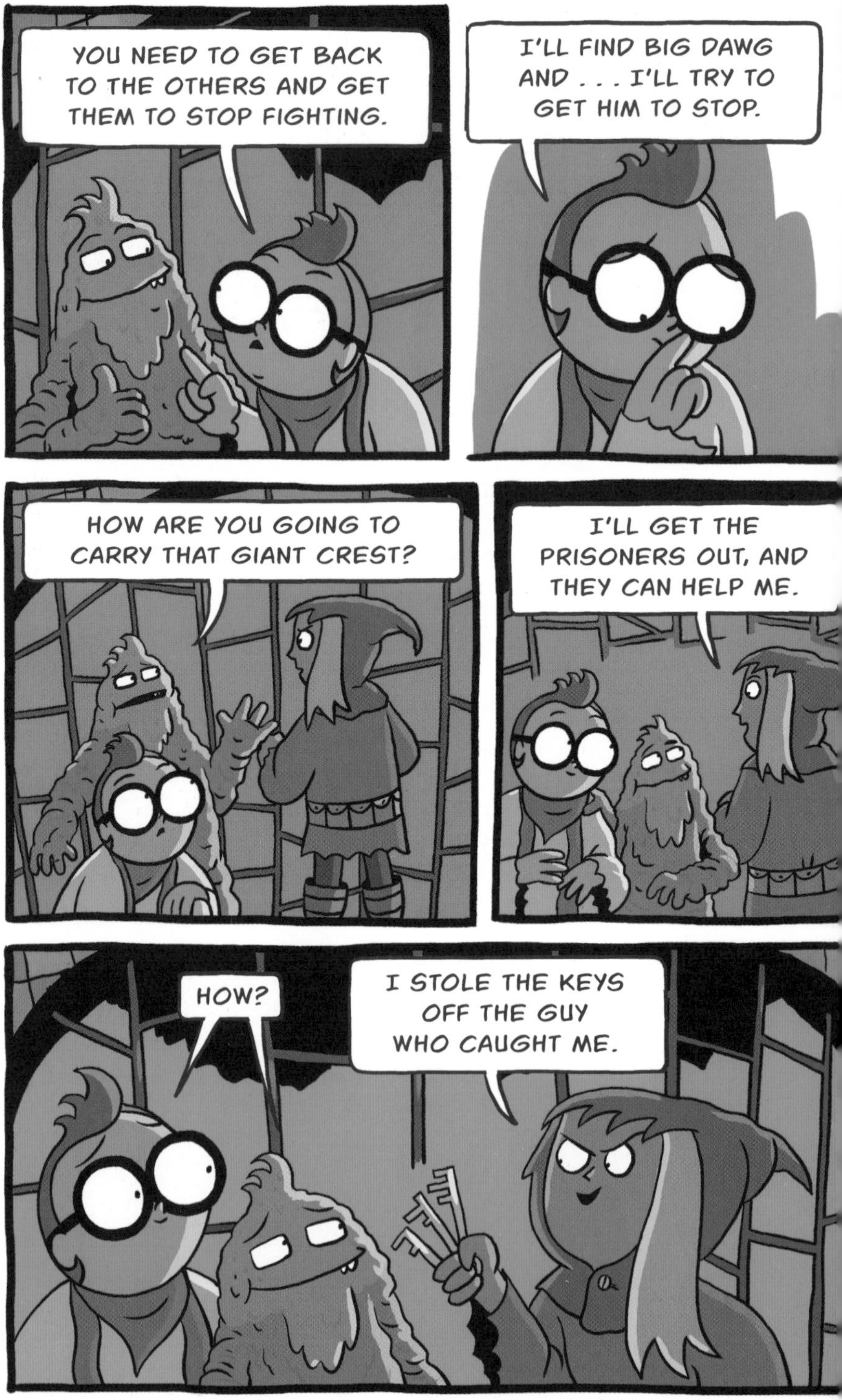
YOU NEED TO GET BACK TO THE OTHERS AND GET THEM TO STOP FIGHTING.
I'LL FIND BIG DAWG AND . . . I'LL TRY TO GET HIM TO STOP.
HOW ARE YOU GOING TO CARRY THAT GIANT CREST?
I'LL GET THE PRISONERS OUT, AND THEY CAN HELP ME.
HOW?
I STOLE THE KEYS OFF THE GUY WHO CAUGHT ME.

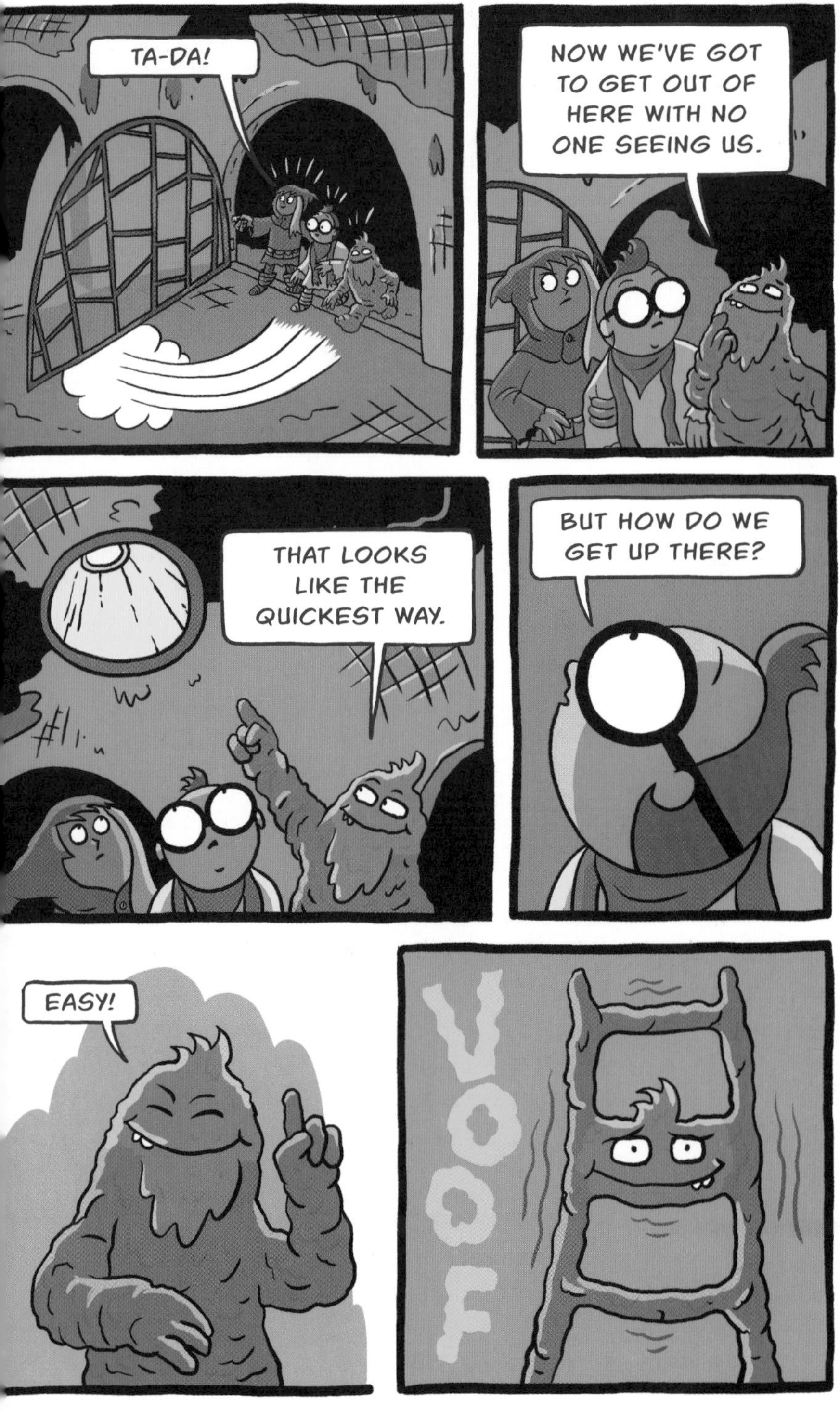
TA-DA!
NOW WE'VE GOT TO GET OUT OF HERE WITH NO ONE SEEING US.
THAT LOOKS LIKE THE QUICKEST WAY.
BUT HOW DO WE GET UP THERE?
EASY!
VOOF

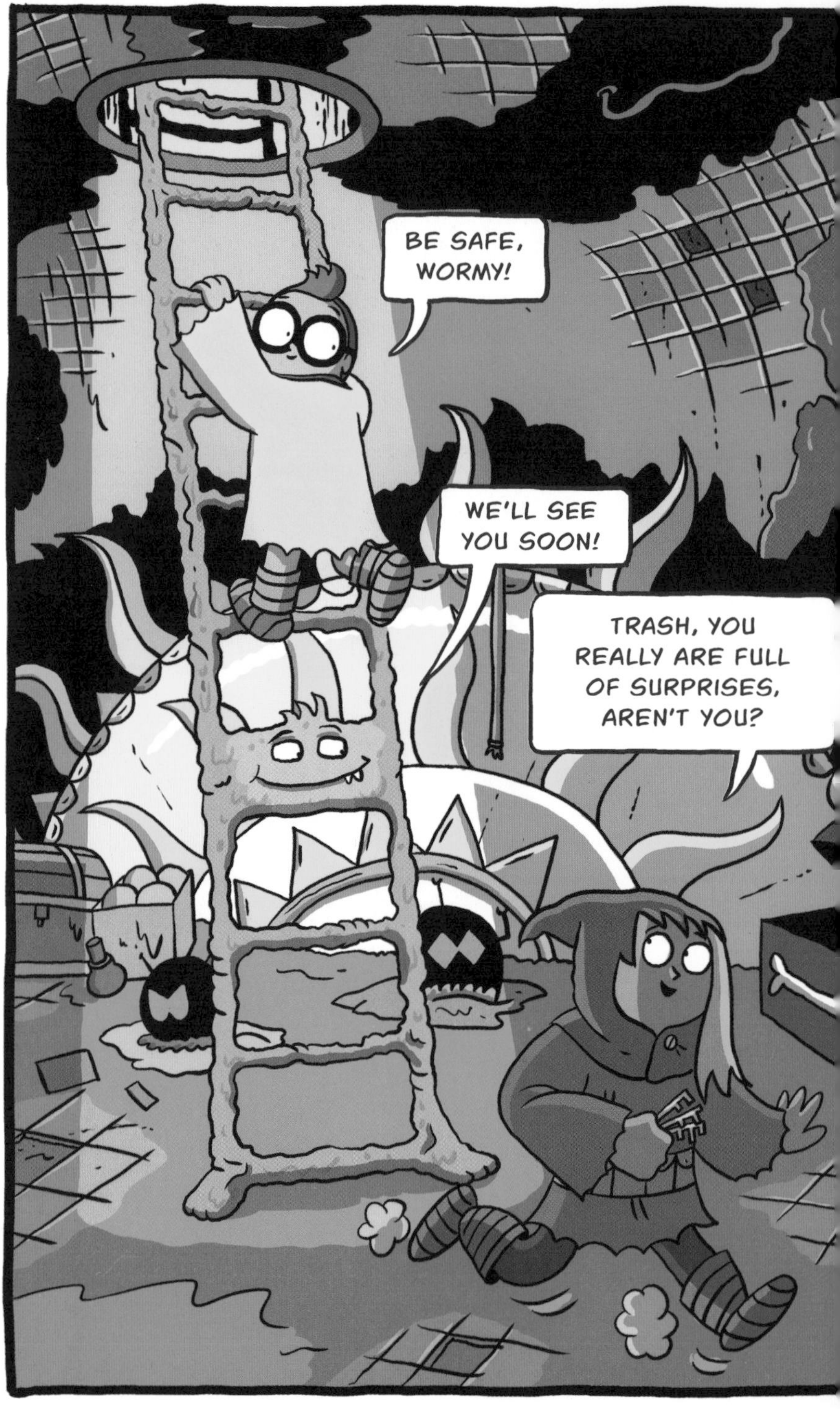
BE SAFE, WORMY!
WE'LL SEE YOU SOON!
TRASH, YOU REALLY ARE FULL OF SURPRISES, AREN'T YOU?

CHAPTER 17

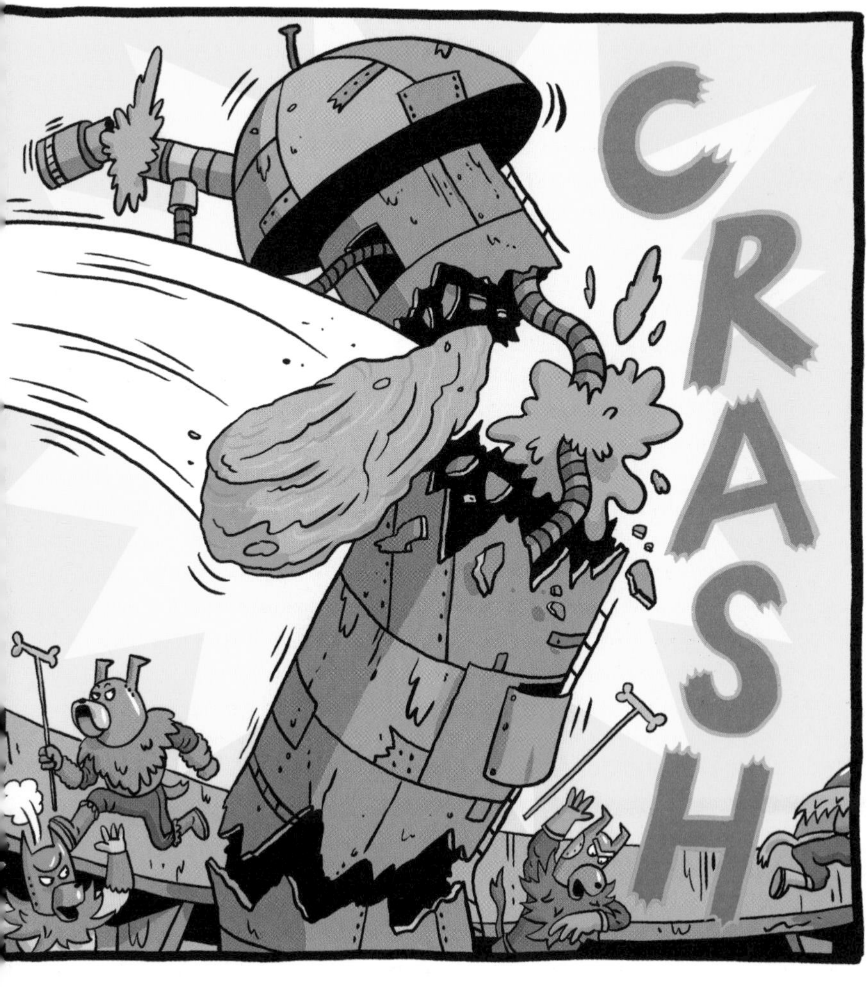
CRASH

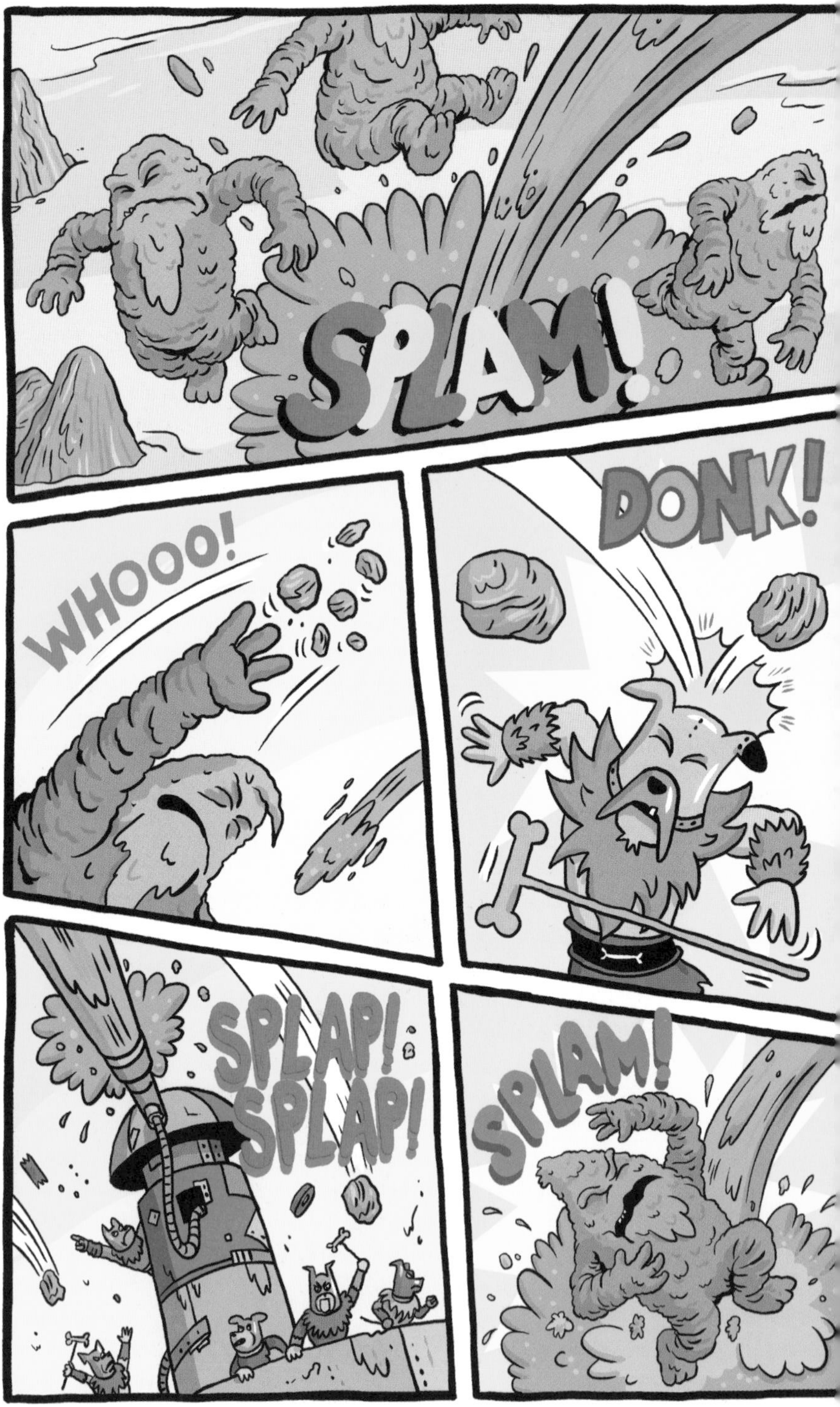
SPLAM!
WHOOO!
DONK!
SPLAP!
SPLAP!
SPLAM!

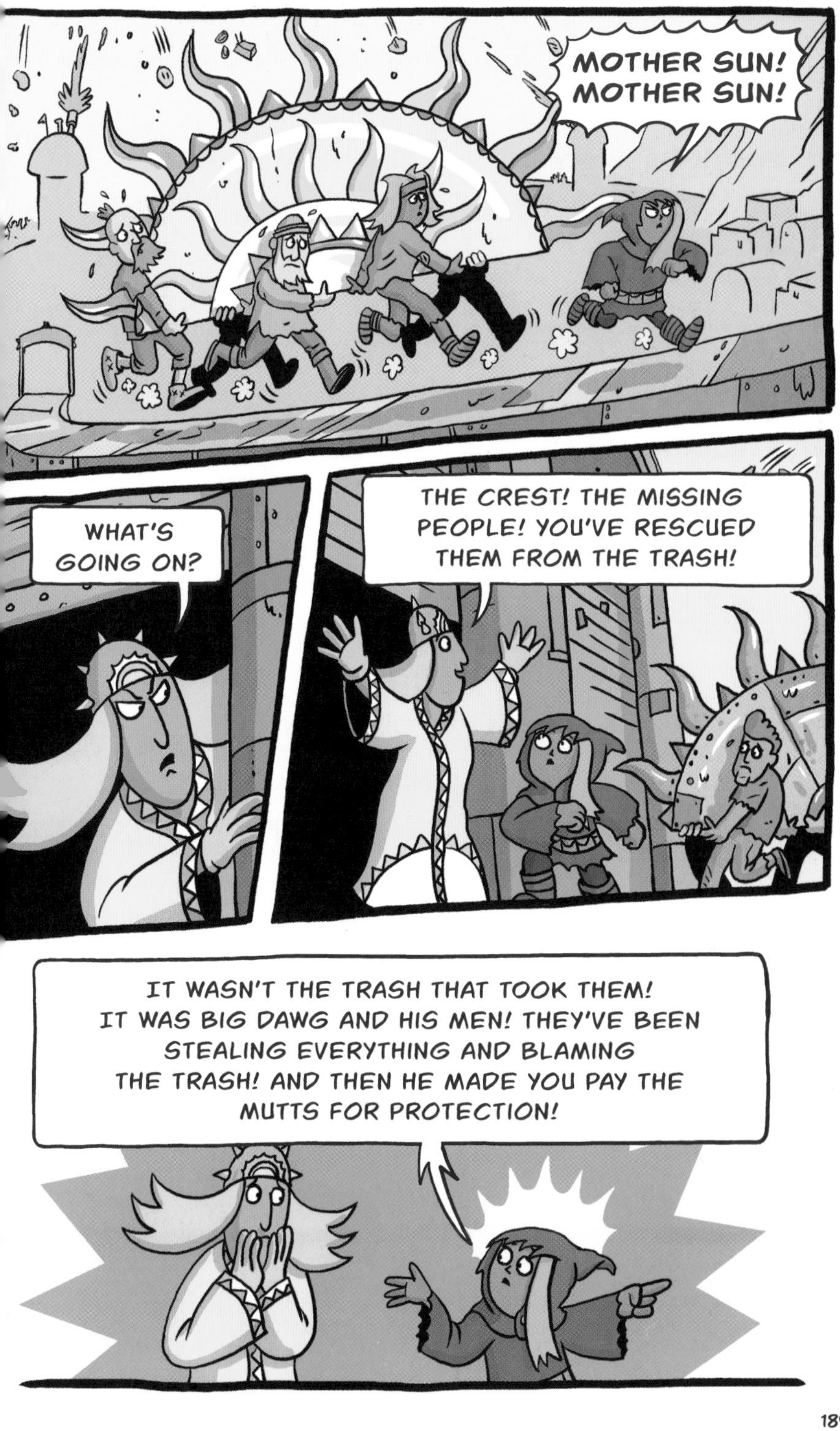
MOTHER SUN! MOTHER SUN!
WHAT'S GOING ON?
THE CREST! THE MISSING PEOPLE! YOU'VE RESCUED THEM FROM THE TRASH!
IT WASN'T THE TRASH THAT TOOK THEM! IT WAS BIG DAWG AND HIS MEN! THEY'VE BEEN STEALING EVERYTHING AND BLAMING THE TRASH! AND THEN HE MADE YOU PAY THE MUTTS FOR PROTECTION!

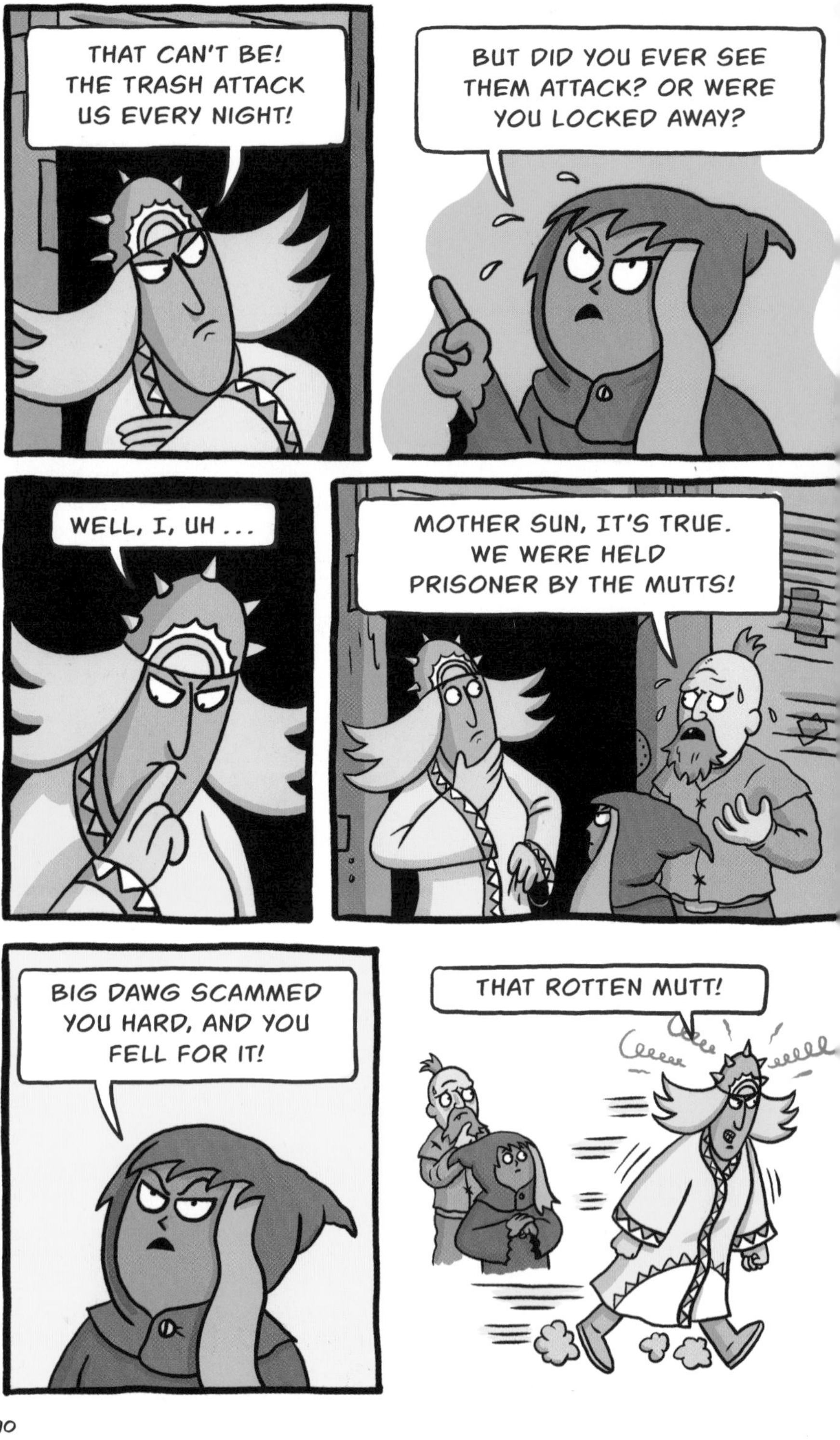
THAT CAN'T BE! THE TRASH ATTACK US EVERY NIGHT!
BUT DID YOU EVER SEE THEM ATTACK? OR WERE YOU LOCKED AWAY?
WELL, I, UH . . .
MOTHER SUN, IT'S TRUE. WE WERE HELD PRISONER BY THE MUTTS!
BIG DAWG SCAMMED YOU HARD, AND YOU FELL FOR IT!
THAT ROTTEN MUTT!

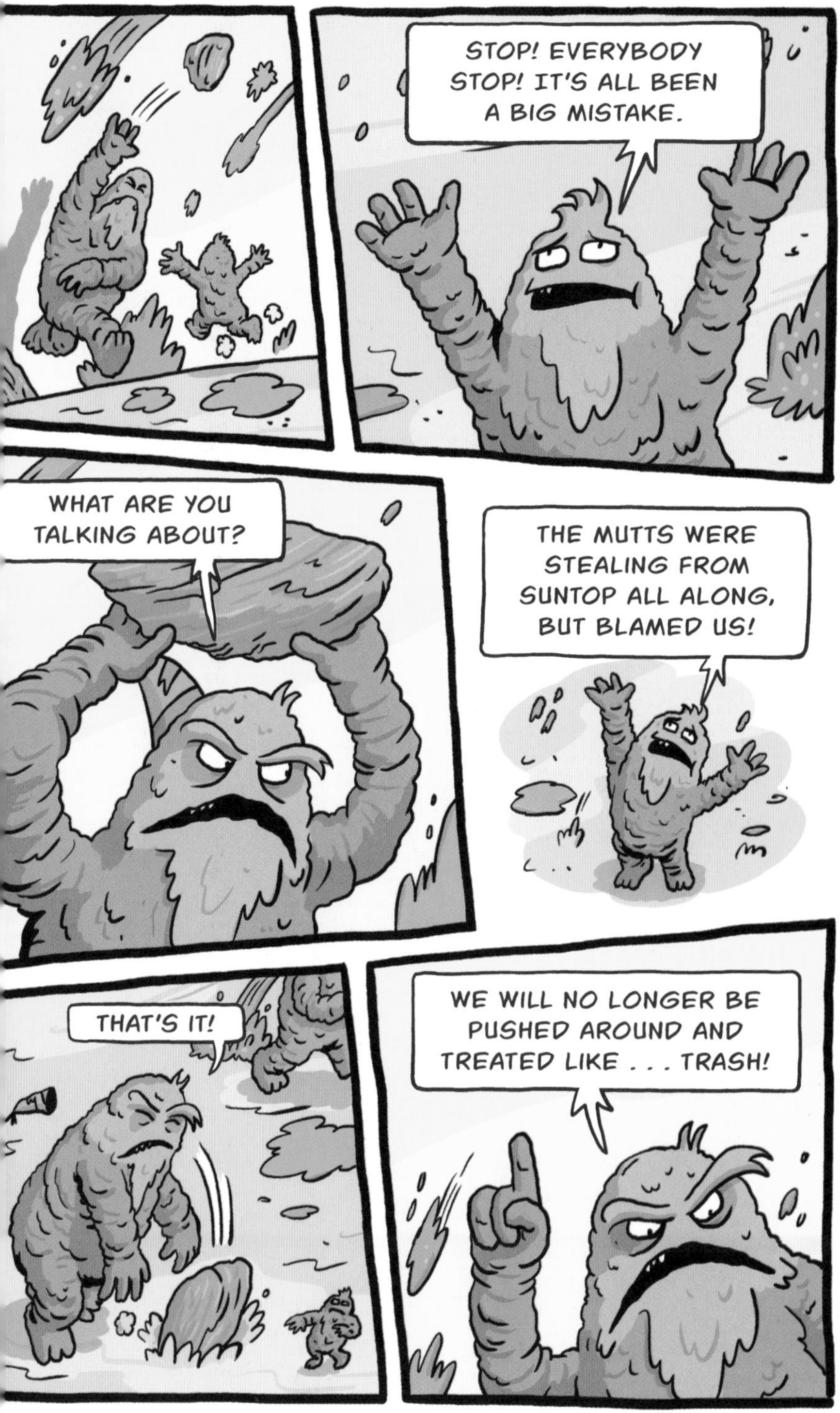

STOP! EVERYBODY STOP! IT'S ALL BEEN A BIG MISTAKE.
WHAT ARE YOU TALKING ABOUT?
THE MUTTS WERE STEALING FROM SUNTOP ALL ALONG, BUT BLAMED US!
THAT'S IT!
WE WILL NO LONGER BE PUSHED AROUND AND TREATED LIKE . . . TRASH!

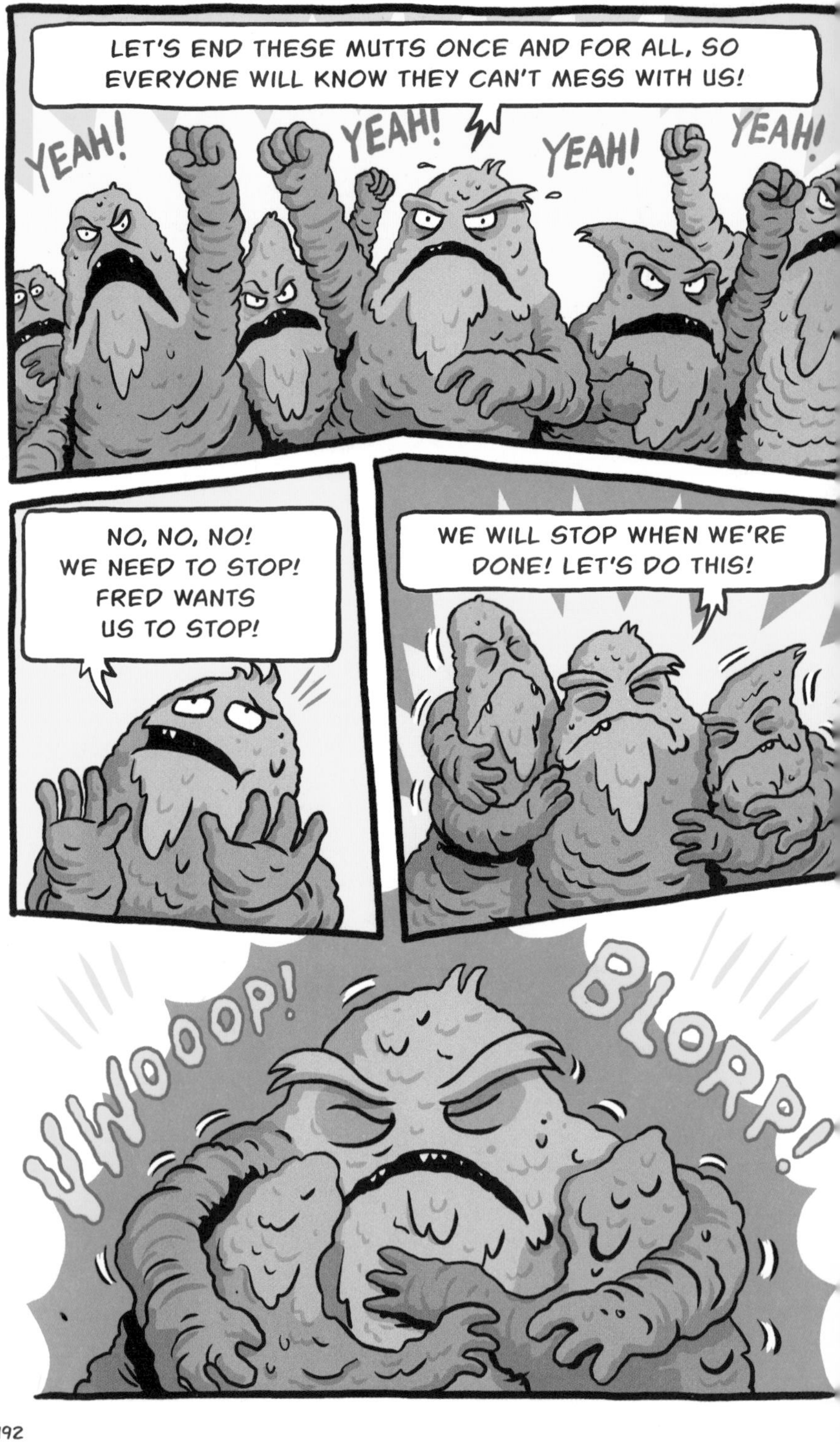
LET'S END THESE MUTTS ONCE AND FOR ALL, SO EVERYONE WILL KNOW THEY CAN'T MESS WITH US!
YEAH!
YEAH!
YEAH!
YEAH!
NO, NO, NO! WE NEED TO STOP! FRED WANTS US TO STOP!
WE WILL STOP WHEN WE'RE DONE! LET'S DO THIS!
WHOOOP!
BLORP!

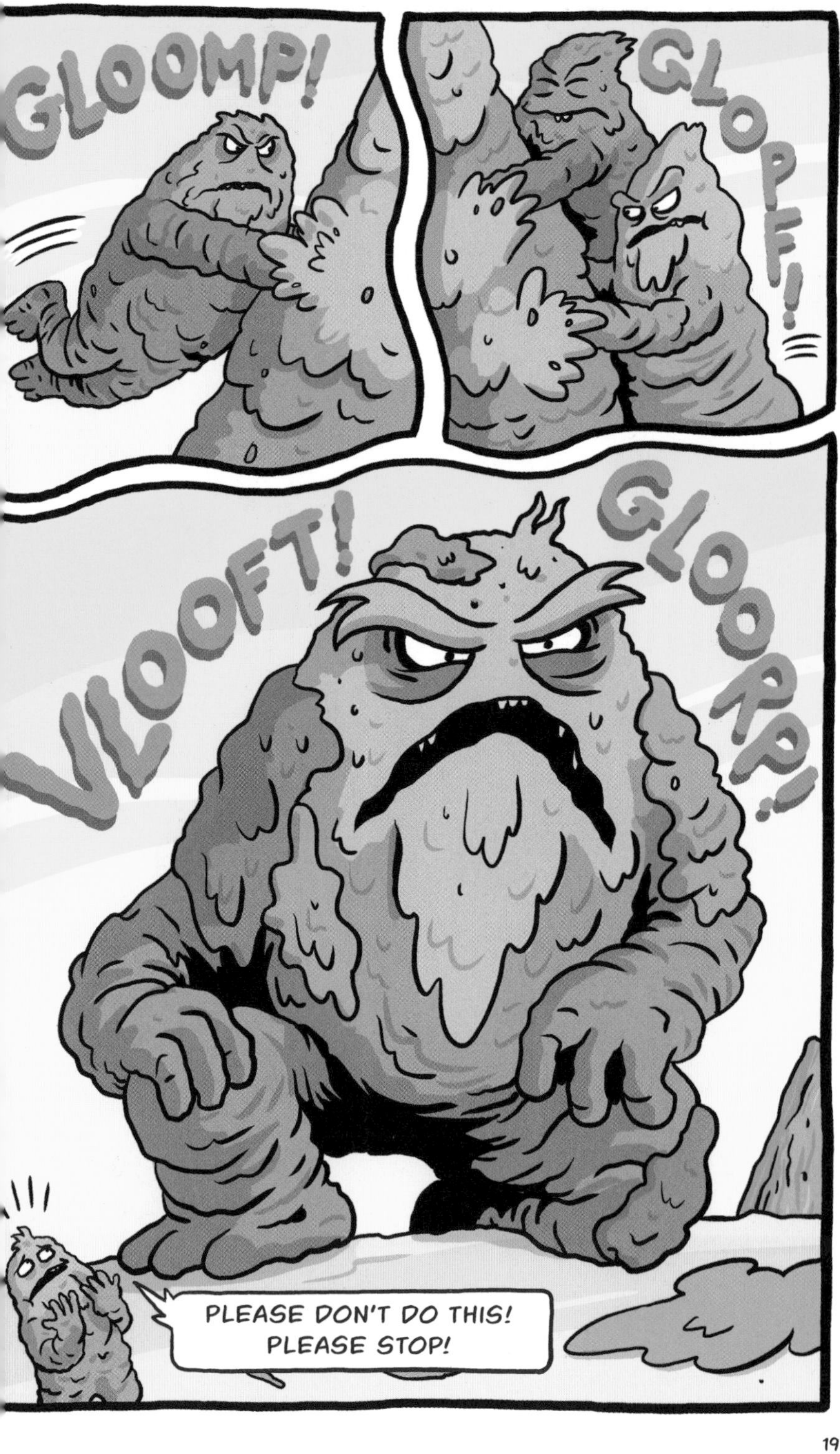
GLOOMP!
GLOPF!
VLOOFT!
GLOORP!
PLEASE DON'T DO THIS! PLEASE STOP!

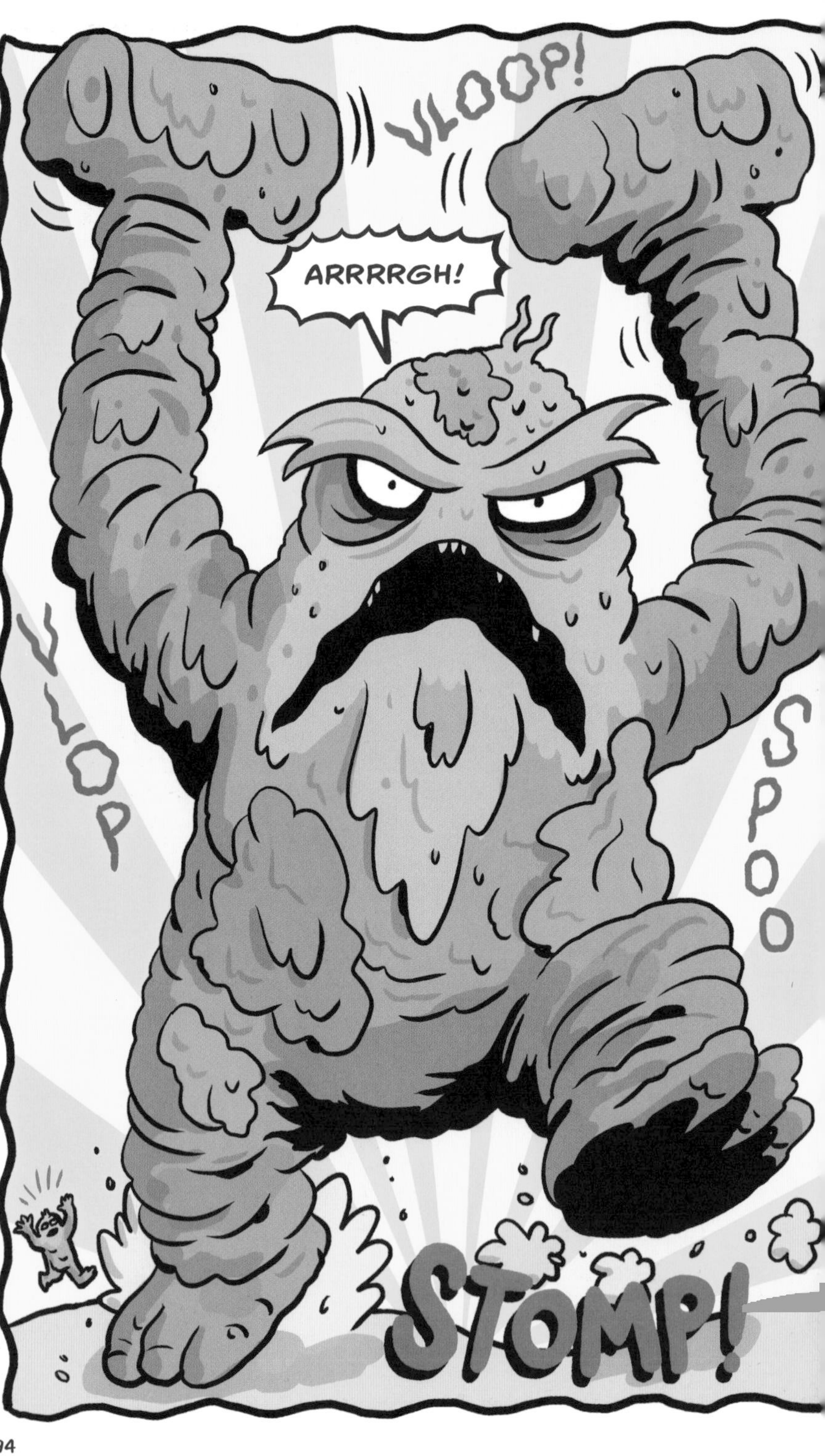
VLOOP!
ARRRRGH!
VLOOP
SPOO
STOMP!

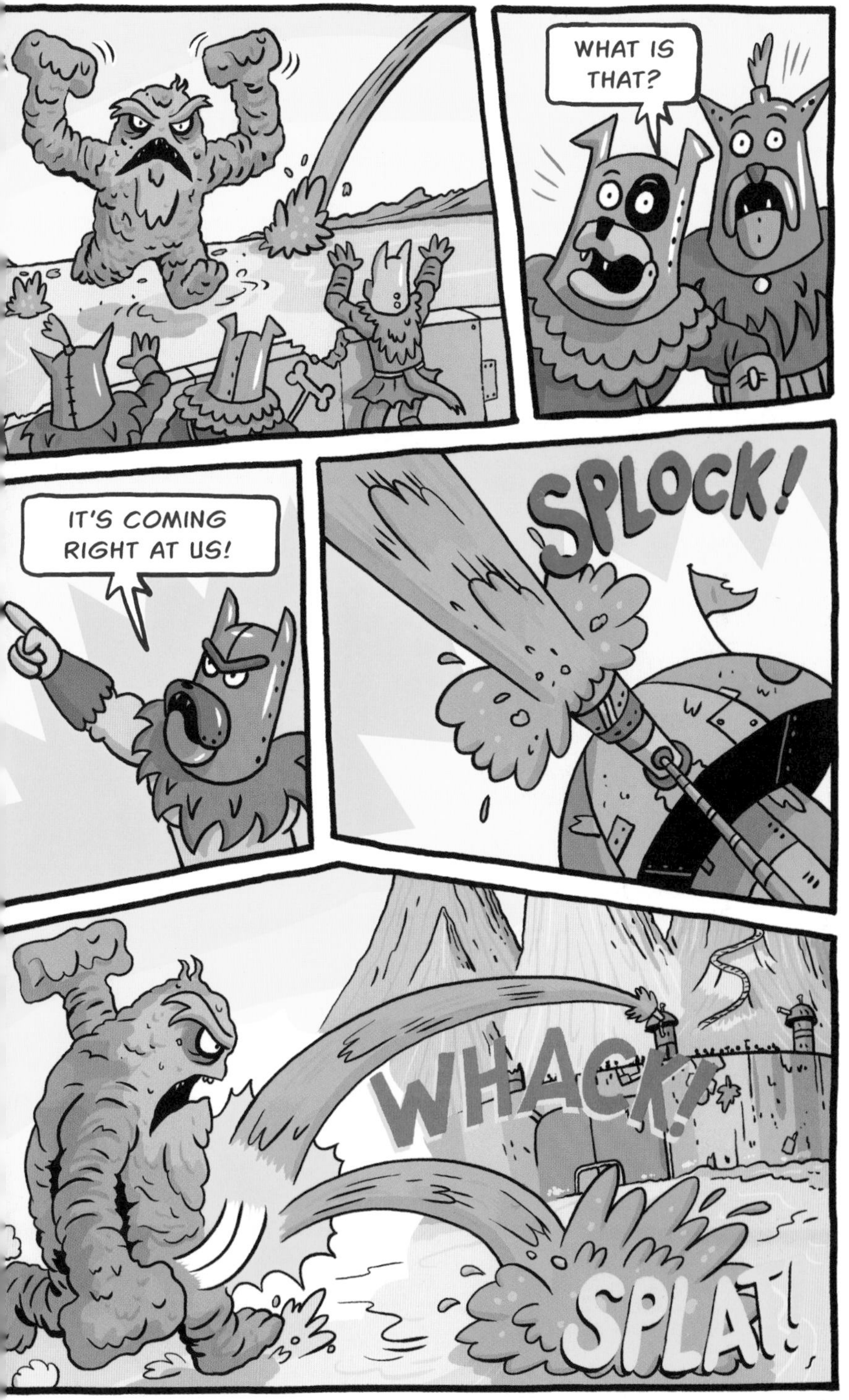
WHAT IS THAT?
IT'S COMING RIGHT AT US!
SPLOCK!
WHACK!
SPLAT!

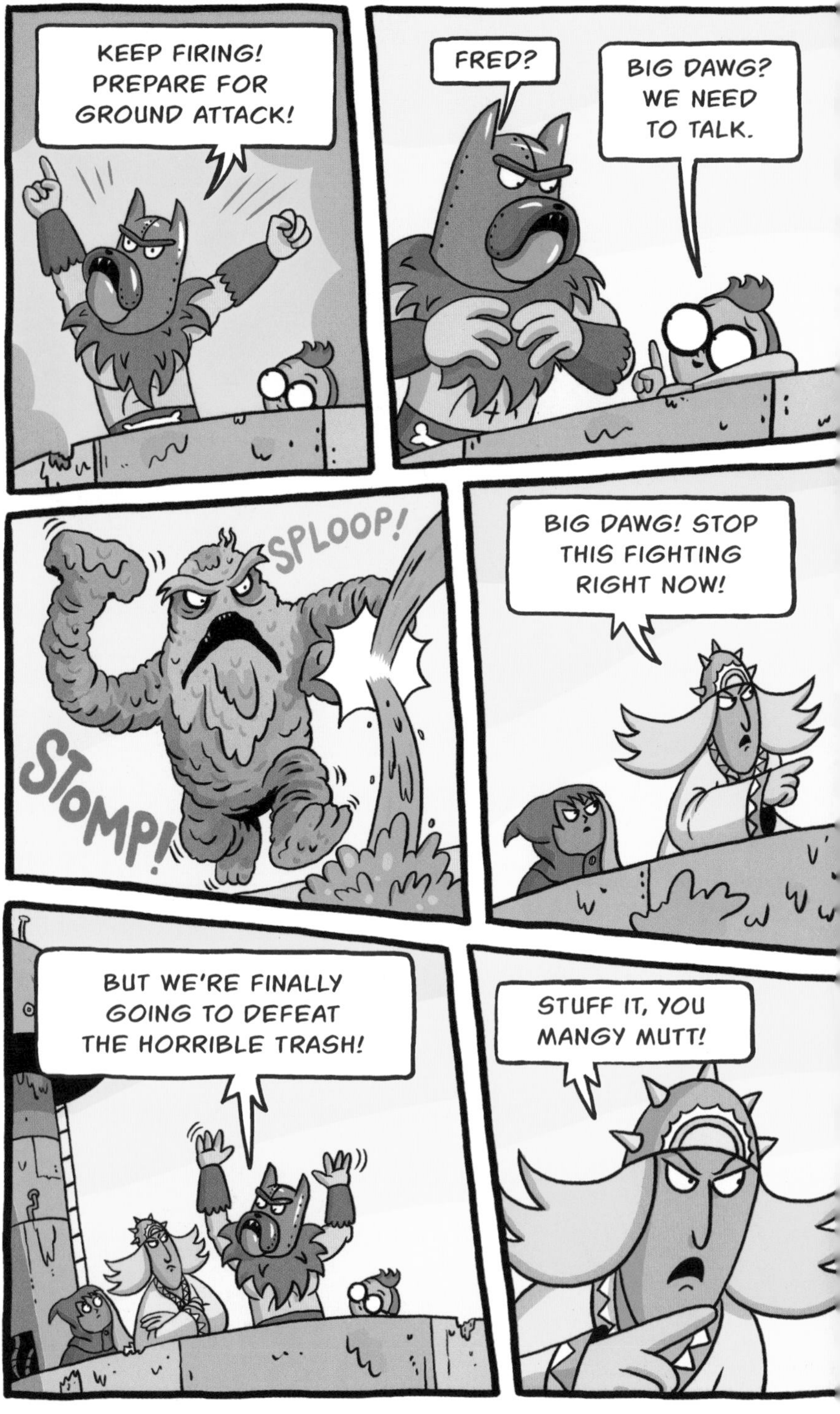
KEEP FIRING! PREPARE FOR GROUND ATTACK!
FRED?
BIG DAWG? WE NEED TO TALK.
SPLOOP!
STOMP!
BIG DAWG! STOP THIS FIGHTING RIGHT NOW!
BUT WE'RE FINALLY GOING TO DEFEAT THE HORRIBLE TRASH!
STUFF IT, YOU MANGY MUTT!

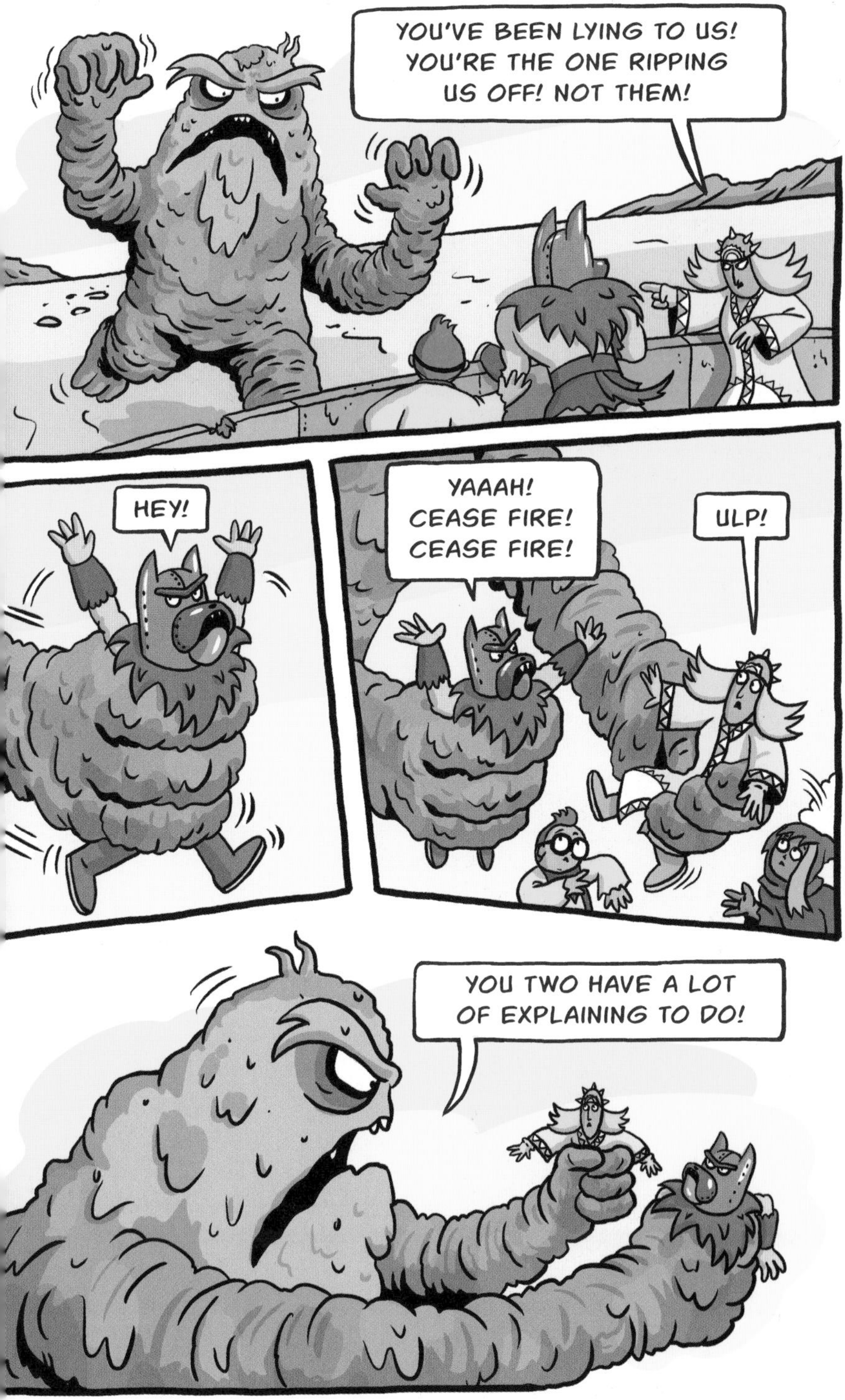
YOU'VE BEEN LYING TO US! YOU'RE THE ONE RIPPING US OFF! NOT THEM!
HEY!
YAAAH! CEASE FIRE! CEASE FIRE!
ULP!
YOU TWO HAVE A LOT OF EXPLAINING TO DO!

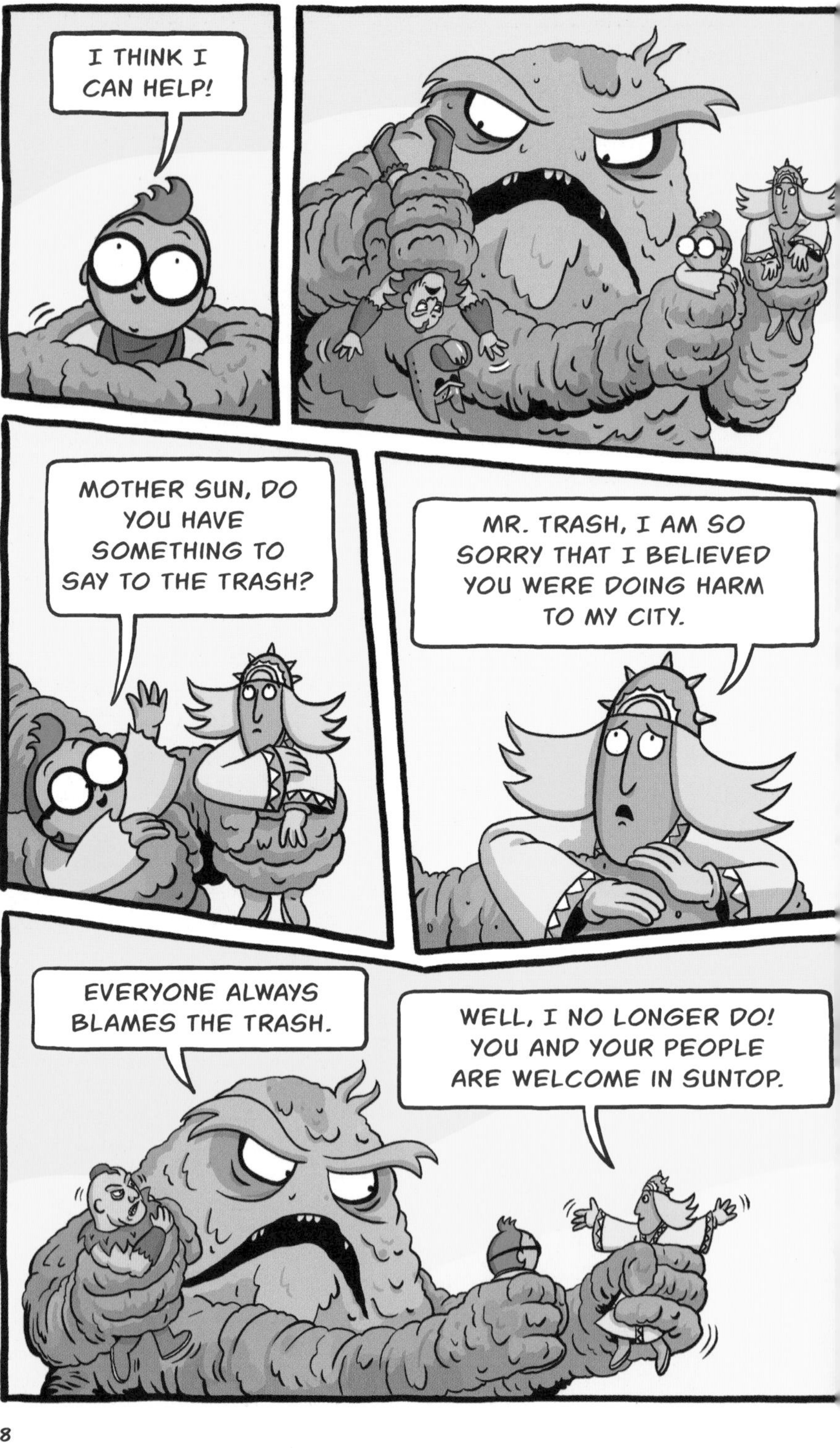
I THINK I CAN HELP!
MOTHER SUN, DO YOU HAVE SOMETHING TO SAY TO THE TRASH?
MR. TRASH, I AM SO SORRY THAT I BELIEVED YOU WERE DOING HARM TO MY CITY.
EVERYONE ALWAYS BLAMES THE TRASH.
WELL, I NO LONGER DO! YOU AND YOUR PEOPLE ARE WELCOME IN SUNTOP.

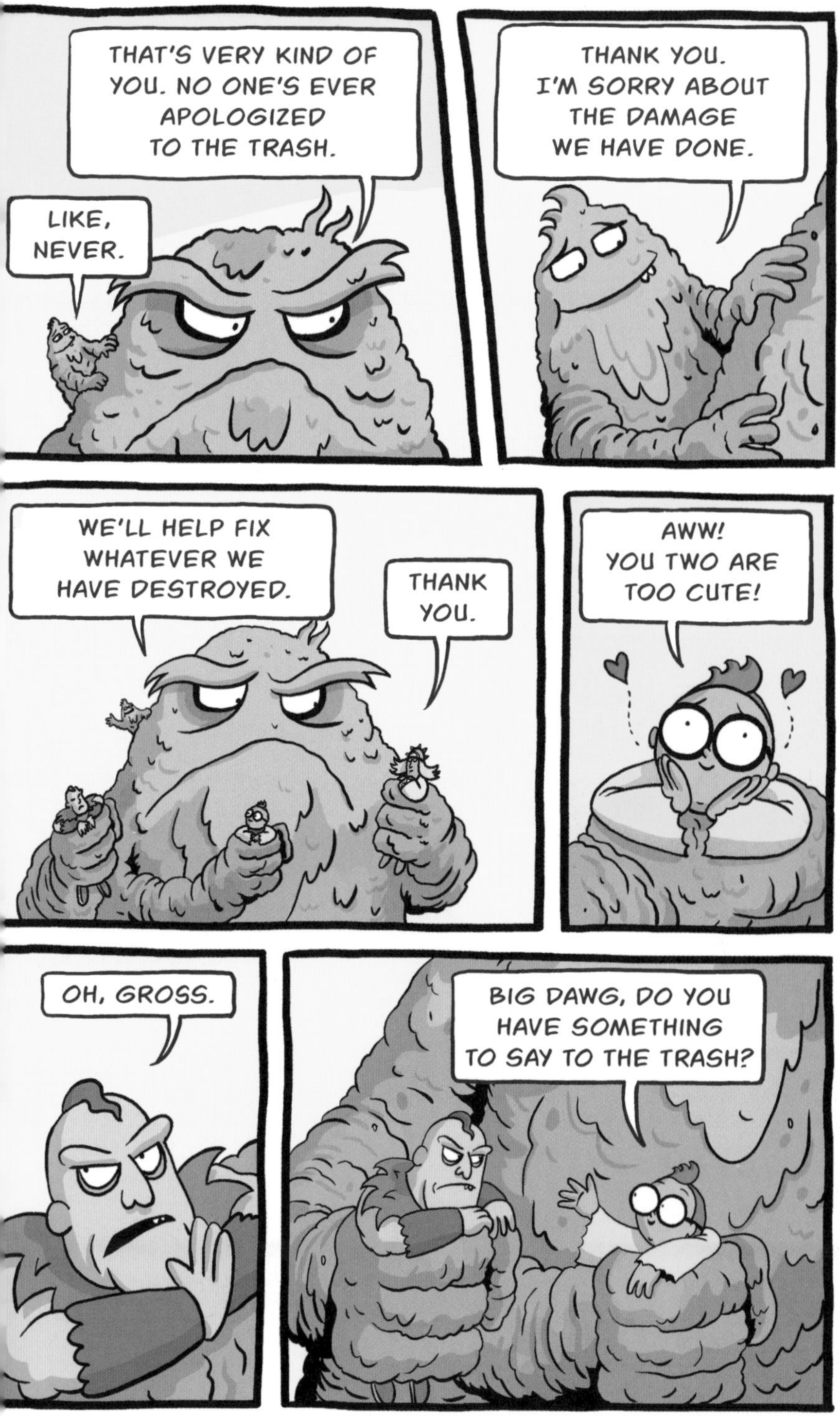
THAT'S VERY KIND OF YOU. NO ONE'S EVER APOLOGIZED TO THE TRASH.
LIKE, NEVER.
THANK YOU. I'M SORRY ABOUT THE DAMAGE WE HAVE DONE.
WE'LL HELP FIX WHATEVER WE HAVE DESTROYED.
THANK YOU.
AWW! YOU TWO ARE TOO CUTE!
OH, GROSS.
BIG DAWG, DO YOU HAVE SOMETHING TO SAY TO THE TRASH?

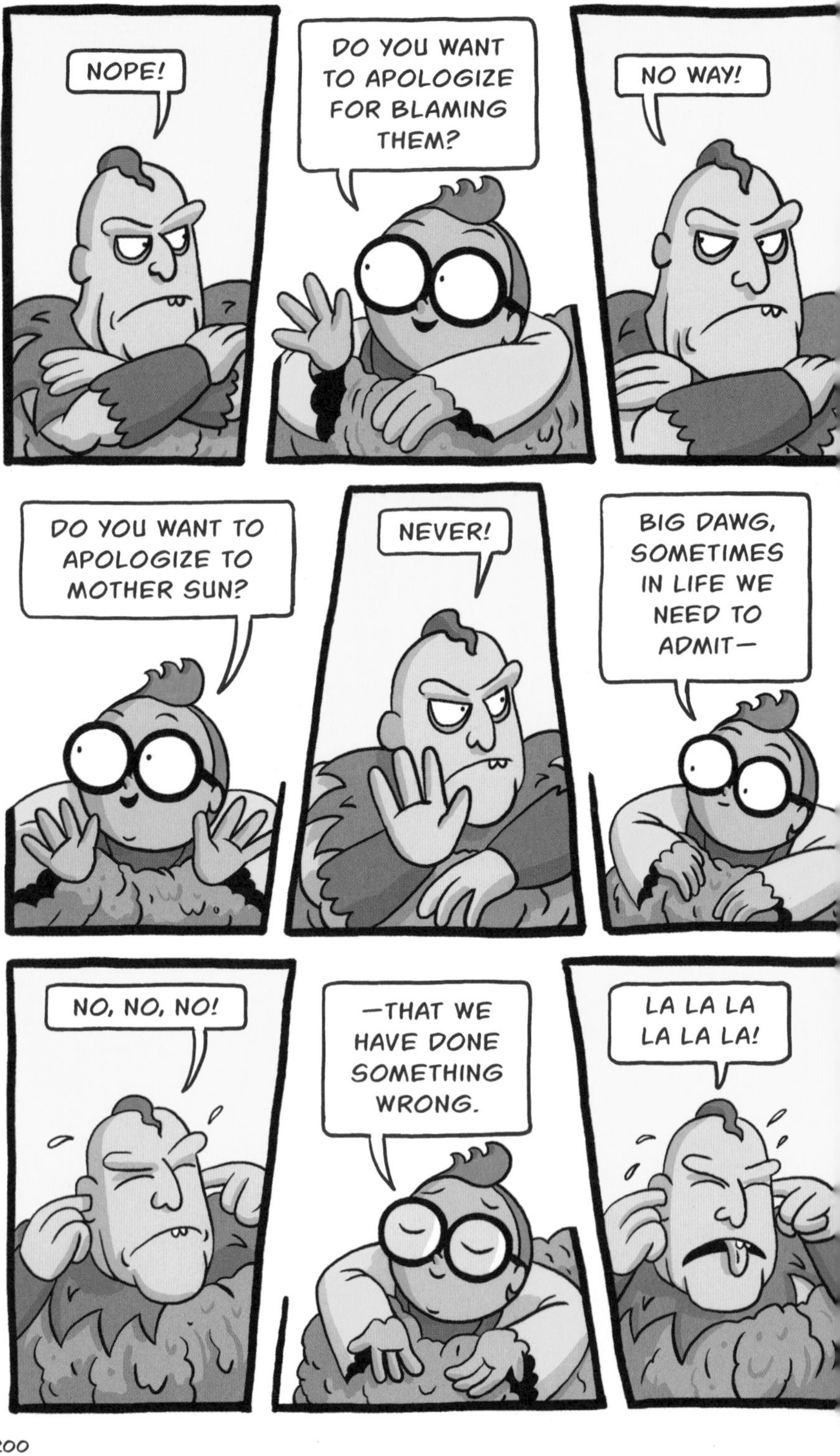
NOPE!
DO YOU WANT TO APOLOGIZE FOR BLAMING THEM?
NO WAY!
DO YOU WANT TO APOLOGIZE TO MOTHER SUN?
NEVER!
BIG DAWG, SOMETIMES IN LIFE WE NEED TO ADMIT—
NO, NO, NO!
—THAT WE HAVE DONE SOMETHING WRONG.
LA LA LA LA LA LA!

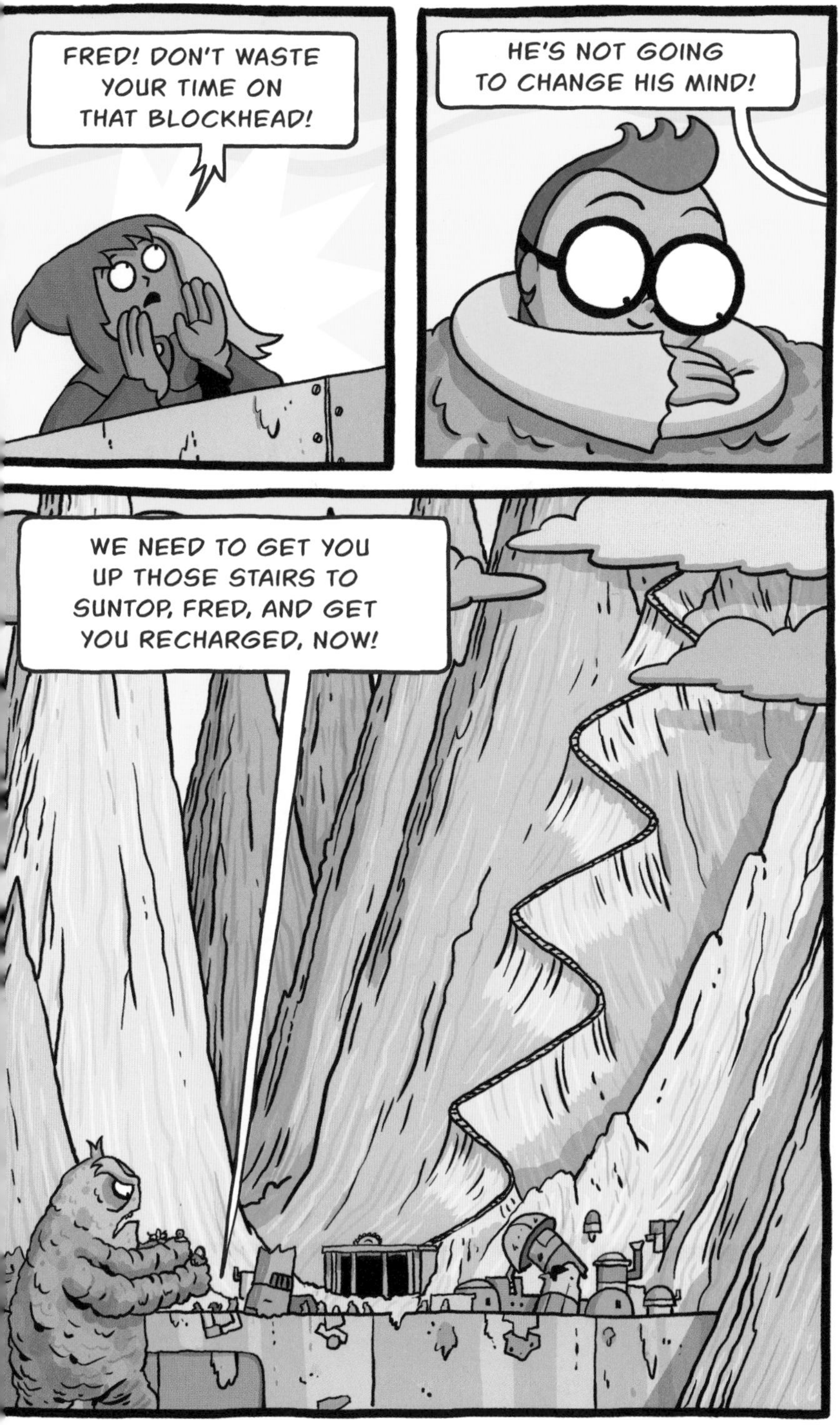
FRED! DON'T WASTE YOUR TIME ON THAT BLOCKHEAD!
HE'S NOT GOING TO CHANGE HIS MIND!
WE NEED TO GET YOU UP THOSE STAIRS TO SUNTOP, FRED, AND GET YOU RECHARGED, NOW!

CHAPTER 18

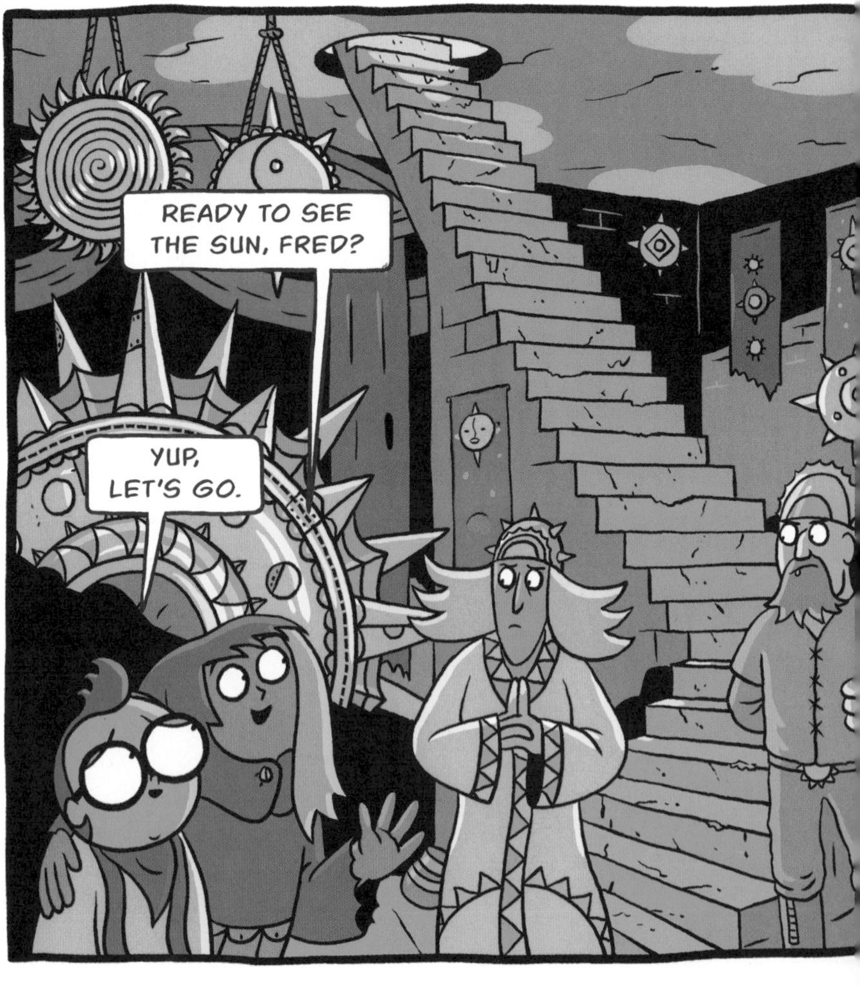
READY TO SEE THE SUN, FRED?
YUP, LET'S GO.

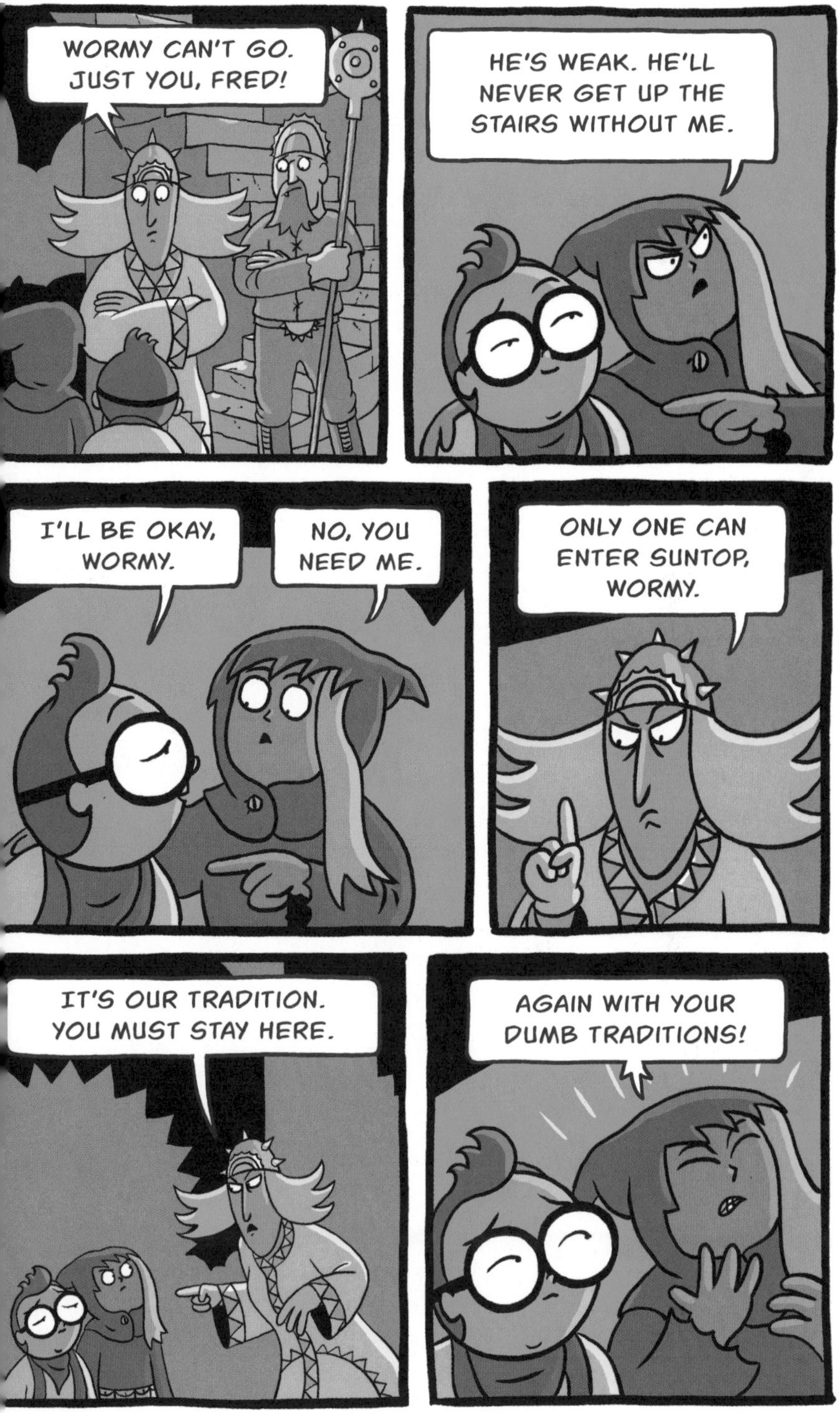
WORMY CAN'T GO. JUST YOU, FRED!
HE'S WEAK. HE'LL NEVER GET UP THE STAIRS WITHOUT ME.
I'LL BE OKAY, WORMY.
NO, YOU NEED ME.
ONLY ONE CAN ENTER SUNTOP, WORMY.
IT'S OUR TRADITION. YOU MUST STAY HERE.
AGAIN WITH YOUR DUMB TRADITIONS!

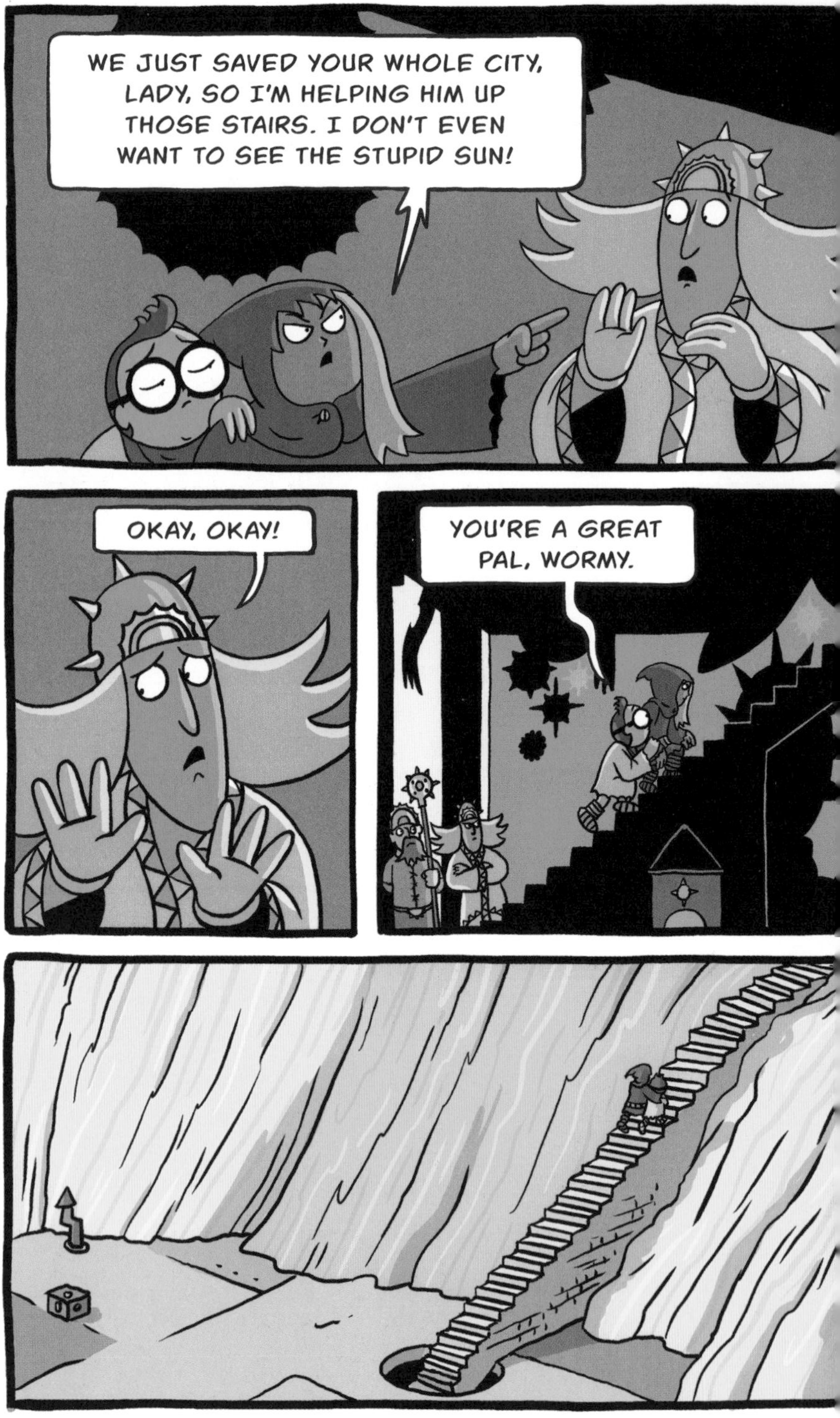
WE JUST SAVED YOUR WHOLE CITY, LADY, SO I'M HELPING HIM UP THOSE STAIRS. I DON'T EVEN WANT TO SEE THE STUPID SUN!
OKAY, OKAY!
YOU'RE A GREAT PAL, WORMY.

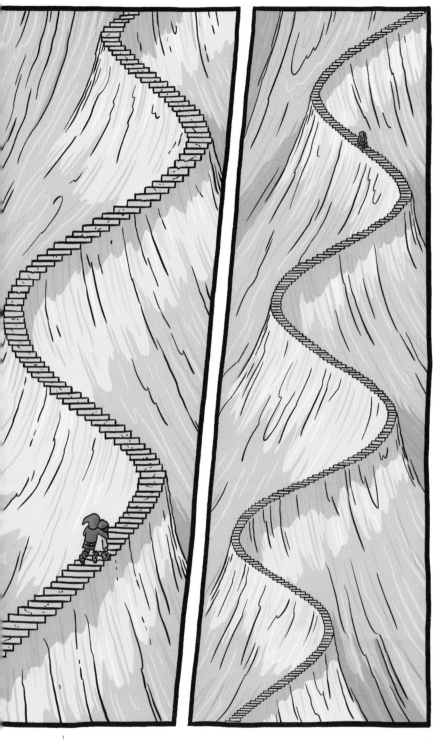

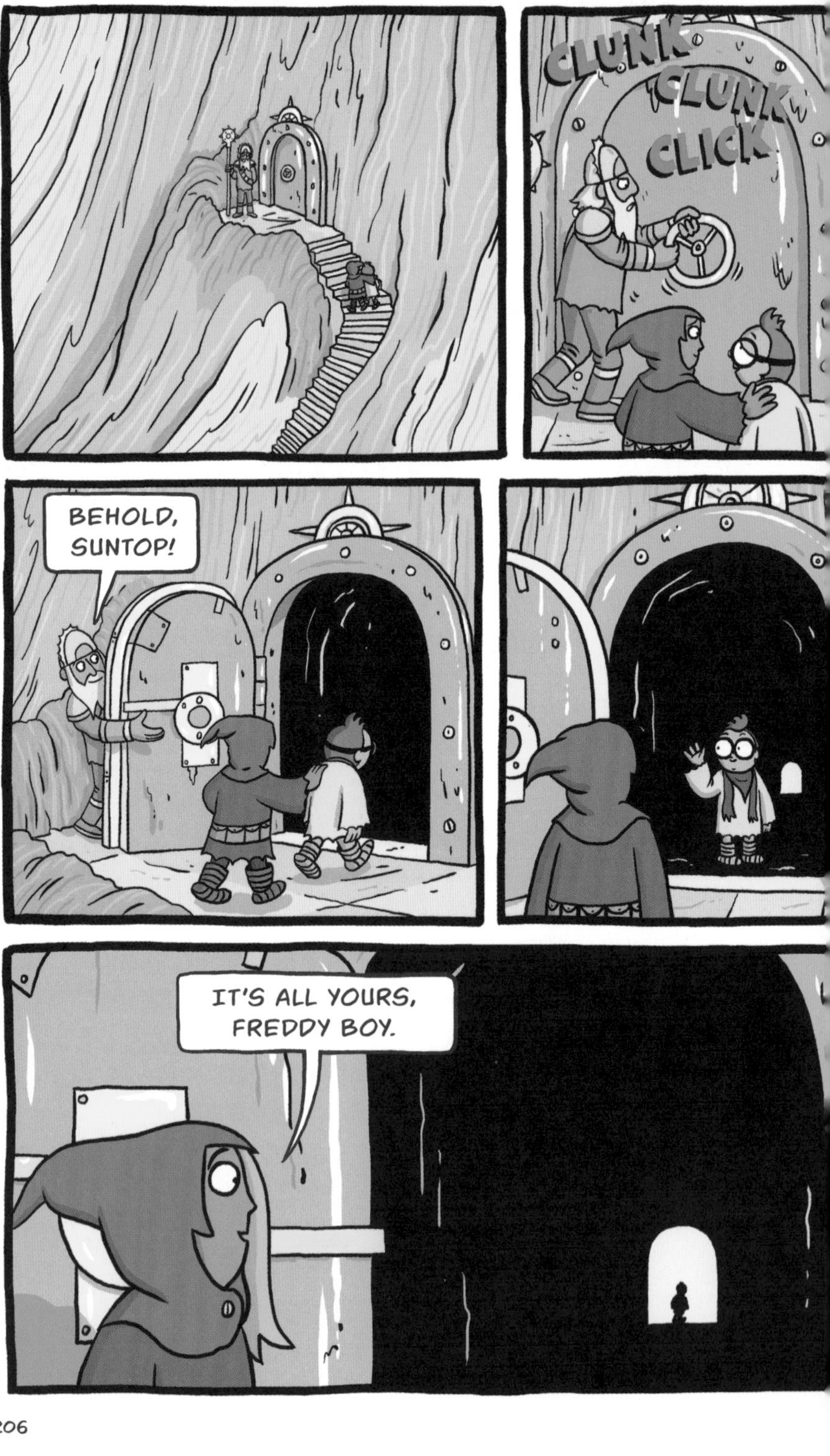
CLUNK
CLUNK
CLICK
BEHOLD, SUNTOP!
IT'S ALL YOURS, FREDDY BOY.

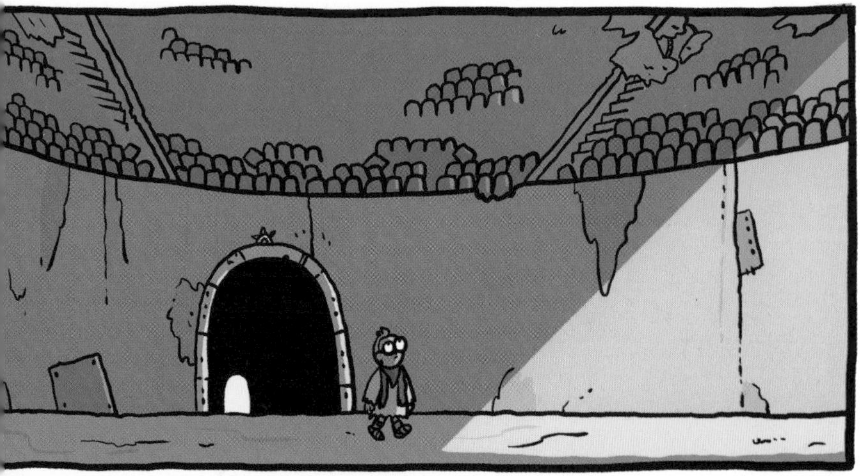

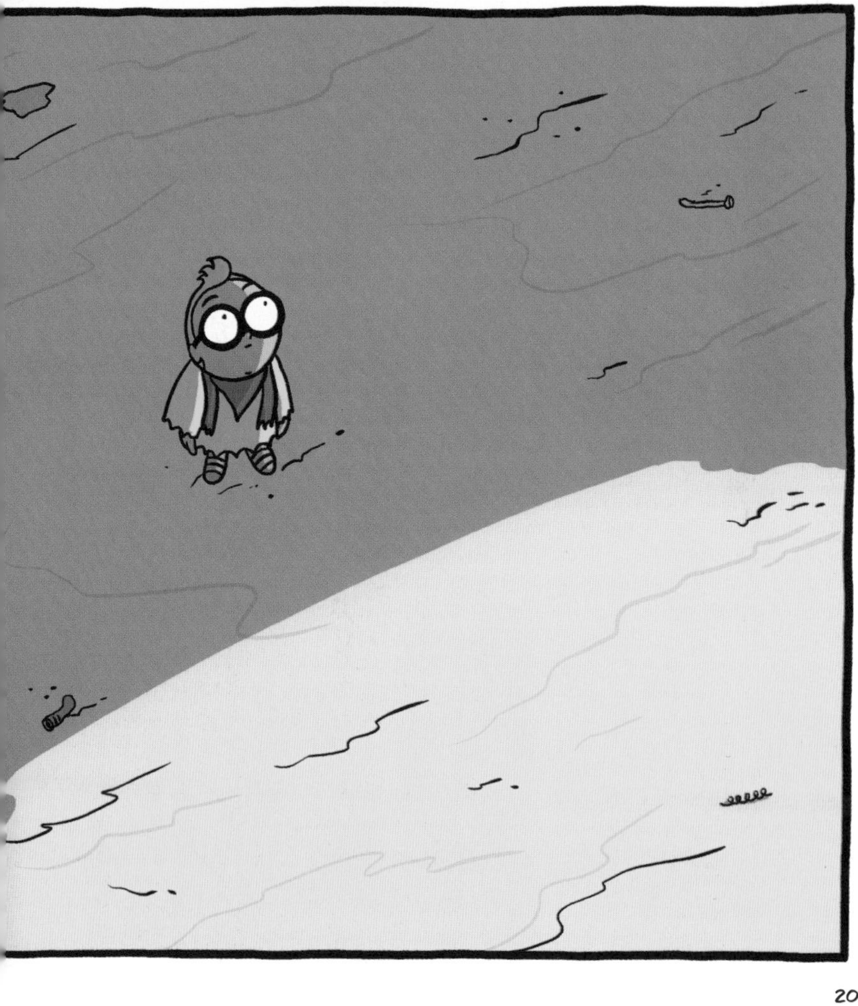

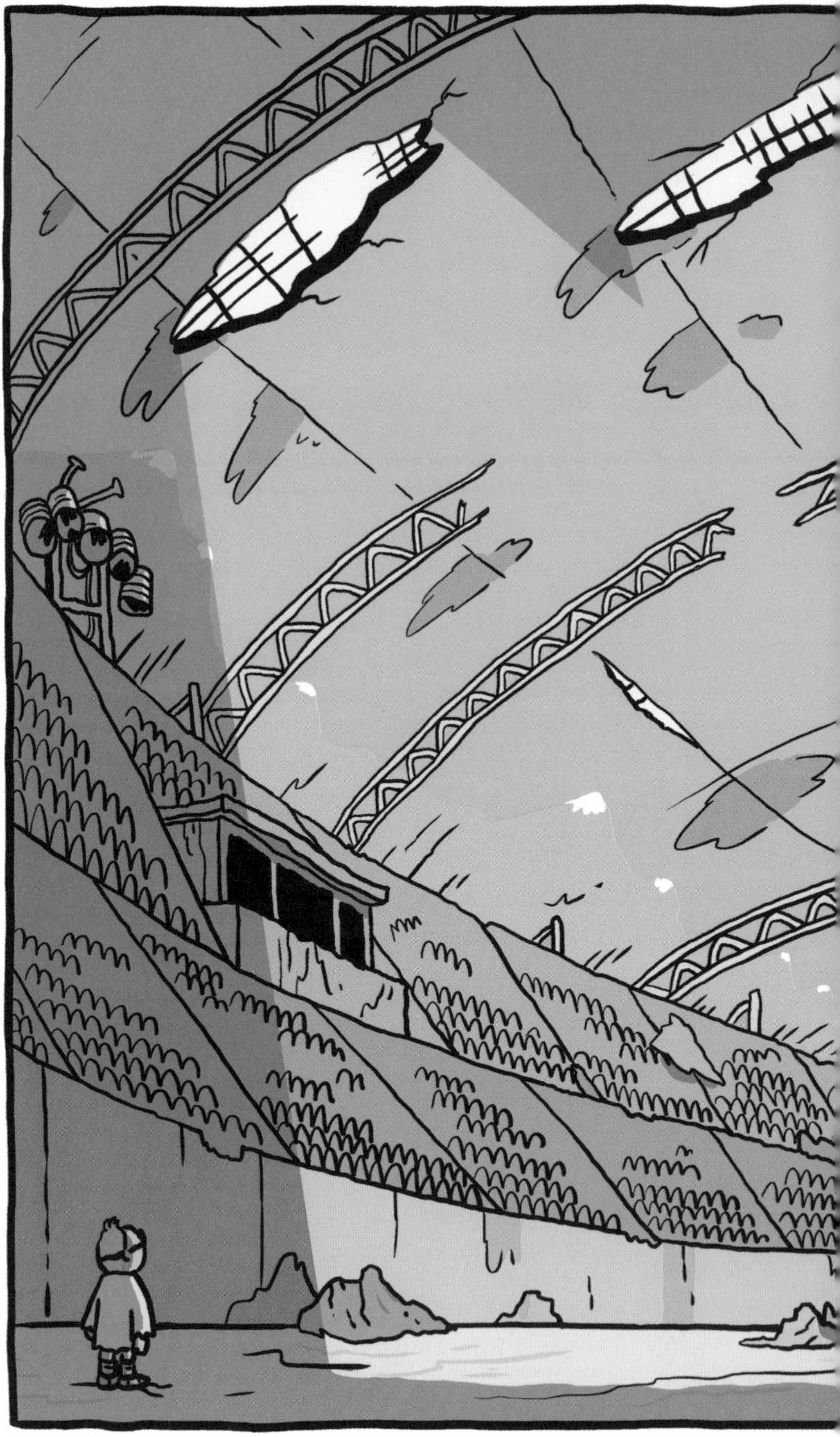

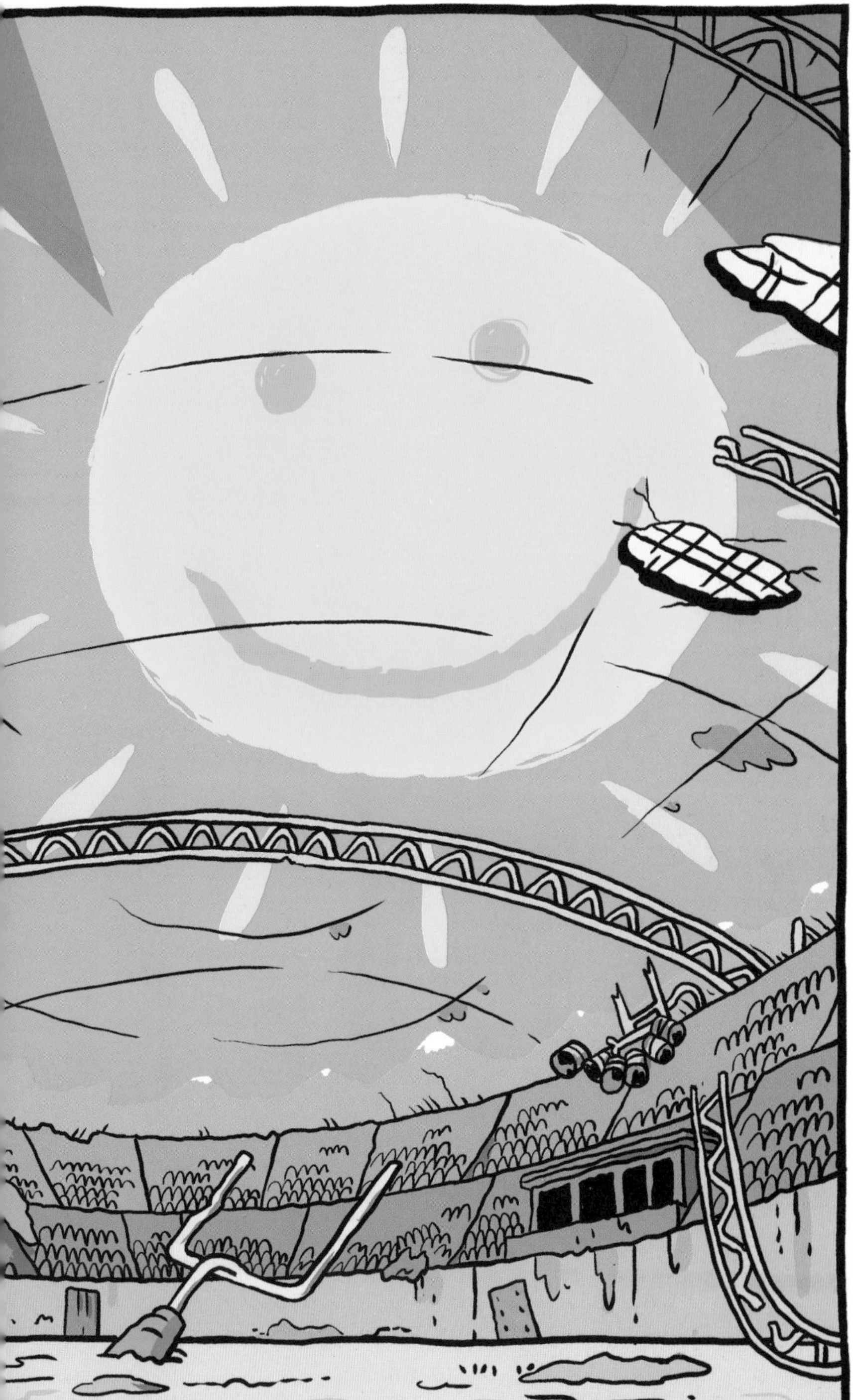

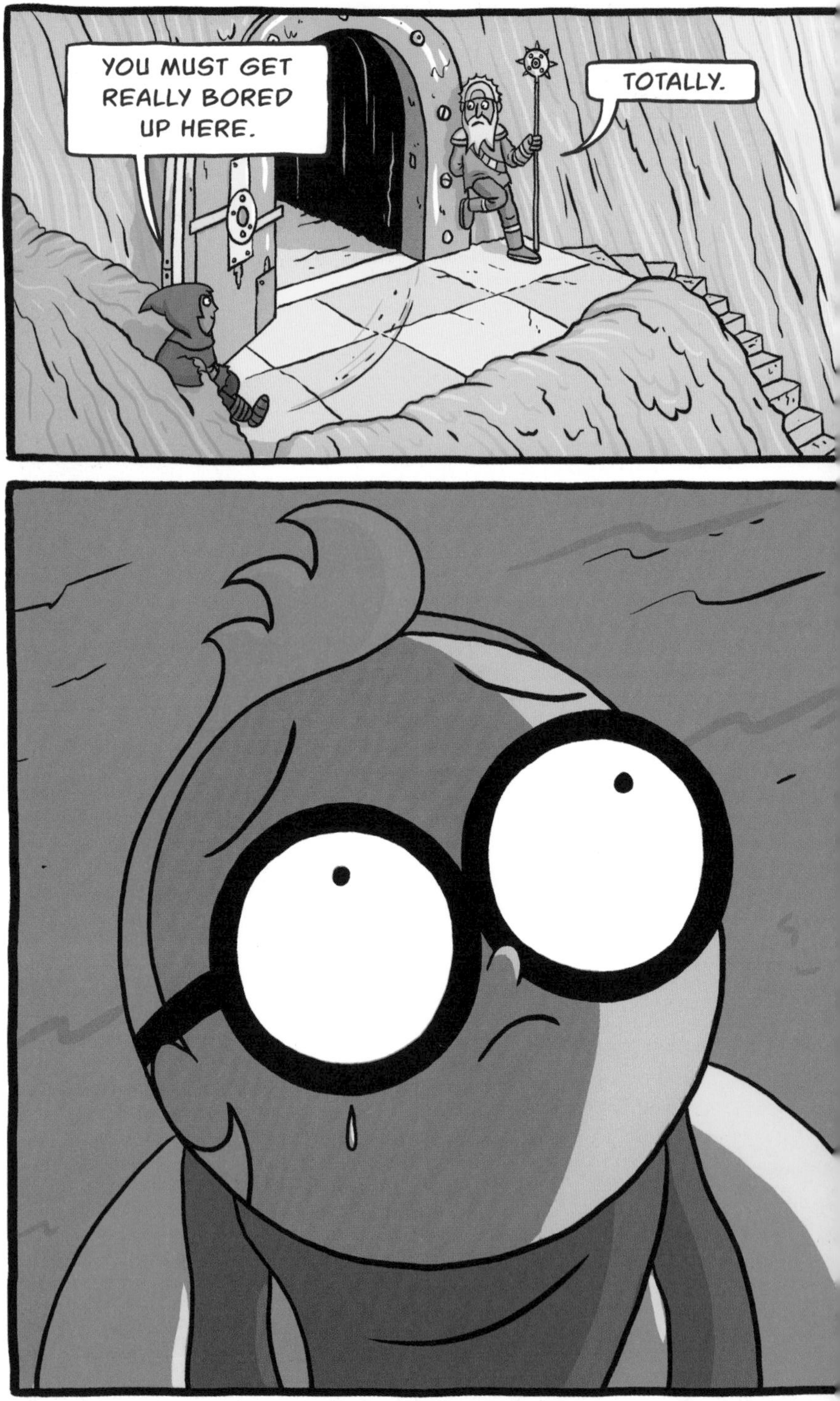
YOU MUST GET REALLY BORED UP HERE.
TOTALLY.

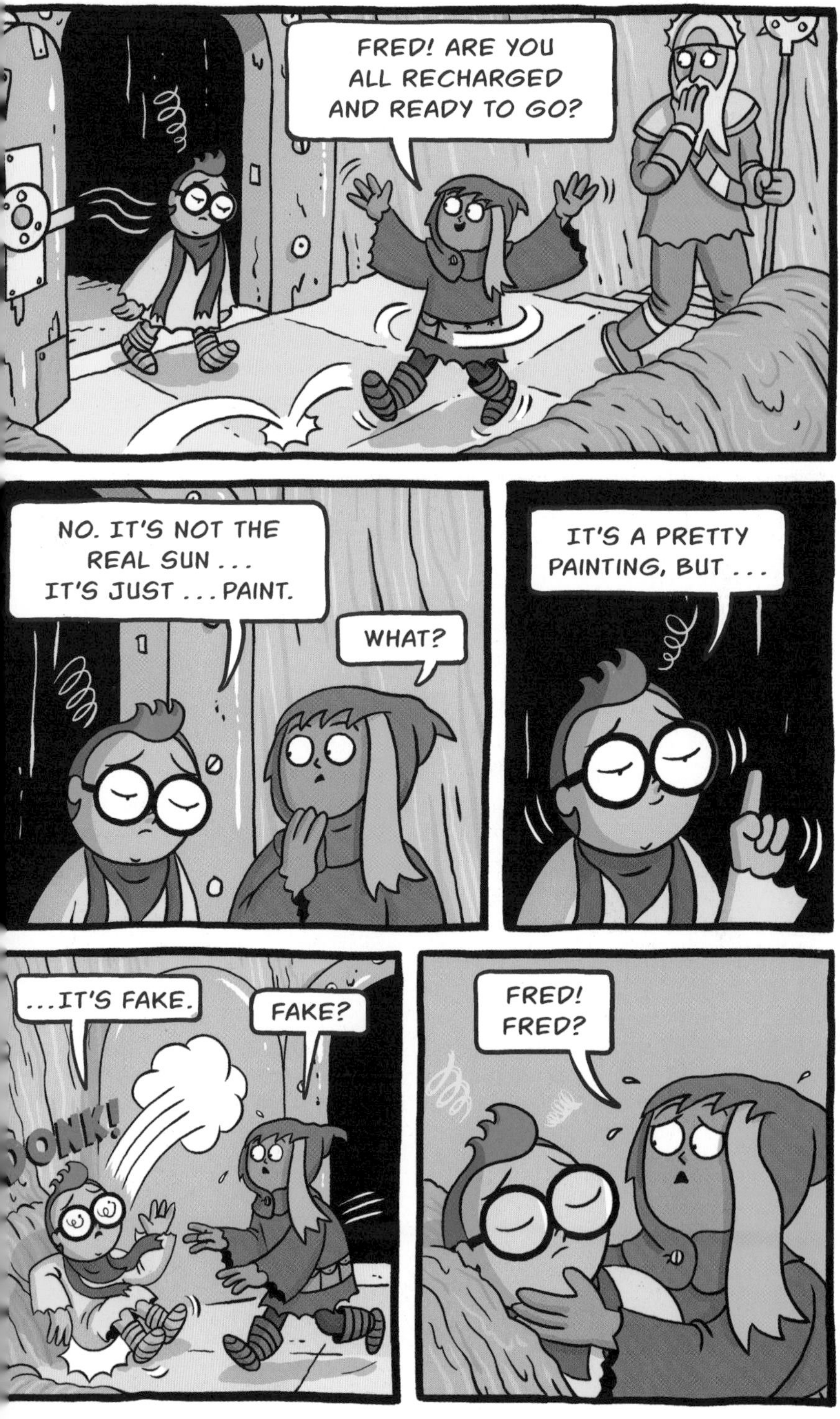
FRED! ARE YOU ALL RECHARGED AND READY TO GO?
NO. IT'S NOT THE REAL SUN . . . IT'S JUST . . . PAINT.
WHAT?
IT'S A PRETTY PAINTING, BUT . . .
. . . IT'S FAKE.
FAKE?
DONK!
FRED! FRED?

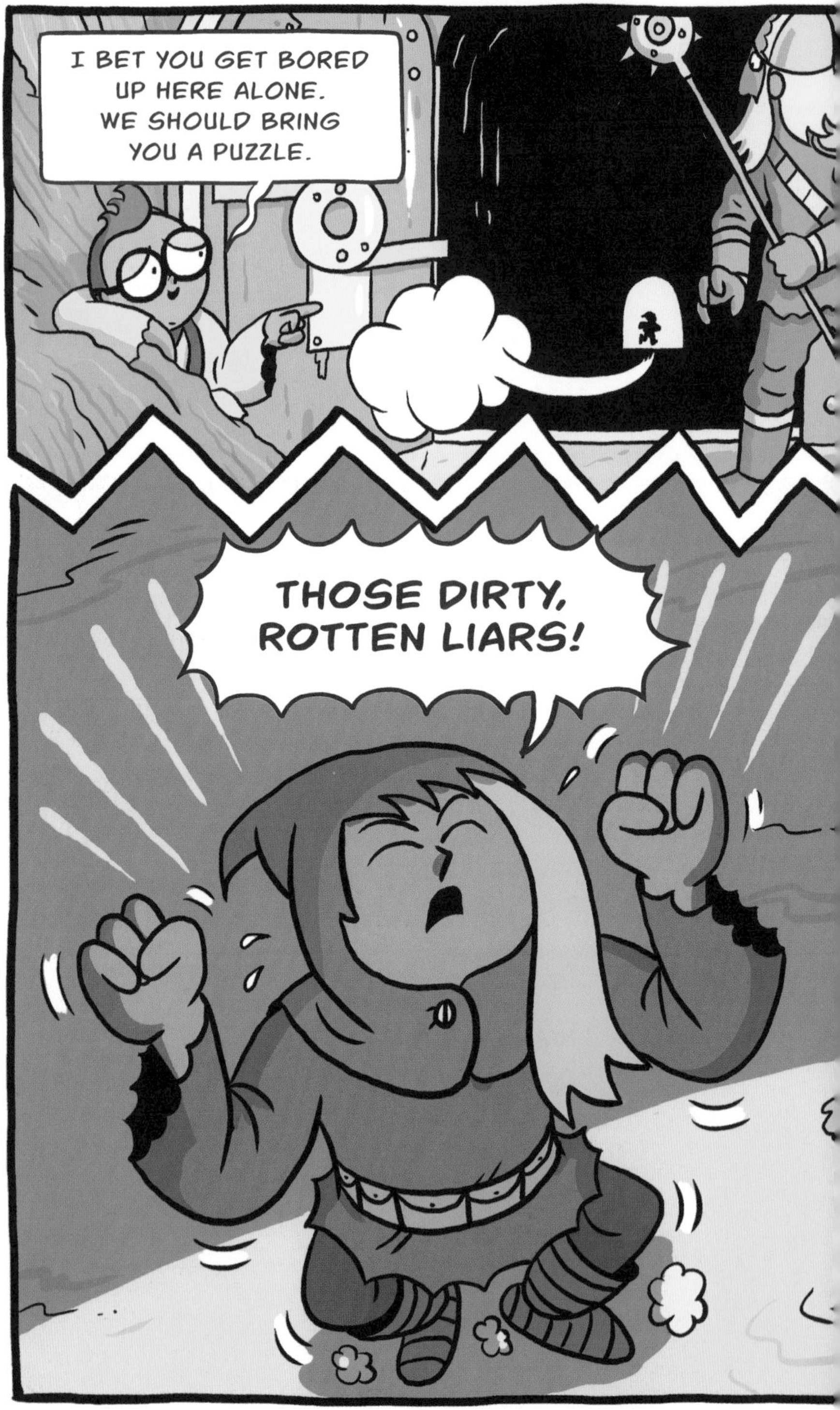
I BET YOU GET BORED UP HERE ALONE. WE SHOULD BRING YOU A PUZZLE.
THOSE DIRTY, ROTTEN LIARS!

CHAPTER 19

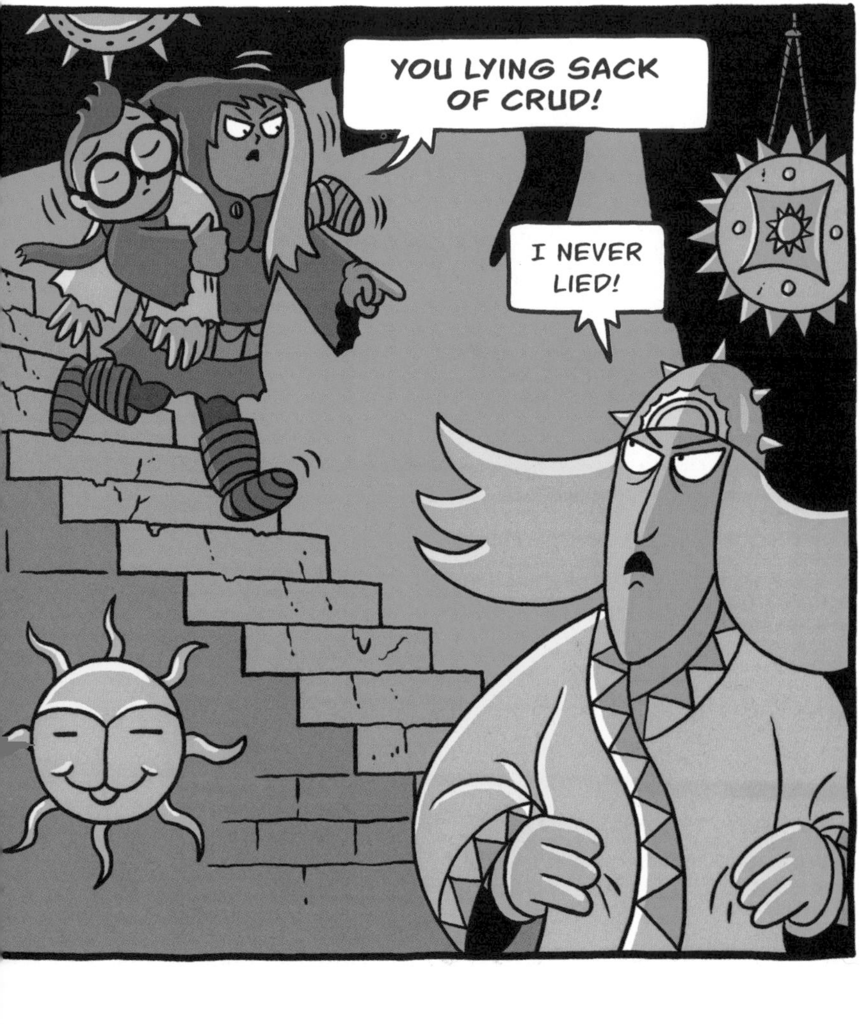

YOU LYING SACK OF CRUD!
I NEVER LIED!

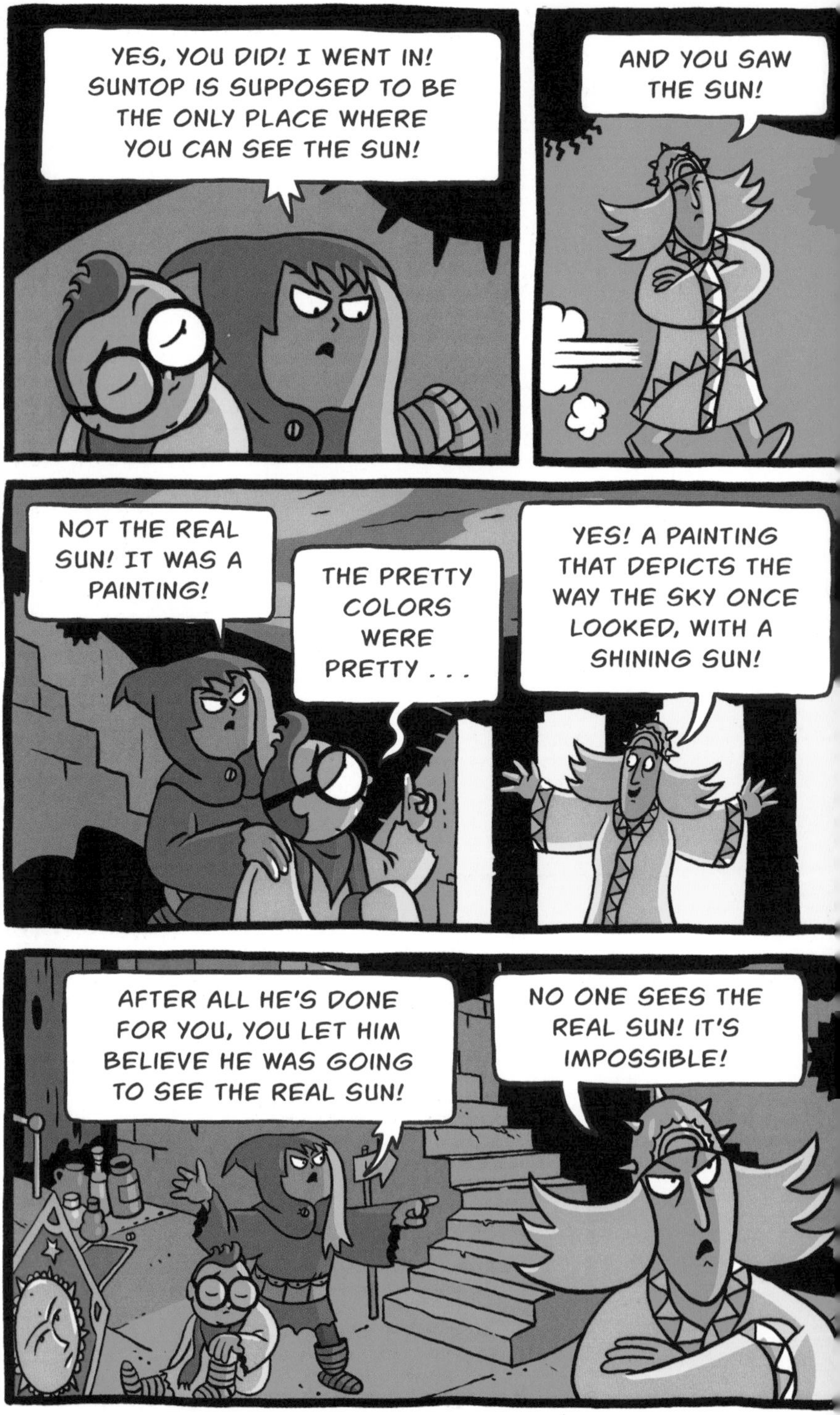
YES, YOU DID! I WENT IN! SUNTOP IS SUPPOSED TO BE THE ONLY PLACE WHERE YOU CAN SEE THE SUN!
AND YOU SAW THE SUN!
NOT THE REAL SUN! IT WAS A PAINTING!
THE PRETTY COLORS WERE PRETTY . . .
YES! A PAINTING THAT DEPICTS THE WAY THE SKY ONCE LOOKED, WITH A SHINING SUN!
AFTER ALL HE'S DONE FOR YOU, YOU LET HIM BELIEVE HE WAS GOING TO SEE THE REAL SUN!
NO ONE SEES THE REAL SUN! IT'S IMPOSSIBLE!

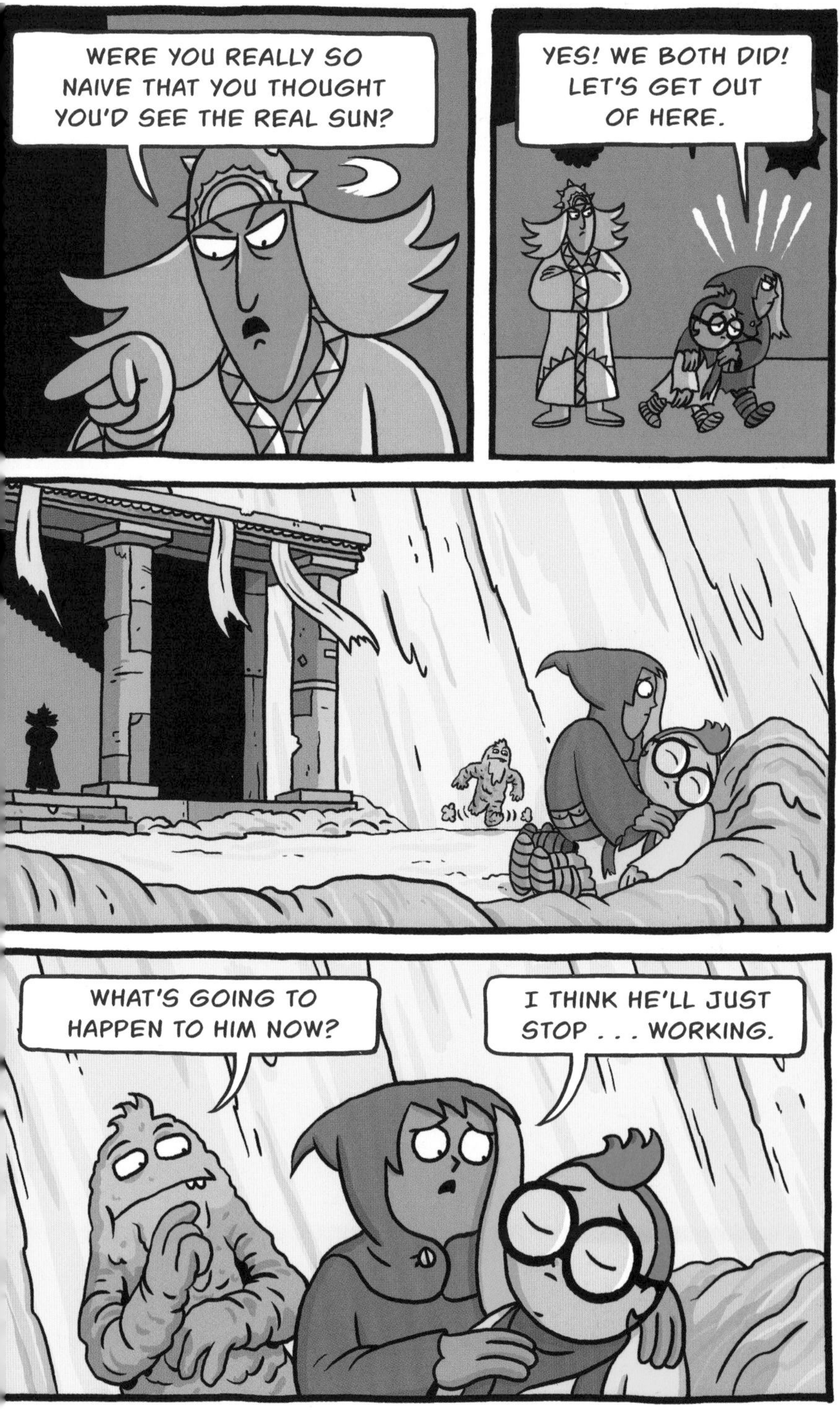
WERE YOU REALLY SO NAIVE THAT YOU THOUGHT YOU'D SEE THE REAL SUN?
YES! WE BOTH DID! LET'S GET OUT OF HERE.
WHAT'S GOING TO HAPPEN TO HIM NOW?
I THINK HE'LL JUST STOP . . . WORKING.

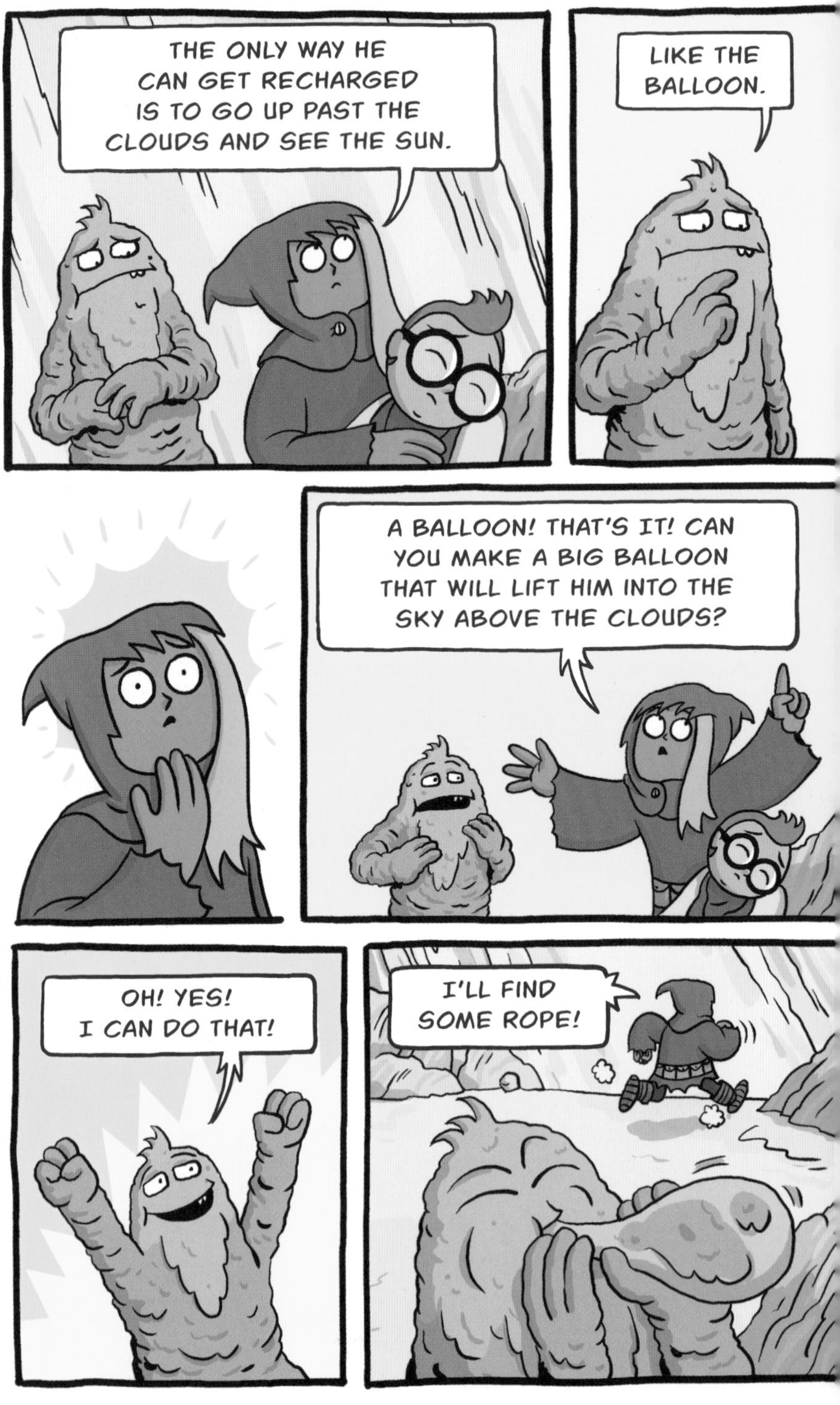
THE ONLY WAY HE CAN GET RECHARGED IS TO GO UP PAST THE CLOUDS AND SEE THE SUN.
LIKE THE BALLOON.
A BALLOON! THAT'S IT! CAN YOU MAKE A BIG BALLOON THAT WILL LIFT HIM INTO THE SKY ABOVE THE CLOUDS?
OH! YES! I CAN DO THAT!
I'LL FIND SOME ROPE!

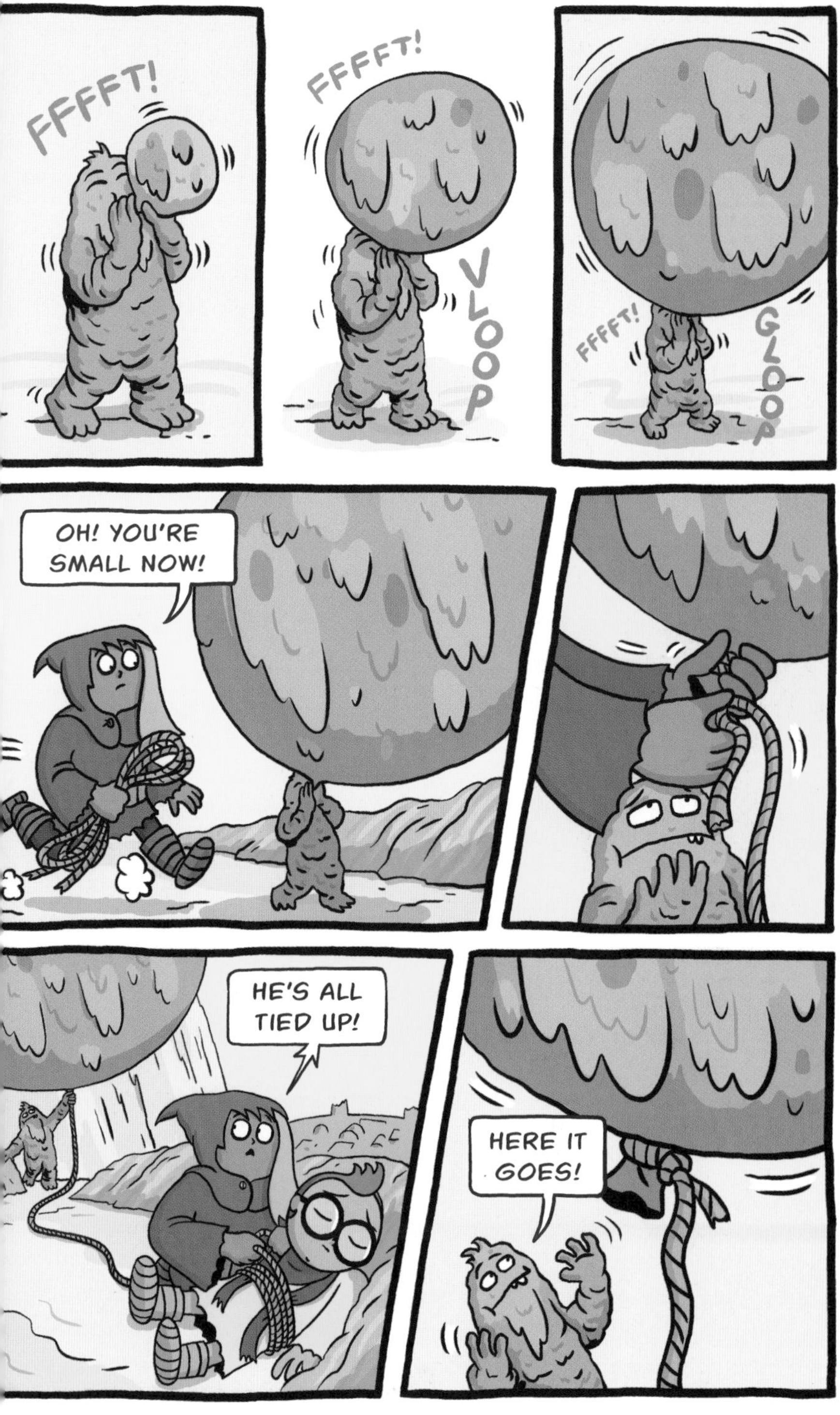
FFFFT!
FFFFT!
VLOOP
FFFFT!
GLOOP
OH! YOU'RE SMALL NOW!
HE'S ALL TIED UP!
HERE IT GOES!

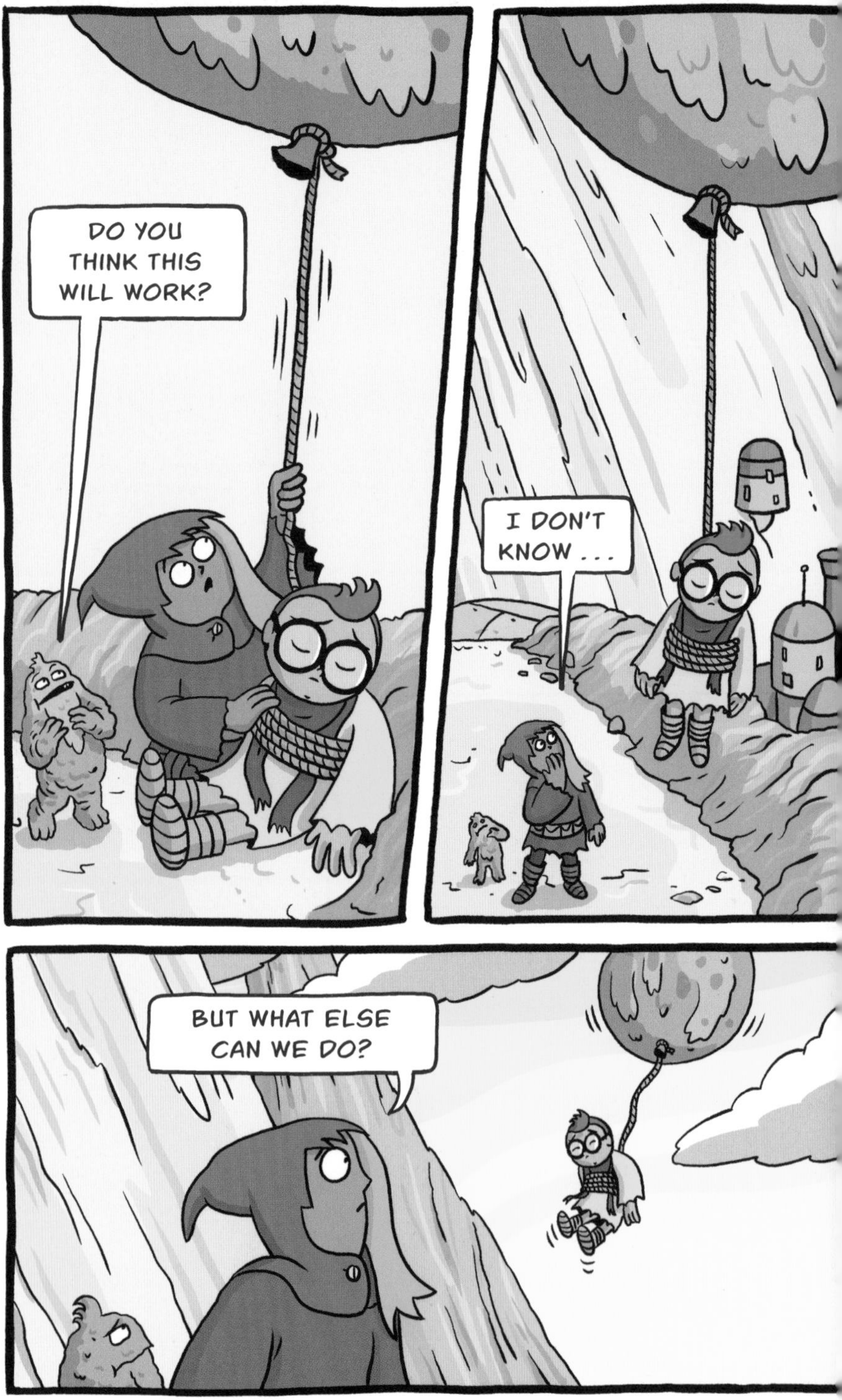
DO YOU THINK THIS WILL WORK?
I DON'T KNOW . . .
BUT WHAT ELSE CAN WE DO?

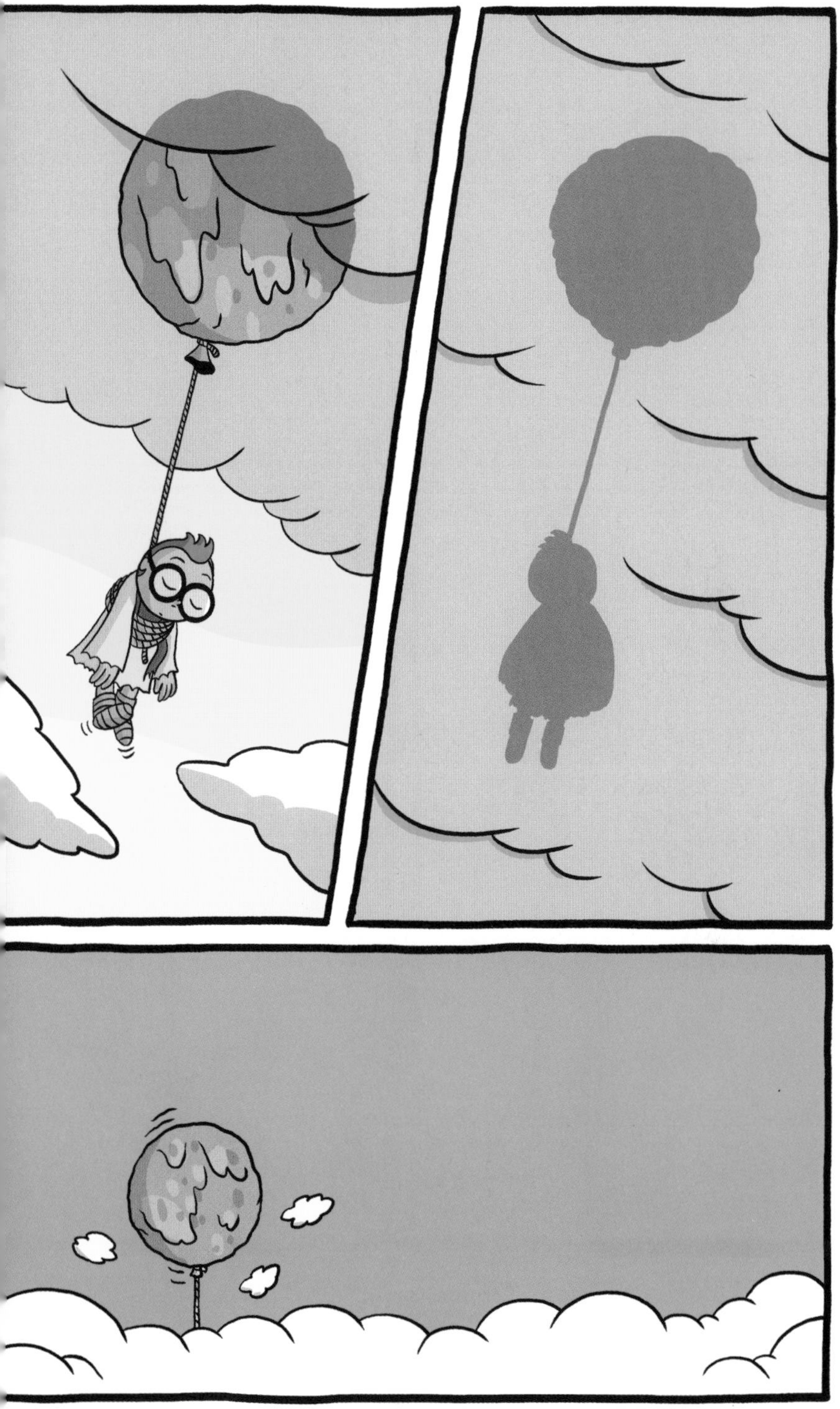

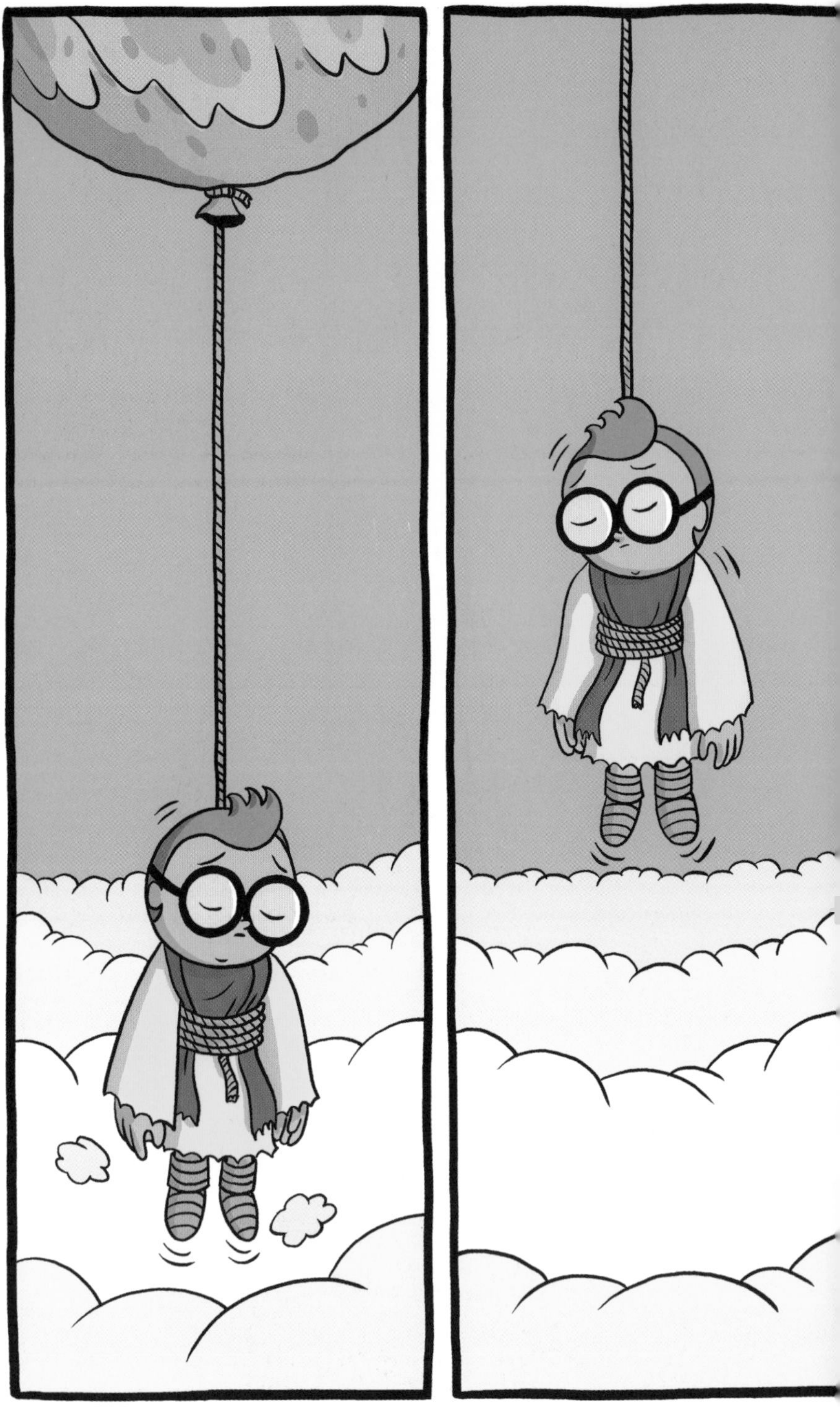

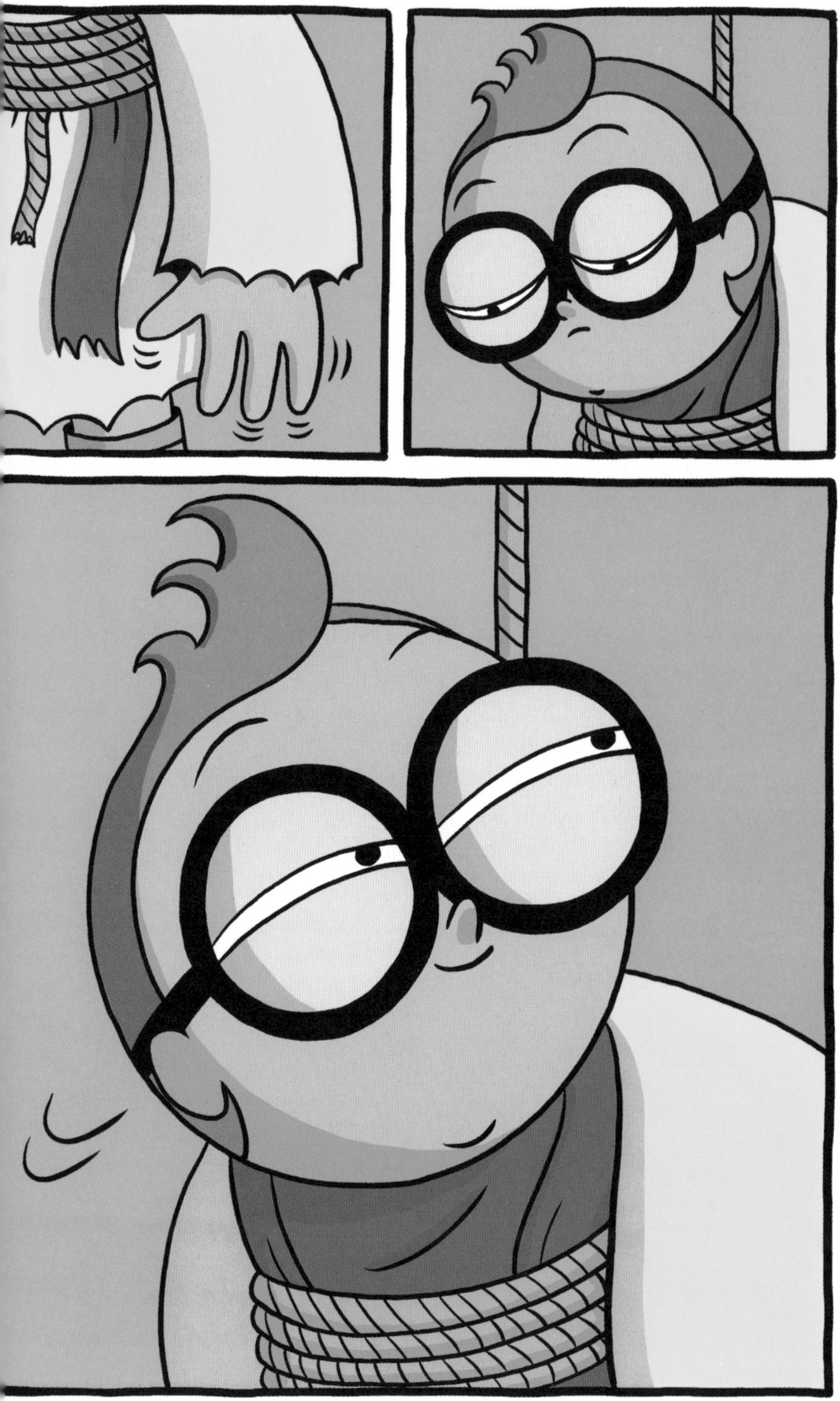

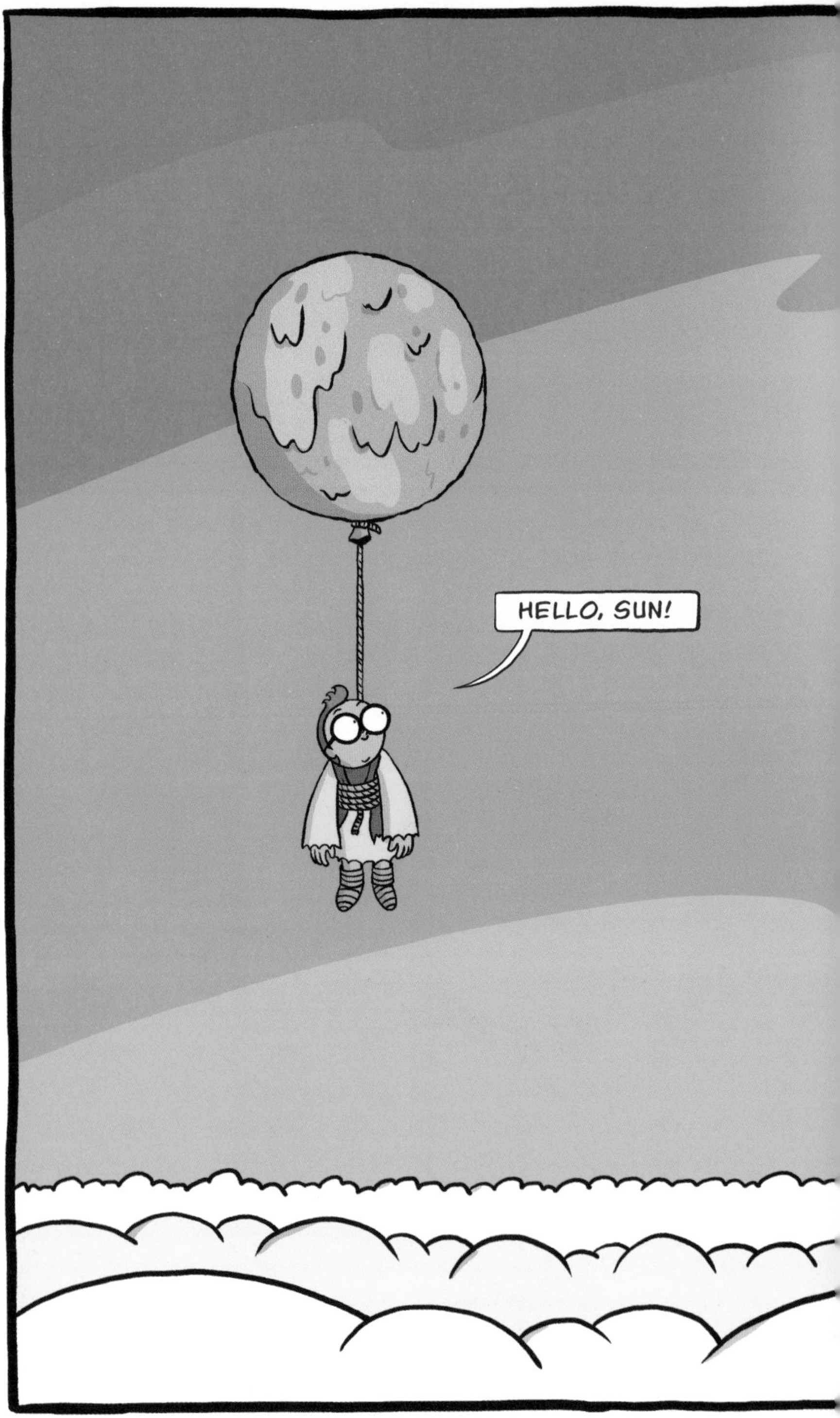
HELLO, SUN!

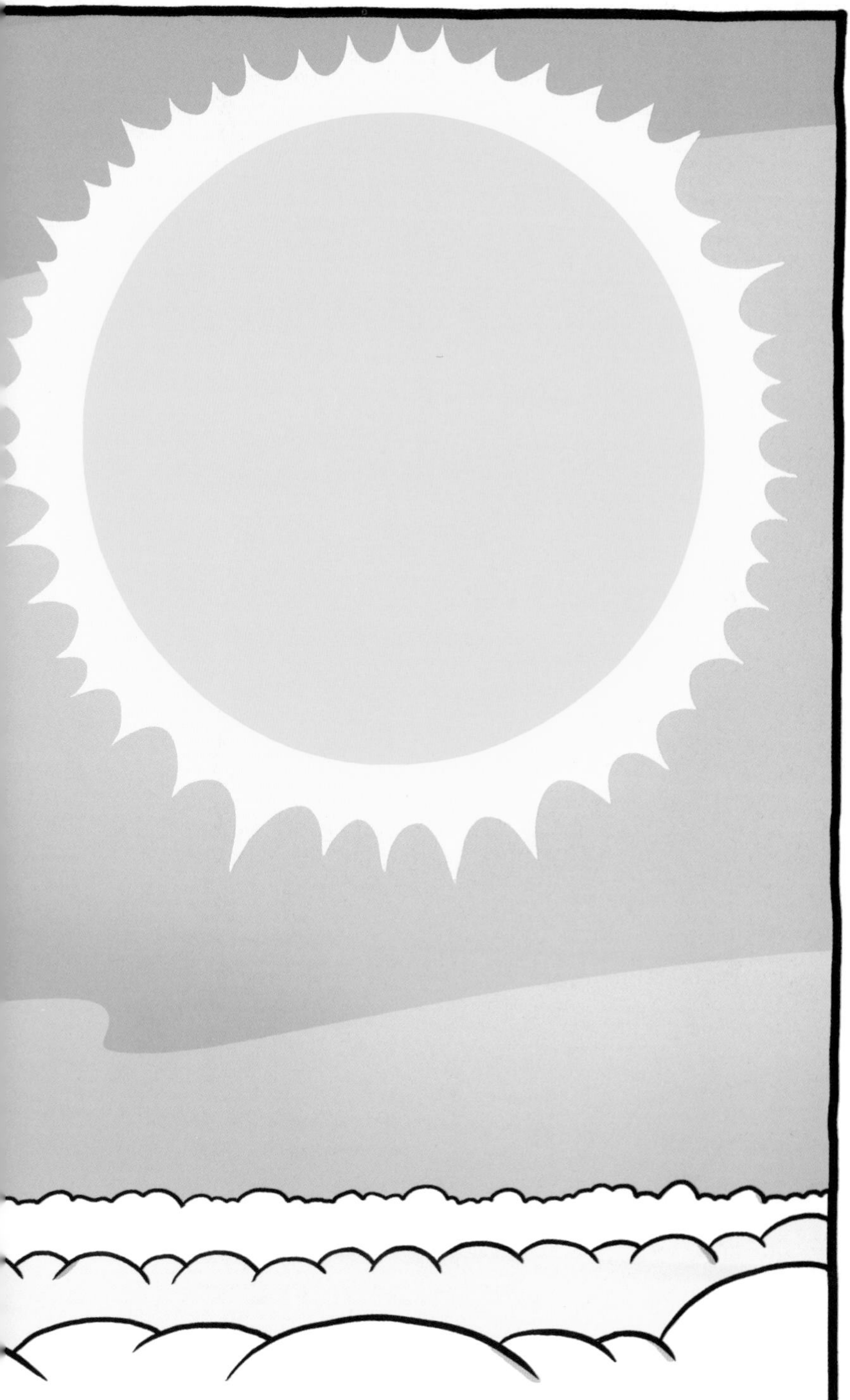

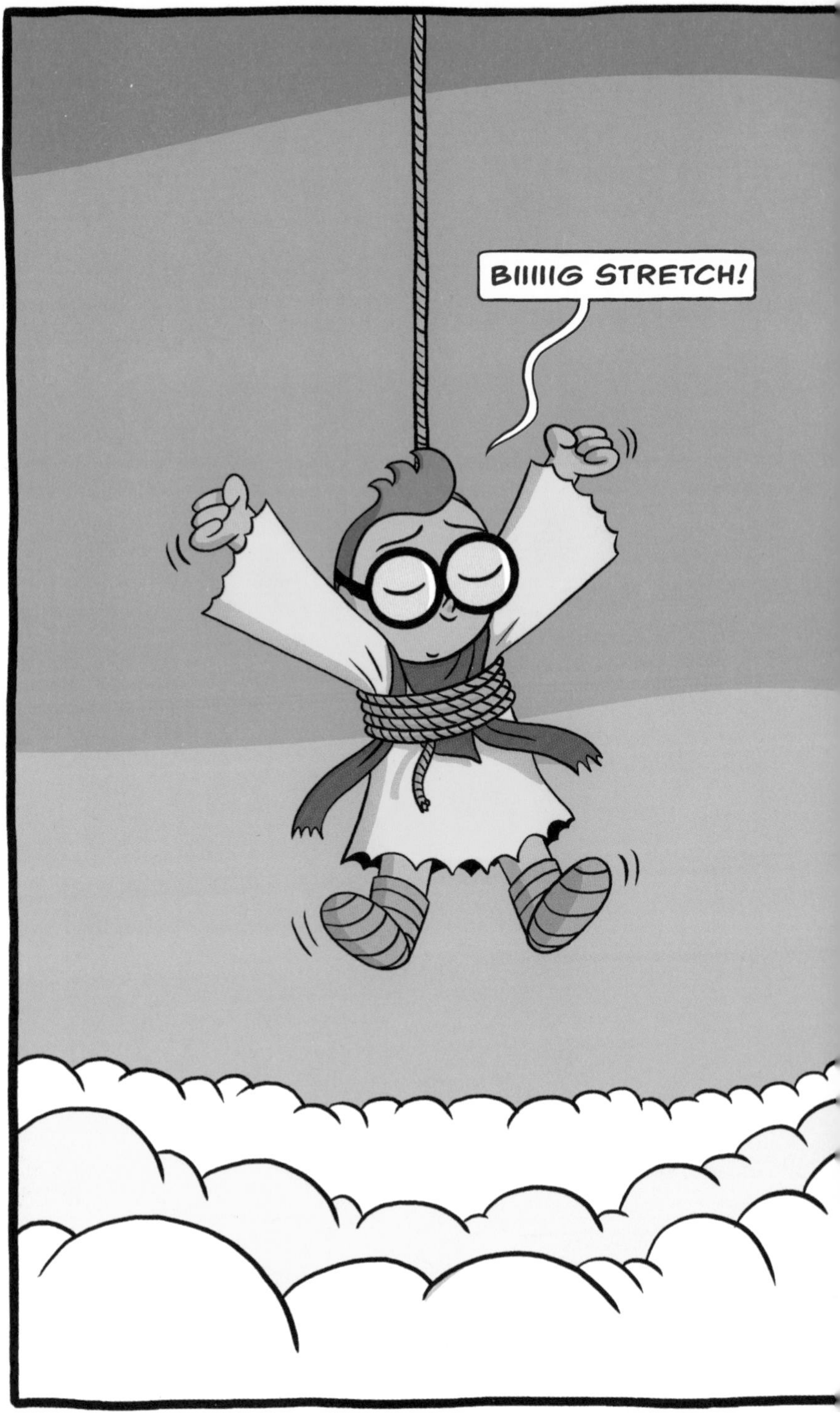
BIIIIIG STRETCH!

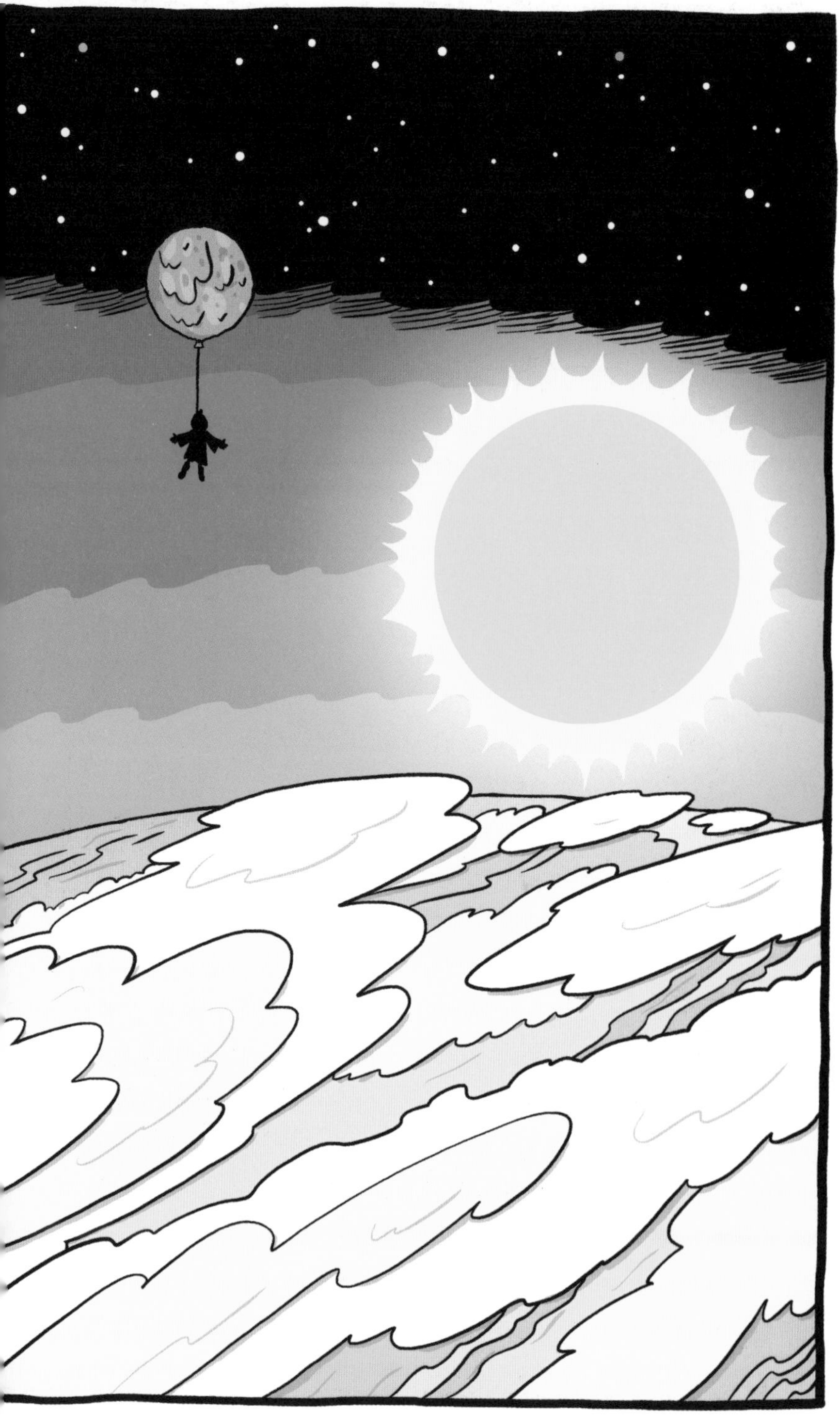

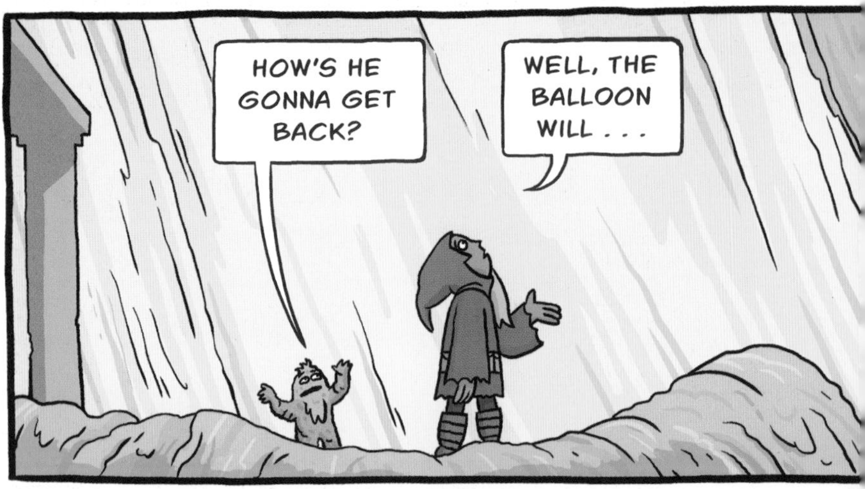
HOW'S HE GONNA GET BACK?
WELL, THE BALLOON WILL . . .

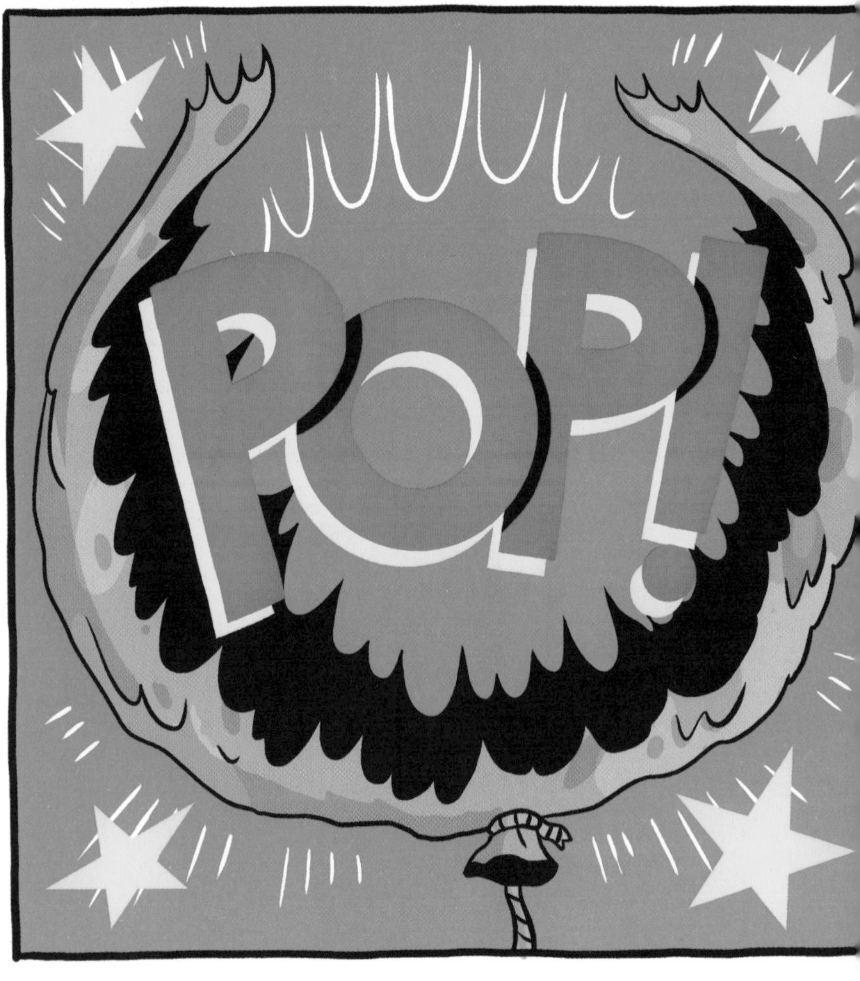
POP!

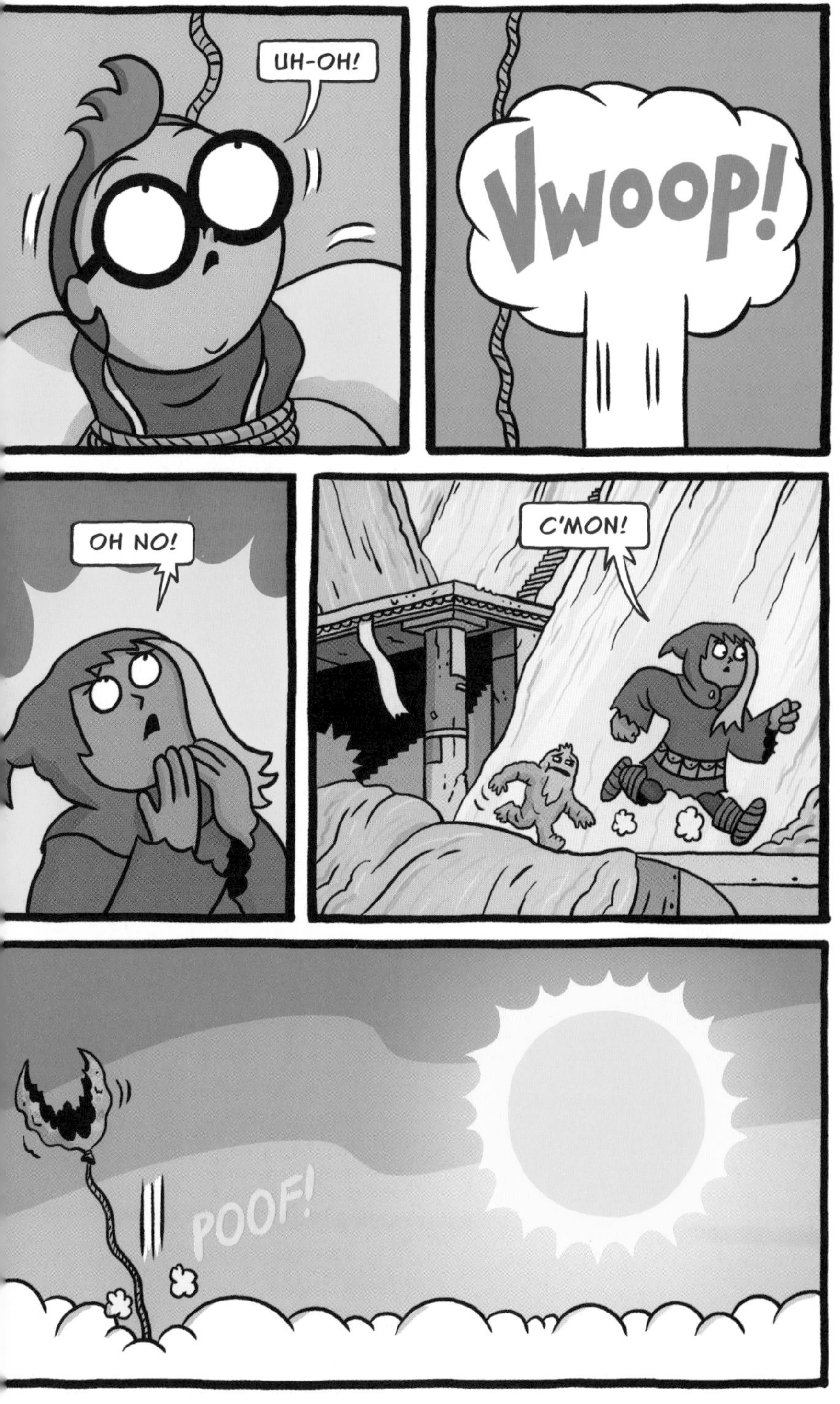
UH-OH!
VWOOP!
OH NO!
C'MON!
POOF!

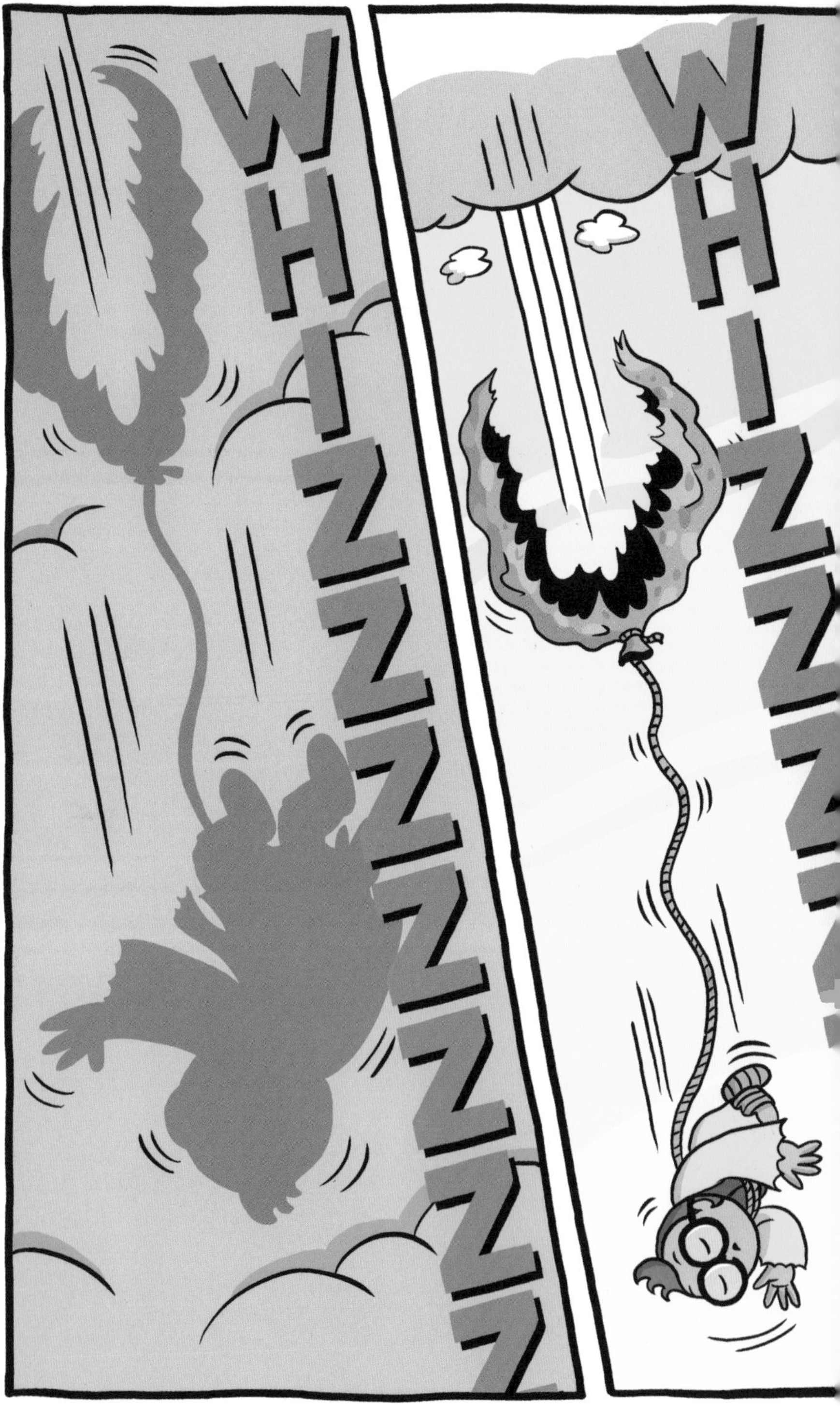
WHIZZZZZZZZ
WHIZZZ

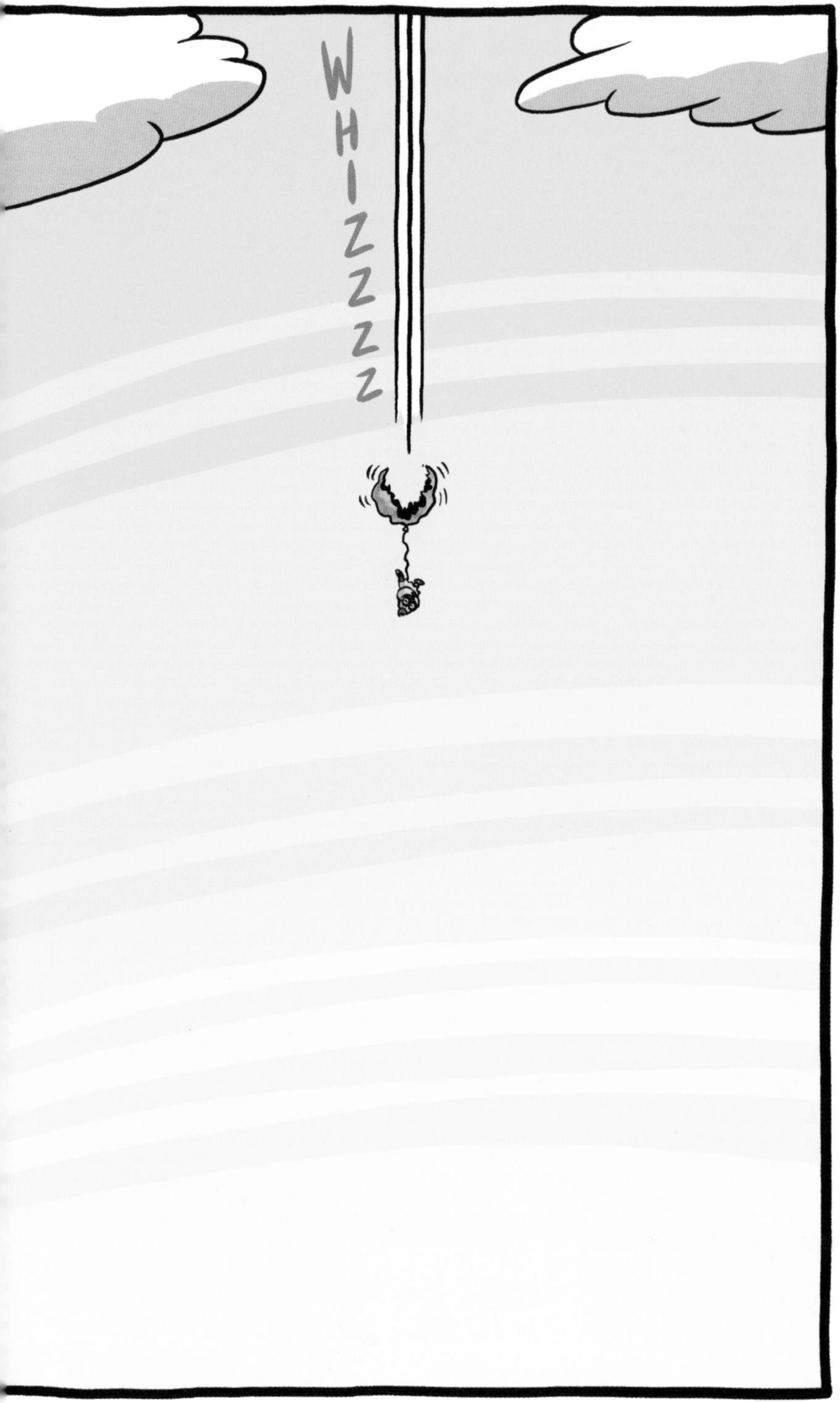
WHIZZZZ

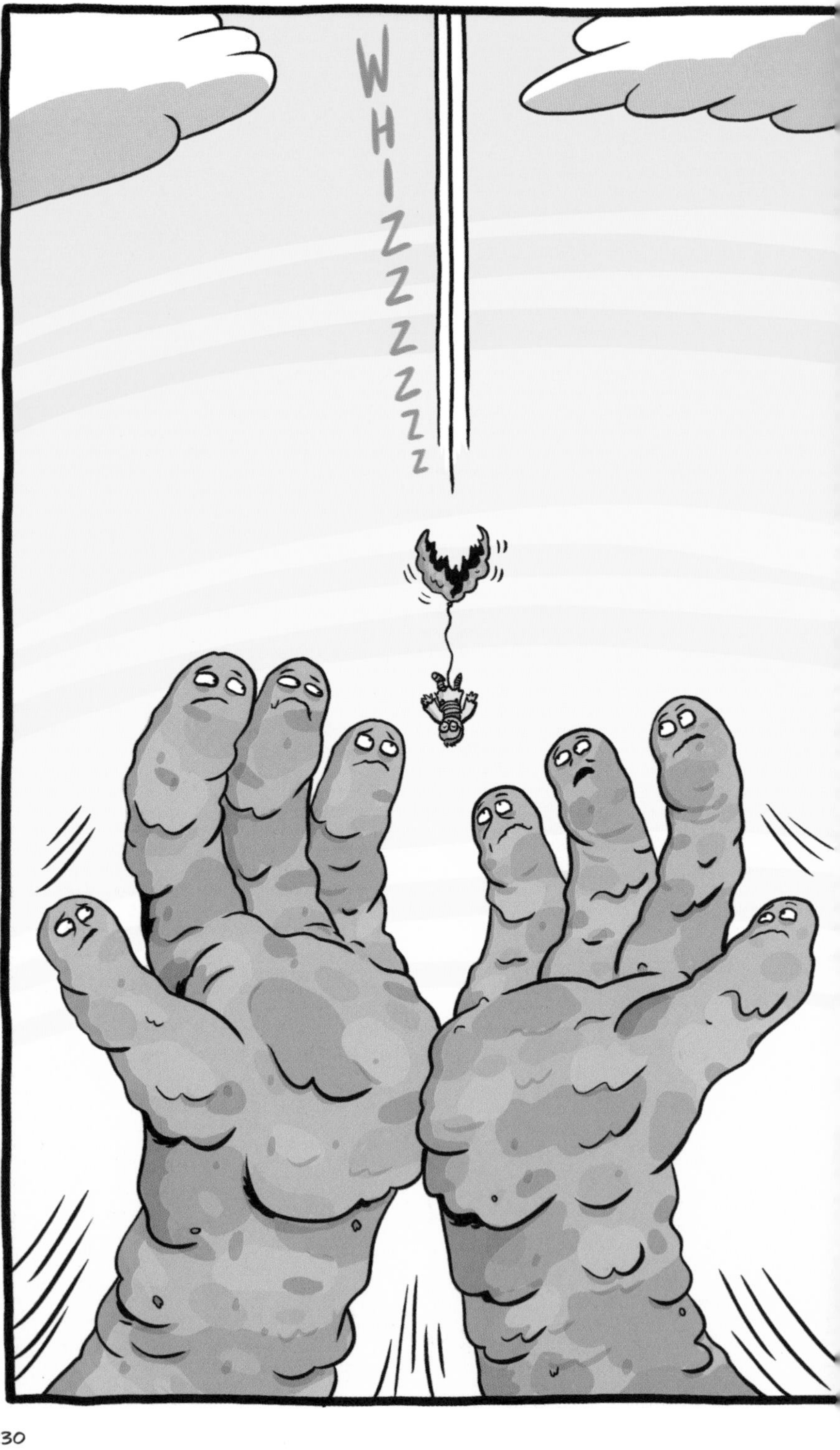
WHIZZZZZZ

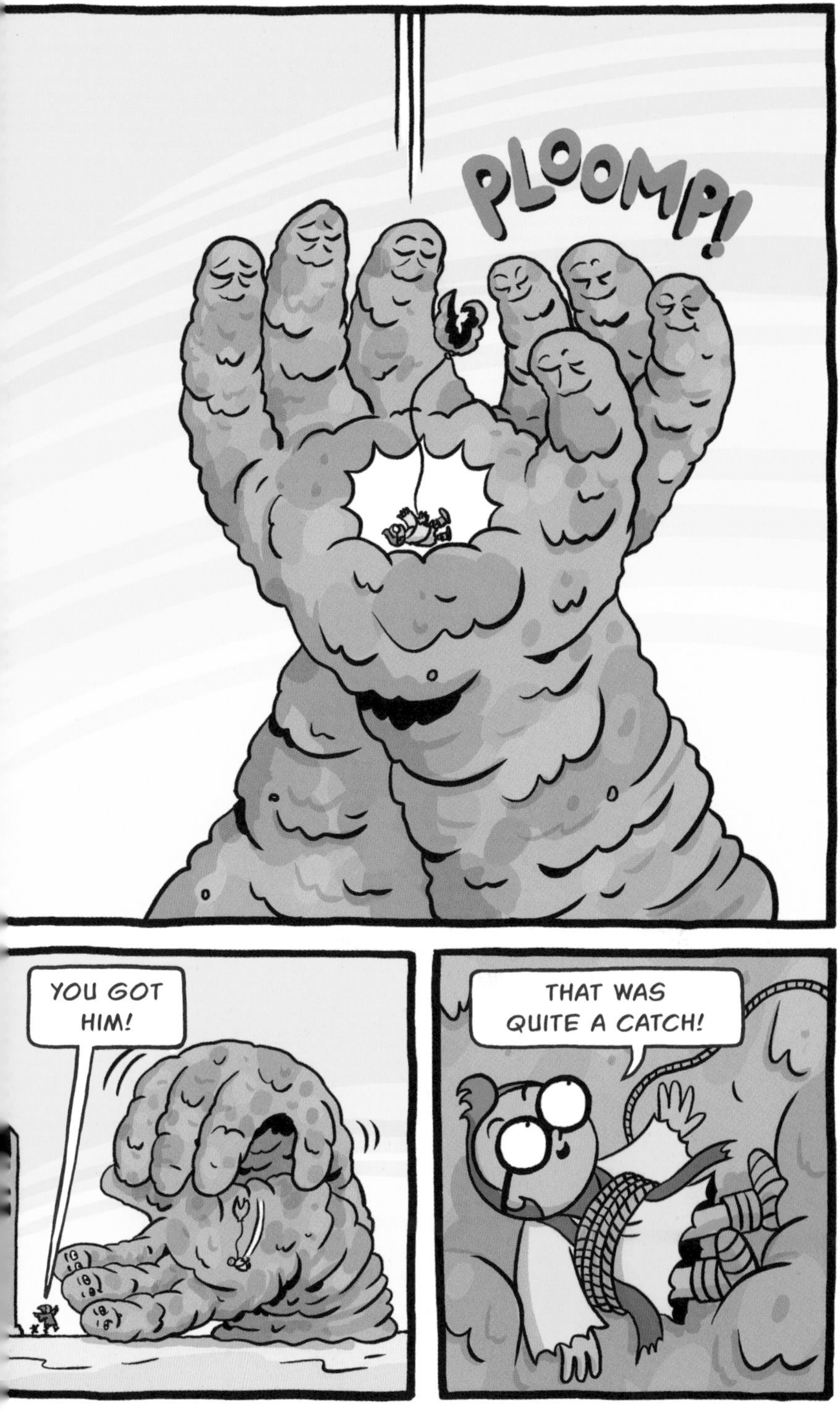
PLOOMP!
YOU GOT HIM!
THAT WAS QUITE A CATCH!

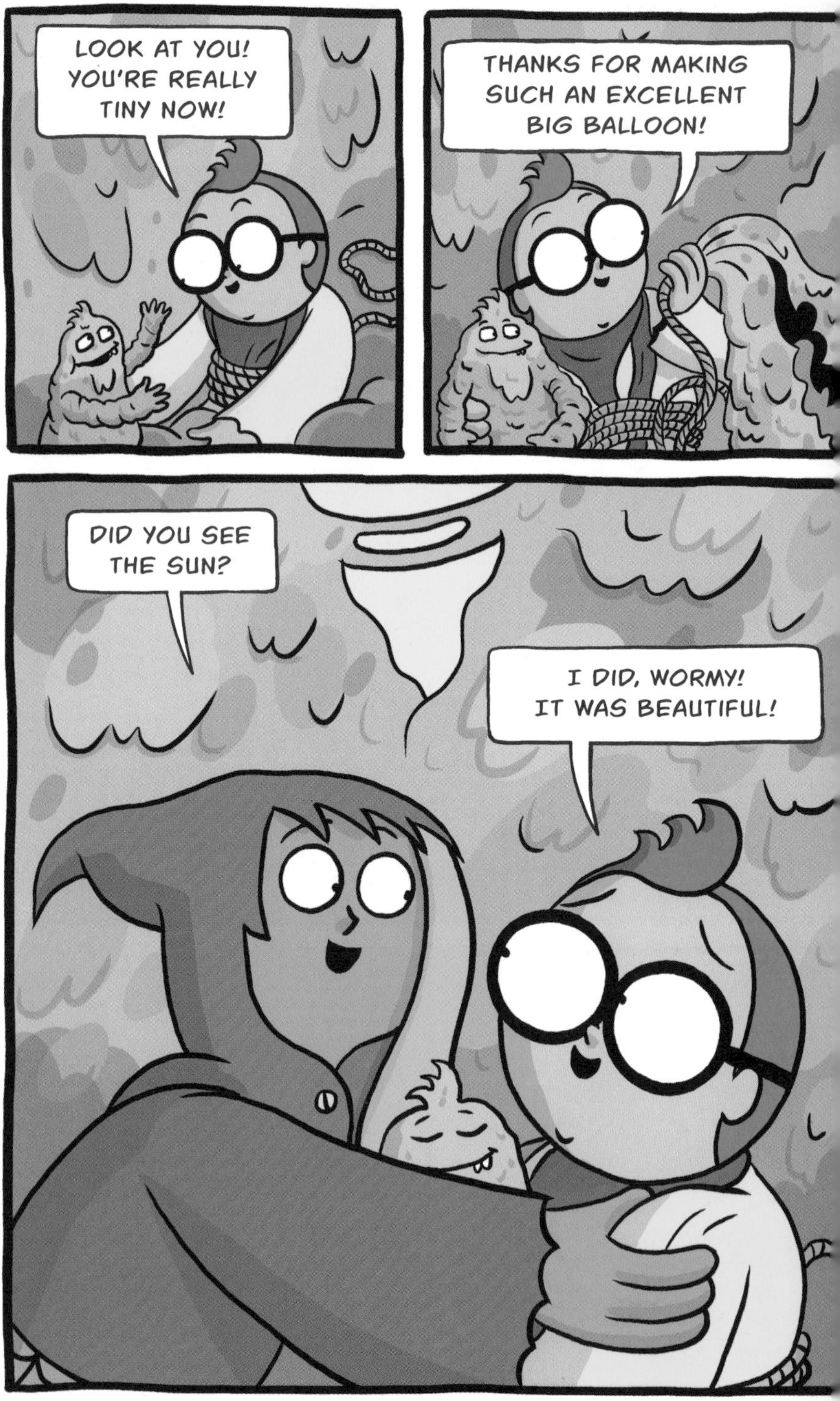
LOOK AT YOU! YOU'RE REALLY TINY NOW!
THANKS FOR MAKING SUCH AN EXCELLENT BIG BALLOON!
DID YOU SEE THE SUN?
I DID, WORMY! IT WAS BEAUTIFUL!

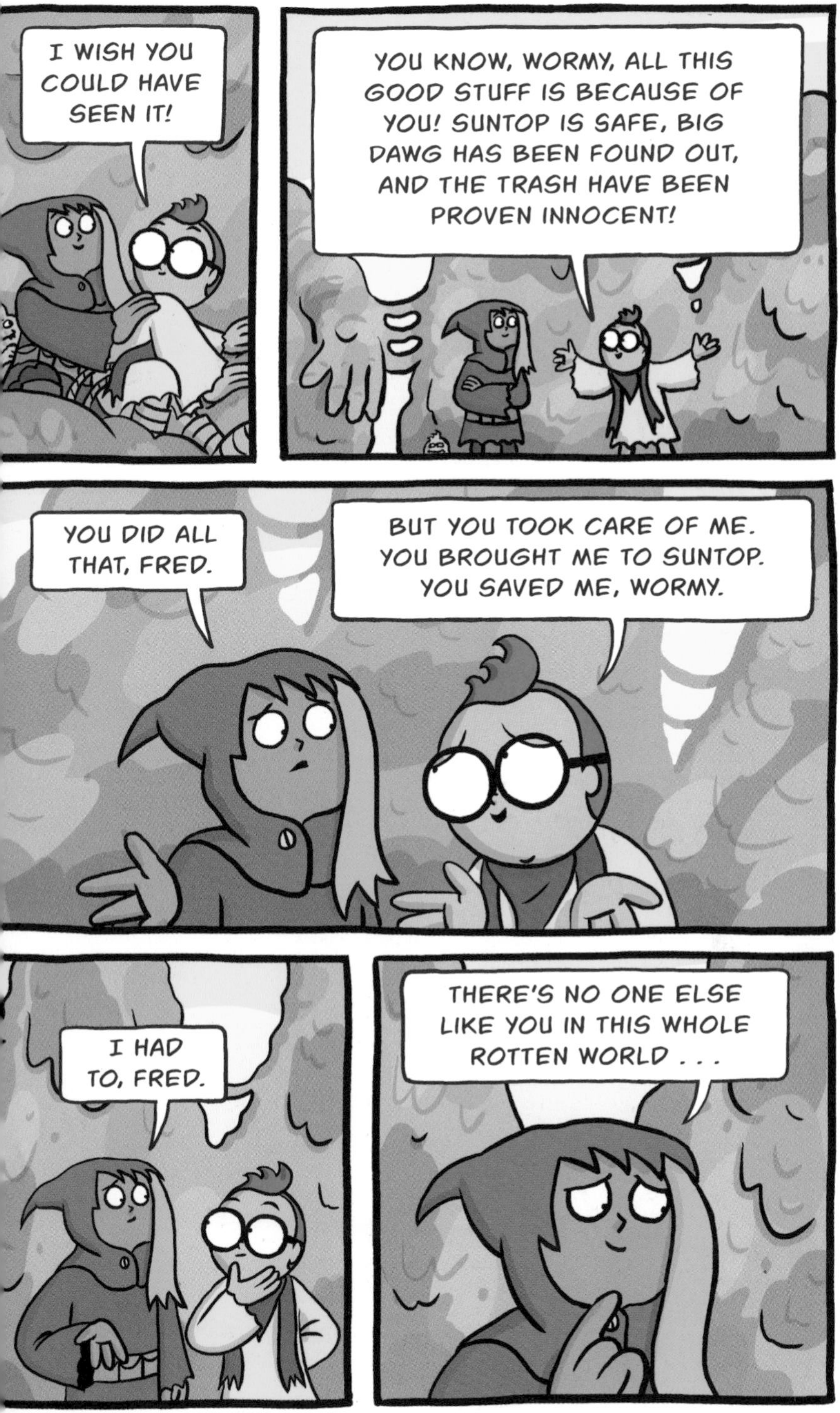
I WISH YOU COULD HAVE SEEN IT!
YOU KNOW, WORMY, ALL THIS GOOD STUFF IS BECAUSE OF YOU! SUNTOP IS SAFE, BIG DAWG HAS BEEN FOUND OUT, AND THE TRASH HAVE BEEN PROVEN INNOCENT!
YOU DID ALL THAT, FRED.
BUT YOU TOOK CARE OF ME. YOU BROUGHT ME TO SUNTOP. YOU SAVED ME, WORMY.
I HAD TO, FRED.
THERE'S NO ONE ELSE LIKE YOU IN THIS WHOLE ROTTEN WORLD . . .

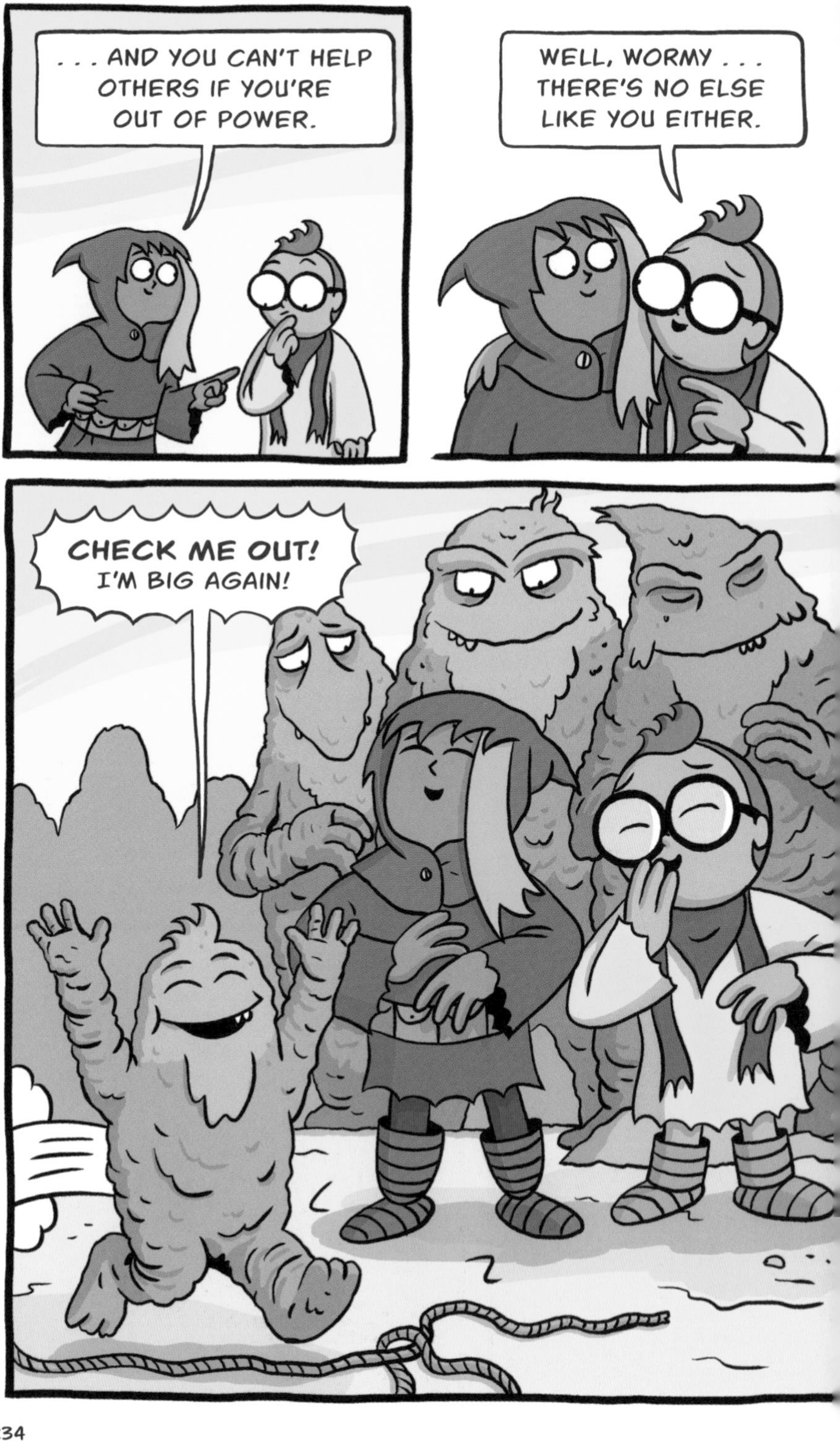
. . . AND YOU CAN'T HELP OTHERS IF YOU'RE OUT OF POWER.
WELL, WORMY . . . THERE'S NO ELSE LIKE YOU EITHER.
CHECK ME OUT! I'M BIG AGAIN!

CHAPTER 20

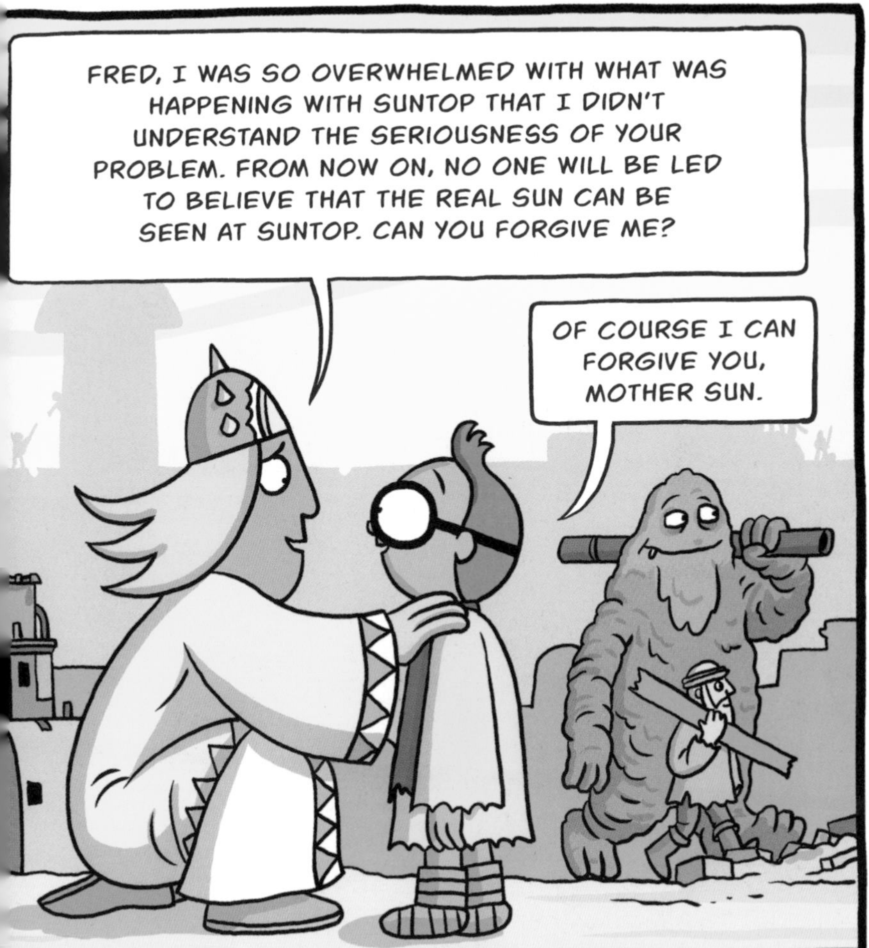

FRED, I WAS SO OVERWHELMED WITH WHAT WAS HAPPENING WITH SUNTOP THAT I DIDN'T UNDERSTAND THE SERIOUSNESS OF YOUR PROBLEM. FROM NOW ON, NO ONE WILL BE LED TO BELIEVE THAT THE REAL SUN CAN BE SEEN AT SUNTOP. CAN YOU FORGIVE ME?
OF COURSE I CAN FORGIVE YOU, MOTHER SUN.

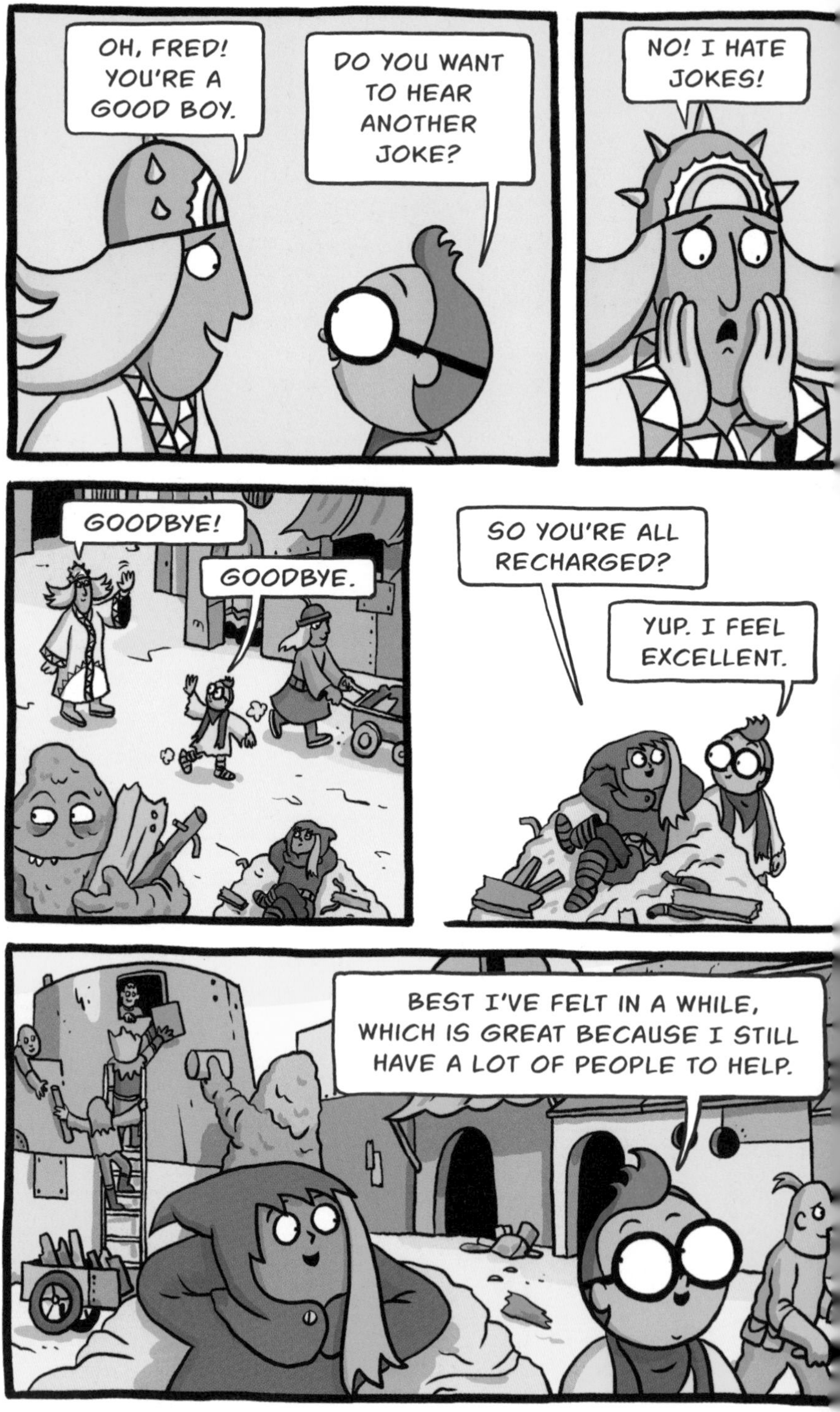
OH, FRED! YOU'RE A GOOD BOY.
DO YOU WANT TO HEAR ANOTHER JOKE?
NO! I HATE JOKES!
GOODBYE!
GOODBYE.
SO YOU'RE ALL RECHARGED?
YUP. I FEEL EXCELLENT.
BEST I'VE FELT IN A WHILE, WHICH IS GREAT BECAUSE I STILL HAVE A LOT OF PEOPLE TO HELP.

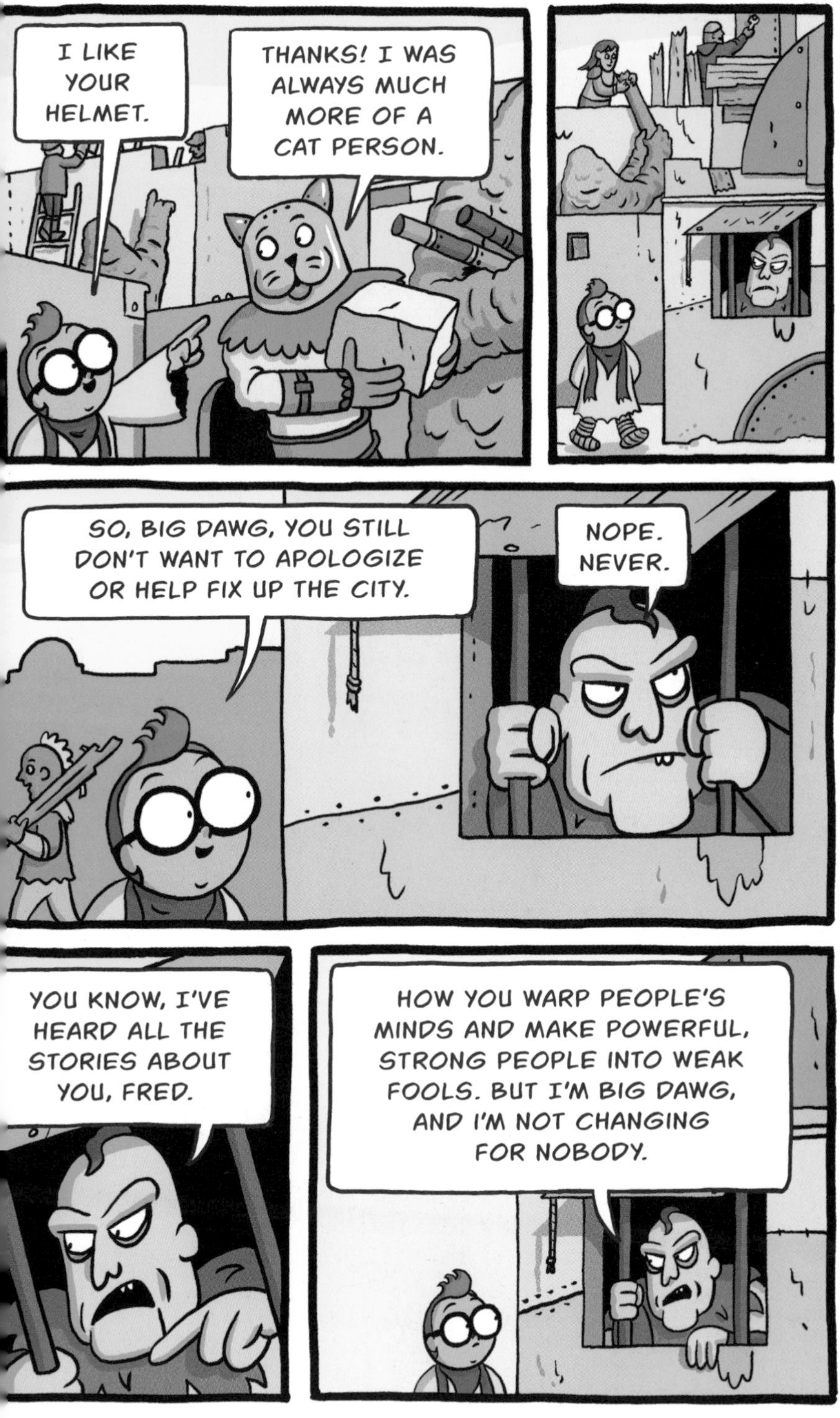
I LIKE YOUR HELMET.
THANKS! I WAS ALWAYS MUCH MORE OF A CAT PERSON.
SO, BIG DAWG, YOU STILL DON'T WANT TO APOLOGIZE OR HELP FIX UP THE CITY.
NOPE. NEVER.
YOU KNOW, I'VE HEARD ALL THE STORIES ABOUT YOU, FRED.
HOW YOU WARP PEOPLE'S MINDS AND MAKE POWERFUL, STRONG PEOPLE INTO WEAK FOOLS. BUT I'M BIG DAWG, AND I'M NOT CHANGING FOR NOBODY.

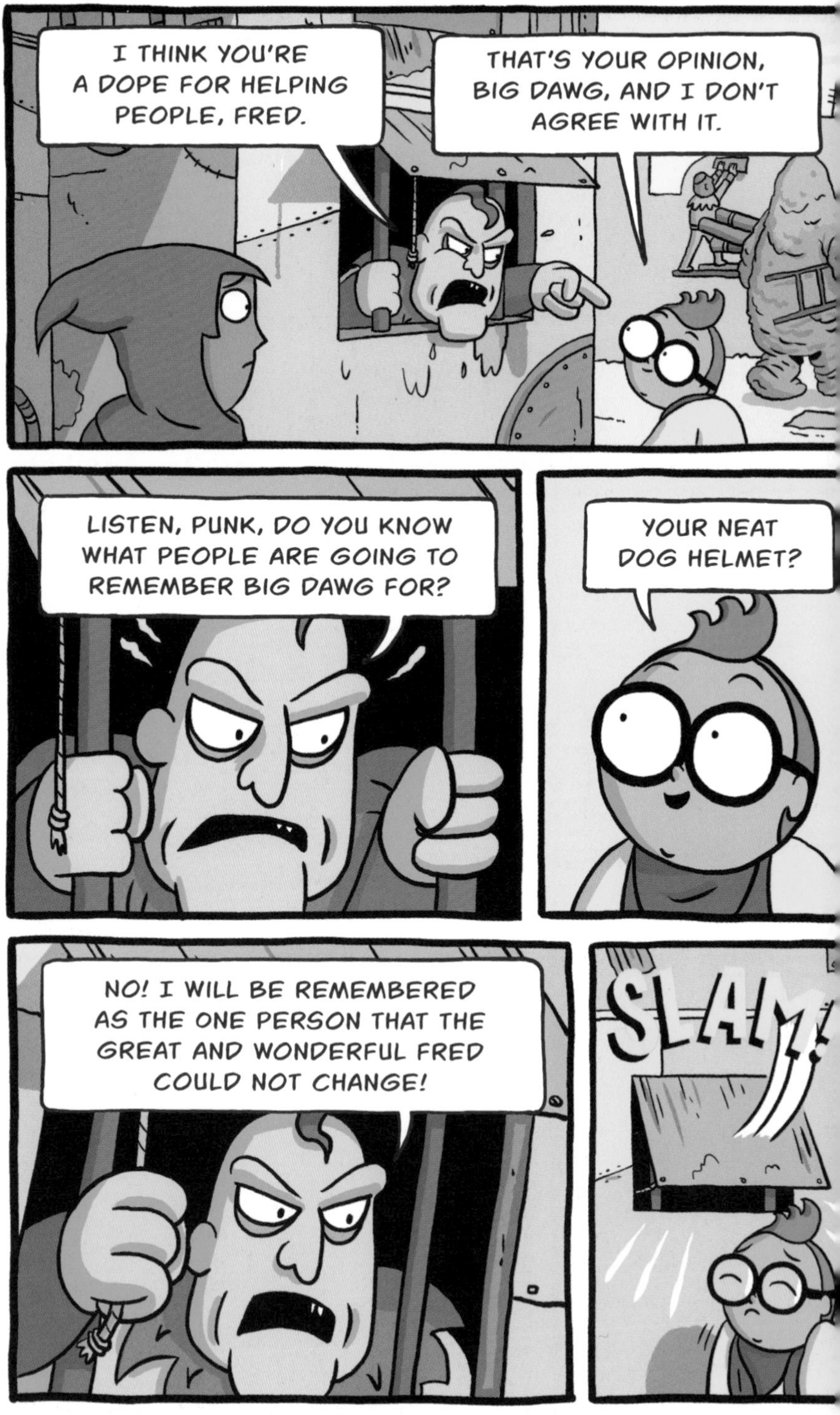
I THINK YOU'RE A DOPE FOR HELPING PEOPLE, FRED.
THAT'S YOUR OPINION, BIG DAWG, AND I DON'T AGREE WITH IT.
LISTEN, PUNK, DO YOU KNOW WHAT PEOPLE ARE GOING TO REMEMBER BIG DAWG FOR?
YOUR NEAT DOG HELMET?
NO! I WILL BE REMEMBERED AS THE ONE PERSON THAT THE GREAT AND WONDERFUL FRED COULD NOT CHANGE!
SLAM!

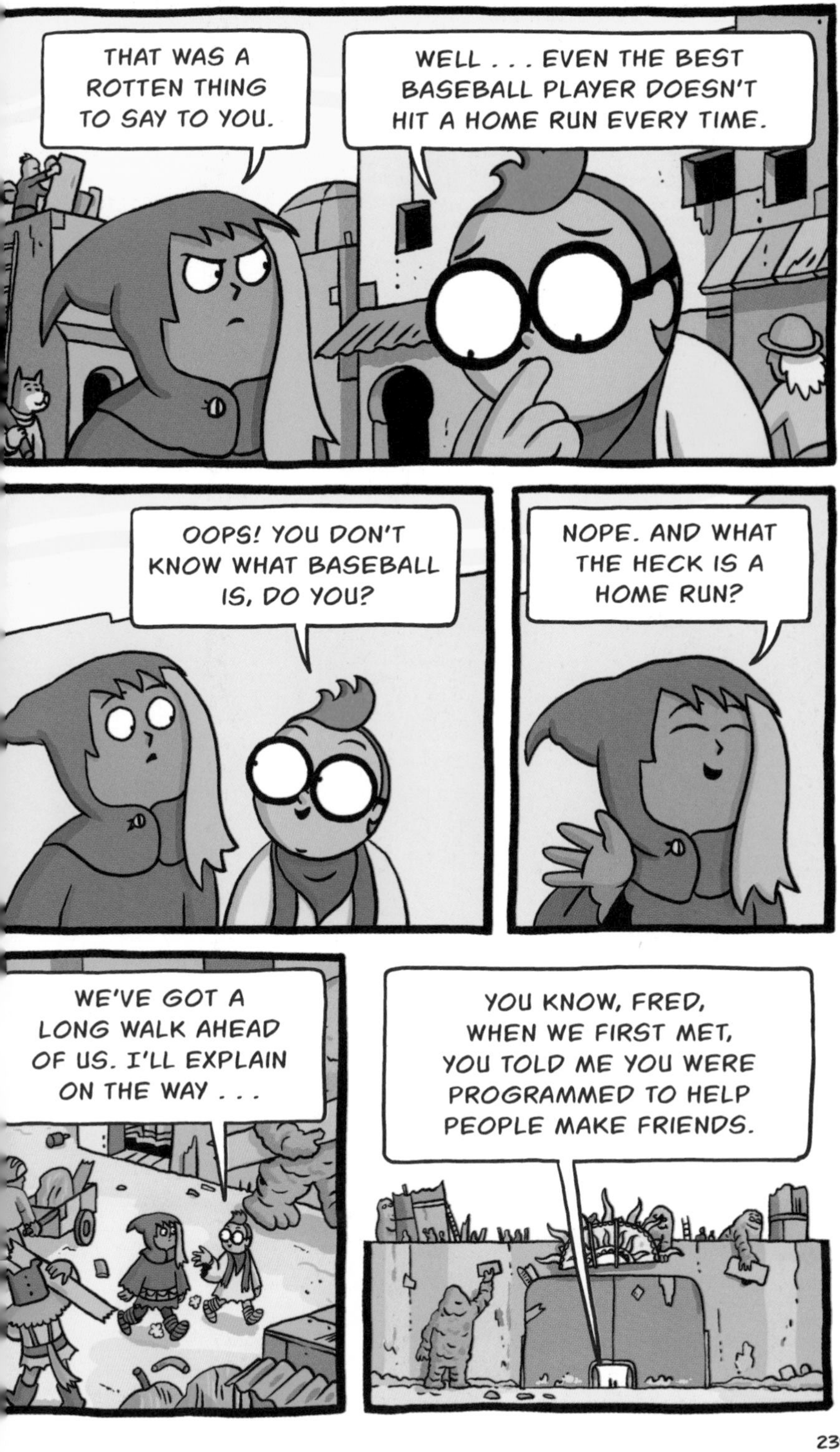
THAT WAS A ROTTEN THING TO SAY TO YOU.
WELL . . . EVEN THE BEST BASEBALL PLAYER DOESN'T HIT A HOME RUN EVERY TIME.
OOPS! YOU DON'T KNOW WHAT BASEBALL IS, DO YOU?
NOPE. AND WHAT THE HECK IS A HOME RUN?
WE'VE GOT A LONG WALK AHEAD OF US. I'LL EXPLAIN ON THE WAY . . .
YOU KNOW, FRED, WHEN WE FIRST MET, YOU TOLD ME YOU WERE PROGRAMMED TO HELP PEOPLE MAKE FRIENDS.

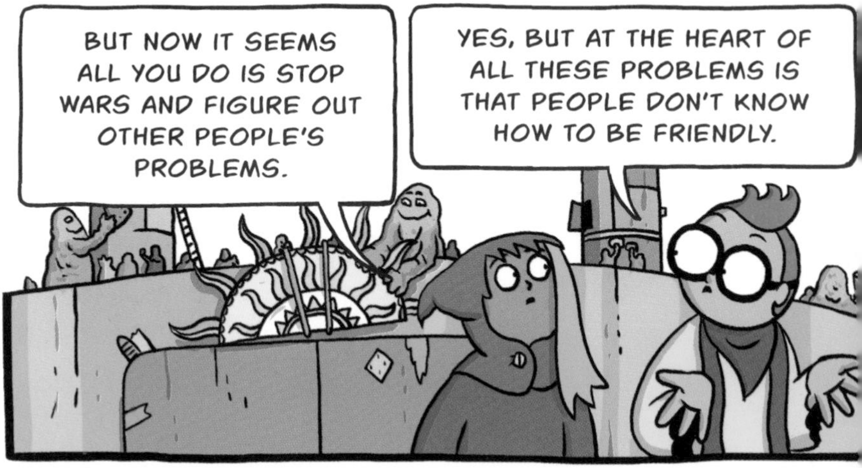
BUT NOW IT SEEMS ALL YOU DO IS STOP WARS AND FIGURE OUT OTHER PEOPLE'S PROBLEMS.
YES, BUT AT THE HEART OF ALL THESE PROBLEMS IS THAT PEOPLE DON'T KNOW HOW TO BE FRIENDLY.

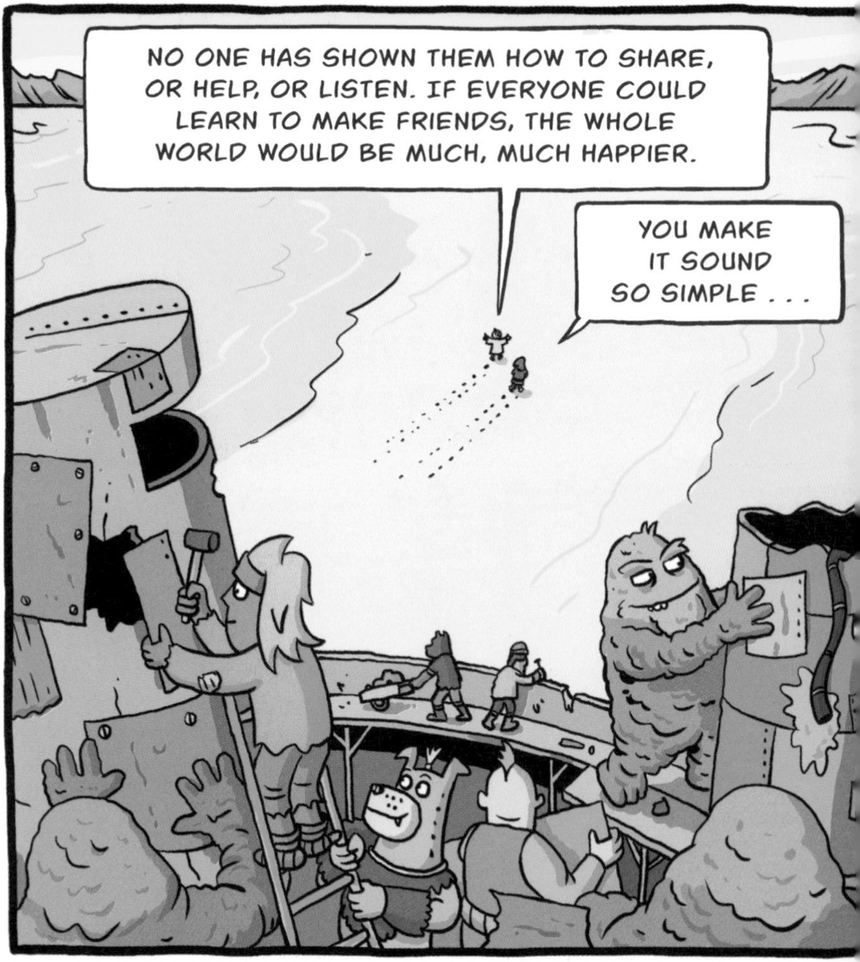
NO ONE HAS SHOWN THEM HOW TO SHARE, OR HELP, OR LISTEN. IF EVERYONE COULD LEARN TO MAKE FRIENDS, THE WHOLE WORLD WOULD BE MUCH, MUCH HAPPIER.
YOU MAKE IT SOUND SO SIMPLE . . .

CHAPTER 21

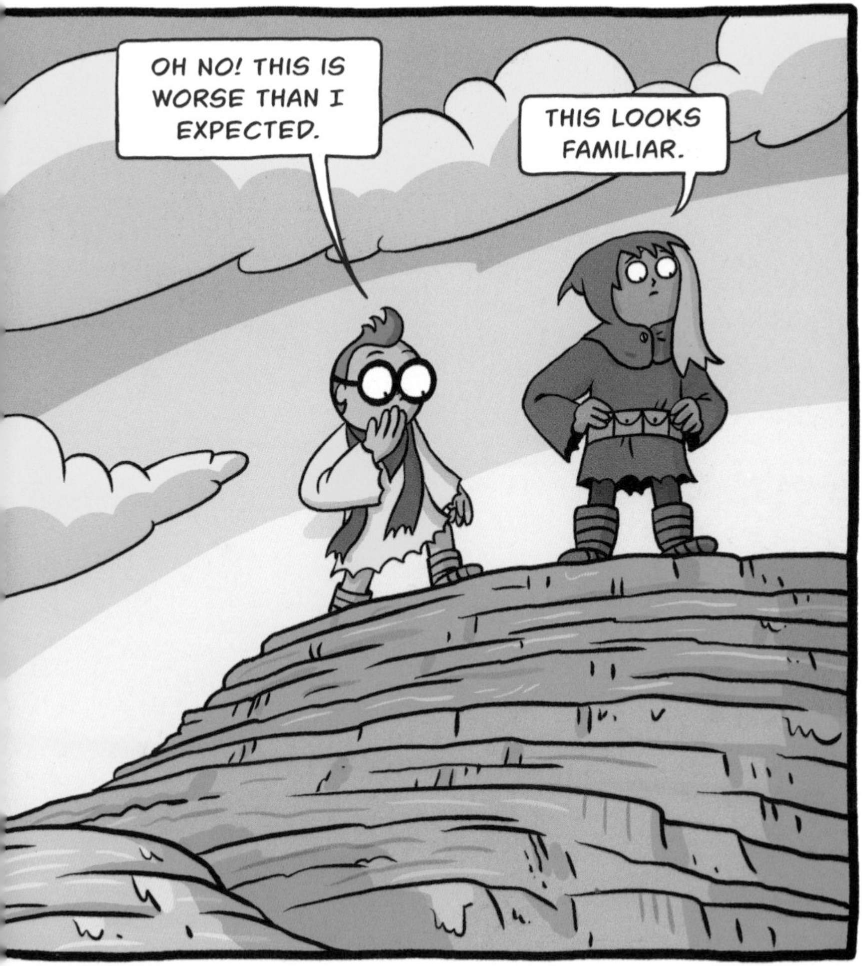

OH NO! THIS IS WORSE THAN I EXPECTED.
THIS LOOKS FAMILIAR.

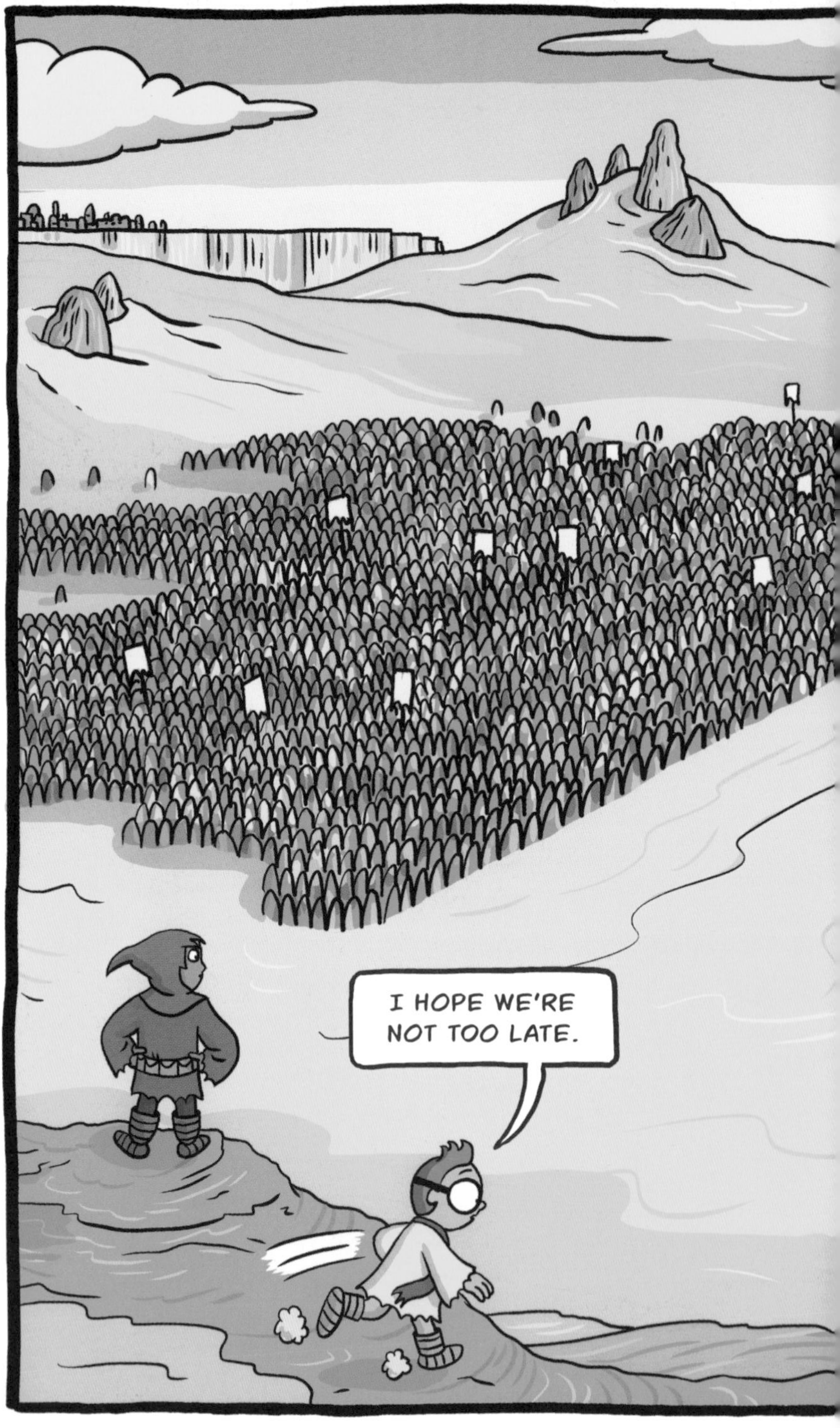
I HOPE WE'RE NOT TOO LATE.

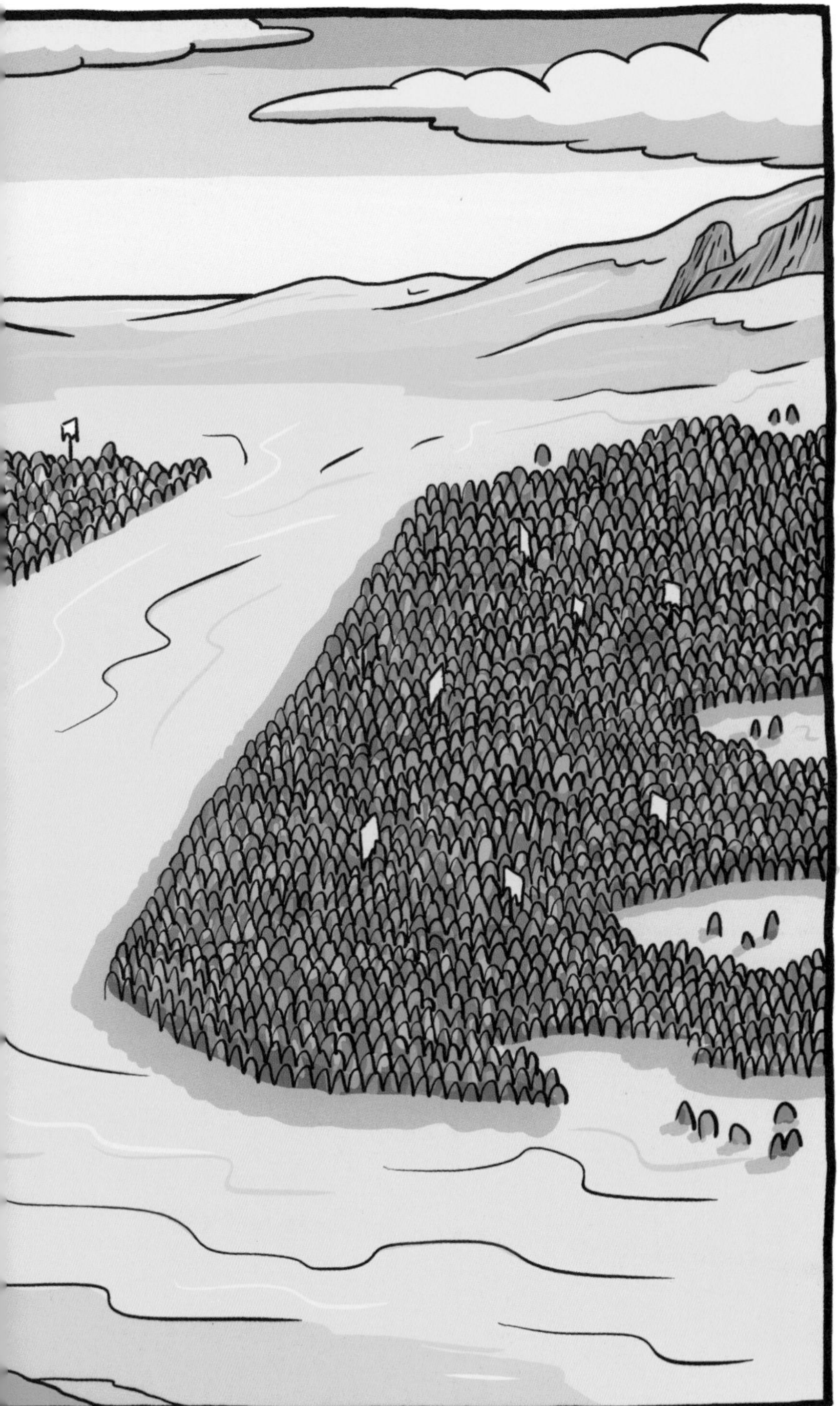

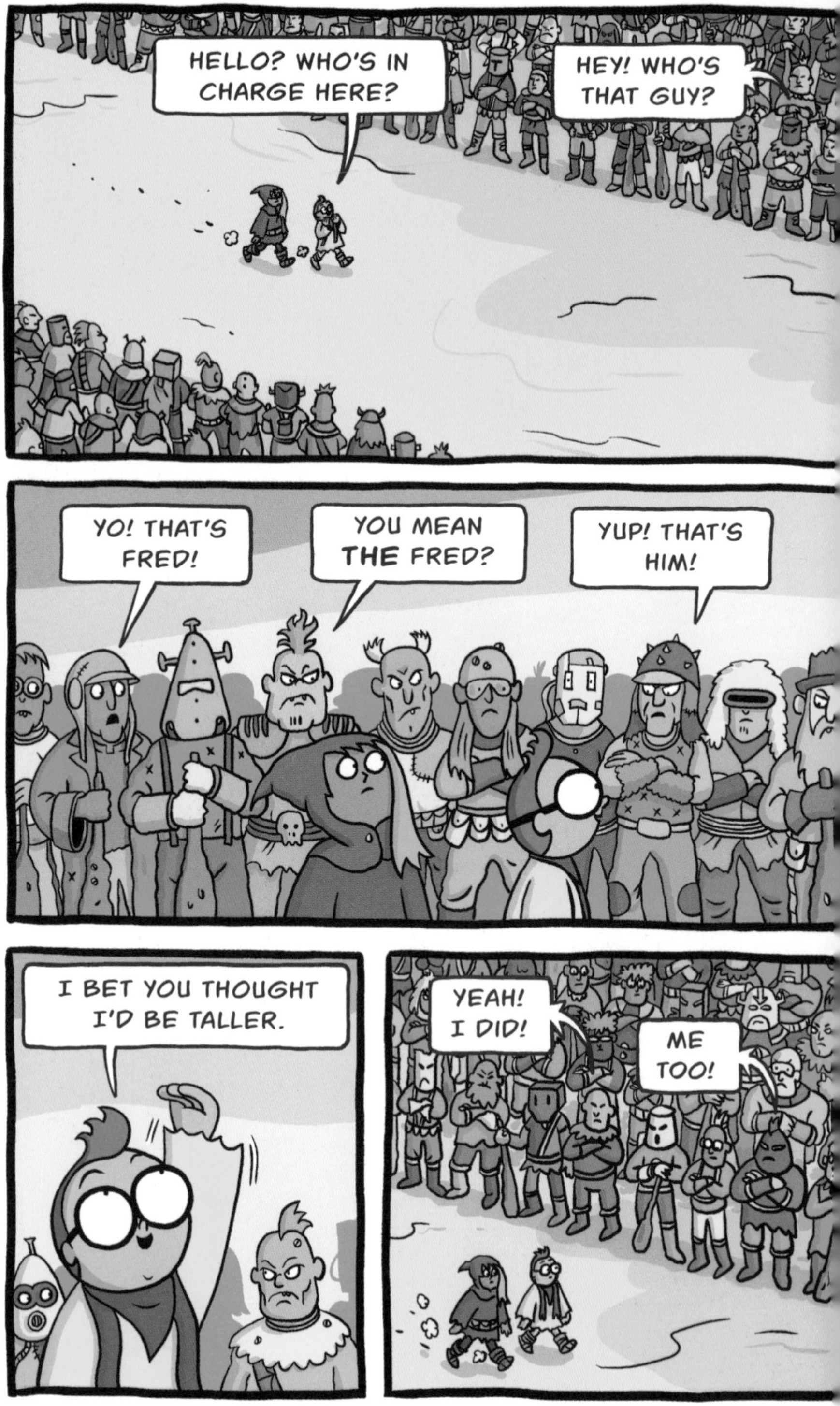
HELLO? WHO'S IN CHARGE HERE?
HEY! WHO'S THAT GUY?
YO! THAT'S FRED!
YOU MEAN **THE** FRED?
YUP! THAT'S HIM!
I BET YOU THOUGHT I'D BE TALLER.
YEAH! I DID!
ME TOO!

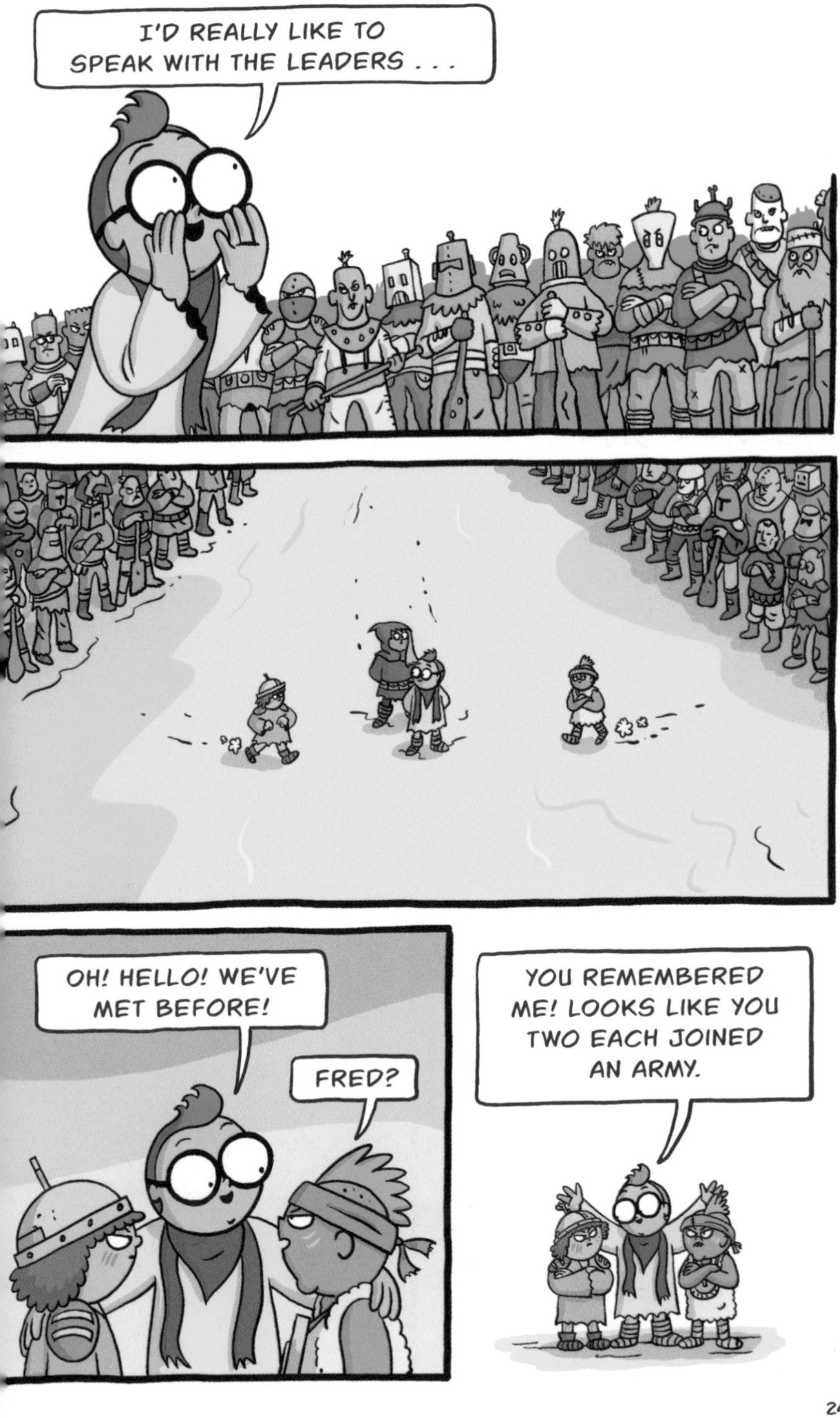
I'D REALLY LIKE TO SPEAK WITH THE LEADERS . . .
OH! HELLO! WE'VE MET BEFORE!
FRED?
YOU REMEMBERED ME! LOOKS LIKE YOU TWO EACH JOINED AN ARMY.

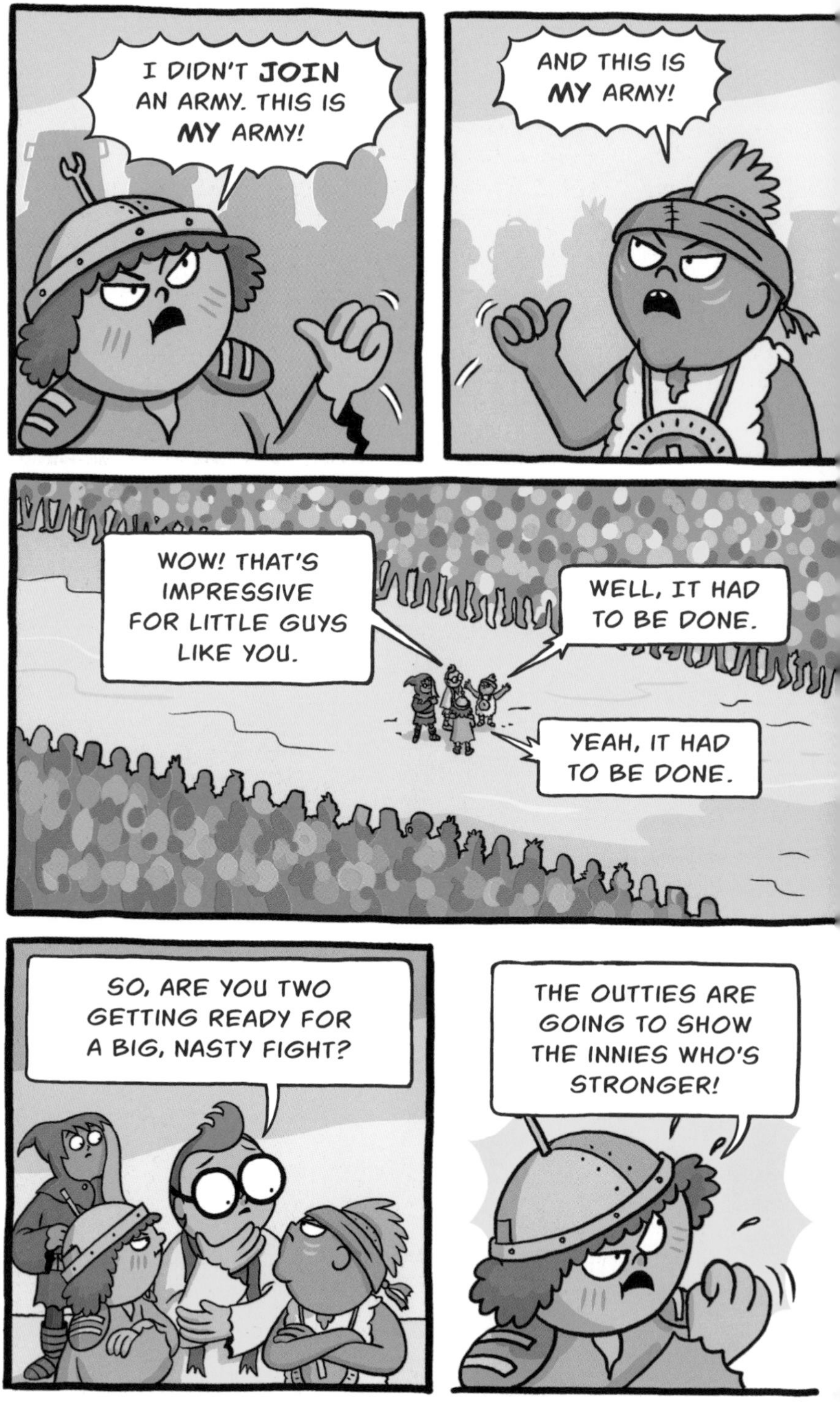
I DIDN'T JOIN AN ARMY. THIS IS MY ARMY!
AND THIS IS MY ARMY!
WOW! THAT'S IMPRESSIVE FOR LITTLE GUYS LIKE YOU.
WELL, IT HAD TO BE DONE.
YEAH, IT HAD TO BE DONE.
SO, ARE YOU TWO GETTING READY FOR A BIG, NASTY FIGHT?
THE OUTTIES ARE GOING TO SHOW THE INNIES WHO'S STRONGER!

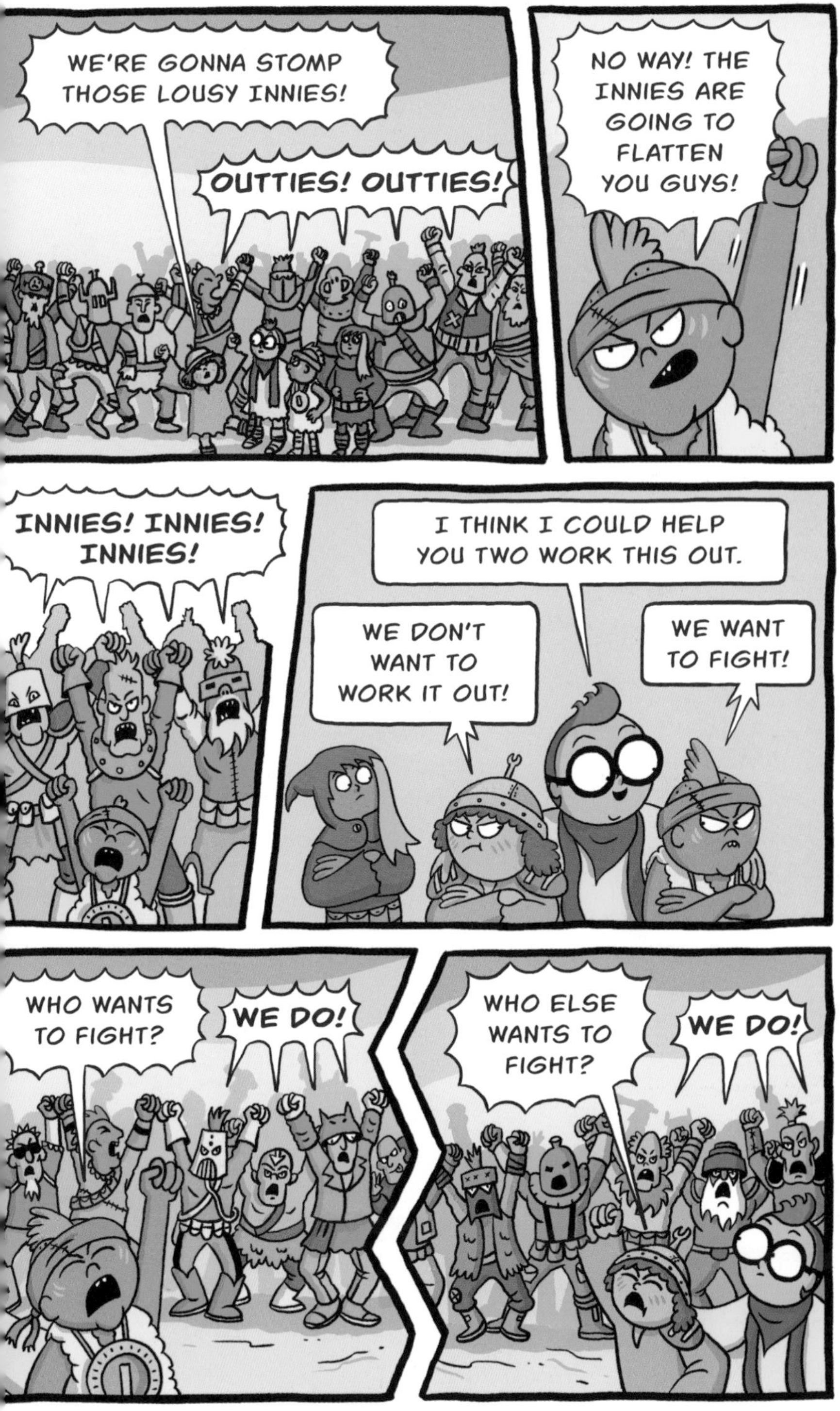
WE'RE GONNA STOMP THOSE LOUSY INNIES!
OUTTIES! OUTTIES!
NO WAY! THE INNIES ARE GOING TO FLATTEN YOU GUYS!
INNIES! INNIES! INNIES!
I THINK I COULD HELP YOU TWO WORK THIS OUT.
WE DON'T WANT TO WORK IT OUT!
WE WANT TO FIGHT!
WHO WANTS TO FIGHT?
WE DO!
WHO ELSE WANTS TO FIGHT?
WE DO!

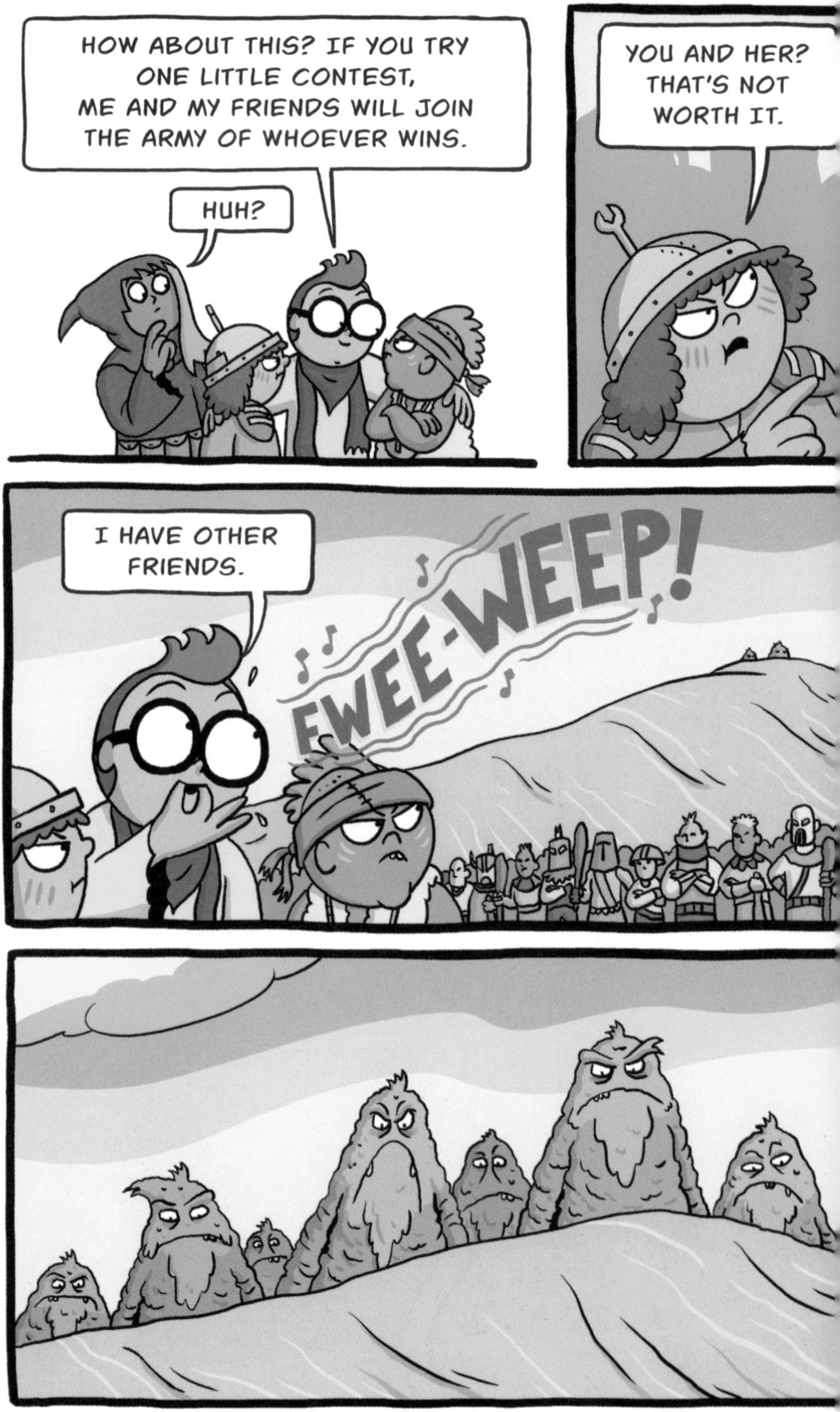
HOW ABOUT THIS? IF YOU TRY ONE LITTLE CONTEST, ME AND MY FRIENDS WILL JOIN THE ARMY OF WHOEVER WINS.
HUH?
YOU AND HER? THAT'S NOT WORTH IT.
I HAVE OTHER FRIENDS.
FWEE-WEEP!

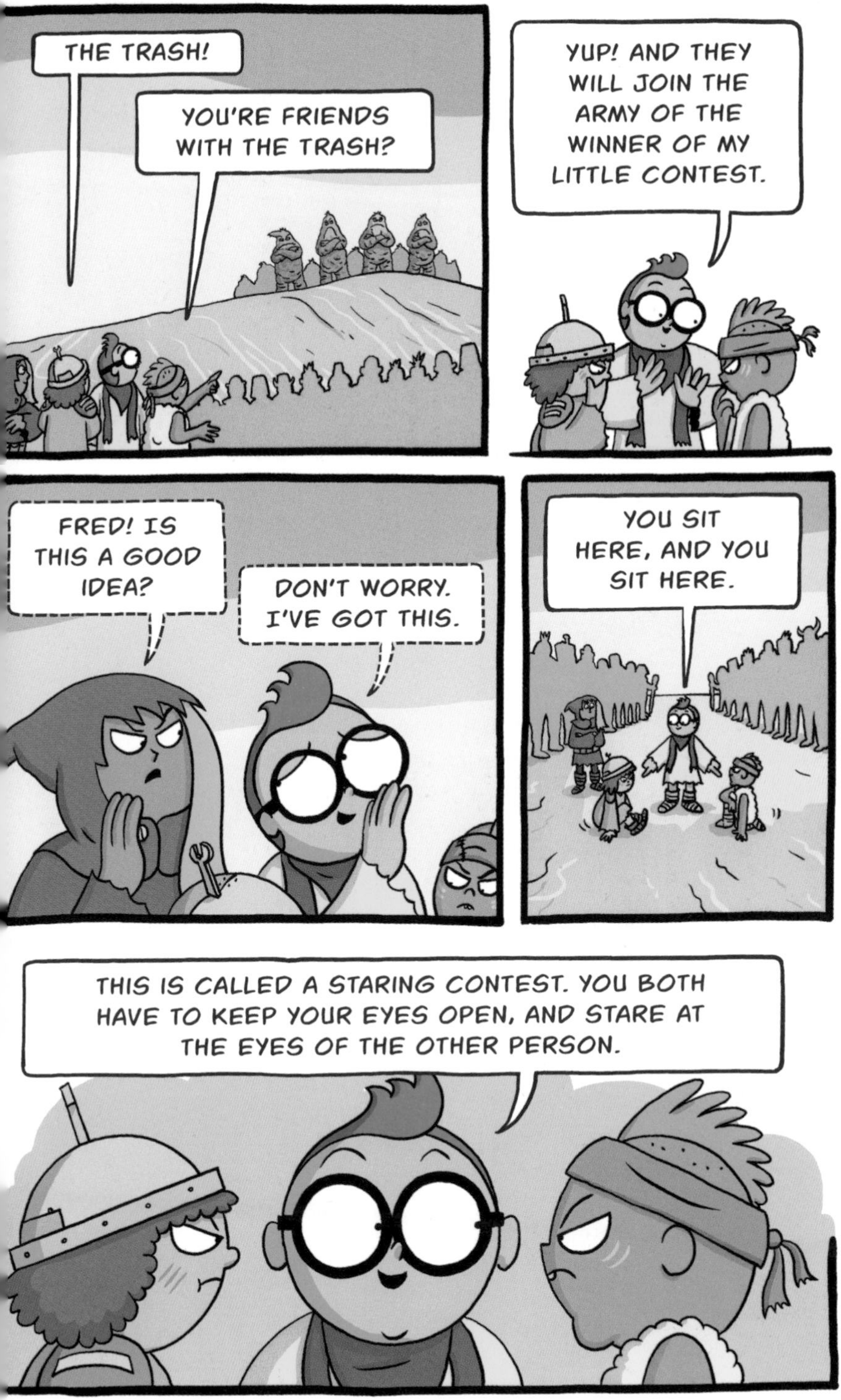
THE TRASH!
YOU'RE FRIENDS WITH THE TRASH?
YUP! AND THEY WILL JOIN THE ARMY OF THE WINNER OF MY LITTLE CONTEST.
FRED! IS THIS A GOOD IDEA?
DON'T WORRY. I'VE GOT THIS.
YOU SIT HERE, AND YOU SIT HERE.
THIS IS CALLED A STARING CONTEST. YOU BOTH HAVE TO KEEP YOUR EYES OPEN, AND STARE AT THE EYES OF THE OTHER PERSON.

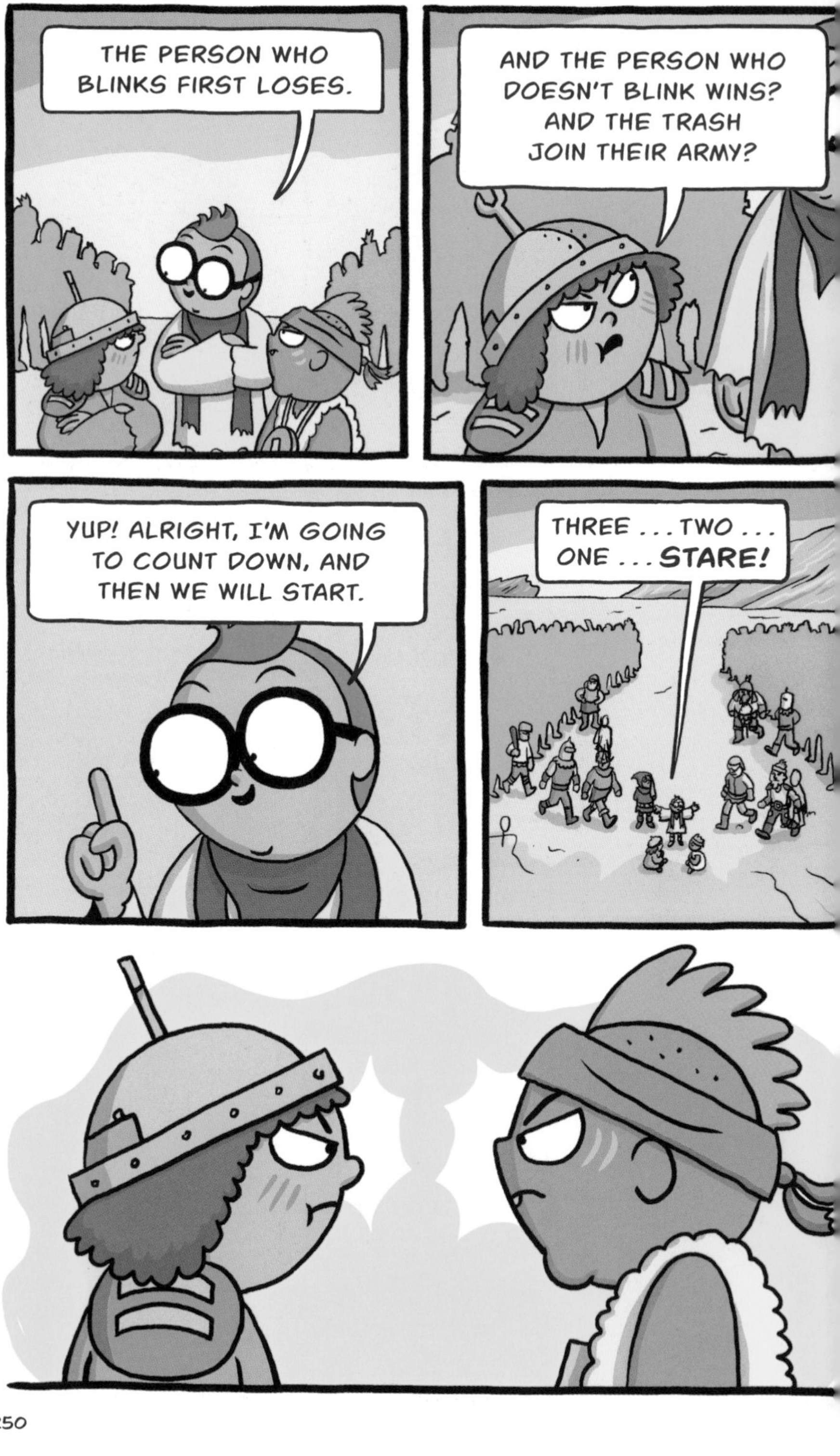
THE PERSON WHO BLINKS FIRST LOSES.
AND THE PERSON WHO DOESN'T BLINK WINS? AND THE TRASH JOIN THEIR ARMY?
YUP! ALRIGHT, I'M GOING TO COUNT DOWN, AND THEN WE WILL START.
THREE . . . TWO . . . ONE . . . STARE!

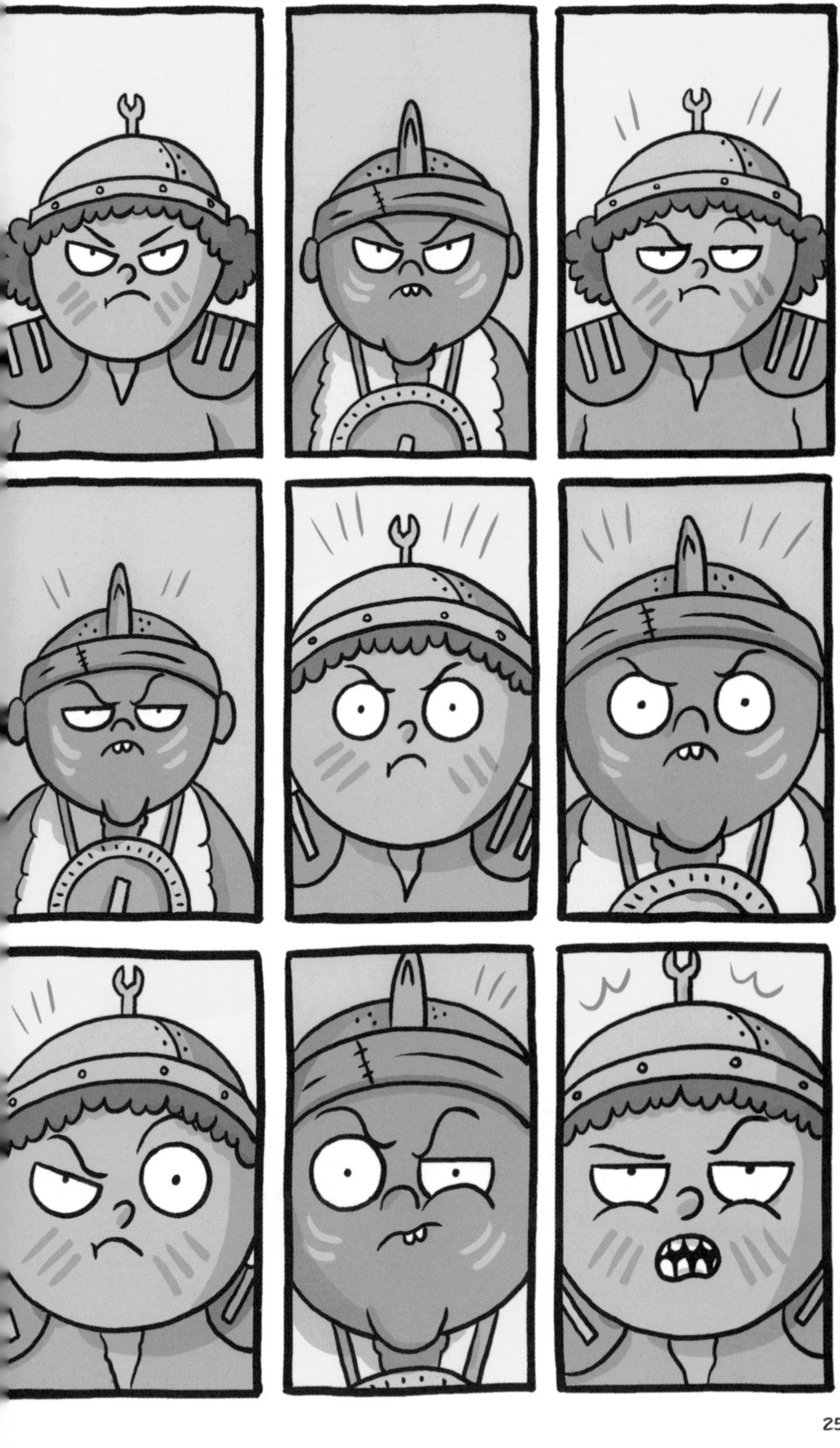

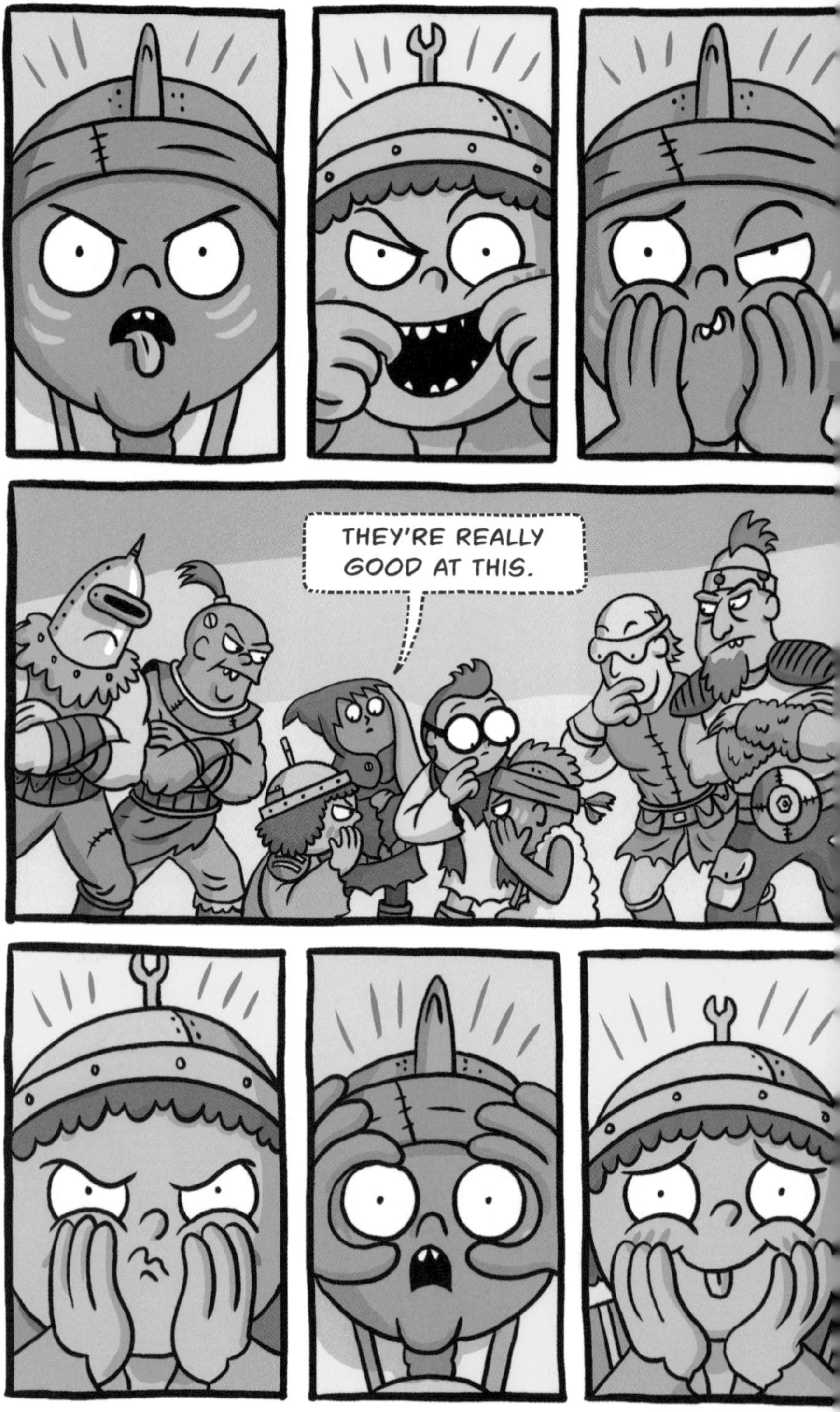
THEY'RE REALLY GOOD AT THIS.

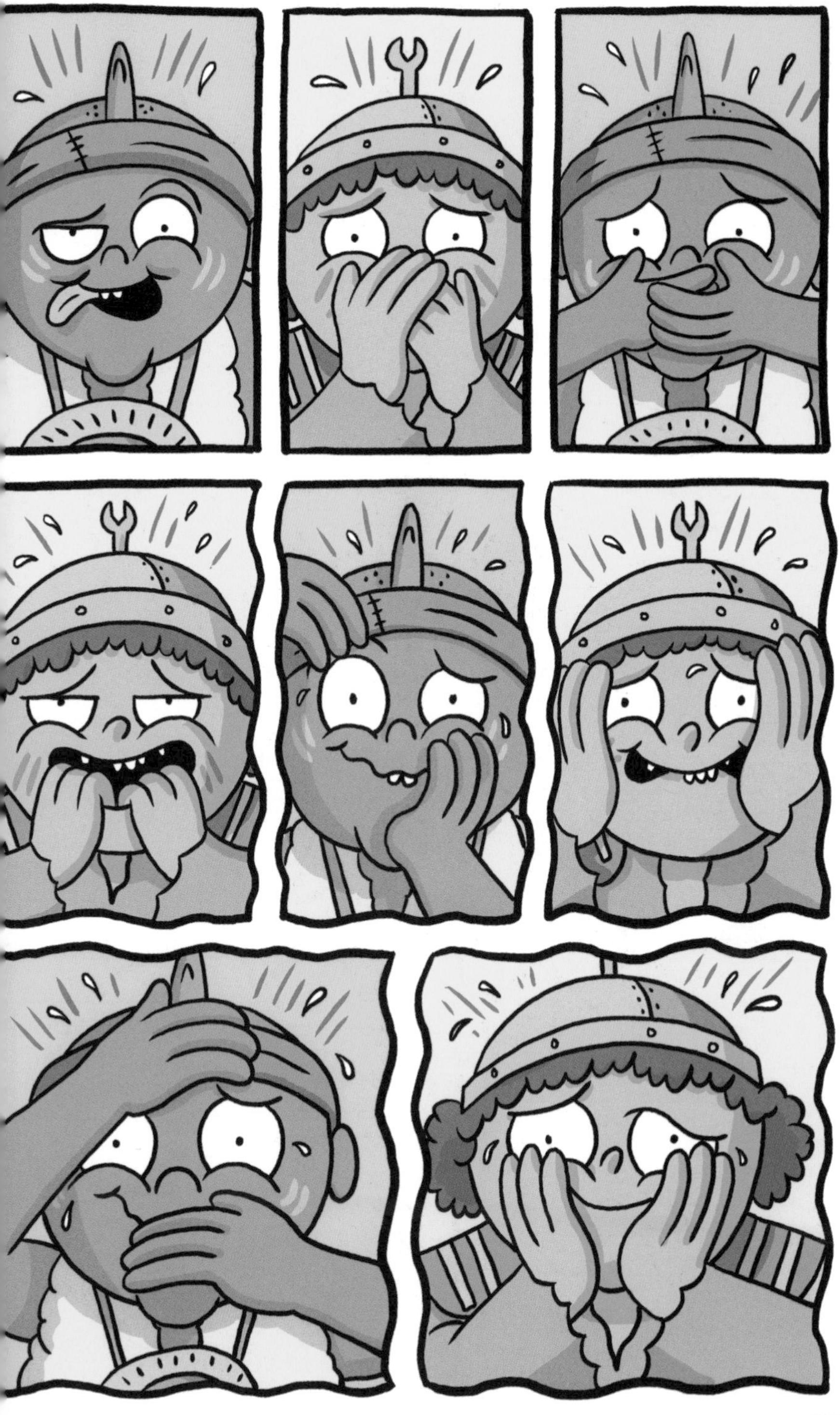

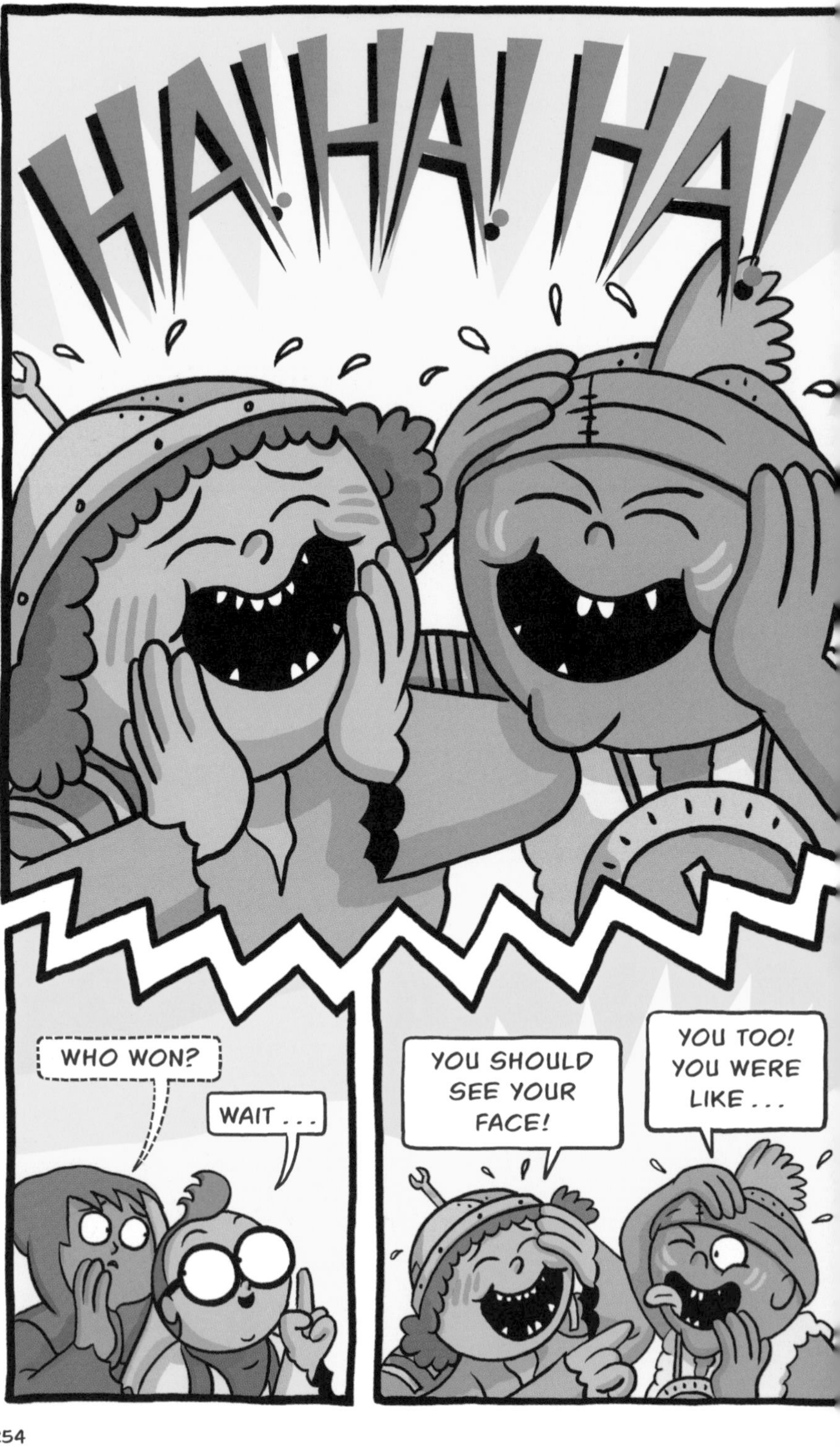
HA! HA! HA!
WHO WON?
WAIT . . .
YOU SHOULD SEE YOUR FACE!
YOU TOO! YOU WERE LIKE . . .

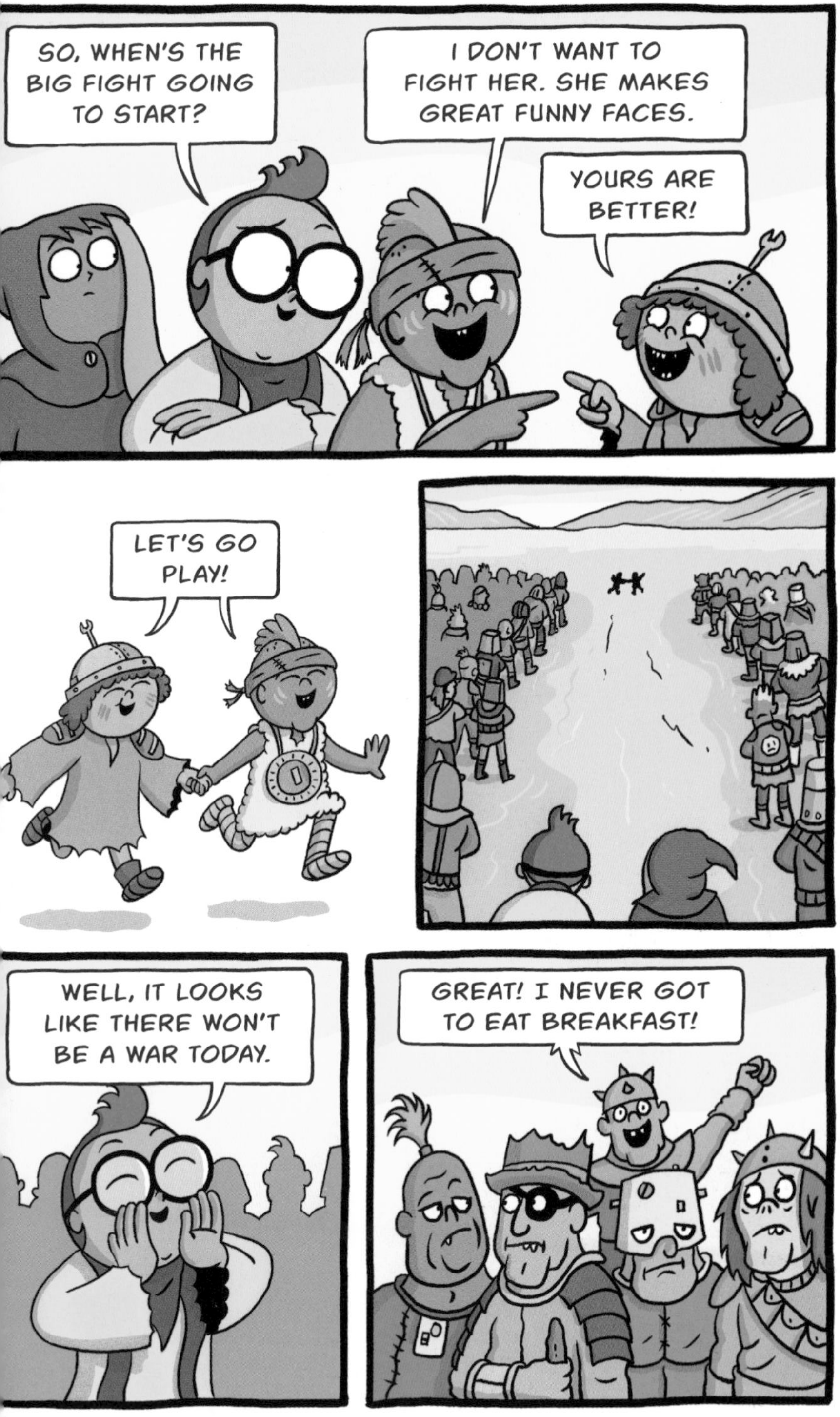
SO, WHEN'S THE BIG FIGHT GOING TO START?
I DON'T WANT TO FIGHT HER. SHE MAKES GREAT FUNNY FACES.
YOURS ARE BETTER!
LET'S GO PLAY!
WELL, IT LOOKS LIKE THERE WON'T BE A WAR TODAY.
GREAT! I NEVER GOT TO EAT BREAKFAST!

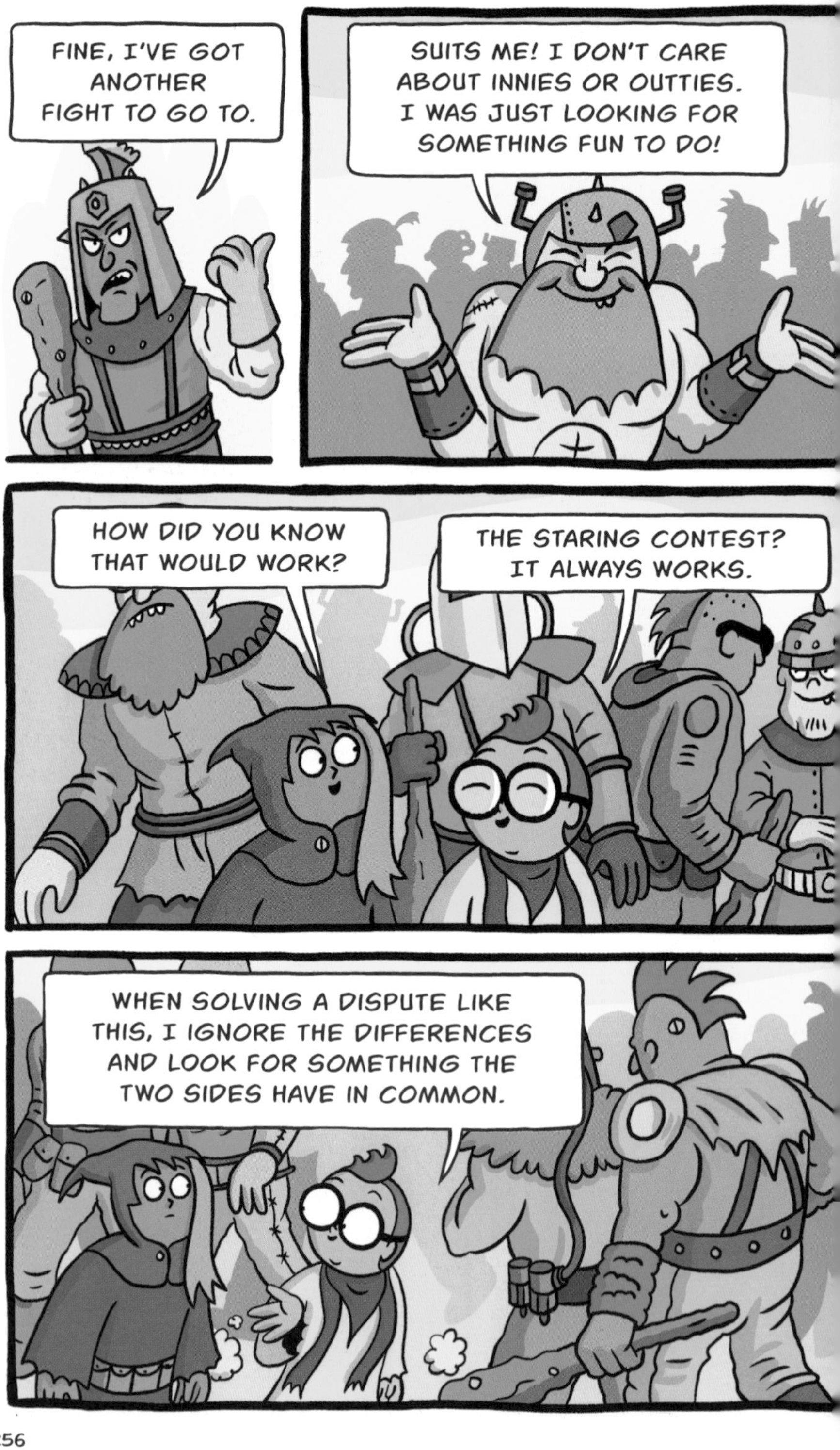
FINE, I'VE GOT ANOTHER FIGHT TO GO TO.
SUITS ME! I DON'T CARE ABOUT INNIES OR OUTTIES. I WAS JUST LOOKING FOR SOMETHING FUN TO DO!
HOW DID YOU KNOW THAT WOULD WORK?
THE STARING CONTEST? IT ALWAYS WORKS.
WHEN SOLVING A DISPUTE LIKE THIS, I IGNORE THE DIFFERENCES AND LOOK FOR SOMETHING THE TWO SIDES HAVE IN COMMON.

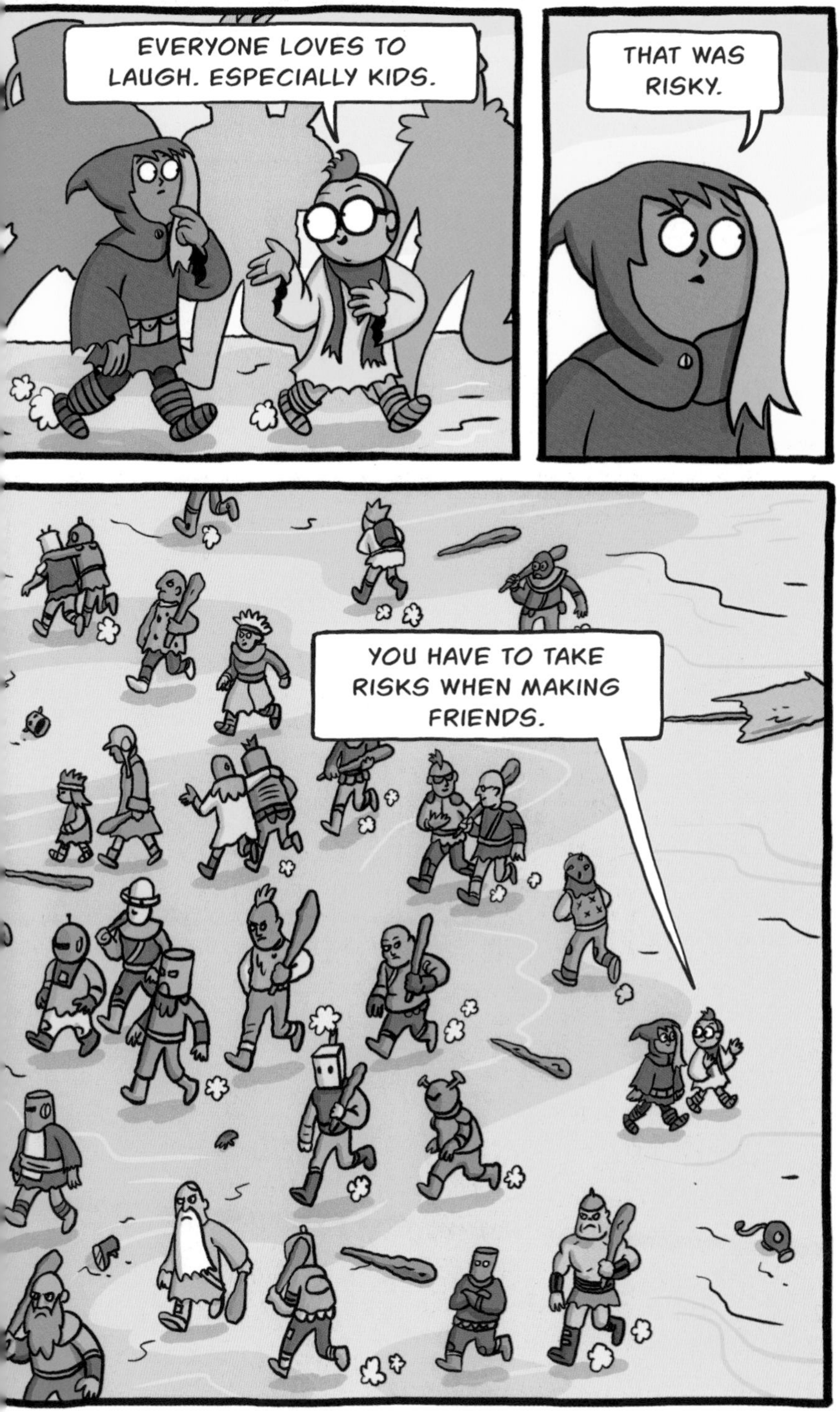
EVERYONE LOVES TO LAUGH. ESPECIALLY KIDS.
THAT WAS RISKY.
YOU HAVE TO TAKE RISKS WHEN MAKING FRIENDS.

CHAPTER 22

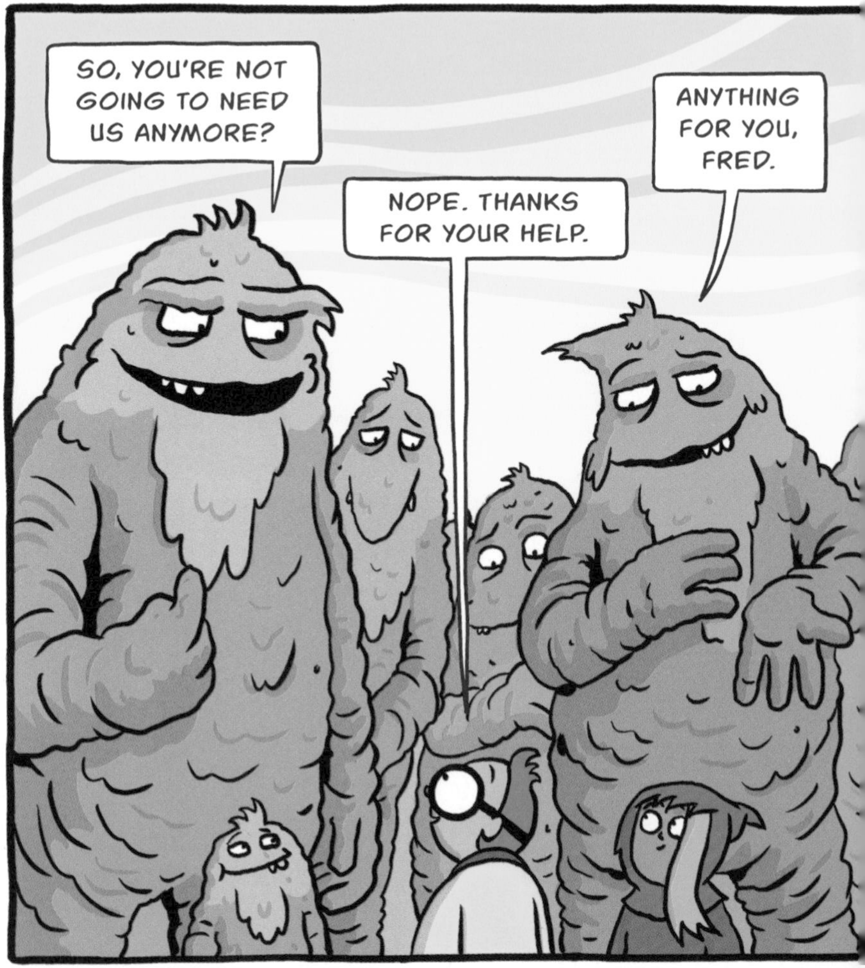

SO, YOU'RE NOT GOING TO NEED US ANYMORE?
NOPE. THANKS FOR YOUR HELP.
ANYTHING FOR YOU, FRED.

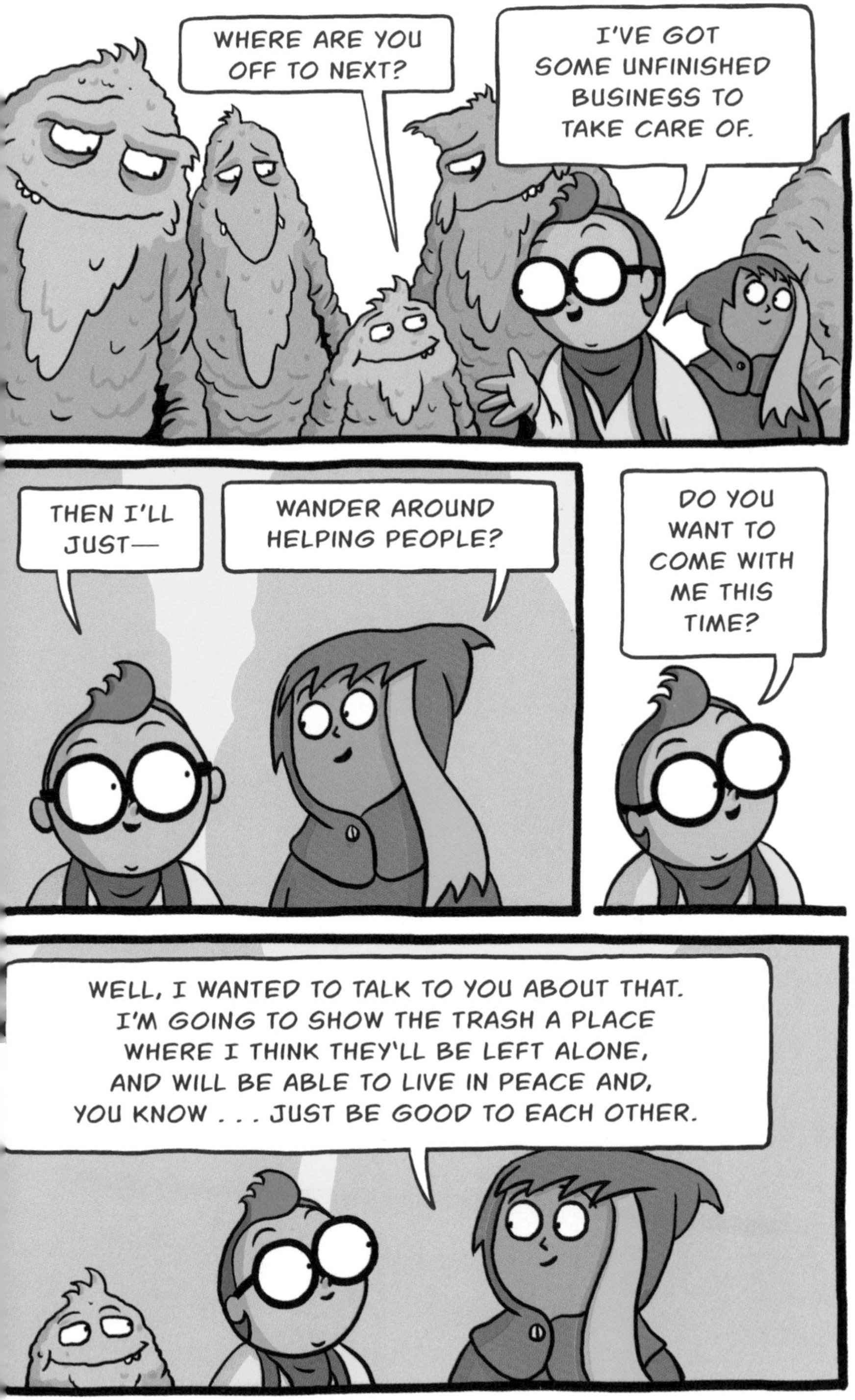
WHERE ARE YOU OFF TO NEXT?
I'VE GOT SOME UNFINISHED BUSINESS TO TAKE CARE OF.
THEN I'LL JUST—
WANDER AROUND HELPING PEOPLE?
DO YOU WANT TO COME WITH ME THIS TIME?
WELL, I WANTED TO TALK TO YOU ABOUT THAT. I'M GOING TO SHOW THE TRASH A PLACE WHERE I THINK THEY'LL BE LEFT ALONE, AND WILL BE ABLE TO LIVE IN PEACE AND, YOU KNOW . . . JUST BE GOOD TO EACH OTHER.

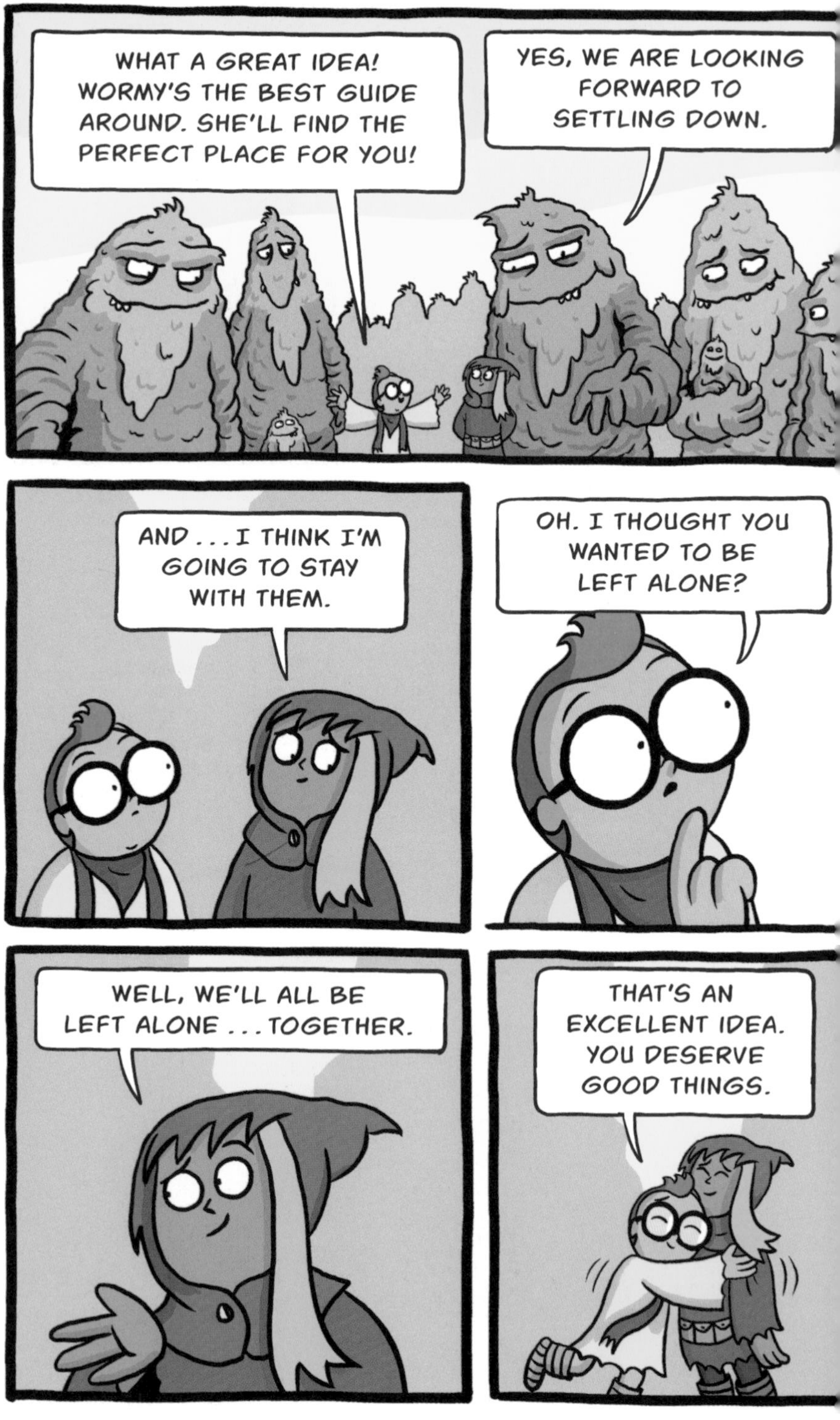
WHAT A GREAT IDEA! WORMY'S THE BEST GUIDE AROUND. SHE'LL FIND THE PERFECT PLACE FOR YOU!
YES, WE ARE LOOKING FORWARD TO SETTLING DOWN.
AND . . . I THINK I'M GOING TO STAY WITH THEM.
OH. I THOUGHT YOU WANTED TO BE LEFT ALONE?
WELL, WE'LL ALL BE LEFT ALONE . . . TOGETHER.
THAT'S AN EXCELLENT IDEA. YOU DESERVE GOOD THINGS.

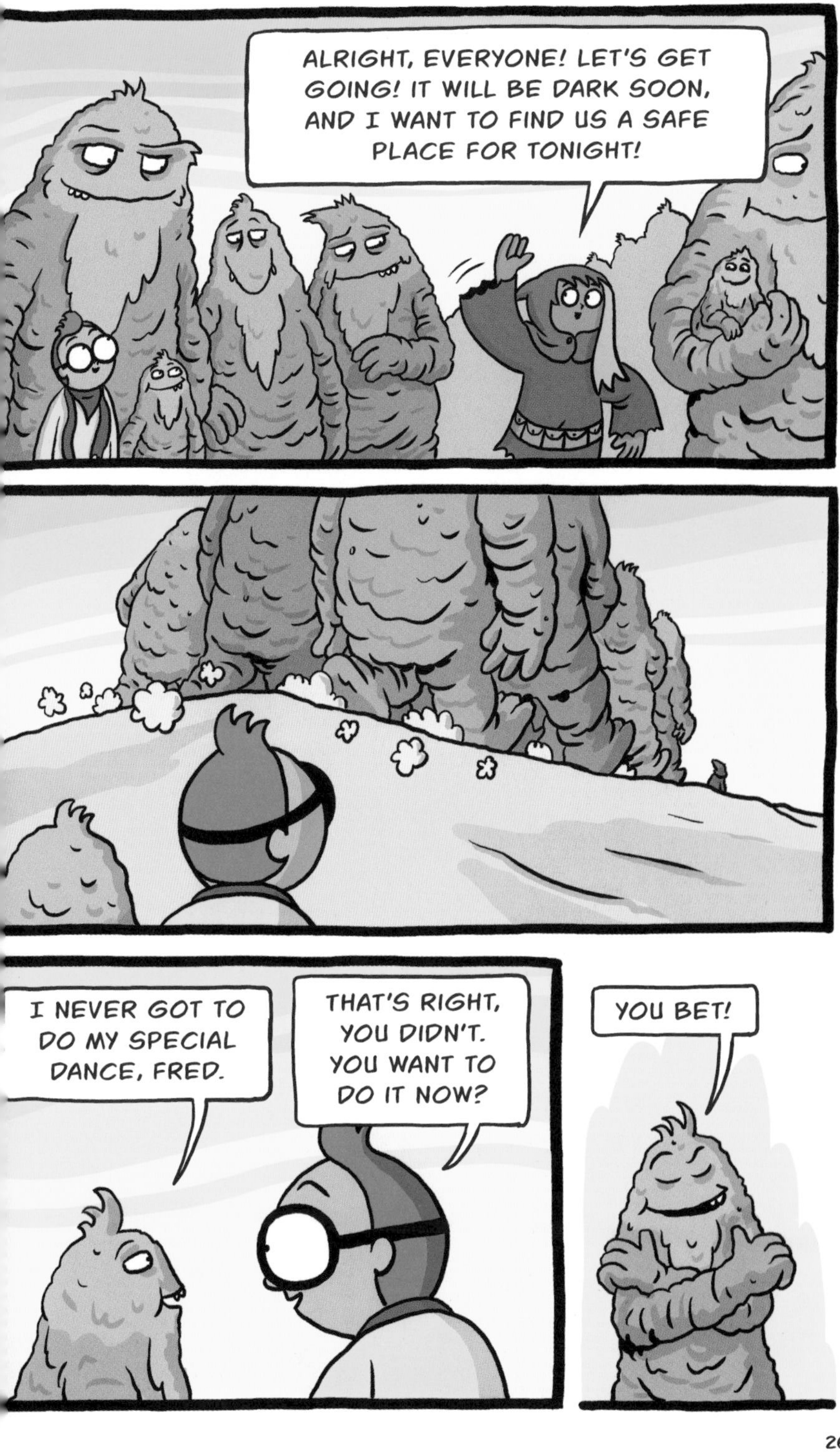

ALRIGHT, EVERYONE! LET'S GET GOING! IT WILL BE DARK SOON, AND I WANT TO FIND US A SAFE PLACE FOR TONIGHT!
I NEVER GOT TO DO MY SPECIAL DANCE, FRED.
THAT'S RIGHT, YOU DIDN'T. YOU WANT TO DO IT NOW?
YOU BET!

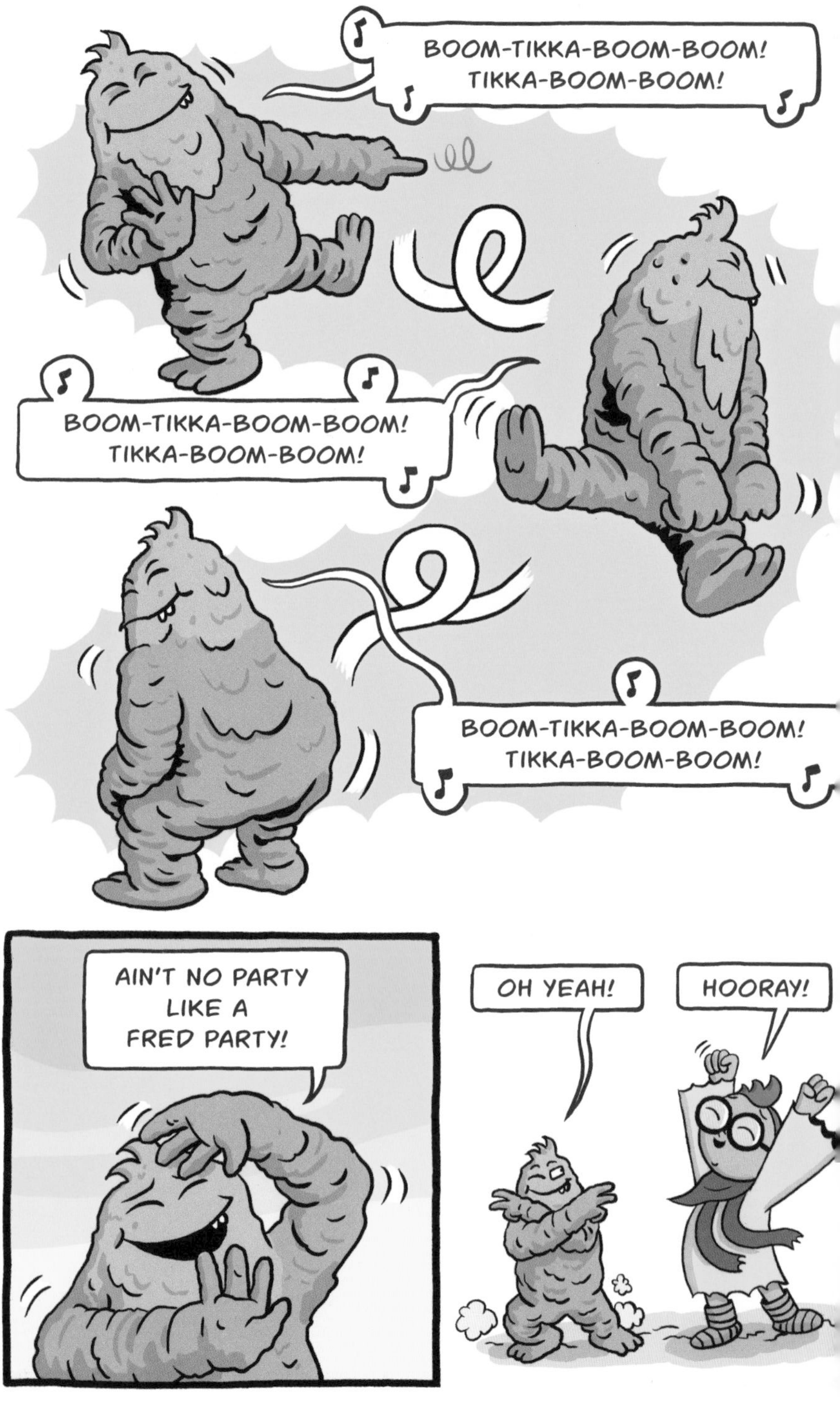
BOOM-TIKKA-BOOM-BOOM! TIKKA-BOOM-BOOM!
BOOM-TIKKA-BOOM-BOOM! TIKKA-BOOM-BOOM!
BOOM-TIKKA-BOOM-BOOM! TIKKA-BOOM-BOOM!
AIN'T NO PARTY LIKE A FRED PARTY!
OH YEAH!
HOORAY!

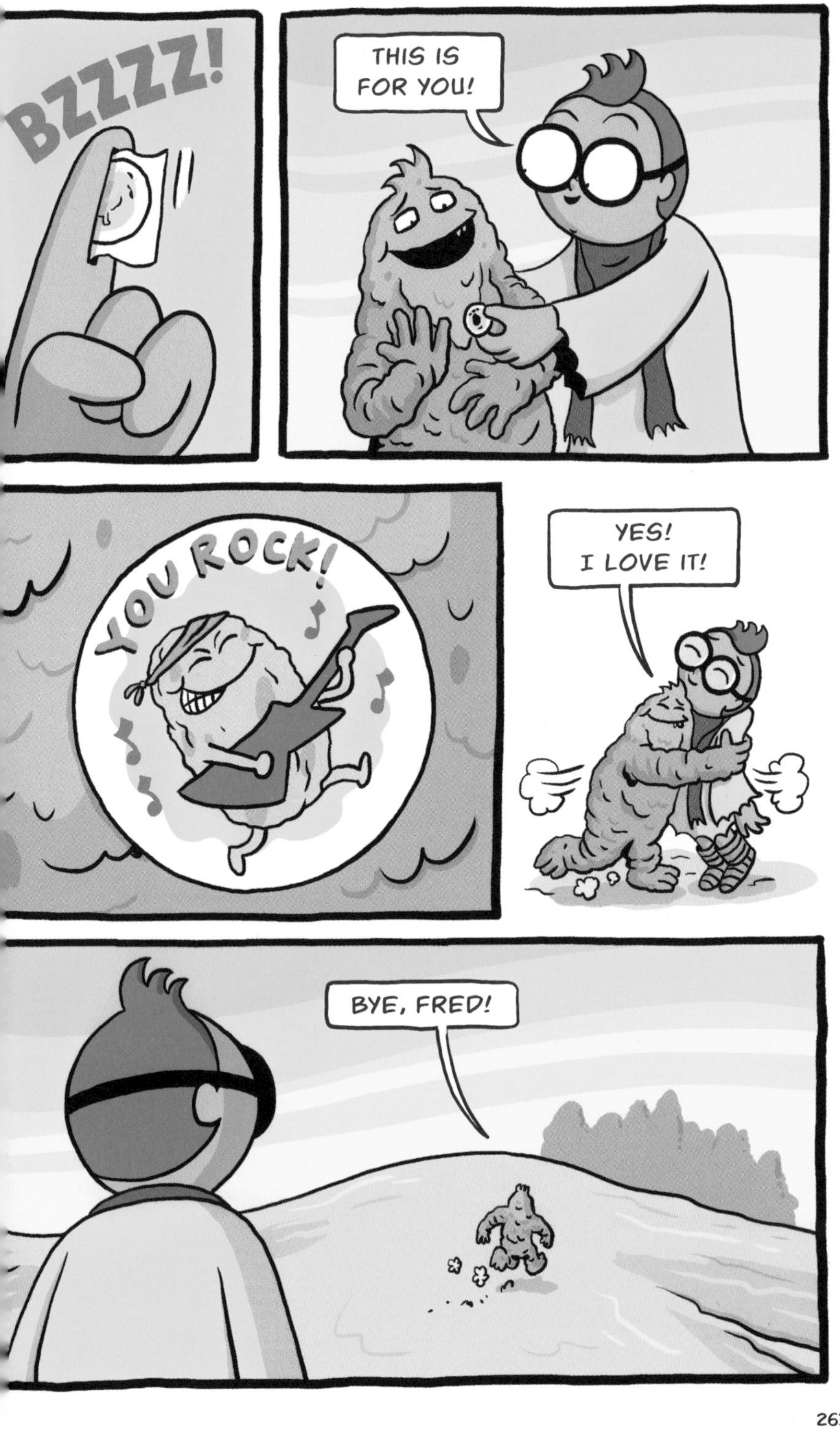
BZZZZZ!
THIS IS FOR YOU!
YOU ROCK!
YES! I LOVE IT!
BYE, FRED!

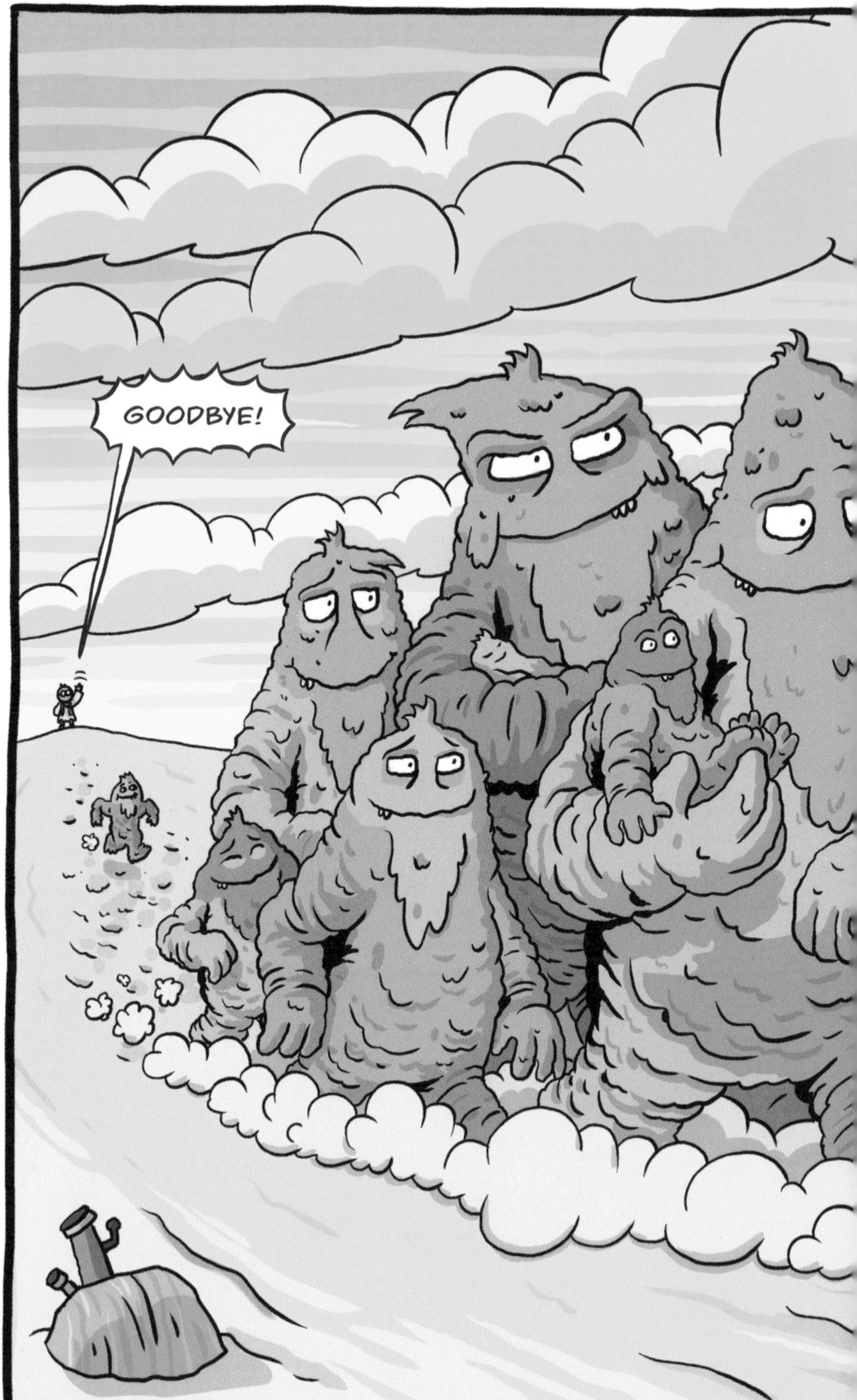
GOODBYE!

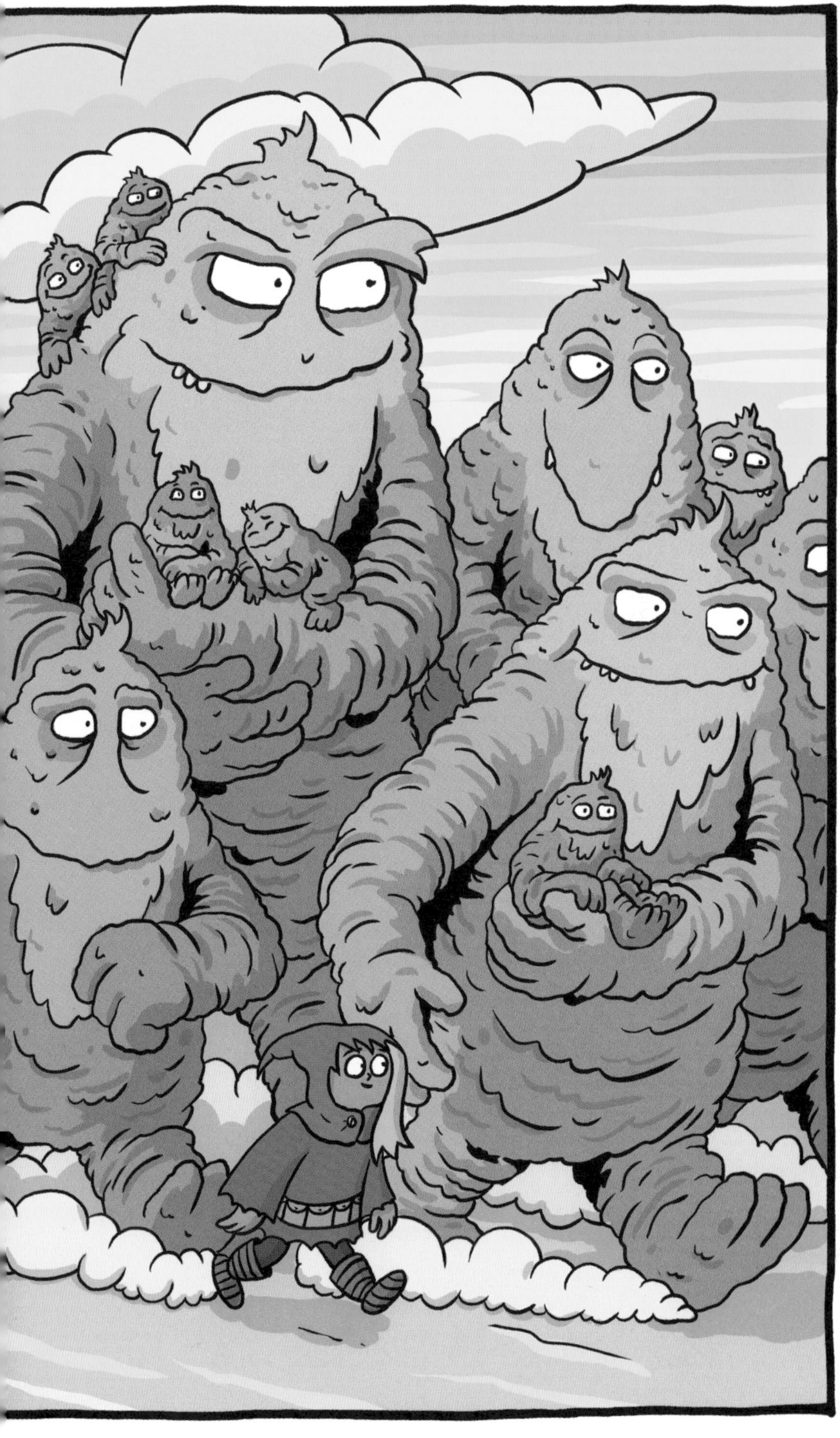

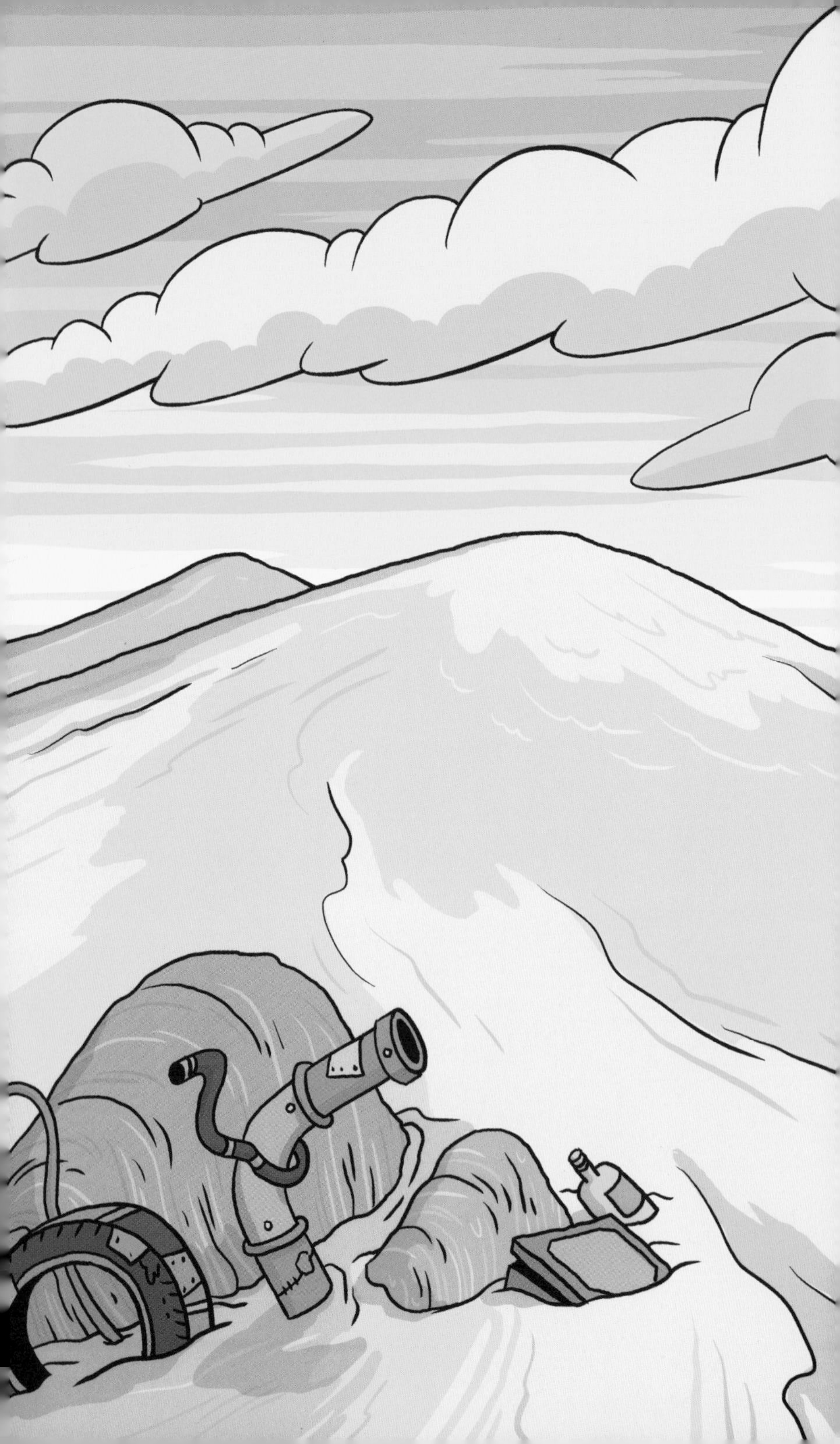

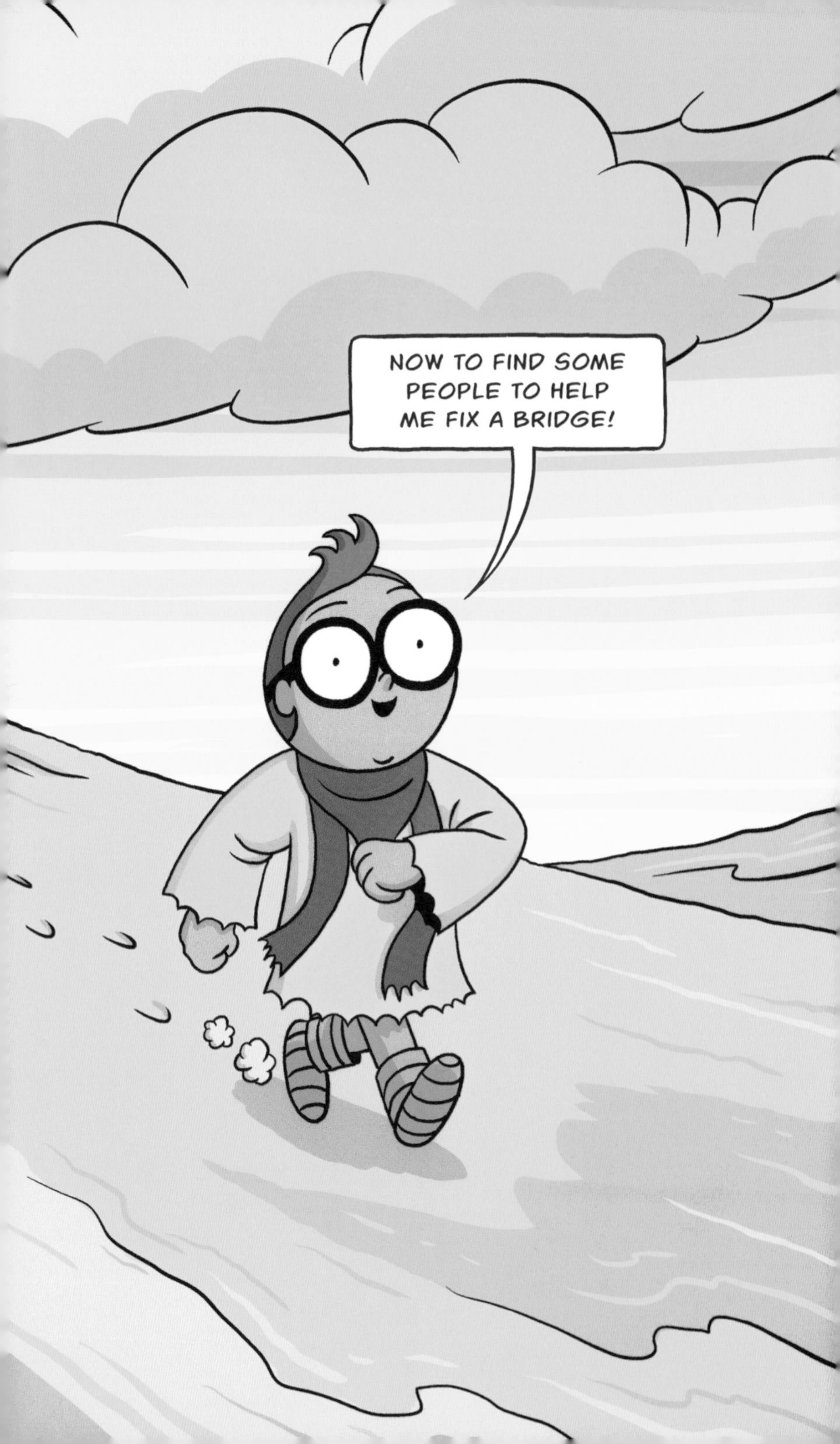
NOW TO FIND SOME PEOPLE TO HELP ME FIX A BRIDGE!

Mike Rex 2022